Schola Cantorum Basiliensis
Scripta

Veröffentlichungen der Schola Cantorum Basiliensis
Fachhochschule Nordwestschweiz / Musik-Akademie Basel
Hochschule für Musik

Band 9

Herausgegeben von Thomas Drescher und Martin Kirnbauer

Anne Smith

Ina Lohr (1903–1983)

Transcending the Boundaries of Early Music

Schwabe Verlag

Publiziert mit freundlicher Unterstützung
der Maja Sacher-Stiftung

MAJA SACHER STIFTUNG

Bibliographic information published by the Deutsche Nationalbibliothek
The Deutsche Nationalbibliothek lists this publication in the Deutsche Nationalbibliografie;
detailed bibliographic data are available on the Internet at http://dnb.dnb.de.

© 2020 Schwabe Verlag, Schwabe Verlagsgruppe AG, Basel, Schweiz
Cover illustration: Ina Lohr, "Ich sah die Unrast der Welt" (Gertrud von Le Fort, *Von den
letzten Dingen*). Reproduction: Paul Sacher Foundation, Ina Lohr Collection.
Copy-editing: Katherine Bird, Berlin
Cover design: icona basel gmbh, Basel
Typesetting: Dörlemann Satz GmbH & Co. KG, Lemförde
Print: Hubert & Co., Göttingen
Printed in Germany
ISBN Print 978-3-7965-4106-3
ISBN eBook (PDF) 978-3-7965-4154-4
DOI 10.24894/978-3-7965-4154-4
The ebook has identical page numbers to the print edition (first printing) and supports full-
text search. Furthermore, the table of contents is linked to the headings.

rights@schwabe.ch
www.schwabe.ch

Table of Contents

List of Illustrations

List of Tables

List of Abbreviations

AJC	Arbeiders Jeugd Centrale
BKO	Basler Kammerorchester (Basel Chamber Orchestra)
CMZ	Collegium Musicum Zurich
FAMB	Freunde Alter Musik Basel (Friends of Early Music, Basel)
ISCM	International Society for Contemporary Music
PGEM	N.V. Provinciale Geldersche Electriciteits-Maatschappij
PSF-ILC	Paul Sacher Foundation, Ina Lohr Collection
PSF-PSC	Paul Sacher Foundation, Paul Sacher Collection
SCB	Schola Cantorum Basiliensis

Acknowledgments

As ever with such endeavors, I am indebted to many people and institutions who helped me during the process of writing this book. Without their generous donation of time, knowledge and financial support, it would have been impossible to draw together the material necessary for fleshing out the figure of Ina Lohr.

The Schola Cantorum Basiliensis served as a basis for the entire project, not only in regards to their archives, but also personally and financially. I wish, in particular, to thank its director, Thomas Drescher, for his warm support of the research for this biography. In addition, it was through this institution that I received a generous two-year grant from the Swiss National Science Foundation, which enabled me to profit from the collaboration on the project with my Schola colleagues, Jeremy Llewellyn and Kelly Landerkin, as well as with Jed Wentz in the Netherlands. Further, Martin Kirnbauer and Martina Papiro of the research department have been of great assistance, both in regard to source material and documentation of my finds. In addition, both Markus Erni and Martina Wohlthat of the Vera Oeri Bibliothek of the Musik-Akademie Basel aided me in the procuring and archivation of documents, and gave me the opportunity of presenting some of my initial results to a more general public. Finally, the Maja Sacher Foundation supported a study day devoted to the link between Basel and the Netherlands through Ina Lohr, as well as sponsoring the recording of some of her early works, which gave many new insights into her musical personality.[1]

It also would have been impossible to write this biography without the Paul Sacher Foundation, as Ina Lohr's estate is found in its archives. Various members of its staff, Carlos Chanfón, Felix Meyer, Ulrich Mosch, Simon Obert, Heidrun Ziems and Heidy Zimmermann, all in their way contributed in a significant manner to the content and style of the book. Simon Obert's careful reading of the final text was particularly valuable.

The staff of the library of the University of Basel, the Zentralbibliothek of Zurich, the archives of Winterthur and Davos all welcomed me and assisted me in finding documents important to my study. I am also grateful to the various libraries and archives in the Netherlands and Sweden which gave me access to their collections: the Amsterdam City Archives, the Netherlands Music Insti-

---

1 www.forschung.schola-cantorum-basiliensis.ch/de/ina-lohr-project

tute in The Hague, as well as the Music and Theater Library of Sweden and the Nydahl Collection of the Stiftelsen Musikkulturens Främjande in Stockholm.

And then there were all of those patient individuals who answered my questions, told me their stories in regard to Ina Lohr, offered me material and insights. Without their personal memories and documents, this book would lack much of its color: Wulf Arlt, Anneke Bailes-van Royen, Anthony Bailes, André Baltensperger, Albert Jan Becking, Henk van Benthem, Elisabeth van Blankenstein, Herbert Blomstedt, Anneke Boeke, Edward Breen, Mieke Breij, Edith Büchi, Peter Bürgi, Jan Crafoord, Arthur Eglin, Tore Eketorp, Stefan Felber, Margrit Fiechter, Veronika Gutmann, Veronika Hampe, Barbara Hasspacher, Christina Hess, Iris Junker, Elisabeth Kiessling, Jolande van der Klis, Jos Knigge, Evelyne Laeuchli, Petra van Langen, Silke Leopold, Jos Leussink, Hans-Martin Linde, Reina Lohr, Marianne Lüthi, Madeleine Modin, Esther Nef, Julia J. G. Muller-van Santen, Christine M. Resink-van der Meer, Hans Adam Ritter, Willy Rordorf, Christina Rufenacht, Katelijne Schiltz, Christian Schmid, Ursula Schmidt, Giselher Schubert, Urs Schweizer, Richard Sparks, Theophil Spoerri, Simone Staehelin Handschin, Hans-Jürg Stefan, Conrad Steinmann, Martin and Esther Stern, Hinrich and Elisabeth Stoevesandt, Marie Sumpf-Refardt, Monica Vischer Richter, Wolfgang Vischer, Henk Waardenburg, Bettina Wehrli, Christin and Walter Wehrli, John Wellingham, Peter Welten, Floris and Aleid Zuidema. I fear that this list is incomplete, but my intent was to include everybody who helped me in the course of writing the book; I beg foregiveness from any whom I may have overlooked.

And last, but by all means not least, are the two people who served as catalysts and later as supporters and advisers in the writing of this book, Christopher Schmidt and Jed Wentz. Christopher not only inspired me in our first interview to uncover more about Ina Lohr, but later his stories and his reactions to my findings were a constant source of both delight and reassurance, the former because of his memories and his ability to make astonishing connections, the latter because he had known Ina Lohr well, both as a student and a colleague. And it was Jed's invitation to write an article together about Gustav Leonhardt's early study years that served as the instigation to write the book. Knowing they were in the wings, so to speak, helped me through many a difficult passage. There is no way I can adequately express my gratitude for the time and thought they gave the project.

Foreword

Flight into the past? I do not know where the present stops and the past begins. Nothing is ever completely over. History can be written and rewritten in a dozen ways. Hidden under the surface of the customary historical picture, in the depths, the mass of that formidable material, lie, never yet 'seen', the connecting points of other pictures with another perspective and completely different forms and dimensions.[1]

On one level, these words of Hella Haasse can be applied directly to my decision to write a biography of Ina Lohr – a woman whose work has by now been largely forgotten – in that her contribution to the world of music, as a co-founder and pedagogical inspiration for the Schola Cantorum Basiliensis, and musical assistant to Paul Sacher, a major patron of contemporary music in the 20th century and conductor of the Basel Chamber Orchestra, gives an entirely new understanding to these institutions. Further, through the investigation of her role in both the Early Music movement and Neoclassicism, new light is shone on the movements themselves.

More personally, however, I recognized in these words a description of the process I went through while sifting through the information and documents concerning Ina Lohr's life. My first intention had been to demonstrate – no matter how strongly this was contested in the latter half of the 20th century[2] – the common roots of the performance ideals of the Early Music movement and Neoclassicism in a single figure, someone who, in addition, possessed a strong sense of religiosity. I saw her as crossing boundaries, moving between fields of activity that were seemingly contradictory. But I soon came to recognize that I, too, in spite of all good intents, was blinkered, only looking for things that I expected to find. The more I opened myself up to the "connecting points of other pictures with another perspective", the more I found them: indeed, I dis-

---

1   "Vlucht in het verleden? Ik weet niet waar het heden ophoudt en het verleden begint. Niets is ooit geheel voorbij. De geschiedenis kan op duizend manieren geschreven en herschreven worden. Verborgen onder de oppervlakte van het geijkte beeld der historie, in de diepte, de massa van dat ontzaglijke materiaal, liggen, nog nooit 'gezien', de verbindingspunten van andere beelden met een ander perspectief en volstrekt andere vormen en afmetingen". Hella S. Haasse, *De tuinen van Bomarzo*, Amsterdam: Em. Querido's Uitgeverij B.V. 1972, 158.

2   See Richard Taruskin, *Text & Act: Essays on Music and Performance*, New York: Oxford University Press 1995, for some of the articles that initiated the whole discourse, as well as his responses to various critics.

covered that it was I who needed to transcend my own boundaries to be able
to do a modicum of justice to a biography about such a multifaceted woman.
In attempting to gain understanding of her life, it was almost as if I had to imagine what it would be like to walk in her shoes. In doing so, my world picture
expanded immensely, as she was involved in so many aspects of life that were
foreign to me, geographically, intellectually and spiritually. I was, as it were, being forced to reconsider all aspects of my understanding of the 20th century,
and my part in it.

One of the most striking differences was that some of the cultural and social boundaries of her age had shifted in our time in such a manner, and at
such a deep level, that I was unaware of the changes, taking my own mores
for granted. This in turn was complicated by the fact that they were also sub-
tly different from those which surrounded me in my youth in the New World.
In writing this biography, I came to see that what for me were boundaries, for
her were part of a continuum, and vice versa; in addition, some of the categories I was using to judge aesthetic processes created divisions that did not necessarily exist for her.

A prime example would be the boundary that I had believed to exist between Early Music and Neoclassicism. When I came of age professionally in
the 1970s as a recorder and baroque flute player, there was a sense of a pioneering spirit, as if we were discovering the essence of music anew, and that the
performance practices we were developing for Early Music had nothing to do
with the conventional ones in the contemporary scene. On a certain level this
was, of course, true, but on another, we were unaware that we were basing this
new practice on the criteria of the conventional approach to music. While the
details of the specific interpretation may have been extraordinarily different,
the fundamental attitude behind the performance remained the same, perhaps
most pithily summed up by Igor Stravinsky when he wrote that "the idea of
execution implies the strict putting into effect of an explicit will that contains
nothing beyond what it specifically commands".[3] Thus, although the results of
the two approaches may have at times radically varied from one another, we
were using the same basic underlying set of criteria for judging all music. The
standards of objectivity, precision, and accuracy we associate with modernism
were being applied to music of earlier eras, even though we now – in particular through the internet – have abundant concrete evidence in the form of his-

---

3   Igor Stravinsky, *Poetics of Music in the Form of Six Lessons*, New York: Vintage Books 1947,
      127.

torical recordings that these standards were still perceived differently as late as the beginning of the 20th century.[4] Nevertheless the conviction gradually arose that the stylistic differences were so great, that musicians needed to decide between early and modern instruments, that it was impossible to play both at the highest standards, as the differences in performance practice were too great. This distinction, with great hubbub, was first called into question by Richard Taruskin in musicological circles, but its implications have yet to be truly understood.

This whole uproar, however, almost becomes irrelevant when we come to view the work of Ina Lohr as the musical assistant of Paul Sacher. On the one hand, she was helping in the preparation of the concerts of the Basel Chamber Orchestra, whose performances were devoted to those works which received little attention from the large orchestras, i.e. works of the early Classical era and before, as well as contemporary compositions for a small chamber orchestra. At the same time they were building up the Schola Cantorum Basiliensis together, now an internationally recognized school for Early Music. They were thus at the forefront of two of the most innovative fields of music in that period. Although original sources were studied in their preparation of early music, so that, for example, questions of instrumentation and ornamentation received new consideration, and Ina Lohr used them as a basis for her analysis and teaching, the basic aesthetic parameters for the century, objectivity and precision, were not called into question. Thus the surface appearance of the two styles differed, but the substrate remained the same.

Aesthetically – and not only in Early Music – the focal point for Ina Lohr lay elsewhere: in the question of function. She was convinced that because the earlier distinctions in functionality, between chamber and concert music on the one hand and between liturgical and concert music on the other, were being disregarded, in that both chamber and liturgical music had become part of the standard fare in the concert hall, that the link between the amateur and professional musician was endangered, with grave consequences on numerous fronts. The social aspect of chamber music, the confessional aspect of liturgical music were both being replaced by a professionalism which deprived the music of its original function. With the removal of chamber music from the realm of amateurs, an important bond with professional musicians was negated; with the ad-

---

4   Neal Peres da Costa, *Off the Record: Performing Practices in Romantic Piano Playing*, New York: Oxford University Press 2012, for example, presents a brilliant analysis of such differences in historical recordings of the piano.

vent of professional musicians in the church, the congregations were no longer being united by their common profession of their faith through music. She was concerned about the disintegration of these elements, seeing it as a cause for the weakening of public support in the modern concert world and of the active participation of the members of the congregation in the church. Thus – apart from her passionate interest in the music itself – in her exploration of the practical and theoretical sources, she was primarily seeking out means of bridging the gap between the amateur and professional, a completely different perspective from that of ours today.

I was also blind to the influence of confessional interests on the 20th-century practice of Early Music. Our practice of Gregorian chant is largely dependent on the battles won by the Benedictine monks of Solesmes, in particular Dom Joseph Pothier and Dom André Mocquereau, who by persuading the Vatican of their ideas in 1904, came to dominate the performance of chant through the omnipresence of their publications. But the same could also be said of the musical reform movements of the Protestant church in the beginning of the 20th century, which in the name not only of musical, but also theological purity, advocated changes in the performance of Johann Sebastian Bach's sacred works, with consequences that still resonate today.[5] Political and social movements also left their traces, from the *Jugendmusikbewegung*, to World War II, and the student protests of the late 1960s.[6] Due to the fact that of all of these trends, I myself was only involved with the protests, and that on a rather minor level – and as far as I was concerned they had no relationship to music – I was oblivious to all of these influences as well.

As a result of my research into a single person who was involved in many different movements, but perhaps paradoxically never really belonged to any, my way of looking at the Early Music movement has been totally revolutionized. I have had to abandon the idea that we were trying to recreate something historical, have gained an entirely new comprehension of the consequences of our inability to escape the culture in which we live. One of the side effects has

5   See Jed Wentz, "On the Protestant Roots of Gustav Leonhardt's Performance Style", in: *BACH: Journal of the Riemenschneider Bach Institute* 48–49, No. 2–1 (2018), 48–92.

6   See Anne Smith, "The Development of the *Jugendmusikbewegung*, its Musical Aesthetic and its Influence on the Performance Practice of Early Music" in: *Basler Beiträge zur Historischen Musikpraxis* 39 (2019), 465–508; and Kailan Rubinoff, "Authenticity as a Political Act: Straub-Huillet's Chronicle of Anna Magdalena Bach and the Post-War Bach Revival", in: *Music and Politics* 5, no. 1 (winter 2011), http://dx.doi.org/10.3998/mp.9460447.0005.103 (23 November 2019).

been that I have not only had to completely revise my understanding of the Early Music movement, but also my view of my role within it, however minor that may have been. This has been not only extraordinarily enriching, but also very liberating.

*   *   *

It cannot be denied that Ina Lohr would have undoubtedly led a different life if she had been a man, other doors would have been opened for her, given her abundance of talent and knowledge. Her music and ideas would have had a more open reception and there is no doubt in my mind that she would have attained a certain recognition as a composer. At the same time it must be acknowledged that her father, a true progressive, had insisted that she have such a broad and thorough education that, if needs be, she could support herself; thus her persona and upbringing were such – even if she did not go out and fight for her rights as a female – that she had no hesitation in insistently demanding that she, including all her ideas and her music, be accepted as an individual. Perhaps it was even because she was a woman that she was able to insidiously realize many of her almost revolutionary ideas concerning music's function. As she required peace and quiet in order to maintain her intense sense of identity, her life was a constant battle between the need of stimulation derived from active participation in the outside world, and of periods of retreat, where she could find herself again. Thus, in all she did, she was intent on maintaining her personal boundaries, while continually making forages in the world around her in search of enlightenment, both earthly and heavenly, and with the intent of changing the world for the better through her singing and teaching.

*   *   *

It is my hope that in this book some of the consequences of these far-ranging boundary shifts will become clear, both explicitly and implicitly, not only in the life of Ina Lohr, but also in the world of music as a whole, and also specifically in Early Music. First and foremost, however, *Ina Lohr: Transcending the Boundaries of Early Music* is intended to be a biography of a remarkable woman, one almost forgotten today, who unknowingly served as a link between various of the important musical movements of the first half of the 20th century.

The origins of the book go back to 2012, to a period where I – in this context somewhat paradoxically – was trying to redefine my own boundaries, my own interests, when Jed Wentz asked me whether I would co-author an article with him on Gustav Leonhardt's student years at the Schola Cantorum Basiliensis.[7] I, of course, saw this as an opportunity to practice saying no, and did so firmly, while at the same time offering to set up some interviews for him, as I knew the people with whom he would need to speak. I then went along on the interviews in order to facilitate the communication. The one with Christopher Schmidt – a fellow student of Leonhardt's as well as a later teacher of ear-training and Gregorian Chant at the Schola – was particularly interesting, or maybe overwhelming is a better word, in that he brought the whole period to life for us. What became crystal clear was that for the three professional students of that time period, Christopher Schmidt, Gustav Leonhardt, and David Kraehenbuehl (Yale University), it was not so much the school's main instrumental teachers (August Wenzinger and Eduard Müller) who captured their interest, but rather Ina Lohr, whose name I recognized as being one of those who, together with Paul Sacher, founded the Schola, but knew little about.

In all honesty, I must admit that I not only knew very little about her, but I also had some clear prejudices against her, based on remarks that I had absorbed from the walls of the school, both during my studies (1973–77) and my subsequent employment there. It is only now that I realize that I came to the Schola at a turning point in its history, at a time where there was a shift away from a focus on the cultivation of early music within amateur and church circles, to one devoted to raising its level of practice to that generally attained in the field of classical music as a whole, i.e. at a time when a new boundary was being established. As I came precisely at the point of change, I was completely unaware of what had gone on before. Needless to say, these ideological and structural changes caused a great deal of upheaval within the institution, most of which also passed me by. Furthermore, it must also be said that I was a product of my time and culture, wanting to distance myself from the standards of organizations such as the American Recorder Society and similar mass gatherings of amateurs in my desire to become a professional musician.

It was thus with a certain amount of surprise that I heard that three people of such penetrating musical ability and intellect had been so fascinated by Ina Lohr and what she had to offer, that they had spent their weekends preparing 15th-century music on two recorders and gamba for those special occasions when she joined them with her voice. Indeed it made me so curious that I began doing a little bit of research at the Paul Sacher Foundation where Ina Lohr's

---

7   In spite of originally saying no, it appeared under both of our names as "Gustav Maria Leonhardt in Basel. Portrait of a Young Harpsichordist", in: *Basler Jahrbuch für Historische Musikpraxis* 34 (2010 which was published in 2014), 229–44.

estate is located, ostensibly to find a bit more information about Gustav Leonhardt's connection with her. In actuality, however, I ended up surveying a large
portion of her estate. In the process I began to discover that she had not only
influenced him, but also Jan Boeke, Kees Vellekoop, Sven-Erik Bäck, and Eric
Ericson. This in turn caused me to read many of her articles and it was through
them I began realizing for the first time the degree to which our performance
practice of Renaissance music was affected by the aesthetic of the *Jugendmusikbewegung*, of the *Singbewegung*, at the beginning of the 20th century, rather than
by our knowledge of the theoretical treatises of the 16th century.

It was about at this point that I, together with Jeremy Llewellyn, Kelly
Landerkin and Jed Wentz, applied to the Swiss National Science Foundation
for a grant to study her life and work within the project "Ina Lohr (1903–
1983), an Early Music Zealot: Her Influence in Switzerland and the Netherlands" at the Schola Cantorum Basiliensis/University of Applied Sciences and
Arts FHNW. We were very fortunate to receive generous funding for our work
for the two-year period 2014–2016. What came to light through our research
with a particular clarity was how some of the specifically Dutch aspects of her
musical training – particularly in regard to the reform of sacred music, both
Catholic and Protestant – were taken to Switzerland, transformed and then
brought back to the Netherlands. In the course of this process, many national,
religious, stylistic, and chronological boundaries were transcended, or perhaps
just ignored, blurred or violated.

Indeed, I have come to realize that the choice of topic could not have been
more serendipitous. First of all, Ina Lohr was far more influential in Early Music than I had originally imagined, in that she seems to have been a link between various important strands of the movement. In addition, by looking at
this movement from the perspective of a single individual my field of vision was
expanded, forcing me to see it in relation to many other cultural tendencies and
phenomena of the 20th century. This has particular validity for Ina Lohr, due
to the above-mentioned link with Paul Sacher in regard to two prominent Basel musical institutions. In connection with this biography, I was the first person given permission to examine their complete correspondence, in which it
becomes clear that she played a highly influential role in the development of
the Basel Chamber Orchestra: she analyzed and marked up the scores, assisted
in the choice of program and soloists, helped rehearse the choir, and provided
general musical advice. Their relationship was at times contentious, in that
their goals were different, Paul Sacher's being the cultivation of music outside of
the mainstream for a chamber orchester in the concert world, whereas her main
focus lay in the praise of God through music wherever she was. No matter what

the issues, however, they found a way to move on, accomodating their working relationship to the new circumstances. Through this work, she also became
acquainted with many notable composers, such as Hindemith, Stravinsky or
Bartók, whose commissioned works were premiered by the orchestra. Thus she
was directly involved with both earlier and later repertoires, living evidence, if
you will, of the closeness of the practice of the two, obviating all need for Richard Taruskin's arguments. But beyond the musical realm, her religious convictions, her focus on the liturgical use of music in earlier centuries, her connections with the church both in Basel as well as in the Netherlands brought her
into contact with some of the foremost theologians of her time, such as Karl
Barth, Wilhelm Vischer, Ernst Gaugler, Gerardus van der Leeuw, and Kornelis Miskotte. Thus an evaluation of her life, of her work, necessitated examining Early Music not only in relation to the Modern Classic but also in relation
to other currents of the time, such as educational reform, the reform of church
music (in both the Catholic and Protestant churches), in addition to various
"modern" responses to Romantic music. Thus Early Music itself is not merely
seen from the point of view of reviving music from earlier eras, but also within
its progressive 20th-century context.

Not surprisingly, given all these connections, I discovered that Ina Lohr herself was a multifaceted, intensely creative individual. She had so many different capabilities and interests that she tended to deal with the world around her
in a compartmentalized fashion. When beginning my research on her, I was
worried that I would only find information about her Early Music contacts, as
she rarely spoke of her family with her professional acquaintances and friends,
or discussed her religious concerns with her musical colleagues, or displayed
her profound interest in *Hausmusik* with the professional students. But rather
each of those with whom I have spoken has automatically assumed that his or
her specific contact with Ina Lohr was that which was central to her life. It has
therefore been particularly gratifying to find certain documents, diaries, extant
correspondence with people very close to her, which have enabled me to build
up a more complete picture of the woman as a whole.

At a certain point in the process I became so overwhelmed by the sheer amount
of disparate information to be analyzed that I began to despair of bringing it
into some sort of cogent form. It was only after I realized that the structure of
the book must of necessity reflect that of her life, must in turn be compartmentalized, that the present order suggested itself. Thus it opens with a chapter on
her formative years in the Netherlands and the first few years in Basel in which
she continued her studies in music theory and composition, while simultane-

ously creating for herself the musical environment that would serve as a basis for all of her later professional activities. The sparse factual information that we have about Ina Lohr's childhood and education stems primarily from a few documents that she herself wrote in the last years of her life: she seems to have gone through a period – perhaps at the request of others – of reflecting upon the circumstances and decisions that led her to come to Basel and caused her to devote herself to the cultivation of vocal music of earlier centuries. I have, in addition, been extremely fortunate with the generosity of some of the descendents of the Lohr family. Not only have Aleid and Floris Zuidema, the executors of the estate of Ina's two sisters, Etty and Sally, placed many family photos and documents at my disposal, but also the historian, Elisabeth van Blankenstein, has been extraordinarily magnaminous in the assistance she has given me concerning the family background.[8]

The following two chapters concern her religious and musical convictions, examing so to speak, where she drew her boundaries, as these are the formative elements of her life. They thus constitute a basis upon which all the day-to-day activities of her professional life can thereafter be discussed in an ongoing narrative. Specifically, the second chapter is devoted to her religious beliefs, which were so central to her persona that it is difficult to understand many aspects of her professional work and career without this knowledge. In this connection, I have been fortunate to have access to her correspondence with two people to whom she turned for spiritual guidance, Ernst Gaugler (through the Paul Sacher Foundation) and Hinrich Stoevesandt (private access).

Her musical convictions are the focus of the third chapter. As with the religious beliefs, it is necessary to look at her musical beliefs in advance, as they are the source of many of her professional choices that are otherwise somewhat incomprehensible for musicians today. It is, for example, hard for us to understand why someone of her caliber of musicianship would prefer to work in the world of amateur music-making, when all the doors to the elite lay open to her. The source lay both in her background and inner needs, in her extreme religiosity and her difficulty in dealing with the emotional turbulence in the world around her. As her primary means of finding inner peace was through song, in particular to God, her musical values were strongly related to the fulfillment of this aspiration. An awareness of these factors enables us thereafter to examine her life both in regard to her own lights, as well as to ours.

8   Elisabeth van Blankenstein, *Dr. M. van Blankenstein: een Nederlandse Dagbladdiplomaat 1880–1964*, The Hague: Sdu Uitgevers 1999.

The subsequent five chapters deal with Ina Lohr's professional life: the first decade in Basel, in which her first experiences as Paul Sacher's assistant as well as the origins of the Schola Cantorum Basiliensis are chronicled; the war years characterized not only by the desolation in the world around her, but also by her internal existential battles which caused her increasingly to turn toward God, not only generally, but also in music; her heyday at the Schola, as it found its place on the map of the world; her final working years at the Schola; and lastly, old age. These periods, of course, were chosen because they represent turning points in Ina Lohr's life, when significant events or decisions affected the course of her activities. As the circumstances changed, both within and without, she came more and more to pursue a life that was in harmony with her goals. This means that over time, different interests received emphasis, which is also reflected in the chapter divisions. In covering the various facets of her work, an endeavor is made to discuss them within the context of the cultural developments in the world around her. It is only by this means that her significance in the world of Early Music can be made visible, that she can be validated in the context of her time; at the same time that context will of necessity also be re-evaluated, be seen within a larger whole.

As with all biographies, the story that one tells is related to the sources available. Thus while her work at the Schola Cantorum Basiliensis is documented primarily by printed texts, either the annual reports of the institution, or articles written by Ina Lohr herself, her cooperation with Paul Sacher is illuminated through their correspondence. This results in a different sort of coverage of the material, one which perhaps does not truly reflect the balance between various aspects of her life, between the more official and the more personal. This can never be known, just as we can never really know how another person ticks. In all cases, however, I have attempted to allow her to speak for herself, so that her views, her insights, her beliefs are not immediately colored by my interpretation of them, so that the reader is free to draw other conclusions than those I have come to in the process of my research. Unless otherwise indicated, all translations are my own.

Table 1: Genealogical Table

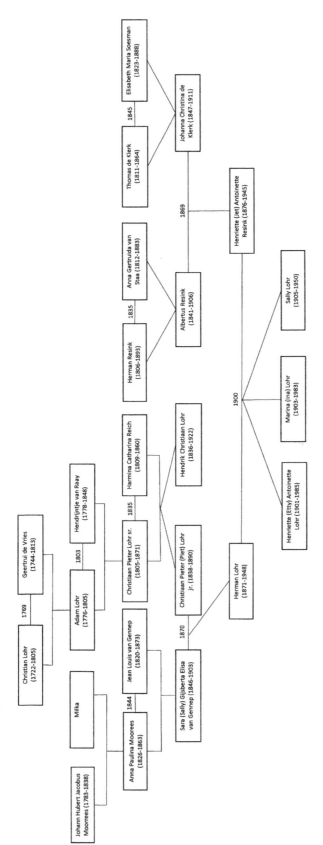

Chapter 1. Ina Lohr: Childhood and Education

1.1 Family and Childhood

It could almost be maintained that Ina Lohr transcended her first boundary more than a decade before she was born, in that she on some level must have vicariously experienced the exotic, culturally-mixed colonial environment in the Dutch East Indies (now Indonesia) where both of her parents, Henriëtte Antoinette (Jet) Resink (1876–1945) and Herman Lohr (1871–1948) spent their formative years.[1] Rob Nieuwenhuys evocatively described its laissez-faire tropical atmosphere as being

> the time of the flattering *sarong kabaja*, of private carriages with Sydneyers [an Australian breed of horse], of hour-long moonlight drives, of *nontonnen* [looking in at festivities as an outsider] in front of the theater called the "Concor[dia]", of fireworks, fountains and mirrors, of French and Italian operas, of big house parties, of gossip and card parties, of *krossie-males* [lounge chairs] and rocking chairs, of the *tong-tong* [a drum made out of a hollow tree trunk], of the *poekel boem* [a ship's time signal] and free gin in the hotels.[2]

Europeans who had been there, or grown up there, for the most part experienced greater freedoms, socially and economically than their peers in the Netherlands; they often participated in a higher class of society than their status in their "home country" would have warranted. Rob Nieuwenhuys also speaks of how

> each white man who came to Indië [the Dutch East Indies] underwent a process of transformation that made him a different person. Certain characteristics in him came to the top and had the possibility of development, others had to be suppressed; he distanced himself from prejudices, but he took on new ones; he almost always lost all illu-

---

1   For the following information concerning both families I am greatly indebted to Elisabeth van Blankenstein. Not only was she extraordinarily helpful in responding to specific questions, she also gave me much of the documentary material, including the genealogy and two of her New Year's letters, from 2012 and 2015 (each containing a nugget of family history). In addition, the entry for "Herman Lohr" by A.B.J. Teulings, in: *Biografisch Woordenboek Gelderland*, Hilversum: Verloren 2002, 94–97, proffers much information concerning Herman Lohr's professional career.

2   "de tijd van de flatteuze sarong kabaja, van eigen rijtuigen met Sydneyers, van het urenlang toeren in de maneschijn, van het 'nontonnen' voor de schouwburg of 'Concor[dia]', van Bengaals licht, fonteinen en spiegels, van Franse en Italiaanse opera's, van grote huisfuiven, van klets- en hombertafels, van de krossie-males en de wipstoelen, van de tong-tong, van poekoel boem en de gratis jenever in de hotels". Rob Nieuwenhuys, "Tempoe Deloe", in: *Tussen Twee Vaderlanden*, Amsterdam: G.A. van Oorschot Uitgever, 2nd edition, 1967, 5.

sion and attached himself increasingly to material things, in that money means power; he could establish himself socially in the Indonesian society and assert himself, [in a manner] which birth had never enabled him to do in Europe; he learned other ideas about the church and marriage, about divorce and living together, he began to apply other moral standards. One man became coarser in his doings, forgot his upbringing, the other polished his language and allowed himself a position of distinction, without being able to fully succeed in the one or the other; the first felt himself to be "sagging", the other felt himself to be rising, but both of them grew increasingly close to one another in the stereotypical "East Indies emigrant". When these East Indies emigrants came back to Holland, with a pension or on a leave in order to "chill out", only then did they notice how they were changed, that they no longer felt at home in the Dutch lifestyle. They felt themselves to be encaged between walls, they became sick of the gray light and even of the long-awaited snow, the "oedijan kapok" seemed merely to fall in order to make the bad atmosphere absolute. Then they thought about Java and about the magnet that according to many tales was hidden in the volcanoes; then they visited one another, at home, on the street and in the foyer of the opera; then they spoke again about promotion and salaries, government mistakes and scandals, about [the] East Indies which maintained its hold on them. They bore the unmistakable Indies "tjap" in their words and gestures, in attitude and appearance and though some did their best to speak quietly and to think differently, they were irrevocably changed, they had become "East Indian", a stereotype which furthermore first came into its own in the East Indies itself.[3]

---

3   "Elke totok die in Indië kwam werd onderworpen aan een omvormingsproces, dat een ander mens van hem makte. Bepaalde eigenschappen in hem kwamen naar boven en kregen de mogelijkheid tot ontplooiing, andere moesten worden onderdrukt; hij deed afstand van vooroordelen, maar hij kreeg er ook nieuwe bij; hij ontnuchterde bijna altijd en hechtte zich hoe langer hoe meer aan het materiële, omdat geld macht betekent; hij kon zich in de Indische samenleving maatschappelijk bevestigen en doen gelden, waar geboorte hem in Europa nooit toe in staat had gesteld; hij leerde andere opvattingen krijgen over kerk en huwelijk, over echtscheiding en samenleving, hij bogon andere morele maatstaven te hanteren. De ene verruwde in zijn doen en laten, vergat wat aan hem opgevoed was, de andere beschaafde zijn spraak en mat zich een houding van voornaamheid aan zonder in het een en ander ten volle te kunnen slagen; de ene voelde zich 'afzakken', de andere voelde zich stijgen, maar beiden groeiden naar elkaar toe in het type van de 'Indischgast'. Kwamen deze Indischgasten in Holland terug, met pensioen of met verlof om 'uit te vriezen', dan pas merkten ze hòe ze veranderd waren, dat ze niet meer thuishoorden in het Hollandse leven. Ze voelden zich beklemd tussen muren, ze werden ziek van de grijze luchten en zelfs de lang verwachte sneeuw, de 'oedijan kapok', scheen slechts te vallen om die nare stemming volledig te maken. Dan dachten ze aan Java en aan de magneet, die volgens veler zeggen in een der vulkanen verborgen moest zijn, dan zochten ze elkaar op, thuis, op straat of in de foyer van de opera, dan spraken ze weer over promotie en traktement, regeringsfouten en schandaaltjes, over Indië, dat hen blééf vasthouden. Ze droegen het onuitwisbaar Indisch 'tjap' in woord en gebaar, in houding en uiterlijk en al deden sommigen nog zo hun best zachter te spreken en anders te denken, ze waren onherroepelijk veranderd, ze waren 'Indischman' geworden, een type dat overigens eerst in Indië zelf tot zijn recht kwam". Rob Nieuwenhuys, "Tempoe Deloe", 32–33.

Thus her parents, who only came to the Netherlands in their adolescence, were among the sizable number of colonial returnees who, with their families, formed a recognizable subset of Dutch society.[4] Ina Lohr herself, to be sure, never experienced Dutch East Indian culture directly, but she must have been aware of her parents' efforts to come to terms with the differences between the cultures. And although her family – through her father's diligence, his education and professional capabilities – became a successful part of Dutch society, it was not without its emotional price.

Herman Lohr was the son of Christiaan Pieter Lohr (1838–1890) who had gone to work in Batavia – as Jakarta was called during the Dutch East Indies period – for the Nederlandsche Handel-Maatschappij (NHM) in 1860. In 1870 Christiaan Pieter Lohr married Sara (Sally) Gijsberta Elisa van Gennep, the oldest daughter of Jan Louis van Gennep, an influential member of the NHM factory there. He was transferred to Semarang in 1871 where their first of nine children, Herman, was born. In 1878 Christiaan Pieter Lohr was appointed the president of the Batavian NHM factory, the highest post attainable for an employee in Dutch East India, thus implying that his family possessed considerable wealth and standing. The family returned to Haarlem in 1886, where Herman Lohr first attended the Hogere Burgerschool before going to Delft in 1890 to study engineering at the University of Technology where he received his degree in 1895.

The family, in line with the society at the time, was well-versed in the arts, with all the children receiving musical instruction, as may be seen from a hand-written concert program of salon music in which the children were to show off their skills on various instruments, Herman on the zither and the mandolin. That he played this instrument is substantiated by Illustration 1.1, in which the family and friends have created a kind of *tableau vivant* on the staircase in front of their house in Haarlem. Herman is the mandolin player half-standing behind the guitarist in the foreground.

Another aspect of the consequences of the colonial experience in the Dutch East Indies is also evident in this image. Due to the fact that from the end of the 16th century until the middle of 19th century – with one exception of short duration in the 17th century – Dutch women were not allowed to emigrate to the Indies, Dutch men established various forms of alliances and marriages with lo-

---

4   A contemporary description of the life of such people, how they dealt with a society that was now foreign to them, may be found in Paul Adriaan Baum's novel, *Indische mensen in Holland*, first published serially in 1888 in Batavia, and later as a book in 1890, and as a modern edition Amsterdam: Em. Querido's Uitgeverij B.V. 1963.

Ill. 1.1: The Lohr family and friends in Haarlem. Photo: courtesy of Aleid and Floris Zuidema, Lochem.

cal women, the resulting children of necessity straddling the two cultures, both in regard to their skin color as well as their upbringing.[5] Thus a social network came into being in the East Indies which was based on the family connections of the young Eurasian brides who married Dutch men. This meant that outside of the administrative affairs, the social life in the East Indies was determined by the local culture; the children were brought up by Asian women, except for the boys who were often sent back to the Netherlands for schooling. The result of this, however, was that the Dutch in the East Indies were exposed to a far greater degree to the local culture, local beliefs, local ways than the English, for example, in India. It may be assumed that this was also the case in the Lohr family in that Herman's great-great-grandmother Milka Room was the indigenous concubine of Johan Hubert Jacobus Moorrees (1783–1838), whom he perhaps later married; in any case, he did legally acknowledge their children as being his own.[6] Her eldest daughter, Anna Paulina Moorrees (1826–1863) gave birth to Herman's mother Sara (Sally) Gijsberta Elisa van Gennep (see Ill. 1.2) in 1846.[7] However that may be, the photograph of family festivities in Haarlem poignantly captures the amalgamation of East Indian delight in such conviviality with the stricter Dutch formality, as evidenced by the elder members on the balcony. This was the context in which Ina Lohr grew up.

The image is perhaps also indicative of the creative streak that ran through the Lohr family. All of its members were highly intelligent, gifted individuals, brilliant in their professional fields or, in the case of the women, married to men who were. Many of them were, however, plagued by what was seen as depression and a certain constitutional weakness, often of the circulatory system. Herman Lohr attributed this to the fact that their father died so young:

5 Jean Gelman Taylor, *The Social World of Batavia: Europeans and Eurasians in Colonial Indonesia*, Madison WI: University of Wisconsin Press 2009², particularly Chapter 6, provides great insight into the cultural cross-currents within the colonial society.

6 Once again I am indepted to Elisabeth van Blankenstein for this information, confirmed by the document found online by André de Jong, "Kwartierstaat van Ing. Hugo, Gustaaf en Mr. Willem de Clercq", http://www.familiedeclercq.nl/fileadmin/declercq/Pdf-bestanden/Genealogie/Kwartierstaat_Willem_de_Clercq.pdf (27 April 2018), 3. De Jong suggests that Milka's last name "Room" may be simply an inversion of the first four letters of Moorrees. This was a common practice according to Rob Nieuwenhuys, who writes in *Tussen Twee Vaderlanden*, 20, that some of these children of East Indian concubines had inverted names of their father, such as "Rhemrev in plaats van Vermeer (of Vermehr), Kijdsmeir in plaats van Van Riemsdijk, Esreteip in plaats van Pieterse".

7 There may also be similar traces of East Indian heritage on the Resink side, but if so they are not documented.

Ill. 1.2: Portrait of Sara (Sally) Gijsberta Elisa van Gennep as a young woman, by Woodbury and Page, famous photographers in the colonial Dutch East Indies. Photo: courtesy of Elisabeth van Blankenstein, Leidschendam.

Later I often very much regretted this [death of my father at an early age], because it is only later that you feel what it is to lack a father in the difficult years of training for later socio-economic life. I am completely convinced that this lack of a 'father' at this time [was the source of the] development in all of us of that so strongly evident *apathy* (I am sorry that I have to use this word) that has slowly become a family trait (in the children!).[8]

He defines this apathy as a kind of floating through life without "thinking about *how* life must be led with greater care, in order to really accomplish our *whole* duty toward oneself as well as to others".[9] Further, Herman Lohr writes of a conversation in which a good friend's success is held to be a product of his father's consistently strict and demanding upbringing rather than that friend's

8 "Ik heb dit later vaak zeer berouwd omdat je later pas voelt wat het gemis van een vader is in die moeilijke jaren van vorming voor het later maatschappelijk leven. Ik ben vast overtuigd dat het gemis van een 'vader' in die tijd, in ons allen heeft ontwikkeld het zo sterk sprekende <u>apathische</u> (het spijt me dat ik dit woord noemen moet) dat langzamerhand een familietrek (in de kinderen!) is geworden". Letter of 15 November 1901 from Herman Lohr to Piet[er] Lohr (1879–1945). Letter in the Lohr Archive, Leidschendam, transcribed and placed at my disposal by Elisabeth van Blankenstein.

9 "nadenken <u>hoe</u> het leven met meer zorgen geleid moest worden, om werkelijk met volle ernst onze <u>volle</u> plicht te doen tegenover onszelf zoals tegenover anderen". Ibid.

formal education, obviously drawing the conclusion that the absence of this paternal solicitude in their own case was the source of the family trait. Today one might be inclined to suspect that this "apathy" was a form of dissociation related to the trauma of being uprooted from the environment in which they had grown up, of being transposed from the warmth of the East Indian island life to the colder, more straitlaced Dutch culture, rather than having its origins in a lack of self-discipline.[10] Indeed this process may have even begun earlier, even in the East Indies itself, during the course of the financial and social upheavals there in the second half of the 19th century: as concubines were increasingly frowned upon, the East Indian Europeans came to be dissociated from the general culture there.[11]

The occasion for this letter had been a conversation with Herman Lohr's mother, Sara van Gennep Lohr, who was worried about what would happen with her younger children upon her death, as she, unbeknownst to the family, had not undertaken the financial restructuring necessary after her husband died. Her eldest son had assured her that he would assume the responsibility of making sure that his younger siblings had the wherewithal necessary to complete their education upon her death and had written to communicate this necessity to his younger brother. As this letter was written in 1901, just after the birth of Herman Lohr's eldest daughter, Henriette (Etty), one can imagine the effect that this had, not only on his dealings with his siblings following his mother's death in 1903, but also on his attitude toward the upbringing of his own children. Indeed it led him to be active, perhaps even over-active, in supplementing and supervising his children's education.

Less is known about the Resink family.[12] Jet Resink's father (see Ill. 1.3a), Albertus (1841–1906), was the son of a confectioner who went to Jakarta as a lieutenant in the army. He was a civil engineer and set up his own company, A. Resink en Co., which serviced the machines required by the sugar industry as well as exporting supplies to the principalities. A freemason, he was one of the ten wealthiest men in Jakarta. He married Johanna Christina de Klerk (1847–1911, see Ill. 1.3b) in Jakarta in 1869, where all their children but the youngest son were born. This family, too, settled in Haarlem upon their return

---

10 I would like to thank Evelyne Laeuchli here for taking the time to discuss the psychological aspects of Ina Lohr's personality with me. It was invaluable to have her professional input and encouragement.

11 See Nieuwenhuys, *Tussen Twee Vaderlanden*, 19.

12 What little I have is from Christine M. Resink-van der Meer, who kindly answered an appeal to all of the Resinks in the Netherlands in the online telephone book, as well as from Elisabeth van Blankenstein.

Ill. 1.3a. and 1.3b: Albertus Resink (left) and Johanna Christina de Klerk [Resink] (right). Photos: Anonymous, Photo Collection RKD – Netherlands Institute for Art History, The Hague.

to the Netherlands in 1894. Albertus Resink joined a lodge there as well and was asked to become a member of the board of trustees of the Colonial Museum. The disposition of the family was liberally progressive with a well-developed interest in the arts. Indeed, Johanna Christina not only had a grand piano, but also played it well. This obviously was an influence on Jet, as like her mother, she was an accomplished pianist, attending the Amsterdam Conservatory, without, however, obtaining a degree in piano.[13] In the mid-1890s the family moved to Alexanderstraat 10, just around the corner from the Lohrs. It was no doubt this proximity which contributed to the marriage of Jet Resink and Herman Lohr in 1900.

In 1902 Herman and Jet Lohr moved to Amsterdam with their first daughter, Etty, where it is said that he had been named the assistant engineering director at the Gemeentelijke Electriciteits Werken. And it is there that Ina was born

---

13   The fact that she did not complete the degree is mentioned by Ina Lohr in a radio interview "Musik für einen Gast: Ina Lohr" on DRS1 on 30 November 1965, archive of Swiss Radio and Television.

Ill. 1.4: Jet Lohr (left) with her daughters Etty and
Ina and an unknown woman. Photo: courtesy of
Aleid and Floris Zuidema, Lochem.

on 1 August 1903 (see Ill. 1.4), a date that was perhaps an omen, as it is Switzerland's national holiday. The youngest child, Sally joined them two years later
in 1905. In 1907 the family moved to Nijmegen where Herman Lohr had taken
on the responsibility of building an electrical plant for the city. In 1915 he became the director of the N.V. Provinciale Geldersche Electriciteits-Maatschap-
pij (PGEM) in Arnhem, thereby assuming the job of overseeing the electrifica-
tion of the entire province of Gelderland. Thus Ina Lohr's childhood was largely
spent in Nijmegen and Arnhem.

In both of these cities the family lived in the apartments for the director
within the complex of the corporation for which her father worked, which were
located on the Waal in Nijmegen (see Ill. 1.5) and on the Lower Rhine in Arnhem (see Ill. 1.6 and 1.7). In each case the view from the windows of the apartments onto the open fields on the other side of the rivers must have been spectacular. The peaceful expansiveness of the Dutch landscape was something that
Ina Lohr later missed in Switzerland.[14]

14   Letter Ina Lohr to Paul Sacher of 29 July 1932, private collection, Switzerland.

Fig. 6. Oostgevel, rechts de directeurs-woning.

Ill. 1.5: PGEM Nijmegen, the director's apartment is on the right. Photo: PSF-ILC.

Although we only have photos of the interior of the family home from a later period, years after Ina Lohr had left the Netherlands, they give an impression of what her environment in her early life must have been like (see Ill. 1.8 and 1.9). In them one sees a rich concatenation of styles and periods. The dark wainscoting, no doubt that from a small synagogue in Prague referred to in Judith Schmitz's memoirs,[15] allied with the wall tapestries and heavy velvet drapes, serve as a background not only for European paintings and works of art from the 16th through the 20th centuries, but also for No masks, chinoiserie and the cupboard full of large, leather-bound books. The freedom with which Asian and European works of art are juxtaposed with one another exemplifies the influence of the colonial experience in the Dutch East Indies on those that returned to the Netherlands.

Ina Lohr sang before she spoke, and remembers her mother singing with her three daughters all day long.[16] It is no doubt due in part to this that she de-

---

15 Memoirs of Judith Schmitz, Elisabeth van Blankenstein's father's sister, written for her children, 154. Lohr Archive, Leidschendam, in the hands of Elisabeth van Blankenstein.

16 From a first version of a text for 27 September 1978 at a program for her 75th birthday, organized by Arthur Eglin in conjunction with the *Oekumenischer Singkreis Basel-Riehen* and the *Stadtposaunenchor Basel*. Many thanks to Arthur Eglin for making all of his documents related to Ina Lohr available to me for this book.

Ill. 1.6 and 1.7: PGEM Arnhem, the Lohr family's apartment was on the top floor. Photos: PSF-ILC.

Ill. 1.8: Interior of the Lohr family home in Haarlem, 1943. Photo: courtesy of Aleid and Floris Zuidema, Lochem.

veloped absolute pitch, even to the degree of being able to differentiate the micro-intervals that her mother used in singing songs from the East Indies.[17] Indeed, singing became her primary mode of expression to the degree that, as she told Elisabeth Stoevesandt, she had not spoken for the first four years of her life. Apparently once when guests had been invited over and were seated at the table, and she was sitting off to the side playing, her mother remarked that they also had "their Ina", who unfortunately could not talk. And then "their Ina" spoke up, saying: "Ina can talk. Ina does not want to talk".[18] This choice of mutism is not only a sign of her great inner willpower, already evincing itself at an early age, but also reflects the necessity she experienced of encapsulating herself from the rest of the world, creating a bubble where she could maintain her own sense of self. It was a battle that she waged for the rest of her life.

Writing in 1958, Ina Lohr speaks of how "the source of the art song lies in singing speech that should remain part of children's experience. Almost every child expresses itself in a singsong manner [*singelt*] as long as he or she is small,

---

17 Interview "Musik für einen Gast: Ina Lohr" on DRS1.
18 Interview with Elisabeth Stoevesandt, 15 January 2015.

Ill. 1.9: Interior of the Lohr family home in Haarlem, 1943. Photo: courtesy of Aleid and Floris Zuidema, Lochem. The portrait above the fireplace is of Sally Lohr, painted by Sierk Schröder (1903–2002).

primarily then when playing alone".[19] This was certainly her own experience – and maybe that was also a source of the late development of her language skills – as in her autobiographical sketch, she writes that although she was a sickly child, she sang all the time, not only children's songs, but fragments of things that she had heard or created. If it became disturbing,

> one sent me with my younger sister, who patiently bore everything, to our dollhouse, where the singing then somehow began being in two parts, and where the more than twenty dolls listened to us benevolently.[20]

Thus at a very early age singing became a mode of expressing herself, perhaps comforting herself, enabling her to give voice to emotions she did not know how to put into words. Its importance to her is exemplified by her answer to a guest who asked her when she was five years old what she wanted to become. Her answer, which came like "a pistol shot", was that she would "make music the whole day or [become] a mother in an orphanage or have twenty children of my own".[21] This in turn may be interpreted as an unspoken expression of her own need of mothering. In this context her choice of music would also make sense, in that it was also where her own mother turned for solace.

Ina Lohr also speaks of how the only way she could successfully "recite" the children's verses she had to learn by heart in school was by singing them. This was more or less accepted there until she was 15 years old when she had to learn Schiller's *Das Lied von der Glocke* as a disciplinary measure. She reports that she memorized the numerous strophes of the poem with varying melodies depending on their content. This first produced astonishment and then such merriment in the class that the teacher decided to let her off the hook. She writes, however, that an illusion was destroyed and her "free singing" was silenced.[22]

---

19 "Und doch liegt die Ursache auch des Kunstgesanges im einfachen singenden Sagen, das den Kindern vertraut bleiben sollte. Fast jedes 'singelt', solange es klein ist, vor allem dann, wenn es allein spielt". Ina Lohr, "Musik aus der Sprache, Musik aus dem Spiel", in: *Singt und spielt* 25 (1958), 67.

20 "schickte man mich mit meiner alles duldenden jüngeren Schwester in unsere Puppen-stube, wo der Gesang dann irgendwie zweistimmig wurde, und wo uns die mehr als zwan-zig Puppenkinder wohlwollend zuhörten". Ina Lohr, "Skizze zum Lebenslauf", 1; Vera Oeri Bibliothek, Basel, Rara Sign. MAB Fb182.

21 "Die Antwort sei [...] wie ein Pistonlenschuss gekommen: Ich werde den ganzen Tag Musik machen oder Mutter in einem Waisenhaus sein oder zwanzig eigene Kinder haben". Ibid., 1.

22 Ibid., 1.

The significance of this emphasis on singing at the beginning of her auto-biographical sketch – written just a year or so before she died – on an innate connection between words and melody cannot be underestimated, as it was an intrinsic part of her attitude towards life, of how she coped with it, as well as of her belief structures; in addition, it served as the foundation of what was to become her profession. Her musical development, however, was also encouraged in other ways within the family home. As she was often ill as a child, her parents did not acquiesce to her desire to play the violin until relatively late. To tide her over this period, her father created an instrument for her from a cigar box, strung with tunable mandolin strings. She spent hours with this instrument searching out accompaniments to her improvised songs, which as she wrote may have been "very primitive, but as [an] expression were authentic and therefore right".[23]

Furthermore in her early years, her parents introduced their children to opera by performing individual scenes from Gounod's *Faust* on mandolin and piano with great verve. In 1912 things changed dramatically, however, when Herman Lohr purchased their first gramophone (see Illustration 10 showing him with one of his later treasured machines for audio reproduction). In his hands it became not only a source of pleasure to the family, but also an extraordinarily effective didactic tool in the musical education of his children. For example, before they were allowed to listen to the first operatic arias, he gave them a summary of the plot of the entire opera as well as a translation of the text in language suitable for children. They then listened to the arias over and over again until they possessed them, had made them their own; they devoured the photographs of the singers and composers, and the liner notes. Ina Lohr even described Marcella Sembrich, Frieda Hempel, Enrico Caruso and Antonio Scotti as being their "first, very patient music teachers, from whom we imitated everything they sang with conscientious exactitude, so that no portamento, no sob, no fermata with tremolo was overlooked".[24]

After that, of course, came Wagner, by means of which they learned their first German by repeating the texts out loud. In addition, they had to learn all

---

23 "die auch sehr primitiv, als Aeusserung aber echt und deshalb richtig waren". Ina Lohr, "Gedanken zum Musizieren in der Freiheit", in: *Basler Nachrichten* 111, Nr. 64, 11 February 1955.

24 "Sie waren unsere ersten, sehr geduldigen Musiklehrer, denen wir alles nachsangen, und zwar mit gewissenhafter Genauigkeit, so dass kein Portamento, kein Schluchzer, keine Fermate mit Tremolo verloren ging". Ina Lohr, "Das Grammophon als Erzieher", in: *Basler Nachrichten* 110, Nr. 494/5, 20–21 November 1954. The description in the following paragraphs of what they learned from recordings is all taken from this article.

Ill. 1.10: Herman Lohr with a later version of his gramophone. Photo: courtesy of Aleid and Floris Zuidema, Lochem.

of the *leitmotiv*'s by heart before they could listen to the recordings, even discussing and being quizzed upon them at the family dining table.[25] The children then, of their own accord, reenacted scenes from the *Meistersinger* in the attic, in particular getting great pleasure from the aria "Wahn, Wahn, überall Wahn" which they sang with their high soprano voices. At that time, Ina Lohr was already concerned with the expression of the text, and as they were unable to achieve the change of timbre she deemed necessary for the phrase "der Frühling [Flieder] war's, Johannisnacht" with their light voices, she convinced her younger sister to lengthen the accented syllable of its last word to "Johaaaaaanisnacht". Their father heard this and felt it then necessary to explain that this was unacceptable, that one was not allowed to alter the rhythm arbitrarily. They were then required to conduct the recordings for awhile until they had acquired a conscious understanding of meter. It was thus with a sense of liberation that she discovered Gregorian chant in her first year of study at the Muziek-Lyceum Amsterdam, in that she was no longer constrained by a regular meter. This, too, was something she could then share with her parents by means of recordings from Solesmes and Beuron.

The gramophone also came to her aid with the violin. She was perfectly happy to practice exercises to reach her goal, but intensely disliked the "character pieces" she was required to learn; she would have preferred improvising, seeking out her favorite opera arias on her violin, rather than playing notated pieces. At the time, however, this was frowned upon by both her teacher and her parents. When her father brought home recordings of Bach and Mozart by Henri Marteau, Fritz Kreisler and Carl Flesch, however, a new world revealed its treasures to her.

She writes that Bach then became "an almost tyrannical friend of the family". Her mother began studying the suites and some of the Well-Tempered Clavier, her sister practiced the small preludes and together with their mother on the piano they sang from Schemelli's *Geistliche Lieder und Arien*. If their mother could not accompany them, they then "improvised" a second vocal part to the songs. Improvised two- and three-part singing became a normal accompaniment of their daily tasks. Thereafter her mother sang Mendelssohn, Abt, and Schumann duets with them, and followed this up with four-part vocal works by Palestrina and other composers of the 16th century. Elsewhere she

---

25 The detail of the discussions at the dining table is taken from the interview "Musik für einen Gast: Ina Lohr" on DRS1.

laughingly remarked on how they, as women, also enjoyed singing the works for men's choir by the Russian composer Dimtry Bortniansky.[26]

As their taste and knowledge expanded, her father put together Sunday evening "concerts", which included not only the obligatory Mozart D major violin concerto, but also *Lieder*, even some by Strauss, and an exploration of works by Debussy, Fauré, and Duparc. They listened to Bruckner and Mahler with the score in their hands. And almost daily they not only listened to a string quartet, but also discussed it, with Herman Lohr persistently asking questions until they could describe in words was was taking place in the piece.[27] It was an unparalleled form of musical education. Given this background, it is no surprise that she decided to pursue music as a profession.

At the same time she was making these musical discoveries, she was, of course, also attending school. Her secondary education took place in Arnhem. She makes particular reference to the pleasure she took in the literature of four different languages, presumably German, French and English, as well as the self-evident Dutch. In the evenings and on Sundays the children not only devoted time to listening to music, but also – sitting around the fire in low chairs specially constructed for them – to the literature their father read aloud to them.[28] In addition, they were taught how to look at paintings and other works of art. In this Herman Lohr was equally dedicated to being a thorough and good teacher, as can be seen by the lectures he wrote on Käthe Kollwitz and on Japanese woodcuts for a general audience.[29] All this was supplemented by frequent visits to Amsterdam for larger concerts and museum exhibitions. She writes that they had a "very full, very happy childhood, which defined our lives".[30] The serious beauty in the expression of all members of the family in

---

26 Interview Ina Lohr with Jos Leussink, 24–25 March, 1983. I first received cassettes with this interview from Henk van Benthem; later Jos Leussink gave me a digital remastering of the original interview, which is now found in the Vera Oeri Bibliothek, Musik-Akademie Basel, Ina Lohr Collection. I wish here to not only thank Henk van Benthem for making me aware of the interview through his gift of the cassettes, but also Albert Jan Becking for his transcription of excerpts from interview.

27 Interview "Musik für einen Gast: Ina Lohr" on DRS1.

28 Interview with Bettina Wehrli, 13 September 2014.

29 "Käthe Kollwitz", lecture for the Dinsdagavondgezelschap in Haarlem, 21 May 1946, from the Lohr Archive, Leidschendam, in the hands of Elisabeth van Blankenstien; and "Inleiding tot de bezichtiging van een collectie japansche houtsneden", lecture September, 1926, Nr. 2041 in the archive of the Broese van Groenou family in The Hague's Gemeentearchief.

30 "reich befrachtete, sehr schöne Jugend, die unser Leben bestimmt hat". Ina Lohr, "Skizze zum Lebenslauf", 2.

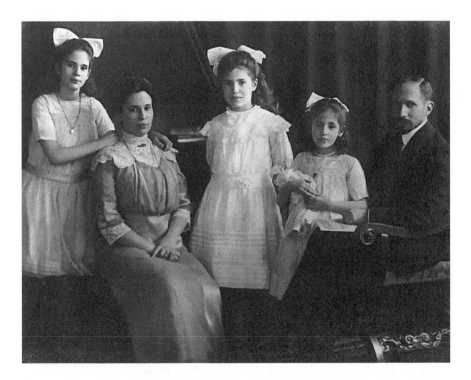

Ill. 1.11: The Lohr family: Etty, Jet, Ina, Sally and Herman (from left to right), 12 January 1913. Photo: courtesy of Aleid and Floris Zuidema, Lochem.

Illustration 1.11, portrayed in front of the piano, representing the importance of music and the arts to the parents, gives an indication of what the Lohr family life might have been like.

The care that Herman and Jet Lohr devoted to the upbringing of their children was exceptional and – partnered with their obvious love – fostered extraordinarily close familial bonds. This can be perceived in various ways. On the one hand it created an intellectually and culturally rich bastion within which the children received boundless support and attention; on the other, it was coupled with Herman Lohr's desire, based on his conviction that his father's early death was the cause of his family's "apathy", to see his children equipped with all the mental and spiritual self-discipline necessary to be successful in the outside world, to be able "to do their duty towards themselves, as well as to others".[31] But it also burdened the children with the obligation of attaining the goals or dreams that their parents had for them, with their success in doing so

31 "om werkelijk met volle ernst onze <u>volle</u> plicht te doen tegenover onszelf zoals tegenover anderen." Letter Herman Lohr to Piet[er] Lohr (1879–1945) of 15 November 1901, courtesy of Elisabeth van Blankenstein.

being felt in some measure to be an indication of their worthiness of this expression of parental love.

Concretely this meant that Etty Lohr had to give up her desire to become an artist and instead study medicine, a field that also interested her, as "she did not have a brother who could support her later".[32] She went on to become a highly successful doctor, opening her own practice in Amsterdam, and later taking on a job as a cardiologist at the hospital of the University of Utrecht, someone the family turned to when no other doctor could offer any hope. This, however, was also a source of great inner conflict for her in those cases where there was nothing that she could do, especially when those she loved were concerned, such as her younger sister Sally Lohr. Her sibling suffered from tuberculosis for the last fifteen years of her life; at that time there was no known cure for it. She had studied art (as she had an older sister who could support her), and was apparently just beginning to have some success in the field when she became sick while visiting Etty Lohr in Switzerland, who herself had gone there to rid herself of the tuberculosis she had picked up in her residency in Groningen. Sally Lohr later lived with her parents and, following their deaths, with her eldest sister; during these years, her sickroom was organized in such a way that she could continue with her artwork within the limits of her illness.

Ina Lohr, on the other hand, was expected to become a professional violinist. Shortly after completing her secondary schooling, however, she was forced to postpone her plans to study music for a year and a half due to a serious illness.[33] Toward the end of her life, she told close friends that she had had a hysterectomy due to a fibroid tumor and that she as a result had had to give up any ideas of marrying, of having children.[34] Although fibroid tumors in young females are still a rarity today, it is nonetheless clear that such an operation must have been an enormous shock to her system, not only seriously deranging her hormonal development and balance, but also impacting her emotional state, her sense of self. It is only in a letter of 11 March 1942 to Paul Sacher that she reveals the degree to which this operation affected her, determined her path. In it she speaks first of what is common knowledge, namely that she was sympathetic to the concerns of others, before going on to describe the further consequences of this long period of illness:

---

32 "Zíj had geen broer die haar later zou kunnen onderhouden!" Memoirs of Judith Schmitz, 165.
33 Ina Lohr, "Skizze zum Lebenslauf", 2.
34 Interviews with Bettina Wehrli 13 September, 2014; with Christin Wehrli 28 November 2014.

[Now] I not only have to listen and help when people pour out their hearts to me, but also complete strangers can deposit their sorrow with me without wanting to. It can happen that I am walking through the city and suddenly somebody looks at me and I know all their troubles and must carry them. I know no details nor the reasons behind it; only the dull feeling of a pain is there and presses upon me. Already as a child I was very "compassionate" [in the etymological sense of the word, as "mitleidig" in German means sharing someone else's pain]; this idiosyncrasy only became significant at the time I was seriously ill at the age of 19 years. When I once again moved among people, I always saw what lay behind them, and for a long time I was afraid and one also avoided me because I was so strange. I could not speak about this, I endured it like a disgrace and like an illness, which would perhaps make me go mad. The Bible helped me there, but I had too little understanding of its language. My salvation at first only lay in music.[35]

Even in her sickbed, music was her consolation, as is evident from her autobiographical sketch, where she writes that

During this time I was never without music, even when I could not play for months at a time. [...] I had a machine [gramophone] next to my bed and listened to string quartets of Haydn, Mozart and Beethoven, which I could follow in Eulenberg scores. Bach's *Matthew Passion* always lay in reach.[36]

Music was thus from her earliest years, in her earliest memories, her source of comfort, her mode of expressing herself. It is just this sense of unquestionable unity of person and musical expression which fascinated those around her in later years.

35 "Ich muss nicht nur zuhören und helfen, wenn die Menschen mir ihr Herz ausschütten, sondern auch wildfremde Leute können mir ihr Elend anhängen, ohne dass sie es wollen. Es kommt vor, dass ich durch die Stadt gehe und plötzlich schaut mich jemand an und ich weiss seinen ganzen Kummer und muss ihn tragen. Ich weiss keine Tatsachen und keinen Grund, nur das dumpfe Gefühl von einem Schmerz ist da und drückt mich. Schon als Kind war ich sehr 'mitleidig', entscheidend wurde dann diese Eigenschaft, als ich mit 19 Jahren schwer krank war. Als ich da wieder unter Menschen kam, sah ich immer, was hinter ihnen stand und ich war lange Zeit erschrocken und man scheute sich auch vor mir, weil ich so fremd war. Ich konnte nicht darüber reden, trug es wie eine Schande und wie eine Krankheit, die mich vielleicht verrückt machen würde. Die Bibel half schon da, aber ich verstand ihre Sprache zu wenig. Meine Rettung war zunächst nur die Musik". Letter Ina Lohr to Paul Sacher of 11 March 1942, private collection, Switzerland.
36 "Während dieser Zeit war ich nie ohne Musik, auch wenn ich monatelang nicht spielen konnte. [...] neben meinem Bett hatte ich einen Apparat und hörte Streichquartette von Haydn, Mozart und Beethoven, die ich aus Eulenburg-Partituren mitlesen konnte. Bachs Matthäuspassion lag immer in erreichbarer Nähe". Ina Lohr, "Skizze zum Lebenslauf", 2.

1.2 Ina Lohr's Studies at the Muziek-Lyceum Amsterdam

Given her background, the all-encompassing nature of her education in music, art and literature, it is not surprising that she decided that she should attend the progressive Muziek-Lyceum in Amsterdam which had opened its doors in 1921 rather than going to the more traditional Conservatory.[37] She later said that someone had told her that "they were stuck at the Conservatory", and used worn-out methods, that she should be someplace where her own thinking was stimulated.[38] The moving force behind the Muziek-Lyceum's inception was the cellist Eugène Calkoen (1881–1947, see Illustration 1.12), who was dissatisfied with the prevailing conditions at the Amsterdam Conservatory where he was then teaching. Under the regime of the pianist Julius Röntgen, who was its director from 1913–1924, there was no sense of community and little possibility for individual teachers to have any influence on the structure and content of the program of study. In addition, there was a lack of awareness of the necessity of giving instruction in anything beyond the mere technical facility required to execute a piece of music.[39]

Calkoen gathered together a group of idealistic musicians and sponsors in an association whose objective was to create a new form of music education. His ambitious educational ideals were revealed in its first prospectus, an educational manifesto of the first degree. As its ideology informed Ina Lohr's approach to music, it is important to examine it in greater detail. The association had, namely,

> set itself the task of educating not only good musicians but also a musically developed general public, and wishes to reach this goal by starting from principles which are directed towards a harmonic link between technical education and inward development.[40]

---

37 Jo Juda, concertmaster of the Concertgebouw Orchestra from 1963–74, writes in his autobiography, *De zon stond nog laag*, Nieuwkoop: Uitgeverij Heuff 1975, 146, that "his parents had heard, however, that one taught in a more modern way at the Muziek Lyceum". "Mijn ouders hadden echter gehoord dat er op het Muziek Lyceum op meer moderne wijze werd lesgegeven".

38 Interview Ina Lohr with Jos Leussink, 24–25 March 1983.

39 Rutger Schoute, *Het Muzieklyceum 1921–1976: een terugblik*, Hilversum: [without publisher] 1976, 14–15.

40 "Zij stelt zich tot taak, zoowel goede toonkunstenaars als een muzikaal ontwikkeld publiek te vormen, en wil dit doel bereiken, door uit te gaan van beginselen, die gericht zijn op een harmonisch verband tusschen technische vorming en innerlijke ontwikkeling". *Muziek-Lyceum*, prospectus of 1921, 4, Staatsarchief Amsterdam, 1079/56.

Ill. 1.12: Eugène Calkoen, presumably supervising some sort of (entrance?) exam. Photo: Amsterdam City Archives: Archive of the Vereniging Muzieklyceum.

Further, these principles

> should in all respects take into account the demands of a serious musical practice which is completely directed towards oneself. Our attitude sees the technical and music theoretical education of the future musician as something undoubtedly necessary, in addition to good instruction in the practice of an instrument for a talented dilettante, and does not want to neglect in any respect the one or the other: but most of all, it wants to direct its attention to the spiritual [*geestlijke*] and aesthetic education as a basis for an artistic development; the one and the other in direct connection to the natural talent and the spiritual needs of each particular individual.[41]

Thus, the Muziek-Lyceum intended to not only educate the ongoing professional in a far more complete manner than the current system allowed, it was

41 "die in alle opzichten rekening houden met de eischen van een ernstige muziekbeoefening welke geheel op het innerlijk is gericht. Onze instelling beschouwt de technische en muziek-theoretische vorming van den aanstaanden toonkunstenaar zeker als iets noodzakelijks, evenals goed onderwijs in de beoefening van een instrument voor den begaafden dilettant, en wil noch het eene, noch het andere, in welk opzicht ook, verwaarloozen: doch vóór alles wil zij het oog gericht houden op de geestelijke en aesthetische vorming, als basis voor een artistieke ontwikkeling: één en ander in onmiddelijk verband met de natuurlijke begaafdheid en de geestelijke behoeften van ieder individu afzonderlijk." Ibid., 10.

also fired by the desire to widen and deepen the cultural base for music within Dutch society as a whole, seeing it as a necessary part of general education.

The emphasis on the spiritual aspects of the teaching and appreciation of music is in line with the reaction at the end of the 19th century and the beginning of the 20th against what was perceived as Romantic excesses in performance. This attitude manifested itself with particular vehemence in both the Netherlands, as well as in German-speaking countries (see Chapter 4 on Ina Lohr's own musical aesthetic), and is, in turn, reflected by the idea(l)s found in the prospectus. It is likely that the formulation of the prospectus was influenced by one of the Muziek-Lyceum's first teachers, Herman Rutters (1879–1961), a musicologist, pedagogue and music critic who through his reviews in the Amsterdam *Algemeen Handelsblad* waged a continuous and influential battle for musical purity.[42]

The almost religious nature of this search for purity is revealed by the final section of the prospectus on "Religion and Philosophy", where their role in the development of future musicians is discussed. In it, the 19th century was seen as being directed toward the precise perception of reality, toward objectivity, to a degree that this "passion for reality" conquered the arts and sciences.

> But now we realize once again that the human consciousness is only human in its entirety when it has been consecrated and deepened by synthetic reasoning. Now we once again realize that it does not benefit man to discover the world, unless he also discovers himself in the central, cosmic sense, through the diversity of the world. The Socratic call to self-reflection rages again through the lonely mind with new clarity and new force. The call is not without danger. If the professional study can no longer be said to be the only salvation, the powerful sense of reality that we received from the 19th century as a precious inheritance threatens to dissipate again into unhealthy dilettantism. It is, therefore, in all truth a spiritual "demand of our time" *to link daily professional studies with philosophic and religious reflection*, and to do so [in such a manner] that this does not remain *adjacent* to the professional studies, but penetrates, deepens and purifies all professional studies as "the centrality of consciousness".
>
> This centralization will naturally first be possible at institutions for instruction in *art*. Whilst a scientific field still has "practical use" without all reflection on life, an artistic field degenerates to a gymnastic [exercise] without this reflection on life, which only results in soulless skill, with neither practical use nor living beauty.[43]

---

42 Cf. Jed Wentz, "H.R. and the Formation of an Early Music Aesthetic in The Netherlands (1916–1921)", www.forschung.schola-cantorum-basiliensis.ch/de/forschung/ina-lohr-project/rutters-and-the-early-music-aesthetic.html (4 February 2020).

43 "Maar thans gaan wij toch weer beseffen, dat het menschelijk bewustzijn eerst vòlmenschelijk is, als het gewijd wordt en verdiept in synthetische gedachten. Thans gaan we weer beseffen, dat het den mensch niet baat, de wereld te ontdekken, tenzij hij met de veelheid der wereld ook zichzelf ontdekt in centraal-kosmisch inzicht. De Socratische roep om zelf-bezinning woedt weer met nieuwe duidelijkheid en nieuwe kracht door de vereenzaamde

Thus the Muziek-Lyceum saw itself as an institution on the forefront of educational and spiritual reform, was highly idealistic in nature, creating new pedagogical structures to attain their goals.[44] Not unsurprisingly this remained a private initiative for many years with charitable donations covering fees for those who could not afford tuition, and with teachers willing to accept lower rates of pay for the satisfaction of teaching at a school where the concept of a complete musical education was paramount. And it is because of the high quality of the musicians associated with it – many of them also playing in the Concertgebouw Orchestra – that it quickly gained an influential position in the musical world of Amsterdam.

This, then, was the school that Ina Lohr attended – entering in the second year of its existence[45] in 1922 or 1923 – one that complemented the esteem with which the arts were regarded within her family. In order to attend it, she had to pass a stringent entrance exam. Beyond having a good general education, she had to demonstrate that her general musical development was sufficient for the school's requirements. In ear-training she was expected to be at home in various keys and meters, have an understanding of the use of clefs, use her organs for respiration and speech well, and know something about the art of performance and phrasing. This was to be tested by:[46]

> gedachten. Zonder gevaar is die roepstem niet. Als de vakstudie niet meer het alleen zaligmakende mag heeten, dreigt het krachtige werkelijkheidsbesef, dat we van de 19de eeuw als kostbare erfenis ontvingen, weer te vervluchtigen in ongezond dilettantisme. 't Is daarom in alle waarheid een geestelijke 'eisch van onzen tijd' *degelijke vakstudie te verbinden met wijsgeerige en religieuze bezinning*, en wel zóó, dat deze niet *naast* de vakstudie blijft, maar als 'centraliteit van bewustzijn' alle vakstudie doordringt, verdiept en verpuurt.
>   Deze centraliseering zal uiteraard het eerst mogelijk zijn bij inrichtingen voor *kunst*onderwijs. Heeft een weteschappelijk vak nog 'praktisch nut' buiten alle levensbezinning om, een kunstvak ontaardt buiten die levensbezinning tot een gymnastiek, die maar ziellooze vaardigheid geeft, zoowel zonder practisch nut als zonder levende schoonheid". *Muziek-Lyceum*, prospectus of 1921, 39.

44 Emblematic for his insistence on this approach is the fact that Calkoen loaned Jo Juda several works by two authors on spiritual and philosophic subjects, Jiddu Krishnamurti and Mathieu Hubertus Josephus Schoenmaekers. Jo Juda, *De zon stond nog laag*, 157.

45 This is the date given by Ina Lohr in an interview with Jos Leussink in 1983. Although in her autobiographical sketch (1981) her training may be understood to have only encompassed two years, 1927–29, this seems unlikely given her knowledge and capabilities by the time she arrived in Basel. Furthermore, in addition to the interview with Jos Leussink, on another cassette tape documenting her memories of "Die Entstehung der Schola Cantorum Basiliensis" (1980), she speaks of having studied several years in Amsterdam, PSF-ILC, CD 4.

46 The following information is found in *Muziek-Lyceum*, prospectus of 1921, 19–21.

1. the accurate singing of scales, intervals and chords (triads and dominant seventh chords with their inversions);
2. the notation, singing and also transposition of one-part dictations of medium difficulty from Lucien Grandjany's *500 dictées graduées* (Paris, 1892);
3. the rhythmical reading and beating of the measure in exercises from Hugo Riemann's *Kathechismus des Musikdiktats* (Leipzig, 1889);
4. the demonstration of ease in the notation of well-known folksongs in c-clefs and the playing of the easiest two-part exercises from Franz Wüllner's *Chorübungen der Münchener Musikschule*, vol. II (Munich, 1877);
5. the sight-singing of a second part, for example Dutch canons, or of one of the two-part songs and cantatas from Angelo Bertalotti's *Solfeggi a Canto e Alto* (Bologna, 1744);
6. the demonstration of knowledge of the most frequently used musical terms.

In harmony, she was expected to be able to make very simple harmonic connections both in writing, and more importantly on the piano, as well as to be able to make harmonic sense of a simple melody.

On the piano she would have to have been able to play all scales, as well as short and long arpeggios, demonstrate that she had thoroughly studied Carl Czerny's *Schule der Geläufigkeit* (composed in the 1830s) or a similar work, and could play some of Johann Sebastian Bach's two-part Inventions.

Finally on her instrument she would have been required

1. to play any scale, also in thirds and sixths and octaves, triads and seventh chords in three octaves with various bowings;
2. to demonstrate her knowledge of left-hand positions, and how to shift from one to another by performing some etude for the left-hand;
3. to demonstrate her knowledge of bowings by playing one exercise from each of the six parts of Otokar Ševčík's *Schule der Bogentechnik* (Leipzig, 1901);
4. to play etudes from Rodolphe Kreutzer's *40 Études et Caprices* (composed ca. 1796) or Federigo Fiorillo's *36 Études ou caprices pour violon*, op. 3 (18th century);
5. to play four concerti by Bach, Nardini, Viotti, Kreutzer, Rode or Bériot; two sonatas from Ferdinand David's *Die hohe Schule des Violinspiels* (Leipzig, 1870); and also a few simple concert pieces.

The musical prerequisites placed by the Muziek-Lyceum more than sufficiently document that although the school was ideologically progressive, it still demanded a high level of traditional technical skills.[47] That these criteria were actually applied is confirmed by Jo Juda – who later became concert master of the Concertgebouw Orchestra after World War II – in his description of his entrance exam: he played Pierre Rode's violin concerto No. 7, had to absolve an ear-training test, and was also examined for his general musical knowledge.[48] One can imagine that Ina Lohr might feel somewhat overwhelmed on entering such a school so soon after recovering from her long illness. It is a tribute to her musical understanding and her skill on the violin that she was able to pass the entrance exam at all under such circumstances.

The program, as delineated in the prospectus, was very demanding.[49] During its first two years, the primary emphasis was on the development of technical skills in the hopes of creating a basis, so that the student's concentration could then be focused on "the inner meaning and pure performance of the various masterworks" in the last two years. This is reflected in the structure of the classes, where there is a shift from more individual training to a stress on music history, analysis, and more ensemble-based instruction:

Table 1.1: Program of study for violinists at the Muziek-Lyceum Amsterdam.

1st Year	2nd Year	3rd Year	4th Year
Violin	Violin	Violin	Violin
Piano	Piano	The Art of Accompaniment	The Art of Accompaniment
Ear-Training	Ear-Training	Music History	Music History
Harmony	Harmony	Ensemble	Ensemble
	Music History	Analysis	Analysis
			Methodology [Pedagogy]

In addition, all students were expected to work regularly in the library, instrumentalists to sing in the choir, and violinists to play viola as needed. Beyond that, you were allowed to participate in other elective courses. Jo Juda confirms the extensive nature of this program, writing that

47 In the process of looking up all the bibliographic information about the works mentioned in the prospectus, I discovered that many of them are still in use today, a fact I found fascinating in relation to the changes in musical style that have taken place in the meantime.
48 Jo Juda, *De zon stond nog laag*, 148–50.
49 *Muziek-Lyceum*, prospectus of 1921, 29–31.

we as violin students had, above and beyond the instruction in our major instrument, also lessons to follow in piano, ear-training, harmony, music history, analysis, orchestra class and chamber music. A few times a week we spent the whole day in the Muziek[-]Lyceum.[50]

This is an extraordinarily different program from that offered by the Amsterdam Conservatory, as described in Rutger Schoute's brochure about the Muziek-Lyceum, and one can understand how it became known as the institution to attend for a complete musical education.[51] Confirmation of this may also be found in the second volume of Jo Juda's biography, where he describes his astonishment at discovering that the orchestra and chamber music classes at the acme of musical instruction, the Berlin Conservatory, where he later studied with Carl Flesch, were of significantly inferior quality than their counterparts at the small, innovative Dutch school.[52]

Thus 1922/23 marked the beginning of Ina Lohr's studies with the violinist Ferdinand Helman (1880–54), who later became the concertmaster of the Concertgebouw Orchestra; today he is primarily remembered as the violinist who premiered Paul Hindemith's (1895–1963) Violin Concerto in 1940 under Willem Mengelberg (1871–1951). Other influential instructors were Anthon van der Horst (1899–1965) and Hubert Cuypers (1873–1960).

Anthon van der Horst's (see Ill. 1.13) exceptional ability as organist, composer and choir director, may be inferred from the fact that he was hired at the age of twenty-one to teach harmony, counterpoint, analysis, and composition at the Muziek-Lyceum at its inception in 1921. He later became known for his direction of annual performances of the Matthew Passion and the B minor mass in Naarden under the aegis of the Bach Vereniging which he took over in 1931. He was one of the formative influences on the Dutch Early Music movement in that he strove to come as close to the original performance practices as possible, going back to the original manuscripts for inspiration. In doing so he was challenging the prevailing romantic view of these works, as reflected by the masterly performances under the baton of Willem Mengelberg.

His instruction took place in small classes as may be seen in Illustration 1.14. According to Jo Juda, there was a relatively free transition between instruction of ear-training and harmony, analysis of compositions, and discussions of re-

50 "wij, als vioolleerlingen hadden, behalve het onderricht in het hoofdvak, ook nog lessen te volgen in piano, solfège, harmonie, muziekgeschiedenis, analyse, orkestklasse en kamermuziek. Enkele malen per week zaten we bijna de hele dag in het Muziek Lyceum". Jo Juda, *De zon stond nog laag*, 186.
51 Rutger Schoute, *Het Muzieklyceum 1921–1976: een terugblik*.
52 Jo Juda, *Voor de duisternis viel*, Nieuwkoop: Uitgeverij Heuff 1978, 33–34.

Ill. 1.13: Anthon van der Horst, ca. 1930. Photo: Netherlands Music Institute, The Hague.

cent performances.[53] This was also the case with Ina Lohr who mentioned in her interview with Jos Leussink that Anthon van der Horst made composition lessons out of her theory classes.

The thorough nature of the training can be gleamed, however, from the extant harmony exercises for his students we have in his hand. One clear example is proffered by Willem Noske's (1918–1995) harmony workbook from 1930–31 (see Ill. 1.15), whose musical talent, based on the extreme nature of these exercises in modulation, must have been formidable. The hand bears great similarity to that found on a free page inserted into one of Ina Lohr's early composition notebooks from 1924, on which the basic elements of functional analysis were applied to J.S. Bach's setting of *Nun ruhen alle Wälder* (see Ill. 1.16). Her assignment, written in her own hand on the top of the page, was to try a similar analysis of her own on *Wer hat Dich so geschlagen* or *O Haupt voll Blut und Wunden*, investigating how they differ from the model. Further we have a workbook full of older Dutch religious melodies for which she wrote organ accompaniments. In addition, her first efforts as a composer were under his wing. Not un-

---

53 Jo Juda, *De zon stond nog laag*, 164–65.

Ill. 1.14: A class of Anthon van der Horst. Photo: Amsterdam City Archives: Archive of the Vereniging Muzieklyceum.

surprisingly almost all the pieces were for voice – usually with piano accompaniment – and display her great sensitivity to the text.

Jo Juda's description of Anthon van der Horst's instruction indicates that although it may have been lacking from a pedagogical point of view, he found it inspiring from a more general musical perspective:

> We were very conscious that Van der Horst was not a particularly good teacher; some students complained behind his back that we learned so little in harmony. But I would not want to have done without his lessons. He made one aware of things that one would not have discovered oneself, or only much later. They were in connection with art and life. He knew how to transmit his respect for this to us in a very special manner.[54]

Anthon van der Horst is one of the people in Ina Lohr's life where I particularly regret that she, when preparing her documents and belongings for the Paul Sacher Foundation, apparently decided to destroy essentially all correspond-

---

54 "We waren er ons heel goed van bewust dat Van der Horst niet een uitgesproken paedagoog was; menige leerling sputterde achter zijn rug dat we zo weinig van het harmonievak leerden. Toch zou ik zijn lessen niet graag gemist hebben. Hij maakte je op dingen attent die je zonder hem nooit of pas veel later zou ontdekken. Zij stonden in verband met de kunst en het leven. Zijn eerbied daarvoor wist hij op een bijzondere manier op ons over te dragen". Jo Juda, *De zon stond nog laag*, 166.

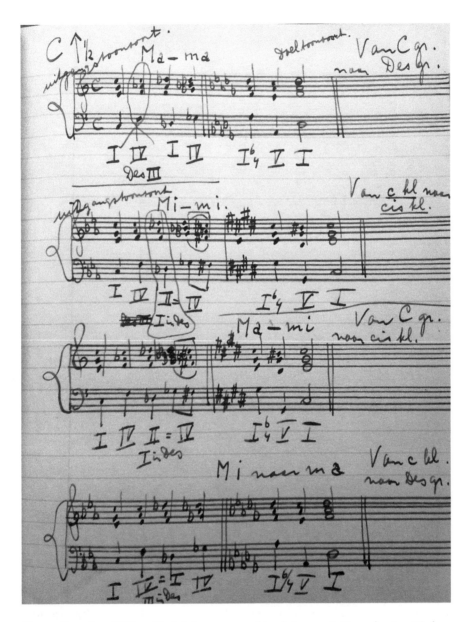

Ill. 1.15: Page from Willem Noske's harmony workbook (1930–31). Reproduction: Netherlands Music Institute, The Hague.

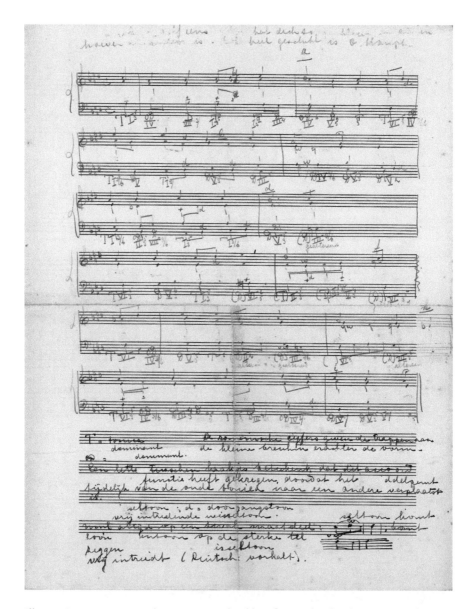

Ill. 1.16: Last page in an early composition booklet of Ina Lohr, dated 1924. Reproduction: Vera Oeri Bibliothek, Musik-Akademie Basel, Ina Lohr Collection.

ence with people she knew before she came to Basel, as if it were only appropriate to leave to the Foundation that which was connected to her life in her role as assistant to Paul Sacher. There are many affinities between Anthon van der Horst and Ina Lohr, and I cannot help but wonder about the degree to which the influence was a two-way street. Only four years separated them in age, both were committed Protestants, Anthon van der Horst having grown up in the conservative Hervormde Kerk, both had had remarkable musical training, both were interested in composition. Her pleasure in writing accompaniments to the traditional hymn melodies and the excellence of her songs must have made her a particularly gratifying student for him. They, together with Hubert Cuypers, also shared a conviction concerning the proper declamation of the text, understanding the melodic line and words to be an integral whole, rather than something where one had precedence over the other.[55]

The closeness of the musical bond between them is exemplified by the fact that in her letters to Paul Sacher from vacations in the Netherlands she occasionly mentions visits with van der Horst and his family. In particular, after her purse was stolen in 1947, she complains that among the things missing was a watch she had received from him.[56] Further, it is extraordinary to see how many of the singers van der Horst accompanied – Jo Vincent, Louis van Tulder, Max Kloos, Ilona Durigo, Berthe Seroen, Charles Panzéra, and Laurens Bogtman – were hired by Paul Sacher for performances with the Basel Chamber Orchestra.[57] Writing in 1939 about the performance practice of Bach's music, van der Horst comments on how outside of the country, "particularly in Switzerland", one has made progress in this regard, but that unfortunately in the Netherlands, with very few exceptions, this lay in the hands of dilettantes.[58] After the war some of van der Horst's students, in particular Gustav Leonhardt and Jan Boeke, went to Basel to study with Ina Lohr, thereby giving the Schola some of its renommé.

Hubert Cuypers' (see Ill 1.17) influence upon her was of an entirely different nature, representing as he did the Catholic tradition. He had studied church music in Aachen, as well as composition and harmony with Bernard Zweers in Amsterdam. There he directed many choirs, including his thirty-year stint at the St. Agnes church. He also played an active role in the revival of Gregorian

---

55 See Chapter 2 concerning Ina Lohr's religious beliefs and Chapter 3 for further discussion of her musical convictions.
56 Letter Ina Lohr to Paul Sacher of 3 August 1947, private collection, Switzerland.
57 See Gerd Oost, *Anthon van der Horst 1899–1965: Leven en werken*, Alphen aan den Rijn: Canaletto 1992, 20.
58 "vooral in Zwitserland". Ibid., 89.

chant in the Netherlands (see Chapter 3). It is no doubt due to his interest that Gregorian chant became an obligatory subject at the Muziek-Lyceum. Ina Lohr tells of how in the third lesson he came in and announced that they would be singing something larger on that day, as there were a few students who could sing very well. He had chosen a chant melody from *Varii canti* (first edition Rome, 1913), the "Salve Regina". As she had already sung it many times, she was able to sing it with ease. Hubert Cuypers was nonplussed and asked her how she could sing it so quickly. She replied that it was not at all quick, since on her own accord she had already studied and practiced it many times at home simply because the music was so beautiful. Upon hearing this, he invited her to "sing with his boys" in the Moses en Aaronkerk. She went on to say that it was from those boys that she learned to sing, that she had not had a single lesson. As her family had been well acquainted with Berthe Seroen, Ina Lohr had once sung for her with the prospect of perhaps having some lessons. The famous Belgian soprano, who had a career both on the opera stage and in the concert hall, and later became a sought-after pedagogue, said to her "Child, you have to promise me that you will never take voice lessons, you sing like a bird, and that you can do for the rest of your life. And we could only ruin it". She was "so grateful to her for this, because [thus] the boys had taught her to sing".[59] I suspect that it was also with these boys that she developed her style of singing chant, taking on some of Hubert Cuypers' preference for a declamation that paid more attention to the word than to the flowing line preferred by the Solesmes' school (see Chapter 3).

The degree to which she attributed her knowledge and background in older music to these two teachers may be seen from a passage in a letter to Paul Sacher written sometime after September 1980 concerning her memories of the founding of the Schola, in which she speaks primarily of how her

> training in Amsterdam had awakened an enthusiasm for the Middle Ages and for vocal music of the 15th and 16th centuries. I had already rehearsed Palestrina's *Missa Papae Marcelli* and the Credo for Josquin's *Missa Pange Lingua* when I was permitted to work with the choirboys in the Moses en Aaronkerk. The choir director, Hubert Cuypers, taught Gregorian chant at the Muziek-Lyceum in Amsterdam and had discovered that he would be able to use me in his rehearsals. Through him I came to know a largish repertoire of early and Cecilian choir music. Cuypers was Flemish and through him I met

59 "De jongens hebben mij dit zingen bijgebracht, ik heb nooit een les gehad. Want toen Berthe Seroen, die mij les wilde geven (die kenden wij goed) me hoorde voorzingen, toen zei ze: kind, zul je me beloven, dat je nooit zanglessen neemt, jij zingt … als een vogel, en dat kun je tot het laatst van je leven doen. En daar zouden wij alleen maar aan kunnen bederven. En ik ben haar daar zo dankbaar voor, want die kinderen hebben me het zingen bijgebracht". Interview Ina Lohr with Jos Leussink 24–25 March 1983.

Ill. 1.17: Hubert Cuypers (1941). Photo: www.geheugen-vannederland.nl/?/nl/items/ SFA02:1002344 (1 March 2015).

the lawyer and musicologist from Brussels, [Charles] van den Borren. [...] He founded "Pro musica antiqua" with his English student and son-in-law, Safford Cape, in 1932. Through this group, already in its initial period of preparation, I had gotten to know English and Dutch choir and keyboard music. My Dutch composition teacher, Anthon van der Horst, had thoroughly trained me in English organ and vocal music of the late 16th and 17th centuries, as well as introducing me to that of the Dutchman Jan Piersz. [sic] Sweelinck.[60]

60 "Meine Ausbildung in Amsterdam hatte eine Begeisterung für das Mittelalter geweckt und für die Vokalmusik des 15. und 16. Jahrhunderts. Palestrina's 'Missa Papae Marcelli' und das Credo aus Josquins 'Missa Pange Lingua' hatte ich schon mit eingeübt, als ich in der 'Moses en Aaronkerk' mit den singenden Buben arbeiten durfte. Der Chorleiter, Hubert Cuypers, unterrichtete am Muzieklyceum in Amsterdam den Gregorianischen Choral und hatte entdeckt, dass er mich in seinen Proben würde brauchen können. Bei ihm habe ich ein ziemliches Repertoire aus der alten und aus der Cäcilianischen Chormusik kennengelernt. Cuypers war Flame und durch ihn habe ich damals den Brüsseler Juristen und Musikforscher van den Borren kennen gelernt [...] Mit seinem englischen Schüler und Schwiegersohn Safford Cape gründete er 1932 die 'Pro musica antiqua'. Durch diese Gruppe hatte ich schon in ihrer Vorbereitungszeit englische und niederländische Chor- und 'Klavier'musik kennen gelernt. Mein holländischer Kompositionslehrer, Anthon van der Horst, hatte mich gründlich in die englische Orgel- und Vokalmusik des späten 16. und des 17. Jahrhunderts, wie auch in die des Niederländers Jan Piersz. [sic] Sweelinck eingeführt". From an undated letter to Paul Sacher, after 1980, PSF-ILC.

Ina Lohr thus clearly perceives Hubert Cuypers and Anthon van der Horst as being those teachers from her studies in Amsterdam who furnished the musical basis for her future work in Basel. In addition, she had already made contact with Charles van den Borren and Safford Cape, two other prominent figures in the renewal of the performance of music from earlier periods who contributed to Herman Rutter's efforts within the Muziek-Lyceum itself to direct her "insatiable interest in music history".[61]

A final figure from her time at the Muziek-Lyceum needs to be mentioned: Willem Mengelberg (1871–1951). The students were allowed to attend all of the dress rehearsals and concerts of the Concertgebouw. In addition, those who were selected by the school were allowed to participate with the orchestra twice a year in their concerts. By this means, Ina Lohr had also had direct experience of what it meant to play in a first-class orchestra under one of the top conductors of the time before she came to Basel.

Despite the musical stimulation she found at the Muziek-Lyceum, her frail constitution meant that she was constantly at the limits of her strength to the extent, as she writes in her autobiographical sketch, that she had difficulty in integrating herself into the school. Although her musical knowledge or understanding was very advanced – how could it not be, given her home environment – she could not practice more than two hours a day and had difficulties playing through an entire string quartet on her viola. She mentioned that "they would have liked to have me as a violist in a quartet because I liked playing chamber music so awfully much. But then, after the second movement, I had to take a break for a quarter of an hour because my strength was gone, [and] thus nothing could come from it. And I was very unhappy about it".[62] Indeed she was so desperate that she actually contemplated suicide, writing:

> I thought that I knew that God would accept me, should I give him back my life. My failure would only disappoint my parents and siblings and the many friends, who expected so much of me. Thus one evening I went into the city, where the water in the canals is so filthy that even if one were saved [from drowning], one would die of poisoning. I was completely calm, continued standing quietly for a little [while], praying and preparing myself for the next world, with which, due to my illness, I was actually already acquainted. Even when a drunkard suddenly appeared and came towards me, he could not take this peacefulness away from me. I just looked at him, and suddenly he was in a state of shock and almost sober, [and] repeatedly stammered that he hadn't

---

61 "onverzadigbare interesse voor muziekgeschiedenis te leiden", Ina Lohr, *Solmisatie en Kerktoonsoorten*, trans. by Henk van Benthem and Jan Boeke, The Hague: Stichting Centrum voor de Kerkzang 1983, foreword.

62 Interview with Jos Leussink, 24–25 March 1983.

realized, no, he really hadn't realized it. I then took his hand and proposed that we go home. He came with me, told of a wife and two children, to whom he now wished to return, and we took leave of one another in front of my door, merely [exchanging words] of thanks. Only when I was seated in my room did it become clear to me that this poor man was sent to me from God as a messenger, as an angel, to show me that helping [others] is also a talent and a task. Two days later, when I pulled back and saved a child who was almost run over by a car, I perceived this as a confirmation of my previous experience and recognized my task: to help where help was needed, but if at all possible within a musical life.[63]

Two aspects of this text are of interest, as they seem to be harbingers for certain facets of her future. Firstly, we know from Ina Lohr's letter to Paul Sacher from 1942 that she found it difficult to go out into the world after her illness. Imagine what it would be like to have to study at a conservatory in that state of health, combined with her desperation and fear of not meeting the expectations of friends and family! Secondly, there was the familial tendency toward depression. Herman Lohr, as we have seen above, believed that this proclivity could be best counteracted by a vigilant and proactive supervision of his daughters' education. It is easy to imagine that the cultivation of music and the arts within the family not only led to the development of extraordinary skills and knowledge, but also to undue pressure on the children, with the concomitant fear of failure on their part. Ina Lohr herself speaks of not being sure whether she was really ill or whether it was a psychosomatic reaction to the demands made upon her.[64] And indeed it cannot be denied that depression and physical weakness

63 "Da meinte ich zu wissen, Gott würde mich annehmen, wenn ich Ihm mein Leben zurückgäbe. Mein Versagen könne doch Eltern und Schwestern und den vielen Freunden, die so viel von mir erwarteten, nur Enttäuschungen bereiten. So ging ich eines Abends in die Innenstadt, wo das Wasser in den Grachten (Kanälen) so schmutzig ist, dass, wer daraus gerettet wird, doch an Vergiftung stirbt. Ich war vollkommen ruhig, stand noch ein wenig still, betete und bereitete mich auf die andere Welt vor, die mir eigentlich von der Krankheit her schon vertraut war. Auch als plötzlich ein Betrunkener auftauchte und auf mich zukam, konnte er mir die Ruhe nicht nehmen. Ich sah ihn nur an, und plötzlich war er nur noch erschrocken und fast nüchtern, stammelte nur immer wieder, das habe er nicht gewusst, nein, er habe das wirklich nicht gewusst. Da habe ich seine Hand genommen und vorgeschlagen, wir würden jetzt heimgehen. Er kam mit, erzählte von einer Frau und von zwei Kindern, zu denen er jetzt zurück wolle, und vor meiner Haustür haben wir uns einfach dankend verabschiedet. Erst als ich in meinem Zimmer sass, wurde mir klar, dass dieser arme Mensch mir als Bote Gottes, als Engel gesandt wurde, um mir zu zeigen, dass auch Helfen eine Gabe und Aufgabe ist. Als ich zwei Tage später auch noch ein Kind, das fast unter ein Auto gekommen wäre, zurückziehen und dadurch retten konnte, empfand ich das als Bestätigung meiner vorigen Erfahrung und kannte meine Aufgabe: helfen, wo es zu helfen gibt, wenn möglich aber doch innerhalb eines Musikerlebens". Ina Lohr, "Skizze zum Lebenslauf", 2–3.

64 Interview with Jos Leussink, 24–25 March 1983.

Ill. 1.18: "Alle, die ihre Hände regen" from *Vom mönchischen Leben* (Rainer Maria Rilke).
Reproduction: PSF-ILC.

Ill. 1.18: (continued)

remained serious health issues throughout her life. At the same time, however, she came to see her chosen profession as a vocation through this experience, always perceiving her work in music in relation to God, to her religious beliefs. Her desire to help people underlay everything she undertook.

Thereafter on a vacation to Switzerland, her father took her to see a specialist in Braunwald who told her to take a break, to throw off her obligations and do just whatever she felt like doing.[65] It was perhaps this that led her and her elder sister, Etty, to decide to spend some time in the mountains of Switzerland to restore their health. Ina was simply exhausted and Etty had come down with tuberculosis in Groningen where she was working as an assistant in a hospital after having finished her studies in medicine. They found a four-room apartment in Davos, complete with a housekeeper, whom they knew from earlier stays in Switzerland, and began a simple life there.

During this period, Ina Lohr immediately found a possibility to continue her musical studies: she took lessons with Willy Rössel (1877–1947), one hour a week being devoted to the analysis of violin sonatas and the other to composition, in which she wrote various songs for her sister with piano, as well as some onomatopoetic piano music for her mother, bringing to life the bells in Davos, Amsterdam, and Lucerne. Whereas the piano music remained within the realm of the conventional, in her songs she seemed to have taken the doctor's words to heart, in that she began finding a voice truly her own, in which elements of French impressionism were blended with elements of harmony more typical of Mahler, to say nothing of modality of earlier music. In it all, the declamation and expression of the text – whether in German, Dutch or French – remained paramount. An example of such a work is "Alle, die ihre Hände regen" on a text by Rainer Maria Rilke from *Vom mönchischen Leben* (see Ill.1.18). Here the voice declaims syllabically, the rhythm and melody accomodating itself to the scansion. This declamation is only interrupted by two melismas, one at the word "flehte" [entreated] creating the image of the prayer of one in great need, and the other at the end of the piece on Frömmigkeit [piety], to bring the whole to a close. The accompaniment is simplicity itself, but with the prevalence of perfect intervals associated with sacred music of earlier time, evocative of the life of a monk, whose main function is to pray.

She wrote similar songs for small chamber ensembles, such as "Der Tod", here also following the lead of her teacher, which were presumably suitable for the cultural life in such a spa. In addition, Rössel encouraged her to play with

65 Interview with Jos Leussink, 24–25 March 1983.

him in the sanatoria, as well as to sing and play with the patients there, something that she would later take up at the end of her life, seeing it as her duty to
use these tools to enliven the days of her fellow inhabitants in the Dalbehof, a
residence for senior citizens, as well as to visit the critically ill in hospitals. She
was, however, forced to leave Davos abruptly, when she discovered that she
could no longer tolerate the cold. Her younger sister, Sally, a budding graphic
artist, took over her place there as Etty's companion with the terrible consequence, mentioned above, that she herself came down with the disease.

On December 17, 1928, on her return to Holland, Ina Lohr stopped off in Basel,
a city that she already knew well, as her family had always stayed there for two
days to prepare for the mountains when they went on vacation to Switzerland
from the lowlands of the Netherlands. This time, however, she was more interested in the people on the streets and in the restaurant at the train station than
in its cultural treasures. She bought a newspaper and read that there was going
to be a choir concert in St. Paul's Church that evening, and decided to fill in
the time before her train's departure at 11 PM by learning more about the concert life in Basel. The concert opened with various works by Bach and concluded with the oratorio *Jephte* by Carissimi. Unbeknownst to all concerned,
this was the beginning of a long-term relationship between Ina Lohr and Basel,
between Ina Lohr and the director of that evening's concert, Paul Sacher, who
later became a celebrated patron of the arts, having commissioned some of the
most significant works of the Modern Classic. All Ina Lohr knew after that
evening, was that she "would like to participate in such an ensemble, singing,
playing and perhaps also on the conceptual level".[66]

Upon her return to the Netherlands she began work on the virtuosic Bruch
Violin Concerto for the completion of her teaching degree on the violin, rather
than the one in E-flat major by Mozart which she would have much preferred.
Having the diploma under her belt, she set off in June or July of 1929 for Davos
for a vacation in order to recover from the demands the preparation for the
exam had made upon her. In the train, however, she suffered such an attack of
weakness that the Dutch friends who had come to greet her at the train station
in Basel took her home with them, and gave her a quiet place to recover her
strength during the subsequent six weeks. At some point, a violinist with whom
she was acquainted came by the house where she was living and saw her cop-

66 "ich würde gerne singend, spielend, und vielleicht auch denkend in einem solchen Ensemble mitwirken". Cassette tape, recording her memories of "Die Entstehung der Schola Cantorum Basiliensis", 1980, PSF-ILC, CD 4.

ying out the parts to her string quartet, which she had composed while studying with Anthon van der Horst (see Ill. 1.19). As the violinist was member of a
good quartet, he suggested that they play it immediately. And thus it came to
be performed at a house concert, to which Felix Weingartner, then the director of both the Basel Symphony Orchestra and the Conservatory, had been invited.[67] Although the work, notwithstanding the singularity of its language and
power of expression, exhibits some inexperience in dealing with larger forms,
he was sufficiently impressed with it – perhaps, as Ina Lohr remarked, "because
a 'Fräulein' who composed was at that time a curiosity"[68] – he proposed that she
just continue studying in Basel, saying that she would be able to get a degree
in composition in a year's time at the Conservatory. In addition, he assured her
that her previous work at the Muziek-Lyceum would be recognized and that
she only need to take classes that were of interest to her.[69] She accepted this invitation and her parents agreed with her decision to stay in Basel to study, as the
climate was better for her there.

1.3 The First Years in Basel

Ina Lohr then found an apartment in a modern house for single women, Spei-
serstrasse 98, which had the sobriquet "Virgin Garage", where she spent her first
four years in Basel. She writes that life in Basel, "where no one knew of me as a
violinist",[70] gave her the possibility of living independently, leaving her free to
imagine that all paths were open to her. Her life was no longer determined by
her family – although she spent all of her vacations with them from 1929–39 –
and she was liberated from the obligation of meeting their expectations and
those of their friends.[71] In spite of the fact that Ina Lohr never expressed a single negative thought about her family, this reaction indicates that she suffered
under what she felt to be the pressure of having to become a soloist. Given the
high value placed on culture in her family, this is more than understandable.
Thus – freed from many subjects she had already completed in Amsterdam –

---

67 Interview Ina Lohr with Jos Leussink, 24–25 March 1983.
68 "weil ein komponierendes Fräulein damals ein Kuriosum war". Cassette "Die Entstehung
    der Schola Cantorum Basiliensis", PSF-ILC, CD 4.
69 Interview Ina Lohr with Jos Leussink, 24–25 March 1983.
70 "wo niemand etwas von mir als Geigerin wusste". From a first version of a text for 27 Sep-
    tember 1978 at a program for her 75th birthday, organized by Arthur Eglin in conjunction
    with the *Oekumenischer Singkreis Basel-Riehen* and the *Stadtposaunenchor Basel*.
71 Ina Lohr, "Skizze zum Lebenslauf", 5.

she thoroughly enjoyed being able to study theory with Gustav Güldenstein and composition with Rudolf Moser on her own terms.

Although her studies at the Conservatory have barely received any notice, seemingly irrelevant for the further course of life, she mentions with gratitude the relatively strict guidance she received from Rudolf Moser, a student of Max Reger – in contrast to the relaxed cooperation with Anthon van der Horst – from whom she learned to write three- and four-part fugues. In the Paul Sacher Foundation there are a canon for a keyboard instrument and a duet for violin and viola, reminiscent of Bach inventions, which were no doubt the product of such studies. She found the work with Rudolf Moser so valuable that she extended her studies for a further year, only completing them in 1931, passing the final exam for a teaching degree in music theory with distinction.[72] They certainly gave her a sense of inner security in relation to her future work in Early Music.

In the context of this program of study, five of her works for choir were performed on 25 June 1931 – in a program with compositions by Reger, Courvoisier, Schumann, Schubert and Mozart – three by the Conservatory choir under the direction of Hans Münch, and two by soloists.[73] In comparison to her other works in the period, these seem relatively stiff and inflexible, although demonstrating her ability to assimilate other styles into her writing. In "Fürchte nicht des Sturmes Toben" (see Ill. 1.20), for example, the outer voices are in canon against the free movement of the middle one, which has its own text, around which the others organize themselves, both musically and expressively, almost as if it were a cantus firmus: the middle voice evokes the omnipresence of God, whereas the outer ones list the dangers from which He alone provides salvation.

Although clever in structure, it lacks the spontaneity and direct impact of both the songs and the string quartet mentioned above. It seems likely that her inner voice was quietened by the institutional constraints. That it was not extin-

---

72 Interview Ina Lohr with Jos Leussing, 24–25 March 1983. The information concerning her degree may be found in the *Jahresbericht über den 64. Kurs 1930/31* of Musikschule und Konservatorium Basel, Vera Oeri Bibliothek, Musik-Akademie Basel, RARA MAB G 1107, 9.

73 Fünf geistliche Chorlieder für dreistimmigen gemischten Chor a cappella
Jetzt wird die Welt recht neugebor'n (Text: Angelus Silesius)
Mir nach, spricht Christus, unser Held (Text: Angelus Silesius)
Fürchte nicht des Sturmes Toben (Text: Paul Zoelly)
Überall wölbt sich das Himmelsgewölbe (Text: Paul Zoelly)
In Ewigkeit, Amen
They were performed at one of the concerts at the end of that school year, with 1, 2, and 5 being sung by the choir and the others by Helene Sandreuter, Pauline Hoch, and Hanns Visscher van Gaasbeek, program leaflet, PSF-ILC.

Streichquartett a-moll 1929

Ina Lohr

Ill. 1.19: Opening of the first movement from Ina Lohr's String Quartet. The parts are in the PSF-ILC.

Ill. 1.19: (continued)

Ill. 1.20: Ina Lohr, "Fürchte nicht des Sturmes Toben". Reproduction: PSF-ILC.

guished is made evident by the small cantata dated 1931, alternating between the movements for three-voice woman's choir, and those for solo voice, which – while remaining penetratingly modal – bring the texts to life through the intersection of harsh vertical clashes with a sense for declamation that allows the import of the words to come forward. This, for example, may be observed in its first movement, "Unwandelbar", with the insistence of the repeated notes of its opening, gaining greater strength by means of the battle between triple and duple rhythms and the entries of the subsequent voices at the interval of a second (see Ill. 1.21). She, too, uses the colors almost impressionistically to create the emotional landscape evoked by the texts, while not foregoing the possibilities of counterpoint.[74]

74 Links to recordings of this and other early works are found at www.forschung.schola-can-torum-basiliensis.ch/de/ina-lohr-project.

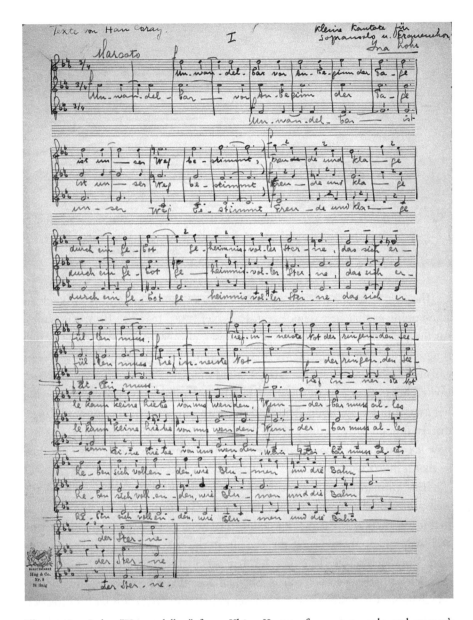

Ill. 1.21: Ina Lohr, "Unwandelbar" from *Kleine Kantate*, for soprano solo and women's choir. Reproduction: PSF-ILC.

Ill. 1.22: Karl Nef, Professor of Musicology, University of Basel. Reproduction: University Library Basel, AN VI 67:71; Photographers: Conrad Ruf and R. Pfützner, Basel.

The Conservatory was not her sole source of musical stimulus in Basel. At some point in that first school year, Karl Nef (1873–1935, see Ill. 1.22), professor for musicology at the University of Basel, also heard her sing some Dutch songs in her own arrangements in a house concert. Like Cuypers and Weingartner before him, he immediately wanted to involve her in his own work and invited her to take part in his seminar, which she did with pleasure. Following her exam in 1931, she continued studying with him with the intent of writing a dissertation on early settings of the Passion, "starting with Gregorian chant and how it continued in the 16th century, but he did one part of it, and I another, so that it didn't work out".[75]

This seminar, under the inspiring direction of Karl Nef, also served as the wellspring for the foundation of the Schola Cantorum Basiliensis (SCB), in that it was there that she met her fellow initiators, Paul Sacher, Arnold Geering and Walter Nef. There were eight students in the class and she usually sat across from Paul Sacher (see Ill. 1.23). Her first personal interaction with him, however, left something to be desired. She had attended a performance by the Basel Chamber Orchestra (Basler Kammerorchester or BKO) under his direction of Honegger's symphonic psalm, *King David,* on 27 September 1929 and had been "powerfully" impressed,

---

75 "Dat ging over de vroege Passies, te beginnen bij het Gregoriaans, en hoe dat in de 16e eeuw verder ging. Maar hij deed er een deel aan, en ik een ander deel, dus dat ging toch niet". Interview Ina Lohr with Jos Leussink, 24–25 March 1983.

Ill. 1.23: Paul Sacher. Photo: Spreng, courtesy of Musik-Akademie Basel.

primarily because you saw, heard and felt that there was an enormous cooperation between the conductor, the choir and the orchestra. And the cooperation communicated itself to the audience. The audience was very much part of it, I was completely hooked by it. And when I said that to him – for I saw him for the first time in that seminar – he immediately became very reserved because he is someone that finds it completely unnecessary to receive praise. He is better at it now, but then he wasn't. And I thought: what an intractable gentleman. Then I won't be wanting to do very much more with him.[76]

This initial impression came to be revised during the course of the seminar, which was on the music of earlier eras. Judging from the anecdotes Ina Lohr tells of the time, the discussions must have been very lively and extraordinarily stimulating, leading as they did to her cooperation with Paul Sacher, both as his assistant in regard to the BKO and with the founding of the SCB.

For example, she told of the moment when Paul Sacher had heard

that I was very much at home in Gregorian chant. And he brought it up in the seminar, [and] he said to Professor Nef: "Did you know that Miss Lohr can sing Gregorian chant? And even very well, apparently". Then I asked where he had that from. Yes, well, he had heard that from the person who lived below me in the house where I live, because every morning I sang chant and she had told others. And then Nef immediately

76 "Vooral daarom, omdat je zag, hoorde en voelde dat er een enorme samenwerking bestond tussen dirigent, koor en orkest. En die samenwerking deelde zich mee aan het publiek. Het publiek deed werkelijk helemaal mee, ik was er helemaal door gevangen. En toen ik hem dat zei – toen ik hem voor het eerst zag, in dat Seminar –, toen deed hij nogal stug, want hij is iemand die het helemaal niet nodig vindt, om zo'n lof in ontvangst te nemen. Nu is hij daar handiger in, maar toen was hij het niet. En ik dacht: wat een stugge meneer. Daar zal ik me verder maar niet veel van aantrekken". Interview Ina Lohr with Jos Leussink, 24–25 March 1983.

said, "Then I would like you to give a talk in the following week, of course on Gregorian chant. Can you do that in a week?". And then I said, "O, yes, I can begin immediately with it". And then I spoke with great pleasure there about Gregorian chant and sang it a lot, too, for example the "Tenebrae factae sunt", by which they were profoundly impressed that so much can be expressed in monody. They simply found it incredible.[77]

She must have similarly impressed them when she analyzed a whole Palestrina mass and presented it to the class, once again illustrating it with her singing. She followed this up by demonstrating her own powers of stimulating and encouraging others, as her reaction to this praise was that she not only wanted to discuss the music in the seminar, but what she really wanted to do was sing it: "We should [be able to sing] the music here as we are eight people; that is also enough in order to sing polyphonic things with one another, if we want to. And my 'fellow students' were in agreement with me".[78] Nef immediately seconded this, saying that in the following week they would then meet in a room with a piano and she would sing for them, asking her what music she would like to choose for the purpose. Her response was immediate: "I would very much like to do that which I have learned from you: Schütz. I have [looked through] the entire complete edition of the *Geistliche Konzerte*. The first is so magnificent and reminds me of Gregorian chant, I can just simply declaim it".[79]

In that class on Schütz, Nef's reaction was to suggest that the beauty of the music lay in her performance, in her interpretation, rather than in the composition itself, and that one could not decide on that basis whether the music were actually also good. Ina Lohr refuted this conclusion, saying

---

77 "En toen kwam het moment dat Paul Sacher gehoord had, dat ik zo thuis was in het Gregoriaans. En dat bracht hij toen te berde in dat Seminar, hij zei Professor Nef: 'Weet U wel dat Fräulein Lohr Gregoriaans zingen kan? En zelfs heel goed, blijkbaar.' Toen vroeg ik waar hij dat vandaan had. Ja, dat had hij gehoord van mijn onderbuurvrouw in het huis waar ik toen woonde, want s'ochtends zong ik altijd Gregoriaans en die had dat verder verteld. En toen zei Nef meteen, 'Dan had ik graag dat U volgende week eens een referaat hield, en wel over het Gregoriaans. Kunt U dat in een week?': Toen zei ik: 'O ja, daar kan ik meteen mee beginnen.' En toen heb ik met groot plezier daar over het Gregoriaans gesproken en heel veel voorgezongen, bijvoorbeeld het 'Tenebrae factae sunt', waar ze dieper dan diep van onder de indruk waren: dat er zo veel uitgesproken kan worden in eenstemmigheid. Dat vonden ze eenvoudig ongelooflijk." Ibid.

78 "we zouden die muziek zo als we hier samen acht mensen zijn [kunnen zingen], dat is genoeg, om meerstemmige dingen ook met elkaar te zingen, als we dat willen. En daar waren mijn 'Kommilitonen' het echt mee eens". Ibid.

79 "En toen zei ik, ja maar ik wou ook erg graag – wat ik door U heb leren kennen: Schütz, ik heb die hele Gesamtausgabe van de 'Geistliche Konzerte' [doorgewerkt], dat eerste is zo prachtig, dat herinnert me aan het gregoriaans, daar kan ik eenvoudig scanderen". Ibid.

I followed the rhythm precisely, I kept entirely to the scansion. And I wrote the accompaniment myself, so that it did not have a dense accompaniment, and I wrote it precisely according to that which he had notated and so [I believe] Schütz is also just as great as the composers of Gregorian chant, and that we thus could discover very much more. And everybody was in agreement with this.[80]

For her, this was the first step toward the founding of the SCB, the step in which a group of interested students decided to investigate the performance of early music from a historical perspective.

Two weeks later Paul Sacher mentioned that he would like to perform older music with his orchestra, asking her what he should choose. She then tells the story of the beginning of her work with the BKO in the following manner:

And it turned out to be a suite by Rosenmüller, totally unknown at the time, totally, and then he asked me to mark up the suite by Rosenmüller for him. Because nothing was [indicated] in it, absolutely nothing. And he was present then, and was very much impressed by it. And at the first rehearsal everybody was so astonished by something so unknown. And there were of course members of the orchestra who asked "is that necessary, there are still such beautiful things by Mozart and Beethoven". "Yes", said Sacher, "but this naturally enriches our repertoire greatly". And with that a really good beginning was made, the concert was a success, and then he asked me, whether for the next choir concert I […] would like to make a program with early music […].

After that came [the program which opened with the Kyrie] by St. Hildegard von Bingen. I was in Wiesbaden for a week to transcribe it all from the big codex and to write about it, and there I overheard [someone say about the concert], "Das ist zum katholisch werden scheen", "[It was] so beautiful, you could become Catholic from it!"

Thus we really had a great enrichment and also an ecumenical expansion of the programming possibilities, and Sacher was open to all these things from the beginning. He had a huge trust [in me] and [thus] asked whether I would take part in the work group [in relation to the BKO]. I said no then, "I can't do that. I am not a person for meetings and those kind of things, I get tired too quickly for them, I can't do that". It thus came to a personal cooperation that has lasted until now, for 54 years, and about which we are both still very happy that it could have happened.[81]

80 "ik heb precies zijn ritme genomen, me precies aan die scandering gehouden. En ik had de begeleiding er zelf bij geschreven, dat er dus niet een dikke begeleiding bij kwam, en die heb ik ook precies naar wat hij aangaf opgeschreven, en [ik geloof] zo is Schütz voor mij zo groot als die Gregoriaanse Komponisten ook, en we zullen nog heel veel zo kunnen ontdekken. En daar waren ze [de deelnemers] het allemaal mee eens". Ibid.

81 "En dat kwam toen neer op een suite van Rosenmüller, volkomen onbekend in die tijd, volkomen, en toen heeft hij mij gevraagd om die suite van Rosenmüller voor hem er aantekeningen in te maken. Want er staat niets in, helemaal niets. En daar was hij ook bij, en was daar helemaal van onder de indruk. En bij de eerste repetitie waren ze allemaal stom verbaasd over zoiets onbekends. En er waren ook wel orkestleden die vroegen, is dat nou nodig, er zijn toch zulke prachtige dingen van Mozart en Beethoven. Ja, zei Sacher, maar dit verrijkt natuurlijk ons repertoire geweldig. En daarmee was werkelijk goed begonnen, dat

This story of the beginning of her cooperation with Paul Sacher is remarkable for various reasons. First of all, the all-too-human details incorporated into her tale – which Jos Leussink conjured out of her, as she was otherwise very reticent about speaking openly about her work with Paul Sacher – give it a kind of verity that the more polished versions she presented to the public do not. For example, in a short text, probably written in relation to a radio broadcast in honor of his 70th birthday in 1976, she speaks of meeting him after a matinee on 11 May 1930 during the Basel Mozart festival, where they first spoke of the concert and thereafter about unknown choir music. Then

> Sacher became all ears when I mentioned Gregorian chant, which at that time I still thought was possible to perform in concert in a program of interrelated works from the field of sacred music. Here the choir director wanted to know more. He came already on [the following] Wednesday to my place for tea and since then Wednesday afternoons have been "devoted to Paul Sacher and his Basel Chamber Orchestra".[82]

Whereas it may be true, it is not the complete story; in its formality it omits all the personal interactions in the seminar with Karl Nef that led Sacher to be able to trust her knowledge and musicality. And most of all, it omits the degree to which her own passionate interest, not only in the music of earlier eras, but also in its performance, stimulated the other members of the seminar, got them – and with them also the professor of the seminar, Karl Nef – to change the direction of the class, to include performance as a part of the study and analysis of the music.

concert had succes, en toen vroeg hij me, of ik voor zijn eerste volgende koorconcert [...] een programma wou maken met oude muziek [...]. Na dat concert kwam van de Hl. Hildegard von Bingen. Ik ben een week in Wiesbaden geweest om uit die prachtige grote codex dat allemaal te noteren en over te schrijven – en daar kreeg ik over te horen: 'Das ist zum katholisch werden scheen': 'zo mooi, dat je er katholiek van zou worden!' Dus toen hadden we werkelijk een grote verrijking en ook een oecomenische uitbreiding van de programmamogelijkheden, en voor al die dingen stond Sacher van het begin af aan open. Hij had een reusachtig vertrouwen, en vroeg of ik mee zou kunnen doen aan de Arbeitsgemeinschaft; toen zei ik nee, dat kan ik niet. Ik ben niet een mens voor vergaderingen en zulk soort dingen, daar ben ik te gouw moe voor, dat kan ik niet. Toen werd het dus een persoonlijke samenwerking, die tot nu toe duurt, 54 jaar lang – en waar we eigenlijk beide toch zeer gelukkig mee zijn, dat dat heeft mogen zijn". Interview with Jos Leussink, 24–25 March 1983.

82 "Sacher horchte auf, als ich den Gregorianischen Choral nannte, den ich damals noch für konzertfähig hielt in einem Programm mit aufeinander bezogenen Werken aus dem Bereich der Kirchemusik. Da wollte der Chordirigent mehr wissen. Er kam schon am Mittwoch zu mir zum Tee und seither ist der Mittwoch-Nachmittag 'Paul Sacher und seinem Basler Kammerorchester gewidmet'". "Zusammenarbeit mit Paul Sacher", 1, PSF-ILC.

But these sorts of ego documents, created 50 years and more after the events took place, also bring their own difficulties with them. In this case the earliest recorded performance of a Rosenmüller suite by the BKO after her advent in Basel, Nr. 2 in D major, took place on 26 November 1933 in honor of Karl Nef's 60th birthday and it was repeated on 4 May 1935 at a memorial marking his sudden death.[83] The question then arises whether she was confusing this work with some other work that she marked up for Paul Sacher, as it was so closely connected with Karl Nef. On the other hand, in Sacher's copy of the volume of *Denkmäler Deutscher Tonkunst* dedicated to the Rosenmüller suites – which was, *nota bene*, edited by Karl Nef – Nr. 11 is marked up in great detail in Ina Lohr's hand with a few additional indications and explanations in the conductor's own hand (see Ill. 1.24).

This page is exemplary for the type of care and thoroughness that Ina Lohr invested into the marking up of scores for the BKO. Although the volume was edited by Karl Nef, she did not shy away from changing the designation of the piece from *Sinfonia* to *Kammersonate,* preferring a literal translation of the title of the original volume, *Sonate da camera* (Venice, 1667), to the generic one chosen by the editor. She added dynamic signs, indications of expression, and ornaments, as well as suggesting an instrumentation for the BKO and the unit in which it should be beaten (*alla breve*, as can be seen in the "cembalo" part). The remarks in Paul Sacher's hand indicate the kind of things they discussed: why there are only 2 flats in the key signature even though the piece is in C minor; that its character should be solemn, as it represented the spirit of antique tragedy, whose successor was the opera; or that the second section, starting in m. 20 was the main section and should be played *cantabile*. It is very imaginable that a young Paul Sacher would have been quite impressed by such a show.

The first performance of this work by the BKO, however, is documented as having taken place on 13 November 1936. Is it possible that the concert referred to by Ina Lohr in the interview with Jos Leussink, was an informal house concert, or simply an open rehearsal of the orchestra? As there is no other recorded work from that time period listed that fits the requirements, it is tempting to think that this C minor suite must be the one to which Ina Lohr was referring in the interview. In any case, already in her first letter to Paul Sacher of 20 July 1930 from Arnhem, she presented her first ideas for a choir concert, starting with Hildegard von Bingen's Kyrie, which then took place on 26 November 1930.[84]

83 *Alte und Neue Musik: das Basler Kammerorchester (Kammerchor und Kammerorchester) unter Leitung von Paul Sacher 1926–1951*, Zurich: Atlantis Verlag 1952, 263–64.
84 Letter Ina Lohr to Paul Sacher of 20 July 1930, private collection, Switzerland.

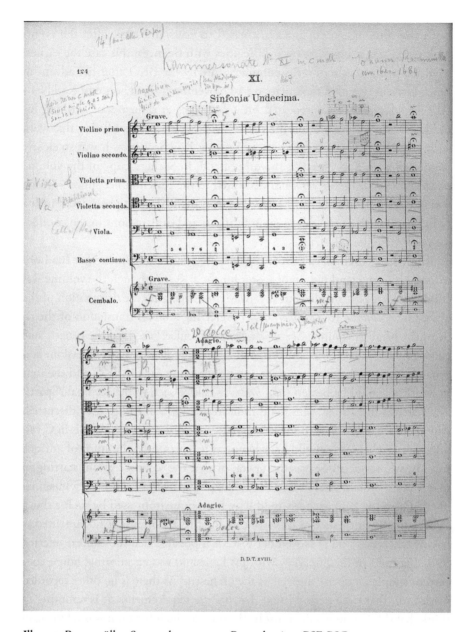

Ill. 1.24: Rosenmüller, Sonata da camera 11. Reproduction: PSF-PSC.

In connection with these memories of the seminar with Karl Nef, Jos Leussink also encouraged her to speak about the founding of the SCB. She speaks of how Sacher suddenly came and suggested, "what about starting to teach this, what about opening a school for early music, and then we did it".[85] She went further, recounting that

> My father thought, well, that will be over in a year, and thus he also put in some money and […] after three weeks we gave an opening concert for the press, where Weingartner also came, and my father came for it from Holland. And I had only played recorder for three weeks, and I had to transpose everything that we played to three different keys […] It was really unbelievable. But the success was overwhelming. And it was naturally so strange [at that time]: that we were devoting ourselves to it so much, and so passionately standing up for it, that we were seriously applying ourselves to early music, that it was beautiful.[86]

This reference to her father investing money in the SCB – together with these stories from the seminar where she truly seems to have been a source of inspiration to the others in regard to the study and performance of early music, as well as the documentation of the early cooperation with Sacher in the marking up of the Rosenmüller suite – places her in a different light in regard to the founding of that institution and indicates that her role in it was greater than believed heretofore.[87] The constrast with her naivité of going out and playing recorder in an inaugural concert after having played it only three weeks, however, is breathtaking, but perhaps that, too, is only a measure of the time.

85 "Want toen opeens kwam Sacher, en zei, als we dat nu eens gingen onderwijzen, als we eens een school openden voor Oude Muziek en dat hebben we toen gedaan". Interview Ina Lohr with Jos Leussink, 24–25 March. This conversation must have taken place two years later, as in a letter of 29 July 1932, Paul Sacher requested that Ina Lohr keep this idea "absolutely secret" [*streng geheim*], PSF-ILC.

86 "Mijn vader dacht, nou ja, na een jaar is dat toch voorbij, dus hij stak er nog wat geld in, en […] Na drie weken hebben we een openingsconcert voor de pers gegeven, waar ook Weingartner bij was, en mijn vader kwam er voor over uit Holland. En ik speelde pas drie weken blokfluit, en ik moest altijd wat we speelden transponeren, in drie verschillend toonsoorten … het was werkelijk ongelooflijk! Maar het succes was overweldigend. Het was natuurlijk zò vreemd, en dat wij ons daar zo voor inzetten, er zo hartstochtelijk voor opkwamen, dat we die oude muziek nu eens ernstig gingen opnemen, dat dat [die muziek] prachtig was.". Interview Ina Lohr with Jos Leussink, 24–25 March 1983.

87 Cf. Wulf Arlt, "Zur Idee und Geschichte eines 'Lehr- und Forschungsinstituts für Alte Musik'", in: *Alte und Neue Musik II*, Zurich: Atlantis Verlag 1977, 37–93 and Martin Kirnbauer, "'Tout le monde connaît la Schola' – Eine Spurensuche zur Vorgeschichte der Schola Cantorum Basiliensis", in: *Basler Jahrbuch für Historische Musikpraxis* 32 (2008), 145–57 and id., "Paul Sacher und die alte Musik", in: *Paul Sacher – Facetten einer Musikerpersönlichkeit*, ed. Ulrich Mosch, Mainz: Schott 2006, 25–56.

But more than this, in these reminiscences of her early life in Basel, she brings to life why so many of the first-class musicians she encountered wanted to work with her – or in one case did not want to work with her – starting with Hubert Cuypers who wanted her to sing in his boys choir; with Anthon van der Horst who changed her theory lessons into "cooperative" composition lessons and with whom she had continuing contact; Berthe Seroen who pleaded with her not to take singing lessons; Felix Weingartner who immediately suggested she come and study at his conservatory; Karl Nef who on hearing her sing invited her to participate in his seminar; or Nadia Boulanger who just a year or two later wanted to have her come to Paris to study a year or two (see Chapter 4). There was an intensity about her interaction with music that was magnetic.

It is difficult to imagine the degree of inner strength and willpower it must have required for Ina Lohr, as a young woman – given her protective family and fragile physical and psychological state – to have gone off on her own to a new country and to establish herself there so successfully in such a short period of time. In Basel, she saw the possibilities of just being herself, of being accepted in her favored means of expression, singing. It offered her the opportunity of combining her emotional needs with her profession. The fact that she did not put up a boundary between the two, but felt connected with a higher sphere through her singing, no doubt contributed to the spell cast by her singing, by her music.

Chapter 2. Religion: "Directing her Heart" to God in Song

Ina Lohr grew up in a complex network of religious influences. In the beginning of the 19th century the Lohr family emigrated from Southern Germany; for the most part, the family retained its Lutheran faith throughout the century, although some were members of the Dutch Reformed and Remonstrant churches.[1] The correspondence between Hendrik Christiaan Lohr (1836–1922), a great uncle of Ina's, and Christiaan Pieter Lohr, her grandfather, gives an indication of the seriousness with which religion was regarded in the family. When looking back at his life in 1902, her great uncle recounted the following:

> I stood under diverse influences, under the influence of intellectual liberalism, of orthodoxy of a pietistic cast, and even of confessional orthodoxy. But nowhere did I find satisfaction for my heart which pined for security or better said: security in relation to transcendental matters. The aridity and numbing coldness of so-called reason horrified me as [something] unnatural, as did the artificiality of pietism, which furthermore was seen to be a great danger, in that it has a stimulating effect on sensuality.[2]

In the end he chose the path of Lutheranism, becoming a pastor in Culembourg from 1863–1875, and thereafter – until his retirement in 1909 – in Rotterdam, where in addition he assumed the presidency of the Lutheran Synod as well as the curatorship of the seminar.

During his working-life in Indonesia, Ina Lohr's grandfather Christiaan Pieter Lohr took a very different path. Although he had established a long-lasting friendship with a Lutheran pastor in Batavia, Johannes Willem Hendrik Ader (1830–1892), he lost all interest in attending church while living there, writing to his sister Harmina Catharina Lohr (1843–1873) on 31 May 1862 that "there is so much that one hears in the church that neither the minister nor the audience believes, but they are not allowed to admit this disbelief, so that it makes one nauseated".[3] He retained his respect, however, for those who gen-

---

1 Elisabeth van Blankenstein, "Nieuwjaarsbrief Lohr, januari 2012".
2 "Ik stond onder allerlei invloeden, onder de invloed van verstandelijke vrijzinnigheid, van piëtistisch getinte orthodoxie, zelfs van confessionele orthodoxie. Maar nergens vond ik bevrediging voor mijn hart, dat smachtte naar zeker of liever: verzekerdheid aangaande bovenzinnelijke dingen. De dorheid en verstijvende koelheid van den zoogenaamden redelijkheid schrikte me af als onnatuur en de gekunsteldheid van het piëtisme, dat bovendien een groot gevaar bleek te zijn, daar het aanwakkerend werkt op de zinnelijkheid". Ibid., 1.
3 "Er is zoveel dat men in de kerk hoort, waar noch dominee noch toehoorders aan geloven, maar voor welk ongeloof zij niet durven uitkomen, dat men er misselijk van word". Ibid., 3.

uinely believed that which is found in the Bible. This stance undoubtedly affected the religious perspective of Ina's father, Herman Lohr. His own mother, Sara (Sally) Gijsberta Elisa van Gennep, was half-Indonesian and thus in all likelihood was influenced by local traditions as well as by the faith of her father, Jan Louis van Gennep, which was probably Calvinism.

As we have seen above, there is much less information on the whole concerning the Resink family. In regard to their spiritual beliefs, all we know is that Jet's father, Albertus Resink, was a freemason and that one of her brothers, Dr. Albertus Johannes Resink (1873–1946) – apart from being a painter, artist, biologist, communist and teacher – was also a theosophist and teacher; her grandmother, Johanna de Klerk, was certainly Protestant, presumably a Calvinist.

Although it is not known whether Ina Lohr's family attended a Calvinist or Lutheran church, they too were clearly Protestant. For example, in the last year of her life she recalled that when the family moved to Catholic Nijmegen from Amsterdam, the children were taught to speak of Catholicism with respect, but they also learned their Bible passages by heart in a very Protestant manner.[4]

As usual, the Lohrs' approach to religion was characterized by an awe-inspiring combination of intensity and intellectual breadth. Musically, for instance, Ina Lohr was not only exposed to Calvinist psalms as a child, but also, as we have seen above, to Palestrina – sung at that time primarily in Catholic Cecilian circles – which she and her sisters and mother sang together. Even before she went to the Muziek-Lyceum, she had come across Gregorian chant through the *Varii Canti*, studying it on her own. Thus before leaving home, she had already become acquainted with some of the most important religious repertoire of both the Catholics and Protestants. In addition, the majority of her early compositions were religious in nature, either for voice and organ, or for a small choir.

The entire family was trained in a skill long-forgotten in our digital age, that of making excerpts from books, which they did in little booklets, several of which still exist today, such as Herman Lohr's complete manuscript copy of Robert Koch's *Zeichenbuch*,[5] a collections of the signs or runes used from Antiquity

---

4   Interview with Jos Leussink, 24–25 March, 1983.
5   *Das ist das Zeichenbuch, welches viele Arten von Zeichen und Sinnbildern enthält, wie sie im deutschen Volk gekannt und angewendet wurden von Handwerkern und Kaufleuten, von Steinmetzen und Apothekern, von Astronomen und anderen weisen Männern und in der heiligen christlichen Kirche und im christlichen Leben zur Ehre Gottes unseres Vaters im Himmel.* Offenbach am M., 1923. A copy of this notebook was placed at my disposal by Floris and Aleida Zuidema, Lochem, Netherlands.

through early Christianity and into medieval times, or Ina Lohr's excerpts from M.C. Nieuwbarn's book on Catholic architecture, *Het roomsche Kerkgebouw*.[6] It was simply taken for granted that the children would take part in the intellectual and artistic interests of the parents on a level that would be considered unusual today.

Sally Lohr, Ina's younger sister, apparently also devoted much time and thought to her faith. There are several notebooks in her hand containing a combination of her own religious meditations as well as quotations she found meaningful. In her letters to Ernst Gaugler, Ina Lohr frequently remarks on how she sends his sermons to her sisters in the Netherlands. She also comments on how her sister Sally's trust [in God] had for years been her own greatest sustenance.[7] Thus while in Basel, she was in constant communication with her sisters on the subject of their faith.

The Lohr family's interest in religion was, of course, not limited to Christianity. In Judith Schmitz's memoirs she speaks of how in the mid-thirties her aunt, Jet Lohr, spoke with her fiancé about her "latest hobby", Eastern faith.[8] And Ina Lohr's older sister, Etty, was so interested in world religions that she kept three statues of Buddah next to her Bible.[9]

Although on the surface – given all these piquant details – it may seem surprising that we know next to nothing of the actual religious observances of the family, it is in line with the mores of the time which considered one's religious affiliation to be a private matter, something not to be discussed outside of one's own four walls. It is not until Ina Lohr herself called her previous religious convictions into question in 1939 that we begin to learn more. On one level, this is understandable, as probably up until that time she had simply accepted her parents' beliefs and religious observance. But it is just this lack of knowledge – together with the vast cultural changes that have taken place in the world in the meantime – which leaves us wondering just what Ina Lohr really meant, when in contemplating the sources of her own religious convictions, she wrote

---

6   Nijmegen, 1908. A copy of this notebook was placed at my disposal by Floris and Aleida Zuidema, Lochem, Netherlands.

7   "Sally's Vertrauen war mir Jahre-lang [sic] die grösste Hilfe". Letter Ina Lohr to Ernst Gaugler of 2 January 1952, PSF-ILC.

8   "Na het inschenken was Tante Jet er natuurlijk bij komen zitten en begon meteen tegen Pappa over het Oosterse geloof dat haar laatste hobby was". As these memoirs were written for her children, she refers to her future husband as "Pappa". Memoirs of Judith Schmitz, 163.

9   I was shown both the Bible and the statues at the home of Floris and Aleida Zuidema, Lochem, Netherlands.

Ill. 2.1: Ernst Gaugler. Photo: courtesy of Christ-katholischer Medienverlag.

And yet my father is a convinced freethinker and even appears to be a nationalist. However, he did that which was demanded of him, and he did it with joy and always acting from an innate philanthropy. And naturally my mother always stood by him. And when I reflect upon it, I do not understand why the Christian idea has overcome me to such a degree, has attacked me.[10]

It is a question that remains difficult to answer today, as for someone so intense in her belief and simultaneously so private in her convictions, she was surprisingly non-dogmatic, active professionally as a musician within both the Catholic and Protestant churches. The following represents an attempt – albeit incomplete and fragmented – to understand the role religion played in her life.

It is only through her correspondence at the end of the thirties and beginning of the forties with Ernst Gaugler (1891–1963, see Ill. 2.1), a member of the Old Catholic church,[11] and her notes for her classes on church songs within the liturgy for the University of Basel that we gain any real insight into her religious motivation.

When Ina Lohr met Ernst Gaugler at the Kurhaus Haltenegg in Heiligenschwendi, where she had gone to for a "cure", he was already a professor of the-

10   "Und doch ist mein Vater ein überzeugter Freidenker und sogar scheint er ein Nationalist. Er hat aber getan, was von ihm verlangt wurde, und er hat es getan mit Freude und immer erfüllt von warmer Menschenliebe. Und natürlich war meine Mutter immer neben ihm. Und wenn ich das überlege, dann verstehe ich nicht, warum mich die christliche Idee dermassen überfallen, ja angegriffen hat". Letter Ina Lohr to Ernst Gaugler, 25 April 1940, PSF-ILC.
11   In Switzerland this is called the "Christkatholische Kirche" in order to emphasize the role of Christ within the denomination.

ology at the University of Berne, noted for his exegesis of the New Testament. In his work he was not so much concerned with

> "spirituality" in the sense of personal Christian piety, as with spiritual impulses toward the creation of a pneumatically founded Church as the Body of Christ. In this regard, his exegetic work blessedly affected the theology of all Old Catholicism. Long before the ecumenical movement constituted itself institutionally, Ernst Gaugler affirmed in the name of the Lord Jesus Christ that the future lay in "one herd under one shepherd".[12]

Influenced by the Christian mystics, both in his theology and his life, Gaugler was drawn to them not only by a sense of religious affinity, but also by an interest in Indian mysticism stemming from his childhood. As he himself suffered from the effects of both tuberculosis and diabetes, many were drawn to him because of his empathy with their own illnesses, own problems. Kurt Stalder, in his eulogy of 23 January 1963, wrote the following about the quality of Gaugler's listening, his ability to hear what was going on in the whole person, not merely comprehend the words:

> If one so hears, with simultaneous acknowledgment and acceptance, with decision, then with the [process of] hearing, a transformation takes place within ourselves. We would not have truly acknowledged and accepted it, had we not at the same time come [ourselves] into a certain congruence with the acknowledgment and acceptance. Taken to the extreme, one would therefore have to say: Man hears what he is. But both clauses belong together. They point us toward the secret of the freedom of God, to the secret of his choice which calls one [person] today to hear and lets another for the moment hear even less. But it is always such that one becomes that which he hears, and thereby experiences that he already was that which he heard. This secret moved and stimulated the deceased again and again to the very depths.[13]

---

12 "'Spiritualität' im Sinne privater christlicher Frömmigkeit, sondern um geistliche Impulse zur Auferbauung einer pneumatisch fundierten Kirche als des Leibes Christi. In dieser Hinsicht wirkte sich sein exegetisches Schaffen segensreich auch auf die Theologie des gesamten Altkatholizismus aus. Lange bevor sich die ökumenische Bewegung institutionell konstituierte, bezeugte Ernst Gaugler im Namen des Herrn Jesus Christus, dass die Zukunft der 'Einen Herde unter dem Einen Hirten' gehört." Hans A. Frei, "Ernst Gaugler (1891–1963): Charismatischer Diener des Wortes", in: *Theologische Profile: Schweizer Theologen und Theologinnen im 19. und 20. Jahrhundert*, ed. Bruno Bürki and Stephan Leimgruber, Freiburg (Switzerland): Universitätsverlag and Paulusverlag 1998, 133.

13 "Wird aber so gehört, in gleichzeitiger Anerkennung und Annahme, also in Entscheidung, so geschieht mit dem Hören immer auch eine Wandlung an uns. Wir hätten ja nicht wahrhaft anerkannt und angenommen, wenn wir nicht zugleich in eine gewisse Entsprechung zu dem Anerkannten und Angenommenen träten. Aufs Äusserste zugespitzt muss man darum wohl sagen: der Mensch hört, was er ist. Aber die beiden Sätze gehören zusammen. Sie weisen uns auf das Geheimnis der Freiheit Gottes, auf das Geheimnis seiner Wahl, die den einen heute zum Hören ruft und den andern zur Zeit noch weniger hören lässt. Aber immer ist es so, dass einer wird, was er hört, und dabei erfährt, dass er zugleich auch schon war, was er hört. Dieses Geheimnis hat den Verstorbenen immer wieder aufs tiefste bewegt

It is apparently in one of these conversations that Ina Lohr – with her constant battle against weakness and illness, and her own knowledge of the effects of tuberculosis, as both of her sisters had the disease, as well as of diabetes from which her mother suffered – had a religious epiphany which caused her to re-examine her life, what she was doing and why. The depth of this experience led to a life-long friendship with Ernst Gaugler, a friendship in which he was constantly expressing his support and appreciation for her chosen path in life. It also led to an intense period of introspection, in which she herself wrote that it was difficult to maintain her relationships with her musician colleagues.[14] Not unsurprisingly, this in turn provoked a certain amount of upheaval in her cooperation with Paul Sacher, as she felt obliged to redefine their working relationship.

The first evidence we have of this epiphany is her first letter to Gaugler, dated 13 October 1939, where she writes:

> I am physically not much better than three weeks ago, but everything has become so much simpler and more joyful because I no longer think that I am sickly or weak, when I choose religion as the "direction of [my] heart".[15]

In an article about 16th-century Easter songs, she makes a passing reference to "piety today still being such a personal affair – a 'direction of the heart' according to Rilke".[16] The likelihood of Rainer Maria Rilke being a source for the phrase in the letter to Gaugler is substantiated by the evident importance of the poet to Ina Lohr. Not only did she have 25 books about or by him in her library – one of which, *Die Aufzeichnungen des Malte Laurids Brigge*, was Paul Sacher's first gift to her – the first four of her compositions which were performed in concert were songs for soprano and piano on texts from his *Stundenbuch*. The phrase stems from a letter – written by the poet to Ilsa Blumenthal-Weiss[17] on 28 December 1921 – devoted largely to the subject of faith and

---

und erregt". Kurt Stalder, Eulogy of 23 January 1963 in: *Ernst Gaugler 1891–1963: Drei Predigten von Prof. Dr. Ernst Gaugler*, Allschwil/Basel: Christkatholischer Schriftenverlag 1964, 12.

14 Letter Ina Lohr to Ernst Gaugler, 26 September 1943, PSF-ILC.

15 "Körperlich geht es mir nicht viel besser als vor drei Wochen, aber alles ist so viel einfacher und freudiger geworden, weil ich nicht mehr meine, ich wäre krankhaft oder schwach, wenn ich die Religion als 'Richtung des Herzens' wähle". Letter Ina Lohr to Ernst Gaugler of 13 October 1939, PSF-ILC.

16 "Frömmigkeit ist auch heute noch so sehr eine persönliche Angelegenheit – eine 'Richtung des Herzens' sagt Rilke". Ina Lohr, "Die Passionslieder des 16. Jahrhunderts", in: *Musik und Gottesdienst* 2 (1948), 45.

17 Ilse Blumenthal-Weiss (1899 – 1987) was a German poet who – as a survivor of both Westerbork and Theresienstadt concentration camps – wrote largely about the Holocaust.

religion. In it, he expresses a mystical approach to God, comprehending the universe as being beyond a specific dogma:

> Faith! – I would almost say that there is none. There is only – love. Forcing the heart to believe this or that which one normally calls faith makes no sense. First you must find God somewhere, experience him as so infinitely, so overall, so immensely present – then whether it is fear, or astonishment, or breathlessness, in the end it is – love, *which* then holds one to him, but that is hardly important; but faith, this obligation towards God, has no place for one who has begun with the discovery of God, in which there is then no more stopping, no matter where one has begun.[18]

Rilke then speaks, almost with envy, of those races where belief is part of the cultural structure rather than something that requires faith; where one needs "faith", religions tend to transform themselves into something moralistic. In Rilke's opinion, however,

> Religion is something endlessly simple, uncomplicated. It is not a knowledge, not the content of feelings (for all contents are to be assumed from the outset, when a person is dealing with life), it is not a duty, nor a sacrifice, it is not a limitation: but rather in the perfect space of the universe, it is: a direction of the heart.[19]

In her epiphany she must have experienced the simplicity and joy of being at one with her God, experienced the mystical feeling of being at one with the universe. This in turn transformed her view of religion, brought her to a space from which there was, as intimated by Rilke in his discussion of faith, no return. Her religious needs and desires were no longer dictated by her weakness and illness, but by the "direction of her heart". Given her constant battles with ill health, with depression, it is understandable that this view of religion not only provided comfort, but also gave her a resource to turn to in need.

---

18 "Glauben! – Es gibt keinen, hätte ich fast gesagt. Es gibt nur – die Liebe. Die Forcierung des Herzens, das und jenes für wahr zu halten, die man gewöhnlich Glauben nennt, hat keinen Sinn. Erst muss man Gott irgendwo finden, ihn erfahren, als so unendlich, so überaus, so ungeheuer vorhanden –, dann sei's Furcht, sei's Staunen, sei's Atemlosigkeit, sei's am Ende – Liebe, *was* man dann zu ihm fasst, darauf kommt es kaum noch an, – aber der Glaube, dieser Zwang zu Gott, hat keinen Platz, wo einer mit der Entdeckung Gottes begonnen hat, in der es dann kein Aufhören mehr gibt, mag man an welcher Stelle immer begonnen haben". *Briefe aus Muzot: 1921 bis 1926 / Rainer Maria Rilke*, ed. by Ruth Sieber-Rilke and Carl Sieber, Leipzig: Insel-Verlag 1935, 65.

19 "Religion ist etwas unendlich Einfaches, Einfältiges. Es ist keine Kenntnis, kein Inhalt des Gefühls (denn alle Inhalte sind ja von vornherein zugegeben, wo ein Mensch sich mit dem Leben auseinandersetzt), es ist keine Pflicht und kein Verzicht, es ist keine Einschränkung: Sondern in der vollkommenen Weite des Weltalls ist es: eine Richtung des Herzens". Ibid., 65.

Nine years later, however, when writing about piety being a "direction of the heart", she continued on to say that it causes each one of us to keep to himself,

> even in the congregation, in the church service [...] and in singing to seek his own private benison. This attitude corresponds from the point of view of content to the [sacred] songs from the 17th and 18th centuries. The sober, but infinitely profitable and deeply faithful factual report upon which the Reformation hymns are based, place demands upon us: firstly, that we believe these facts and sing out of a sense of thankfulness; secondly, that we do not do this as a private person, but rather as members of the congregation of Jesus Christ.[20]

She came to see it as her vocation to integrate two seemingly disparate aspects of the Protestant church, the "sober facts", that is the Word, the theology, the dogma, with profound thankfulness for the eternal unifying mystery more often associated with mysticism. And this she did again and again in her singing both without, but especially within the church, bringing the congregation to sing – in Jean Calvin's words – "from one mouth". Perhaps this is the source of her particular love of psalms, as according to Jean Calvin and Guillaume Farel, they "can stimulate us to raise our hearts to God and arouse us to an ardor in invoking as well as in exalting with praises the glory of His name".[21]

And from this perspective of religion being a "direction of the heart", her intense pursuit of bringing a new sense of community within the Christian Church, no matter what the denomination, is completely comprehensible. It finds its most precise expression in a lecture Ina Lohr wrote for a class on liturgical singing and playing of music at the University of Basel in which she speaks of why one attends church, remarking that it is

> the profession of a Christian in acknowledgment of the denomination within which he was born or which he has chosen. In this manner, there are ever new congregations – from the Catholic church to the [anthroposophical] Christian Community – which embrace Jesus Christ as their Lord. This profession, which manifests itself in the attendance of church, joins everybody, everybody turns to the same Lord who heals, saves, the Re-

---

20 "dass sogar in der Gemeinde, im Gottesdienst jeder gerne für sich bleibt und im Singen seine eigene, private Erbauung sucht. Dieser Haltung entsprechen inhaltlich die Lieder aus dem 17. und 18. Jahrhundert. Der nüchterne, aber unendlich dankbare und glaubensstarke Tatsachenbericht, der den Reformationsliedern zu Grunde liegt, stellt Anforderungen an uns: Erstens: dass wir diesen Tatsachen glauben und aus Dankbarkeit singen; zweitens: dass wir das nicht als Privatmenschen tun, sondern als Glieder der Gemeinde Jesu Christi". Ina Lohr, "Die Passionslieder des 16. Jahrhunderts", 45.

21 "Les psaulmes nous pourront jnciter a esleuer noz cueurs a Dieu et nous esmouoyr a ung ardeur tant de linuocquer que de exalter par louanges la gloyre de son nom". The translation is by Charles Garside, Jr., "The Origins of Calvin's Theology of Music: 1536–1543", in: *Transactions of the American Philosophical Society* 69 (1979), 10. I wish to thank Hans-Jürg Stefan for pointing out this connection to me.

deemer, the Savior. This Lord promised us to be with us every day until the end of the world, but also that He would be among us whenever two or three people assemble in His name. There He is present in substance, and therefore every church service in the congregation should be a celebration.[22]

This stance led her to be able to participate musically in churches of various Christian denominations. What was important to her was that she be able to facilitate the profession of faith. Thus for her, although the message of the text was always of greater importance than the music with which it was associated, the music served to create a sense of community in the congregation and thereby unity with the sublime.

It is also this which enabled her to not only teach classes on Gregorian chant for the regular students but also for Catholic priests. Furthermore, in order to make it possible for her regular students to experience the chant in its liturgical function, she also went to Catholic services with them. In doing so, however, she had set very clear confessional boundaries for herself, as becomes evident in a letter to Hans Urs von Balthasar to whom she had written in regard to the possible publication of some quotations of Augustine concerning music that she frequently used in her teaching. In his response, he questioned her interest in Gregorian chant, wondering how it could be reconciled with her Protestant faith. She replied, in a letter written on Easter Sunday, 6 April 1947 in the following manner:

> I cannot share your belief that we should make "the" path manifest, i.e. the path of one *church*. I can sing Et unam sanctum in the Credo with the greatest conviction, because I believe in one church that is the Corpus Christi. But it is no longer a unity here in this world, and I cannot believe that *one* of its forms possesses the entire truth. All are searching, but from the beginning of time, [all] have been found by God [...]
>   Nonetheless, thanks to God, a large portion of our articles of faith and professions are the same. And it is for this reason that I believe I have the right to sing chant and old polyphony with Catholics and Protestants. For it is just then that we are part of this

22 "Bekenntnisakt des Christen, der zu seiner Konfession, in die er hineingeboren wurde, oder die er gewählt hat, steht. Es bilden sich in dieser Art immer von neuem Gemeinden von der katholischen Kirche bis zur Christengemeinschaft, die sich zu Jesus Christus als ihrem Herrn bekennen. Dieses Bekenntnis, das im Kirchgang sichtbar zum Ausdruck kommt, verbindet alle, alle kommen zum gleichen Herrn, dem heilenden, rettenden, dem Erlöser, Heiland, 'Seligmacher'. Dieser Herr hat uns verheissen bei uns zu sein, alle Tage, bis an der Welt Ende, aber auch, Er würde mitten unter uns sein, wo zwei oder drei in seinem Namen zusammen sind. Dort ist Er real präsent, und darum sollte jeder Gottesdienst in der Gemeinde ein Fest sein". There is a marginal note "Mt. 28, 20b, Mt. 18, 20" to the Biblical texts she paraphrased. It is taken from a lecture entitled "Vom liturgischen Singen und Spielen. WS [Wintersemester] 1965", PSF-ILC.

One Church which comes into existence in such forms. That which I can sing only as an artist, but not as a professing Christian are the Marian texts, the Stabat Mater, the Salve Regina, Ave Maria, etc. [...] I know and respect these texts better than most, and precisely because of this, I know how much doctrinal strength lies within them, I cannot approve of only singing them as "beautiful words", as mere forms. [...] As a profession we cannot and may not sing them in the Protestant church; this has a different doctrine, which is, to be sure, not all that different in the most important points. Therefore, it is unproblematic for us to sing a mass. We were always permitted to do that.[23]

This passage demonstrates a great knowledge in doctrinal differences, as well as her own standpoint, and a willingness to express them openly if asked to do so. In her letter, Ina Lohr not only reacted sensitively to Balthasar's religious scruples, but of her own accord, she informed him that she would, in this case, pursue a different course of action in regard to the Augustine quotations.

The extraordinary degree to which she lived these ideals of religious tolerance is documented by her being willing to be responsible for the music in an investiture ceremony in the Dominican church in Riehen on 25 January 1957. On its eve, she noted in her diary that "the mass and investiture must be as good as possible". On the following day, however, after remarking on how well everything had gone, she once again revealed the clarity with which she perceived her own religious position:

But I am still a convinced Protestant. The mass, as it is now, is so overloaded, that it is impossible to follow all of the ideas consciously. It operates through the feelings and through the perceptions. Is that enough?[24]

23 "ich kann nicht mit Ihnen glauben, dass wir 'den' Weg, d.h. wohl den Weg einer <u>Kirche</u> zeigen sollten. Ich kann mit tiefster Ueberzeugung im Credo das Et unam Sanctam singen, weil ich glaube an die eine Kirche die Corpus Christi ist. Sie ist aber hier auf Erden keine Einheit mehr, und ich kann nicht glauben, dass <u>eine</u> ihrer Formen die ganze Wahrheit besitzt. Alle suchen, sind aber von jeher von Gott gefunden. [...]
    Nun sind aber, Gott sei gedankt dafür, ein grosser Teil unserer Glaubensäusserungen und Bekenntnisse gleich. Darum meine ich doch das Recht zu haben, den Choral und die alte Polyphonie mit Katholiken und Protestanten zu singen. Gerade dann sind wir Teil dieser Einen Kirche, die in solchen Formen in Erscheinung tritt. Was ich nur als Künstlerin, nicht als bekennende Christin singen kann, das sind die Marientexte, das Stabat Mater, das Salve Regina, Ave Maria u.a. [...] Dabei kenne und achte ich diese Texte besser als die meisten, und gerade deshalb, weil ich weiss, wie viel Bekenntniskraft in ihnen liegt, kann ich es nicht billigen, dass wir sie als 'schöne Worte', als blosse Form singen würden. [...] Als Bekenntnis können und dürfen wir sie in der protestantischen Kirche nicht singen; diese hat ein anderes Bekenntnis, das allerdings in den wichtigsten Punkten gar nicht so verschieden ist. Darum können wir ohne weiteres eine Messe singen. Das wurde uns auch immer erlaubt". Letter Ina Lohr to Hans Urs von Balthasar of 6 April 1947, PSF-ILC.
24 "Maar ik ben toch overtuigd Protestant. De mis, zooals die nu is, is zoo overladen, dat het onmogelijk is al die gedachten bewust te volgen. Het gaat uitsluitend door het gevoel en door de waarneming. Is dat genoeg?", Diary entry of 26 January 1957, PSF-ILC.

Thus, while participating in the service, she was open to all that was going on, but in the end, however, she made use of it to reaffirm her own personal beliefs.

In spite of this, Ina Lohr was nonetheless forced to reconcile the strength and direction of her faith in relation to the attitude of those in the religious or musical circles in which she was active, as she was very aware that it did not always meet with complete approbation. In retrospect this can perhaps be traced to her upbringing in the Netherlands and the very different atmosphere that prevailed in Protestant circles there. Although the Reformed Churches in the Netherlands and Switzerland stem from the same movement in the 16th century, over time they had come to manifest themselves differently in the local cultures. In addition, Basel had become a prominent center for Protestant theology with the return of Karl Barth (1886–1968) to Switzerland in 1935, where he assumed a chair in systemic theology at the university.[25] Through his active stance against Nazism as author of the Barmen Declaration, in which the influence of Nazism on German Christianity was rejected, and his 13-volume masterpiece of systemic theology, *Church Dogmatics*, his work had a significant impact on Protestantism throughout the world. The eminent Princeton theologian, George S. Hendry, wrote that Barth's

> evangelical theology is essentially modest; for it speaks of the God of the Gospel who transcends all human enterprises, including that of theology. This God relates himself to man by his own deed, and theology, therefore, must always speak of this relationship in the direction from God to man and not from man to God [...] Above all it must remember that the supreme act of God is his relating himself to man in love. The God of the Gospel is Immanuel, God with us, and therefore evangelical theology must be "the most thankful and happy science".[26]

This approach, however, did not match that of Ina Lohr, as may be seen from a letter to Ernst Gaugler:

> I still profit from our meeting in the fall and winter '39 and how much has happened since then! I called perhaps then more "from the depths" than now; it seemed to me that "my world", with its many external events, stood in the way of my reaching God, even stopped me from calling to him. Now I am laboriously on my path and I have learned to call and to pray and feel myself to be strongly connected, even often pain-

---

25 I am indebted to Christopher Schmidt for introducing me to this very foreign world. As son of Karl Ludwig Schmidt (1891–1956), professor of theology at the University of Basel from 1935–1953, brother of Martin Anton Schmidt (1919–2015), who received his degree in 1948 from the University of Basel and taught there from 1967–89, and for all intents and purposes the godson of the family friend Karl Barth, he proffered me a perspective which was at one and the same time both intimate and detached. In our many conversations, he helped me place Ina Lohr within this highly complex context.

26 George S. Hendry, "Barth for Beginners", in: *Theology Today* 19 (1962), 267.

fully and mysteriously, to my beloved ones. But this mysteriousness separates me from much that others expect from me. It is a daily struggle. And in addition, there is the whole new world of theologians in Basel, who have now given me their trust and accept me, but whom I often cannot understand at all. Professor Barth and also Pastor Lüthi can downright scare me.[27]

Her perception that her profound faith isolated her from her musician friends is something that she was forced to contend with over a longer period of time, as we will see in the discussion of her cooperation with Paul Sacher. In addition, however, with an idiosyncratic stringency particular to her being, she also chose an independent religious path. This choice was based partly on the call of her own heart, but also on extensive reading in theology, as may be seen from the following passage from a letter to Hinrich Stoevesandt[28]:

> In the last, also for me more difficult weeks, I have occupied myself intensely with Miskotte[29] and have grasped very well (which has now been confirmed by your letter) why K[arl] B[arth] cannot relate to him. His [Miskotte's] sensitivity is that of an artist, but it also stems from the threat of depression, with which he is no doubt constantly confronted. The miracle is that he overcomes this depression again and again through his faith and through everything that he knows to say about this faith. There the C[hurch] D[ogmatics] has been a blessed help to him, the C.D. that Karl Barth wrote, not the human Karl Barth, who with his healthy commonsense approach to life [Bauernnatur] does not have the understanding for this great uncanny, profound knowledge of human suffering. M[iskotte] speaks to me directly, often almost terrifyingly so, because I know this threat only too well. He is just for that reason a great help for me at the moment, because he can say from the knowledge of the C.D. (and also that of M[iskotte] himself!) how one should live in daily life, [how one] can better endure this daily life.[30]

---

27 "Ich schöpfe immer noch aus diesem Zusammentreffen im Herbst und Winter '39[,] und wie vieles ist seither geschehen. Damals rief ich vielleicht mehr 'aus der Tiefe' als jetzt; es kam mir vor, als stehe 'meine Welt' mit dem vielen äusseren Geschehen mir im Weg um zu Gott zu gelangen, ja verhinderte mich sogar daran Ihn anzurufen. Jetzt bin ich mühsam auf dem Weg und ich habe gelernt zu rufen und zu beten und fühle mich dadurch mit meinen Lieben stark, ja oft sogar schmerzhaft und unheimlich verbunden. Aber dieses Unheimliche trennt mich von vielen, die hier anderes von mir erwarten. Das ist ein täglicher Kampf. Und dazu kommt die ganz neue Welt der Basler Theologen, die mir jetzt Vertrauen schenken und [mich] aufnehmen, die ich dann aber oft gar nicht verstehen kann. Professor Barth und auch Pfr. Lüthi können mir regelrecht Angst machen". Letter Ina Lohr to Ernst Gaugler of 1 January 1944, PSF-ILC.

28 Born in 1931, Hinrich Stoevesandt was director of the Karl Barth Archive, Basel, and from 1971–1997 he was main editor of the complete works of Karl Barth.

29 Kornelis Heiko Miskotte (1894–1976) was a well-known Dutch Protestant theologian.

30 "In den letzten, auch für mich etwas schweren Wochen habe ich mich intensiv mit Miskotte beschäftigt und doch sehr gut verstanden (was Ihr Brief mir nun bestätigt), dass K.B. keine Beziehung zu ihm findet. Seine Sensibilität ist die eines Künstler, aber sie geht auch an die Bedrohung durch die Depression zurück, der er wohl ständig ausgesetzt ist. Das Wunder

Through this passage in a letter to a personal friend and spiritual adviser, we gain a glimpse into the depths of Ina Lohr's struggles with her own personal demons. It becomes manifest that in religion she found the means to deal with her black periods of depression, with the weakness of her constitution. It gave her the strength to go on, and to continually renew her faith and joy by directing her heart, her whole self – in particular through song – to God. In what we shall see to be characteristic for her approach to life in general, she has chosen spiritual guidance from those who can help her deal with these issues from a practical point of view, who give her the means to continue along her chosen path: "to help where help was needed, but if at all possible within a musical life".[31]

ist, dass er diese Depression immer von neuen durch den Glauben und durch alles, was er über diesen Glauben zu sagen weiss, überwindet. Da ist ihm die K.D: eine segensreiche Hilfe gewesen: die K.D., von Karl Barth geschrieben, nicht der Mensch Karl Barth, der mit seiner gesunden Bauernnatur das Verständnis für soviel fast unheimliches hintergründiges Wissen um menschliches Leiden nicht aufbringt. Mir spricht M. unmittelbar, oft fast beängstigend an, weil ich diese Bedrohung nur zu gut kenne. Er ist mir augenblicklich aber eben darum auch eine grosse Hilfe, weil er sagen kann, wie man aus den Erkenntnissen der K.D. (und auch eigenen von M!) im Alltag leben soll, diesen Alltag besser bestehen kann". Letter Ina Lohr to Hinrich Stoevesandt of 25 June 1961. I wish here to express my appreciation for Elisabeth and Hinrich Stoevesandt's interest in my project, which is reflected in their generosity in placing Ina Lohr's letters to the family at my disposal.

31 Cf. Chapter 1, p. 37.

Chapter 3. Ina Lohr's Musical Convictions

Ina Lohr's attitude toward music, her music aesthetic if you will, was very idiosyncratic, quite different from those around her. We will first consider her innate sense of the pre-eminence of the singing voice, which subsequently led her to place an inordinate importance on melody, particularly in relation to text, in her perception of music. It also led to a love of Gregorian chant, the world of sacred monophony, and, of course, affected how she approached the singing of the pre-Reformation and Reformation melodies that were so close to her heart. The following section investigates the influence of the *Jugend-musikbewegung* (German youth music movement) and the *Singbewegung* (Singing movement) upon her musical approach. Stemming from youthful protest against the mechanization of society, these movements came to push for purity and objectivity in performance, almost as a moral duty. In Chapter 2, we saw how strongly she had been affected by her religious experience in 1939, and we will consider next how this in turn colored her stance on the role of music and the musician in the church and in the liturgy. Closely related to this is the subject of *Hausmusik* (house music) in which she became increasingly active at about the same time, in that she saw in it the possibility of strengthening communal ties. And lastly, we will examine her approach to solmization and the church modes, which was a cardinal – and by no means universally accepted – aspect of her musical identity, providing a musical theory for her melodic focus.

3.1 The Role of the Voice in Personal Development

In the first chapter we saw how she could sing before she could speak and how she later came to consider this sort of innocent crooning as an innate, treasured source for all music. For her, the (singing) voice was an expression of a person's personality, and therefore to be cultivated throughout life. To underline the importance she attributed to this form of music-making, I want to quote two extensive passages taken from articles she wrote for two widely disparate journals, one for Swiss kindergarten teachers, the other for the Swiss Catholic Women's Association:

> Tomorrow the month of March begins and already very early today, I heard birds singing. Their song was still weak and tender, but it filled me with great joy. Yesterday I had the same experience when a child on the street – completely lost in thought – was singing to himself, without words, without a specific form, but authentically, without artificiality. In earlier days, when many children came to me each week to sing and play

recorder, we called this "singele" [singing in a singsong manner], and we meant this kindly, not contemptuously. And this means of expressing oneself should remain available to an adult, as a help in our often dismal lives. For our voice is our most personal instrument, that we always have with us, that we do not need to take out or put away, that we do not even need to tune. Purity of intonation and key are not so important, as long as we are only crooning to ourselves, not to learn, but to liberate that which lives within us.[1]

This was her means, from a very early age, of giving tongue to her thoughts, emotions, of comforting herself, of coming to term with the difficulties in her life. As it was such a powerful mode of expression for her, an aid in any and every difficult situation, she wanted to ensure that it was available to everyone.

In the second article, she encouraged her readers to make their own attempt at setting text to music, suggesting that they read

a poem or a consciously formed passage of prose aloud – in any case "setting" high and low, long and short notes – and make a singing out of this declamation, in that the beginning of the syllable at the onset of the note is sustained, not allowed to fall, as is usual in speaking. The length of this "sounding" is determined by the poetic verse and leads to a musical rhythm. [...] Every child can and should come from speaking to singing, and from singing to more conscious speaking. We adults can learn from children.

This kind of musical creativity is and remains dependent on language. Is a pure, wordless musical art therefore to be valued more highly? It comes about through the play with rhythms and notes. Such a play seems to bestow more freedom, but presupposes a discipline that was provided by the words in a texted melody. And one's self-criticism will have to be stricter, because the particular significance inherent to the text is lacking. But these warnings should not hinder us in making the attempt of singing like a child until a melody has formed itself, giving it to someone else, perhaps singing a counter-voice to it, beginning to move in its rhythm, liberating ourselves from worries and stress through a purposeless joy in the sound of our activity. But even this liberation should not be the purpose of a so-called rhythmization, which utilizes this singing

---

1   "Morgen beginnt der Monat März und schon heute in aller Frühe, hörte ich Vogelgesang. Er klang noch dünn und zart, erfüllte mich aber mit grosser Freude. Gestern hatte ich das gleiche Erlebnis, als ein Kind auf der Strasse ganz in sich versunken sang, ohne Worte, ohne bestimmte Form, aber echt und ungekünstelt. Ein solches Singen nannten wir früher, als noch jede Woche viele Kinder zu mir kamen, um zu singen und Blockflöte zu spielen, 'singele', und zwar liebkosend, nicht etwa verachtend. Und diese Äusserungsmöglichkeit sollte dem erwachsenen Menschen erhalten bleiben als Hilfe im oft so düsteren Leben. Ist doch die Stimme unser eigenstes Instrument, das wir immer bei uns haben, nicht aus- oder einpacken, nicht einmal stimmen müssen. Sogar die Reinheit und die Tonart sind nicht so wichtig, solange wir ganz für uns 'singele', nicht um zu lernen, sondern um frei zu geben, was in uns lebt". Ina Lohr, "Was ist unser 'eigenes' Instrument?", in: Der schweizerische Kindergarten 73/6 (1983), 2.

and playing with notes. Every human can and should be able to express himself freely and according to his ability and desire with the help of his voice or an instrument for "the glory of God and recreation of his soul" (J.S. Bach).[2]

For her, this was an extraordinarily fruitful approach not merely to music, but to life, demonstrating her belief in the intrinsic relationship between speech and song, with or without words. It gave her a source for channeling her thoughts and emotions, a means of expressing them beyond words, and above all, it gave her a means of adequately praising God.

It is also the source of her fascination with melody, with one-part music, both as a composer as well as a practical musician, in a world that found single lines insufficient, lacking, when harmony and counterpoint offered so much more variety. This is made clear in a newspaper article she wrote shortly before the premiere, on 9 May 1941, of the only compositions from her hand performed by the Basel Chamber Orchestra and Chamber Choir: her three songs for unisono choir and strings on texts by Heinrich von Laufenberg.[3] In this article, Ina Lohr openly admits that

---

2 "Eigentlich sollten alle, die diese Überlegungen lesen, einmal den Versuch machen, ein Gedicht oder einen bewusst geformten Prosatext laut zu lesen und aus diesem Sagen, das auf alle Fälle hohe und tiefe, lange und kurze Töne 'ansetzt', ein Singen zu machen, indem der Anfang der Silbe angesetzte Ton ausgehalten, nicht fallen gelassen wird, wie das beim Reden üblich ist. Die Dauer dieses 'Tönens' ergibt sich aus dem Vers und führt zum musikalischen Rhythmus. [...] Jedes Kind kann und sollte vom Sprechen zum Singen, vom Singen zum bewussteren Sprechen kommen. Wir Erwachsene können bei den Kindern lernen.
Diese Art der musikalischen Kreativität ist und bleibt abhängig von der Sprache. Ist darum eine reine, wortlose Ton-Kunst höher einzuschätzen? Sie entsteht aus dem Spiel mit Rhythmen und Tönen. Ein solches Spiel verleiht scheinbar mehr Freiheit, setzt aber eine Zucht voraus, die bei der Wortmelodik durch den Text vorgegeben war. Und die Selbstkritik wird strenger sein müssen, weil der Eigenwert des Textes wegfällt. Aber diese Warnungen sollen uns nicht daran hindern, den Versuch zu machen, wie ein Kind zu trällern, bis sich eine Melodie bildet, sie einem andern weiter zu geben, vielleicht eine Gegenstimme dazu zu singen, uns nach dem Rhythmus in Bewegung zu setzen, uns durch eine zwecklose Freude am klingenden Tun von Sorgen und Verkrampfung zu befreien. Aber auch diese Befreiung sollte nicht Zweck einer sogenannten Rhythmik werden, die das Singen und Spielen mit Tönen für sich in Anspruch nimmt. Jeder Mensch kann und soll sich mit Hilfe seiner Stimme oder eines Instrumentes frei und seinem Können und Wollen gemäss äussern können 'zur Ehre Gottes und zur Recreation des Gemütes' (J.S. Bach). Ina Lohr, "Musikalische Kreativität", in: *Schritte ins Offene* 5 (1975/4), 5.

3 *Drei Lieder für einstimmigen Chor und Streicher nach Texten von Heinrich v. Laufenberg*, Basel 1940. These were the first and only pieces by a woman to be premiered by Sacher until the 1980s when he inaugurated four works by Patricia Jünger, as pointed out by Jürg Erni, *Paul Sacher, Musiker und Mäzen: Aufzeichnungen und Notizen zu Leben und Werk*, Basel: Schwabe 1999, 145.

years ago, when I heard unisono, unaccompanied singing for the first time in a Catholic church in Amsterdam, a burden fell from from my shoulders. The Gregorian melodies seemed to me to be sublimated musical truth. From that time on, I was captivated by Gregorian chant, and I will undoubtedly and happily remain in this captivity. In addition, I discovered for myself our old Dutch folk songs, whose melodic lines are in part so perfectly beautiful that they do not require any accompaniment. The need for penetrating the mysteries of pure melody and writing my own melodies became increasingly urgent. My songs for choir, which will soon be performed here, stemmed from this need and first belonged to my collection of "musical exercises". One can train one's fingers, or one's ears, but one can also train one's mode of expression. It is my greatest joy to listen to a text until a melody emerges.[4]

Her entire musical and expressive focus thus was directed towards melody, towards line and its relationship to text. There were various factors that led to this almost obsessive singularity of approach. First of all, it was certainly in part due to her own sensibilities that she was so consumed by melody. Her inclinations, however, were certainly strengthened and shaped by her choral experiences at the Muziek-Lyceum with Hubert Cuypers, who not only, as we have seen above, taught Gregorian chant, but also directed the school choirs. In addition, through Cuypers she had become acquainted with a broad repertoire of early and Cecilian choir music.[5] Moreover, the more general popular interest in old folk songs and in *Hausmusik* (or *huismuziek* in Dutch) taken over from the *Jugendmusikbewegung* in Germany by the socialist youth organization, *Arbeiders Jeugd Centrale* (AJC) in the Netherlands, certainly did not escape her notice. In what follows, we will examine the influence of her studies with Hubert Cuypers upon her musical approach, particularly in regard to Gregorian chant, seeking to ascertain her own particular stance in the acrimonious battles concerning its performance in the first decades of the 20th century.

---

4 "Als ich vor Jahren in einer katholischen Kirche in Amsterdam zum erstenmal einstimmig, unbegleitet singen hörte, fiel eine Last von mir ab. Die gregorianischen Melodien kamen mir vor wie die musikalisch sublimierte Wahrheit. Von dem Tag an hatte mich der gregorianische Choral gefangen, und ich werde zweifellos und gerne in dieser Gefangenschaft bleiben. Dazu entdeckte ich für mich unsere alten, holländischen Volksmelodien, die zum Teil so vollendet schön sind in ihrer schlichten Melodik, dass sie keiner Begleitung bedürfen. Immer dringender wurde dann das Bedürfnis, in die Geheimnisse der reinen Melodik einzudringen und eigene Melodien zu schrieben. Die Chorlieder, die demnächst hier aufgeführt werden, sind aus diesem Bedürfnis heraus entstanden und gehörten zunächst zu meiner Sammlung 'Melodische Uebungen'. Man kann seine Finger oder seine Stimme oder seine Ohren üben, man kann aber auch seine Ausdrucksweise üben. Es ist meine grösste Freude, in einen Text hineinzuhorchen, bis aus ihm eine Melodie entsteht". Ina Lohr, "Wie ich meine Lieder schrieb", in: *Basler Nachrichten*, 3 May 1941, PSF-ILC.

5 Letter Ina Lohr to Paul Sacher about founding the Schola Cantorum Basiliensis, ca. 1980, PSF-ILC.

3.2 The Influence of Hubert Cuypers: Gregorian Chant and Cecilianism[6]

After the turbulences of the Reformation, Counter-Reformation, the Council of Trent, and the negation of the church during the Age of Enlightenment in France, with their concomitant effects on the singing of Gregorian chant, a need was perceived by certain members of the clergy in the 19th century to reform its performance as a means of consolidating faith within the Church. This involved a search for a form of the chant deemed to be most suitable for unifying the members of the congregation. As the Vatican considered it to be desirable for liturgical unity within the church that chant and its performance be uniform throughout the world, this led to considerable battles as to the content and execution of its melodies, particularly between the German faction associated with the Friedrich Pustet *Neo-Medicaean* editions and the French schools of Dom Joseph Pothier and Dom André Mocquereau associated with Solesmes *Vatican Editions*. Hubert Cuypers grew up during this period of renewal, taking an active part in it. It seems reasonable to assume that Ina Lohr's particular musical style in regard to chant reflected that of her teacher and mentor in that subject, Hubert Cuypers, especially as she speaks of him with such appreciation.

As we have seen, Hubert Cuypers was a highly successful, prize-winning choir director, organist and composer in the Netherlands, and as a result, prominent in Catholic music circles. Born only twenty years after the restoration of the diocesan hierarchy in the Netherlands in 1853, he grew up in a period of active cultivation of a new Catholic identity within the country, including the revival of chant as the sole true church music. Michael Johann Anton Lans, one of the primary figures in the renewal of chant in the Dutch Catholic church, founding the *Gregoriusblad* journal in 1876, and the associated organization of those interested in propagating chant, the *Gregoriusvereniging* in 1878, was an adherent of the Cecilian movement and thus also of the *Neo-Medicaean* edition of Pustet. Accordingly, Hubert Cuypers' original training was strongly influenced by the chant practice in Germany, in particular as his formal professional training took place at the *Gregoriushaus* in Aachen from 1889–91. There he studied with Franz Nekes who was known for the particular emphasis he placed on chant and the music of Palestrina. An idea of what his training might have entailed – and thus also an indication of what he may have passed on to Ina

6   I would not have been able to write this section without the extensive help of Kelly Landerkin (Schola Cantorum Basiliensis, Basel), Edward Nowacki (Cincinnati, Ohio), and Petra van Langen (Utrecht) who generously shared their knowledge of Gregorian chant with me.

Lohr – can be gained from the basic books on chant and polyphony utilized in seminaries at that time: Michael Johann Anton Lans's *Handboekje ten gebruike bij het onderwijs in den gregoriaanschen zang*, Leiden: van Leeuwen Verlag 1874, and Franz Xaver Haberl's *Magister Choralis*, Regensburg: Pustet 1866. He did not by any means remain limited to these ideas in his further musical development, however, writing of a performance of chant in Rome in 1904, according to the ideas of Solesmes, that it was "the first time in my life that the total impression came close to that of my own imagination".[7] Throughout his career he was renowned for the excellence of his choirs and, in particular, for the attention he gave to the appropriate presentation of the text. For example, Herman Leonard Berckenhof, in reviewing a performance of Gregorian chant wrote that

> the accent of the word, the meaning of the content, determine the declamation, an immaculate, pure declamation with the right accentuation of the syllable, which also receives the stress in the spoken language, but everything connected with a flowing musical rhythm. In order to obtain this smoothly and yet in an unaffected manner from the entire choir […] a long period of preparation, of singing together, is necessary under the direction of an artist in whom this music has entered his blood. Such a person is Mr. Hubertus Cuypers.[8]

Further, the eminent music critic, Herman Rutters, wondered whether Hubert Cuypers' highly successful melodramas were not influenced by his knowledge of chant declamation.[9] This – together with Cuypers' later articles on the performance of chant – gives an indication of the composer's concern for the correct and expressive declamation of the text, a concern that was later advocated by Ina Lohr.

---

7   "De totaalindruk kwam mijn phantasie voor 't eerst van mijn leven nabij". Various authors, *Hubert Cuypers 80 Jaar*, Amsterdam: N.V. Drukkerij J. K. Smit & Zonen 1953, 28.

8   "Het accent van het woord, de beteekenis van den zin, bepaalt de declamatie, een vlekkeloos zuivere declamatie met het juiste accent op dat woorddeel, hetwelk ook in de spreektaal den nadruk ontvangt, maar alles gebonden in een vloeiend muzikaal rhytme. Om dit gelijkmatig en toch ongedwongen van een heel koor te vorderen […] een lange tijd van voorbereiding, van samenzang noodig is, onder leiding van een kunstenaar, dien deze muziek in het bloed is gevaren. Zóó iemand is de heer Hubertus Cuypers". Herman Leonard Berckenhoff, *Kunstwerken en Kunstenaars (Muziek)*, Amsterdam: Maatschappij voor goede en goedkoope lectuur 1915, 67–68.

9   Letter Herman Rutters to Hubert Cuypers of 23 September 1909 (Netherlands Music Institute, The Hague) in which he speaks of a performance of Cuypers' melodrama *Adam in Ballingschap*, asking whether he is greatly mistaken in thinking that "within the characteristic use of rhythm, the secret of a thoughtful connection lies hidden and that your study of the Gregorian chant has contributed very much to it?" ("Vergis ik mij erg, als ik meen dat juist in die eigenaardige aanwending der rhythmiek het geheim schuilt van een gezinde verbinding en dat Uw studie van het Gregoriaansch daartoe veel heeft bijgedragen?").

As the question of how the chant was to be performed was not merely a matter of performance practice, but also of liturgical unity within the Catholic church, the decision on which editions were to be used – the German *Neo-Medicaean* or the French Solesmes (with and without Mocquereau's rhythmic indications) – ended up being in the hands of the Vatican. This in turn had significant financial consequences for the publishing houses concerned. As a result, these issues were sources of much internal strife on various levels within the church. Petra van Langen has examined the specifically Dutch aspects of these conflicts in her book, *Muziek en religie: katholieke musici en de confessionalisering van het Nederlandse muziekleven 1850–1948*. There she describes the various organizations in the Netherlands which were responsible for maintaining the liturgical, religious and musical order within the Catholic church, carefully delineating the lines both linking and separating clerical authority and professional music-making.[10] In the mid-1920s, there was considerable pressure, particularly from the clerical side, for the use of Dom Mocquereau's *Vatican Edition* with his added rhythmic markings, as these markings were perceived to facilitate a coordinated declamation of the text. Hubert Cuypers vehemently contested Dom Mocquereau's conclusions in 1930–31, not only in a radio broadcast, but also in an article in the Catholic newspaper *De Tijd* and three articles in *Caecilia*, a journal on music, in which he called the markings' veracity into question, in particular concerning the rhythmic interpretation of the neumes in relation to the text. Although he was certainly against Dom Mocquereau's ideas, the ferociousness of Hubert Cuypers attack was mainly directed at the efforts he perceived on the part of the clergy, as represented by the *Gregoriusvereniging*, to influence the interpretation of chant through their restriction of the flow of information concerning current scholarly research, thereby encouraging certain aspects of musical practice with which he did not agree. One can understand the sharpness of his writing both from the point of view of having his musical authority questioned by clerics, but also more concretely from the specific manifestations of this performance practice which were being advocated in the Netherlands at the time. In one of the responses to the article in *De Tijd*, the conductor and composer Theo van der Bijl wrote that Hubert Cuypers' manner of performing chant "instead of possessing manly seriousness and worth, had a charming, feminine character, too much concerned with concert effects, which in regard to the holiness of this music are popularly said to be: affected in performance, too weak, too sweet" as opposed to the recordings of Eliseus Bruning and his choir of the Minor Friars in Vernay which demon-

10 Hilversum: Verloren 2014.

strated the appropriate "manly, worthy and serious character of this music".[11] About these self-same recordings, the chant scholar Mary Berry later wrote in 1979 that the Vernay singers "sing quite fast, gliding from note to note in a weirdly mannered and unnatural way. They are typical of those many singers who strove, almost against nature, to follow the French example to the letter without quite bringing it off".[12] With his protracted offensive, Hubert Cuypers may not have won over all chant scholars, but he did succeed in re-establishing his own authority to make musical decisions and implicitly his artistic freedom.

In Ina Lohr's first years in Basel, however, she was constantly seeking to widen her own horizons in regard to chant, was by no means limiting herself to what she had learned in Holland. From the interview with Jos Leussink, we not only know that she went to Wiesbaden to transcribe Hildegard's Kyrie, but also went for "a good week" to the archabbey of Beuron and to the abbies of Maria Laach, Engelberg and Einsiedeln. It was her very practical method of exploring the performance practice of chant in that

> everywhere I asked whether they would show me how they sang [...] and everywhere I received the nicest help. Most of the time I was shut up in a room, alone with a lot of manuscripts, marvelous [...] but afterward we also spoke about them, that was really great. And there [...] I believe it was in Einsiedeln, there someone told me: "No, we don't sing that, we simply can't do it" [perhaps referring to the Phrygian gradual *Tu es Deus*, which she had been discussing just previously].[13]

By going to all of these monasteries, she was not only able to examine the manuscripts herself – and knowing her, sing from them – but she was also able to hear for herself how chant was being sung in some of the foremost abbeys of

11 "in plaats van mannelijken ernst en waardigheid te bezitten, een charmeerend, vrouwelijk karakter draagt, te veel op concerteffect gericht, wat, ten opzichte van de heiligheid dezer muziek in den volksmond genoemd wordt: een gemaakte voordracht, te weekelijk, te zoet" and "op het mannelijk-waardige en ernstige karakter van deze zang". Theo van der Bijl, "Gregoriaansche Gramophoonplaten uit Venray. De Strijd van Hub[ert] Cuypers tegen de Methode-Solesmes", in: *De Tijd*, 26 November 1930, as quoted in Petra van Langen, *Muziek en religie*, 207.

12 Mary Berry, "The restoration of the chant and seventy-five years of recording", in: *Early Music* 7 (1979), 204. Selections from the recordings, which indeed are rather eccentric, are found on the CD: *Gregorian Chant Early Recordings*, Parnassus 2013.

13 "overal heb ik gevraagd, of ze me wouden wijzen hoe ze zongen [...] alleraardigst, ik heb overal hulp gekregen. Ik werd meestal wel opgesloten in een kamer, alleen met een hele-boel manuscripten, heerlijk [...] maar daarna werd er ook over gesproken, dat was werkelijk fijn. En daar heeft [...] het was geloof ik in Einsiedeln, daar heeft iemand me gezegd: nee, dat zingen wij niet, dat kunnen we eenvoudig niet". Interview Ina Lohr with Jos Leussink, 24–25 March 1983.

the time, to experience chant in its liturgical place. This, no doubt, was of assistance in the formation of her own ideas on the performance of this music, leading as we see here to the singing of chants that were avoided in the monasteries. It also is an indication of the verve and determination with which she was exploring her own personal musical interests.

While doing so, she developed an idiosyncratic manner of singing chant, in line with her own ideas not only of how chant came into being, but also in relation to her self-identification with song and song forms, particularly in relation to those of the pre-Reformation and Reformation church. It was not that she was unaware of what was going on around her, as is made very evident by what she writes about chant and the bibliography she assembled for her teaching which contained all the latest research. She seemingly remained detached from the controversy as far as her own performance was concerned, as her main interest lay in how it was later assimilated by the Protestant church. It is as though the knowledge that one cannot know how it was actually sung, and the fact that she was for the most part not making use of it liturgically, gave her the freedom to shape the lines in her own manner.

She was very aware of the differences in approach, however, as is obvious from a text concerning rhythm in chant where she writes that

> on this subject, the sources as well as the theorists are not clear. And the result of the efforts of many scholars and practical musicians during the past 50 years is so diverse, that it is difficult to give preference to a specific theory. That the Catholic church was searching for a generally applicable solution is understandable and to be welcomed. Without the theory of the equality of the dots and of grouping in groups of two and three, the Latin monodic sacred song would not have sounded again. It is explained by Dom Mocquereau in his great work, *Le Nombre musical grégorien*, substantiated and expanded to a system which is generally recognized in the practice of the church today. Dom Mocquereau proceeds from the theory that the melody controls the word, that the word accent hardly had an influence on the "ictus". In an ingenious manner, he developed the theory of the smallest, indivisible unit, notated as a punctum, which leads to the melodic line of a group. The ictus, which at one and the same time is the conclusion of the movement of one part and the beginning of the next, has no weight, must have no accent, but rather only the vitality, the impulse to sum up the completed movement and to lead to the next. This theory breaks with any doctrine of accented and unaccented beats. It was necessary at the beginning of our century. It brought freedom from a system which many musicians (also those who did not occupy themselves with Gregorian chant) perceived as a constriction. One spoke of "free" rhythm in contrast to metric or mensural rhythm.[14]

14 "Auf diesem Gebiet lassen uns die Quellen wie die Theoretiker im Unklaren. Und das Resultat der Bemühungen vieler Wissenschaftler und Praktiker der letzten fünfzig Jahre ist so uneinheitlich, dass die Entscheidung für eine bestimmte Theorie schwer fällt. Dass die katholische Kirche eine allgemein durchführbare Lösung suchte, ist begreiflich und erfreu-

This passage, from a text obviously conceived as a summary of the material she presented in her teaching at the Schola, clearly indicates the importance that Dom Mocquereau's work had at his time – that it was necessary for a restoration of chant in the Catholic church – while at the same time revealing the above-mentioned detachment on her part from this approach. In particular, it seems as if she sees his theory within a larger context or framework than the study of chant, as being a valuable but not the sole answer to the question of rhythm.

Indeed, Christopher Schmidt – who not only studied with Ina Lohr, but later taught chant at the Schola himself – recalls that she found it difficult to explain how chant should be sung, but came into her own when she sang it herself, that it was then simply a thing of beauty. She approached those chants, such as antiphons – whose forms were more similar to songs, and where her modal concepts functioned – with a deep inner conviction; it was easy to understand her fascination with them, as their connection with the later Protestant hymns was obvious. It was quite different with the melismatic responsorial chants, such as the graduals and the alleluias, where Christopher Schmidt sensed a certain unease on her part, stemming from their ecstatic nature, something that she could come to terms with as a singer, but not as a theoretician or teacher. It was simply too far from her Protestant upbringing, as well as from the new call for objectivity stemming from both the *Singbewegung* and Neoclassicism, somehow a boundary she found difficult to breach. Her own discomfort with this aspect of chant seemed to lead her to fall back on Mocquereau's grouping in twos and threes for the melismas. While absolutely convincing

lich. Ohne die Theorie vom Gleichwert der Punkte und vom Gruppieren in Gruppen von zwei und drei wäre der lateinische einstimmige Kirchengesang nicht wieder zum Klingen gekommen. Sie ist von Dom Mocquereau in seinem grossen Werk 'Le Nombre musical grégorien' erklärt, begründet und zu einem System ausgebaut worden, das heute in der kirchlichen Praxis allgemein anerkannt wird. Dom Mocquereau geht von der These aus, dass die Melodie das Wort beherrscht, der Wortakzent kaum einen Einfluss auf den 'Ictus' hat. In genialer Weise entwickelt er die These von der kleinsten, unteilbaren Einheit, als Punkt notiert, die zur Gruppenmelodik führt. Der Ictus, der zugleich Abschluss einer Teilbewegung und Anfang er nächsten ist, hat keine Schwere, muss keinen Akzent haben, sondern nur die Vitalität, den Impuls zum Zusammenfassen der gewesenen Bewegung und zum Antreiben der kommenden. Diese Theorie bricht vollständig mit jeder Lehre vom schweren und leichten Taktteil. Sie war am Anfang unseres Jahrhunderts eine Notwendigkeit. Sie befreite aus einem System, das von vielen Musikern (auch von solchen, die sich nicht mit dem gregorianischen Choral befassten) als Zwang empfunden wurde. Man sprach vom 'freien' im Gegensatz zum taktgebundenen und zum mensurierten Rhythmus". It is one of three texts on her music theoretical beliefs that obviously served as a basis for some lectures, PSF-ILC.

when she was singing the more song-like chants, where the structure was given by the text, she was less so in the more melismatic ones, where at times the Mocquereau groupings seemed to obscure their sense. As a result, she was more effective as a precentor than a director, coordinating by example rather than by conducting. The students, as a consequence, found it rather puzzling in the chant exams that everybody was required to conduct the groupings of twos and threes. Everyone managed to get through it, but all were left wondering why they had to do it.[15]

This ambiguity may perhaps be a result of, or an explanation for, some of the difficulties Ina Lohr experienced when she gave her first course in Gregorian chant in Basel in 1932 under the auspices of the Basel Chamber Choir (*Basler Kammerchor*). The organist at the Heiliggeistkirche, Otto Rippl, after only attending a half an hour of the second session, sent a virulent letter of protest to the editor of the Catholic *Basler Volksblatt,* in which he maintained that "in these choir courses mistakes are made, wherever possible. The beautiful voice with which Miss Lohr sings is not sufficient alone!"[16] This was rebutted in a highly objective manner by a letter from the BKO, in which the general public was not only informed of Ina Lohr's background in chant, but also of the discussions within scholarly circles concerning its performance:

> Miss Ina Lohr [...] was introduced to chant by the director of the Schola Cantorum in Amsterdam, Hubert Cuypers, and since then, in the last seven years, has thoroughly studied the history of chant and the manner of singing it according to the method of the Benedictines of Solesmes, while simultaneously taking the German teachings of Peter Wagner and of P. Dom Johner (Beuron) into consideration. It is well known that the scholarly opinions in regard to the transcription of the chant notation and the performance of chant diverge greatly from one another, so that one can in good faith agree to disagree.[17]

---

15 Interviews with Christopher Schmidt, 7 December 2015, 9 January 2017 and 24 February 2017.
16 "Es werden also in diesem Chorkurs Fehler gemacht, wo nur möglich. Die wunderschöne Stimme, mit welcher Frl. Lohr vorsingt, die alleine tut's nicht!" Letter Otto Rippl to the *Basler Volksblatt* of 10 June 1932.
17 "Fräulein Ina Lohr [...] wurde vom Direktor der Schola Cantorum in Amsterdam, Hubert Cuypers, in den Choral eingeführt und hat seither, in den letzten sieben Jahren, die Geschichte des Chorals und die Gesangsart nach der Methode der Benediktiner von Solesmes eingehend studiert, unter gleichzeitiger Berücksichtigung der deutschen Lehren von Peter Wagner und von P. Dom Johner (Beuron). Bekanntlich gehen die wissenschaftlichen Anschauungen inbezug auf die Uebertragung der Choralnotation und die Gesangsart des Chorals weit auseinander, so dass man in guten Treuen verschiedener Meinung sein kann". Letter in *Basler Volksblatt*, 21 June 1932. That she stood by her stylistic independence may

In spite of the declaration of her adherence to Solesmes here, it is striking how much closer her ideas concerning the performance of music are to those of M. J. A. Lans, as expressed in his *Handboekje ten gebruike bij het onderwijs in den gregoriaanschen zang* (Handbook for Use in the Instruction of Gregorian Chant) than the solely aesthetic views of those of Dom Pothier and Dom Mocquereau. M. J. A. Lans insists, namely, that

> the words are not there for the music, but the music for the words. The spoken word is the foundation of our religious ceremonies, the expression of our reverence. It is the language of the Holy Bible, the language of tradition and the saints, the language of the church. The sole reason that chant was introduced by the church, was to give its elevated words a stronger, more solemn expression.[18]

He further insists that "there must be expression in the performance, and this expression differs in accordance with the character of the feast and with the content of the text".[19] As we have seen in Chapter 2, this concept of music also corresponded to Ina Lohr's view of music within the Christian church, one that enabled her to express her own personal faith in Jesus Christ in accordance with Protestant thought, while at the same time unifying the congregation to speak, as it were "from one mouth".

There is evidence from the end of her life that Ina Lohr was very aware of the idiosyncratic nature of her own personal stance towards the performance of chant, indeed openly stating that it was even perhaps questionable from a musicological point of view. In the "Conclusion as a Foreword to the Fourth Edition [1981]" of her book, *Solmisation und Kirchentonarten*, which appeared just two years before her death, she wrote namely that she had

---

    be seen from a comment she made to Jos Leussink in 1983, asking whether he could really send her commentary on the singing of chant in the Netherlands, remarking that Professor Hélène Wagenaar-Nolthenius of Utrecht University, while acknowledging that Ina Lohr sang the melodies beautifully, had declared that it had "nothing to do with Gregorian chant", ["maar dat heeft met Gregoriaans niets te maken!"].

18 "niet de woorden zijn voor de muziek, maar de muziek is voor de woorden; het uitgesproken woord is de grondslag onzer godsdienst-plegtigheden, de uitdrukking van onze eeredienst; het is de taal der H. Schrift, de taal der Overlevering en der Heiligen, de taal der Kerk; alleen daartoe werd de zang door de Kerk ingevoerd, om aan haar verheven woord eene meer krachtige, meer plegtige uitdrukking te geven". Michael Johann Anton Lans, *Handboekje ten gebruike bij het onderwijs in den gregoriaanschen zang*, Leiden: van Leeuwen 1874, 70.

19 "In de voordragt moet uitdrukking wezen; en die uitdrukking is verschillend naar het karakter van het feest en naar den inhoud van den tekst". Ibid., 72.

intensely devoted herself to Gregorian and to medieval chant for about fifty years, and concerned myself again and again and ever increasingly with its rhythm, which is not obviously definable through its notation. Today I know that I cannot know or prove anything, but that the songs have formed themselves in me, that for me they can only sound in this manner and in no other.[20]

The knowledge that scholarly transcriptions of these melodies now existed gave her the strength to notate her own versions of them in this late edition, thus also substantiating Christopher Schmidt's description of her as a moderate mensuralist.

In addition – in one of the few emendations she made for this edition – she spoke of some principles she adhered to in the performance of monophonic music, for example that it is necessary

to sing toward an important syllable, particularly toward a final syllable, also toward the end of a melodic phrase. This does not, however, mean that this note should be "accented". It is not about dynamics, but rather about agogics, about movement with a goal. The goal itself should then be comparatively light, so that a new flow will not be impinged upon.[…]

In addition, it appears to me to be improbable that medieval music theorists, with their mathematical training, would have been satisfied with note equality (isochronie). With the hymns, sequences, also with metric poetic texts, such as "Salve Regina" and "Ave Regina coelorum", the melodic rhythm is a product of the meter, assonance or rhyme. The melismatic Gregorian melodies give rise to too many unresolved questions that I would dare to stray from the grouping in groups of two or three notes, such as it was and is usual in the Catholic church.[21]

20 "Mit dem Gregorianischen und mit dem mittelalterlichen Choral habe ich mich ungefähr fünfzig Jahre intensiv beschäftigt und mich immer wieder und immer mehr um den aus der Notation nicht eindeutig sichtbar werdenden Rhythmus gekümmert. Heute weiss ich, dass ich nichts wissen oder beweisen kann, dass aber die Gesänge sich in mir geformt haben, dass sie für mich nur so und nicht anders klingen können". Ina Lohr, *Solmisation und Kirchentonarten*, Zurich: Hug & Co. 1981, unnumbered.

21 "das Hinsingen auf eine wichtige Silbe, vor allem auf die Schlussilbe(n), auch auf den Schluss einer melodischen Phrase. Das bedeutet darum noch nicht, dass dieser Ton 'betont' sein soll. Es geht nicht um Dynamik, eher um Agogik, um Bewegung mit einem Ziel. Der Zielton selber soll dann eher leicht sein, damit ein neues Fliessen nicht aufgehalten wird. […]
Es scheint mir übrigens unwahrscheinlich, dass sich die mathematisch geschulten Musiktheoretiker des Mittelalters mit dem Gleichwert der Töne (Isochronie) begnügt hätten. Bei den Hymnen, Sequenzen, auch bei metrisch poetischen Texten, wie 'Salve Regina' und 'Ave Regina coelorum', ergibt sich der melodische Rhythmus aus Metrum, Assonanz oder Reim. Die melismatischen Gregorianischen Gesänge geben zu viel Rätsel auf, als dass ich es wagen würde von der Gruppierung in Gruppen von zwei oder drei Tönen, wie sie in der katholischen Kirche üblich war und ist, abzuweichen". Ibid., 38.

Thus her continuous and deep musical investigation of chant, combined with her own inner freedom in dealing with it, stemming perhaps both from her Protestantism as well as from her compositional training, led her to her highly personal style in singing chant, a style that fascinated and inspired those around her.[22]

It also seems that M. J. A. Lans, with Hubert Cuypers as a conduit, could have been a source for her concept of "singing speech" or "speaking song", in that he describes the *cantus accentus*, or the melodies declaimed in accordance with their punctuation, as being "not much more than a solemn reading, which bore as much resemblance to speaking as to singing".[23] In 1954, at a workshop about practical work with religious song, she questioned why we sing Biblical texts, rather than merely reading them, reflecting on them. Her answer was that the

> song form allows us [the congregation] to speak and to reflect upon the text together, so that in singing we come to [...] the praise of God. If this is so, then the singing needs to remain quite close to the speaking of the text, to its actual scansion. The quiet metric-rhythmic speaking of a verse is an exercise that has largely been forgotten now. The reading of verse is usually adapted – for the benefit of personal interpretation and shaping – to the reading of prose. With this, however, the essence of verse is lost. In verse, each line stands on its own even when the sentence continues on into the next line; the various lines of a strophe create a whole. The rhyme favors both the independence as well as the unity of the lines, the meter and rhythm keep the verse and strophe "in order". Only by means of this order, does communal reading actually become possible. We will only attain clear, communal speaking with difficulty, if rhythm and rhyme are lacking.[24]

22 For an example of her singing, see https://soundcloud.com/user-802211739-365337350/puer-natus-est-sung-by-ina-lohr. That this appreciation was also, at least in part, shared by the musicological world can be seen from Ina Lohr's description of her encounter with Amédée Gastoué in 1940 – on a visit to Basel at the invitation of Jacques Handschin – in her interview with Jos Leussink on 24–25 March 1983: "And Gastoué immediately asked whether there was anybody who knew Gregorian chant already, and then Handschin said himself [her relations with him were decidedly limited in nature], yes, that I was there, and he knew my name already [...] thus then I represented the choir as a completely different voice. And he was then the soloist. And that really worked with one another, it was unbelievable" ("En Gastoué vroeg toen opeens, of er al iemand was, die al Gregoriaans kende, en toen heeft Handschin zelf gezegd, ja, dat ik er was, en hij kende mijn naam al [...] dus toen heb ik het koor voorgesteld, als heel andere stem. En hij was dan de solist. En dat klopte nou toch met elkaar, het was ongelooflijk").

23 "niet veel meer dan eene plegtige oplezing, en geleek evenzeer op spreken als op zingen". Michael Johann Anton Lans, *Handboekje*, 88.

24 "weil die Liedform es uns ermöglicht gemeinsam einen Text zu sagen und zu überlegen, um so, singend, [...] zum Loben Gottes zu kommen. Wenn es sich so verhält, müsste dieses Singen recht nahe am Sagen des Verses, beim eigentlichen Skandieren bleiben. Nun ist das

For Ina Lohr then, the epitome of song was attained in a communal "sing-ing-speaking" of a text; it is what made her reject performance where the message of the text was not foremost. This does not mean that she put music on a lower level than the words, as is made clear by her insistence on the equivalence of "singing speech" and "speaking song". It is more a reflection of her advocacy of function. If the primary goal of sacred music in her eyes was the praise of God, it was this message, as revealed by the words, that needed to come through in the music. Thus her approach to the pre-Reformation and Reformation hymns was strongly influenced by her experience in singing Catholic chant.

3.3 The Influence of the *Jugendmusikbewegung* and the *Singbewegung*

A parallel substrate for these attitudes may perhaps be found in the ideals lying behind the German *Jugendmusikbewegung* (German youth music movement) and the *Singbewegung* (Singing Movement), and other movements throughout Europe seeking to reform society through communal singing. These movements turned to romanticized visions of the past, including its music, in order to cure what they saw to be the ills of modern civilization, its drive toward mechanization, its love for superficiality, virtuosity, sentimentality. About the same time that Ina Lohr was about to begin her music studies, the Dutch social-democratic party or Sociaal-Democratische Arbeiderspartij (SDAP), and an association of trade unions, the Nederlands Verbond van Vakverenigingen (NVV), created the Arbeiders Jeugd Centrale (AJC), a socialist organization for young people based on the various German youth movements. By means of it, they wished to cultivate the sense of community and, in the process, stem the per-

ruhige, metrisch-rhythmische Sagen eines Verses eine Uebung, die uns weitgehend verloren gegangen ist. Das Lesen von Versen wird heute fast immer zu Gunsten der persönlichen Deutung und Gestaltung dem Lesen von Prosa angepasst. Damit geht aber das Wesen des Verses verloren. Im Vers steht jede Zeile für sich da, sogar, wenn der Satz in die nächste Zeile hinübergeht, die verschiedenen Zeilen einer Strophe bilden ein Ganzes. Der Reim begünstigt sowohl die Selbständigkeit, wie auch die Zusammengehörigkeit der Zeilen, Metrum und Rhythmus halten Vers und Strophe 'in Ordnung'. Durch diese Ordnung wird das gemeinsame Lesen erst wirklich möglich. Fehlen Rhythmus und Reim, so werden wir schwerlich ein klares gemeinsames Sagen erreichen." Taken from a lecture, "Praktische Arbeit am Kirchenlied", held on 22/23 September 1954 in Boldern-Männedorf, Switzerland, PSF-ILC.

ceived societal shift toward individualism and materialism.[25] As part of this process, a new interest in Dutch folk songs arose, with young people getting together for large outdoor festivals or group hikes through the countryside, passing their time with the singing of folk songs. No doubt Ina Lohr's discovery of Dutch folk songs in this period was related to the increased general interest in them due to the AJC.

More importantly, however, all of these movements came to have a quasi-religious aspect in their approach to music. Olga Pokorny Hensel, the wife of the German *Singbewegung*'s leader, Walter Hensel, formulated this in a very succinct manner when she asserted that

> Art is only then real art when it brings us spiritual growth. [...] Only when we experience something divine in music and recognize the creator of a work of art as a vessel through which the divine flows, is there noble music at all. [...] The artist must be the mediator and obey – in the true meaning of the word – God.[26]

Because of this outlook on music, the experiences of the *Singbewegung* came to be seen as something that could be emulated in the reform of sacred music, particularly within the Lutheran church, as a means of increasing the participation of the congregation in the services.[27] Indeed, we have seen in the first chapter how the Muziek-Lyceum incorporated these ideas in its program of instruction, creating structures in which its initiators hoped a new attitude toward music could be inculcated in its students.

It is not known whether Ina Lohr had any connection with the Dutch AJC before she came to Switzerland, but by 1939 she was certainly a member of the *Schweizerische Vereinigung für Volkslied und Hausmusik* (Swiss Association for Folk Songs and House Music), as that was the year when the first of the 35 articles she wrote for their journal appeared (initially called *Volkslied und Haus-*

25 Information about the AJC may be found in Jolande van der Klis, *Oude muziek in Nederland: Het verhaal van de pioniers 1900–1975*, Utrecht: Stichting Organisatie Oude Muziek 1991, Chapter 7. It is the vade mecum of the Dutch Early Music movement, an invaluable resource for all research on the topic.

26 "Kunst ist nur dann wirkliche Kunst, wenn sie uns geistiges Wachstum bringt [...] Nur wenn wir in der Musik etwas Göttliches empfinden und im Schöpfer eines Kunstwerkes das Gefäss erkennen, durch das ein Göttliches strömt, gibt es überhaupt eine edle Musik [...] Der Künstler muss der Mittler sein und im wahren Sinn des Wortes Gott gehorchen". Olga Pokorny, "Erneuerung und Veredlung der Hausmusik", in: *Die Laute* 3 (1919), 39.

27 See Anne Smith, "The Development of the *Jugendmusikbewegung*" for general information and Wilhelm Stählin, "Die Bedeutung der Singbewegung für den evangelischen Kirchengesang", in: *Die deutsche Jugendmusikbewegung in Dokumenten ihrer Zeit von den Anfängen bis 1933*, ed. Wilhelm Scholz and Waltraut Jonas-Corrieri, Wolfenbüttel and Zurich: Möseler Verlag 1980, 836–40.

musik but changing its name to *Singt und spielt* in 1942). We are very fortunate to have these articles and those she later wrote for *Musik und Gottesdienst*, the journal of the church musicians' association in the German-speaking cantons of Switzerland, and for similar Protestant organizations in the Netherlands, as it is in them that she openly speaks about her musical beliefs. She did not perceive her articles as being scholarly – although she had no qualms about displaying her knowledge of the subject at hand – but rather as a means of animating others to follow her musical path, the path of her heart.[28] As such they offer a window on her own practice.

Throughout her life, Ina Lohr was concerned with the functional aspect of music, with the set of circumstances, the social context for which it had been written. This is perhaps a consequence of her deep interest in the liturgical function of sacred music, her perception that when this music is performed on the concert stage it no longer fulfills its original purpose. However, she also extended this concept of functionality to chamber music, remarking on how its name originally also referred to its location of performance, namely in a small, intimate room, often executed by amateurs. When these pieces gradually were taken over by professional musicians at the end of the 18th and beginning of the 19th centuries and performed on the concert stage, amateurs came to have less and less space to participate actively in the musical world.

> We possess rich art music [*Kunstmusik*] from the 17th, 18th and 19th centuries, and up until now, one only meant this genre with the word "music". Because such pieces only then really sound beautiful when they are executed perfectly from the technical point of view, the role of music-making increasingly has devolved upon musicians and talented amateurs. The crowd of those that listen in silence has grown. If they began to sing, then they sang from editions of art music [*Kunstmusik*] "for the people"; real folk and church music was in danger of disappearing.[29]

28 In a letter probably to Walter Nef of January, 1942 (on the basis of its place in the file), she wrote namely: "There is no way that I can promise an article for the book [10 years SCB]. If I happen by chance to be able to write one during the holidays, it will be a matter of luck. It is my job to teach. Thus, I can at most write a textbook, or an informative or 'stimulating' article. That is all right for Volkslied und Hausmusik, but not for the scholarly Schola book". ("Einen Aufsatz für das Buch kann ich unmöglich versprechen. Wenn mir zufällig in den Ferien einer gelingt, ist das ein Glücksfall. Es ist meine Aufgabe zu unterrichten. Darum kann ich höchstens ein Lehrbuch, oder einen belehrenden, oder 'anregenden' Aufsatz schreiben. Das ist recht für Volkslied und Hausmusik, nicht für das wissenschaftliche Scholabuch".) Archive of the Schola Cantorum Basiliensis, Basel.

29 "Wir besitzen eine reiche Kunstmusik aus dem 17., 18. und 19. Jahrhundert, und unter 'Musik' verstand man bis vor kurzem nur diese Gattung. Weil ein solcher Satz aber nur dann wirklich schön klingt, wenn er technisch einwandfrei zu Gehör gebracht wird, fiel die

Although Ina Lohr herself was a trained professional musician, she never really enjoyed being on the concert stage; as we have seen above, it seemed to her to require too much from her. This is corroborated by a passage in which she proclaims that

> a top prerequisite in a concert today is excellence in performance, and that a very spoiled audience compares the performances, judging and evaluating [them]. The musician must have something of the medieval juggler who pleased, touched and amazed [the crowd]; he must conquer the favor of the audience through great effort.[30]

Comparing the musician onstage with a medieval juggler reveals her aversion to having to meet the standards and taste of an audience, when her musical ideals lay elsewhere. Apart from serving as Paul Sacher's assistant, a task which we will see was accompanied by its own difficulties in just this realm of functionality, Ina Lohr's focus in her work was on those genres of music that she felt called upon to support and promote ideologically: true church music, and, allied with this, *Hausmusik* (house music), a specific form of chamber music designed to nurture the cultivation of music within the family or close circle of friends. The following two sections will be primarily devoted to a discussion of aspects of her approach to the performance of music in these two categories, aspects which are displayed in all her activities as a professional musician.[31]

Rolle des Musizierens immer mehr den Musikern und den begabten Musikfreunden zu. Die Schar derer, die schweigend zuhörten, wuchs. Wenn sie auch anfing zu singen, dann sang sie 'Volksausgaben' der Kunstmusik; die echte Volks- und Kirchenmusik drohte unterzugehen". Ina Lohr, "Von einem Lied", in: *Volkslied und Hausmusik* 6 (1939), 117.

30 "sicher ist dass, im heutigen Konzert die hervorragende Leistung eine erste Voraussetzung ist, und dass ein sehr verwöhntes Publikum die Leistungen verschiedener Konzertgeber messend und urteilend einander gegenüberstellt. Der Musiker muss also etwas vom mittelalterlichen Jongleur, der ergötzte, rührte und verblüffte, an sich haben; er muss sich die Gunst des Publikums durch eine grosse Anstrengung erobern". Ina Lohr, "Einige Gedanken zum Thema 'Hausmusik – Konzertmusik'", in: *Singt und spielt* 19 (1952), 17.

31 It must be mentioned here that Ina Lohr was not blind to the fact that the *Singbewegung* was absorbed into the Nazi machine, being used to create an intense sense of community among young people. In her notes for a lecture sometime after the war, she wrote "But the organizing of a singing movement that does not also reach the individual and make it clear to him that just singing along can also be an escape from life and just move him from one large group to another, appears to me to be very dangerous today". ["Aber das Organisieren einer Singbewegung, die nicht auch den Einzelnen erreicht und ihm klarmacht, dass ein nur-Mitsingen eine Flucht aus dem Leben bedeuten kann und ihn nur von der einen Masse in die andere stellt, scheint mir heute sehr gefährlich".] She went even further, claiming that "its right to existence is questionable, when it does not involve singing in the church". ["ihre Existenzberechtigung [ist] fraglich, wenn es sich nicht um ein kirchliches Singen handelt".] PSF-ILC.

3.4 The Performance of Sacred Music

In an article in 1942, Ina Lohr examined in some depth the role of the musician in the church in the past and today, speaking about how there had always been two kinds of music in the church, *Kunstmusik* (art music) and the singing of the congregation. She maintained that at first art music – particularly that of sacred solo song and mensural music – was not there merely for beauty's sake. Instead the singers assumed a duty of great responsibility. Taking the early Christian cantor as an example she explained that

> his function was to sing as a representative of the congregation, to express and give form to that which each individual felt. His "ecstatic" song performed the service of bringing the prayer of all believers to God. What is involved here is, in the deepest sense, a priest's task, so that a cantor in the old church had to be a member of the priesthood.[32]

This she then contrasted with what she perceived to be the current state of affairs, speaking of the gap between what a cantor should be able to do, and the actual activities of the church musician of her own day.

> Such a cantor should have a *vocation*, but also the *talent* and the technique that his office demands of him. […] In the reformed church, the organist with the choir director and the members of the choir have come to fulfill [this office]. The personal responsibility of this group may scarcely be compared to that of the old cantor, and also the trust of the pastors and the congregation is unfortunately no longer great […] But the cause of this condition cannot solely be sought in the church. Again and again, and increasingly often, the means of a singer's talent and technique have become his goal. Because of this, he had to distance himself from the church. In the [secular] world his task would have actually been the same one: to sing the joys and sorrows vicariously for others, which the average person cannot express and bring into a form. Every great artist fulfills this task, consciously or unconsciously. Only in the church, we have lost the sense, the understanding of this, because we are afraid of the secularized, "egotistic" singing artist. Musicians then created church concerts for artistic church music, without always being clear that with this music, they also assumed the role of the church singer. When, however, they understand this office, the old "priestly" singing will again be able to flourish in that context. […] The question is only whether we will be able to assume this responsibility, that is: to not only work very soberly and in a goal-oriented fashion on our technique, but also on our liturgical duty.[33]

32 "Seine Funktion war: stellvertretend für die Gemeinde zu singen, das auszudrücken und in Form zu bringen, was jeder einzelne empfand. Sein 'ekstatischer' Gesang ist dienend, er trägt das Gebet aller Gläubigen zu Gott. Es handelt sich hier im tiefsten Sinne um einen priesterlichen Dienst, so dass der Kantor in der alten Kirche dem Priesterstande angehören musste". Ina Lohr, "Etwas von der Kirchenmusik im allgemeinen [sic] und von dem Kirchenlied im besonderen", in: *Singt und spielt* 9 (1942), 99.

33 "Ein solcher Vorsänger soll die *Berufung* haben, aber auch die *Begabung* und die Technik, die sein Amt von ihm verlangt. […] In der reformierten Kirche sind der Organist mit dem

This text is an extraordinary expression of the goal that Ina Lohr had set for herself within the reformed church. She wanted to have music once again fulfill the role of conveying the praise and thankfulness experienced by the congregation; they, however, needed the assistance of a "cantor" to enable them to express it adequately in song. Indeed, as we saw in Chapter 2, this is a reflection of her religious beliefs and the basis of her vocation. As such, she was indefatigable in her efforts to demonstrate in her person how this might be achieved. With her passion for monophony and her faith, it is not surprising that she turned to Gregorian chant and monophonic pre-Reformation and Reformation songs, as these repertoires brought together her fascination with melody with what she came to see as her religious vocation as a cantor.

Above we have seen the importance that she attributed to the communal declamation of a text, in observation of its rhythm and rhyme. Indeed, she was of the unsubstantiable opinion that "Gregorian chant originated from the common recitation of Latin texts and from the ecstatic embellishment and intensification of such declaimed melodies".[34] Its strength lay in the joint affirmation in a single melodic line. She often uses the word "Einstimmigkeit" in this context, a noun referring to one-part music or melodies, regardless of the forces performing them, which is perhaps best translated as monophony. The word "einstimmig", however, is also an adjective meaning "in unison". When she uses these words, she is often using them with a mixture of these meanings, at times

---

Chorleiter und den Chorsängern seine Träger geworden. Die persönliche Verantwortung dieser Gruppe ist aber kaum zu vergleichen mit der des alten Kantors, und auch das Vertrauen der Pfarrherren und der Gemeinde ist leider nicht mehr gross [...] Die Schuld für diesen Zustand liegt nicht nur bei der Kirche. Immer wieder und immer mehr wurde dem Sänger das Mittel seiner Begabung und seiner Technik zum Zweck. Dadurch musste er sich von der Kirche trennen. In der Welt wäre seine Aufgabe allerdings eine gleiche gewesen; sie war es anfänglich bei den alten Barden und wird auch heute noch oft so verstanden: die Freuden und Leiden, welche die Menschheit im allgemeinen nicht äussern und in Form bringen kann, stellvertretend für sie zu singen. Jeder grosse Künstler erfüllt bewusst oder unbewusst diese Aufgabe. Nur in der Kirche haben wir den Sinn, das Verständnis dafür verloren, weil wir den verweltlichten, 'sich' singenden Künstler fürchten. Die Musiker haben dann für die kunstvolle Kirchenmusik das Kirchenkonzert geschaffen, ohne sich immer darüber klar zu sein, dass sie mit der Musik auch das Amt des kirchlichen Sängers übernahmen. Wenn sie dieses Amt aber verstehen, sollte an dieser Stelle das alte, priesterliche Singen wieder aufblühen können. [...] Die Frage ist nur, ob wir imstande sein werden, die Verantwortung auf uns zu nehmen, das heisst: sehr nüchtern und zielbewusst nicht nur an unserer Technik, sondern auch an der liturgischen Aufgabe zu arbeiten". Ibid., 99–100.

34 "Es lässt sich nachweisen, dass der Choral entstanden ist aus dem gemeinsamen Rezitieren der lateinischen Texte und aus extatischem Umspielen und Steigern solcher Deklamationsmelodien". Handwritten notes in booklet, PSF-ILC.

speaking of music which is monophonic, that is, music which manifests itself as a melodic line, and at times of the performance, which might either be by a soloist or a choir or congregation. In what follows I will be translating "Einstimmigkeit" as "monophony" when it refers to the stylistic phenomenon and as a "unisono choir" when a unisono execution by more than one singer of the "monophony" is concerned.

Ina Lohr's particular interest lay in the psalms, no doubt partially due to her Dutch reformed religious background, but also because in her studies with Karl Nef, she had come to realize that sacred music from earlier centuries was dominated by them.[35] In the introductory words to a concert of the *Oekumenischer Singkreis Basel* (Ecumenical Singing Circle Basel) and the *Stadtposaunenchor Basel* (Trombone Choir of the City of Basel) on 21 Februar 1971, she averred that

> The human being in the psalms is the human being of here and now. The human being of today, no matter where he lives, what nationality or race he is, has the same joys, the same anxieties, the same afflictions as the ones in the Old Testament, although he is in a "changed world". And he rejoices, praises, laments and calls out, just as the human being in the psalms did. But he did it *in song* and he laid all his concerns down in front of the living God.[36]

As the first Reformation songs and psalms by Luther and Calvin were monophonic, they had a particular attraction for her; she felt that they possessed an innate ability – in part a result of the circumstances surrounding their origin – to unify the faithful, thereby creating a true congregation. Indeed, this links up with Jean Calvin's conviction, as expressed in the articles of 16 January 1537 for the organization of the church and its worship in Geneva, in which he declares that

> it is a thing most expedient for the edification of the church to sing some psalms in the form of public prayers by which one prays to God or sings His praises so that the hearts of all may be roused and stimulated to make similar prayers and to render similar praises and thanks to God with a common love.[37]

---

35 From a speech concerning Protestant church music, PSF-ILC.
36 "Der Mensch in den Psalmen ist der Mensch hier und jetzt. Der Mensch heute, wo er auch lebt, welcher Nationalität oder Rasse er auch angehört, hat die gleichen Freuden, den gleichen Kummer, die gleichen Nöte wie der aus dem Alten Testament, wenn auch in einer 'veränderten Welt'. Und er jauchzt, lobt, klagt und schreit wie der Mensch in den Psalmen. Aber der hat alles das <u>singend</u> getan und: er hat alle seine Anliegen vor den lebendigen Gott gebracht". Introductory words to a concert of the *Oekumenischer Singkreis Basel, Bläser des Stadtposaunenchors Basel*, 21 February 1971, PSF-ILC.
37 "Dauantage cest vne chose bien expediente a ledification de lesglise de chanter aulcungs pseaumes en forme doraysons publicqs par les quelz on face prieres a Dieu ou que on chante

To this purpose, Jean Calvin advocated the singing of the psalms in unison. Moreover, Claude Goudimel in his *Pseaumes mis en rime francoise* (Geneva, 1565) specifies in his letter to the readers that he has taken the melodies, as sung in the church, and added three polyphonic voices to them for one's devotion at home. This naturally resonated with Ina Lohr's musical affinity for monophony in the church setting, allowing her to investigate the possibilities for monophonic choral music within the Protestant church. She suggests that some rare person searching for the jewels among the Protestant hymns

> will perhaps find that it is most satisfying when all who are there together sing as if from a single mouth, because all of them have the same need of calling to God, of pleading to Him, of praising Him, of thanking Him. That is the simplest, most basic, even the most authentic way of singing. Unfortunately, it has almost been lost by our congregations. Various of our most beautiful airs came into being as monophonic, unaccompanied song. The accompaniment of voices which weave around the melody or of a simply-set organ part creates a new form, which can of itself be very beautiful, but does not enhance the beauty of the melodic line itself, but instead perhaps undermines it. The composers in the 16th century knew this so well![38]

Ina Lohr was unflagging in her attempts to revitalize congregations by encouraging them to sing these early Reformation melodies without accompaniment, believing that some of their original power of renewal would be assumed, taken over by the faithful today, when they were brought together and unified by the joint declamation of significant texts. She was of the opinion that an organ accompaniment all too often allowed the congregation members to entrust the expression of their faith, of their praise of God to the professional organist, thereby weakening both the musical and religious impact of the music.

ses louanges affin que les cueurs de tous soyent esmeuz et jncites a former pareilles oraysons et rendre pareilles louanges et graces a Dieu dune mesme affection". In: *Ioannis Calvini Opera Quae Supersunt Omnia*, ed. Johann-Wilhelm Baum, Edouard Cunitz, and Eduard Reuss (Brunswick: C. A. Schwetschke and Sons 1863–1900), Vol. 11, 6. Translation by Calvin Garside, "The Origins of Calvin's Theology of Music: 1536–1543", 7–8.

38   "ja, vielleicht findet er sogar, dass es das Allerschönste ist, wenn alle, die da zusammen sind, wie aus einem Munde einstimmig singen, weil in allen das gleiche Bedürfnis ist, zu Gott zu rufen, Ihn zu bitten, Ihn zu loben und Ihm zu danken. Das ist die einfachste, die ursprünglichste, ja die echteste Art zu singen. Leider ist sie in unseren Gemeinden fast verloren gegangen. Verschiedene unserer schönsten Lieder sind aber noch als einstimmiger, unbegleiteter Gesang entstanden. Die Begleitung von umspielenden Stimmen oder vom einfachen Orgelsatz schafft eine neue Form, die an sich sehr schön sein kann, die aber die Schönheit der melodischen Linie an sich nicht steigert, sondern möglicherwiese nur herabsetzt. Wie gut haben das die Komponisten aus dem 16. Jahrhundert gewusst!" Ina Lohr, "Vom Reichtum des Kirchenliedes", in: *Volkslied und Hausmusik* 7 (1941), 169.

Because of their function, as described by Jean Calvin, she also believed that they required a very different kind of execution than was standard for the first half of the 20th century:

> The psalm melodies are primarily vehicles for the text and therefore have very little in common with "our music making". Everything that makes our music attractive and interesting for the listener – the individual timbre of the voice, the personal interpretation, which primarily comes from the dynamic differences and rhythmic freedom (rubato) – are either minor details or even strange coincidences. The concern [instead] is about notes which are grouped such that the syllables of the text receive their full weight, whereby they give us the possibility of singing the text [as if] from one mouth.[39]

She makes it clear here, that her choice of practice is a result of the function of the music, the purpose of its performance. Therefore, for the comprehension of the text, she considered it important that the rhythmic unit of counting be shifted from the quarter that was usual at the time, to the half note. "The old rule, according to which two syllables make up the beat, can very suddenly lead to the correct singing from speaking. Real help can be derived from the common, calm, metric declamation of the text, from which the tempo for the singing also emerges".[40] From various statements, it seems that she considered that the half note should be beaten somewhere between 60 and 80 MM; like many other earlier theorists, she related it to the beat of the heart.

But for her, it was not merely a matter of a faster tempo, it was an entirely different conception of rhythm, one directly related to the text:

> Rhythm is primarily *movement*. And this movement is not arbitrary, but *ordered*. Each movement has a *goal*. Then each line of a song must have a note which is its goal. If I move toward a goal, I will do so with larger or smaller steps, faster or slower, depending on how far away I am from it, and how great my desire is to reach this goal. In music, the *tempo*, the "slow" or "fast", depends on how far the goal is from the opening note and the degree of the tension between these two notes. All of this manifests itself as the rhythm, as the shape of a melody, and has very little to do with our concept of

---

39 "De psalmmelodieën zijn in de eerste plaats vehicula voor de tekst en hebben in zoverre met ons 'muziek maken' maar weinig gemeen. Alles, wat ons musiceren aantrekkelijk en voor de hoorder interessant maakt, de persoonlijke stemklank, de persoonlijke interpretatie, die vooral ontstaat door dynamische verschillen en rhythmische vrijheden (rubato), zijn bij het psalmzingen of bijzaak of zelfs vreemde bijkomstigheden. Het gaat om tonen, die zo gegroepeerd zijn, dat ze de lettergrepen van de tekst in hun volle waarde dragen, waardoor ze ons de mogelijkheid geven, die tekst uit één mond te zingen". Ina Lohr, "Haspers Psalmberijming", in: *Kerk en Eredienst* 4/2 (1949), 117.

40 "Die alte Regel, nach der zwei Silben einen Schlag geben, kann ganz plötzlich zum richtigen Singen aus dem Sagen führen. Eine wirkliche Hilfe leistet auch das gemeinsame ruhige metrische Sprechen des Textes, aus dem dann auch das Tempo für das Singen entsteht". Ina Lohr, "Das Gesangbuch in der Hausmusik", in: *Singt und spielt* 22 (1955), 75–76.

meter. For a greater, superior liberty prevails in this ordered movement which we poor humans – caught in meter, i.e. in the set order, in the written rules – take at first glance as arbitrariness.[41]

She saw this declamatory freedom as being an enlivening feature of the monophonic Reformation songs, one which could be utilized in the cultivation of the active mental and spiritual presence of the congregation. Seemingly finding it easier to write about her musical beliefs in her native language, she describes in greater detail in Dutch why this might be:

> Through the regular downward movement of a finger, the beat (tactus) is made clear to all of the singers. The singing with rubato which we know so well, that is sometimes faster, and then slower, in accordance to the nature of our temperament or what the content of the song requires, cannot be given by the movement of a finger, and thus did not happen. But that does not mean that singing in that manner cannot seem spontaneous and lively. It depends more upon whether the singers experience the rhythmic order as a constraint or as a benevolent organic flow. It is not a loveless "lex", which we have to take upon ourselves, but a possibility to let ourselves be led along with all of the other members of our Christian congregation by means of the same "movement": Musica est ars bene movendi![42] [Music is the art of moving well!]

It was this conviction that the congregation could be unified that spurred her activity in the circles surrounding the choice and presentation of the songs in the

---

41 "Rhythmus ist in erster Linie B e w e g u n g . Und diese Bewegung ist nicht willkürlich, sondern g e o r d n e t . Jede Bewegung hat ein Z i e l . Dann muss auch jede Liedzeile einen Zielton haben. Wenn ich mich auf ein Ziel hin bewege, werde ich das mit grösseren oder kleineren Schritten, schneller oder langsamer tun, je nach dem, wie weit ich davon entfernt bin, und wie gross mein Verlangen ist, dieses Ziel zu erreichen. In der Musik hängt das T e m p o , das 'Langsam' oder 'Schnell' davon ab, wie weit der Zielton vom Anfangston entfernt ist und wie gross die Spannung zwischen diesen beiden Tönen ist. Das alles ergibt den Rhythmus, den Ablauf einer Melodie, und hat zunächst mit unserem Begriff vom Takt nichts zu tun. Denn in dieser Bewegungsordnung herrscht eine grosse, eine überlegene Freiheit, die wir armen, vom Takt, d.h. von der erstarrten Ordnung, vom geschriebenen Gesetz gefangenen Menschen auf den ersten Blick für Willkür halten". Ina Lohr, "Rhythmische Probleme im Choral", in: *Singt und spielt* 9 (1942), 51. The italicized words in the translation represent the expanded spacing of specific words in the original text.

42 "Door het gelijkmatig op en neer bewegen van een vinger werd die slag (tactus) voor alle zangers zichtbaar gemaakt. Het ons zo vertrouwde rubato zingen, d.w.z. nu eens vlugger, dan eens langzamer, al naar mate ons temperament, of de inhoud van het lied dat verlangt, is door een vingerslag niet aan te geven, kwam dus niet voor. Maar dat wil niet zeggen, dat een zingen op die manier niet spontaan en levendig werken kan. Het hangt er maar van af, of de zingenden de rhythmische orde als dwang of als weldadig organisch stromen voelen. Het is niet een liefdeloze 'lex', die we op ons moeten nemen, maar een mogelijkheid om ons met alle andere leden van onze Christelijke gemeente door dezelfde 'beweging' te laten leiden: Musica est ars bene movendi!" The final statement is a traditional medieval definition of music going back to Augustine. Ina Lohr, "Haspers Psalmberijming", 116.

trial volume of the new church hymnal (*Probeband* of the *Gesangbuch der evangelisch=reformierten Kirchen der deutschen Schweiz*, Zurich, 1941; see pp. 192–94 for further information). As she believed the pre-Reformation and Reformation songs to be of utmost importance for the church of her own day, she invested much time into introducing these forgotten melodies, in the attempt to overcome the resistance in the local congregations to their foreignness of style and notation in comparison to the later and better-known versions of the previous hymnal. These later melodies were simpler rhythmically, as they had become more regular metrically, in order to compensate, in Ina Lohr's opinion, for their richer harmonizations. She deemed that the older melodies with their text-related syncopations were more appropriate for a congregation than harmonic complexities.[43] And it would not be surprising if it were partially due to her advocacy that these melodies were printed in the trial volume in their original form, without barlines and without accompaniment. The degree of her investment in the task may be gleaned from a reproduction of Psalm 130, "Aus tiefer Not schrei ich zu Dir", from her own personal copy of the volume (see Ill. 3.1), in which she entered a variant of the melody in the margin, "bar lines" indicating the focal points of the text, plus other commentary. This was just one of numerous hymns that received this sort of attention. The congregations, however, felt lost on the whole without their accustomed forms of orientation. To counter this, Ina Lohr gave courses on these hymns[44] and came to church services with her students, taking on the role of the precentor she so missed in the church of her day. At the same time, she felt that it was important that her students experience sacred music within the liturgical context, and thus this activity served two purposes.[45] Christopher Schmidt remembers her standing in front of the congregation, clearly not there as an individual, but in her role as a church musician serving her function within the church, while simultaneously remaining completely herself.[46]

Although the introduction of unison singing without organ accompaniment in Switzerland was not without its difficulties and opponents – also be-

---

43   Ina Lohr, "Rhythmische Probleme im Choral", 51.
44   She went together with Walter Nef to various congregations in the cantons Basel-Stadt and Basel-Land. Walter Nef first presented the ideas behind the choices found in the trial hymnal and she followed up with an introduction of how to sing some of the original Reformation melodies, complete with their more complex rhythms. Interview with Esther Nef, 17 February 2016.
45   See Ina Lohr, "Die Kirchenmusik als Lehrfach an der Schola Cantorum Basiliensis", in: *Musik und Gottesdienst* 7 (1953), 112.
46   Interview with Christopher Schmidt, 10 November 2015.

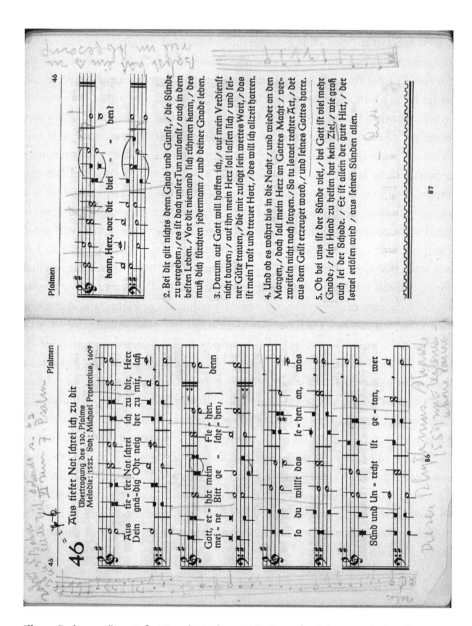

Ill. 3.1: Psalm 130: "Aus tiefer Not schrei ich zu Dir", *Gesangbuch der evangelisch=reformierten Kirchen der deutschen Schweiz*, Zurich: Fretz AG 1941 [Probeband]. Reproduction: PSF-ILC.

cause there was a long-standing tradition in certain regions of the country to sing in four parts – her teaching had an immediate and intense effect in the Netherlands after World War II, perhaps due to the fact that there the entire congregation was accustomed to sing the melodies in equal note values in a very slow tempo to the accompaniment of the organ. Jan Boeke who was present at her first workshop of 6 June 1946 wrote that her manner of "speaking song" and "singing speech" had all of the power of a bomb, "all confusion about questions concerning how music can or should function in the service were suddenly put into perspective by the resounding power of an existential singing in unison".[47] This, as we will see later in Chapter 6, had a compelling effect on the musical reform within the Dutch Protestant church during the following years.

The short articles in the various journals mentioned above also make repeated reference to a variety of other aspects of performance practice in regard to sacred music. For example, Ina Lohr was a great believer – not only in her writing, but also in her concert programming – in *alternatim* performances of strophic songs, maintaining that in this manner the singers paid more attention to what was actually being said. This practice can perhaps be traced back to the Dutch Cecilian influence in that M.J.A. Lans in his *Handboekje* writes that one should

> divide the choir into half-choirs, precentors, boys' and men's voices, high (soprano and tenor) and low (alto and bass) voices, [or] sopranos, altos, etc. alone. The alternation between these different parts and the unification now and then of several of them, or of all, not only brings the singing richly to life, but also prevents many of the difficulties that would otherwise be unavoidable when singing for relatively extended periods of time.[48]

This is exactly the usage one finds in Ina Lohr's scores and arrangements for larger events within the church.

In accordance with her desire for a regular rhythm, her avoidance of rubato, she was also restrictive in her use of the louder side of the dynamic range.

---

47 "Alle verwarring over de vragen hoe muziek in de eredienst mocht of moest functioneren werd hier plotseling gerelativeerd door de klinkende kracht van een existentieel eenstemmig zingen". In Arie Eikelboom and Jaco van der Knijff, "De vrouw van de kerktoonsoorten", 31 March 2008, http://www.refdag.nl/muziek/de_vrouw_van_de_kerktoonsoorten_1_252438 (9 May 2018).

48 "Men verdeele het koor in halfkoor, voorzangers, jongens- und mannenstemmen, hoogere (Sopraan en Tenor) en lagere (Alt en Bas) stemmen, Sopraan, Alt enz. alléén; de afwisseling tusschen deze verschillende partijen en de vereeniging nu en dan van meerdere of van alle brengt niet alleen een rijk en vol leven in den zang, maar voorkomt ook vele bezwaren, die anders bij een tamelijk lang voortgezet zingen onvermijdelijk zijn". Michael Johann Anton Lans, *Handboekje*, 76.

We should know that the mensural rhythm in the Reformation remained strict, that the expression in the Baroque, however, demanded small freedoms, which are nonetheless not yet rubato in the sense of the Classic or the Romantic. With dynamics it is the same thing: it is good and prudent not to make music too loudly, so that one hears one another and attains an in-tune result. But the "piano" cannot be a goal in and of itself, and in a time that knew solo singing, the singers and also the instrumentalists made dynamic nuances, even if these are not to be compared with our possibilities (which are often impossible!).[49]

Most of these ideas concerning performance can be traced back to her Cecilian training with Hubert Cuypers, combined with her own reading of historical theorists. Thus practices of her own time came to be infused with her own interpretation of the sources.

She, of course, did not limit herself to the monophonic repertoire of church music, but followed the development of German church music from Luther's songs through the four-part chorale arrangements to the more complex music of Heinrich Schütz, which she particularly prized, and Johann Sebastian Bach. Her approach, however, remained the same, with attention devoted to how the text's message could best be brought out in performance through the joining together of the individual lines into an integral whole.

3.5 The Performance of *Hausmusik*

The concept of *Hausmusik* is somewhat foreign to us today, as it was a phenomenon particularly characteristic for its time. Its origins may be found in the ideal of music-lovers – amateurs in the true sense of the word – coming together in the circle of the family and friends and making music together. As Ina Lohr expressed it, in trying to distinguish between "concert music" and "house music",

---

49 "Wir sollten es wissen, dass der mensurale Rhythmus in der Reformationszeit straff bleibt, dass der Ausdruck im barocken Zeitalter aber kleine Freiheiten verlangt, die zwar noch kein Rubato im Sinne der Klassik und Romantik ergeben. Mit der Dynamik ist es gleich: es ist gut und vorsichtig, wenn man ja nicht zu laut musiziert, damit man einander hört und zu einem sauberen Resultat kommt. Aber das 'leise' kann nicht ein Zweck an sich sein, und in einer Zeit, die den Sologesang kannte, kamen die Sänger und auch die Spieler zu dynamischen Nuancen, auch wenn diese nicht zu vergleichen sind mit unseren Möglichkeiten (die oft unmöglich sind!)". Ina Lohr, "Stilfragen in der Hausmusik", in: *Singt und spielt* 13 (1946), 10.

it concerns those, who know or suspect that at all times, and in all countries and portions of the world, there have been people who came together in order to sing and play with the conscious or unconscious intention of finding something of that which lies behind and above all human thinking and activity. We probably choose to seek *Hausmusik* in the so-called "early music" because it opens up something of the spirit of former generations for us, which, to be sure, lived differently than we do, were also acquainted with other musical forms and rules, but in the end were still trying to express the same thing.[50]

For her this form of music-making was enormously important for various reasons. If, for example, one thinks about her own upbringing and the important place that music and music-making in the family circle held within it, it is understandable that this was something that she desired for everybody, believed was important for everybody's development. In addition, she saw the cultivation of *Hausmusik* as a means of encouraging a congregation's musical participation in the liturgy, believing that if the church members sang the hymns at home, they would sing them with increased intensity during the services. To this end, she was constantly inquiring of her pastor friends, whether they were continuing to make music in the home.[51]

She described the delights of *Hausmusik* in the following manner:

Hausmusik is above all an intimate music, which is meant for a small, close circle [of people]. The performers and auditors know one another, can therefore discuss that which is played and sung with one another, can repeat it and enjoy it in a cognizant community. As the performers are usually not "professionals", the technical demands cannot be too high; the musical ones, however, can be even greater than those of concert music, just because the possibility of discussion and repetition is given. The beauties may lie deeper, be more hidden than in the concert hall, where the performer must first overcome the obvious gap between himself and the audience, in order to shape that unknown group [of people] into a uniform, listening public. Every musician must want and dare to engage in this battle, but it is only fought in the concert hall, not in the domestic circle. It is for that reason that virtuosity, whose intent is first to amaze and then enchant, cannot find its place in the chamber. This virtuosity is, however, only an intensified kind of playfulness, which in its normal form is indeed an important element of *Hausmusik*. There are so many pieces that delight us to the point of laughter, and it so wonderful when we can just laugh uninhibitedly at home when the music provokes

---

50 "Es geht um solche, die wissen oder ahnen, dass es zu allen Zeiten und in allen Ländern und Weltteilen Menschen gegeben hat, die zusammenkamen, um miteinander zu singen und zu spielen in der bewussten oder unbewussten Absicht, etwas von dem zu finden, was hinter und über allem menschlichen Denken und Tun steht. Wahrscheinlich suchen wir darum die Hausmusik gerne in der sogenannten 'alten Musik', weil sie uns etwas vom Geiste früherer Generationen erschliesst, die zwar anders lebten als wir, auch andere musikalische Formen und Gesetze kannten, letzten Endes auch doch das gleiche auszudrücken bemüht waren". Ina Lohr, "Einige Gedanken zum Thema 'Hausmusik – Konzertmusik'", 19.

51 Interview Hans-Jürg Stefan, 8 January 2015.

it! Part of this intimacy are the smaller forms, ones which do not quite have the desired "effect" in the concert hall. The musician on stage needs time, and therefore also somewhat longer pieces, in order to compel his audience to concentrate. At home we can absorb a single chorale strophe, a little song or a short dance and make it our own.[52]

This passage is illustrative of some of the problematic aspects of her advocacy of *Hausmusik*. In contrast to it, music of the concert hall is clearly depicted here as being more superficial, a genre in which virtuosity is used to dazzle listeners into submission. The musician on stage must wage a battle to engage the attention of the audience, thereby turning his performance into an act of bravery. *Hausmusik*, however, is for the domestic circle, where all can and are expected to participate. The technical difficulty of the music must therefore be commensurate with the ability of the weakest musician. Because one can repeat and discuss the music, she claims that those involved in the performance experience the music more deeply. One does not need virtuosity, as one can hear the playful aspects of the music without being overwhelmed by a surfeit of notes. One is not constrained by the demands of the concert hall and can be satisfied with smaller musical forms.

Ina Lohr did not stand alone with these convictions, but was part of a larger quest to bring music back to the people. This is reflected in an article with much the same tenor written by the composer Max Butting in which he demands that

---

52 "Vor allem ist die Hausmusik eine intime Musik, die sich an einen kleinen, nahen Kreis wendet. Ausführende und Hörer kennen sich, können darum über das Gesungene und Gespielte miteinander reden, können es wiederholen und sich in bewusster Gemeinschaft daran freuen. Da die Ausführenden meistens nicht 'vom Fach' sind, dürfen die technischen Anforderungen nicht zu gross sein; die musikalischen können aber sogar grösser sein als bei der Konzertmusik, gerade deshalb, weil die Möglichkeit der Verständigung und des Wiederholens besteht. Die Schönheiten können etwas tiefer, versteckter liegen als im Konzertsaal, wo der Ausführende zuerst die äussere Kluft zwischen sich und dem Publikum überwinden muss, um dann die fremde Menge zu einer einheitlichen, lauschenden Hörerschaft umzubilden. Diesen Kampf muss jeder Musiker auf dem Podium wollen und wagen, er wird aber nur im Saal, nicht im häuslichen Kreis ausgekämpft. Darum kommt die Virtuosität, die zuerst verblüffen, dann bezaubern will, im Zimmer nicht zu ihrem Recht. Diese Virtuosität ist aber nur die gesteigerte Spielfreudigkeit, die in ihrer Normalform wieder ein wichtiges Element der Hausmusik ist. Wie viele Spielstücke gibt es, die uns zum Lachen ergötzen können, und wie herrlich, wenn wir zu Hause ungeniert lachen dürfen, wenn die Musik uns dazu reizt! Zur Intimität gehört auch die kleine Form, die im Konzertsaal oft nicht recht 'wirken' will. Der Musiker auf dem Podium braucht Zeit, darum auch eine etwas längere Musik, um seine Hörerschaft zur Konzentration zu zwingen. Zu Hause können wir eine einzige Choralstrophe, ein kleines Lied oder einen kurzen Tanz aufnehmen und uns zu eigen machen". Ina Lohr, "Stilfragen in der Hausmusik", 9.

composers stop writing only for the concert hall, for the [professional] musicians. They must at least in part make the attempt to limit the technical difficulties of their works so that the musical amateur can occupy himself with them. It does not need to become popular music. To the contrary, that which the dilettante studies at home can often be more profound than the piece that has to be successful in the concert hall. But one cannot demand from the dilettante the technical capabilities of the professional musician. As long as every new composition only can be played by a professional, a deep abyss will, in essence, separate the dilettante from new art.[53]

In contrast to Butting, however, Ina Lohr did not see this form of music-making as a bridge to new art, to music performed on the concert stage, but rather regarded it as a developmental and moral necessity. Thus many of her first courses at the Schola Cantorum Basiliensis were devoted to *Hausmusik*, indeed the first diplomas were for leaders of *Sing- und Spielgruppen* (vocal and instrumental groups) and teachers of *Kirchenmusik und Hausmusik* (church and house music) and it came to take an increasingly important position in her life.

3.6 Solmisation und Kirchentonarten

In the summer of 1941, under the auspices of the Swiss Organist Society (Schweizerischer Organistenverband), Ina Lohr gave six two-hour lectures on the subject of solmization and modes in Winterthur, which thereafter appeared in organization's journal, *Der Organist*, in 1942–43, and later as a separate offprint. In 1948, an extended version was published in book form as *Solmisation und Kirchentonarten*, which then reappeared in two further editions in 1967 and 1981. From this publication record alone, we can get a sense of the excitement with which this book was received. The reception, however, was directly coupled to her own personal charisma and to the success with which she had presented the material in Winterthur. We get an inkling of what the week was like from the letter that the pastor Arnold Odermatt wrote to Ina Lohr's parents on 15 August 1941:

---

53 "Ferner müssen die Komponisten aufhören, ganz allein für den Konzertsaal, für den Interpreten zu schreiben. Sie müssen den Versuch machen, die technischen Schwierigkeiten ihrer Werke wenigstens teilweise so zu begrenzen, dass sich der Musikfreund mit ihnen beschäftigen kann. Das braucht keine populäre Musik zu werden. Im Gegenteil, was der Dilettant zu Hause studiert, kann oft tiefer sein, als das Stück, das im Konzertsaal Erfolg haben muss. Aber es darf vom Dilettanten nicht die technischen Fähigkeiten des beruflichen Interpreten verlangen. So lange jede Komposition nur vom Berufsmusiker gespielt werden kann, trennt praktisch den Dilettanten eine tiefe Kluft von neuer Kunst". Max Butting, "Die Musik und die Menschen", in: *Melos* 6 (1927), 63.

In addition, however, I promised Ina to write to you about what Ina achieved in Winterthur. There were about 370 organists, choir directors, singers collected there to receive an introduction to our new hymnal. All of them more or less good musicians. There she introduced us to the otherwise so feared secrets of Gregorian chant in such a lively, lucid, clear manner, that afterwards, for example, a dental technician from Chur, already in his mid-sixties, attending the course at the request of the local church board, enthusiastically told me that now he had understood something. What more does one want? But this was true for many others also, certainly almost everybody. And afterwards we all besieged her in order to hear more and to find a possibility of meeting with her again and continue working [with her]. And her voice continued to resound in us all, a Gregorian voice.[54]

Thus, with one fell swoop, Ina Lohr's name came to be associated with solmization throughout Switzerland. It is evident that also here her personality played a role, as the book's explanations of solmization and modes disconcertingly fall short of our expectations today. Perhaps it can best be described as an insightful collection of notes and thoughts about the repertoire, one that could only be understood fully in accompaniment with Ina Lohr's personal explanations, and most of all, with her singing. Once again, people were mesmerized by her voice. This leaves the reader of today, however, with a curious sense of unease.

There is, for example, no succinct explanation of the gamut, the hexachords and their relationship to one another, nor an explanation for the names of the notes within the gamut or of how one should mutate from one hexachord to the next. Instead the book, written in dialogue form as so many of the older treatises, opens with a chapter on the Dorian mode, immediately placing the question of why there is music,[55] why we are not satisfied with a single note.[56] Her answer was that any sustained tone over time begins feeling high, needs to fall, is a *Rufton* (calling or recitation note) that is seeking its *Ruheton* (peaceful

54 "Dann aber habe ich Ina versprochen, Ihnen davon zu schreiben, was Ina in Winterthur geleistet hat. Es waren da etwa 370 Organisten, Chorleiter, Sänger versammelt, sich in unser neues Kirchengesangbuch einführen zu lassen. Alles mehr oder weniger gute Musici. Da hat sie in so lebendiger, anschaulicher, klarer Art in die sonst so gefürchteten Geheimnisse der Gregorianik eingeführt, dass mir nachher z. B. ein mehr als 60-jähriger Zahntechniker aus Chur, abgeordnet an diesen Kurs durch den dortigen Kirchenvorstand, begeistert erzählte, jetzt sei ihm etwas aufgegangen. Was will man mehr? Aber so ist es noch vielen andern, gewiss fast allen ergangen. Und nachher fielen wir über sie her, um noch mehr zu hören und eine Möglichkeit zu finden, wieder mit ihr zusammenzukommen und weiterzuarbeiten. Und wie hat uns allen ihre Stimme nachgeklungen, eine gregorianische Stimme", Letter Arnold Odermatt to Jet and Herman Lohr of 15 August 1941, PSF-ILC.

55 Early treatises seek instead to define music by asking, "What is music?", rather than searching for the reason of its existence.

56 "Warum gibt es *Musik*, warum genügt uns nicht der *Ton*?" Ina Lohr, *Solmisation und Kirchenmusik*, Zurich: Hug 1981, 1.

tone or final). The natural interval between these two notes, in her opinion, was the fifth. Thus, from the very beginning her attention was not directed towards solmization as a tool for sight-singing, the purpose for which it was originally developed, but instead towards its use as an instrument for comprehending the melodic relationships or tensions between the individual notes of each mode. In so doing, she was creating a melodic theory, a means of analyzing melody in accordance with the functional relationships of the notes in a line, as opposed to the omnipresent harmonic approach represented by Hugo Riemann (1849–1919). She was one of the pioneers of melodic analysis, proceeding however in a much different fashion than Ernst Kurth (1886–1946), professor of musicology in Berne, generally acknowledged as being the first to create a melodic theory of music. According to Ernst Kurth, that which was essential in a melody was the "sensation of the relationship of the notes". In turn, the manner of this relationship of the notes was determined by our psyche, the source of all human creativity; it was also primary, taking precedence over harmony.[57] Ina Lohr did not even speak of such things, for – as we have seen above – she considered it to be self-evident that singing was an elemental urge, shared by all.

Ina Lohr's interest lay in understanding how the melodies of chant, of pre-Reformation and Reformation hymns worked, why they were so effective, were able to express the affects found in their texts with such clarity. That these melodies had this capability was something that she did not question, perhaps because of her innate receptivity to their influence, but certainly also due to her training. It seems likely that this attitude can be traced back to M.J.A. Lans, as he emphasized the importance of modal affect by discussing this aspect at both the beginning and the end of his respective chapter, going to the extent of citing three different theorists' modal descriptions in their entirety. Indeed, in the concluding section on the character of the modes, he writes that

> although the writers do not all agree with one another when they give the particular characteristics of the different modes, that which they claim is, however, in no way to be attributed to pure fantasy or subjective opinion; the different location of the semitones in the scales and the different sequence of the intervals, in relation to the final, undoubtedly give to each mode a particular character.[58]

57 "Das Wesentliche ist die Empfindung der Verbindung der Töne und die Art dieser in unserem Empfinden vorliegenden V e r b i n d u n g der Töne ist durch jene Kraft bestimmt, welche die Erscheinung des Melodischen überhaupt gründet". Ernst Kurth, *Grundlagen des linearen Kontrapunkts: Einführung in Stil und Technik von Bach's Melodischer Polyphonie*, Berne: Akademische Buchhandlung von Max Drechsel 1917, 2.

58 "Ofschoon de schrijvers niet alle juist overeenstemmen, wanneer zij het eigenaardig karakter der verschillende kerktoonen opgeven, is toch hetgeen zij zeggen geenzins louter aan phantasie of subjektieve opvatting toe te schrijven; de verschillende ligging der halve

It seems likely that this was the background which informed Ina Lohr's desire for understanding how these melodies worked, for understanding the relationship between the individual tones. She found it fruitful to associate the function of a note in a given mode with a specific solmization syllable, as this gave her a structural framework for a mode in which one (or more) note(s) were exclamatory, another was the final, and yet others neighboring notes to these primary centers. Together with the placement of the semitones, these relationships gave each mode its individuality. Close to the beginning of the book, she describes how each note has its own pitch name (such as a, b, c) which however reveals nothing of its function. She finds it peculiar that most people are only interested in the name of the notes, but not in their melodic function. She complains that

> it is only in music theory, or more precisely in analysis, in the investigation of musical syntax that we only concern ourselves with function. But the knowledge of the function, in any case for vocal music without the accompaniment of instruments, is one of the most important things. It is not the pitch of the first note which determines what is essential in our short melody, but [the fact] that after this note, whichever one it might be, the other notes follow *in the correct relationship* to one another.[59]

She then provided trapezoidal diagrams for each mode which illustrated the specific function of the notes in the mode (see Ill. 3.2).

This diagram of Dorian, for example, illustrates a far greater understanding of the melodic tugs within the mode than that provided by the more usual scale patterns found in lexica. For example, it gives the ambitus of the mode as it was actually used, from *c* to *c*. The importance of *D* and *A*, as the final and recitation tones, is indicated by their capitalization; the *f* between them linked the two together. This *f*, however, on occasion could take on the function of the dominant, of the recitation tone; *c* and *g* only appear as neighboring and passing notes in Dorian melodies, and therefore are in the lower row and possess lesser inherent strength than those in the upper one. The lines between the notes give an indication of the dependence of these notes upon one another, as do the dotted lines to the solmization syllables above the diagram. She also

toonen in de toonladders en de verschillende opvolging der intervallen, van den grondtoon uit gerekend, geven ontwijfelbaar aan elken kerktoon een eigen karakter". Michael Johann Anton Lans, *Handboekje*, 28.

59 "[U]m die Funktion kümmern wir uns höchstens in der Theorie, genauer gesagt in der Analyse, in der Zergliederung. Und doch ist die Kenntnis der Funktion, auf alle Fälle für die nicht instrumental begleitete Gesangsmusik, etwas vom Allerwichtigsten. Nicht die Höhe des ersten Tones bestimmt das Wesentliche an unserer kleinen Melodie, sondern dass nach diesem Ton, welcher er nun auch sei, die anderen Töne *im richtigen Verhältnis* zueinander folgen". Ina Lohr, *Solmisation und Kirchentonarten*, 2–3.

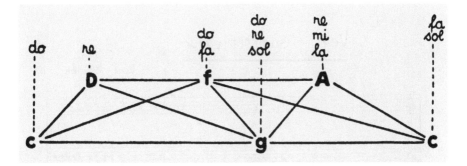

Ill. 3.2: Dorian Mode. Ina Lohr, *Solmisation und Kirchentonarten,* Zurich: Hug 1981, 12.

pointed out that these five notes are those of the pentatonic system. Both *b* and *b-flat* are possible, as far as she was concerned, because both *f* and *g* could mutate to "do".[60]

This linking up of the solmization syllable to a function within a mode, however, imbues it with a meaning that can lead to a dissociation from the original significance of the syllable as a means of locating oneself in the gamut, within the tonal system. As a result – particularly evident in the 16th-century Reformation melodies where a relatively rigid system of solmization was employed to further humanistic goals in music education – her hexachord mutations were inconsistent, were in line with her own personal functional analysis of the particular melody, but not with the rules found in the treatises of the time (see Appendix 1 for a more detailed discussion of these differences).

Whereas this coupling of syllable and function in her teaching and singing of modal music led to greater understanding, it was smiled upon when she insisted on applying it to later music, such as Arthur Honegger's *Jeanne d'Arc au bûcher* or Sven-Erik Bäck's motets, or Ernst Krenek's *Veni sanctificator* (see Ill. 3.3), where it had little or no relevance.[61] While this way of thinking, of hearing expanded her students' capacities for analyzing and understanding melodic relationships, it remained sufficiently idiosyncratic that it could only be thoroughly understood within the context of her teaching, thus limiting its general acceptance.

---

60 This use of "do" instead of "ut" is irritatingly anachronistic, as she took it from an unnamed source from 1659 (the date of 1559 in the 1981 edition is no doubt just an error), and thereafter made use of it, as she preferred its vocal nature. Ina Lohr, *Solmisation und Kirchentonarten,* offprint of *Der Organist,* Zurich, 1943, 3; 4th edition, Zurich: Hug 1981, 5.

61 Honegger: Interview Jos Leussink, 25 March 1983; Bäck: letter Karl Gösta Engquist to Ina Lohr of 6 April 1982, PSF-ILC; Krenek: PSF-ILC.

Ill. 3.3: Ernst Krenek, *Veni sanctificator*. Reproduction: PSF-ILC.

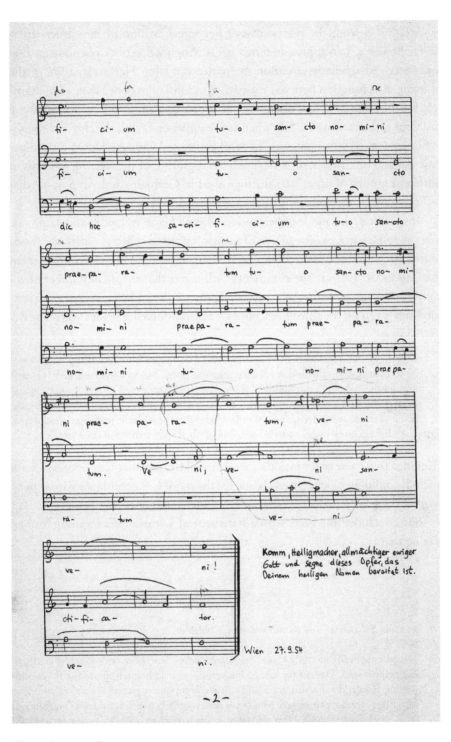

Ill. 3.3: (continued)

Examined from the perspective of her interpretation of the earlier repertoire, however, her approach shows great insight, describes phenomena that
only received scholarly attention many decades later. Her explanation of the
difference in function between the two *c*'s in Dorian may be taken as an example for this. She describes the lower *c* as supporting the notes of its triad above
it, *e* and *g*, thus calling it "do", whereas the upper one, with the closure brought
by its associated semitone, was "fa", and connected with the fifth and third below it, *f* and *a*.[62] This is, on some level, a recognition of the layering in thirds of
different groups of notes later distinguished in German scholarship on medieval monody by the concepts of *Hauptklang* and *Gegenklang*.

In addition, this mode of perception allowed her to recognize and name various melodic patterns – by means of their solmization syllables – that were associated with the individual modes, were characteristic for them, and gave them
their individual affect. She comments with regret that the small number of examples does not allow her to demonstrate the rich abundance of expressive possibilities given by the three hexachords.[63] She reinforced this idea when she declared that

> the sum of the notes does not result in music, no matter how beautifully these notes
> are sung or played. This is true for every musical genre, but to a special degree for vocal
> monophony, which in the Middle Ages was not first "composed", fixed in notation and
> then "performed", but was improvised by a singer on a given text and in a given mode.
> Text and mode were given, and with the mode, also the melodic motifs associated with
> it. And these motifs were ornamented, embellished with figuration (flowers).[64]

This idea that these older melodies were assembled together (com-ponere) from
melodic building blocks characteristic for the modes, in accordance with expression of the text, remained a pillar of her understanding of this music.

She concluded the book with a statement of solmization's meaning for her,
saying that it

---

62 Ina Lohr, *Solmisation und Kirchentonarten*, 4th edition, 8.

63 Ibid., 28.

64 "Die Summe der Töne ergibt keine Musik, auch wenn diese Töne noch so schön gesungen
     oder gespielt sind. Das gilt für jede Musikgattung, aber in besonderem Masse für die ein-
     stimmig-vokale, die im Mittelalter nicht zuerst 'komponiert', schriftlich fixiert und dann
     'aufgeführt', sondern von einem Sänger aus dem vorgegebenen Text und der vorgegebenen
     Tonart improvisiert wurde. Text und Tonart waren gegeben, mit der Tonart auch die ihr
     eigenen Wendungen. Und diese Wendungen wurden von den Sängern mit Floskeln (Blu-
     men) geschmückt, umspielt". Ibid., 30.

creates order in one's musical entity, which is all too often determined by feelings. Solmization teaches us that the notes are always searching out and finding a new order
among themselves, always building a new community, always obeying the same law of
the falling [fifth]. When we accustom ourselves to listening untiringly for this order, it
will have an ordering and cleansing effect not only in our music-making or in music lessons, but also in our lives and in the lives of our students.

For "discipline and moderation" are required of every musical performance which
stems from a "community", whether it be that of the church, home or concert, and di-
rects itself to a listening community. Solmization should show us how we can bring our
singing and playing – as our most true inner expression – "to order", so that we can better pray, praise and give thanks. May God help us in this.[65]

This coupling of solmization, order and religious belief was emblematic for the
inseparability of music and faith in her mind, she could barely conceive of musicality without faith, the one was so intrinsically intertwined with the other. This
led to an expectation, a desire on her part that all musicians see their profession from this perspective, hoping that solmization and singing could help others along this path, as it had her. This attitude, not unsurprisingly, was accepted
wholeheartedly by those with similar convictions, but led others to distance
themselves from her, even if they had an appreciation of her musical abilities.
This, too, was not conducive to a general acceptance of her melodic theory, as
those who understood music as an independent art form were alienated by this
approach.

We have seen that her development of her own conception of solmization was
in accordance with her desire to raise the analysis of melody to a higher level,
to match it more adequately with the more common functional analysis of harmony associated with Hugo Riemann, to re-calibrate, as it were, what she perceived as an imbalance between the three moments of music: rhythm, melody and harmony. Her background, her education at the Muziek-Lyceum in

---

65 "Dass er Ordnung schaffe in seinem oft sehr vom Gefühl geleiteten musikalischen Inneren.
Die Solmisation lehrt uns, dass die Töne unter sich immer von neuem Ordnung suchen
und finden, immer wieder eine neue Gemeinschaft bilden, immer wieder der dem gleichen
Gesetz des Fallens gehorchend. Wenn wir uns daran gewöhnen, unermüdlich auf diese
Ordnung zu hören, so wird sie nicht nur in unserem Musizieren, oder nur im Musikunterricht, sondern zuletzt auch in unserem Leben und im Leben unserer Schüler ordnend und
säubernd wirken.
    Für jede Musikausübung, die von einer 'Gemeinde', sei es eine Kirchen-, Haus-, oder
Konzertgemeinde, ausgeht und sich an eine zuhörende Gemeinde wendet, sind 'Zucht
und Mass' Gebot. Die Solmisation soll uns zeigen, wie wir unser Singen und Spielen als
unsere echteste, innerste Äusserung, 'in Ordnung' bringen, damit wir besser beten, loben
und danken können. Gott helfe uns dazu". Ibid., 84.

Amsterdam and in Basel make it eminently obvious that she was not unaware of what was going on in world of music, but rather that she had made a conscious, independent choice to pursue a path no longer trodden, identifying herself with an earlier musical culture which bore some similarity to her highly personal vision of what music is and can achieve. Indeed, it could be claimed that her interest in earlier music is a product of her faith and her own fascination with the relationship between word and melodic line.

* * *

In this overview of Ina Lohr's musical convictions, what is evident is how her whole musical world was colored by text and faith, by music's function as a mediating force between members of a community, a congregation, and God. And whereas this was characteristic for various movements of the time – the *Jugendmusikbewegung/Singbewegung* and the movements to renew the music of both the Protestant and Catholic churches – what is unusual is that she participated in all of them, did not let herself be limited to a single organization, but rather sought opportunities within all these organizations to realize her own personal musical and religious goals. Her own interest, from her earliest childhood, lay in the expressive possibilities of text in relation to music, using these elements even in her earliest compositions to express her thankfulness and faith in God. In contrast to the general trend of the time towards objectivity – and notwithstanding her own advocacy of accuracy and constancy of rhythmic interpretation – in her own performance there was such an integrity, oneness of word and melodic line, that the music was infused with an overwhelming subjective expressivity that her students and audiences were captivated.

Chapter 4. Her New Life: Ina Lohr's First Decade in Basel

With this information concerning her childhood and her extraordinary musical training, as well as her theological and musical convictions, we can now turn to Ina Lohr's career and – while following her path – observe where and how these ideals influenced her professional choices when she first came to Basel. To be sure, the two major projects to which she devoted her time, the Basel Chamber Orchestra and the Schola Cantorum Basiliensis were, in reality, inextricably intertwined with one another, as both Paul Sacher and she – as his assistant – were intensely involved in the development of both of them. In this chapter, however, these entities will be treated separately, in order to more easily discuss their individual growth.

4.1 Ina Lohr's Assistantship to Paul Sacher, Director of the Basel Chamber Orchestra

We can only gain comprehension of why the cooperation between Paul Sacher and Ina Lohr was so fruitful, if we examine the qualities and capabilities each of them brought into the working relationship, investigate how they complemented one another, compensated for deficits on both sides, enabling both to get further in the attainment of their personal goals. Paul Sacher's were on a more public, international level, while Ina Lohr's were on a more local, more private one, which one might even describe as a transcendental plane. This necessitates a short review of Paul Sacher's background and education in regard to the parallels that drew them together, as well as for the differences that made their work at times tempestuous, but in the end served the needs of both.[1]

Paul Sacher

Paul Sacher was born in 1906 in Basel. He came from a family of farmers and artisans, people who worked hard merely to survive. His mother, Anna Dürr Sacher, wished to escape from the land and established herself as a seamstress. It was she who assumed financial and social control of the family, while his

---

[1] The information on Paul Sacher's early years is largely taken from the biographies by Lesley Stephenson, *Symphonie der Träume*, Zurich: Rüffer & Rub 2001 and Jürg Erni, *Paul Sacher: Musiker und Mäzen*.

father, Oswald August Sacher, worked for a logistics company, gradually moving upwards in its ranks. They were quite a poor family whose budget allowed no luxuries. Nonetheless Paul Sacher was able to have violin lessons from the age of six. When his parents enrolled him in the *Obere Realschule*, the higher level secondary school for the sciences in Basel, they also expected him to work hard in order to ensure that the sacrifices they made for him were worth the effort. At the age of 16,he decided that he wanted to become a conductor. Realizing that he lacked many of the necessary skills for that profession, he began tutoring fellow students at the *Realschule* to earn the money required to enable him to take private instruction in music theory from Rudolf Moser (1892–1960) – ear-training, harmony and counterpoint. At that age, therefore, he was already intent on his goal and working to attain the musical prerequisites for his future.

Aware that he could only gain the experience necessary to be a conductor by participating in an orchestra, both as a player and its leader, he founded one with other members of his school class in 1922, one that was entirely independent of the school administration. "There was no intention other than making music together for several hours [per week], thereby taking a break from the demanding schoolwork, and interacting in a different way with one another than was possible in the school".[2] Only five years later he would give voice to his aesthetic motivation for creating this orchestra:

> Today people have no connection with art. Stringency, greatness and devotion to the art are no longer required in music, nor the fulfillment of duties and cooperation, but rather stimulation and artistic enjoyment, a heightening of the emotions to sensual, sentimental wallowing in art and snobistic pleasure. The cultural dearth of our artistic efforts manifests itself most strongly in the concert business. In conjunction with a lack of recognition of the true content of the music, an over-valuation of technical capabilities has come, in general, to prevail. Anybody who through sheer [technical] skill provokes astonishment is called an artist. The sensitivity toward art and artists – and thus also a just evaluation of that which is merely technically virtuosic – is missing. The audience lacks the feeling of an inner responsibility toward the art, its position is disrespectful; and therefore, it also has no right to criticize. Music should not only be – as

---

2   "Es bestand kein anderer Zweck als der, gemeinsam einige Stunden zu musizieren, dabei von der anstrengenden Schularbeit auszuruhen, und in anderer Form, als dies in der Schule möglich war, miteinander zu verkehren". The quotation stems from the section entitled "Geschichte" (History) of a small brochure, *Orchester Junger Basler*, Basel: Haupt 1927, 6, which documents the activities of this orchestra. The first section "Musik und Schule" is clearly by Paul Sacher himself, the content and the style indicate that the documentation of the orchestra's history may perhaps have been written by H.B. or Hermann Bots, the president of the association at the time, whose initials are found at the end. See also Wulf Arlt, "Zur Idee und Geschichte", p. 39–41, and Martin Kirnbauer, "Paul Sacher und die alte Musik", 27–29.

it is today – something for a guild of performers, but for the whole population [Volk]. Only for a few is music still a spiritual happening above man, a spiritual force, in which a point of balance is sought, just as in a spiritual world, which man penetrates with his own longing and striving and receives something already formed, objective. Art, like religion, can be redemption.[3]

In this he gave tongue to the sentiments and ideals of the German *Jugendmusikbewegung*, in a fashion not dissimilar to that of Ina Lohr, before she had even arrived in Basel.

With a charisma and efficiency that would remain characteristic for Paul Sacher throughout his life, he led his first orchestra, originally as its concertmaster and later as its conductor, from one success to another. In his review of the final concert within the context of the school in 1924, a critic for the *Neue Basler Zeitung* commented that "Mr. Sacher is serious about his task and has complete control over his players. The discipline was good, the intonation pure, and in everything one felt the dashing, spirited temperament of the conductor".[4]

Due to the acclaim the orchestra received and the eager participation of the players, the group decided to continue to work together under the name of "Orchester Junger Basler" after the completion of their secondary education. They were joined by the members of a similar female orchestra led by Annie Tschopp at the girls' school, the *Töchterschule*. As many of the players had begun their studies at the Basel Conservatory, the orchestra offered them the possibility of continuing to work in the ensemble – a highly pleasurable prospect –

---

3 "Heute steht das Volk der Kunst fern. In der Musik wird nicht mehr Strenge, Grösse und Hingabe an die Kunst verlangt, nicht Erfüllung von Pflichten und Mitarbeit, dafür Anregung und Kunstgenuss, Erhitzung der Gemüter bis zum sinnlich-sentimentalen Kunstschwelgen und snobbistisches Geniessen. Die Kulturlosigkeit unserer Kunstübung manifestiert sich am stärksten im Konzertwesen. Entsprechend der Verkennung des wirklichen Inhaltes der Musik macht sich auch allgemein eine Überschätzung der technischen Fertigkeiten breit. Künstler wird jeder geheissen, dessen glattes Können in Staunen setzt. Das Sensorium für Kunst und Künstler und damit die gerechte Einschätzung des Nur-Technisch-Virtuosen fehlen. Dem Publikum fehlt das Gefühl der inneren Verpflichtung gegenüber der Kunst, seine Stellung ist ehrfurchtslos, und deshalb auch ist ihm ein Anrecht auf Kritik abzusprechen. Musik sollte nicht, wie heute, nur die Angelegenheit einer Zunft von Ausübenden, sondern des ganzen Volkes sein. Musik ist nur für wenige noch ein über dem Menschen stehendes geistiges Geschehen, eine geistige Macht, in der ein Ruhepunkt gesucht wird, als in einer Welt des Geistes, die der Mensch mit seinem eigenen Sehnen und Streben durchdringt und empfängt als ein bereits Gestaltetes, Objektives. Kunst kann wie Religion Erlösung sein". Paul Sacher, "Musik und Schule", 3.

4 "Herr Sacher ist mit Ernst bei seiner Aufgabe und hat seine Spieler fest in der Hand. Die Disziplin war gut, die Intonation rein, und aus allem spürte man das rassige, frische Temperament des Dirigenten". *Neue Basler Zeitung*, 29 September 1924 as quoted in Lesley Stephenson, *Symphonie der Träume*, 86.

as well as an unparalleled opportunity to explore a repertoire little played at the time. Sacher's express desire was, namely, to perform compositions for string orchestra from the 17ᵗʰ and 18ᵗʰ centuries, as well as contemporary pieces, both genres of music otherwise neglected then. These musicians formed the nucleus of the Basel Chamber Orchestra, founded in November of 1926. Like many of the members of his orchestra, Paul Sacher was still studying, both at the Conservatory and the university. Although he never received a formal degree in music, he was enrolled at the Conservatory for three years, in the first year with voice as a major (with Arthur Althaus) and violin as a minor (with Fritz Hirt), and then in the following two years, with the advent of Felix Weingartner, he switched his major to conducting.[5] From the latter he learned a great deal, as he himself carefully specified, about "conducting technique".[6] In addition, he participated in classes in a wide range of subjects at the university, among them courses in musicology taught by Karl Nef and Jacques Handschin.

In comparing Paul Sacher's upbringing with that of Ina Lohr, it is the differences that are most evident. Whereas Paul Sacher's mother worked hard to gain a place for her family in the Basel bourgeoisie, Herman Lohr took his social position for granted. He too, however, as we have seen above, was concerned that his children be able to function well in society, that they would be able to support themselves financially as adults. He accordingly took an inordinate interest in their education, with a particular emphasis on the arts, in spite of the fact – or because of it? – that he was an engineer. As a result, Ina Lohr had a musical education of breathtaking breadth and depth. In comparison, Paul Sacher's training was less profound, lacking the knowledge and training that Ina Lohr had absorbed as part of her existence in her family. He, however, was propelled by the desire to be a conductor, a desire that he set about realizing by founding his own orchestra, thereby actively creating the setup needed to train himself. Ina Lohr, on the other hand, plagued by ill health, had an entirely different personal goal, that of helping "where help was needed, but if at all possible within a musical life".[7] Thus in their very orientation their perspectives were different, Paul Sacher's being much more individualistic, more egocentric, while Ina Lohr's view was focused on the well-being of those around her. This

5   Simon Obert, "Der Direktor – zunächst aber Student und Anwärter: Paul Sacher und die Musik-Akademie der Stadt Basel", in: *Tonkunst macht Schule: 150 Jahre Musik-Akademie Basel 1867–2017*, ed. Martina Wohlthat, Basel: Schwabe Verlag 2017, 192–194.

6   *Paul Sacher: Ein Filmportrait*, a documentary film by Leo Nadelmann, Swiss Television, 3 October 1971.

7   Ina Lohr, "Skizze zum Lebenslauf", 3.

does not mean that Paul Sacher was not aware of the needs of those around him; to the contrary, as we shall see, he was not only sensitive to them, but at times helped alleviate them; and similarly, Ina Lohr, in her search for herself, was driven by her own issues.

Assistantship to Paul Sacher

These differences not withstanding, there were certain similarities of personality, of musical interest that brought them together, enabled them to create a working relationship that lasted more than 50 years. One has always known of Ina Lohr's work as his assistant, indeed Paul Sacher refers to it on occasion in his speeches, speaking of her "invaluable aid",[8] and how she had helped him particularly with the programming of early music:

> She knew this early music very well. She brought many suggestions and I actually discussed all of the programs with her during my entire life until she died. It doesn't all come from me – neither the program ideas nor the pieces themselves. Everything was mixed, so that one could not say: that was now Lohr's [choice], that was mine. And Lohr was not the only one who worked with me, there were other people too. But she was the most important [one].[9]

What form her assistance took, however, has always remained rather murky, largely because neither of them spoke of it, as both of them were very reserved about talking about their lives, both of them limiting communication about their inner worlds to family and a small group of friends. Nonetheless, the evidence revealed by their correspondence, by her markings in both Sacher's scores and in the orchestral and choral parts, and by her work in preparing the Basel Chamber Choir indicate that her participation in the activities of the Basel Chamber Orchestra went considerably further than that of a program adviser.

Beyond their singular determination in the pursuit of their personal goals, they had both studied the violin and abandoned it, choosing instead to use

---

8 "unschätzbaren Dienste". "Basler Kunstpreis 1972 an Paul Sacher", in: *Alte und Neue Musik II: Das Basler Kammerorchester (Kammerchor und Kammerorchester) unter Leitung von Paul Sacher 1926–1976*, ed. Veronika Gutmann, Zurich: Atlantis Verlag 1977, 314.

9 "Sie hat diese alte Musik sehr gut gekannt. Sie hat viele Vorschläge gebracht, und ich habe eigentlich alle Programme mit ihr besprochen, mein Leben lang, bis sie gestorben ist. Es kommt also nicht alles von mir – weder die Programmideen noch die Stücke selbst. Das war alles gemischt, so dass man nicht sagen konnte: das war jetzt die Lohr, das war ich. Und die Lohr war nicht die einzige, es hat ja auch noch andere Leute gegeben, die da gearbeitet haben. Aber die Lohr war die wichtigste". Lesley Stephenson, *Symphonie der Träume*, 124. Lesley Stephenson generously gave me access to the two passages in her interviews from fall of 1985 in which Paul Sacher spoke of Ina Lohr. This is a slightly expanded version of what appears in her biography of him.

their studies on that instrument as a foundation for that which truly interested them in the field of music. Furthermore, they were both sympathetic to the social and spiritual ideals of the *Jugendmusikbewegung*, Paul Sacher both through his awareness of the writings of Fritz Jöde and his implementation thereof with his school orchestra, Ina Lohr through the explicit philosophy of the Muziek-Lyceum and her own convictions. In addition, they shared a common enthusiasm for early music, Paul Sacher's stemming from the possibilities it offered for a string chamber orchestra, Ina Lohr's coming more from her fascination for sacred music, in particular Gregorian chant in relation to the musical and liturgical changes demanded by the Reformation. In this, both were more concerned with the practice of this music than the underlying theory. This meant that their interest in musicology lay not in systemic or philological considerations, but in how that which they learned could be applied directly in practice. This, in particular, led the eminent musicologist Jacques Handschin to question some of their musical decisions, causing him to say that Ina Lohr was not a musicologist, but rather a "Nützlichkeitsfanatikerin" (a fanatic only interested in things of practical significance).[10] In part, of course, it was just the manner in which the differences between Paul Sacher and Ina Lohr complemented one another that brought them together. Ina Lohr's great knowledge of music of all periods, but particularly that of earlier eras, combined with her aversion for standing in the limelight, made her an ideal associate for Sacher. In addition, as we saw in Chapter 1, it was her ability to bring the music to life with her voice that fascinated him, was what initially caused him to inquire whether she might be interested in helping him. Linked with this was their joint interest in creating good programs, programs that presented unfamiliar music to audiences within a context which grabbed their attention, was informative, and placed the music in a good light. All these factors contributed to the success of their long cooperation.

What little knowledge we do have concerning their cooperation comes almost exclusively from their correspondence. Although one might ask why they wrote about such questions when they lived in the same city, this is explained by the fact that the documents are largely written in the summer months when both were, at least in theory, on vacation. As, however, the BKO's annual program needed to be published by the beginning of September, complete with the programming and the names of the soloists for the individual concerts, in truth much preparatory work needed to be done during July and August. The extent of the correspondence, however, does not lend itself to a purely chron-

10   Interview with Jos Leussink, 24–25 March 1983.

ological discussion. Instead, what follows will orient itself around certain individual topics, chosen to illustrate the various aspects of their work together, both from the musical as well as the psychological perspective.

Programming

In order to illustrate the degree to which Ina Lohr was involved in all aspects of the planning of the BKO's concerts, we will begin by examining the correspondence concerning their first joint concert. Ironically enough, the cooperation began with an absolute failure, in that Ina Lohr was unable to read Paul Sacher's handwriting and was forced to go to the secretary of the BKO for help in deciphering his first letter of 28 June 1930. In it he had requested suggestions for the choir concert in November and asked her to take up contact with the singer she had recommended for the performance of André Caplet's *Miroir de Jesus* in December 1930.[11] On 16 July 1930, he redoubled this request in a typed letter, in which he also asked whether she wanted to realize the continuo part of the Buxtehude mass for strings, while encouraging her to suggest to the singer that she accept the engagement at a low fee, as it would be a form of introduction to the Basel music world.

Ina Lohr responded on 20 July 1930 with the following program suggestion:[12]

I. St. Hildegardus [sic] (12th century)	Kyrie
II. Palestrina	Sicut Cervus
	Dies Sanctificatus
III. Buxtehude	Missa Brevis
IV. Bach	Concerto A minor
V. Bach	Motet

She accompanied this with an explanation of her reasoning, questions, and other information and suggestions:

– With only a string orchestra at their disposal, it would be impossible to perform a Bach cantata; for closure, however, one needed another of his works at the end.
– The Kyrie would be sung *in alternatim* by a women's or men's choir.
– Although the texts of *Sicut Cervus* and *Dies Sanctificatus* were contrasting in character, she understood the latter to be an answer to the former.

11   Letter Paul Sacher to Ina Lohr of 28 June 1930, PSF-ILC.
12   Letter Ina Lohr to Paul Sacher of 30 June 1930, private collection, Switzerland.

- She informed him where the music could be obtained, saying that she would prefer to write out the parts and have them copied, that it would not increase the costs significantly.[13]
- She planned to visit a Catholic choir director in Arnhem to look through a complete edition of Palestrina, mentioning various desirable editions, if there were a budget for such things; the Sweelinck edition was out-of-print, but it would perhaps be possible to copy some pieces in Amsterdam later.
- There were only two possibilities for the Buxtehude: either singing it *a cappella* or having the strings accompany the voices *colla parte* with the continuo being played by an organ or harpsichord.
- She had written to the singer, Berthe Seroen, who had not yet replied. Should she contact other singers in the North, should Berthe Seroen not be able to take the engagement, or did he know of someone in Basel who would be able to sing it?
- And finally, in connection with another program for the upcoming concert season, she suggested complementing Caplet's *Miroir* with his *Prières* and *Messe à trois Voix*.

In a letter of 25 July 1930, Paul Sacher responded to this proposal in detail:[14]

- First, he preferred only one motet by Palestrina, together with one or two by other less well-known masters, perhaps Lechner's *Deutsche Sprüche von Leben und Tod*, or something of her suggestion. From the chronological point of view, an additional piece between Hildegard and Palestrina would be possible. He disliked the idea of concluding with a Bach motet. He asked if an old Italian violin concerto or a modern choral work would not be better, as we must not "forget the need of continually increasing the tension throughout the program".[15]
- He requested that she copy out the Hildegard and send it to him, so that it could be printed, remarking that "with all of these pieces, one needs to watch out that the text does not disturb the nerves of our bigoted pastors".[16]

---

13 Martin Kirnbauer in "Paul Sacher und die alte Musik", 42, speaks of how in contrast to other groups of the time, the BKO insisted on performing music from printed editions rather than manuscript transcriptions. As we shall see later, this was more of a concern of Paul Sacher's than Ina Lohr's.
14 Letter Paul Sacher to Ina Lohr of 25 July 1930, PSF-ILC.
15 "Nur dürfen wir die Steigerung im Programm nicht vergessen". Ibid.
16 "Bei allen diesen Werken ist darauf zu achten, dass der Text unseren bigotten prot. Pfarrherren nicht auf die Nerven geht". Ibid.

In addition, all of the parts needed to be marked up from the point of view of the agogic and dynamics.
- He requested a marked-up score of *Sicut cervus*, so that one could copy out the parts for the choir and have them printed.
- In the Buxtehude mass the strings would play *colla parte*; the continuo would be performed by a harpsichord and a string bass, as in the *secco* recitatives in Bach; he wanted to avoid the cost of the organ.
- He needed the choir parts by the beginning of September and would order those for the Buxtehude from Bärenreiter and see whether they were acceptable.
- "One has to watch out that the whole program is not too severe. The audience can only stand absolute music to a certain degree. At least one number must have an expressive and sentimental effect on the naiver souls".[17]
- If Berthe Soroen could not come for the Caplet, he would let Berthe de Vigier or some young Swiss woman sing it.
- Caplet's *Miroir* should be coupled with a work by another composer unless she found his other compositions particularly beautiful. Could she obtain the scores for other works?
- A further composition was needed for the June concert with Purcell's *Dido and Aeneas*.
- "I am still happy to have found such a knowledgeable assistant in you",[18] assuring her that all costs in association with her work would be covered by the BKO.

This first exchange gives a glimpse of the profound nature of the cooperation between the two of them. They had obviously already discussed the basic nature of the program before the summer; Ina Lohr in her letter was simply furnishing it with a provisional outer form. In addition, she spoke of practical matters, from the need of parts for the choir and/or orchestra to the impossibility of a realization of a continuo for strings for the Buxtehude mass. Her letter also reveals the comparative scarcity of modern scores for older music at that time, compounding the programming difficulties. Paul Sacher, on the other hand, reviewed the suggestions from the conductor's perspective, making sure that they would serve the needs of his ensembles, and also asking her to mark up the

17 "Man muss darauf achten, dass das ganze Programm nicht zu streng wird. Das Publikum erträgt die absolute Musik nur bis zu einem gewissen Grad. Es muss wenigstens eine Nummer auch für naivere Seelen ausdrucksvoll und empfindsam wirken!" Ibid.
18 "Ich bin nach wie vor sehr froh, in Ihnen eine so wissende Mitarbeiterin gefunden zu haben". Ibid.

scores for performance. Further, they were concerned about finding good vocal soloists for the concert.

Ina Lohr's response of 9 August 1930, delayed due to work on a commissioned composition, was to the point:[19]

- She reported what she had found out about the various editions of Palestrina, both as far as their contents were concerned, their publishers, the availability of parts, and their price.
- She suggested inserting Sweelinck's *Dies sanctificatus* between Palestrina and Buxtehude.
- She proposed further that one might place Févin's *Descende in Hortum meum* between Hildegard and Palestrina, also mentioning the availability of its score and parts.
- If he would prefer Lechner, then it would become a three-part program and one could sing something at the end from the new choir book.
- A Bach concerto would be better than an old Italian one.
- The Kyrie would be included in her letter and she hoped that everything was clear.
- Finally, she inquired whether the orchestral parts for the Buxtehude needed to be finished by mid-August, saying that this would be impossible at home, where she had so many other duties.

We have the printed version of Hildegard's Kyrie that she made for this performance (see Ill. 4.1), from which we can draw certain conclusions about the interpretative decisions she was making. First of all, the handwritten remark suggests that the transcription was originally made from a manuscript in Ghent and in its present form taken from an unspecified print found in Amsterdam.[20] The piece is transposed down a semitone, from F to E, with the result that the score has the forbidding and anachronistic staff signature of four sharps. The melismas have been carefully divided up into groups of two and three, according to the school of Solesmes, with the dynamics meticulously stipulated. Additional commas were inserted, partly by hand, to indicate which groups belonged together, the even larger units being divided by vertical lines through the staff. Later in this chapter, we will see how she came to chafe under the necessity of specifying this level of perfomance in chant transcriptions. Finally, a performance *in alternatim* is suggested, with the first Kyrie and the Christe each being

19 Letter Ina Lohr to Paul Sacher of 9 August 1930, private collection, Switzerland.
20 It was only after the concert that she went to Wiesbaden to examine the manuscript there, see p. 51.

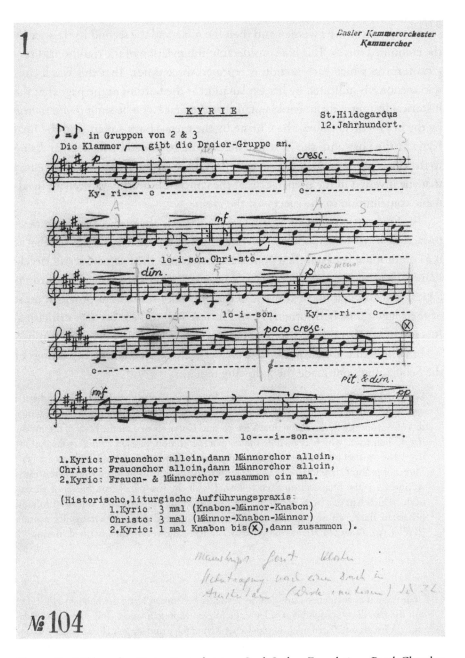

Ill. 4.1: St. Hildegardis, Kyrie. Reproduction: Paul Sacher Foundation, Basel Chamber Orchestra Collection.

sung twice, first by the women and then the men, and the second Kyrie once by the combined forces. This is a considerable abbreviation of the traditional liturgical form in which each section is repeated three times. That this was a conscious choice is indicated by her explanation at the bottom of the page that the historical liturgical form would entail that the first Kyrie be sung *in alternatim* by the boys – men – boys, the Christe by the men – boys – men, and the final Kyrie by the boys until the X, where they would be joined by the men and sing to the end. Assuming the work on this short piece is representative for the effort that she invested in the preparation of the concert, it must have been an invaluable contribution to the success of the event.

The final version of the program (see Ill. 4.2) was obviously worked out face-to-face, as it has undergone considerable further alteration. We can see that it is a compromise between their approaches: although the first part is still largely Franco-Flemish and the second German, what prevails is a sense of a chronological tour through music history. In the discussions, Ina Lohr provided most of the suggestions, both originally and in response to Paul Sacher's criticisms. It is fair to say that this program would not have come into being without her.

In reminiscing about the concert on a cassette tape about the beginnings of the Schola, Ina Lohr made the following remarks:

> We dared to begin it with the Kyrie – now known once again – of the holy Hildegard von Bingen, who lived from 1098 to 1179. It was followed in chronological order by motets of Antoine de Févin, Palestrina, Victoria and Corsi, chosen on the basis of the meaning of their texts, which as a whole made up a meditation, or even a non-traditional liturgy. The six-part piece of the Dutch [composer] Jan Pieterszoon Sweelinck on the 134th Hugenot psalm *Or sus serviteurs du signeur* served as a transition to a more conventional section [...] The final section then followed with the five-part Missa brevis of Buxtehude, which had just been published, and by the violin concerto in A minor of Johann Sebastian Bach, whose name could not be missing, and the somewhat older cantata [BWV] 150, *Nach Dir Herr verlanget mich*, which is, however, only ascribed to him.[21]

21 "Wir wagten es anzufangen mit dem jetzt wieder bekannten Kyrie der heiligen Hildegard von Bingen, die von 1098 bis 1179 lebte. Es folgten Motetten von Antoine de Févin, Palestrina, Vittoria und Corsi in chronologischer Reihenfolge und ausgesucht nach der Aussage ihrer Texte, die als Ganzes eine Meditation, sogar eine nicht traditionelle Liturgie bildete. Als Überleitung zu einem mehr konventionellen Teil wirkte der sechsstimmige Satz des Niederländers Jan Pieterszoon Sweelinck über den 134. Hugenotten Psalm, *Or sus serviteurs du signeur* [...] Als letzter Teil folgte dann die fünfstimmige Missa brevis von Buxtehude, die gerade herausgekommen war, und von Johann Sebastian Bach, dessen Name nicht doch fehlen durfte, das Violinkonzert in a-moll und die ihm allerdings nur zugeschriebene, etwas ältere Kantate 150, Nach Dir Herr verlanget mich". Cassette "Die Entstehung der Schola Cantorum Basiliensis", PSF-ILC, CD 4.

BASLER KAMMERORCHESTER
KAMMERCHOR UND
KAMMERORCHESTER
LEITUNG PAUL SACHER

MITTWOCH 26. NOVEMBER 20.15 UHR IN DER MARTINSKIRCHE

3. KONZERT *1930*
IM ABONNEMENT

SOLIST **STEFI GEYER** VIOLINE

PROGRAMM

ST. HILDEGARDIS 12. JAHRHUNDERT	**KYRIE ELEISON**[x]
ANTON FEVIN 1473—1515	**DESCENDE IN HORTUM MEUM**
G. P. DA PALESTRINA 1526—1594	**SICUT CERVUS**[x]
T. L. DA VITTORIA UM 1540—1611	**ET INCARNATUS EST**[x] **AUS DER MISSA QUARTI TONI**
GIUSEPPE CORSI 17. JAHRHUNDERT	**ADORAMUS TE**
JAN PZN SWEELINCK 1562—1621	**PSALM 134 „OR SUS, SERVITEURS DU SEIGNEUR"**[x]
DIETRICH BUXTEHUDE 1637—1707	**MISSA BREVIS**[x]
JOH. SEB. BACH 1685—1750	**VIOLINKONZERT A-MOLL** **KANTATE No. 150 „NACH DIR, HERR, VERLANGET MICH"**[x] Soli: MARIANNE LÖW Sopran, EMILIE WACKERNAGEL Alt, AUGUST SUMPF Tenor, KARL THEO WAGNER Bass Cembalo: MARTHA HAMM-STOECKLIN

[x] Erstaufführung in Basel.
CEMBALO PLEYEL DES B. K. O. (Alleinvertretung HUG & Co.).   Texte umstehend.

KARTEN zu Fr. 6.60, 4.95, 3.30 und 2.20 bei HUG & Co., Freiestrasse 70a und an der Abendkasse 19.30 Uhr. VERKAUF ab Freitag, 21. November. Für Mitglieder Preisermässigung und Vorbezugsrecht ab Donnerstag, 20. November. Programm mit Text 40 Cts.

4. KONZERT IM ABONNEMENT (Kammerchor u. Kammerorchester) am 14. Dezember im Münstersaal.
Solist: BERTHE SEROEN (Amsterdam), Sopran. CAPLET, Miroir de Jésus.
VORANZEIGE der J. G. N. M.: Am 30. November JULIUS WEISMANN (Klavier) mit eigenen Werken.

Ill. 4.2: BKO program of 26 November 1930. Reproduction: PSF-PSC.

Two aspects of this commentary jump out at us. First, we get a glimpse of the courage it took to perform a program of music almost completely unknown to the Basel audience. Even the Buxtehude had just appeared in a new edition and thus was also a novelty. This was presumably also why the need for the Bach violin concerto was felt so strongly. And secondly, we can see that Ina Lohr was already then grouping pieces in accordance with their textual meaning, striving on some level to find a spiritual order for them, to the degree that 50 years later she speaks of it being "a non-traditional liturgy".

That these first discussions were not without their difficulties is made abundantly evident in a missive sent to Paul Sacher by Ina Lohr on 28 September 1930. She made her intentions clear from the very beginning: "this letter is addressed not to the nitpicker [Mengelmeyer] but to Paul Sacher with the intent of creating clarity in a couple of issues".[22] This use of the nickname "Mengelmeyer" was an indication that they had in all likelihood spoken about his perhaps abrasive insistence on details, resolving the issue on some level by his acceptance of this moniker. In the further course of the letter, it becomes apparent that she had also been asked to help another musician by the name of [Rudolf?] Moser with his concerts, and turned him down, saying that she was working for the BKO. Paul Sacher had evidently spoken to her about this in a somewhat disparaging manner. She explained she was unwilling to reject Moser without giving a reason, speaking of how some people can delegate better than others, giving their burdens to the accompanying drivers and cyclists who assist the competitor during a race. Further that

> every true artist should be a bit of a prophet; *he* [Moser] has the need to create, but not the strength; you have the strength, but at the moment do not exactly know what and to whom you wish to evangelize. This is where my sympathy lies with Moser and why I must tell him that I also belong to the cyclists [accompanying you]! Do you object to this, do you perhaps object that I speak of this work at all? I must then also clear up something here: it is of no importance to me to see my name on the program, but I also feel that I myself am a bit of a prophet, and I want to be able to stand up for my work before the entire world. In the meanwhile, nobody believes that I have lots to do, because my work gives me such great pleasure: it is then always a help when I can point to practical results. I also only recently found out that I will only have very little money in the future; I am happy about this, because it gives me the right to count myself among the working people and that is my pride. You will perhaps not really understand this; you are thus a poor rich man and I am a rich poor woman. If one – like me namely – has always been ill or half-ill and on the sidelines, then it is something particularly won-

---

22 "Dieser Brief ist nicht an Mengelmeyer aber an Paul Sacher gerichtet und dient dazu in ein Paar Punkten Klarheit zu schaffen". Letter Ina Lohr to Paul Sacher of 28 September 1930, private collection, Switzerland.

derful to be able to be of assistance in the practical world, even if in such minor way. I wish to be able to express this joy now and then, and you may not take that from me. I do not demand any official recognition (for that, my part in the work is far too small), but I want to be able to work quietly, but not, however, in secret.[23]

This passage is remarkable for many reasons. First, there is an astonishingly bold immediacy in her willingness to address issues that are important to her. While acknowledging Paul Sacher's strength as a leader, his ability to delegate, she questions the depth of his musical vision. In saying that she feels herself to be "a bit of a prophet", she is in a sense acknowledging that she is providing something necessary to the success of Paul Sacher's project, giving the programs a message that might otherwise have been lacking. And this is followed by the poignancy of her remarks concerning her joy of being able to work, to have a job that is meaningful, and the necessity of being able to speak of her activities. It brings to the fore, however, the degree to which her work for the BKO had been shrouded in secrecy up until that point. It becomes evident here that Sacher would have preferred to keep quiet about it, but that she was insisting on her right to speak of it. Sadly, however, in the last year of her life, in her interview with Jos Leussink, she speaks of how she had only recently overcome her reticence about speaking of their cooperation. Indeed, in this interview she relishes telling about her experiences and work with such figures as Nadia Boulanger, Igor Stravinsky, Arthur Honegger, Paul Hindemith, Béla Bartók, and Ernst Krenek, just to mention a few of the most well-known. I suspect that her

---

23 "Jeder wahre Künstler soll ein bischen [sic] Prophet sein; er hat das Bedürfnis zu zeugen aber nicht die Kraft; Sie haben die Kraft aber vorläufig wissen Sie noch nicht genau was und wem Sie verkündigen müssen. Es ist hier, dass meine Sympathie an Mosers Seite ist und eben darum muss ich es ihm sagen, dass ich auch zu den Radfahrern gehöre! Ist Ihnen das nicht recht und ist es Ihnen vielleicht überhaupt nicht recht, dass ich von dieser Arbeit rede? Auch da muss ich dann etwas auseinandersetzen: ich lege keinen Wert darauf meinen Namen im Programm zu sehen aber auch ich fühle mich ein Bischen [sic] Prophetin und ich will zu meiner Arbeit stehen dürfen vor der ganzen Welt. Dabei glaubt man mir nie, dass ich viel zu tun habe weil meine Arbeit mir nun einmal sehr viel Freude macht; es hilft dann immer, wenn ich auf praktische Resultate hinweisen kann. Auch weiss ich seit kurzer Zeit, dass ich später nur sehr wenig Geld haben werde; ich bin froh deshalb, denn es gibt mir die Berechtigung mich zu den arbeitenden Menschen zu rechnen und das ist mein Stolz. Sie werden das vielleicht nicht genau verstehen; Sie sind hier nml. ein armer Reicher und ich eine reiche Arme. Wenn man nml. wie ich immer krank oder halbkrank und abseits gewesen ist, dann is [sic] es etwas sonderbar Herrliches in der Praxis mithelfen zu dürfen, wenn auch noch so wenig. Diese Freude möchte ich dann und wann mal äussern und Sie dürfen mir das nicht nehmen. Ich verlange also [sic] gar keine offizielle Anerkennung (dafür ist ja mein Teil in der Arbeit viel zu gering) aber ich möchte zwar im Stillen aber nicht im Geheimen schaffen". Ibid.

work with Paul Sacher was something that she spoke of only with her family and one or two of her close friends, if it at all. And finally, in referring to herself as a "rich poor woman" while calling Paul Sacher a "poor rich man", she speaks not only of the differences in their financial situation, but also of their difference of attitude towards their work, she being happy at the opportunity of participating usefully in society, whereas he was moving powerfully forward in his career. Yet – as it was before his marriage with Maja Hoffmann-Stehlin – it is almost as if she foresaw that he would be a financially successful man, who at the moment simply lacked funds.

Advice on Music and Musicians

Another example of the type of influence she wielded over Sacher, were her detailed instructions concerning Luigi Cherubini's *Requiem*, a work that the BKO never performed, although Ina Lohr had prepared the score.

> The whole thing may be divided into psalms with the antiphons that belong to them. The Dies irae stands for itself alone. The psalms are very dramatic, the antiphons contemplative, pleading. Also the Dies irae is in part dramatic, in part very introspective. One has to set these contrasts off from one another, and this more agogically than dynamically. I've written in quite a bit, but you have to involve yourself with the text and use your fantasy. Imagine a funeral in the late Middle Ages [...] The basic tenor of the entire work is a mixture of the fear of death, and the fear of and trust in God [...] The mass of the dead is a restrained plaint, in which fear flares up in each of the psalm verses. The opening movement of the Cherubini must, for example, be very restrained, but never overladen with sorrow and pain.

She then goes through the entire piece, characterizing the individual movements and concluding with "so, I hope that you are not bothered by the bad and sentimental German. The main thing is that the job is finished".[24] One gets a whiff of a bit of impatience that it is actually necessary to explain these things,

---

24 "Das Ganze lässt sich einteilen in Psalmen mit jeweils dazu gehörenden Antiphonen. Das Dies Irae steht für sich. Die Psalmen sind sehr dramatisch, die Antiphonen beschaulich, flehend. Auch das Dies Irae ist teils dramatisch, teils sehr versunken. Man muss diese Gegensätze ziemlich stark gegen einander abheben und das mehr durch Agogik als durch Dynamik. Ich habe verschiedenes eingetragen, aber Sie müssen sich mal mit dem Text auseinandersetzen und Ihre Phantasie gebrauchen. Stellen Sie sich eine Totenfeier im späten Mittelalter vor [...] Grundstimmung von dem ganzen Werk ist ein Gemisch von Todesangst, Gottesfurcht und Gottesvertrauen. [...] Die Totenmesse ist eine verhaltene Klage, darin in den Psalmversen jedesmal die Angst auflodert. Der Anfangssatz bei Cherubini muss z. B. sehr zurückgehalten sein, aber nie geladen mit Trauer und Schmerz [...] So, hoffentlich stört Sie das schlechte und sentimentale Deutsch nicht. Hauptsache ist, dass die Sache erledigt ist". Letter Ina Lohr to Paul Sacher of 8 July 1932, private collection, Switzerland.

to have to discuss the reciprocal influence of text and music. These instructions also make it manifest where the value of Ina Lohr's input for the performance of such works lay for Paul Sacher.

Whereas her involvement with the actual choice of pieces was greater in the realm of music of earlier eras, it does not mean that Paul Sacher did not ask for her opinion about contemporary music. For example, in August 1935, she studied Arthur Lourié's *Concerto spirituale* [1928–29] with great enthusiasm, finding it fascinating in its use of chant, hence also its cantabile and gripping melodic lines, but inappropriate for them, because of the instrumentation and the difficulty of the choir parts. She did believe, however, that

> one should hear the cantata by René Matthes, at least in a study performance [...] Everything sings, even under the influence of [Gregorian] chant. The tonality is not always clearly delineated and I am bothered by the lack of style in the collection of texts, which is only made on the basis of content. That results in a textual stew, like the one that Mahler cooked so beautifully in the 8th symphony. The melodic lines are unfortunately not always interesting.[25]

This discussion is illuminating, in that it shows an ability to characterize and analyze a work in an extraordinarily precise fashion, illustrates the degree to which she was interested in the contemporary music of the time. In addition, the manner in which she complains about the lack of textual style or unity shows an engaging sense of humor, an ability to make pithy metaphors. Although she may not have had the same knowledge and passion for this music as that of earlier times, Paul Sacher obviously prized her ability to evaluate compositions in his continual search for new music. He maintained a notebook, in which such remarks – made by a number of musicians and scholars associated with him – were entered alphabetically by composer. Ina Lohr's are noteworthy, both for their succinctness and her clarity in stating whether a piece was appropriate for the BKO or not.

The choice of vocal soloists was another area of programming in which her expertise was called upon. The degree to which she participated in their selec-

---

25 "Die Kantate von René Matthes sollte man, mindestens in einer Studienaufführung einmal hören [...] Alles singt und zwar auch unter dem Einfluss von Choral. Die Tonart ist aber nicht immer deutlich getroffen und mich stört die stillose Textzusammenstellung, die nur vom Inhalt aus getroffen ist. Das gibt ein Textgemüse, wie es auch Mahler so schön gekocht hat in der 8. Sinfonie. Die Melodik ist leider nicht immer interessant." The letter from Ina Lohr to Paul Sacher is undated, but from its place in the correspondence and the location it was written, it is clear that it must be from the first half of August 1935, private collection, Switzerland.

tion is illustrated by a passage from a letter of 21 July 1933 written in Haslemere, England, in which she first mentions that she has spoken with the Jo Vincent's agent, but has been told that the minimum fee for the singer would be fr. 600. She writes Sacher that

> she is naturally much better and more reliable than Siegrist, but I think that even fr. 500 would be too much in comparison with our other fees. We should not give a Dutch woman more than the fr. 350 [or 250 as mentioned in a letter of 7 August 1931?] that Seroen and Kloos received [...]
>
> La Roche likes to sing Handel, but she drags the tempi awfully and we do not know how she sings in English. Shouldn't one actually consider Gradmann? Her voice is very beautiful and she works well. I am not enthusiastic about Cron, but it might be good to take him for diplomatic reasons. His part, however, is extraordinarily important. Don't you want to wait with the inquiry until the concerts are over [both] here and in Cambridge? Perhaps there is a good tenor here and then it would not be dumb to have an English soloist. We heard a good bass here. I still go to him for pronunciation.
>
> *Paris.* Why would Fahrni not be good for the Parisians? She can hardly be more German than Merz-Tunner. By the way, I have heard that the latter does not work well independently and that is why she is so variable in her singing. I know of a Dutch woman who sang the part in Antwerp, but her personality is awkward and stiff. And someone from the opera? Prechtl? We haven't heard her for a long time and she is said to have learned a lot. Rutters, the critic from Amsterdam, has recommended Annie Quistorp of Leipzig to me, but his taste is very idiosyncratic and I have never heard her myself.[26]

As with the evaluation of the modern works, what is surprising here is the freedom with which she expresses her opinion about the singers, the manner in which she speaks of them. Musicians can only write in this way about other

---

26 "Natürlich ist sie viel besser und zuverlässiger als die Siegrist, aber ich finde auch fr 500 viel im Verhältnis zu unseren sonstigen Honoraren. Wir sollten einer Holländerin nicht mehr geben als fr 350, was Seroen und Kloos bekamen. [...]

Die Laroche singt gern Händel, nur zieht sie die Tempi furchtbar und wir wissen nicht, wie sie Englisch singt. Wäre eigentlich nicht mal an die Gradmann zu denken? Die Stimme ist sehr schön und sie arbeitet gut. Von Cron bin ich nicht begeistert, aber aus diplomatischen Gründen wäre es vielleicht gut ihn zu nehmen. Seine Partie ist aber ungeheuer wichtig. Wollen Sie nicht noch warten mit der Anfrage, bis hier und in Cambridge die Konzerte vorbei sind? Vielleicht ist hier ein guter Tenor und dann wäre es nicht dumm, einen englischen Solisten zu haben. Einen guten Bass haben wir hier gehört. Ich gehe noch zu ihm für die Aussprache.

Paris. Warum wäre die Fahrni nichts für die Pariser? Sie kann doch kaum deutscher sein als die Merz-Tunner. Uebrigens habe ich hier gehört, dass diese nicht gut selbständig arbeitet und darum unterschiedlich singt. Ich weiss eine Holländerin, die die Partie in Antwerpen gesungen hat, aber sie ist als Persönlichkeit ungeschickt und steif. Und eine von der Oper? Die Prechtl? Wir haben sie lange nicht gehört und sie soll viel gelernt haben. Rutters, der Kritiker aus Amsterdam hat mir schon einige Male die Annie Quistorp aus Leipzig empfohlen, aber er hat ein sehr eigenwilliges Urteil und selber habe ich sie nie gehört". Letter Ina Lohr to Paul Sacher of 21 July 1933, private collection, Switzerland.

musicians if they have absolute trust that their correspondents will both understand what they write and treat it with circumspection, to avoid repercussions
from colleagues. It is also clear that Ina Lohr expects her opinions to be taken
very seriously, knows that they will be important in the decision-making process.

Preparation of Conducting Scores and Parts

In the first chapter, we saw that her cooperation with Paul Sacher began when
she marked up a Rosenmüller *sonata da camera* for him, complete with explanations of modal influence and hemiolas. She was to continue doing this for earlier music for him for most of her life, as this was where the necessity for such
work showed itself most, as the convention of notating all articulation, dynamics, tempi, etc. only established itself in the 19th century. Very early on, in order
to simplify things for herself, she made up a trill chart for the orchestra in which
various forms of baroque trills were identifiable by letter (see Ill. 4.3).

This meant that instead of having to notate the form of each trill explicitly,
she could get by with only placing a letter in the parts, thus greatly simplifying
her task. We can see an example of this in Philipp Heinrich Erlebach's Suite in
D minor, first performed by the Basel Chamber Orchestra on 15 October 1942
(see Ill. 4.4). Not only are the trills in m. 3 marked with *a*, and those in m. 4–6
with *d*, she has also added and altered slurs, marked the bowings, indicated that
as an overture the upbeats should be overdotted. In addition, the dynamics and
phrasing have been clarified. Once again, we can see the methodical thoroughness with which she approached her task.

In addition, she at times made her own realizations of the thorough bass for
the orchestra for such works as Marc-Antoine Charpentier's *Le Reniement de
Saint Pierre*. We have the evidence for this not only in the fact that it receives
explicit mention in the concert program of 27 April 1932, but also from the vocal score in the Ina Lohr Collection of the Paul Sacher Foundation in which her
manuscript version has been pasted over the printed one.[27] Both realizations reflect a lack of awareness of the French sources of thorough bass playing of the
period, depart from a strict four-part texture, taking the liberty of making leaps
with the right hand, and in the case of Ina Lohr, extending the range up much
higher than deemed suitable by the treatises.[28] The printed version lies better

---

27 See Martin Kirnbauer, "Paul Sacher – Facetten einer Musikerpersönlichkeit", 41, with the
    commentary on 43–44.
28 See Jesper Bøje Christensen, *Die Grundlagen des Generalbassspiels im 18. Jahrhundert: Ein
    Lehrbuch nach zeitgenössischen Quellen*, Kassel and Basel: Bärenreiter 1992, 10–11.

Ill. 4.3: Trill Chart for the Basel Chamber Orchestra. Reproduction: Paul Sacher Foundation, Basel Chamber Orchestra Collection.

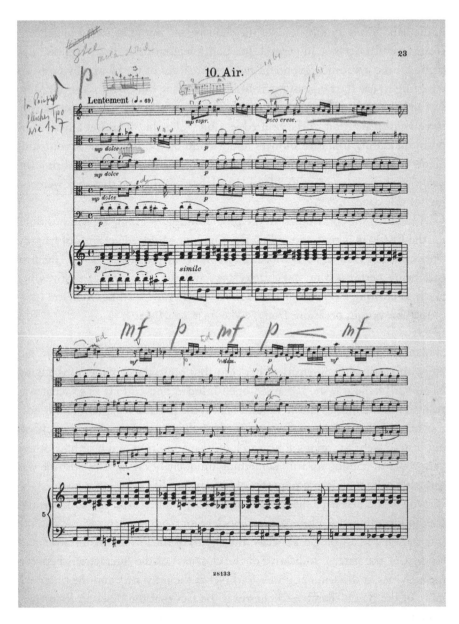

Ill. 4.4: Philipp Heinrich Erlebach, Suite in D minor. Reproduction: Paul Sacher Foundation, Basel Chamber Orchestra Collection.

in the hand, often simply doubles the choir voices, but in its use of full chords creates parallel octaves. In general, Ina Lohr's realization is decidedly less idiomatic for the instrument, contains many more leaps of the hand, obviously attempting to use the range of the realization to bring out the musical phrasing. At Omnes vos (see Ill. 4.5), for example – in comparison to the sparse, mostly three-voice realization of the printed version – she almost creates a new composition, adding imitative motives and a sense of vocality to the accompaniment. It seems likely that some of her choices were also designed to bring the qualities of the relatively new Pleyel harpsichord to the fore that they were using for this concert.[29]

And lastly, she contributed to the programming by arranging compositions for the BKO, an activity extending from making abridged versions of lengthy works, such as Handel's oratorio, *L'Allegro, il Pensieroso ed il Moderato* (the first part being performed on 7 February 1933 and the second on 20 November 1935), to creating a version of Bach's *Art of the Fugue* for string orchestra (performed on various occasions from 13 May 1936 to 18 March 1950).

Widening Her Horizons

Notwithstanding the intensity of her contribution to the activities of the Basel Chamber Orchestra, she remained open-minded and curious as to what was going on in the musical world around her. In the previous chapter, we saw how she did not limit herself to Cuypers' or the Solesmnes interpretation of chant, but instead went to various abbeys to look at manuscripts and hear how others performed it, coming up with something uniquely her own. This attitude was something she took into other areas of her musical life as well.

One of the first trips she took, from 1–6 September 1930, was to Liège and the joint meeting of the International Society for Contemporary Music and the International Musicological Society, the eighth of the former organization and the first of the latter.[30] Indicative of the closeness of the interactions between the activities in the seminar under Karl Nef at the university and the programming of the Basel Chamber Orchestra is the fact that the Basel professor presented a paper on the above-mentioned oratorio by Charpentier, *Le Reniement de Saint Pierre*.

29 This instrument had been officially inaugurated the previous year by Wanda Landowska. Martin Kirnbauer, "'aufs eindrücklichste für das Cembalo werben' – Wanda Landowska in Basel", in: *Notenlese: Musikalische Aufführungspraxis des 19. und frühen 20. Jahrhunderts in Basel*, ed. Martina Wohlthat, Basel: Schwabe Verlag 2013, 103.

30 There is a program of the event, with the sessions she was interested in marked in pencil, in PSF-ILC.

In retrospect, one of the most startling of these forays into the greater musical world was a trip she took to Paris in 1931 together with Paul Sacher and the Swiss composer Conrad Beck, who at that time was taking lessons with Nadia Boulanger. She told Jos Leussink that her

> father decided that it would be a good if I were also to go to her. So I went to Paris to hear the first performance [the work was premiered in Brussels on 13 December 1930; this was the Parisian premiere] of the *Symphonie de psaumes* by Stravinsky – with Sacher and Beck. And Lili[31] [Nadia] Boulanger had invited me to visit her in the Avenue [Rue] Ballu to take part [...] in a large class she had there; and there I was in a real Paris salon, full of all kinds of little – I also have such little useless knick-knacks standing round about, which is sometimes found frivolous in my line of work – but at Lili [Nadia] Boulanger's it really was to the point that you didn't know how to sit on your chair. The place was completely full. But she had a presence that was really unbelievable.
>
> And then we went together to the rehearsal, the dress rehearsal that Stravinsky himself was conducting, and I ended up sitting next to her and I looked into the large first manuscript score by Stravinsky, and she asked me what I thought there and there, and [she] immediately said that she wanted to keep me one or two years. To which I replied: "You know, I do not feel at all at home in your salon, I am not someone for salons. And as far as that goes – I really love Paris, I know Paris pretty well, I always came here with my parents in May, and stayed a month to hear the premieres, I know all about it – but I could never put down roots here. Yet I felt at home in the little city of Basel from the very first moment, to me that is very important. I do not need to become famous". With that she was so surprised that I said: "*C'est pas necessaire, pas necessaire d'être celèbre, pas du tout*". She was dumb-struck by that.[32]

31 In one of old age's forgetful moments, she was obviously confusing Nadia Boulanger with her younger sister Lili, who had died in 1918.

32 "En toen vond mijn vader, dat ik daar ook nog maar eens naar toe moest gaan. En toen ben ik voor de eerste uitvoering [in Parijs] van de Symphonie de psaumes van Strawinsky – met Sacher en met Beck – naar Parijs gegaan om dat daar te horen. En Lili [Nadia] Boulanger had me toen uitgenodigd, om bij haar een keer in de Avenue [Rue] Ballu mee te doen ... in zo'n grote klas die ze daar had, en toen kwam ik in een echte Parijse salon, vol met alle mogelijke kleine – ik heb ook van die kleine dingetjes, die daar zo rondstaan, die niet nodig zijn, wat natuurlijk wel eens onnodig gevonden wordt in mijn beroep – maar dat was bij Lili [Nadia] Boulanger nu werkelijk zo dat je niet wist, hoe je op je stoel moest zitten. Het was alles vol. Maar er ging iets van haar uit, dat was werkelijk ongelooflijk.
En toen zijn we met elkaar naar de repetitie geweest, de generale repetitie die Strawinsky zelf dus dirigeerde, en toen kwam ik naast haar te zitten en keek in de eerste grote handgeschreven partituur van Strawinsky, en ze vroeg wat ik daar vond en daar vond, en (ze) zei meteen, ze wou me wel één, twee jaar houden. Waarop ik zei: 'maar weet U, ik voel me helemaal niet thuis in uw salon, ik ben geen salonmens. En in zoverre – ik houd erg veel van Parijs, ik ken Parijs vrij goed, ben altijd met mijn ouders hier geweest, in mei, een maand om premières te horen, dat weet ik allemaal – maar ik zou hier niet kunnen aarden. Terwijl in het kleine stadje Basel heb ik me van het eerste moment af aan thuis gevoeld, dat is voor mij heel gewichtig. Ik hoef niet beroemd te worden'. Daar was ze zo stomverbaasd over, dat ik zei: 'c'est pas necessaire, pas necessaire d'être celèbre, pas du tout'. Toen was ze zo stom verbaasd". Interview Jos Leussink, 24–25 March 1983.

Ill. 4.5a: Marc-Antoine Charpentier, *Le Reniement de Saint Pierre*, Paris: Éditions musicales de la Schola Cantorum, ca. 1925, 4. The copy with Ina Lohr's realization is found in the Paul Sacher Foundation, ILC.

Ill. 4.5b: Marc-Antoine Charpentier, *Le Reniement de Saint Pierre*, Paris: Éditions musicales de la Schola Cantorum, ca. 1925, 4. The copy with Ina Lohr's realization is found in the Paul Sacher Foundation, ILC.

Once again we have evidence that one of the most prominent musical personalities of that period was immediately so captivated by Ina Lohr's musical personality that she wanted to have her come and study with her. Ina Lohr was
clearly also aware of the honor inherent in this invitation and that acceptance
could lead to a brilliant future as a composer, but despite this, she responded
that it was more important for her to feel at home in her life than to be famous.
That Nadia Boulanger extended the invitation at all, however, is also a sign of
the degree that Ina Lohr was at home in the world of contemporary music of
the time, in that she could instantly provide adequate responses to Nadia Boulanger's questions about the newly composed *Symphonie de psaumes*. So not
only do we have Ina Lohr desiring to avoid the limelight as a violinist, but also
as a composer. This impression is reinforced in a comment made shortly thereafter in the selfsame interview, when she speaks of how at the beginning she
had avoided being around Stravinsky, saying that "I really just wanted to be
alone with myself and really to become myself and that was successful, and I
kept true to that".[33] This again seems to be an indication that she was actively
choosing a place in the background, wanting to have an influence, but not
to stand in the front ranks. And although this was certainly partly a consequence of the society around her discouraging women from excelling professionally, she obviously saw also the positive side of it, that it gave her the freedom to be the person she chose to be, rather than the one desired by the outside
world.

She not only was in contact with the most influential people in contemporary
music, but also sought out those involved in the Early Music movement. For
example, after attending the congress of the International Musicological Society in Cambridge in 1933, she went to Haslemere together with Annie Tschopp
and August Wenzinger to visit the workshop of Arnold Dolmetsch, from where
she wrote on 21 July 1933, that they had spent a lot of time with Hans Eber-
hard Hoesch, a collector of instruments and a founder of the series of chamber
music concerts with historical instruments in Kabel, Germany. She also speaks
of the pleasant encounter with an early maker of historical string instruments,
Eugen Sprenger. Although she regretted that Paul Sacher was not there to share
the experience, she wrote that he would often have been irritated, as the performances were often quite awful. But she also commented that the old man had

---

33 "Ik wilde nu werkelijk eens helemaal voor mezelf zijn, en helemaal mezelf worden, en dat
    is ook gelukt, en daar ben ik ook bij gebleven". Ibid.

something, namely "a strong inner connection with older music and the possibility of being alone with the music in front of an audience".[34]

Participation with the Choir

There is another largely unknown aspect of Ina Lohr's work for Sacher: she was the assistant director of the Basel Chamber Choir until 1946. Her job, however, was not that of a usual assistant conductor, in that they actually, on a certain level, jointly prepared the choir, something that was not always conducive to the most amicable of working relationships. The positive side of it is revealed in the interview with Jos Leussink, when she speaks of how they would divide up the choir. Using the *Symphonie de psaumes* as an example, she describes how she took the basses and tenors with her and rehearsed without a piano with them, while at the same time Paul Sacher, with the assistance of a pianist, would work with the women:

> I only finally got into contact with Stravinsky when I became involved in his music, when I had to work with the chamber choir here on a performance of the *Symphonie de psaumes* [on 25 January 1932]. I was responsible for the preparation of the men, for which I needed no piano, I simply cannot bear it while people are singing; Sacher had a pianist with him to prepare the ladies [...] We did the initial rehearsals this way and it was very helpful.[35]

She goes on to say how she trained the choir to sing the *a cappella* section through the use of solmization syllables, one of the occasions in which her anachronistic application of this historical practice to music for which it was not conceived fueled the discomfort of her contemporaries:

> The *Symphonie de psaumes* [...] is a glorious work, but very difficult. In the second part the orchestra suddenly stops and so it's a bit mean to the choir, in that the orchestra plays a tremendous role, so you unintentionally always listen to the orchestra and suddenly the orchestra stops, [...] so it becomes a cappella and that is very difficult. And sure enough, I used solmization syllables for all of that, in every voice. I rehearsed each

34 "Sie würden sich aber anderseits sehr viel ärgern, weil die Aufführungen oft herzlich schlecht sind. Etwas hat aber dieser alte Mann und auch die Familie hat es bisweilen: eine starke innere Bindung mit der alten Musik und die Möglichkeit vor einem Publikum mit der Musik allein zu sein". Letter Ina Lohr to Paul Sacher of 21 July 1933, private collection, Switzerland.

35 "Dus met Strawinsky kwam ik eigenlijk pas in kontakt, toen ik met zijn muziek ook te maken kreeg, eraan mee moest doen de Symphonie des psaumes met het kamerkoor hier uit te voeren. Ik kreeg voor mijn rekening het instuderen met de heren, dan had ik geen piano nodig, dat verdraag ik nu eenmaal niet als er gezongen wordt. Sacher nam met een pianiste de dames [...] De eerste deel van de repetities brachten we zo door, en dat hielp enorm". Interview with Jos Leussink, 24–25 March 1983.

voice with solmization. And they really enjoyed it! Then they knew it so well, they could add the text to it, then they had the melody.[36]

It is obvious here that she was deeply involved in the preparation of the choir, identified herself with the performance. She did not merely make sure that they knew the notes, but actively searched for means to make it work well and took pride in her success in doing so!

But the first strains in their cooperation also came from their joint preparation of the choir. In Chapter 3, we saw how in 1932 her understanding of Gregorian chant was publicly called into question by Otto Rippl in the Catholic *Basler Volksblatt*, with an objective response in defense from the BKO. For Paul Sacher that finished the issue, but it continued to trouble Ina Lohr on various levels for a longer period of time. The first knowledge we have of this is in her letter of 14 July 1932 where she makes a fleeting reference to an as yet undiscovered text – it is not clear whether it is a letter or an article – about the chant course by a spokesman for the choir, Jacques Wildberger, who is not to be confused with the Basel composer of the same name. She then goes on to say that

> music [brought] me to you and the BKO. It has now become entirely clear to me that I cannot expect any understanding of my work and for my attitude toward music from you and I will therefore search for more of my own work, so that I will not suffocate mentally, because I have no expression of my own. I am really not being impatient here, only sad that this course has divided us so. My trust and my attitude toward you and the BKO, however, have not changed since our last conversation.[37]

Paul Sacher's response of 19 July 1932 is remarkable. He first asks what was wrong with Wildberger's text, saying that he had only skimmed through it, and that by now everybody would have forgotten it. He then goes on, saying

---

36 "De Symphonie des psaumes [...] is een prachtig werk maar heel moeilijk. En in het tweede deel houdt opeens het orkest op en het is daroom so een beetje gemeen tegenover de koor, omdat het orkest een geweldige rol speelt, dus onwillekeurig luister je all naar het orkest en opeens houdt het orkest op [...] en daar wordt dus a capella en dat is heel moeilijk. En warempel, dat heb ik helemaal gesolmiseerd, in iedere stem. In iedere stem solmiseerend instudeerd. En ze vonden het leuk! Toen wisten ze het zo goed, ze konden de tekst erop zeggen, toen hadden ze de melodie". Ibid.

37 "Die Musik hat mich an Sie und an das B.K.O. [gebracht]. Ich bin mir nun ganz klar darüber geworden, dass ich von Ihnen kein Verständnis für meine Arbeit und für meine Einstellung zur Musik erwarten kann und darum werde ich mehr eigene Arbeit suchen sodass ich nicht geistig ersticken muss, weil ich keine eigene Äusserung habe. Ich bin jetzt wirklich nicht unduldsam, nur traurig, dass dieser Kurs uns so auseinander gebracht hat. Mein Vertrauen und meine Einstellung zu Ihnen und zum B.K.O. haben sich aber seit unserem letzten Gespräch nicht mehr geändert". Letter Ina Lohr to Paul Sacher of 14 July 1932, private collection, Switzerland.

I only regret that I must assume from this remark, and from the others which follow, that you do not feel well. If you were not ill, such depressed thoughts would not rise to the surface. I can distance myself *completely* from such remarks. In such moments I do not take things personally. You could even insult me in your affliction [...] and I would not respond. For it concerns *you* alone. In such moments, no matter what I did, I would only depress you further or even precipitate angry outbreaks. I do not take anything of that amiss (even though you do not spare me at times). When you are well once again and restored, the world will no longer seem so dark and unjust to you. I must only repeat that I do perhaps have some understanding for your work and your attitude towards music! And should I not yet have it, I am at least trying to [attain it]. How could I appreciate your cooperation, if this were otherwise? Or do you still not believe *that* I do so? That would be a shame and sad. My first hope is that you will now find good health and peace. Once this has been attained, I am unconcerned about everything else. And believe me, all mistrust toward me is misplaced, for you can count on my friendship. I even request you to fight against it, for through it, your strength is compromised. Our relationship will only bear fruit and be satisfying, if you have trust. You can only have trust when you are well and have regained your strength. But I cannot prove to you with words what you must feel.[38]

This response shows not only insight into Ina Lohr's character, but also that Paul Sacher was willing to invest himself personally in the continuation of this cooperation, to speak directly to the questions of friendship and trust. It is a reflection, I believe, of an awareness that they could depend on one another. On 29 July 1932, Ina Lohr thanked him for this paragraph, admitting

---

38 "Ich bedaure einzig, dass ich dieser Bemerkung und anderen, die Sie daran anschliessen entnehmen muss, dass Sie sich wenig wohl fühlen. Wenn Sie nicht krank wären kämen nicht so deprimierte Ansichten zum Vorschein. Ich kann mich bei diesen Ueberlegungen völlig ausserhalb stellen. Ich beziehe in solchen Augenblicken nichts mehr auf mich. Sie könnten mich aus Betrübtheit sogar insultieren [...] ich würde mich nicht regen. Denn es handelt sich dabei nur um S i e. In solchen Augenblicken könnte ich tun was ich wollte, ich würde Sie nur weiter deprimieren oder gar zu Ausfällen verleiten. Ich nehme Ihnen von all dem nichts krumm (wenngleich Sie mich manchmal nicht schonen). Wenn sie erst wieder gesund und erholt sind wird sich Ihnen die Welt nicht mehr so trübe und gegen Sie ungerecht zeigen. Ich muss Ihnen nur wiederholen, dass ich vielleicht doch einiges Verständnis für Ihre Arbeit und Ihre Einstellung zur Musik habe! Wenn ichs noch nicht haben sollte, so bemühe ich mich wenigstens darum. Wie könnte ich Ihre Mitarbeit schätzen, wenn das anders wäre? Oder glauben Sie mir noch immer nicht, d a s s ich das tue? Das wäre allerdings schade und traurig. Ich hoffe zuallererst, dass Sie jetzt dann Gesundheit und Ruhe finden. Wenn das erst einmal gelungen ist habe ich um alles weitere keine Sorge. Und glauben Sie mir, jedes Misstrauen das Sie mir entgegenbringen ist unnötig, denn Sie können auf meine Freundschaft zählen. Ich bitte Sie sogar, bekämpfen Sie es, da dadurch nur Ihre Kräfte in Mitleidenschaft gezogen werden. Unser Verhältnis wird erst Früchte tragen und erfreulich sein, wenn Sie Vertrauen haben. Vertrauen haben können Sie erst wenn Sie gesund und wieder bei Kräften sind. Nur kann ich Ihnen nicht mit Worten beweisen, was Sie fühlen müssten". Letter Paul Sacher to Ina Lohr of 19 July 1932, PSF-ILC.

Yes, I was in a very bad state, and had not wanted to admit it and fought desperately [against it] until I couldn't go on. I found peace again in bed. I never doubted your friendship, only your understanding, but I am now once again convinced that that perhaps does not even exist and that only trust counts.[39]

She went on to also explain what had disturbed her so much in Wildberger's text:

the quoted terminology was wrong: the psalmodies are recitative songs and are not melodically charming and there is no tone painting in the ordinary [of the mass], only in the proper, and chant never luxuriates! Catholics made great fun of this, as I have heard. Rippl was triumphant because somebody from our side admitted that the spirit of this music had first been understood from records! Just in this regard, it would have been very important to me that somebody had defended me, as he [Rippl] spoke of something he himself had not experienced.[40]

She did not have the tools to fight against this sort of criticism: it ate into her self-confidence to such a degree that she became ill.

Paul Sacher again responded thoughtfully to this, writing on 27 July 1932 that he regretted not having taken Wildberger's commentary seriously. He went on to suggest – while explicitly stating that in saying this, he is not attempting to exculpate himself – that she perhaps takes all criticism too seriously.

Only what *we ourselves* think is of substance; we cannot do things in a way that contradicts our sensibilities! I also try to learn from others. – You are appearing in public more than before. Take the conviction with you, already from the beginning, that what others say is of no importance. We should only accommodate ourselves to them, if we admit they are right … and then we do not need the others as a reason any more, for it is then our own opinion.[41]

39 "Ja, es ist mir sehr schlecht gegangen und ich wollte es nicht zugeben und kämpfte verzweifelt weiter, bis ich nicht mehr konnte. Im Bett kam dann die Ruhe wieder. Ich zweifele nicht an Ihre [sic] Freundschaft, nur an Ihr [sic] Verständnis, aber ich bin jetzt auch wieder davon überzeugt, dass es das vielleicht überhaupt nicht gibt und dass nur das Vertrauen zählt". Letter Ina to Paul Sacher of 29 July 1932, private collection, Switzerland.

40 "die angeführten Termen [waren] falsch: die Psalmodien sind rezitativische Gesänge und nicht melodisch reizvoll und Tonmalereien gibt es nirgends im Ordinarium nur im Proprium und schwelgen tut der Choral doch nie! Darüber haben sich, wie ich hörte, die Katholiken recht lustig gemacht. Rippl hat triumphiert, weil einer aus unserem Lager zugegeben hat, dass man erst aus den Platten den Geist dieser Musik gehört hätte! Gerade daran wäre mir soviel gelegen gewesen, dass man mich in dieser Hinsicht verteidigt hätte, nachdem er von einem nicht eigenen Erlebnis gesprochen hatte". Ibid.

41 "Massgebend ist doch nur was wir selber denken; wir können ja doch nicht anders handeln als wir selber empfinden! Ich versuch auch von den andern zu lernen. – Sie treten jetzt mehr in die Oeffentlichkeit als früher. Nehmen Sie, schon am Anfang, die Ueberzeugung mit, dass es wurst ist, was andere sagen. Wir dürfen nur nach ihnen gehen, wenn wir ihnen recht geben … und dann brauchen wir die andern als Begründung nicht mehr, dann ist es schon unsere eigene Meinung". Letter Paul Sacher to Ina Lohr of 27 July 1932, PSF-ILC.

But he did not leave it at that. He also saw to it that an article she had written for an obscure journal on the importance of Gregorian chant today, "Der Gregorianische Choral und seine Bedeutung für die Gegenwart", would appear in the *Schweizerische Musikzeitung*, as well as a review of some of the earliest recordings of this music.[42] In addition, he initiated a survey that appeared in the same journal, in which various theologians, priests, musicians and musicologists examined, from their specific perspective, the question of whether Gregorian chant could be performed in concert.[43] And of those asked, Ina Lohr was certainly not the only one who was of the opinion that it was appropriate, as long as the original liturgical nature of the music was taken into account. In going on this offensive, Paul Sacher effectively gave Ina Lohr the status of an expert and the legitimation to continue performing this music in concert.

Another source of irritation in all this was the fact that she was required to prepare a modern edition of some chant melodies for the use of the choir, in which their rhythmization was precisely indicated. It is obvious from what she writes on 12 July 1932 that she was exasperated by the necessity of notating things that she felt should be left open to the freedom of the singer:

> Why does one have to add the quarter note rests when it has expressly been said that every | and every ‖ (except in the sequences) is a quarter note rest? The image of the music just appears more complex. I have really put in all the rests for you that I myself make. If you think more are necessary, you can put them in. Don't take the improvisatory character away from chant in your desire to mark up everything, even that which stems from a faulty vocal technique. The music on the page then no longer corresponds with the original in the end. I do not even intend to prescribe all of the rests which you have [in your edition] for others. Levy already has found the rhythmization to be a limitation and thus a disadvantage of our edition. The more that is in it, the less will conductors be attracted to these pages.[44]

---

42 Ina Lohr, "Der Gregorianische Choral und seine Bedeutung für die Gegenwart", in: *Die Besinnung* 6 (1932), 79–84, and shortly thereafter reprinted in: *Schweizerische Musikzeitung* 72 (1932), 673–79. Ina Lohr, "Der Gregorianische Choral auf Schallplatten", in: *Schweizerische Musikzeitung* 72 (1932), 594–96.

43 Paul Sacher, "Zur Frage der Verwendbarkeit liturgischer Musik im Konzert: Rundfrage durchgeführt von Paul Sacher", in: *Schweizerische Musikzeitung* 73 (1933), 11–15 and 51–55.

44 "Warum muss man aber alle Viertelpausen eintragen, wenn ausdrücklich gesagt wird, dass jeder | und jeder ‖ (ausser in den Sequenzen) eine Viertelpause bedeutet? Das Notenbild wird nur kompliziert. Bei Ihnen habe ich wirklich alle Pausen eingetragen, die ich selber immer mache. Wenn Sie mehr für nötig halten, so können Sie die eintragen. Nehmen Sie dem Choral doch nicht den improvisierten Character [sic], dadurch dass Sie alles, auch das was nur aus einer mangelhaften Gesangstechnik entsteht, eintragen wollen. Das Notenbild korrespondiert dann schliesslich gar nicht mehr mit dem ursprünglichen. Ich habe sogar nicht vor, alle Pausen, die bei Ihnen stehen auch anderen vorzuschreiben. [Ernst?] Levy hat

And two days later after having corrected the proofs, her lack of patience with the task showed itself again:

> The explanations for the chant are now, in my opinion, unambiguous. It is, however, really impossible to establish exact rules or indicate everything. I have added a couple of regular rests to your score, but they seem superfluous to me, if you were to memorize what each stroke means.[45]

Only a year later, she felt obliged to take an open stance concerning her belief that it is inappropriate to perform chant and polyphony in a modern concert hall. The BKO had been invited to perform two concerts in Paris, the first with some works for *a cappella* choir, followed by Gluck's *De Profundis* and Stravinsky's *Symphonie de psaumes,* the second with Mozart's *Idomeneo.* The organizers decided that the first concert would also have to take place in the Salle Pleyel, which she felt that would give such emphasis to the second part of the program that the first would become almost pointless. After much inner turmoil, she wrote on 31 August 1933 to say that she could not take part in the concert:

> I have, however, always emphasized that I can only imagine this music in a church and a festive concert of this nature is a monstrosity for me. I consider it tasteless and without respect. This sounds awful again, but you know how much everything is a matter of the heart for me. I do not expect you to change anything or to cancel it, but I cannot participate in it or come along. Our cooperation cannot go so far that I have to deny my convictions. Since our first fight, after the spring concert [27 April 1932] before the Italian festival in 1932, I have had to fight for my intellectual independence again and again, and my work for the BKO last year was often routine and menial. For that reason, I am now looking in all directions for an activity which is completely mine. The problem lies with me, not you, that I know. Perhaps and hopefully we will be able to once again find common ground in the Scola [sic!], should I still be in Basel. Annie [Tschopp] will have told you that I am once again negotiating with Amsterdam.[46]

sogar die Rhythmisierung schon eine Beschränkung und darum ein Nachteil unserer Ausgabe gefunden. Je mehr drin steht, je weniger die Dirigenten sich zu diesen Blättern angezogen fühlen werden." Letter Ina Lohr to Paul Sacher of 12 July 1932, private collection, Switzerland.

45 "Die Erläuterungen zum Choral sind jetzt m.e. eindeutig. Es ist übrigens wirklich unmöglich entweder genaue Regeln aufzustellen oder alles anzugeben. In Ihre Partitur habe ich noch ein paar regelmässige Pausen eingetragen aber die scheinen mir überflüssig, wenn Sie sich einprägen, was jeder Strich bedeutet". Letter Ina Lohr to Paul Sacher of 14 July 1932, private collection, Switzerland.

46 "Ich habe aber immer betont, dass ich mir diese Musik nur in der Kirche denken kann und ein solches Festkonzert ist für mich ein Monstrum. Ich finde es geschmacklos und ehrfurchtlos. Das klingt wieder schlimm, aber Sie wissen, wie sehr das alles mir Herzenssache ist. Ich erwarte gar nicht, dass Sie etwas ändern oder absagen, nur kann ich nicht mitmachen und mitkommen. Unsere Zusammenarbeit kann nicht so weit gehen, dass ich meine Ueberzeugung verleugnen muss. Seit unserem ersten Kampf, nach dem Frühjahrskonzert

Here we clearly see the internal battle raging within her about her work for Paul Sacher, a battle which will continue to smolder with intermittant flare-ups for another fifteen years. The question always remained the same: how much can she do for him and still retain her own personal musical integrity. In this period, she was continually trying to delineate the boundaries of her work, both in quantity and quality, searching for what was uniquely her own, while at the same time recognizing his need for her contribution, should he wish to reach his goals.

In this same letter, she also wrote about her compunctions about trying to convince Karl Vötterle of Bärenreiter to publish the Basel Chamber Choir's transcriptions of various chant melodies.

> As I contemplated the upcoming discussion with Vötterle yesterday in the train, everything came to mind which I myself objected to in the chant edition. Primarily, that one should not fix an improvisatory art in this manner and that with these pages now everybody, without having to make the effort himself to understand the material, can sing chant in some fashion. I now more than ever believe in this point of view and if I defend your point of view, I deny myself.[47]

Luckily, she was traveling with August Wenzinger, who suggested that she say that the edition had been made for practical reasons for the course she had given. That she could easily do. She was received enthusiastically by Karl Vötterle, but had to report that he was against marked-up scores, that "he found them completely awful and maintains that most conductors would prefer unmarked up ones".[48] In all likelihood this was the source of a certain amount of satisfaction to her.

[27. April 1932] vor dem ital. Festspiel habe ich immer wieder um meine geistige Selbständigkeit kämpfen müssen und meine Arbeit für das B.K.O. war im letzten Jahre oft Routine und Pflichtarbeit. Darum suche ich jetzt nach allen Seiten nach einer Betätigung, die ganz meine Sache ist. Das Problem liegt bei mir, nicht bei Ihnen, das weiss ich. Vielleicht und hoffentlich können wir in der Scola [sic] wieder ein gemeinsames Gebiet finden, wenn ich dann noch in Basel bin. Die Annie wird Ihnen gesagt haben, dass ich wieder mit Amsterdam verhandle". Letter Ina Lohr to Paul Sacher of 31 August 1933, private collection, Switzerland. It is unknown with whom or what institution she was negotiating, perhaps the Muziek-Lyceum?

47 "als ich mir gestern im Zug auch das kommende Gespräch mit Vötterle überlegte, kam mir alles in den Sinn, was ich selbst gegen unsere Choralausgabe einzuwenden hatte. Hauptsächlich, dass man eine Improvisationskunst nicht so festlegen darf und dass durch diese Blätter jedermann jetzt, ohne dass er sich Mühe geben muss selber in die Sache einzudringen, schlecht und recht Choral singen kann. Auf dem Standpunkt stehe ich jetzt mehr als je und wenn ich Ihren Standpunkt verteidige, verleugne ich damit mich selbst". Ibid.

48 "Die findet er überhaupt schrecklich und er behauptet, dass die meisten Dirigenten eine unbezeichnete wünschen". Ibid.

Upon her return to Basel they continued this dialogue in person, the results of which were so dispiriting to Ina Lohr that she felt it necessary to write again on 15 September 1933 and fix the conditions of her further cooperation with him.

> Our discussion still leaves me no peace. When I say that for me, music stands above the person, that means that I will always be interested in all early music that is being played in Basel and elsewhere. I will not be able to say yes to everything that the Scola [sic!] does, just because I belong to it and, by the same measure, I will be unable to reject everything else. That is not a new point of view for me; from the beginning of our discussions I have pointed to the Academy in Berlin, the Scola [sic] in Paris and the *Singbewegung* and have never been able to understand why all of that should not be good. To be sure, Walter Nef was also far less radical in this than Geering and you. I was just in Kassel and have come to know the *Singbewegung* and some people from the Academy and I still see no reason why we should turn against these people. I want to participate in the Collegium musicum, because it gives me the opportunity of interacting with the people directly through music and for the same reason I want to compose more. I am just an artist "at heart" [Gemütsartistin] and in the BKO you only need my head. My heart cannot bear this and that makes me increasingly intolerant.
>
> If you give me fr. 100 per month at the Scola [sic], I will either give 4–5 hours of lessons or work in some other way one day a week for the Scola [sic]. I will also reserve one day a week for the BKO. My other time then will belong to me and it is up to me [to decide] how I make use of it. This all sounds very blunt and you will once again think that I possess no softness. That is not true; I have only lost it a bit in relation to you, but will certainly find it once again, when I have work that satisfies me and when I no longer feel myself to be exploited and exhausted. It is not at all in my nature to be in a bad mood, and for a year now I have often been so![49]

49 "Unser Gespräch lässt mir noch keine Ruhe. Wenn ich sage, dass die Musik mir über die Person geht, dann heisst das, dass ich mich immer interessieren werde für alle alte Musik, die in Basel und anderswo gemacht wird. Ich werde nicht von vornherein ja sagen können zu allem, was die Scola [sic] tut, nur weil ich dazu gehöre und ich werde ebensowenig alles andere ablehnen können. Das ist für mich kein neuer Standpunkt; ich habe vom Anfang unserer Besprechungen an auf die Akademie in Berlin, an die Scola [sic] in Paris und auf die Singbewegung hingewiesen und nie verstehen können, warum das alles nichts Rechtes sein könne. Übrigens war auch Walter Nef darin viel weniger radikal als Geering und Sie. Jetzt war ich in Kassel und habe die Singbewegung und einige Leute von der Akademie kennen gelernt und ich sehe immer noch keinen Grund, warum wir uns gegen die wenden sollten. Ich möchte im Collegium musicum mitmachen, weil es mir die Gelegenheit gibt direkt mit der Musik zu den Menschen zu kommen und aus demselben Grunde möchte ich wieder mehr komponieren. Ich bin nun einmal nur eine 'Gemütsartistin' und im B.K.O. brauchen Sie nur meinen Kopf. Das hält mein Herz nicht aus und das macht mich immer unduldsamer.
    Wenn Sie mir an der Scola [sic] fr. 100 im Monat geben, dann werde ich dafür 4–5 Stunden geben oder einen Tag in der Woche sonst für die Scola [sic] arbeiten. Für das B.K.O. werde ich auch einmal in der Woche einen Tag reservieren. Meine übrige Zeit gehört dann mir und es ist meine Sache, wie ich darüber verfügen werde. Das klinkt [sic] alles furchtbar schroff und Sie werden wieder finden, dass ich gar keine Weichheit habe. Das ist nicht wahr; ich habe sie nur Ihnen gegenüber ein wenig verloren, werde sie aber be-

This is a remarkable letter considering that the Schola Cantorum Basiliensis was just about to open its doors (see pp. 169–72). At its very inception, the person who in the end was responsible for holding the institution together during its first thirty years was endeavoring to establish working conditions for herself, ones which would ensure both her musical freedom as well as time to pursue her own musical goals, even when they did not necessarily match those of the school. She obviously felt hemmed in by the ideals of her colleagues which did not match her own. She wanted to secure time for herself for interacting directly with people through music and for composition, as these were the two areas of her work that kept getting infringed upon in her work with Paul Sacher. It is not without irony that just those features that caused him to ask her to be her assistant in the beginning – her ability to communicate through singing and her inspired approach to music and text – are those that come to be sources of contention within her first two or three years' work with the choir.

Recordings in Paris

One of Paul Sacher's major coups in the thirties was the establishment of a fruitful contact with Curt Sachs, a foremost musicologist of the time and one of the founders of the field of organology. In 1933, Sachs was forced to flee Berlin, leaving behind one recording project, *Parlophone* – "2,000 years of music, a concise history of the development of music from the earliest times through the 18th century"[50] – only to start a new one a year later in Paris, *L'Anthologie sonore*. By 1935, Paul Sacher was negotiating with Curt Sachs concerning a series of recordings for *L'Anthologie sonore*, for the most part 16th-century *a cappella* music. On 14 August 1935, following up on a meeting they had had at the end of May, he wrote to Curt Sachs that he had just returned to Basel a few days before and promising to work out his suggestions for the recordings in the coming days, requesting that he be patient.[51] Not unsurprisingly, we find that Ina Lohr had

---

stimmt zurückfinden, wenn ich eine Arbeit habe, die mich befriedigt und wenn ich mich nicht mehr ausgenützt und erschöpft fühle. Es liegt gar nicht in meiner Natur schlechter Laune zu sein und seit einem Jahr war ich das öfters!" Letter Ina Lohr to Paul Sacher of 15 September 1933, private collection, Switzerland.

50 Background information may be found in Ulrich Mosch, "Paul Sacher und die Schallplatte", in: *Paul Sacher – Facetten einer Musikerpersönlichkeit*, ed. Ulrich Mosch, Mainz: Schott 2006, 94–99; and Pierre-F. Roberge "L'Anthologie sonore", http://www.medieval. org/emfaq/cds/ans99999.htm (13 May 2018).

51 "ich bin vor einigen Tagen nach Basel zurückgekehrt und habe meine Arbeit wieder aufgenommen. Die Vorschläge für Choraufnahmen werde ich in allernächster Zeit ausarbeiten, ich bitte Sie noch für kurze Zeit um Geduld". Letter Paul Sacher to Curt Sachs of 14 August 1935, PSF-PSC.

already done most of the preparatory work in regard to these suggestions, as is seen from an excerpt from her letter to Paul Sacher of 22 July 1935:

> In recent days, I spent much time in the library and looked through everything. I erred again with the *Missa Caput* (it is time that I take a vacation, otherwise I will be of no use!), had looked at Dufay's rather than Obrecht's. Today I read through the Obrecht, which is very beautiful and just the right length. The suggestions of Professor Sachs are good actually, only somewhat impractical. The 6-voice piece by Josquin would be difficult for us to master, the 5-voice would work. I'll take the 4-voice motets of the complete edition with me to Flims and make you a suggestion soon. Also, the Obrecht does not lie well […] Therefore, I quickly copied out another 3-voice Kyrie from the *Missa Forseulement* (3 minutes, 20 seconds). It is somewhat shorter, perhaps too short. This magnificent music needs to be rehearsed like chant, in a very relaxed manner, with each voice singing to the highpoint and then falling again. A delightful work.[52]

This is then followed by proposals for seven different recordings, by Josquin, Finck, Obrecht, Gombert, Notker / Hildegard von Bingen, Bach and Schütz. Presumably they then put together the proposal for four different recordings, including many of the pieces selected by Ina Lohr, as well as some works already in the repertoire of the Basel Chamber Choir. In the end, three recordings were pressed: 1) Ludwig Senfl / Heinrich Finck (*L'Anthologie sonore* 51); 2) Heinrich Schütz / Johann Philipp Krieger (*L'Anthologie sonore* 60); and 3) Michael Praetorius / Hans Leo Hassler (*L'Anthologie sonore* 72) from these selections. In all of the negotiations with Curt Sachs, Ina Lohr's name is never mentioned.

Curt Sachs retained a certain critical detachment in his evaluation of the recordings writing on 3 June 1936 that

> the Finck-Senfl recording is finally finished and a copy will be sent to you. You will be pleased with the Senfl; in particular, the *Glocken von Speyer* sounds magnificent. The Finck is not quite as good: it is a bit unsettled and perhaps not clear enough in the delineation of the lines. Choral recordings demand something that is fundamen-

---

52 "Diese Tage war ich lange auf der Bibliothek und habe alles durchgesehen. Mit der Missa Caput hatte ich mich wieder geirrt (es wird Zeit, dass ich Ferien mache, sonst bin ich nicht mehr zu gebrauchen!), hatte Dufay statt Obrecht angesehen. Heute las ich Obrecht durch, der sehr schön und in der länge [sic] gerade recht ist. Eigentlich sind also die Vorschläge von Prof. Sachs schön, nur etwas unpraktisch. Das 6-stimmige Stück von Josquin ist für uns schwer zu bewältigen, das 5st. geht. Ich nehme jetzt die 4 stimmigen Motetten der Gesamtausgabe mit nach Flims und mache Ihnen bald noch einen Vorschlag. Auch Obrecht liegt ungünstig […] Darum schrieb ich in alle[r Eile] noch eine 3 stimmiges Kyrie aus der Messe Forseulement ab (3 min 20 sec) Es ist etwas kürzer, vielleicht zu kurz. Diese prachtvolle Musik muss man üben wie Choral, so ganz locker und in jeder Stimme auf den melodischen Höhepunkt hinsingen und wieder fallen lassen. Eine herrliche Arbeit". Letter Ina Lohr to Paul Sacher of 22 July 1935, private collection, Switzerland.

tally impossible: that regular clarity down to the last sixteenth, which nonetheless remains light. And this is particularly difficult just in this early style with its many cadential formulas.[53]

It was certainly a feather in the cap of the Basel Chamber Orchestra and Choir that their work was documented at such an early date. The recordings were of music largely unknown at the time and – in comparison to many of the other albums in the series – at a very high standard of performance.

The Balancing of Interests

Just as these recordings were appearing, a new storm in their cooperation was brewing. The two of them had decided to perform Palestrina's *Missa Papae Marcelli* in their concert of 19 December 1937. At the behest of Ina Lohr, they tried out a new format in which the five movements of the ordinary of the mass were interlaced with some organ intonations by various composers and some chorales by Michael Praetorius. These pieces served as placeholders for the music from the proper which, as it was part of the liturgy, was deemed inappropriate for a concert. Their function was to provide some variety from relentless polyphony. As Ina Lohr wrote later in an article about programming,

> in the case of Palestrina, everybody will rejoice in the wonderful vocal lines, but notice a certain monotony in regard to harmony. In a church service, the vocal lines are beautiful – as in a concert – but only because the words of the texts concerned connect together meaningfully and are conveyed into the ear and the heart of the congregation. The downside of the monotony is of no consequence, as no variety of affect is demanded or expected. The attempt of at least putting the movements of the proper in the right place, albeit without the readings and prayers, leads to an unusual form of concert, which has proved its value several times.[54]

53 "Die Finck-Senfl-Platte ist endlich fertig, und ein Exemplar geht an Sie ab. Sie werden Ihre Freude an dem Senfl haben; namentlich die Glocken von Speyer klingen herrlich. Der Finck ist nicht ganz so gut geraten: er ist ein wenig unruhig und vielleicht in der Linienführung nicht klar genug. Chorplatten verlangen etwas im Grunde kaum Erfüllbares; jene ebenmässige Deutlichkeit bis ins letzte Sechzehntel hinein, die dennoch leicht bleibt. Und gerade in diesem Frühstil mit seinen vielen Kadenzschleifen ist das besonders schwer". Letter Curt Sachs to Paul Sacher of 3 June 1936, PSF-PSC. These early recordings may be heard here: https://soundcloud.com/user-802211739-365337350/sets/basel-chamber-choir-recordings.

54 "Im Falle Palestrina wird jedermann sich an den wundervollen Gesangslinien freuen, aber auch eine gewisse Monotonie im Harmonischen feststellen. Im Gottesdienst sind die Gesangslinien schön, wie im Konzert, aber ausschliesslich, weil sie die Textworte, um die es geht, sinnvoll zusammenschliessen und in das Ohr und Herz der Gemeinde tragen; der Nachteil der Monotonie fällt weg, weil keine abwechslungsvolle Wirkung verlangt oder erwartet wird. Der Versuch, unter Verzicht auf Lesungen und Gebete, wenigstens die

Eventually they decided that the Protestant chorales by Praetorius clashed stylistically with the mass and they were replaced by Gregorian chant in later concerts; to further unify the program, all the organ intonations were by Girolamo Frescobaldi.

It should be clear by now, however, that this program would have been very close to Ina Lohr's heart, as she had sung the mass under Cuypers and thus knew it very well. In addition, she was attempting to create a new concert form by putting it into a quasi-liturgical context. In the Paul Sacher Foundation there is a score – stamped on the front with "Basler Kammerorchester, Basler Kammerchor" – which has been meticulously marked up by her for performance. Illustration 4.6 shows the opening of the Credo. Above the title she writes in Dutch that it should be slower and more intense and that one should observe the diminuendo marks. It is evident here that she is using the differences in dynamics to bring out the text; by tapering off the ends of phrases, space is made for new entries; finally the dissonance in m. 7 is brought out by the swell in the cadential voice. The care with which she treats the declamation is also evident on the following page, in which the text "Et in unam Dominum", is grouped by brackets, the ends of the phrases being enunciated lightly. The syncopated "Jesum Christum" in mm. 18–20 is to be "sehr gehalten" or "very sustained". At mm. 23–27 the grouping of the notes at "Et ex patre natum ante omnia saecula" is clearly determined by the scansion of the text. The entire composition is marked with this level of care. It does not take much imagination to realize that this set-up was almost begging for conflict with Paul Sacher.

It did indeed come and, based on the exchange of letters after the fact, it must have been vehement, shaking them both profoundly. Although they both acknowledge that the concert was a success – something which is also confirmed by the reviews in the press – they both speak of the difficulties they experienced during rehearsal. In a letter of 23 December 1937, Ina Lohr opens by writing that she knows of no present for him and that

> just this year I would have liked to have given you I-know-not-what, because I am so happy that we have so victoriously survived our difficulties. Yet I am so thankful for your patience with it and for your trust, for I really know that it is not always easy to get on

Propriumsteile an den richtigen Ort einzusetzen, führt zu einer ungewöhnlichen Form des Konzertes, die sich aber verschiedene Male bewährt hat". Ina Lohr, "Zur Programmgestaltung", in: *Alte und Neue Musik [I], Das Basler Kammerorchester (Kammerchor und Kammerorchester) unter Leitung von Paul Sacher 1926–1951*, Zurich: Atlantis Verlag 1952, 36–37.

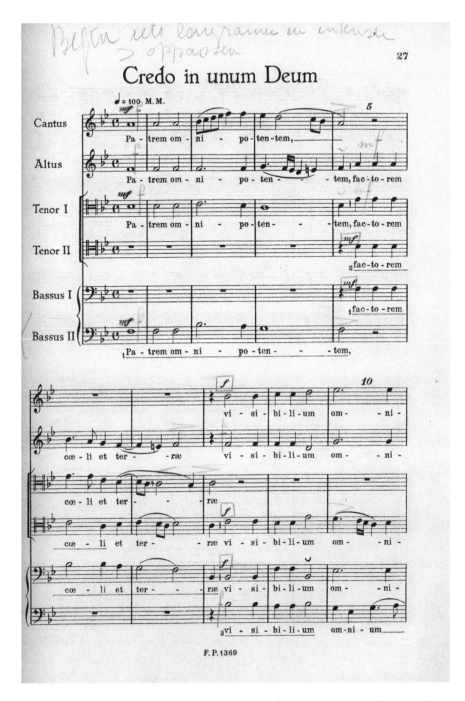

Ill. 4.6: Giovanni Pierluigi da Palestrina, Credo from the *Missa Papae Marcelli* in an edition in the Paul Sacher Foundation, ILC.

Ill. 4.6: (continued)

F. P. 1369

Ill. 4.6: (continued)

with me. But, even when I rebel on occasion and search for something else, the work with you, however, does come first, if I only know that you have need for it.[55]

On Christmas Day of that year Paul Sacher responded in the following manner:

A project that began with such difficulty and without hope has ended with such gratification and uplift. A new proof – if one was at all needed – that one should not abandon something precious before its absolute infeasibility can no longer be denied. You write to me that you were happy about it. I am not less so. It is unnecessary to thank me for my patience in this regard, for one can hardly summon up more patience than you have shown toward me. Our cooperation requires trust and faith. Only when they are lacking, do the real difficulties begin. Where is the boundary between talent and willpower to be drawn? With artistic people and in art, the one can hardly be distinguished from the other. In the end, the personality, in all of its aspects, decides. Talent is so often equated with a skill and is in reality something completely different. Therefore, there is also no need to despair about the future. Much greater is the question of whether a so independent and in a certain sense so expansive person as yourself [will] in the long run want to serve another for the fulfillment of your nature. I am exaggerating. But you indubitably understand me, you wild, fanatic missionary! The only chance may be found in your femininity. A man would never do it, a woman in her position can attain, as an undreamt-of enhancement of that which she desires, something else that she also desires![56]

55 "Gerade dieses Jahr hätte ich Ihnen gerne ich weiss nicht was geschenkt, weil ich so froh bin, dass wir unsere Arbeitsschwierigkeiten so siegreich überstanden haben. Dabei bin ich Ihnen sehr dankbar für Ihre Geduld und für Ihr Vertrauen, denn ich weiss genau, dass es nicht immer leicht ist mit mir auszukommen. Aber, auch wenn ich hie und da rebelliere und etwas anderes suche, die Arbeit mit Ihnen kommt doch zuerst, wenn ich nur weiss, dass Sie sie nötig haben". Letter Ina Lohr to Paul Sacher of 23 December 1937, private collection, Switzerland.

56 "Eine Arbeit die so schwierig & aussichtslos begann hat so erfreulich & beglückend geendet. Ein neuer Beweis – wenn es dessen überhaupt noch bedürfte – dafür, dass man nicht Kostbares aufgeben darf ehe die völlige Undurchführbarkeit nicht abzustreiten ist. Sie schreiben mir, dass Sie darüber glücklich waren. Ich bin es nicht weniger. Sie haben es nicht nötig sich in diesem Zusammenhang für meine Geduld zu bedanken, denn mehr Geduld als Sie mir gegenüber bewiesen haben kann man wohl kaum aufbringen. Unsere Zusammenarbeit verlangt Vertrauen & Glauben. Erst wenn es daran fehlt beginnen die eigentlichen Schwierigkeiten. Wo ist die Grenze zwischen Begabung & Willen mit Sicherheit anzugeben? Bei künstlerischen Menschen & in der Kunst ist der eine vom andern oft kaum auseinander zu halten. Letzten Endes entscheidet die Persönlichkeit in allen ihren Aspekten. Begabung wird zu oft einer Fertigkeit gleich gesetzt & ist in Wirklichkeit etwas ganz anderes. Darum liegt auch für die Zukunft kein Grund zur Verzweiflung vor. Viel grösser ist die Frage ob ein so selbständiger & in einem bestimmten Sinne so expansiver Mensch wie Sie sich auf die Dauer zur Verwirklichung seines Wesens eines anderen bedienen will. Ich spreche zugespitzt. Aber Sie verstehen mich zweifellos, Sie rabiater, fanatisierender Missionar! Die Einzige [sic] Chance liegt in Ihrer Weiblichkeit. Ein Mann würde es nie tun, eine Frau kann in Ihrer Lage zum einen was sie will als ungeahnte Steigerung noch ein anderes dazubekommen, was sie auch will!" Letter Paul Sacher to Ina Lohr of 25 December 1937, PSF-ILC.

This exchange reveals as much about their mode of working with one another, as about the differences in expectation and in their goals. Ina Lohr, when she invested herself in a project, was trying to realize the music in accordance with her ideals, insisting that the message carried by the text in sacred music be foremost. Paul Sacher had originally sought her out because of her greater knowledge of music, her ability to bring earlier music to life through her singing; at the beginning, thus, her influence on their performance of this music must have been far-reaching. Seemingly, as time went on, Paul Sacher began insisting on his own path with this music, that it be formed according to his musical ideals, continuing to see her as an assistant in this cooperation rather than as an equal partner. In this letter he speaks openly about their conflicts, wondering whether she will be content to remain his assistant – thereby making it clear that this is how he still regards her – given her creative and evangelistic nature. He suggests that a woman might be willing to do this in order to gain something else in addition to reaching her own goals. Ina Lohr, on the other hand, chafed under this, was unhappy that her own musical ideals were not always fulfilled or striven for to the degree she desired. This was a constant source of contention throughout the first 20 years of their cooperation. What she received in return, as we shall see in the following chapters, was a kind of beneficent friendship and support that carried her through life, allowing her to reach many of her own personal goals. What is less obvious, however, is where Paul Sacher set their own individual boundaries between talent and willpower.

Although she wrote on 29 December 1937 that she looked forward to "everything that can still come and will come", she also shared her thoughts about her own projects for the coming year. First of all, she mentioned that she had turned down August Sumpf's proposal that she take over the choir in the Theodorskirche. In doing so, she also referred to the choir of the Matthäuskirche for whom she wrote the music for a lay theater production in honor of Pastor Benz, who left the congregation in 1936. In its review of this performance, a local newspaper wrote that Ina Lohr "with the simplest means, composed deeply moving accompanying and choral music. Above all, however, with an immense effort, she brought the simple amateur actors to a level of vocal accomplishment which will ensure that we shall never forget her settings of the psalms we heard".[57] With

---

[57] "mit den einfachsten Mitteln eine tief ergreifende Begleitmusik und Chöre komponiert hat. Vor allem aber hat sie mit ungeheurer Arbeit die einfachen dilettantischen Darsteller zu einer Gesangsleistung erzogen, die uns die gehörten Psalmen in ihrer Vertonung nie wieder vergessen lassen werden". Clipping from the *Basler Nachrichten* [?], PSF-ILC.

this choir and with the choir of the Theodorkirche she desired to perform her cantata once again, striving for "an entirely personal and independent accomplishment". She continued on to say that she believed that her

> completely independent expression will always be composition and everything connected with it. For everything else I am glad to stand behind you, am very thankful for this possibility. Only I can promise so little. I am often so helpless in relation to my own development. "C'est plus fort que moi!"⁵⁸

Thus in her answer she was very honest, not promising anything but to follow her own inclinations, which included her wish to continue composing and to direct her own choirs within the context of the church. And follow her inclination she did, as is cooborated by her autobiographical sketch, where she confirmed the significance of her work with the choir of St. Theodor, in that it led her into her true world, "into the world of the church, in which I could express my faith without resistance or inhibitions".⁵⁹

It is clear that the difficulties had not completely dissipated by the summer, for it is then that Paul Sacher took up the subject once again. In a letter of 28 July 1938, the following paragraph is found:

> I often ask myself whether you are on the right path with your conducting career. And I am naturally inclined to say no, if our joint work is placed into question as a result of it. You combine a natural humility with such a strong personality and ambition (a drive to let your being manifest itself), that difficulties will be unavoidable. But I still cannot see – and will never do so – why there should be no room for our musical marriage. To be sure, there is no one-sided wedded bliss. Unfortunately, you were not always happy. I have always hoped that you will be able to make that which is most true to you reveal itself through composition or teaching. But now your development appears to be taking a different – and in regard to us more dangerous – direction. The only thing that I absolutely cannot stand, or only with great difficulty, is when you cold-bloodedly speak of a possible abrogation of our relations [...] I think that all good and worthwhile things have a high price. These difficulties and troubles are no doubt the price for a personally and artistically satisfying and fruitful relationship.⁶⁰

---

58 "Wohl möchte ich im Herbst mit dem Chor und mit dem Chor vom Laienspiel meine Kantate noch einmal machen. Ich glaube, dass meine ganz selbständige Äusserung immer das Komponieren sein wird und was damit zusammenhängt. Für alles andere stehe ich gerne hinter Ihnen, bin sehr dankbar für diese Möglichkeit. Nur kann ich so wenig versprechen. Ich stehe oft sehr hilflos gegenüber meiner eigenen Entwicklung. 'C'est plus fort que moi!'", Ibid.

59 "in die Welt der Kirche, in der ich meinen Glauben ohne Widerstand oder Hemmungen äussern konnte". Ina Lohr, "Skizze zum Lebenslauf", 6.

60 "Ich frage mich ja oft, ob Sie mit Ihrer Dirigentenlaufbahn auf dem rechten Weg sind. Und ich bin natürlich geneigt nein zu sagen wenn dadurch unsere gemeinsame Arbeit in Frage gestellt wird. Sie verbinden eine natürliche Bescheidenheit mit so starkem Persönlichkeits-Ehrgeiz (Drang zur Manifestation Ihres Wesens), dass Schwierigkeiten nie vermeidbar sein

The reference he made here to a musical marriage is a startling one, an indication of the closeness of their working relationship. The passage also reflects his awareness of all Ina Lohr's conflicting interests: her teaching, composition, choir directing on the one hand and her work for him on the other. He underlined here that he is not expecting everything to be easy, but that he strongly desired to find a solution that would enable their musical partnership to continue.

Ina Lohr responded immediately on 30 July 1938, in a quite remarkable manner:

> I also always make the comparison with a marriage and it appears to me, as if our musical household has grown so big and time-consuming that we have had no time at all to notice that in many things we have grown apart from one another. And our children, the BKO and the Schola, have grown up and have developed [in a manner] such that I also often feel alienated from them as well. That is, you see, what often makes me insecure and apparently "hard-hearted". When I answer evasively, or say, that is your decision, then it is really because everything seems so alien to me. But cold-blooded, never, that I am not, otherwise I would not be so exhausted now![61]

The fact that she not only understood his allusion to a "musical marriage" but then took it to a further level is astonishing, and a confirmation of the depth of their cooperation. What she expressed was a sense of detachment to what is going on around her, a sense of not belonging to the current musical world, not unlike the dissociation from the world around her referred to in Chapter 1. And further, she pointed out that her gruff responses came not from lack of

---

werden. Aber ich kann trotzdem nicht einsehen – & werde es nie – warum kein Platz für unsere musikalische Ehe sein soll. Nun gibt es kein einseitiges Eheglück. Sie waren ja leider nicht immer glücklich. Ich habe immer gehofft, dass Sie Ihr Eigenstes im Komponieren oder Unterrichten werden manifestieren können. Nun zielt die Entwicklung auf eine andere – in Bezug auf uns gefährlichere – Seite. Das einzige was ich gar nicht, oder doch nur sehr schlecht ertrage ist wenn Sie kaltblütig über eine ev. Aufgabe unserer Beziehungen sprechen […] Ich denke aber immer dass auf allen guten & wertvollen Dingen ein hoher Preis steht. Diese Schwierigkeiten & Mühen sind wohl der Preis für eine menschlich & künstlerisch schöne & fruchtbare Verbindung". Letter Paul Sacher to Ina Lohr of 28 July 1938, PSF-ILC.

61   "Auch ich ziehe immer den Vergleich mit der Ehe und es kommt mir so vor, alsob [sic] unsere musikalische Haushaltung so gross und zeitraubend geworden wäre, dass wir gar keine Zeit hatten zu bemerken, dass wir einander in vielen Sachen fremd geworden sind. Und unsere Kinder, B.K.O. und Schola sind gross geworden und haben sich so entwickelt, dass ich mich oft ganz fremd fühle auch ihnen gegenüber. Sehen Sie, das ist es, was mich oft unsicher macht und scheinbar 'lieblos'. Wenn ich ausweichend antworte, oder sage, das sei Ihre Sache, dann ist das wirklich, weil mir vieles so fremd vorkommt. Aber kaltblutig, nein, das bin ich nicht, sonst würde ich jetzt nicht so kaputt sein!" Letter Ina Lohr to Paul Sacher of 30 July 1938, private collection, Switzerland.

emotion, but because she felt removed from her environment. Her letter continued on as follows:

> I only really became aware of the gulf between us in the last rehearsals of *Jeanne d'Arc* [*au bûcher* by Arthur Honegger]. It was a brilliant and thrilling accomplishment and you were totally in your element. And just this brilliance and sense of thrill make me terribly afraid; I am not afraid for myself, but for everything that is and what still is to come. You once aptly said yourself that we would live and give concerts "as if there were nothing [to be concerned about]". It is just this that makes me desperate; and I only find the courage and justification to live in this time, if I do something, by means of which I can give something as a human. And that I can only do in small and simple [contexts]. This is why I turn increasingly to the laity and feel myself less and less at home in concerts. This is why I often think that you no longer need me, in that I will lag ever further behind on your path to great accomplishments.[62]

Here, for the first time, we get a glimpse of the upheaval within her caused by her sensitivity to the world around her, an inkling of the despair and hopelessness that she took on from others. The only way she successfully knew to deal with it was through song.

Paul Sacher did not shy away from seeking a solution for their difficulties. In a letter of 7 August 1938, he began by remarking that

> all of your qualities which you lament are your merits, your difference from me is just that which makes a fruitful whole. What you can do is a mystery to me and what I can perhaps do is impossible for you. Should it not be that way? We should be – with all our differences – ourselves and not try to be like the others. If you could simply accept me, just as I acknowledge you and admire you in your essence, then there is no place for worry and questioning.[63]

---

62 "Wirklich zum Bewusstsein kam mir die Kluft zwischen uns erst in den letzten Proben der Jeanne d'Arc. Das war eine glänzende und sensationelle Leistung und Sie waren ganz darin. Und mir machen eben der Glanz und die Sensation eine furchtbare Angst; Angst nicht für mich, sondern für alles was ist und was noch kommen wird. Sie haben selber einmal treffend gesagt, wir würden leben und Konzerte geben 'alsob [sic] nichts wäre'. Eben das ist es, was mich verzweifelt macht; und den Mut und die Berechtigung in dieser Zeit zu leben finde ich nur, wenn ich etwas tue, wobei ich menschlich etwas geben kann. Und das kann ich nur im Kleinen und Einfachen. Darum suche ich immer mehr die Laien und fühle mich im Konzert immer weniger zu Hause. Darum denke ich oft, dass Sie mich nicht mehr nötig haben, weil ich auf dem Weg zur grossen Leistung immer weiter zurückbleiben werde". Ibid.

63 "Alle Ihre Eigenschaften die Sie beklagen sind ja eben Ihre Vorzüge, Ihr Anders sein als ich ist gerade die fruchtbare Ergänzung. Was Sie können ist mir verschlossen & was ich vielleicht vermag ist Ihnen versagt. Soll es nicht so sein? Wir sollen ja in aller Verschiedenheit uns selber sein & nicht versuchen wie der andere zu werden. Wenn Sie mich gelten lassen können, wie ich Sie anerkenne & in Ihrem Eigensten bewundere dann ist doch kein Platz für Kummer & Bedenken". Letter Paul Sacher to Ina Lohr of 7 August 1938, PSF-ILC

He then went on to say that she had not become strange for him, and that if they just had a few minutes together, then they would be able to resolve their household problems, even if they were twice the size. He wondered whether she simply did not lose trust in him on occasion.

> Certainly, the sensational aspect with which some events come to be associated is a danger, even when the instigator has not intended that at all. What moves the people, however, is the essence of the thing and not its sensational exterior. People give and receive as humans, also there where foolish minds only see brilliance, [and] not any less than in the simplest surroundings. You should never lose your belief in this truth, even when the superficialities disturb you, at least not the belief that this is my deepest conviction. It would be faint-hearted to forget the inner truth on the basis of the outer appearance".[64]

It is evident here that he is endeavoring to see the situation from Ina Lohr's perspective, and searching for arguments that could change her mind, that could affect her attitude towards their work not only on a personal level, but also on a more abstract one. He goes on to more practical aspects of their cooperation, saying that for them the biggest difficulty lies in the difference of their energy levels. "I must not give you too much to do – but you must also refuse [work] even there where you would often be necessary!"[65] This latter is, of course, easier for the stronger person to say than for the weaker to execute.

In spite of this conflict – whose source in part was the horrifying madness of the forces moving slowly towards war in the world around them – a conflict, which kept Ina Lohr constantly searching for something beyond her own self-realization, she remained fascinated by the new forms of art she came into contact with through Paul Sacher. This is part of what made her dilemma of whether to go or to stay so difficult for her. We get a glimpse of this positive side of the coin from the interview with Jos Leussink in 1983, in which she describes her contacts with various modern composers, among them Arthur Honegger, whom she met for the first time during the preparations of *Jeanne d'Arc*. In listening to her speak about it, the excitement of being part of the project infuses her voice:

---

64 "Gewiss ist das Sensationelle der manchen Ereignissen anhaftet eine Gefahr, selbst wenn es der Urheber gar nicht beabsichtigt. Was aber die Menschen rührt ist der Kern einer Sache & nicht das sensationelle Gewand. Menschlich gegeben und empfangen wird auch da noch wo törichte Wesen nur des Glänzende sehen, nicht weniger sogar als im schlichtesten Rahmen. Den Glauben in dieser Wahrheit dürfen Sie nie verlieren, selbst wenn Aeusserlichkeiten Sie stören, mindestens nicht den Glauben, dass dies meine tiefste Ueberzeugung ist. Es wäre Kleingläubigkeit über dem äusseren Schein die innere Wahrheit zu vergessen". Ibid.

65 "Ich darf Ihnen nicht zu viel aufbürden – aber auch Sie selbst dort müssen abweisen wo Sie oft nötig wären!" Ibid.

And that was really satisfying, to be able to experience the creation of that work. We received sketch after sketch, now this came, now that, and then there were the discussions with the three of them: Honegger, Ida Rubinstein, Sacher and the result came first – because Honegger wrote everything first, he worked at the piano, which was entirely new to me, I can only write in directly on paper. So I never sit at the piano when I write something. But he worked entirely at the piano, and only when the piano score was finished, did he begin with the orchestration.[66]

The fact that she was totally involved in the project from beginning to end, from discussions about its conception to its execution, becomes evident from a later passage:

And it was a magnificent work. There are some very difficult passages in it, as you well know [...]: it took awhile until I had pumped that into my tenors and basses! [...] And that was then a very great success.[67]

So also here, with modern music, just as with Stravinsky's *Symphonie de psaumes*, she was participating actively in the preparation of the choir. Although the original big manuscript score does contain some of her mark-ups, there is a later printed score from 1939 (see Ill. 4.7) which she marked up in detail similar to that which we saw in the Credo of Palestrina's *Missa Papae Marcelli*. Here she has not only corrected the spelling of *factae*, but throughout the entire piece altered the rhythmization of the choir passages in Latin to meet her own, personal standards of declamation, obviously finding the French approach to this language lacking. As these markings actually change the substance of the composition, one can't but imagine that this might also have caused considerable discussion between Paul Sacher and Ina Lohr.

In a later performance in 1942 in Zurich,[68] she was also responsible for the choirboys. In a speech she gave at the 35th anniversary of the Basel Chamber Choir in 1963 she recalls:

---

66 "En dat was nu werkelijk fijn, om het ontstaan van dat werk mee te beleven. We kregen telkens schetsen, nu komt dat en nu komt dat, en dat waren dan besprekingen, met z'n drieën, Honegger, Ida Rubinstein, Sacher en het resultaat was eerst – want Honegger schreef alles eerst, hij werkte aan de piano, wat voor mij volkomen nieuw was, ik kan alleen in lijnen schrijven. Dus ik zit nooit aan de piano, als ik iets schrijf. Maar hij werkte helemaal aan de piano, en pas als het hele klavieruittreksel klaar was, dan ging hij het orkestreren". Ibid. This portion of the interview may be heard online: https://soundcloud.com/user-802211739-365337350/ina-lohr-about-bartok-interview-1983.
67 "En dat was een reusachtig werk. Er zijn heel moeilijke gedeelten in, dat weet U wel [...]: tot ik mijn tenoren en bassen dat ingepompt had duurde het wel even! [...] En dat werd toen een heel groot succes". Ibid.
68 The first scenic performance of the oratorium took place on 13 and 19 June, 1942 in the Stadttheater (now known as the Opera House) Zurich.

Ill. 4.7: From Arthur Honegger's *Jeanne d'Arc au bûcher* (Paris 1939), from an edition in the Paul Sacher Foundation, PSC.

I stood with the choirboys in one of the proscenium loges and discovered that this group only kept quiet if I sang the entrances of all the voices and also imitated [the soloists'] movements, [as if I] actually gave a cabaret performance. Mrs. Hirsig, for example, threw her head to the side in a very particular way at a high entrance, Mr. Fürst wrinkled his brow upwards when it became very beautiful, and for the low notes, Mr. Herold let his jaw sink down to his tie. I have rarely been so part of the choir and felt myself to really belong to it; and the children sang like birds.[69]

It is just this integration in a larger unit, the experience of being a useful member of a larger team that was so valuable to her and made it so difficult to decide to set off on her own. On 8 July 1939, she wrote to Paul and Maja Sacher, who had sent her a present in honor of her 10th anniversary in Switzerland, speaking of how her friends in Basel "had succeeded in making a useful and confident member of society" out of her.[70] For a person who perceived herself as always being on the outside, this must have been of major importance.

Her contact with major composers as musical assistant to Paul Sacher, however, did not always bring such joy, as may be seen in her description of her interactions with Béla Bartók in the period leading up to World War II:

For me he was a bit scary, because Bartók had so violent a character, and a tremendous power. He was a very delicate man, and also looked so refined and elegant. But even just his eyes, [seemed like] they pierced through you – that made me uncomfortable. And, in addition, he was powerful. And at that time I had a copy of a little pianoforte such as Mozart had for traveling, a very beautiful Stein-pianoforte, copied to the millimeter by Hoesch in Kabel. […At that time] I had organized the library of the industrialist Hoesch, who was a great music-lover and who had a collection of instruments, of music and of I know not what else: and I organized the library and my salary was this little pianoforte. And it was lovely […] Bartók went suddenly over to that little keyboard and struck it so hard and three hammers were broken. Actually, I could never entirely forgive him for that – it was such a shock. I had to send the hammers to Kabel, and it was all very complicated before I finally got them back. He hadn't the slightest feeling for that, he thought it a shame that Sacher also devoted time to early music. He sim-

---

69 "Ich stand mit den Chorbuben in einer Proszeniumsloge und entdeckte, dass diese Bande nur ruhig blieb, wenn ich alle Einsätze in allen Stimmen mitsang und auch Bewegungen imitierte, eigentlich eine Cabaretvorstellung gab. Frau Hirsig z.B. warf bei einem hohen Einsatz den Kopf in einer ganz bestimmten Art auf die Seite, Herr Fürst runzelte die Stirn nach oben, wenn es ganz schön wurde und Herr Herold liess bei den tiefen Tönen den Unterkiefer bis auf die Krawatte sinken. Ich habe mich selten so in den Chor einverleibt und so zugehörig gefühlt; und die Kinder sangen wie die Vögel", untitled speech, PSF-ILC.

70 "Ich habe in der letzten Woche immer wieder über die 10 Jahre nachdenken müssen und wurde immer dankbarer gestimmt, weil es meinen Basler Freunden gelungen ist ein brauchbares und zuversichtliches Mitglied der Gesellschaft aus mir zu machen". Letter Ina Lohr to Paul and Maja Sacher of 8 July 1939, private collection, Switzerland.

ply found it a waste of time [...] He therefore could not at all understand what I was doing there, what my role was in it. It never worked between the two of us. So I don't have so many memories about that, only a great admiration, for an attitude such as his.[71]

Such encounters, however, were compensated for by other, more felicitous events, such as the concert of the Basel Chamber Choir on 10 June 1939 in the Abbaye de Royaumont in Paris. There they once again performed Palestrina's *Missa Papae Marcelli*, in the version using Gregorian chant for the proper between the movements of the ordinary of the mass. The concert was an enormous success, as documented by both the Swiss and French reviews. For example, the following review by Heinrich Strobel left the Basel citizens in no doubt about the success of their Chamber Choir:

> The artistic impression was extraordinarily strong. One says nothing new when one remarks that the Basel Chamber Choir under Paul Sacher is one of the most ideal interpreters of early music in Europe today. In what does this perfection lie? Firstly, in the expunging of all aspects of sentimentality from the performance practice, in the liberation of classical polyphony from the rigidity of the bar line and from virtuoso, decorative dynamics. Secondly, in the transparence of its sonority, which allows the lines of this music to be heard in a way hardly ever experienced and at the same time communicates the simple beauty of its harmonic order. This singing of the choir is just as far from dramatic interpretation as from bloodless formalism. It is neither "Pre-Raphaelite" nor "Wagnerian". The spirit of the music is caught in its essence, the spirit of noble harmony and of classical moderation.
>
> In between we heard Gregorian melodies which Ina Lohr directs with incomparable vibrancy and floating figuration. The singular combination of ornament and melodic tension (again distinct from all later differentiation between light and heavy metric accentuation), this connection between orientalism and Christianity, this endless

---

71 "Voor mij was hij een beetje een schrik, want Bartók had zo'n geweldig temperament, en een geweldige kracht. Hij was een heel fijn mannetje, zag er ook zo fijn en elegant uit. Maar zijn ogen al, die waren zo, alsof ze door je heen gingen – dat vond ik ook niet zo prettig. En verder had hij een kracht. En ik had in die tijd om me heen een nagebouwd klaviertje zoals Mozart had voor zijn reizen, een heel mooi Stein-klaviertje, millimeterprecies nagebouwd bij Hoesch in Kabel [a neighborhood of the city of Hagen]. Ik heb [toendertijd] de bibliotheek van de fabrikant Hoesch, die een groot muziekliefhebber was, een verzameling had van instrumenten, muziek en weet ik wat, en ik heb toen de bibliotheek georganiseerd en mijn honorarium was zo'n klaviertje. En dat was iets prachtigs [...] Bartók liep meteen naar dat klaviertje toe, sloeg zo erop en drie hamertjes waren kapot. Dat heb ik hem eigenlijk nooit helemaal kunnnen vergeven – dat was zo'n schoc, de hamertjes moest ik insturen naar Kabel, en voordat ik die weer terug kreeg was het natuurlijk een heel gedoe. Daar had hij niet de minste zin voor, hij vond het helemaal doodjammer dat Sacher ook tijd gaf aan de oude muziek. Dat vond hij eenvoudig tijdverlies [...] Hij kon daarom ook helemaal niet begrijpen wat ik daar allemaal mee te maken had, wat ik daar voor een rol speelde. Tussen ons is het nooit tot klappen gekomen. Dus daar heb ik niet zo heel veel herinnering aan, alleen een geweldige bewondering, voor zo'n houding". Interview with Jos Leussink of 24–24 March 1983.

variety of melodic form in a strictly diatonic framework, this incomprehensible rich-
ness within the limitations of unaccompanied monody was never so purely experienced
as in this hour in Royaumont.[72]

The musical and social significance of this concert can be measured by the fact
that it was attended by the Swiss ambassador to France, Walter Stucki, as well
as the composers Igor Stravinsky, Florent Schmitt, Arthur Honegger and Darius
Milhaud, among others. Judging from what she said about it in the interview
with Jos Leussink, Ina Lohr also looked back upon it as one of the musical
highlights of her life, reporting that in the intermission Stravinsky had sought
her out and given her such a powerful embrace that she thought "her last hour
had struck"; because both she and he were more or less skin and bones, it was
"pretty awful". She continued on with "but Milhaud was standing next to him,
who said ..." We shall, unfortunately, never know how this sentence ended, as
the tape ran out at that moment.[73]

In the review, moreover, the anti-Romantic, unsentimental, transparent
performance style is highly praised. In this regard it represented ideals typical
of the *Jugendmusikbewegung*, which were also gradually being assumed by the
nascent Early Music movement, ideals that were, as we have seen above, shared
by Paul Sacher and Ina Lohr. At the same time, the freedom from the barline

---

72 "Der künstlerische Eindruck war ausserordentlich stark. Man sagt nichts Neues, wenn
man feststellt, dass der Basler Kammerchor unter Paul Sacher einer der idealsten Interpreten alter Musik ist, die es heute in Europa gibt. Worauf beruht diese Vollendung? Erstens
auf der Reinigung der Aufführungspraxis von allen Elementen der Sentimentalität, auf der
Befreiung der klassischen Polyphonie vom Schematismus des Taktstrichs und von der virtuos dekorativen Dynamik. Zweitens auf einer klanglichen Transparenz, welche die Stim-
migkeit dieser Musik in einer kaum erlebten Art hörbar werden lässt und zugleich die
schlichte Schönheit der harmonischen Ordnung vollkommen vermittelt. Dieser Chorge-
sang ist ebensoweit von der dramatisierenden Auslegung wie von blutlosem Formalismus
entfernt. Er ist weder 'prä=raffaelitisch' noch 'wagnerisch'. Der Geist der Musik ist wesen-
haft begriffen, der Geist der edlen Harmonie und des klassischen Masses.
     Dazwischen hörten wir gregorianische Weisen, die Ina Lohr mit einer unvergleich-
lichen Beschwingtheit und schwebender Figuration vortragen lässt. Die eigenartige Mischung von Ornament und melodischer Spannung (wiederum jenseits aller späteren Un-
terscheidung von leichten und schweren Taktzeiten), diese Verbindung von Orientalischem
und Christlichem, diese unendliche Vielfalt der melodischen Gestalt in einem streng dia-
tonischen Rahmen, dieser unbegreifliche Reichtum in der Beschränkung auf die unbeglei-
tete Einstimmigkeit wurde noch nie so rein erlebt wie in dieser Stunde in Royaumont".
Heinrich Strobel, "Der Basler Kammerchor in Paris", in: *Basler Nachrichten*, 13 June 1939.
73 "en toen kwam Strawinsky en heeft me zo omarmd, dat ik dacht, nu heeft mijn laatste uur
geslagen. Strawinsky [...] was, en is, en gebleven is, niet veel meer dan huid en beende-
ren, en ik was ook niet veel meer; dus dat was heel erg. Maar daarnaast stond Milhaud, die
zei...". Interview with Jos Leussink, 24–25 March 1983.

is emphasized, both in the polyphony and the chant, a freedom which was certainly a product of Ina Lohr's conviction that this music must be sung in a declamatory manner. This is also what lay behind her marking of the score, as for her the communication of the message was of primary importance. It is also what led the French critic, Émile Vuillermoz, to declare in his review that "this manner of conceiving sung prayer is extremely moving".[74]

This innate ability to fuse a text – its syntax, accentuation, and above all its meaning – with a soaring musical line was characteristic for all of Ina Lohr's music-making, and was that which captivated both her fellow musicians and audiences. And while she adhered to the objectivity, the transparency, the clarity demanded by the anti-Romantic tendencies of the time, her music-making remained imbued with meaning through her insistence on the text within the context of the musical fabric.

Following this profound experience, she went to the Netherlands for her summer vacation, hoping to recover from the exertions of the year. She, however, became seriously ill, being forced to spend several weeks in St. John's Hospital in Laren, luckily being able to stay in the same institution as her sister Sally, who suffered from tuberculosis. It is there that Paul Sacher sent her a birthday greeting on 1 August 1939, in which he expressed his hopes that she would begin feeling better soon, although he was skeptical that the doctors would find a simple, organic source for her illness. He believed namely that

> with sensitive and passionate people all illnesses have a psychological cause. […] I often ask myself and now once again for the source of this disturbance of your soul, given that your life fulfills so much of what you desire professionally and personally. Unfortunately, our ego is often more mysterious than the power of knowledge and more idiosyncratic than our reason. Therefore, I wish you strength & patience & the courage that has never yet abandoned you. Not only for your birthday, but for all days.[75]

Ina Lohr, gradually recovering her strength in the hospital, responded on 5 August 1939 with gratitude.

---

74 "Cette façon 'éolienne' de concevoir la prière chantée est extrêmement émouvante". Émile Vuillermoz, "A l'Abbaye de Royaumont", in: *Excelsior*, 12 June 1939, PSF-ILC.

75 "bei sensiblen & leidenschaftlichen Menschen alle Krankheiten psychisch bedingt sind […] Ich frage mich oft, & jetzt wieder nach der Ursache dieser seelischen Störung, wo doch Ihr Leben beruflich & menschlich so viel ersehntes [sic] erfüllt. Leider ist unser Es oft geheimnisvoller als die Kraft der Erkenntnis & eigenwilliger als unsere Vernunft. Darum wünsche ich Ihnen Kraft & Geduld & den Mut, der Sie noch nie verlassen hat. Nicht nur zum Geburtstag, sondern für alle Tage". Letter Paul Sacher to Ina Lohr of 1 August 1939, PSF-ILC.

It is your irrational belief and your trust that again and again make it possible for me to continue and it is my greatest worry that I will at some point put your trust too much to the test, or that I could lose it. As long as you, a healthy and vital person have the courage to continue working with me, I will not give up the struggle and perhaps sometime even find a lasting balance.[76]

That Paul Sacher was right in his judgment that her illnesses also had a psychological component will be seen in the following chapter about the wartime years. As can be imagined, Ina Lohr was beset not only with the general difficulties of the wartime situation, but also almost intolerably oppressed by the lack of contact with her family in the Netherlands; indeed, the next time she was to see them was only after the war. During this entire period, when the structures of the world known up until then were sundered, and also afterwards, his trust in her remained unshaken.

4.2 The Founding of the Schola Cantorum Basiliensis

Parallel to her cooperation with Paul Sacher in regard to the BKO came the germination of the seed sown in the seminars with Karl Nef, namely the founding of a school dedicated to the study and performance of early music, the Schola Cantorum Basiliensis (SCB). As with so many things in life, one cannot claim that there is linear history of its founding, but rather that it was a conjunction of interests that came together at a certain moment in time. As the institution very quickly came to represent different things to different people, we need to distinguish the sparks of inspiration that led to its foundation from its organizational and administrative history, its intent from its reality, as well as to differentiate between the various goals of those actively involved in the school. In comparison to the BKO, we have relatively little documentation about its beginnings and as a consequence, the major studies of its history by Wulf Arlt and Martin Kirnbauer have devoted themselves primarily to its organizational and ideological underpinnings.[77] Further information concerning financial and personnel issues gleaned from the school's annual reports and meetings of the

---

76 "Ihr irrationeler [sic] Glaube und Ihr Vertrauen sind's, die es mir immer wieder ermöglichen durchzuhalten und meine grösste Sorge ist, dass ich Ihr Vertrauen einmal zu sehr auf die Probe stelle, oder gar verlieren könnte. So lange aber Sie, gesunder, vitaler Mensch den Mut haben mit mir weiter zu arbeiten, werde ich den Kampf nicht aufgeben und vielleicht sogar einmal ein dauerhaftes Gleichgewicht finden". Letter Ina Lohr to Paul Sacher of 5 August 1939, private collection, Switzerland.

77 Cf. p. 55, footnote 87.

board, as well as from letters between those active at the Schola, will be drawn upon here to give a more complete picture of the institution's early years and Ina Lohr's role within it. We have little direct information concerning this, however, as there are few references to the Schola in her correspondence with Paul Sacher, due to the fact that the letters were primarily written during the school vacations, and for the most part concerned immediate issues involving the BKO. Thus we are left to infer much from the few extant documents. In addition, I have also collated a table of information found in the SCB's annual reports for the years 1933–39 concerning the roster of teachers, courses taught, workshops and concerts given, plus any further activities in which the school was involved (see Appendix 2). From this factual information, a picture of the Schola at that time emerges, one much different from that of the institution today, much different than our conceptions of what early music practice and its musicological foundations require.

In the first chapter we saw what an enlivening experience Karl Nef's seminar at the University of Basel was for Ina Lohr, that it stimulated her to display her knowledge, as well as demonstrated her ability to convince through song. She perceived the turn from solely studying and analyzing the music to performing it with her fellow students – which she had initiated in the class – as being the source of inspiration for the founding of the Schola. In addition, this approach was no doubt spurred on by Karl Nef's specific interest in the historical collegium musicum. Indeed, she mentioned in a home-made cassette recording made in 1980 how "our benevolent mentor, Karl Nef, often had to restrain us. He was the one that made us aware of the different sound of old instruments; also of another kind of singing that adapted itself to the instrumental sound".[78] Further, it was in that very first seminar that Paul Sacher asked Ina Lohr about further early music for the BKO, watched her mark up a chamber sonata of Rosenmüller for his orchestra, leading to her becoming his musical assistant. In the selfsame recording she recalls their first choir concert of 26 November 1930 which opened with Hildegard's Kyrie, saying that "Paul Sacher and I were, however, absolutely committed to continuing to work in this manner. But we were also aware of the fact that we would continue to need singing and playing, thinking and seeking colleagues".[79]

---

78 "Unser gütiger Mentor Karl Nef musste oft bremsend eingreifen. Er war es, der uns auf den anderen Klang der alten Instrumente aufmerksam machte. Auch auf ein anderes Singen, das sich dem Instrumentalklang anpasste", Cassette "Die Entstehung der Schola Cantorum Basiliensis", 1980, PSF-ILC, CD-4.

79 "Paul Sacher und ich aber waren fest entschlossen in dieser Art weiter zu arbeiten. Aber wir waren uns dessen bewusst, dass wir singende und spielende, denkende und suchende

The first unmistakeable indication we have that they were concretely thinking of founding a school is a postscript at the end of a letter of 29 July 1932
from Paul Sacher to Ina Lohr in which he rejoices "All this [the publication of
their edition of chant melodies and Ina Lohr's articles for the *Schweizerische
Musikzeitung*] is at the same time the best publicity for our editions, your work
and the school for early music! But please keep the last point in particular, absolutely secret".[80] This, however, did not mean that Paul Sacher kept quiet on the
subject. To the contrary, he was speaking and corresponding with many others
about it, as exemplified by a remark made by the musicologist Walter Nef – not
only a member of the seminar at the university, but also a good friend, and a
nephew of the above-mentioned Karl Nef – that he is "eager for the latest news
about the Schola", to which Paul Sacher responded on 2 September 1932, that
he had spoken with most of the people concerning the Schola and received
"from all of them, particularly from [the singer and musicologist Arnold] Geering and [the singer Max] Meili, enthusiastic approval and acceptance".[81] Walter
Nef replied on 6 September, expressing his pleasure in this state of affairs and
wondering how things stood "on the financial side and with the gentlemen who
come into question for the board?"[82] Shortly thereafter Paul Sacher set down
some basic ideas for the "Schola cantorum basiliensis", dated Thursday, 22 September, perhaps after conferring about it with Ina Lohr on the previous day
during their regular meeting for tea on Wednesday afternoon.[83] There was one
paragraph devoted to the intent of the school, a long list of possible courses and
teachers, and two pages concerning organizational necessities.

Paul Sacher met with Arnold Geering and Ina Lohr on 23 September for
a "discussion about the plans for an exposé on the intent and program of his

Mitarbeiter auch weiterhin brauchen würden", Cassette "Die Entstehung der Schola Cantorum Basiliensis", 1980, PSF-ILC, CD-4.

80 "Das alles ist ja gleichzeitig die beste Propaganda für unsere Noten, Ihre Arbeit & die
Schule für alte Musik! Aber halten Sie bitte besonders den letzten Punkt streng geheim".
Letter Paul Sacher to Ina Lohr of 29 July 1932, PSF-ILC.

81 "Ich bin gespannt auf die neuesten Nachrichten über die Schola" and "Trotzdem habe ich
nebenher mit den meisten Leuten betr. Schola gesprochen und von allen, hauptsächlich
auch von Geering und Meili begeisterte Zustimmung und Zusage erhalten". Letter Paul
Sacher to Walter Nef of 2 September 1932, PSF-PSC. See also Martin Kirnbauer, "'Tout le
monde connaît la Schola'", 146.

82 "Wie steht es mit der finanziellen Seite und den Herren, die für das 'Praesidium' in Frage
kommen?". Letter Walter Nef to Paul Sacher of 6 September 1932, PSF-PSC.

83 This dating was found on a copy of the document examined by Wulf Arlt, "Zur Idee und
Geschichte eines 'Lehr- und Forschungsinstituts für Alte Musik'", 45. An undated copy
thereof is found PSF-ILC.

school."[84] As we know from a letter of 26 September written on Paul Sacher's behest by Arnold Geering to Walter Nef, who had been unable to be there, Paul Sacher had first informed them of the organizational structure he had in mind for the school. He foresaw two boards, one for administrative-financial affairs and the other for the scholarly-artistic matters, both presided over by him as the director of the Schola. His fellow students from Karl Nef's seminar, Ina Lohr, Arnold Geering and Walter Nef, were the prospective members of the scholarly-artistic board. For the purposes of research and the dissemination of its results, a journal, a library and a record archive were to be placed at their disposal. Ina Lohr was to be in charge of the record archive and the two men were to choose between the journal and the library. Arnold Geering was to write the introductory words concerning the motivation for the founding of the Schola. Walter Nef was to receive this document and add in his own suggestions and ideas. The two of them were also to order and complete the list of subjects to be taught. Much time in the meeting was also spent discussing the list of teachers.

On that same 22 September on which he wrote down his ideas for the Schola, Paul Sacher also wrote a long letter to August Wenzinger, a friend from the early days of the BKO who was later to become one of the foremost viola da gamba players of the 20th century, whom he wished to entice to Basel to participate in the (ad)venture:

> Dear August,
> A plan, that has long engaged me, can now perhaps be realized in the foreseeable future. I would like, namely, to found a school for early music, in which scholars and artists, hand-in-hand, engage with the problems that concern us all. My train of thought is more or less the following: the enormous amount of material brought to light by musicology can only poorly be roused to sounding life in practice, as musicologists, when they undertake such attempts themselves, usually do so without the necessary musical-technical tools; and as, on the other hand, most practical artists, if they are interested in early music at all, lack the historical knowledge which is nonetheless necessary. The "Schola Cantorum Basiliensis" would have to have the sub-title: Artistic-Scholarly Institute for the Teaching and Research of Early Music. That sounds awful and if at all possible should never appear in print in this formulation. But it concisely expresses most closely what I have in mind. I know, of course, that in many places, attempts in this direction have been made, and also are [still] being pursued with energy today. The only thing that would presumably be really new in Basel is the great foundation and the all-encompassing nature of the goal which I wish to set for us. Those in Basel who come into question, with whom I have taken up provisional contact, have mostly reacted to

---

84 "Zu einer Besprechung seines Planes für ein Exposé über Zweck und Programm seiner Schule". Letter Arnold Geering to Walter Nef of 26 September 1932. University Library Basel, NL 212 (Estate Karl Nef). See also Martin Kirnbauer, "'Tout le monde connaît la Schola'", 147.

this plan with great enthusiasm. Also, the financing should be possible, although extraordinarily high sums will be necessary. Globally seen, I am by no means disregarding the extraordinary difficulties that the execution of this plan will bring with it, and am, for all that, convinced that everything will depend on the staff of the projected school. I believe that it will be possible to find young and good people for this purpose. One of my particularly heartfelt wishes would be to include you in this effort. Would this project be of sufficient interest to you, and is there a possibility that you would give up your job in Bremen in order to invest your entire energy here?[85]

This letter demonstrates, in conjunction with all the other indications above, the degree to which Paul Sacher was the motivating organizational force behind the founding of the Schola, that it was he that took it upon himself not only to find a collection of teacher/scholars dedicated to the purpose of the institution, but also to put together an administrative and financial structure that would make it viable.

Although all the initial contacts took place on a one-to-one level, there began to be meetings of larger groups to discuss basic issues. For example, from

85 "Lieber August,

Ein Plan, der mich schon lange bewegt, kann nun vielleicht in absehbarer Zeit Wirklichkeit werden. Ich möchte nämlich eine Schule für alte Musik gründen, an der Wissenschaftler und Künstler Hand in Hand den Problemen, die uns alle beschäftigen, zu Leibe rücken. Mein Gedankengang ist ungefähr folgender: Das riesige von der Musikwissenschaft zu Tage geförderte Material kann praktisch nur schlecht zum klingendem Leben erweckt werden, da die Musikwissenschaftler, wenn Sie selber solche Versuche unternehmen, gewöhnlich ohne das musikalisch-technisch nötige Rüstzeug ans Werk gehen, und da umgekehrt den meisten ausübenden Künstlern, wenn sie für alte Musik überhaupt Interesse haben, die immerhin notwendigen historische Kenntnisse fehlen. Die 'Schola Cantorum Basiliensis' müsste demnach den Untertitel tragen: Künstlerisch-wissenschaftliches Lehr- und Forschungsinstitur [sic] für alte Musik. Das klingt scheusslich und soll wenn möglich auch nie in dieser Formulierung gedruckt werden. Es drückt aber am ehesten in Kürze das, was ich meine, aus. Ich weiss wohl, dass an vielen Stellen Versuche in dieser Richtung unternommen worden sind, und auch heute mit Energie weiter geführt werden. Das Einzige, was in Basel voraussichtlich aber wirklich neu wäre, ist die grosse Basis und das allen Stoff umfassende Ziel, das ich uns stellen möchte. Die in Frage kommenden Basler Kräfte, mit denen ich vorläufig Fühlung genommen habe, sind durch diesen Plan grösstenteils in hohe Begeisterung versetzt worden. Auch die Finanzierung dürfte sich lösen lassen, obwohl ausserordentlich hohe Summen nötig sein werden. Im Ganzen verhehle ich mir die ausserordentlichen Schwierigkeiten, die die Ausführung dieses Planes mit sich bringen wird, keineswegs, immerhin bin ich überzeugt, dass alles von den Mitarbeitern der zu gründenden Schule abhängen wird. Ich glaube, dass sich zu diesem Zweck junge und tüchtige Kräft [sic] auftreiben lassen [werden]. Es wäre mein besonders herzlicher Wunsch, dich bei dieser Arbeit dabei zu haben. Interessiert Dich das Projekt genügend und besteht eine Möglichkeit, dass Du Deine Stellung in Bremen aufgibst, um hier Deine ganze Kraft einzusetzen?" Letter Paul Sacher to August Wenzinger of 22 September 1932, PSF-PSC. See also Martin Kirnbauer, "'Tout le monde connait la Schola'", 149.

letters to Ina Lohr and Walter Nef on the 26 October 1932, we know that he
held a meeting with them and Arnold Geering, his future "scholarly-artistic
board", about the final version of the exposé describing the intents and structure of the Schola. Further, we know from the correspondence with August
Wenzinger and Max Meili that Paul Sacher was planning larger meetings of almost all the staff at the end of January and the beginning of May 1933.

The financial and administrative side was obviously more difficult to organize than Paul Sacher had anticipated in his letter to August Wenzinger. It is evident from the financial overview of the first three years of the Schola that the
support for the institution – beyond the income deriving from the enrollment
fees – came primarily from eight donors, presumably Maja Sacher (at the time
still Maja Hoffmann), Alfred Von der Mühll, Werner Reinhart, Benedict Vischer, Dr. Ruth Witzinger, a Frau Morel, Dr. Roland Ziegler, and finally Herman Lohr, Ina Lohr's father, although I suspect he may have only made a contribution in the first year to ensure his daughter's livelihood in that period.[86]
Finding these eight people, however, was no easy task. Originally he had placed
his hopes in significant financial support from Werner Reinhart (1884–1951), a
patron of music based in Winterthur, with whom he presumably had discussed
the matter at the end of October 1932.[87] He apparently went away from this discussion with the feeling that Werner Reinhart would be willing to provide sub-
stantial, if not the greatest support for the SCB of all those he had approached.
His disappointment over Werner Reinhart's response to his letters of 27 June
1933 was as a result quite bitter, perhaps made doubly so by the somewhat pa-
tronizing words that accompanied it:

> You will remember that I felt it necessary at our past discussion to recommend that you
> ensure the approval and support of all the leading musical circles in Basel. It was also
> not your intent to compete with any of the present institutions, but only to supplement
> existing ones. I therefore considered it essential and necessary that you should first win
> over the leading figures of the Allgemeine Musikgesellschaft as well as the Basel Conserv-
> atory for it. From your accounts to date it is not evident how successful you have been in
> this. As our Music Collegium, as well as myself, have maintained long-term friendly rela-
> tions with the gentlemen of the Allgemeine Musikgesellschaft, particularly to Mr. Spei-

---

86 "Rückblick in Zahlen auf die ersten drei Schuljahre S.C.B". *Bericht über das dritte Schuljahr
    der SCHOLA CANTORUM BASILIENSIS*, Archive of the Schola Cantorum Basiliensis.
87 Letter Paul Sacher to Werner Reinhart of 18 October 1932, Winterthur Libraries, Study
    Library, Depot Archive of the Music Collegium Winterthur. See also the discussion of Paul
    Sacher's correspondence with Werner Reinhart concerning the Schola Cantorum Basilien-
    sis in Ulrike Thiele, *Musikleben und Mäzenatentum im 20. Jahrhundert: Werner Reinhart
    (1984–1951)*, Diss. Phil. University of Zurich, 2016 doi.org/10.5167/uhz-13409, publication
    forthcoming, 51–54.

ser, it is also in a certain way, a matter of tact for me not to be involved in an enterprise that is not welcomed and supported by these authorities and circles. You will therefore understand that I would have liked to have received some further information in this regard. The whole thing, as we discussed it, should be also begun modestly, as far as the means are concerned, and also be able to sustain itself as soon as possible. In regard to my possible contribution, I had thought of it being in the range of 1000 francs, whereby the distribution over the first three years can be determined by the needs of the Schola.[88]

In addition, Werner Reinhart turned down his invitation to become a member of the Schola's supervisory board.[89] Paul Sacher gave expression to this setback in a letter to Max Meili of 8 September 1933:

Unfortunately, things look very bad for the Schola. In order to be able to start, I am still lacking a sum of about 10,000 francs a year, although I have already reduced the budget to the very minimum required. The decision of Werner Reinhart was particularly disappointing, who wishes to give 333.33 francs annually for the first three years! From his oral promises in the fall of last year, I had assumed that he would be the strongest financial patron of the Schola, an assumption which has been catastrophically undermined by this decision. *Werner Reinhart's attitude is totally incomprehensible to me, and I request you urgently not to speak to a single person about it. The other members of the Schola have only been informed generally on this subject.* As I want under no circumstances to begin the work of the Schola without being financially backed for three years in advance, I have

88 "Sie werden sich erinnern, dass ich Ihnen damals bei unserer Unterredung glaubte, anraten zu müssen, sich von vornherein der Zustimmung und Unterstützung aller massgebenden musikalischen Kreise Basels zu versichern. Es war ja auch nicht Ihre Meinung, mit der Schola irgend eine der jetzigen Institutionen zu konkurrenzieren, sondern Bestehendes nur zu ergänzen. Darum hielt ich es für unumgänglich und notwendig, dass Sie vor allem die leitenden Persönlichkeiten der Allgemeinen Musikgesellschaft, sowie des Basler Konservatoriums dafür gewinnen sollten. Aus Ihren soweitigen Mitteilungen ist nun nicht ersichtlich, wie weit Ihnen das gelungen ist. Da sowohl unser Musikkollegium als auch mich langjährige freundschaftliche Beziehungen zu den Herren der Allgemeinen Musikgesellschaft, namentlich zu Herrn Speiser, verbinden, ist es für mich auch gewissermassen eine Taktfrage, mich nicht an einer Unternehmung zu interessieren, die nicht auch von diesen Stellen und Kreisen begrüsst und unterstützt wird. Darum wäre es, wie Sie verstehen werden, mir erwünscht gewesen, von Ihnen noch einige Aufschlüsse in dieser Hinsicht zu erhalten. Die ganze Sache sollte ja auch anfänglich, wie wir dies besprachen, was die Mittel anbetrifft, bescheiden aufgezogen werden und sich eben möglichst bald auch selbst erhalten können. Was meine allfällige Zuwendung anbetrifft, so hätte ich mir dieselbe in der Höhe von total Fr. 1000.– gedacht, wobei die Verteilung auf die 3 ersten Jahre je nach den Bedürfnissen der Schola noch geregelt werden könnte". Letter Werner Reinhart to Paul Sacher of 27 June 1933, Winterthur Libraries, Study Library, Depot Music Collegium Winterthur, 365/41.

89 He did, however, donate CHF 600 for a set of Dolmetsch recorders. See Ulrike Thiele, *Musikleben und Mäzenatentum*, 52–53 and letters of 21 September 1933 and 27 September 1933 between Werner Reinhart and Paul Sacher, Winterthur Libraries, Study Library, Depot Music Collegium Winterthur, 365/27 and 365/14 respectively and the letter of 14 December 1933 from Werner Reinhart to the Schola Cantorum Basiliensis, Winterthur Libraries, Study Library, Depot Music Collegium Winterthur, 365/20.

no choice but to continue to collect money and wait until the necessary sum has been attained. All these difficulties have given me much to do during the course of the summer, they are unfortunately not to be overcome just like that by means of energy alone.[90]

Whilst he was searching for money to enable the school to be put on a stable footing, however, some of his prospective teachers, such as August Wenzinger, Max Meili and Herman Leeb, were seeing it as a means of enhancing their income and were eagerly making their needs known. Thus Paul Sacher also was in his turn in the position of the bringer of bad tidings to August Wenzinger when on 26 March 1933 he wrote that "enough money has been gathered that we can certainly begin modestly in autumn, but I see no possibility of including a guarantee sum for you in the budget, such as we discussed earlier in Basel".[91] By 16 September, however, he was able to state that the budget would just allow him to offer a guarantee of 100 francs, but for this August Wenzinger would have to commit himself for three years for the project, as well as have sufficient free time in Basel to make it worthwhile for the school. In juxtaposition to this toughness in negotiation with the gambist on the part of Paul Sacher, it is noteworthy to recall the letter mentioned above, written just the previous day by Ina Lohr to the future director of the Schola (see pp. 144–45), in which she valiantly attempted to define her obligations to the SCB and the BKO. Due to her difficulties in preventing the work for Paul Sacher from encroaching upon her own interests, she had felt the necessity there of explicitly stating that she will neither limit herself to the Schola's ideals nor reject others from the outside, merely

90 "Mit der Schola steht es leider sehr schlecht. Um starten zu können, fehlt mir noch immer eine Summe von jährlich ca. 10'000 Franken, obwohl ich das Budget bereits auf das allernotwendigste Minimum reduziert habe. Ganz besonders enttäuschend war der Bescheid von Werner Reinhart, der in den ersten 3 Jahren jährlich Fr. 333.33 geben will! Seinen mündlichen Versprechungen im Herbst vor einem Jahr habe ich seinerzeit entnommen, dass er der finanziell stärkste Gönner der Schola sein werde, eine Annahme, die durch diesen Bescheid katastrophal enttäuscht worden ist. Die Einstellung Werner Reinharts ist mir vollständig unverständlich, und ich bitte Dich dringend, davon zu keinem Menschen zu sprechen. Die übrigen Mitglieder der Schola sind von dieser Tatsache nur ungenau orientiert. Da ich unter gar keinen Umständen die Arbeit der Schola beginnen möchte, ohne vorher finanzeill [sic] auf 3 Jahre gesichert zu sein, bleibt gar nichts anderes übrig, als weiter Geld zu sammeln und abzuwarten bis die notwendige Summe beieinander ist. Diese ganzen Schwierigkeiten haben mir im Laufe des Sommers viel zu schaffen gegeben, sie sind leider mit Energie allein nicht ohne weiteres zu überwinden". Letter Paul Sacher to Max Meili of 8 September 1933, estate of Max Meili, Zentralbibliothek Zurich, Mus NL 100: A13.

91 "Bis heute ist so viel Geld beieinander, dass wir in bescheidenem Rahmen im Herbst auf alle Fälle anfangen können, aber ich sehe keinerlei Möglichkeit, eine Garantiesumme, wie wir es seinerzeit in Basel besprochen haben, für Dich im Budget unterzubringen". Letter Paul Sacher to August Wenzinger of 26 March 1933, PSF-PSC.

because she belongs to the institution. And that for the 100 francs she will either teach 4–5 hours or reserve a day per week for the Schola. So, on the one side, Paul Sacher was trying to ensure that August Wenzinger would be sufficiently present at the school for the 100 francs that were available and, on the other, Ina Lohr was endeavoring to delimit her involvement, both time-wise and musically. Notwithstanding the scant funding, by mid-September Paul Sacher had clearly made the decision to embark on the new project.

As members for his institutional board, he was able to win over Alfred Von der Mühll and Wilhelm Merian. Alfred Von der Mühll was the wealthy owner of a ceramics firm in Lausen, who had already proved his value as the second president of the BKO board.[92] Wilhelm Merian was a musicologist who had studied with Hermann Kretzschmar and Johannes Wolf in Berlin, as well as with Karl Nef in Basel, writing his dissertation on early German organ tablatures; later he initiated the first complete edition of Ludwig Senfl. He was the first secretary of the International Musicological Society from 1927–48 and also the president of the Basel section of the Swiss Musicological Society from 1919–32, and of the whole organization from 1935–46.[93] He was thus ideally placed in the musicological world, both locally and internationally, to be able to give strategic advice in regard to the Schola's development.

As Martin Kirnbauer already concluded in his article on the early Schola, this documentary evidence demonstrates clearly the degree to which the practical foundation and organization of the institution were in Paul Sacher's hands – that it was really his school – although he was only in the roster of teachers in the first year, as a coach for ensembles.[94] In this sense, the notice to the press of November 1933, written by Arnold Geering, concerning its founding reflects the reality:

> The initiator of the Schola Cantorum Basiliensis is Paul Sacher, co-founders are Alfred Von der Mühll and Prof. Dr. Wilhelm Merian, who together with him constitute the board. The entire faculty served in an advisory capacity in its foundation: Claire Levy, Ina Lohr, Annie Tschopp, Dr. Arnold Geering, Walter Kägi, Hermann Leeb, Max Meili, Dr. Fritz Morel, Walter Nef und August Wenzinger.[95]

92 Lesley Stephenson, *Symphonie der Träume*, 107.

93 This information is taken from the obituary written by Walter Nef, "Wilhelm Merian zum Gedächtnis", in: *Die Musikforschung* 6 (1953), 143–44.

94 Martin Kirnbauer, "'Tout le monde connaît la Schola'", 147.

95 "Der Initiant der Schola Cantorum Basiliensis ist Paul Sacher, Mitbegründer sind die Herren Alfred Von der Mühll (Präsident) und Prof. Dr. Wilhelm Merian, die mit ihm zusammen den Vorstand bilden, und beratend stand bei der Gründung der gesamte Lehrkörper zur Seite: Claire Levy, Ina Lohr, Annie Tschopp, Dr. Arnold Geering, Walter Kägi, Hermann Leeb, Max Meili, Dr. Fritz Morel, Walter Nef und August Wenzinger". *Basler*

In fact, it seems likely that it was this form of organization, in which the links to all those involved ran through him, allowing him to keep the diverse agents within the school working together by means of his force of personality, that ensured its long-term success.

The Intentions and the Reality of the First Years of the Schola

The grandeur of Paul Sacher's thinking is illustrated by the extent of the proposed program, and intended infrastructure, which included not only a library but also a collection of instruments that was already included in his first document of 22 September. The final exposé, written primarily by Arnold Geering, as is made clear by the above-mentioned letter, dates from 30 November 1932.[96] Noteworthy here is not only the elevation of the language, but also the increased prominence of the scholarly side of the venture, perhaps a reflection of Arnold Geering's interests, as indicated by the inversion of the placement of the words "teaching" and "research" in the description of the school.[97]

> There is the intention of the foundation of a research and teaching institution for early music under the name of the *Schola Cantorum Basiliensis*. Its task is the investigation and practical testing of all questions which are connected with bringing early music back to life again, with the goal of creating an active communication between scholarship and practice. The *Schola Cantorum Basiliensis* will communicate its results by means of performances and new editions, as well as through articles in its own journal. Instruction in playing early instruments and exercises in the performance of earlier works in the spirit of their age will offer the student, as well as the professionally active musician, the opportunity of expanding their education and of getting advice in all questions pertaining thereto.[98]

Nachrichten, 21 November 1933. My thanks to Simon Obert for bringing this notice to my attention. The press report appears in its entirety in Arnold Geering, "Schola Cantorum Basiliensis", in: *Mitteilungen der schweizerischen musikforschenden Gesellschaft* 1(1934–36), 16–17.

96 Wulf Arlt, "Zur Idee und Geschichte eines 'Lehr- und Forschungsinstituts für alte Musik'", 45. The text of the entire exposé may be found on pages 45–48.
97 This inversion was already noted by Wulf Arlt, Ibid., 45.
98 "Es besteht die Absicht, in Basel ein Forschungs- und Lehr-Institut für alte Musik unter dem Namen *Schola Cantorum Basiliensis* ins Leben zu rufen. Seine Aufgabe ist die Erforschung und praktische Erprobung aller Fragen, welche mit der Wiederbelebung alter Musik zusammenhängen, mit dem Ziel eine lebendige Wechselwirkung zwischen Wissenschaft und Praxis herzustellen. Die *Schola Cantorum Basiliensis* wird ihre Ergebnisse kundtun durch Aufführungen und Neuausgaben, sowie durch Berichte in einer eigenen Zeitschrift. Unterricht im Spiel auf alten Instrumenten und Übungen in der Wiedergabe älterer Werke im Geist ihrer Epoche werden dem studierenden wie auch dem beruflich tätigen Musiker Gelegenheit bieten, sich weiterzubilden und in allen einschlägigen Fragen Rat zu holen". Wulf Arlt, "Zur Idee und Geschichte eines 'Lehr- und Forschungsinstituts für alte Musik'", 45–46.

Clear from this description is that their targeted audience was the conservatory student or already active professional musician. Structurally, the core of the school was to be the "colloquium of the teachers, in which the common tasks shall be discussed and tested".[99] Further,

> parallel to this central common work of the whole institute, the instruction of the playing of early instruments, voice, theoretical, historical and other fields shall take place, in as much as they are connected with the interpretation of early music. The instruction shall transpire in two divisions, one an external one for special subjects, and an internal, one-year course, which shall provide a general, well-founded introduction into the musical performance of the pre-Classical period. A completed conservatory education is the prerequisite for the participation in the internal division.[100]

Thus their goals were very high, both intellectually and practically: in essence they desired to bring together the crème de la crème of musicology with the foremost performing musicians of the time to create a musical hotbed devoted to the performance of music of earlier eras in a historical manner, an aim still doggedly sought after by all such institutions today. Besides their lack of resources, however, this goal was simply unattainable at the time, as there was not a pool of trained, interested musicians in Basel, apart from those already involved in the school, which could be drawn upon as pupils. As a result, the Schola initially devoted itself to two areas of activity: giving concerts preceded by work weeks involving all the teachers; and teaching the amateurs, both adults and children, that would come to form their audience. In looking back at the founding of the Schola in 1980, Ina Lohr reflected that

> It took courage to perform early music at that time, that is, music from the time before Bach. It therefore also required a lot of courage to open a music school that would occupy itself solely with this music. We had the required innocence and the vitally crucial enthusiasm simply to try it. Apart from the loyal help from some lovingly smiling friends who supported us, the *Singbewegung* for young people in Germany was useful to us. It had met with much criticism in Switzerland. But now, however, trained musicians took valuable old instruments and also ones carefully copied [from the originals],

---

99 "Den Kern der Schule bildet das Colloquium der Lehrer, in welchem die gemeinsamen Aufgaben besprochen und durchgeprobt werden sollen". Ibid., 47

100 "Neben dieser zentralen gemeinsamen Arbeit des ganzen Institutes soll der Unterricht im Spiel älterer Instrumente, Gesang, theoretischer, historischer und anderer Fächer einhergehen, insofern sie mit der Interpretation älterer Werke zusammenhängen. Der Unterricht soll in zwei Abteilungen erteilt werden, einer externen für Spezialfächer, und einem internen, einjährigen Kurs, welcher eine allgemein fundierte Einführung in die Musikübung der vorklassischen Zeit vermittelt. Bedingung für den Besuch der internen Abteilung ist eine abgeschlossene, konservatorische Ausbildung". Ibid., 47.

even into smaller churches and concert halls, as well as giving lessons to both older and younger amateurs who wanted to play and sing music because they loved it.[101]

Whereas Ina Lohr relished the task of teaching amateurs, this was not true for all of the young and upward striving professionals Paul Sacher had engaged. On 21 November 1933, Max Meili wrote the following to the director in apology for an emotional scene during the working meeting in preparation for the school's opening in the following month:

> It was a shame that it was no longer possible, after our somewhat explosive encounters, to again emphasize our personal, friendly contact in a more extended manner. But perhaps that will be possible during my next visit. I am aware that it could never have come to such a misunderstanding, if we had already spoken about all of these small and larger difficulties earlier in a friendly way. What I desire to bring to the Schola is free from any personal ambition, is the essence of my artistic personality. I am primarily interested in bringing music of earlier artistic eras back to life, mainly that of the baroque and pre-baroque, together with good musicians. And as at the moment at least, there are too few good, stylistically sure musicians, it will be necessary to educate such [people]. These intentions, I assume, are also shared by the other Schola employees. Certainly, it will be necessary, at least for the moment, also to teach other less talented [individuals], because we, given the present financial situation, cannot yet afford to be so exclusive, unfortunately![102]

101 "Es brauchte damals Mut, alte Musik, das hiess damals die Musik aus der Zeit vor Bach aufzuführen. Es brauchte darum auch sehr viel Mut eine Musikschule zu eröffnen, die sich ausschliesslich mit dieser Musik beschäftigen würde. Wir hatten die nötige Unbefangenheit und die dringend notwendige Begeisterung es einfach zu wagen. Abgesehen von der treuen Hilfe einiger allerdings liebevoll lächelnder Freunde als Unterstützer, kam uns die Jugend Singbewegung aus Deutschland entgegen. Sie war in der Schweiz auf viel Kritik gestossen. Jetzt aber brachten ausgebildete Musiker zum Teil kostbare alte Instrumente und auch sorgfältig nachgebaute, sogar in die kleineren Kirchen und Konzertsäle und gaben auch den grossen und kleinen Dilettanten, die aus Liebe zur Musik spielen und singen wollten, Stunden". Cassette "Die Entstehung der Schola Cantorum Basiliensis", PSF-ILC, CD-4.

102 "Schade, dass es nicht mehr möglich war, nach unseren etwas explosiven Zusammenkünften unseren persönlichen, freundschaftlichen Kontakt in ausgiebigerem Masse wieder zu betonen. Aber vielleicht ist das bei meinem nächsten Besuch möglich. Ich bin mir bewusst, dass es nie zu einem derartigen Missverständnis hätte kommen können, hätten wir uns über alle diese kleinen u. grösseren Schwierigkeiten schon früher in freundschaftlicher Weise aussprechen können. Was ich in die Schola mitbringen will, ist frei von jedem persönlichen Ehrgeiz, ist mir das Wesentliche meiner künstlerischen Persönlichkeit. Es liegt mir vor allem daran, Musik aus frühen, vor allem barockern und vorbarocken Kunstepochen mit guten Musikern gemeinsam wieder lebendig zu machen. Und da es im Augenblick wenigstens zu wenig gute, stilsichere Musiker gibt, wird es eben nötig sein, solche heranzubilden. Diese Absichten, nehme ich an, werden auch die anderen Schola-Mitarbeiter haben. Gewiss, es wird nötig sein, wenigstens vorläufig, auch an weniger Berufene Unterricht zu geben, weil wir es nun in den jetzt gegebenen finanziellen Verhältnis-

It is not difficult to imagine, given the lack of money and accomplished musicians, that Paul Sacher may have felt quite some gratitude toward Ina Lohr's attitude toward teaching lay people, stemming from a combination of a certain financial independence and a genuine interest in teaching lay musicians. In an otherwise difficult situation, her contribution at the Schola's inception was both generous and effective.

From the very beginning, the activities of the school were divided up between regular instruction, special courses of limited duration and concerts. These were supplemented with various other events, such as lectures, participation at exhibitions, fairs, and conferences (see Appendix 2). In the first four years, the subjects that received the largest enrollment were recorder, Gregorian chant, thorough bass, and the ensemble classes of Ina Lohr and August Wenzinger. During these first years, the tuition fees for regular instruction covered not only the wages of the teachers, but also a great deal of the costs of the infrastructure. The special courses showed neither loss nor profit financially, but served as advertisement for the Schola, both in Basel and throughout Switzerland. The concerts were, of course, the primary source of the deficit for which the board was responsible for finding the funding.

Regular Instruction

Ina Lohr was the main pedagogical motor of the school, in that her classes generated the most interest and therefore the greatest income. In the first three years, for example, she brought in four times more than August Wenzinger, and indeed she remained the best paid teacher at the Schola until the end of the 1950s when she was superseded by Hans-Martin Linde, a sign that her classes were perennially full. Her popularity as a teacher was already a "problem" by 13 January 1935 when Walter Nef wrote to Paul Sacher, asking his opinion about whether Ina Lohr could be a recorder teacher in her own right at the SCB, instead of merely appearing in parentheses after August Wenzinger's name as a substitute when he was unable to be there:

> We have already received requests several times from people explicitly interested in enrolling in recorder lessons with Miss Lohr. When they heard that Miss Lohr serves as a substitute for Wenzinger for us, they usually found some threadbare argument not to enroll, and instead signed up with Miss Lohr for private lessons.[103]

sen noch nicht leisten können, so exclusiv [sic] zu sein; leider!" Letter Max Meili to Paul Sacher of 21 November 1933, PSF-PSC.

103 "Wir erhielten schon mehrmals Anfragen von Interessenten, die sich ausdrücklich bei Frl. Lohr für Blockflötenunterricht anmelden wollten und dann, als sie hörten, dass Frl. Lohr nur als Vertreterin Wenzingers bei uns tätig ist, gewöhnlich mit irgend einer fadenschein-

She, of course, saw this as a welcome contribution to her living costs and was unwilling to forego it. An obvious solution was to allow her to teach these people through the school. This brought problems with it, in that on the one hand, rightly or wrongly, "certain teachers had misgivings about Ina Lohr's recorder playing (particularly Geering)", and, on the other, it might create a situation where even more students would prefer her teaching to that of August Wenzinger.[104] Paul Sacher decided that she be allowed to teach recorder to those explicitly wanting her as a teacher, on the condition that all of her private group classes (ideally each with five students) be taught through the Schola.[105] And indeed she went from one guaranteed lesson per week on 3 January 1934 to twelve on 15 September 1936, being one of the few teachers who brought in a profit.[106]

At the beginning she still took part in the concerts stemming from the joint work of the staff:

> Already from 1934 we gave concerts in suitable locations, even in the cloister of the Munster. It was at that time directed by August Wenzinger, who before the first concert contended that one could not play recorder in tails, nor the women in an evening gown. All were in agreement. We therefore played in our Sunday best and felt comfortable with it. [See Ill. 4.8] But we had success! and that changed this pleasant situation. Already in the following year we were invited to Zurich for a real concert in a beautiful old guild-house. But then concert tenue was prescribed. And we were not allowed to introduce the various works with explanations. It was simply supposed to be a festive concert. For me everything changed on that evening in relation to our music-making in public. The execution was suddenly primary, and I had no interest in performing as a soloist.[107]

igen Ausrede sich nicht eingeschrieben haben, sondern sich später bei Frl. Lohr als Privatschüler anmeldeten". Letter Walter Nef to Paul Sacher of 13 January 1935, PSF-PSC.

104   "Die Lösung der Angelegenheit ist nicht ganz einfach, da einerseits gegen das Blockflötenspiel des Frl. Lohr von Seiten gewisser Lehrer (vor allem Geering), ob mit Recht oder Unrecht, kann ich nicht entscheiden, Bedenken bestehen und wir anderseits verhindern müssen, dass alle Blockflötler mit der Zeit zu Frl. Lohr gehen und Wenzinger weniger Stunden hat". Ibid.

105   Letter Paul Sacher to Walter Nef of 15 January 1935. University Library Basel, NL 212 (Estate Karl Nef).

106   Letters Paul Sacher to Ina Lohr of 3 January 1934 and 15 September 1936, Archive of the Schola Cantorum Basiliensis. Minutes of the board meeting of 15 May 1937, PSF-PSC.

107   "Aber schon seit 1934 gaben wir auch Konzerte in passenden Räumen, sogar im Kreuzgang vom Münster. Die Leitung hatte dann August Wenzinger, der vor dem ersten Konzert die These vorlegte, man könne nicht im Frack Blockflöte spielen, die Damen auch nicht im Abendrock. Einverstanden waren alle. Wir spielten also im Sonntagsgewand und fühlten uns wohl dabei. Wir hatten aber Erfolg und das änderte diese angenehme Situation. Schon [nach] einem Jahr wurden wir für ein richtiges Konzert nach Zurich eingeladen in ein

Ill. 4.8: August Wenzinger, Ina Lohr, and Valerie Kägi. Photo: R. Jeck, Basel.

She went on further to say that she also

> soon noticed that one has to give unstintingly of oneself both in making music in a
> concert and in teaching, if one is to do justice to it. It is a responsibility to communi-
> cate that which one has discovered oneself and considers to be full of wonder to others.
> And the effort that this requires is naturally very great and can lead to exhaustion and
> perhaps to flagging strength. I could not afford that and so already after two years I said
> that I would no longer participate in the concert group. It was more important to me
> that I work with children and with adults, also with whole groups, in courses, Saturday
> and Sunday workshops, *Hausmusik* and church music, to bring it all closer to the peo-
> ple, and to get them to take part in the singing and playing. For that we put in a lot of
> time and effort. And then I left the concert group completely to the real instrumental-
> ists, which was also certainly better.[108]

wunderschönes altes Zunfthaus. Da wurde dann aber Konzerttenue vorgeschrieben. Auch
durften [wir] nicht wie bisher die verschiedenen Werke mit einigen Erklärungen einleiten.
Es sollte einfach ein festliches Konzert sein. Für mich änderte sich an dem Abend alles im
Bezug auf unser Musizieren in der Öffentlichkeit. Die Leistung stand plötzlich im Vor-
dergrund und mir fehlte die Freude am solistischen Auftreten". Cassette "Die Entstehung
der Schola Cantorum Basiliensis", PSF-ILC, CD-4.

108 "Aber da habe ich schon bald gemerkt, dass man sich sowohl beim Musizieren im Konzert
wie im Unterricht enorm ausgeben muss, um seiner Sache gerecht zu werden. Es ist eine
Verantwortung, das, was man selber entdeckt und wundervoll findet, anderen weiter zu
geben. Und diese Anstrengung, die es dafür braucht, ist natürlich sehr gross und kann

We see, thus, that already within the first two years a certain polarization had taken place, a division that went through the school, and that was to continue until Ina Lohr retired. Further evidence of this is found in a letter Max Meili wrote to Paul Sacher on 29 April 1936 in which he complains that

> the influence that our dear friend Lohr exercises over the programming is somewhat too powerful. She may have a wide knowledge of the literature and many enthusiastic recorder and Gregorian chant students at the Schola, she may also be very musical and be able to sight read the wildest and most distant clefs, but she is nonetheless not an artistic person.[109]

In this letter a sense of unease over the direction the Schola was taking is expressed; whereas Ina Lohr was primarily concerned with music's role in building a community, stemming largely from her religious background, but also in part from the philosophical ideals lying behind the Muziek-Lyceum's program, the concert group under the direction of August Wenzinger was interested in the professionalization of Early Music. On a documentary level, the depth of the gulf between them is perhaps best reflected by the fact that the Schola concert programs were archived according to which group was involved rather than chronologically for the entire school and, even more significantly, that the music in the original library was catalogued in accordance to which of the two used it.

From the very beginning there were four subjects that Ina Lohr taught regularly: Gregorian chant, recorder, ensemble, and thorough bass. The foundation for the Gregorian chant classes had already been laid by the controversial course she had taught in 1932 in connection with the Basel Chamber Choir. Evidence of her approach to the subject in her instruction may not only be drawn from *Solmisation und Kirchentonarten*, but also from a notebook copied out by

---

dazu führen, dass man ermüdet, erlahmt vielleicht. Das konnte ich mir nicht leisten und so habe ich schon nach zwei Jahren mitgeteilt, ich würde in der Konzertgruppe nicht weiter mitmachen. Mir sei mehr daran gelegen mit Kindern und mit Erwachsenen, auch mit ganzen Gruppen, in Kursen, Samstag-, Sonntagkursen, Hausmusik, Kirchenmusik, alles das den Leuten näher zu bringen, und zu machen, dass sie mitsingen und mitspielen. Da drauf haben wir sehr viel Zeit und Kraft verwendet. Und ich hab' dann eben die Konzertgruppe ganz und gar den wirklichen Instrumentalisten überlassen, das auch sicher besser war". Ibid.

109 "Und dann ist mir persönlich der Einfluss, den unsere liebe Freundin Lohr auf die Programmgestaltung ausübt, etwas zu mächtig. Sie mag ja eine grosse Literaturkenntnis und viele Blockflöten- u. Gregorianik-Begeisterte als Schüler an der Schola haben, sie mag auch ganz musikalisch sein und die wildesten u. fremdsten Schlüssel vom Blatt lesen können, aber sie ist trotz alldem kein künstlerischer Mensch". Letter Max Meili to Paul Sacher of 29 April 1936, PSF-PSC.

hand by a former Schola student, Margrit Fiechter, from material Ina Lohr had assembled expressly for that purpose.[110] The latter included a table of neumes, with suggestions of how they should be transcribed; basic information about the form of the mass, and of its individuals parts; a discussion of Marian antiphons; a list of chant melodies that could later be found in various Reformation hymns; a discussion of individual forms, such as tropes, hymns, sequences, responses; a section on medieval Easter plays; and a discussion of the forms found in Gregorian chant with commentaries to specific pieces. Although it is from a much later time, it gives an idea of the dimensions of Ina Lohr's thinking in regard to her chant course. This was supplemented by the modal analysis proffered in her book.

We have already seen above that she was sufficiently sought after as a recorder teacher that potential students were choosing to study with her privately, rather than with August Wenzinger. In 1935, Ina Lohr was considering offering autumn courses in September, as she was anyway going to be making up some lessons she had missed in spring. In this context, Walter Nef expressed some concern to Paul Sacher that it might make it even more difficult to encourage people to sign up with August Wenzinger, saying that "he also knew that W. was rather sensitive in this regard, even if he does not show it", but that

> she has a great ease in interacting with the students. Wenzinger is often absent, which is not exactly advantageous for regular instruction, and on the other hand, some students are a bit shy of the virtuoso that he is, and believe that he is not really interested in teaching (which is not the case at all).[111]

It was then decided that on this occasion she should offer recorder classes for children, so that she would not be perceived as creating competition with August Wenzinger. Through such recorder classes, the number of her students continually increased, as culturally conscious bourgeois families began sending their children to the Schola for recorder lessons, for *Hausmusik*. In this manner, a large portion of her work at the school came to be invested in *Hausmusik*.

---

110 I am grateful to Margrit Fiechter of Basel, who studied at the Schola from 1962–66 and later taught recorder there, for the loan of this notebook, as it gave practical insight into Ina Lohr's instruction.

111 "und ich weiss auch, dass W. in dieser Hinsicht ziemlich empfindlich ist, wenn er es auch nicht so zeigt […] aber Du weisst ja, dass sie eine grosse Leichtigkeit hat, mit den Schülern zu verkehren. Wenzinger ist häufig abwesend, was natürlich einem regelmässigen Unterricht nicht gerade förderlich ist, andererseits haben manche Schüler eine gewisse Scheu vor dem Virtuosen, der er ist, und glauben, der Unterricht interessiere ihn nicht recht (was ganz nicht der Fall ist)". Letter Walter Nef to Paul Sacher of 7 July 1935, PSF-PSC.

During the 1930s and 1940s she was perhaps on the forefront with this approach to Early Music, as she was using the latest editions from Bärenreiter and Kallmeyer and applying her theoretical knowledge of solmization and modes, of diminution, etc. to them. As with the German *Jugendmusikbewegung* and *Singbewegung*, however, the emphasis lay on the group participation, the collective experience of the music rather than on the music itself.

In all of these early Schola reports there is seemingly a general lack of consciousness of the recorder as an instrument. Because of its apparent simplicity, there was no sense of the necessity of having to invest work in it. In this, Ina Lohr was no different than the rest of her generation; all with whom I have spoken are in agreement about her modest abilities on the instrument.[112] Maria Sumpf-Refardt, who received the first diploma for recorder from the Schola Cantorum in 1943, remembered that within only a matter of weeks she could play better than Ina Lohr, who was uninterested in improving her own technical dexterity. What she did possess was a knowledge of the music and how it should sound.[113] This is confirmed by Christopher Schmidt's recollection that she never demonstrated anything on the instrument for her recorder students, but always sang the passages.[114] As a result, however, he learned how to play in a cantabile manner on an instrument, learned the innate connection between a melody and the voice.

These recorder ensembles led to the inscription in 1936 of the first internal, professional student for a course of instruction leading to a degree as leader of *Hausmusik* groups ("Leiter von Sing- und Spielkreisen und Lehrer für Hausmusik"). This in turn led to the creation of recorder and gamba courses for the "people" [Volk], which were then used as practica for ongoing teachers, supervised usually by Ina Lohr.[115] Between 1933 and 1957, the last year such a degree was awarded, ten were for *Hausmusik*, two for recorder (Ina Lohr), two for gamba (August Wenzinger), and five for organ (Eduard Müller (1912–1983) who began teaching at the Schola in 1939).

---

112 See Chapter 1, p. 55, where she speaks of playing her first concert on the recorder after only having played it three weeks.

113 Interview with Marie Sumpf-Refardt, 2 October 2013.

114 The information concerning recorder instruction and *Hausmusik* at the Schola Cantorum Basiliensis stems largely from conversations with Christopher Schmidt, 18 and 21 January 2016.

115 This supervision only began receiving remuneration at a later date, its introduction being communicated in a letter of Paul Sacher to Ina Lohr of 18 March 1942, Archive of the Schola Cantorum Basiliensis.

She also taught the theoretical aspect of thorough bass, a rather surprising fact, as she was not noted for her keyboard playing. Her knowledge in this field no doubt stemmed from her work with Anthon van der Horst, with his background as an organist and his interest in early music. From another hand-copied study notebook of Margrit Fiechter, we can see what the course entailed. The book had eight sections:

1. A general introduction, including remarks on the advantages of improvised performance and a discussion of the meaning of the figures;
2. Voice-leading;
3. Cadences and connections to functional harmony, complete with Jean-Philippe Rameau's subdominant;
4. Sixth chords;
5. The subdominant as a sixth chord;
6. Six-four chords;
7. Seventh chords;
8. Chords with ninths and seconds.

Each section was complete with exercises and appropriate quotations from historical sources, such as the treatises by Lodovico Grossi da Viadana, Michael Praetorius, Christoph Bernhard, Heinrich Albert, Johann Sebastian Bach, Johann Mattheson, and Georg Philipp Telemann. It is, in sum, a complete introductory course in thorough bass. Indeed, Christopher Schmidt recalls that the harpsichordist Gustav Leonhardt felt that he gained far more from Ina Lohr's courses on thorough bass than from the instruction of his organ teacher Eduard Müller, as she gave him an historically differentiated basis that the latter could not provide.[116] It is extraordinarily different in approach from that of her realization of Charpentier's *Le Reniement de Saint Pierre* (see pp. 129–32), where she allowed her compositional fantasy to reign.

Other Courses and Workshops
As we can see from the table in Appendix 2, workshops for "Alte Haus- und Kirchenmusik" (Early House and Church Music) were already held in the first year with the hope of providing a low-threshold enticement to potential students who were curious, but not willing to commit themselves to a semester-long course. In each of the first two years, Ina Lohr gave two courses together with August Wenzinger, who in that second year also established a separate summer

116   Interview with Christopher Schmidt of 8 January 2014.

course of his own in Rigi-Klösterli. Thereafter Ina Lohr was joined by Walter
Nef for these courses, of which there were four to seven a year, attracting from
16–60 participants. In 1935 she also initiated the first fall courses in September,
a month's instruction before the regular semester began in October. These, too,
were very successful. In the summer of 1936 they had hoped to hold a course
for professionals, but unfortunately the registration was insufficient to carry it
out. It took until the summer 1939 for August Wenzinger's name to have sufficient pull that he was able to fill his summer course with professional musicians.

In addition, she gave courses at the Vincentianum, a local orphanage and,
as mentioned above in relation to her work for the BKO, took over a choir
in Kleinbasel, the working-class area of Basel, as well as building up the recorder classes for the people. And finally, in an effort to reach out to schools, to
awaken their interest in early music, she gave a highly successful, month-long
course of "Early Music for Schools" in the fall of 1938, which formed the beginning of a long-term fruitful interaction with elementary school teachers.

It becomes very obvious when one looks at this evidence that Ina Lohr was
the motor behind the pedagogical activities of the Schola, that the institution
would have failed without her contribution. At the same time, without the concert activities of August Wenzinger and the "Konzertgruppe", the school would
have not received the international recognition that was also necessary to ensure its existence. In this sense, Paul Sacher's innate ability to select people appropriate for specific tasks paid out: with Ina Lohr, he had the moving force
necessary to bring the Schola into the public eye in Basel, with August Wenzinger, the professional musician, driven by the desire to take his place on the
world stage, and with Walter Nef, the softer, mediating individual necessary to
keep the poles from drifting too far apart.

It is no surprise, however, given her investment both emotionally and time-
wise in both the BKO and the SCB, that she was in a state of utter exhaustion
by the time the summer of 1939 rolled around. Together with the threat of war
looming over Europe and her generally weak constitution, she no longer had
the physical and mental resources to draw upon to continue in this manner,
something had to change.

Interregnum: Prelude to War

Ina Lohr, "Ich sah die Unrast der Welt" (Gertrud von Le Fort, *Von den letzten Dingen*).
Reproduction: PSF-ILC.

Ich sah die Unrast der Welt in einer Wolke dahin fahren:
Die Stille des Abends war wie Sturm in ihrem Segeln, sie floh vor dem Untergang der Sonne
   wie in grossen Ängsten.
Denn wohin soll sie sich wenden, wenn der mächtige Schlaf kommt, und wo soll sie Obdach
   suchen, wenn er sie aus ihrem Zelt treibt?
Es ist um sonst, dass sie die Menschen peinigt und die Gier ihrer Leidenschaft wider ihn anjagt.
Er brauet ihnen dennoch den Trank, davon sie stumm werden!
Die Städte brausen wohl noch eine Weile, aber das grosse Schweigen sickert schon durch ihre
   Mauern.
Der Purpur ihrer Schmerzen verdunkelt, und der Purpur ihrer Lüste wird grau wie die Däm-
   merung.
Ihre stolzen Geister werden grau wie Vergessen. Alles Wollen wird zu Nebel, und alles Wirken
   wird zu Träume eines Traums.
Die Könige müssen schlafen, und die Gewaltigen müssen sich hinlegen wie kleine Kinder:
Alle sinken an die Brust der Notdurft, da wird ihre Hoffart wie der schlichte Sand.
Da werden sie alle wie einst in ihren Gräbern.
Herr, erbarme dich der armen Seelen!

I saw the restlessness of the world moving by in a cloud:
The silence of the evening was like a storm in its sails. It fled from the setting of the sun as if
   in great fear.
For where should it turn, when overpowered by sleep and where should it seek shelter when
   driven out of its vault?
It is in vain that it punishes mankind and sets the greed of its passion upon it.
It brews them the potion, by which they turn deaf!
The cities will yet still rage for awhile, but the great silence already seeps through their walls.
The purple of its pain grows dark, and the purple of its lusts turns gray like the dusk.
Its proud ghosts turn gray like forgetfulness. All will turns to fog, and all effect to dreams of
   a dream.
The kings must sleep, and the powerful must lie down like small children:
All sink to the breast of necessity, there their arrogance is like the simple sand.
There they all become as they will once be in their graves.
Lord, have mercy upon the poor souls!

Chapter 5. The War Years

With World War II, the foundations of society throughout the world were torn asunder by a battle of heretofore unparalleled dimensions. Everything was called into question, something no less true for Ina Lohr than anyone else: the horror of the external battles exacerbated her own internal struggles and conflicts. Given her extreme sensitivity to the emotions of those around her, it is not surprising that, as we saw in Chapter 2, she sought solace through her faith. This in turn entailed an entire redefinition of her work with Paul Sacher, as well as an increased concentration of her focus on religious music. In the course of this process, she made choices which – although they led her further away from mainstream concert music – enabled her to better embody her ideals, both on musical and socio-religious levels.

In this chapter, the story of the SCB will first be continued, building upon its pre-war origins, thereby revealing how the war not only demanded creativity and sacrifices from all involved to keep the institution alive, but also gave her work an impact it might otherwise not have received. The structure for her life during this time period, as well as her interactions with the outside world, will thereby become evident. Only then will we turn to her internal battles – physical, psychological and spritual – as documented by her correspondence with Paul Sacher. In her perception, these battles were existential, becoming on some level commensurate to the one going on in the world outside her. They, therefore, will receive particular attention, giving as they do, a window on her ardent convictions, her emotional upheavals, which came to determine the rest of her life.

5.1 The Schola Cantorum Basiliensis: 1939 to 1941

Although it had originally been feared by all concerned that the war would have a negative effect on the Schola by making regular instruction impossible and decreasing the number of students, this anxiety turned out to be unwarranted.[1] The beginning of the school year, to be sure, fell together with the first general mobilization of the Swiss militia army on 1 September 1939, but the number of students dropped only momentarily in that first semester of the war,

---

[1]   Unless otherwise indicated the information about the curriculum and concerns of the SCB is taken from the respective annual reports, Archive of the Schola Cantorum Basiliensis.

and thereafter continued to increase gradually. In view of the circumstances, the students in that year were gracious in their acceptance of lesson cancellations or substitutes for the teachers that were called up, among them August Wenzinger, who was almost continuously on duty, and Arnold Geering, who was called up for occasional reserve service. This mobilization, however, had grave consequences for the concert activities of the institution: in that first academic year during the war, all concerts were canceled, either due to the lack of availability of the artists in question, or the reluctance of the organizers to schedule events that they were not sure could take place. In addition, the absence of the male faculty members also affected the distribution of influence within the faculty of the SCB, in that those courses which could be maintained with regularity throughout the war gained greater ascendancy. Thus, Ina Lohr's own specific interests came to have an increased importance in the structural development of the SCB during this period.

On the surface, however, everything at the Schola just took its natural course, with the third diploma in the leading of "Hausmusik" groups being awarded, complete with a definition in the annual report of what this degree entailed:

> As opposed to a vocal or instrumental diploma, this program demands versatility. The student must show that he is capable of finding appropriate material for a group of singers and players and rehearse it accordingly. That necessitates that he know the basics of singing and the playing of various instruments and, in addition, possess extensive knowledge of theoretical and historical disciplines. The demands are different than that of a vocal or instrumental training, but hardly smaller. The more pedagogically and less virtuosically inclined student will turn gladly to this training possibility, which is designed to give any budding musician and, in particular, any music teacher a good and broad general basis.[2]

On the basis of their experience with the first three candidates for this degree, the SCB decided to raise the standards of the diploma by requiring future can-

---

2   "Im Unterschied zu einem Gesangs- oder Instrumentaldiplom verlangt diese Ausbildung Vielseitigkeit. Der Schüler muss sich ausweisen, dass er fähig ist, für eine Gruppe von Singenden und Spielenden den geeigneten Stoff auszusuchen und ihn sinngemäss einzustudieren. Das bedingt, dass er die Grundlagen im Singen und im Spiel auf verschiedenen Instrumenten und dazu ausgedehnte Kenntnisse in den theoretischen und historischen Disziplinen besitzt. Die Anforderungen sind anders als bei einer Gesangs- oder Instrumentalausbildung, aber kaum geringer. Der mehr pädagogisch und weniger virtuos begabte Schüler wird gern zu dieser Ausbildungsmöglichkeit greifen, die geeignet ist, jedem angehenden Musiker und vor allem Musiklehrer eine gute und vielseitige allgemeine Grundlage zu geben". *Bericht über das siebente Schuljahr der Schola Cantorum Basiliensis*, 1 September 1939 – 31 August 1940, 2. Archive of the Schola Cantorum Basiliensis.

didates to take an internal exam on their instrument after the first year (waived for conservatory graduates), before joining the main course. This is of significance on two levels: first of all, it demonstrates an awareness that the inadequate standard of musicianship in those attaining these degrees could harm the reputation of the SCB; and secondly, it established a stronger foundation for Ina Lohr's work in this field, something which will be of consequence for her work in the Netherlands after the war.

All of the normal courses were taught during the first year of the war, with Ina Lohr expanding her instruction in Protestant hymns to include those of the 17th and 18th centuries. Together with Walter Nef, she also taught a workshop on "Old Christmas music" and her students not only participated in four normal student recitals, but also a vespers service, and four concerts for soldiers in Lucerne.

Of greater consequence for her future, was her creation of a new musical entity – primarily made up of former and current Schola students and her church choir – the *Ensemble für Kirchenmusik* (Ensemble for Church Music), which then became her vehicle for the performance of the sacred repertory in accordance with her convictions over the next 25–30 years. Its inauguration took the form of two radio recordings, thereby giving her a far wider platform than heretofore. In her interview with Jos Leussink she speaks of how the second one, of 18 February 1940, *Aus ernsten Zeiten*, came about. She recalled that the composer Conrad Beck had been appointed head of the music department at the radio in Basel in 1939. As part of the ritual of acceptance, it was necessary for him to put together a radio program exemplifying his ideas for the medium. Ina Lohr told the story as follows:

> He had already asked a local poet to gather together 17th-century poems from the time of the Thirty Years War. [...] First he asked Sacher if he had any music that could accompany them, then Sacher said, "You can't accompany them with any suites by Rosenmüller, it's impossible. You'd better ask Ina Lohr". And that was just the thing for me, of course, because I had my choir, I had an excellent recorder ensemble. They could accompany beautifully when the melody was in the tenor, and then a bass recorder underneath and two recorders above [...] That was called *Aus ernsten Zeiten*, and we were on the brink of war [...] And I had one of the best actors here as the reader, [together with,] alas, an overly-emotional female voice [...] That was a very great success and that gave me suddenly a chance with the radio, for which I am very grateful.[3]

---

3   "toen had hij al een dichter hier de opdracht gegeven om gedichten bij elkaar te zoeken uit de 17e eeuw, uit de tijd van de Dertigjarige Oorlog. Eerst vroeg hij Sacher, of hij daar muziek bij had; toen zij Sacher, 'daar kun je geen suites van Rosenmüller bij spelen, dat is onmogelijk. Dan moet je Ina Lohr vragen'. En dat was voor mij een kolfje naar mijn hand natuurlijk, want ik had mijn koor, ik had een uitstekend blokfluitensemble. Die konden

From this time on, her *Ensemble für Kirchenmusik* performed regularly for the radio, thus extending her reputation beyond the city limits of Basel.

By the time the 1940/41 school year began, the SCB had gained experience in improvising in accordance with the demands placed on them by circumstances. As in the previous year, three of the male teachers, August Wenzinger, Arnold Geering and Walter Nef, were not always available, and one made do by making up lessons later or finding a substitute for the occasion. In addition, the lutenist Fritz Wörsching was unable to teach for a while, as he did not have the correct work permit. Another difficulty arose from the rationed heating, necessitating a re-organization of the teaching schedule, so that instruction only took place on five days of the week, Tuesday through Saturday. Further, the Christmas holidays were extended by a week and a two-week "heating vacation" in February was introduced to further save on fuel. Additional reductions were attained by creating a heating plan, so that the minimal number of rooms was in use at any time. The students, understanding the reasons behind these changes, graciously accepted these conditions, in particular as many of the teachers made up some of the canceled lessons by teaching at home. One can imagine that these hours devoted to something so other-wordly were particularly treasured by the pupils in this time of deprivation and hardship. Although the details were modified over the course of time to better meet the needs of the school, this plan remained in effect throughout the war. In spite of all these difficulties, demand continued to increase, so that over a hundred students were enrolled in the summer semester of 1941. Of these, only three were participating in degree programs.

Ina Lohr was once again very active during this school year, teaching four autumn courses and two well-attended weekend workshops in Basel, as well as one in Zurich, and her students took part in four student recitals and twice played live examples in adult education classes taught by Walter Nef. In the winter semester 1940/41 she taught a new course, "Introduction to the Music Theory of the 17th and 18th centuries: Counterpoint Exercises in accordance with examples found in Schütz/Bernhard and Fux". Her *Ensemble für Kirchenmusik* made two radio broadcasts, on 6 November and 8 December [see Ill. 5.1],

prachtig begeleiden als de stem in de tenor lag, en dan een basblokfluit eronder en twee blokfluiten erboven [...] Dat heette *Aus ernsten Zeiten*, en wij stonden voor de oorlog [...] [E]en van de beste toneelspelers hier had ik als de man die het las; helaas een pathetische vrouwenstem [...] Dat is een heel groot succes geworden en dat gaf me opeens een kans in de radio, waar ik heel dankbaar voor ben". Interview with Jos Leussink of 24–25 March 1983.

Ill. 5.1: Ensemble at radio recording, with Anita Stange, student of Ina Lohr, on the left and Ernst Denger and Ina Lohr singing. Photo: courtesy of Arthur Eglin, Basel.

as well as performing together with August Wenzinger's gamba consort in a Schola benefit concert for refugees on 30 March 1941, organized by the Protestant church.

The most significant addition to the Schola's program, however, came from another direction, one for which it seems likely that Ina Lohr provided the initial impulse. Walter Nef described the path leading to the "Introductory Courses in Protestant Church Music" (*Einführungskurse in die evangelische Kirchenmusik*) in the following manner:

> We had long regretted that the SCB had, for all practical purposes, no contact with the church and church circles. In order to initiate contact, and primarily in order to give budding theologians – the students of the theology department – the possibility of taking courses in Protestant church music, designed to match their needs, parallel to their university studies, we presented several proposals for cooperation to the dean of the theology department of the University of Basel, Professor Dr. Ernst Staehelin, in the late fall of 1940. They met with a very warm reception, and in a meeting at which, in addition to the dean, various representatives of the theology department, as well as the director and assistant director of the SCB [Paul Sacher and Walter Nef himself] took part, it was decided to announce, as a first trial run, a five-hour course on the subject of "Old Church Hymns and their Melodies" (led by Ina Lohr). Through the intercession of Professor Staehelin, the board of the Protestant Church of the City of Basel became a joint-sponsor together with the theology department of the University of Basel.

Thus, the course was not restricted solely to the students of the theology department, but was also open to theologians, church musicians and music lovers. It took place in May and June 1941 at the SCB with 50 participants, most of whom came into contact with our work for the first time. Although the large number of participants was gratifying, it must, however, be taken into consideration that the subject had been imbued with a particular attraction, as shortly before the beginning of the course the trial volume of the new church hymnal [*Probeband*] had appeared.[4]

Walter Nef was correct in his assessment that the effect of the introduction of the *Probeband* could not be underestimated in relation to the enrollment. In addition, one would have to add that the effect of both the movement leading to the introduction of the *Probeband* and the inception of these courses at the SCB at this moment of time had indelible consequences for the further development of the institution.

The Introduction of the *Probeband*

The *Probeband* came about through the decision of the Swiss Protestant Church in 1928 to produce a single hymnal for use throughout the German-speaking cantons. According to Andreas Marti, it oriented itself

consistently on the strict linguistic, theological and musical criteria of the German reform movement of the 1920s and 1930s. In addition to the pronounced historical emphasis, however, contact with contemporary poetry and music of the "1st Modern" [era]

---

4   "Schon lange bedauerten wir, dass die S.C.B. mit der Kirche und den kirchlichen Kreisen so gut wie keine Verbindung hatte. Um den Kontakt zu suchen und vor allem für die werdenden Theologen, die Studierenden der theologischen Fakultät, die Möglichkeit zu schaffen, parallel mit dem Universitätsstudium Kurse in evangelischer Kirchenmusik besuchen zu können, die auf ihre Bedürfnisse zugeschnitten wären, unterbreiteten wir dem Herrn Dekan der theologischen Fakultät der Universität Basel, Herrn Prof. Dr. Ernst Staehelin, im Spätherbst 1940 einige Vorschläge zur Zusammenarbeit. Sie erhielten eine sehr freundliche Aufnahme, und in einer Sitzung, an der neben dem Herrn Dekan verschiedene Vertreter der theologischen Fakultät sowie Direktor und Assistent der S.C.B. teilnahmen, wurde beschlossen, als ersten Versuch im Sommersemester 1941 einen fünfstündigen Kurs mit dem Thema 'Alte Kirchenlieder und ihre Melodien' (Leitung Ina Lohr) anzukündigen. Auf Vermittlung von Herrn Professor Staehelin trat als Veranstalter zur theologischen Fakultät der Universität Basel auch der Kirchenrat der evangelisch-reformierten Kirche Basel-Stadt. Der Kurs blieb deshalb nicht nur den Studenten der theologischen Fakultät vorbehalten, sondern stand auch Theologen, Kirchenmusikern und Musikfreunden offen. Er konnte im Mai und Juni 1941 in der S.C.B. mit 50 Teilnehmern geführt werden, von denen die meisten zum erstenmal mit unserer Arbeit in Berührung kamen. Wie erfreulich die hohe Teilnehmerzahl auch war, so muss dabei berücksichtigt werden, dass das Thema eine besondere Anziehung erhalten hatte, weil kurz vor Kursbeginn der Probeband zum neuen Kirchengesangsbuch erschienen war". *Bericht über das achte Jahr der Schola Cantorum Basiliensis*, 6. Archive of the Schola Cantorum Basiliensis.

was a desideratum. In place of the continuous four-part scoring of the previous hymnals, several of the (psalm) melodies were once again printed without accompaniment.[5]

There is little information about how Ina Lohr came to be involved in the propagation of the *Probeband*, beyond her obvious identification with the ideas that lay behind it. There is, however, one clear point of interaction: Walter Tappolet (1897–1991). He came into contact with the *Singbewegung* after World War I, seeing in it a source of bringing meaning to life through the serious cultivation of all the arts, with the intent of shaping the whole person. In the thirties he became one of the first Swiss brothers of the *Michaelisbruderschaft*, an organization which emerged from the Berneuchen Movement, in which certain aspects of the *Singbewegung* were cultivated in the attempt to bring about renewal within the German Protestant Church. Of central importance to him was the religious "folk song".[6] It was a consequence of these activities that he was chosen as one of the two representatives of the *Singbewegung* within the commission responsible for the *Probeband*.[7] In 1935, he was already writing articles in which he expressed very similar opinions to those of Ina Lohr concerning the renewal of music in the church through a return to older Reformation songs as well as a rethinking of its role in the services. Among the factors he discussed were the need of a faster tempo in singing the hymns, the development of the singing congregation, and its liberation from the dominance of the organ. In addition, he even spoke of the necessity of returning to the original rhythmization and modal form of the melodies as a means of communicating their inner force.[8] Thus in Walter Tappolet, Ina Lohr clearly found someone who shared her visions in regard to the place of music within the Protestant

---

5   "Der Probeband (Pb), 1941 publiziert, […] orientierte sich konsequent an den gestrengen sprachlichen, theologischen und musikalischen Kriterien der deutschen Reformbewegung der 1920er- und 1930er-Jahre. Neben der betont historischen Ausrichtung wurde jedoch auch der Kontakt mit der zeitgenössischen Dichtung und der Musik der '1. Moderne' gesucht. Anstelle der durchgehenden Vierstimmigkeit der Vorgängergesangbücher sind einige (Psalm-)Lieder wieder einstimmig abgedruckt". Andreas Marti, "Gesangbücher in der reformierten Deutschschweiz: Ein Überblick mit Auswahlbibliographie", in: *Ökumenischer Liederkommentar zum Katholischen, Reformierten und Christkatholischen Gesangbuch der Schweiz*, ed. by Peter Ernst Bernoulli, Freiburg: Paulus Verlag and Zurich: Theologischer Verlag 2001–2009, 6th part, unpaginated.

6   Information about Walter Tappolet is taken from Max Schoch, "Dem Echten verpflichtet", in: *Quatember* 1987, 234–35.

7   Hanspeter Zürcher, "Die Probeband-Text-Kommission rein menschlich gesehen", in: *Reformierte Schweiz* 1, Heft 2 (February, 1944), 25.

8   See Walter Tappolet, "Über das Probeheft zum neuen schweizerischen Kirchengesangbuch", in: *Volkslied und Hausmusik* 2 (1935), 55–59 and 69–71.

church. Whereas there is no evidence that he was a source of her own ideas –
she seems to have had so many of them even before she came to Basel – it seems
obvious that within the Swiss *Singbewegung*, of whose journal Walter Tappolet
was the editor, she found a circle of like-minded individuals eager to create a
new sense of commonality in the congregation through song. The fact that she
was actively involved in the compilation of the *Probeband* can be deduced from
the following passage in the letter to Paul Sacher of 5 October 1939:

> Tappolet sent me back my songs for the new church hymnal with the request that I
> write 4-part accompaniments to them, as the commission still does not want any pure
> melodies. I wrote the accompaniments in my deck chair and played them through to-
> day on the piano; to my horror, they sound suspiciously like Reger![9]

Unfortunately, it is not possible to determine which songs were hers, as the
musical material for the publication has not been yet subject of an investigation.
We do have evidence, however, that she was very active in its propagation, not
only by writing numerous articles for *Volkslied und Hausmusik*, *Singt und spielt*
and *Gottesdienst und Musik*, but also by going to the source and teaching those
that would be responsible for its utilization within the church: the theology students, ministers, organists and interested lay people. She began with the course
on "Old Church Hymns and their Melodies", jointly sponsored by the SCB, the
theology department of the University of Basel and Protestant Church in Basel.

The Schola Cantorum Basiliensis: 1941 to 1944

In the school year of 1941/42, the Schola continued having the mobilized male
teachers make up their lessons whenever they got the chance and cutting back
on heating due to lack of fuel. Nevertheless, the student numbers continued
to grow, particularly in the winter semester of 1941, when a group of rhyth-
mics and gymnastics teachers from the Zurich Conservatory attended some of
the courses, most likely those of Ina Lohr. It is also noteworthy that at the end
of the first semester, the institution's first instrumental diploma, for the organ,
was awarded.

Ina Lohr taught all of her regular courses, one autumn course, and two
workshops in Basel, as well as one at the Conservatory of Berne. She gave a
lecture in Zurich in October of 1941, as well as a three-part introduction to

---

9   "Tappolet hat mir meine Lieder für das neue Kirchengesangbuch zurückgeschickt mit der
    Bitte 4 stimmige Begleitungen dazu zu schreiben, da die Kommision [sic] immer noch
    keine reine Einstimmigkeit will. Ich machte die Begleitungen auf dem Liegestuhl und
    spielte sie heute am Klavier durch; zu meinem Entsetzen klingts [sic] verdächtig nach
    Reger!" Letter Ina Lohr to Paul Sacher of 5 October 1939, private collection, Switzerland.

the *Probeband* in Riehen, a suburb of Basel, in spring. In addition, she gave five courses on church songs under the sponsorship of the University and the Protestant Church: a continuation of "Early Church Hymns and their Melodies"; "The Songs of the Reformation Period in their Connections to Gregorian Chant and to Secular Song"; "The Liturgical Songs of the Catholic Church and their Influence on Protestant Church Music"; "Rhythm and Tempo in the Protestant Hymn"; and finally, "The Modes in the Church Music of the 16th and 17th Centuries".[10] These courses, again one hour a week over a five-week period, were attended by between 18–45 students, indicating their high degree of popularity and relevance at the time for those encountering the *Probeband*. By bringing together students, pastors, and interested lay people in such numbers, these courses brought increased weight to the study and performance of sacred music at the school.

In addition, her students took part in five recitals, as well as in a bazaar at the Fine Arts Museum of Basel organized by the Red Cross under the auspices of their Children's Aid program. Further, her *Ensemble für Kirchenmusik* performed a Christmas concert on 14 December 1941 in Arlesheim, a town in the environs of Basel, as well as a benefit concert for refugees on 21 May 1942, together with several soloists, in the city itself.

By the summer semester of the 1942/43 school year, in spite of all the constraints, the number of students had increased even further to 134, with 174 inscriptions, that is to say, some individuals were enrolled in more than one course. In addition, the Schola's concert group under August Wenzinger was beginning to gain ground again and was able to give several concerts. Given the situation in the surrounding countries, this is a truly astonishing state of affairs. In addition, due to the lack of teachers, some of those who wished to study recorder had to be turned down. Nonetheless, a landmark was set when a pupil of Ina Lohr, Marie Sumpf-Refardt, became the first Schola student to receive an instrumental degree in recorder.

Complementing her customary instruction in 1942/43, her five student recitals, and her usual participation in a weekend workshop for *Hausmusik* in November, Ina Lohr was once again pursuing her activities for the furtherance of church music through the courses sponsored together with the theol-

---

10 "Alte Kirchenlieder und ihre Melodien", "Die Lieder der Reformationszeit in ihren Beziehungen zum gregorianischen Choral und zum weltlichen Lied", "Liturgische Gesänge der katholischen Kirche und ihr Einfluss auf die evangelische Kirchenmusik", "Rhythmus und Tempo im evangelischen Kirchenlied", "Die Kirchentonarten in den Kirchenliedern des 16. und 17. Jahrhunderts".

ogy department of the University and the Protestant Church of the City of Basel. With the exception of the first course in which the lessons were twice the
usual hourly length, these courses retained the one hour for five weeks format
that had been deemed suitable in the context of the theology students' very full
academic program. Three of the courses were devoted to subjects related to the
Probeband and the first, in September 1942 – "How Shall We Sing from the
Probeband?" ("Wie singen wir aus dem Probeband?") – was particularly successful, drawing no fewer than 56 participants. Also related to the propagation
of this hymnal, were two concerts with children's recorder ensembles of "*Hausmusik* with songs from the *Probeband*" on 21 March 1943 in the City Mission's
Vogesen Chapel and on 1 April 1943 in Binningen, on the outskirts of Basel.

During this period, she was also active with her *Ensemble für Kirchenmusik*,
taking part in a celebration of the Eucharist at a meeting in Rheinfelden, a
town just 15 kilometers up the Rhine from Basel, of the Schweizerischer Pfarr-
vereins (Swiss Association of Pastors) on 28 September 1942 and in an evening
of singing for the congregation of St. Paul's church in Basel on 9 October 1942.
And finally, on 24 June 1943 they participated in a vespers service in St. Alban's
church, Basel.

In the 1943/44 school year, in spite of all of the constraints, the SCB still
managed to not only maintain, but also increase their numbers, and this in
spite of the fact that the teachers were granted a 20% increase in wages due
to inflation. The continual rise in the number of students also caused an increase in student recitals. Ina Lohr's students took part in eight such events, as
well as two radio programs, one for a school broadcast, "We Sing and Play on
Instruments" ("Wir singen und spielen auf Instrumenten") on 19 November
1943 and a special transmission for the ill on 16 December 1943, "What Shall
We Sing at Advent and Christmas?" ("Was singen wir in der Advents- und
Weihnachtszeit?"). And, in addition, her students performed Gregorian chant
and 15th-century polyphony for a tour of the musical instrument collection led
by Walter Nef on 25 June 1944. She also gave three of the six fall courses.

Above and beyond her regular course work, however, her main focus at the
SCB lay with the introductory courses in Protestant hymns and in the *Ensemble
für Kirchenmusik*. The three courses of this nature given by the SCB in this year
endeavored to make a connection between the course content and the actual
musical practice, the intent of the enterprise. The first course, taught by Eduard Müller and Ina Lohr, was made up of three lectures which paved the way
for three musical events in St. Paul's Church: a concert of "Organ Music" by
J.S. Bach (played by Eduard Müller's students), and two liturgical services, on
20 February and 23 April 1944, each presided over by pastors associated with the

Basel Mission, Emanuel Kellerhals and Hans Huppenbauer respectively, with music of Schütz, Schein, Frescobaldi as well as from the Reformation period. In the summer semester, Ina Lohr gave two courses in parallel, "Kunstlied und Gemeindelied" ('Art' Song and Congregational Singing), and the second, "Wie üben wir die Lieder aus der Reformationszeit ein?" (How do We Rehearse the Reformation Songs?), both of which were brought to a close by lectures in the St. Nicholas Chapel. These well-attended courses continued to be supported by the theology department of the University of Basel as well as by the Protestant Church of the City of Basel.

Furthermore, they were very closely connected to her work with her *Ensemble für Kirchenmusik*, which according to the annual report, was "a choir of ca. 15 to 20 voices for the cultivation of church music which developed out of an ensemble class of Ina Lohr while remaining integrated in her regular teaching".[11] Not only did it perform in the above-mentioned lectures in the St. Nicholas Chapel, but earlier in the school year, in September and November of 1943, it also participated in two church services of Pastor Wilhelm Vischer in St. Jacob's Church.

The Cooperation with Wilhelm Vischer

The degree to which Ina Lohr prized this work together with Wilhelm Vischer (1895–1988, see Ill. 5.2) can hardly be underestimated. He had received recognition as a scholar through his work on the Old Testament, as a result of which he was offered a position at the Bethel School of Theology in Germany. He soon drew the antipathy of the supporters of the Nazi's, as he saw the Old Testament as essential to the Christian faith and interpreted it accordingly. The conflict escalated until Wilhelm Vischer called Hitler a "Balkan" in 1933, at which point he was forced to give up his job in Germany. He first went to Lugano for three years before coming to Basel in 1936 as pastor at the St. Jacob's Church, where he remained until he left Basel in 1947 to teach at the University of Montpellier.

In Basel he soon became known for the quality of his sermons, to the degree that additional trams ran on Sunday morning to accommodate all those wishing to attend his services. He also made minor changes in the service – adding a modicum of liturgy and creed – which met with some protest in the congregation. It is reported that one member said "As long as Helmi continues with

---

11 "ein Chor von ca. 15 bis 20 Stimmen zur Pflege der Kirchenmusik, der sich aus einer Ensemble-Klasse von Ina Lohr entwickelt hat, dem regelmässigen Unterricht aber eingegliedert bleibt". *Bericht über das elfte Jahr der Schola Cantorum Basiliensis*, 6. Archive of the Schola Cantorum Basiliensis.

Ill. 5.2: Wilhelm Vischer in Gwatt, Switzerland, ca. 1944. Photo: courtesy of
Monica Vischer Richter, Biberstein.

this theater, I won't go there any more".[12] Karl Barth was also infuriated by these
changes, although he continued to recognize the quality of Wilhelm Vischer's
sermons, writing that "he was a born poet-translator [...] with an amazing ability of assimilating such a text to the point that the atmosphere and the random
contour of its intonation, as it really is, [seems to] emanate from his pulpit".[13]
In addition, Vischer was a gifted amateur musician.

Given what we know about Ina Lohr, it is not surprising that she also was
drawn to the St. Jacob's Church in this period. Wilhelm Vischer's children,
Wolfgang Vischer und Sonja Chazel, remember that she was highly regarded
by their father. In particular, his daughter recalls that Ina Lohr often sang in

12   "Solange der Helmi dieses Theater macht, gehe ich nicht mehr hin". The information about
     Wilhelm Vischer is largely taken from Stefan Felber, *Wilhelm Vischer als Ausleger der Hei-
     ligen Schrift: Eine Untersuchung zum Christuszeugnis des Alten Testaments*, Göttingen: Van-
     denhoeck & Ruprecht 1999, 101–02.
13   "Er war der geborene Nach-Dichter [...] mit einer erstaunlichen Fähigkeit, sich einen sol-
     chen Text sozusagen zu assimilieren, sich bis in die Stimmung und Tongebung hinein in
     seiner zufälligen Kontur, wie sie nun einmal ist, auf seiner Kanzel zu Wort kommen zu las-
     sen". Ibid., 102.

and for the congregation.[14] Evidence that he was equally interested in her work is given by a passage in a letter of Ina Lohr to Ernst Gaugler on 26 September 1943 that Paul Sacher was of the opinion that she

> should be less active in concerts this winter and finish the work on the *Probeband*, which is generally regarded by musicians as an unnecessary hobby of mine. I am now doing that and meet together a lot with Pastor Vischer, who for quite a while now has been a very loyal course participant.[15]

Their cooperation went still further in that Pastor Vischer invited her, along with Lili Wieruzowski and Trudi Sutter, to write settings for his edition of selected psalms. Ina Lohr gladly acquiesed in this and contributed eighteen pieces to the eight volumes. This work meant a great deal to her, in that he was the only theologian in Basel who identified on that level with her work. But it was still not what she was really searching for, as can be seen from a letter to Ernst Gaugler of 29 December 1943:

> I see much of Pastor Vischer, because we are making an edition of songs together. He is also singing in my ensemble (he even sings very beautifully) and we understand one another very well. His book also says a lot to me [perhaps *Die früheren Propheten* which has a handwritten dedication to her in the author's hand],[16] but I miss that which speaks from your entire person: that not only your head, as well as your desire and deed (that is all present in Vischer, too), but also your heart is entirely consumed and must express itself. Then that which is difficult to understand also becomes clear and simple.[17]

She must have seen Wilhelm Vischer's participation in the ensemble as an honor, that a theologian of his caliber join her ensemble. The closeness of the relationship can also be judged by the fact that they appear to have been on "Du" terms – something rare for her – in that there is an entry in her diary on

---

14　Interview with Wolfgang Vischer and his daughter Monika Vischer Richter of 1 June 2017, and a communication of Monika Vischer Richter of 6 June 2017.

15　"Er [Paul Sacher] fand sogar, ich solle ruhig diesen Winter im Konzert weniger mitmachen und dafür die Arbeit am Probeband, die von den Musikern im allgemeinen als unnötige Liebhaberei meinerseits wird angesehen, fertig machen. Das tue ich jetzt und komme dafür viel mit Pfarrer Vischer zusammen, der jetzt schon ziemlich lange ein sehr treuer Kursteilnehmer ist". Letter Ina Lohr to Ernst Gaugler of 26 September 1943, PSF-ILC.

16　Zollikon: Evang. Verlag 1942, PSF-ILC.

17　"Pfarrer Vischer sehe ich viel, weil wir zusammen eine Liedausgabe machen. Auch singt er in meinem Ensemble mit, (er singt sogar sehr schön) und wir verstehen uns sehr gut. Auch sein Buch sagt mir viel, aber es fehlt mir doch das, was bei Ihnen aus allem spricht: dass nicht nur Ihr Kopf und auch Ihr Wollen und Tun (das ist bei Vischer alles da), sondern auch Ihr Herz gänzlich ergriffen ist und sich ausgeben muss. Dadurch wird auch das Schwerverständliche klar und einfach". Letter Ina Lohr to Ernst Gaugler of 29 December 1943, PSF-ILC.

5 January 1957, speaking of a visit of Maria and Helmi Vischer, indicating that
she was used to calling him by his nickname.

It is tempting to place the sum total of these remarks in connection with
Christopher Schmidt's memory that Karl Barth had complained that Wilhelm
Vischer's church services had come to contain too much music, necessitating
the shortening of the sermon. It is easy to imagine that this might have been as
a result of Ina Lohr's courses. In addition, Karl Barth was bothered by her influence over the theology students, telling Christopher Schmidt that she was a
"dangerous person", albeit with an ironic twinkle in his eye.[18]

This remark must also be placed in relation to the fact that there was considerable general opposition to the *Probeband*. This stemmed not only from the
usual difficulties in countenancing change in a highly traditionalized facet of
life, but also from specific aspects of its contents: its texts were considered to be
too old-fashioned, difficult to understand; the original rhythmization too complex; unison singing was seen as being deficient in comparison to that in four
parts, customary in Swiss churches; and finally, the modal hymns were too severe in character and arduous to sing. As a result, the Swiss Protestant Church
decided to revise the *Probeband* in order to make it more attractive to a wider
public while retaining some of these compositions. It was, however, just these
aspects which Ina Lohr was particularly propagating. So, in her support of the
Probeband, she was openly taking an uncomfortable position, something of
which the world around her was certainly cognizant.

The Schola Cantorum Basiliensis: 1944/45

The school year 1944/45 coincided with the end of the war, which had an effect
on its activities; this is particularly evident in the increase in the number of concerts given by the concert group under August Wenzinger. Ina Lohr was as busy
as usual, giving three fall courses in addition to her regular instruction. Her students played not only in 11 student recitals, but also one of her ensembles for
Hausmusik played in a celebratory event of the Zurich organization of *Sing- und
Spielkreise* (Singing and Playing Circles) on 14 October 1944. Further, her *Ensem-
ble für Kirchenmusik* performed a vespers service on 31 March 1944 in Arlesheim.
Her three introductory courses on Protestant church music – "Lieder aus dem
Probeband im Gottesdienst" (Songs from the *Probeband* in the Church Service),
"Praktische Übungen am Kirchenlied" (Practical Exercises with Hymns) and
"Gregorianische Quellen zum Kirchenlied" (Gregorian Sources for Hymns) –

---

18   Interview of 24 May 2017 and also Christopher Schmidt, "Erinnerungen an Ina Lohr", in:
     Basler Jahrbuch für Historische Musikpraxis 32 (2008), 160.

Ill. 5.3: Rehearsal of students at the Alumneum under the direction of Ina Lohr. Photo: PSF-ILC.

continued to be successful. Indeed, participants from her courses took part in the 100th anniversary of the Basel Alumneum, a house for theology students (see Ill. 5.3). Max Wyttenbach (1921–2015) recalls that this celebration

> appears to have been the catalyst for the organization of regular practice sessions for singing for us alumni. It was then that Ina Lohr of the Schola Cantorum Basiliensis was able, in regularly scheduled singing lessons, to stimulate our enthusiasm for joyful singing, particularly of church hymns. We thus learned, in view of our future activity as pastors, the importance of communal singing in the church service.[19]

With this activity Ina Lohr increased her contact and influence within the Protestant theological community in Basel, perhaps, as we have seen above, something that was not observed with pleasure by all members of the university faculty.

19   "Die früher erwähnte Jubiläumsfeier unseres Hauses scheint übrigens den Anstoss gegeben zu haben, mit uns Alumnen regelmässige Gesangsübungen zu organisieren. Es war dann Frau Ina Lohr von der Schola Cantorum Basel, die uns in regelmässig angesetzten Gesangsstunden zu freudigem Singen, vor allem von Kirchenliedern, zu begeistern vermochte. Wir lernten so, im Blick auf unser einstiges Wirken in einem Pfarramt die Wichtigkeit gemeinsamen Singens im Gottesdienst kennen". Taken from an account of the history of the Basel Alumneum which no longer appears online.

It is interesting to note in this context that the Schola initiated an introductory course for Catholic church music given by August Wenzinger from May through October of 1945, similar to those given by Ina Lohr for Protestants. It also received outside support, in this case from the Commission for Roman Catholic Religious Instruction of the Canton of Basel-Land. There were no immediate follow-up courses until Ina Lohr began teaching them in 1948.

5.2 The Cooperation with Paul Sacher for the BKO: the War Years

1940

What the above description of her activities at the Schola during the war does not reveal, however, is the extent of her desperation at the state of the world, that such bloody battles were being fought, that hatred and destruction were prevailing. Nor does it give any indication of the willpower it must have taken her just to get through her daily activities. As before, it is the correspondence between Ina Lohr and Paul Sacher that is most informative about the issues involved because he was one of the few people she felt she could turn to in her moments of despair and physical weakness. In addition, as she became increasingly convinced of her mission in life, she felt forced to speak out about musical issues that were not part of the picture when their cooperation began.

Her excessive workload, her fragile emotional and physical constitution, together with the excitement of the performance of Palestrina's *Missa Papae Marcelli* in Paris had led, as we saw in Chapter 4, to a lengthy stay in the hospital in the Netherlands in the summer of 1939. Concerned about her health, and desirous that she regain her strength, Paul Sacher welcomed her suggestion that she not give any autumn courses at the Schola that year, but instead go on a cure, commenting that this provided a "wonderful perspective for quiet and contemplation and unhurried work".[20] Their letters from the end of September when Ina Lohr was in Heiligenschwendi (see Chapter 2) were devoted almost solely to work for the BKO, thus revealing – by their very existence – the dilemma in which the two of them stood, their seemingly irreconcilable differences. On the one hand, they were in agreement that she needed to recuperate her strength, for which she needed peace and quiet. Part of her recovery, however, was dependent also on having undisturbed time to work, as this was also a source of renewal for her. But this inner drive to be useful to others came time

---

20 "Welch schöne Perspektive auf Ruhe & Sammlung & unüberhetzte Arbeit". Letter Paul Sacher to Ina Lohr of 9 August 1939, PSF-ILC.

and time again – most obviously in her work with Paul Sacher – to collide with her own projects, her own ideals. He, on the other hand, was aware not only of her physical limitations, but also of the value of her work in the pursuit of his own goals, which, however, had a different orientation than those of Ina Lohr. Their work on the joint projects thus came from divergent perspectives, and was dominated by Paul Sacher, as the employer and organizer.

It was at Heiligenschwendi, through her encounters with Ernst Gaugler with whom she "philosophized" daily at meals,[21] that Ina Lohr came to increasingly trust herself, began to have confidence in her need to turn to God directly in song. This made verbal communication with Paul Sacher more difficult, as she admitted in a letter of 31 October 1939 to Ernst Gaugler:

> Unfortunately, my acknowledgement of "another world" is a disturbance as long as Sacher sees it as *escapism*. The strange thing is that, in spite of this, we are working on a kind of icon together in rehearsing Purcell's *Te Deum* and Bach's *Magnificat*. There everything is then good, and perhaps it is not so important that we understand one another verbally, as long as we can find one another in such work.[22]

This discrepancy in intent, however, was bothersome enough for her that she was dissatisfied with her own work with the choir, as it met neither of their needs completely. She was worried that he might take offense if she were to want to find her own expression in their music, thereby displaying a kind of disloyalty; nonetheless, she had such "an 'urge to profess' musically" that it had to find an outlet.[23] This notwithstanding, in a letter to Paul Sacher of 22 December 1939, in which she included her *Laufenberg Lieder* for unisono choir and string orchestra as a Christmas present, she felt the need to declare

> My inner bond to you is greater than that to any other person, but that it in no way places you under any obligation and if you do not need me so much for awhile, then I could earn my living in some other way for that time. But I am, no matter if I often seem recalcitrant, always there for you, whenever you need me.[24]

---

21 Letter Ina Lohr to Paul Sacher of 28 September 1939, private collection, Switzerland.
22 "Leider stört aber mein Bekenntnis zur 'anderen Welt', solange Sacher diese Hinwendung als <u>Weltflucht</u> ansieht. Das Merkwürdige ist, das[s] wir trotzdem zusammen an einer Art Ikone arbeiten, wenn wir Purcells Te Deum und Bachs Magnificat einüben. Da ist dann alles gut und vielleicht ist es gar nicht so wichtig, dass wir einander in Worten verstehen, solange wir uns in solcher Arbeit finden". Letter Ina Lohr to Ernst Gaugler of 31 October 1939, PSF-ILC.
23 "Ich habe allerdings gerade jetzt einen fürchterlichen musikalischen 'Bekenntnisdrang'". Letter Ina Lohr to Paul Sacher of 22 December 1939, private collection, Switzerland.
24 "Innerlich bin ich Ihnen vor allen anderen Menschen verbunden, aber das verpflichtet Sie zu nichts und wenn Sie mich eine Zeit lang weniger brauchen können, dann könnte ich in

He, of course, reassured her on 1 January 1940 that he was very happy with her work. In addition, he made it clear that he was intending to include her composition in a future concert of the BKO:

> The *Laufenberg Lieder* are very personal and so strongly confessional that I cannot really imagine them with Krenek & Bartók. They belong in the St. Martin's church. There is a real connection here with early music. Would not this be a reason for a mixed program?[25]

This decision to perform these songs is noteworthy, represents a real commitment on his part, in that it is the first and only composition by a woman that he would direct until those of Patricia Jünger from 1981 onwards.

This peaceful state of affairs only lasted until the next project tried their nerves, namely the premiere of Arthur Honegger's *La Danse des morts* on 1 March 1940. In a letter of 8 March, Paul Sacher apologized to Ina Lohr, saying that he had not realized until that morning the degree to which the project had taxed her; in addition, he wished her good luck in a concert of her own on the coming Sunday. She was apologetic in her response of 11 March, while nonetheless declaring that until things were cleared up between them, she would not touch her wages. This state of emotional upheaval was no doubt heightened by her concerns for her family, as not only was communication irregular, but she was also forced to decide whether or not to return to Holland for her vacation. As the potential for "difficulties with the return trip" was high, she felt she could not risk leaving her colleagues and students in the lurch for weeks.[26] She thus chose to remain in Switzerland, disappointing her family, not foreseeing the immense personal torment that would ensue from this choice.

A month later, on 25 April 1940, hoping to receive some support and resolution regarding the question which had come to dominate her life, she wrote Ernst

---

der Zeit in anderer Weise für meinen Unterhalt sorgen. Aber ich bin, wie bockig ich auch oft scheine, immer für Sie da, wenn Sie mich notig [sic] haben". Ibid.

25 "Die *Laufenberg Lieder* sind sehr persönlich & so stark bekenntnishaft, dass ich sie mir neben Krenek & Bartok noch nicht gut vorstellen kann. Sie gehören in die Martinskirche. Hier besteht nun eine echte Verbindung mit alter Musik. Wäre das nun nicht ein Anlass zu einem gemischten Programm?" Letter Paul Sacher to Ina Lohr of 1 January 1940, PSF-ILC.

26 "Sie verstehen daraus wohl schon, dass ich nicht nach Hause kann. Die Schwierigkeiten mit der Rückreise sind zu gross und ich darf es nicht riskieren meine Mitarbeiter und Schülerinnen Wochen lang im Stich zu lassen, weil mir die Rückreise vielleicht nicht bewilligt wird. Es fällt mir schwer, dass ich meinen Eltern diese Enttäuschung bereiten muss". Letter Ina Lohr to Ernst Gaugler of 17 March 1940, PSF-ILC.

Gaugler a long letter in which she laid out her predicament: namely, whether it was reasonable to insist on her religious vocation, or whether it was more important to do her duty. She spoke of how

a great portion of our work is very virtuoso, even brilliant, but therefore dangerous in our times, which is undermined by technique, superficial brilliance and inner emptiness. It is most dangerous there where, for example, Honegger, or rather Claudel [in *La Danse des morts*], takes a religious topic, pours it into a [poetic] form in a virtuoso manner, which is then set by Honegger using colorful effects. Then we again employ all of our means in order to bring the thing to resound in all its fullness and when I listened to the thrilling loud piece in the first orchestra rehearsal, it seemed to me that I had betrayed the best of that which I had come to understand in the recent months. It seems forbidden and dangerous to me today, when an unengaged soloist with the most beautiful voice sings: "Je crois que mon rédemptor vit" [I know that my Redeemer lives] and when the choir shouts out in fortissimo: "souviens toi homme que tu es pierre et que sur cette pierre je bâtirai mon église" [remember, man, that you are stone and that on this stone I will build my church] when the church has no meaning any more for the majority of the participants. In the end, everything is then created for the effect and for the truly great performance. After the concert, I was then so demoralized that I suggested to Sacher that I would search for another choir director for him and only work on historical things with him. Indeed, a week had gone by before I could even talk with him. But then he did not leave me in peace any more. We had endless discussions; they, in any case, made *it* clear to me that I cannot and may not abandon him. Now, however, the work with him requires so much time and strength that my work with amateurs comes too short [...] What is better anyway, that one does one's duty without questioning, i.e. that which people expect from us, or that one does that for which one feels "the call", whereby, however, we leave others in the lurch? I am often no longer sure [...] And Sacher's patience is something extraordinarily good. He does not understand at all what is going on in me, although he is trying very hard; but he has unlimited trust in me. Then I do have to support him, don't I?[27]

27 "ein grosser Teil von unserer Arbeit ist sehr virtuos, glänzend sogar, aber darum gefährlich in unserer Zeit, die an Technik, äusserlichem Glanz und innerer Leere zu Grunde geht. Am gefährlichsten ist es dort, wo z.B. Honegger, oder vielmehr Claudel ein religiöses Thema nimmt, das virtuos in eine Form giesst, die dann mit farbigen Mitteln von Honegger vertont wird. Wir wenden dann auch wieder all unsere Mittel an um die Sache gross zum Klingen zu bringen und als ich in der ersten Orchesterprobe dem packenden Krachstück zuhörte, kam es mir vor, als ob ich das Beste, was mir in den letzten Monaten aufgegangen is[t] verraten hätte. Es kommt mir verboten und gefährlich vor, wenn heute ein gleichgültiger Solist mit schönster Stimme singt: 'Je crois que mon rédempteur vit' und wenn der Chor im ff. schreit: 'souviens toi homme que tu es pierre et que sur cette pierre je bâtirai mon église', wenn die Kirche dem allergrössten Teil von den Mitwirkenden nichts mehr bedeutet. Es geht dann schliesslich alles um den Effekt und um die wirklich grossartige Leistung. Ich bin dann nach dem Konzert so zusammengeklappt, dass ich Sacher vorgeschlagen habe, ich würde ihm einen anderen Repetitor suchen und nur noch für historische Sachen mit ihm arbeiten. Es ging allerdings eine Woche bevor ich überhaupt mit ihm reden konnte. Dann liess er mir keine Ruhe mehr. Wir hatten endlose Gespräche, die mir auf alle Fälle das klargemacht haben, dass ich ihn nicht im Stich lassen kann und darf. Nun

This, in a nutshell, is the dilemma in which she felt herself trapped: she could neither follow her own "calling" completely and simply work with amateurs, nor could she forgo what she perceived as her obligations to Paul Sacher. This concert brought these issues to the surface and once there, they were a constant object of discussion and negotiation between them for years until a resolution was seemingly found sometime after the war.

In his response of 29 April 1940, Ernst Gaugler encouraged her to stand by her work, as he felt that the source of her musical strength was all-important, also for Paul Sacher, even though the latter may not have realized it on a conscious level. He claimed, namely, that

> One thing is clear to me: you still have to serve the Schola for the moment. In Haltenegg someone who knows the Schola well said to me [...] that *you* are the "*soul* of the Schola". That without you, it would be *nothing*.
>
> I believe that the manner in which you *experience* early music, how you also *experience* the eternal in new [music], how you hear it, what it is, and give yourself up to it completely, want to *serve* it, that makes you the *soul* of this work. If Mr. Sacher cannot or cannot yet do this, there is no blame. But, there is something *great* that he apparently *feels* that you have. And therefore, I do believe that you *must* continue to do it.[28]

Ina Lohr's response to him of 5 May 1940 is very telling: "Don't worry at all that I will ever give up the Schola. I couldn't do that, for the work there is certainly part of my calling".[29] It also highlights her comparative discomfort with the work with Paul Sacher, for at the Schola, too, she went beyond her limits, but there her activities fulfilled some deep inner need.

nimmt aber die Arbeit mit ihm mir soviel Zeit und Kraft, dass ich zur Laienarbeit immer weniger komme [...] Was ist überhaupt besser, dass man ganz ohne zu fragen seine Pflicht tut, d.h. das, was unsere Mitmenschen von uns erwarten, oder das[s] man das tut, wozu man sich 'berufen' meint, wodurch man aber die Mitmenschen im Stich lässt? Ich komme oft nicht mehr draus [...] Und etwas sehr schönes ist Sachers Geduld. Er versteht gar nicht was in mir umgeht, obwohl er sich alle Mühe gibt; aber er hat ein grenzenloses Vertrauen zu mir. Da muss ich doch zu ihm halten?" Letter Ina Lohr to Ernst Gaugler of 25 April 1940, PSF-ILC.

28 "Eines ist mir klar: Sie müssen vorerst noch der Schola dienen. Auf der Haltenegg sagte mir jemand, der die Schola gut kennt, [...] dass Sie 'die Seele der Schola' seien. Ohne Sie wäre sie nichts. Ich glaube, dass eben die Art, wie Sie die alte Musik leben, wie Sie auch in der neuen das Ewige leben, wie Sie das hören, was sie ist und sich ihr ganz unter-stellen [sic], ihr dienen wollen, dass eben dies Sie zur Seele dieser Arbeit macht. Wenn Herr Sacher das nicht oder noch nicht kann, so ist das nicht Schuld. Aber, es ist schon etwas Grosses, dass er offenbar spürt, dass Sie das haben. Und so glaube ich wohl, daß Sie das vorläufig auch müssen". Letter Ernst Gaugler to Ina Lohr of 29 April 1940, PSF-ILC.

29 "Haben Sie keine Angst, dass ich die Schola je aufgeben werde. Das könnte ich nicht, denn die Arbeit dort ist sicher ein Teil von meiner Berufung". Letter Ina Lohr to Ernst Gaugler of 5 May 1940, PSF-ILC.

In any case, by the summer vacation they had achieved some sort of truce, when Ina Lohr wrote to Paul Sacher on 19 July 1940 that

> I know with my head that you "urgently need" me, my odd heart just does not always believe it. The last weeks before your departure, however, have done my heart good. Perhaps we really will get so far that everything will work more smoothly. For that I must primarily learn that my pride often stands in the way of our trust in one another and that it therefore would be much better if I were to complain humorously when something is no longer possible. That is certain to be better than forcing something, which then ruins my mood. If only you could believe that I am never trying to avoid any task![30]

In confirmation of this change in their *modus operandi*, she also wrote to Ernst Gaugler on 21 July 1940 that

> the other difficulties are still there, but they are much less difficult than they were. Sacher has proved again and again in the last weeks that his friendship is indestructible. He does not come close to understanding me all the time and I must often make it difficult for him in his work, because for me making music is always the means and for him it is the goal. I am often intolerant and impatient, but he stands by me through thick and thin, so that I am ashamed of myself. He has reduced my workload considerably for the next season; I only have to lead half as many rehearsals and can work more at home.[31]

That Paul Sacher was eager to clear the air, to once again return to simpler days, may be seen from his letter of 27 July 1940, in which he asked, "Why should your heart not believe that I need you?" and "Why do you insatiably desire to proselytize, when the hungry are so nearby?" He assured her that he was endeavoring to uncover, understand the reasons for their difficulties with one another, that he really wished to ban any aspect of mistrust from their cooperation, for the only thing that he "could not tolerate between us is that deathly atmos-

---

30 "Ich weiss mit meinem Kopf, dass Sie mich 'dringend brauchen', mein merkwürdiges Herz glaubts [sic] nur nicht immer. Die letzten Wochen vor Ihrer Abreise haben aber auch meinem Herzen gut getan. Vielleicht kommen wir wirklich einmal so weit, dass alles reibungsloser geht. Dafür muss ich vor allem lernen, dass mein Stolz unserem gegenseitigen Vertrauen oft im Wege steht und dass es darum viel besser ist, dass ich möglichst mit Humor reklamiere, wenn etwas nicht mehr geht. Das ist sicher besser als das Forcieren, was dann meine Stimmung kaput [sic] macht. Wenn Sie nur nie meinen, dass ich mich um irgend eine Aufgabe drücken will!" Letter Ina Lohr to Paul Sacher of 19 July 1940, private collection, Switzerland.

31 "Die anderen Schwierigkeiten sind immer noch da, aber sie sind viel weniger schwierig als sie waren. Sacher hat in den letzten Wochen immer wieder bewiesen, dass seine Freundschaft unerschütterlich ist. Er versteht mich lange nicht immer und ich muss es ihm in seiner Arbeit oft schwer machen, weil bei mir das Musizieren immer nur Mittel ist, während es bei ihm Zweck ist. Ich bin oft unduldsam und ungeduldig, aber er steht durch dick und dünn zu mir, sodass ich mich schämen muss. Für die nächste Saison hat er mich sehr entlastet; ich muss nur noch halb soviel Proben leiten und kann mehr zu Hause arbeiten". Letter Ina Lohr to Ernst Gaugler of 21 July 1940, PSF-ILC.

phere of diminishing trust".[32] With this in mind he once again requested that she turn to no one else other than him with these concerns.

This letter provoked a quite blunt response from Ina Lohr on 29 July 1940, one in which she answered these questions in a very direct manner, in the process clearly presenting her side of the situation.

> If my proselytizing only had the goal of helping others, then the whole thing would be simple enough and I would then surely be an ideal employee. But music is for me, time and again and solely, the means by which I profess my Christianity and convince others of these truths. [The reason] why – in my heart – I don't believe that you need me is this: you need my musicality, my head, my voice, yes even my enthusiasm for the music; the other, my "conviction" – for me the main thing – is only a somewhat bothersome adjunct for you. I say this not as a reproach, only as an observation. For this reason, I tend increasingly, particularly in stressful times – for example, this year when we were rehearsing the Honegger – to undertake something with the *Ensemble für Kirchenmusik*. As long as the two projects run parallel to one another, things work comparatively well, I am tired, but satisfied, because I am true to both of my obligations, my work with you and my "confessional work". The catastrophe then occurs when *my* obligation – which naturally required some effort – stops, and the work with you then speedily nears its end and almost "robs" me [of all remaining strength]. You are at that moment not aware – and therein lies your strength! – of how much you demand of your employees when you only have eyes for your goal. In such a moment, it is impossible for me to tell you that I can do no more. [For] that disturbs your schedule and you perceive it almost as a betrayal.[33]

32 "Warum soll Ihr Herz nicht glauben, dass ich Sie brauche? [...] Warum wollen Sie unersättlich andere missionieren wo doch so nahe Hungrige sind? [...] Das einzige was ich keinesfalls zwischen uns dulden würde ist jene mordende Atmosphäre des schwindenden Vertrauens". Letter Paul Sacher to Ina Lohr of 27 July 1940, PSF-ILC.

33 "Wenn mein Missionieren nur als Ziel hätte anderen zu helfen, dann wäre die Sache einfach genug und dann wäre ich sicher eine ideale Mitarbeiterin. Aber die Musik ist für mich immer wieder, und immer nur, das Mittel, mich zum Christentum zu bekennen und andere von diesen Wahrheiten zu überzeugen. Warum ich mit dem Herzen nicht glaube, dass Sie mich brauchen, ist dieses. Sie brauchen meine Musikalität, meinen Kopf, meine Stimme, ja sogar meine Begeisterung für die Musik; das andere, meine 'Gesinnung', für mich die Hauptsache, ist für Sie nur eine etwas lästige Beigabe. Ich sage das nicht als Vorwurf, nur als Feststellung. Aus diesem Grunde komme ich immer mehr dazu, gerade in den Stosszeiten, (dies Jahr z. B. als wir für Honegger probierten), etwas mit der Kirchenmusikgruppe zu unternehmen. Solange die beiden Arbeiten nebeneinander laufen, geht es verhältnismässig gut, ich bin müde, aber befriedigt, weil ich meinen beiden Aufgaben, der Arbeit mit Ihnen und meiner 'Bekenntnisarbeit' treu bin. Die Katastrophe tritt dann ein, wenn meine Aufgabe (die natürlich doch Kräfte verbraucht hat) aufhört und die Arbeit mit Ihnen dann im Eiltempo dem Ende zugeht und mich fast 'ausraubt'. Sie sind sich auch nicht darüber klar, (und darin liegt Ihre Kraft!), wieviel Sie von Ihren Mitarbeitern verlangen, wenn Sie nur noch Ihr Ziel sehen. Ich kann Ihnen in einem solchen Augenblick unmöglich sagen, dass ich nicht mehr kann. Das stört Ihr Programm und Sie empfinden es fast als Verrat". Letter Ina Lohr to Paul Sacher of 29 July 1940, private collection, Switzerland.

This forthrightness in the expression and description of her emotions and experiences provoked a thoughtful, almost philosophical response on 1 August 1940, extraordinary on all terms, but certainly as a birthday greeting. Also noteworthy about it are the marginalia in Ina Lohr's hand, obviously written in contemplation of how to respond to the letter. As Paul Sacher pointed out

> The crux is this issue: music and religion. Already for the Greeks, beauty was […] very close to goodness. And Christianity is, among other things, the doctrine of goodness. Music is, in a certain sense, the doctrine of beauty. Must a Christian, when he is pursuing beauty, always at the same time preach goodness? Can he not, with wisdom and discretion, do the beautiful and *think* the good? Must every Christian, as a Pauline zealot, force beauty into the good, all the time and everywhere? My mode of expression is deliberately primitive, because otherwise I would have to write a book and not only a letter. But do you not understand the concept anyway?[34]

Whereas with the previous letters, one might question the degree with which he was really trying to enter into Ina Lohr's thought processes, into the reasons why she was having difficulties as his musical assistant, with this one a new level of discussion is opened, in which he is endeavoring to clarify the sources of their problems. He was not being selfless in this, but had come to understand that without discussion or resolution of these questions, further cooperation was almost impossible. The most poignant of Ina Lohr's marginal notes shows her divided mind: she scribbled "I would like to let you be, but then it would be impossible to be so involved in the work. No, it would be betrayal then, if I had to simulate indifference, or only work technically, even if I should always begin with it".[35] Even in her notes to herself, her internal battle made itself manifest.

She opened her response on 6 August 1940 by saying that whenever she did not know what to do, she turned to him for help. On the previous day she had completed her preparations for her fall course on sacred music and then her heart had gone on strike again. It was obvious to her that it was a psychoso-

---

34 "Der Kernpunkt ist das Thema: Musik und Religion. Das Schöne war schon für die Griechen […] sehr nahe beim Guten. Und das Christentum ist u. a. die Lehre vom Guten. Die Musik nun ist gewissermassen eine Lehre vom Schönen. Muss ein Christ, wenn er sich mit dem Schönen beschäftigt, immer gleichzeitig das Gute predigen? Kann er nicht in Weisheit & Ueberlegenheit das Schöne tun & das Gute denken? Muss jeder Christ als paulinischer Eiferer das Schöne in das Gute zwängen, immer & überall? Meine Ausdrucksweise ist bewusst primitiv, weil ich sonst ein Buch schreiben müsste & nicht nur einen Brief. Aber, verstehen Sie den Gedanken nicht trotzdem?" Letter Paul Sacher to Ina Lohr of 1 August 1940, PSF-ILC.

35 "ich will Sie gerne gewähren lassen, aber kann mich dann unmöglich so sehr um die Sache kümmern. Nein, aber es ist Verrat, wenn ich Gleichgültigkeit vortäuschen muss, aber nur technisch arbeite, wenn ich immer mit dem auch anfangen sollte". Marginal note in letter Paul Sacher to Ina Lohr of 1 August 1940, PSF-ILC.

matic reaction, a consequence of her inability to deal with the mounting correspondence from people who turned to her for sustenance. And on top of
this, his letter, too, had made her so sad, for if she had been able to conceive,
choose and stay on her path, "then we would have clearly achieved it in the past
year".[36] This was followed by a further attempt to clarify her position in a manner that Paul Sacher could comprehend:

> I really do acknowledge that your mode of working and making music has just as much
> justification as mine, and in no way do I think that my way is better. This is true only
> for me. I am happy to let you be, but you cannot expect that I will then at the same
> time participate with heart and soul. And that is what you want, because otherwise
> you don't get much from it, since I can only work technically and make explanations,
> if I have delved into something wholeheartedly. If another project which would be di-
> rectly suited for "my way" cannot be accepted because of this, then I get into this grim
> state, which is the absolute worst for me. As an example, I can tell you that the work
> on my cantata is liberating because it gives a kind of answer to the questions and pleas
> from these people that think I can help them. First, the composition gives me the right
> answer, and then I can again go on [...] I am not really a composer, but only write in
> notes what another would say or do. By the way, I know well that one can come from
> beauty to goodness. If one treats each note with the greatest love and care, then it be-
> comes beautiful and good, no matter whether it is a mass, or secular songs or a dance.
> It hurts me, therefore, when modern composers no longer have respect for the individ-
> ual notes, for the human voices and for the possible instrumental sonorities, and that it
> is why it disturbs me so greatly when you rehearse in fortissimo.[37]

36 "Wenn das möglich wäre, dann hätten wir es im vergangenen Jahr sicher zustande ge-
    bracht". Letter Ina Lohr to Paul Sacher of 6 August 1940, private collection, Switzerland.
37 "Ich sehe wirklich ein, dass Ihre Art zu arbeiten und zu musizieren genau soviel Berechti-
    gung hat wie meine und ich bilde mir gar nicht ein, dass meine Art besser ist. Sie ist das
    nur für mich. Ich will Sie gerne gewähren lassen, aber Sie können nicht erwarten, dass
    ich dann gleichzeitig mit Leib und Seele mitmache. Und das wollen Sie doch, denn sonst
    haben Sie nicht viel davon, weil ich auch Technisches nur kann und erklären kann, wenn
    ich mich ganz in etwas vertiefe. Wenn dann dafür eine andere Aufgabe, die sich direkt an
    'meine Art' stellen würde, nicht angenommen werden kann, dann komme ich in diesen
    grimmigen Zustand hinein, der für mich am allerschlimmsten ist. Als Beispiel kann ich
    Ihnen sagen, dass die Arbeit an meiner Kantate darum erlösend ist, weil sie eigentlich eine
    Antwort gibt auf diese Fragen und Bitten von diesen Leuten, die meinen ich könnte hel-
    fen. Zunächst gibt diese Komposition mir die richtige Antwort und ich kann dann wieder
    weiter. Seitdem Sie nach der Einleitung zu den *Laufenberg Liedern* gefragt haben, arbeite
    ich nur noch mit schlechtem Gewissen und für die Einleitung finde ich überhaupt den
    Rank nicht. Es ist das wieder gar kein Vorwurf. Sie habe recht zu fragen und für die mei-
    sten Komponisten wäre es eine Aufmunterung. Ich bin eben keine Komponistin, sondern
    ich schreibe in Noten auf, was ein anderer sagen oder tun kann. Übrigens [sic] weiss ich
    gut, dass man vom Schönen zum Guten kommen kann. Wenn man jeden Ton mit gröss-
    ter Liebe und Sorgfalt behandelt, dann wird es schön und auch gut, ganz gleich ob es sich
    um eine Messe, um weltliche Lieder oder um einen Tanz handelt. Darum tut es mir weh,
    wenn moderne Komponisten gar keine Ehrfurcht mehr vor den einzelnen Tönen, vor den

She then comments that she has not let herself be inhibited by either "pride or decorum" in this letter, she just needs to know whether she should begin to teach again at the end of August. Indeed, there is a sense that both of them are speaking very openly about their difficulties with one another, trying to find a way forward. In this regard, it is very typical that at the end of this letter, Ina Lohr abruptly changed the subject and reported that she has not yet marked up Haydn, Biber, C.P.E. Bach, and Staden, although she had worked two to three hours a day with the exception of four days when she had a visitor. It again shows also the dimensions of her dilemma, for in the period in which she should, at least in part, have been recovering from the strains of the previous year, she was devoting a significant amount of time to preparing for the following concert season and school year, an inherent conflict in itself.

On 10 August 1940, she wrote thanking Paul Sacher for telephoning her, and recommending that she stay a bit longer in Crans/Sierre, that they could then prepare everything quietly together when she returned to Basel. This is followed by a passage which makes it so clear why Sacher valued her cooperation so highly; her enthusiasm for a musical work simply lights up the page:

> At the moment everything is still a mountain, but it is already better than it was. Chiefly because with the Haydn symphony [Nr. 26, "Lamentatione"], I forgot to brood. Imagine, I think it is almost as beautiful as the "Passione", only that its beauty is more hidden, more intimate. In the slow movement, the simultaneous presentation of the severe, serious chant melody together with the light, floating Rococo theme is something very unique. But also the first movement becomes very three dimensional, if one understands it entirely from the perspective of the chant melody. By the way, I think it is not from the John Passion, but from the Matthew Passion. Otherwise is does not correspond with the syllables. This is not unimportant for the phrasing. I am also not sure about the lamentation melody, although I have compared all lamentations with the movement. I should now read the article by Schering, perhaps he has a solution, or? In any case, I must continue to investigate it in Basel, and we must then discuss the phrasing very exactly. Also, Trudy Flügel should check the bowing, particularly with the Biber. And you the trills! I will now send you everything with this, so that you already have something, but everything will be looked at again in Basel.[38]

menschlichen Stimmen und vor den klanglichen Möglichkeiten der Instrumente haben und darum macht es mich so kaputt, wenn Sie fortissimo üben". Letter Ina Lohr to Paul Sacher of 6 August 1940, private collection, Switzerland.

38   "Augenblicklich ist nur alles noch ein Berg, aber es ist schon besser als es war und hauptsächlich habe ich über der Haydnsymphonie alle Grübeleien vergessen. Denken Sie, ich glaube, sie ist fast so schön, wie die 'Passione', nur ist ihre Schönheit viel versteckter, intimer. Im langsamen Satz ist das Zusammengehen von dieser herb-ernsten Choralmelodie mit diesem duftigen Thema aus dem Rokoko etwas ganz einzigartiges. Aber auch der erste Satz wird plastisch, wenn man ihn ganz von der Choralmelodie aus nimmt. Uebrigens [sic] glaube ich, dass es sich nicht um die Johannes-, sondern um die Matthäuspassion han-

The combination of her enthusiasm, plus her willingness to investigate the background and structure of the music must have been a great assistance to Paul Sacher, providing a stimulus and support to his activities. But as Ina Lohr came increasingly to see how her work for him was preventing her from pursuing her own goals, her reluctance to continue involving herself in this manner became a source of contention between the two of them. In Paul Sacher's letter of the same day, he spoke directly to these issues, searching to find a solution which would enable a continuation of the cooperation, while at the same time providing Ina Lohr with more space for her own projects. He first addressed her attack of weakness resulting from the emotional demands made upon her by family and friends. He tried to find a means of explaining to her that she could best help these people by not taking on their problems, but instead by showing them – to be sure with great compassion – the path they needed to follow:

> But beyond that you cannot allow the whole misery of this world to beleager you and carry it on your shoulders. You provoke these numerous letters yourself namely, because you often overload yourself with work & then (because you naturally cannot deal with the excess) you complain about it! Both are wrong in my opinion. How does it help the other [people] anyway, when they unburden their hearts and weigh you down with their worries? Each person must deal with his concerns *himself*! It is not something more humane and better to allow oneself to be burdened with all of that. To the contrary, you have to tell the people that they should try to come to terms with themselves on their own & that they can only be relieved if they overcome their pains through their own experience. Weakness may never be answered with weakness; this means that one can only endeavor to show the path to someone seeking help, but one should not burden oneself, in addition, with the weight of the other's fate, as one then no longer has the capacity to help.[39]

delt. Es stimmt sonst nicht mit den Silben. Das ist für die Phrasierung nicht unwichtig. Auch mit der Lamentationsmelodie komme ich nicht ganz nach, obwohl ich alle Lamentationen mit dem Satz verglichen habe. Ich sollte jetzt dann auch den Aufsatz von Schering lesen, vielleicht gibt der die Lösung, oder? Auf alle Fälle muss ich in Basel das noch weiter nachsehen und wir müssen die Phrasierung dann genau besprechen. Auch sollte Trudy Flügel die Striche kontrollieren, hauptsächlich bei Biber. Und Sie die Triller! Ich schicke jetzt alles mal damit, dass Sie schon etwas haben, aber es kommt dann alles [in] Basel noch einmal dran". Letter Ina Lohr to Paul Sacher of 10 August 1940, private collection, Switzerland.

39 "Aber Sie dürfen darüber hinaus nicht auch noch das ganze Elend dieser Welt an sich herankommen lassen & mit sich herumtragen. Sie provozieren diese zahlreichen Briefe nämlich selber, weil Sie sich auch oft mit Arbeit überladen & dann (weil Sie das Uebermass naturgemäss nicht mehr bewältigen können) darüber klagen! Beides ist nach meiner Ansicht falsch. Was hilft es den anderen schon, wenn Sie [sic] Ihnen das Herz ausschütten & Sie mit fremden Sorgen belasten? Jeder Mensch muss mit seinem Kummer selber fertig werden! Es ist nicht etwas menschlicher & besser sich das alles aufladen zu lassen. Man muss den Menschen im Gegenteil antworten, dass sie versuchen sollen mit sich selber fertig zu werden & dass sie nur erlöst werden können, wenn sie ihre Schmerzen aus eigenem Erleben überwin-

This, however, was Paul Sacher's means of dealing with the needs of others – now a wealthy young man just recently arrived in the top circles of both the cultural and business world of Basel – not those of a woman raised in a highly protected environment seeking self-realization through religion. The rest of the letter remains true to this model, in that he laid out his perception of the situation and the possible outcomes. He attempted to remain on an objective level, with the aim of making it easier for Ina Lohr to make whatever decision she needed to make, even if it were to his own disadvantage.

He first investigated the question of the difference between desiring and having to do something:

> If you have *really* been pervaded by an insight or epiphany, then nothing other than reflection, examination & consistent adherence, and disciplined desire is necessary. True desire is *also* obligation. Obligation is only stronger when the desire was not real.
>
> Therefore, one cannot be critical and tenacious enough in questioning *before* a decision [is made]. Afterwards, however, feelings and understanding must become one! Something "patched together" is never an "insight". If, therefore, our possibilities of cooperation only lead to a "sought after" & "thought out" path, then they are built on sand. But if they, having been examined by your *heart* and mind, remain tempting, then afterwards they are worth every tribulation of their thorny realization. It is then important not to lose your head in the whirlwind of events, [but] to find the starting point again, when it wants to slip away, to relax, take a breath & continue on calmly.[40]

Thus, he first asked Ina Lohr to test her "insight", her "epiphany", to make sure it was something that she really whole-heartedly desired, something that she could really not forgo, because it was so much part of her. On a certain level, he was challenging her belief in its validity, as in his perception, she did not seem to be able to stick to the decision she had made; she was vacillating

---

den. Schwäche darf nie mit Schwäche beantwortet werden, d. h. man kann nur versuchen einem der Hilfe sucht den Weg zu weisen, aber man darf nicht die Schwere des fremden Schicksals auch noch auf sich laden, sonst ist man nicht mehr im stande zu helfen". Letter Paul Sacher to Ina Lohr of 10 August 1940, PSF-ILC.

40 "<u>Wenn</u> Sie von einer Erkenntnis <u>wirklich</u> durchdrungen sind, braucht es nichts als nachdenken, überprüfen & konsequentes Festhalten, diszipliniertes Wollen. Wahres Wollen ist <u>auch</u> müssen. Das müssen ist nur stärker, wo das Wollen nicht echt war.
      Darum kann man <u>vor</u> der Entscheidung nicht kritisch & hartnäckig genug prüfen. Nachher aber müssen Gefühl & Verstand in Eines fallen! Etwas 'Zusammengedachtes' ist niemals eine 'Erkenntnis'. Wenn also unsere Möglichkeiten der Zusammenarbeit nur auf einen 'ausgesuchten' & 'ausgedachten' Weg hinausführen, sind sie auf Sand gebaut. Wenn sie aber mit <u>Herz</u> & Kopf geprüft, verlockend bleiben, sind sie nachher in der dornenvollen Verwirklichung jeder Mühsal wert. Dann gilt es im Trubel der Geschenisse den Kopf nicht verlieren, den Ausgangspunkt wieder finden, wenn er verloren gehen will, ausruhen, Atem holen & ruhig weiter machen". Ibid.

between wanting to continue her assistantship with him and with desiring to work solely within the church community. He was asking her to review seriously whatever decision she made, as success could only come from one that she fully embraced. It was only then that he proceeded to analyze the difficulties between them:

> After all our experiences, I can only see the conflict in the following manner: you prefer doing your own work that stems entirely from you. This appears to me to be completely normal. You value our general cooperation. You would like to assist with the choir, but you no longer have the strength for it when your own [work] suffers from it, whether it be because you are too tired for it, or primarily when something of your own is made impossible by the cooperation.
>
> This honest & simple definition certainly eliminates uncertainties and complications. You then no longer need to "objectify" your aversion & to clothe [them] in thoughts, which match the actual facts less well. In certain situations, you clearly no longer *wish* to participate. Then you should really go on strike. You should really let me down, otherwise there would be no reason to assure me of the opposite![41]

He was willing to say things outrightly that Ina Lohr, with her bourgeois upbringing, was less able to express in such simple terms, willing to admit that it would be natural for her to follow her own inclinations, her own musical desires, rather than spending so much time with his, rather than taking part in musical activities that came into conflict with her own beliefs.

He then made the following proposal:

> Let us therefore not be complicated. Let us take the things as they really are. The assistance with the choir is often a burden to you because you would much rather do other things. If you want to do *only* your own things, then we have to forgo this. If you can keep yourself in check, then the solution lies in the correct dosage.[42]

---

41 "Nach all unseren Erlebnissen kann ich den Konflikt nur so sehen: Sie machen Ihre eigene, allein von Ihnen ausgehende Arbeit weitaus am liebsten. Das scheint mir durchaus natürlich. Unsere allgemeine Zusammenarbeit ist Ihnen wertvoll. Die dienende Mitarbeit im Chor möchten Sie schon machen, Sie bringen aber dann keine Kraft mehr dafür auf, wenn das Eigene darunter leidet. Sei es, dass Sie dafür zu müde sind, vor allem aber wenn etwas eigenes durch die Mitarbeit etwas verunmöglicht wird.

   Diese ehrliche & simple Definition schafft sicher Unklarheiten & Komplikationen aus der Welt. Sie haben es dann auch nicht mehr nötig Ihren Ueberdruss zu 'objektivieren' & in Gedanken zu kleiden, die den einfachen Tatsachen weniger nahe kommen. Sie wollen in gewissen Situationen ganz sicher nicht mehr mitarbeiten. Sie streiken dann tatsächlich. Sie lassen mich wirklich sitzen, sonst bestünde kein Grund mir das Gegenteil zu versichern!" Ibid.

42 "Seien wir darum nicht kompliziert. Wir wollen die Dinge annehmen wie sie wirklich sind. Die Mitarbeit im Chor ist Ihnen oft eine Last, weil Sie viel lieber anderes unternähmen. Wenn Sie nur eigenes machen wollen, müssen wir das aufgeben. Wenn Sie sich im Zaum halten können, besteht die Lösung in der richtigen Dosierung". Ibid.

By making it clear that their work cooperation could not bring the desired results, if she were only participating half-heartedly, that a good friend needs also to be able to say "No", he thus left the door open for her to stop her work with the choir.

The letter comes across as an enormous vote of confidence, in that it sought to make it easier for her to choose the path best for her own needs, based on the conviction that the cooperation would only work if were good for both of them. To lend weight to his argumentation, he also included her pay for September, so that she could afford to stay longer to recuperate more fully if she so desired. In this way, too, he lived the theory expressed at the beginning of the letter, namely that it was unnecessary for him to take on her emotional turmoil in order to provide her a basis for moving on in her decision-making process.

This letter naturally provoked a great deal of self-reflection on the part of Ina Lohr on all sorts of levels, as well as an extraordinarily open response on 14 August 1940. First of all, she thanked him both for the letter and for the money which she hoped she would not need, as it was already budgeted for later. She then remarked on how they both so stubbornly remained true to type, perceiving things in the other, while remaining unable to conceive their true source. She first addressed the question of her inability to detach herself from the concerns of those around her, speaking of her innate loneliness which is overcome by reaching out to other people, and that this need had become even greater through the separation from her family due to the war. She herself saw this in relation to her unfulfillable childhood dream of having many children, a family of her own to care for. It only became a problem for her when it came into conflict with her work, when she no longer knew what came first.

She then continued on to deal with the other issues raised by Paul Sacher in his letter:

> It is correct [to say] that I do not always reflect [over things] but come to my insight through my feelings. But it is always the same insight and I always experience the same "obligation": to make music with simple people and primarily in the field of sacred music. Our cooperation came into being in a completely different way and then only because *you* wanted it, and wanted it again and again. Our cooperation is not built on sand because *you* unequivocally wanted it and sacrificed enough for it. When *I* try to find the starting point and examine it with my heart and mind, then I stumble over a problem, since for me, everything at the beginning was at least as problematic as now and these confusions were already there after the first year!
>
> If I base my [decision] on this insight, I would have to ask you, to be consistent, to let me resign. But when I get that far in my thinking, then something else comes to my aid: our common experience in our work, and everything that is simply there and ties me to it tightly. Therefore, I must repeat what [I said] already in my second-to-last let-

ter: we are tied to our work in very different ways. You basically believe in the concert and today's musical life. I also believe in it for you, but my own work is in another field. The only solution, therefore, lies in the correct dosage.[43]

Also here, she had the strength to stick to her own convictions, pointing out that in her eyes the difficulties – as we also saw in the previous chapter – had already been there in the first year, thereby not letting herself simply to be pressed into Paul Sacher's attempt to deal with her emotional needs "objectively". She had no qualms about admitting the lack of consistency in her reactions, an extraordinarily human behavioral trait, in that all of us can house contradictory emotions. This, in turn, gave her the strength to withstand the pressure to simplify her affective world through denial. She had always had a vision of her musical goals, but simultaneously had to acknowledge the emotional importance, for her, of the work together with him – a cooperation which he had initiated and maintained – and the bonds that it had created.

She then went onto outline her ideas of what her work with the choir might entail:

> I certainly cannot take up the work with the choir like last year. It is too foreign to me, too tiring. But I will, of course, always come when it is necessary to clean up the voices, or to listen. Further, I believe the choir will also be glad for such an agreement. I would prefer to work musically in a more general fashion, which will also be to your advantage. In all of the preparation I did in the last weeks, there were also things that would be useful to you. I wish to make them available to you in some form. The question is only, whether you will be satisfied with that. Already now, I am often sad that you are never actually satisfied, and that you want either everything or nothing. Yes, I have to be able to do my own work at the same time, and I would have to not be obliged to partic-

---

43 "Es ist richtig, dass ich nicht immer denke, sondern von der Empfindung aus zu meiner Erkenntnis komme. Aber es ist immer die gleiche Erkenntnis und ich 'muss' immer dasselbe: mit einfachen Leuten einfache Musik machen am ehesten auf dem Gebiet der Kirchenmusik. Unsere Zusammenarbeit ist ganz anders entstanden und zwar nur, weil Sie sie wollten und immer wieder wollten. Unsere Zusammenarbeit ist darum nicht auf Sand gebaut, weil Sie sie auf alle Fälle wollten und Opfer genug dafür bringen. Wenn ich versuche den Ausgangspunkt wieder zu finden und mit Herz und Kopf zu prüfen, dann stosse ich auch da auf ein Problem, denn für mich war das alles am Anfang mindestens so problematisch wie jetzt und diese Verwirrungen gab es schon nach dem ersten Jahr!

Wenn ich von der Erkenntnis ausgehe, müsste ich konsequenterweise Sie bitten mich gehen zu lassen. Wenn ich aber soweit denke, dann kommt mir etwas anderes zu Hilfe: unsere gemeinsamen Arbeitserlebnisse und alles, was jetzt einfach da ist und mich fest bindet. Darum muss ich wiederholen, was schon im vorletzten Brief stand: wir sind an unsere Aufgabe ganz verschieden gebunden. Sie glauben für sich an das Konzert und an das heutige Musikleben. Ich glaube auch für Sie daran, aber mein eigenes Arbeitsfeld liegt auf einem anderen Gebiet. Darum ist die einzige Lösung die richtige Dosierung". Letter Ina Lohr to Paul Sacher of 14 August 1940, private collection, Switzerland.

ipate when something was involved that goes so against the grain for me, such as Honegger. I admit that I should be able to do it in my function, but I "can" only really do it when I participate in everything! Therefore, I still believe that it will be possible for you to find an assistant who has sufficient technique so that he can participate in everything without exhausting himself mentally. Until then, I will do it to the best of my powers, if you can be content with that.[44]

With this, she was beginning to place her own demands, namely that she was no longer willing to regularly rehearse with the choir, reducing her assistance to working with specific voices that were having difficulties mastering the notes, and listening to rehearsals and giving her input. She also felt convinced that her own musical analysis and research, put in a useful format, would be of benefit to him. Her final conclusion was that he would most likely be better off with a trained conductor who – through his professionalism and personality – was less involved with the musical outcome, and that she would continue on as best she could until he found such a person. She ended the letter by saying that her composition, the *Laufenberg Lieder*, worried her: "There is a sketch for the introduction and it will be done in September with the new score. The whole thing, however, has too little drama for you, even though while working [on it] I always thought of you and the orchestra".[45] This again is a statement about the ambivalence she felt about working for Paul Sacher, investing her heartblood in a composition, while being convinced it would not really meet his musical taste.

On 18 August 1940, after he had clearly also responded to the letter by telephone, Paul Sacher once again chose to write about some of his basic convic-

---

44 "Ich kann die Chorarbeit sicher nicht wieder aufnehmen, wie im vergangenen Jahr. Sie ist mir zu fremd und zu anstrengend. Aber natürlich werde ich immer kommen, wenn es nötig ist Stimmen auszuputzen, oder zuzuhören. Ich glaube übrigens, dass der Chor auch froh sein wird über eine solche Regelung. Ich möchte mehr allgemein musikalisch arbeiten, was Ihnen dann auch zu gute kommt. Bei allen Vorarbeiten, die ich in den letzten Wochen gemacht habe, kamen Sachen, die für Sie wertvoll wären. In irgend einer Form will ich die für Sie sichern. Die Frage ist nur, ob Sie damit zufrieden sind. Schon jetzt macht es mich oft traurig, dass Sie eigentlich nie zufrieden sind, und dass Sie alles oder nichts wollen. Ja, ich muss meine eigene Arbeit daneben tun können und ich müsste nicht mitmachen müssen, wenn es sich um etwas handelt, das mir so gegen den Strich geht, wie z. B. Honegger. Ich sehe ein, dass ich das in meiner Funktion können sollte, aber ich 'kann' wirklich nur, wenn ich alles mitmache! Darum glaube ich immer noch, dass es möglich sein wird, dass Sie einmal einen Assistenten finden, der soviel Technik hat, dass er alles mitmachen kann, ohne sich seelisch zu erschöpfen. Bis dahin werde ich es tun nach meinen besten Kräften, wenn Sie sich damit begnügen können". Ibid.

45 "So macht mir meine Komposition Angst. Die Einleitung ist skizziert und wird dann im September mit der neuen Partitur fertig. Das Ganze hat aber zu wenig Effekt für Sie, obwohl ich bei der Arbeit immer an Sie und an Ihren Apparat gedacht habe". Ibid.

tions about life, thereby revealing a side of himself that few people were allowed to see:

> A good human relationship is simple, both in content & form (as is everything that is
> important in life). I have never understood why you speak of "pride" and similar things!
> I am always there for you in a self-evident way, which grew from within over time, so
> that I have no idea what mental states you would need to hide from me. The best friend-
> ship seems to me to be that in which one presents oneself without make-up, just how
> you are. Women are more complex in this, I am aware of that. But after everything,
> I could almost be your brother, so that all hiding, keeping of secrets, or transposition
> of ideas in other (than their original) form, etc., etc., almost seems unnatural to me.
> I would like it if you had more trust, particularly in this relationship. You must start
> from the premise that I want nothing *against* you, that I do *not* intend to exploit you,
> in short, that I am not trying to bluff you. I really do want the best for you, and have a
> lot of patience, much more than men usually do, because I know that the most beauti-
> ful fruit ripen only slowly. As in nature. And only in the sun. The sun in this case is the
> personal connection & to be sure, the trust. (My daily impatience, or intolerance & in-
> satiability at work has nothing to do with this).[46]

This is a remarkable statement concerning his conception of an ideal friendship.
At the same time, with it he is saying that he had seen Ina Lohr in her despair,
anger, weakness, and still wanted to work together with her, that he valued the
relationship, felt a closeness akin to that of a brother; that he was not trying to
exploit her. At the same time, he admitted to his most obvious defects, clarifying, however, that they did not reflect a lack of trust in her, that they were on a
different plane. He went on with the following confession:

> I admit that I often treat people as a clever rider does his horse. Certainly, but I make
> exceptions. You are such an exception. Please believe this without the slightest trace of
> mistrust.

46 "Eine gute menschliche Beziehung ist einfach, in Inhalt & Form (wie alles wichtige im
   Leben). Ich habe ja nie begriffen warum Sie von 'Stolz' & ähnlichem reden! Ich bin für
   Sie in einer so selbstverständlichen, innerlich gewachsenen Art ständig vorhanden, dass
   ich nicht weiss, welche Seelenzustände Sie vor mir verbergen müssen. Die beste Freundschaft scheint mir die, in der man sich ungeschminkt gibt, genau so wie es einem zu Mute
   ist. Frauen sind darin komplizierter, das ist mir bewusst. Aber nach allem könnte ich nun
   beinahe Ihr Bruder sein, sodass mir alles Verbergen, Geheimhalten, in andere Gedanken-
   gänge (als die ursprünglichen) transponieren etc etc beinahe unnatürlich vorkommt. Ich
   hätte gerne, wenn Sie gerade in dieser Beziehung noch mehr Vertrauen hätten. Sie müssen
   einmal von der Voraussetzung ausgehen, dass ich nichts gegen Sie will, dass ich nicht vor-
   habe Sie auszubeuten, kurz, dass ich Ihnen nichts vormache. Ich will wirklich Ihr Bestes &
   habe viel Geduld, vielmehr als Männer sonst aufbringen, weil ich weiss, dass die schönsten
   Früchte nur langsam reifen. Wie in der Natur. Und nur in der Sonne. Die Sonne ist in diesem Fall die unmenschliche Verbundenheit & eben das Vertrauen. (Meine tägliche Unge-
   duld, oder Unduldsamkeit & Unersättlichkeit in der Arbeit hat damit nichts zu tun)". Letter Paul Sacher to Ina Lohr of 18 August 1940, PSF-ILC.

> Try to understand that I am meeting you like a father or brother, i.e. as a friend. You will make that much more possible, or better said, you will only make it possible, if you accordingly enter in on it with trust and security.[47]

Implicitly with this he is admitting that he often acted out of mere egotism, but that in her case he really felt the closeness of a family relationship, perhaps even in the chivalrous sense of taking over the supervisory, care-taking role that her father could no longer carry out due to the war. This does open the more far-reaching, unanswerable question of whether there was some intrinsic basic similarity between him and Herman Lohr which led her to be drawn into the cooperation initially and left her fighting for her own space, just as she had done with her father through the act of coming to Basel.

Paul Sacher wondered further, why she felt such reluctance about the *Laufenberg Lieder*, asking whether she thought he "criticized something about her work, do[es] not like it, or find it virtuoso or dramatic enough?" to which he answered resoundingly "By no means!"[48] He then went on to say, led on perchance by the openness of Ina Lohr's letter and the degree to which she was willing to speak of her own motivations for her behavior, to speak of himself, his own perception of how he encountered the world:

> Don't let yourself be deceived: I do not speak much. My objectivity is not so much related to a lack of warmth or fantasy, but lies in a strong sense for reality, a marked dislike for mere talk or prettied-up feelings; and (in another context) in an unerring instinct for what is possible. This is all in considerable contrast to your effervescent temperament. One can be sensitive and at the same time a farmer. That's how I am. That, however, does not at all exclude my getting on with your sparkling [literally Champagne] vitality.[49]

---

47 "Ich gebe zu, dass ich sehr oft Menschen behandle, wie ein geschickter Reiter sein Pferd. Gewiss, aber ich mache Ausnahmen. Sie sind eine solche Ausnahme. Glauben Sie das bitte ohne jedes Misstrauen.

   Versuchen Sie einzusehen, dass ich Ihnen wie ein Vater oder Bruder, eben als Freund begegne. Sie machen das viel möglicher, ja geradezu: Sie ermöglichen das erst, wenn Sie entsprechend vertrauensvoll & selbstverständlich darauf eingehen". Ibid.

48 "Und warum die Hemmung mit den Lauffenberg [sic] Liedern? Glauben Sie, ich kritisiere etwas an Ihrer Arbeit, fände sie nicht schön, oder virtuos & effektvoll genug? Keineswegs!" Ibid.

49 "Lassen Sie sich nie täuschen: Ich mache wenig Worte. Meine Nüchternheit entspricht weniger mangelnder Wärme oder Fantasie, sie ruht in einem ausgesprochenen Tatsachensinn, einer betonten Abneigung gegen Phrasen oder zur Schau gestellte Gefühle, und (in anderem Zusammenhang) einem unbeirrbaren Instinkt für das Mögliche. Das alles kontrastiert erheblich mit Ihrem sprudelnden Temperament. Man kann susceptible sein & gleichzeitig ein Bauer. So bin ich. Das schliesst keineswegs aus, dass ich mit Ihrer Champagner-Lebendigkeit nicht auskäme". Ibid.

With these words, he wanted to be sure that Ina Lohr understood certain aspects of his behavior that he feared she may have misconstrued, wanting to make clear that an apparent lack of reaction on his part did not mean that he was unaware or untouched by what was going on in her.

This letter broke through Ina Lohr's reserves, so that on 22 August 1940 she could only write:

> I have been vanquished: the hardness in me, which we have called pride, cannot with-stand so much "sun". I will try to hold on to this trust and not defend myself against imagined attacks against my last and most inner possession and against my last strength. I just cannot give everything and am so often under the impression that you want everything and still more. But you now know my limits and I hope to prove my will-ingness to give, even if I begin cautiously. I never had such a feeling of coming "home", as when I returned to Basel this time.
>
> That is also a good sign. I thankfully accept your brotherly friendship.[50]

In any case, these letters cleared the air sufficiently to enable them once again to take up their work together in the following season. The extent of Paul Sacher's insight into Ina Lohr's dilemma and her suffering due to being separated from her family, and the effect of the sensitive way in which he spoke of it – not in any way making a claim that he could replace her family, but only reflecting on the nature of the bond between the two of them – may be seen by a passage in a letter from Ina Lohr to Ernst Gaugler of 5 September 1940. Here she spoke of how her father had admitted in a letter that he had to just accept the fact that both he and his wife will not see Ina until the war was over. Only after receiv-ing this, did she feel able to

> take the second step and feel and declare myself to belong here completely. A protracted and often difficult correspondence with Sacher contributed to this. Both of us fought with ourselves and with one another, and in it he mustered up far more courage and more friendship than I did. This really very rare friendship has in the end won out. My pride has been vanquished. I no longer play the role of the independent Dutch woman

---

50 "Ich gebe mich gewonnen: gegenüber soviel 'Sonne' hält eben diese Härte in mir, die wir Stolz genannt haben nicht stand. Ich werde versuchen dieses Vertrauen fest zu halten und mich nicht zu wehren gegen vermeinte Angriffe auf meinen letzten und innersten Besitz und gegen meine letzte Kraft. Ich kann eben nicht alles hergeben und stehe zu oft unter dem Eindruck, dass Sie alles und noch mehr möchten. Aber Sie kennen jetzt meine Gren-zen und meine Gebensbereitschaft hoffe ich zu beweisen, auch wenn ich noch vorsichtig anfange. Noch nie habe ich so das Gefühl gehabt 'nach Hause' zu kommen, als ich nach Basel kam, wie diesmal.
     Auch das ist ein gutes Zeichen. Ich nehme Ihre brüderliche Freundschaft dankbar an". Letter Ina Lohr to Paul Sacher of 22 August 1940, private collection, Switzerland.

who helps out with the work, but otherwise manages to get through alone. I am letting myself be spoiled and am happy when one helps me in practical things.[51]

This did not mean, however that she found it easy to deal with the situation of being separated from her family. In her Christmas wishes to Paul Sacher of 27 December 1940 she wrote:

> I can only write you that which I cannot easily say: that I am always thankful for your friendship, even then when I am seemingly unapproachable and closed. The struggle with homesickness in the fall was very hard. Things are now better, and I hope to not lose my courage again.[52]

Her difficulty was not only the homesickness itself, but her inability to speak of it with those around her, feeling obligated to maintain the armor of an "independent Dutch woman".

The *Laufenberg Lieder* and 1941

On 9 May 1941, Ina Lohr's *Laufenberg Lieder* were performed and received with appreciation. These songs form a kind of bridge between her intensely personal compositional approach for solo voice and her work with the BKO (see Ill. 5.4).

Two of the melodies were written much earlier, as they are found interspersed in a manuscript together with other songs dated between 1933–38. It is therefore clear that they were originally conceived independently from the string parts. A review of the concert in the national music journal, *Die Schweizerische Musikzeitung*, commented that

> the unisono singing, the core of the composition, is divided between the women's and men's voices, which at times alternate with one another, at times come together in a beautiful richness. The gossamery string-writing, from which sometimes two bright solo violins emerge, accompanies and joins with the song. The first strophe begins narratively, similar in tone to that of an old ballad; the second continues with greater joy,

---

51 "hat es mir ermöglicht den zweiten Schritt zu tun und mich hier ganz zugehörig zu fühlen und zu erklären. Dazu hat auch eine ausgiebige und oft sehr schwierige Korrespondenz mit Sacher beigetragen. Wir haben beide mit uns selbst und miteinander gekämpft und er hat dabei entschieden mehr Mut und auch mehr Freundschaft aufgebracht als ich. Diese wirklich ganz seltene Freundschaft hat schliesslich gewonnen. Mein Stolz ist besiegt. Ich spiele nicht mehr die selbständige Holländerin, die in der Arbeit mitmacht, aber sonst alleine durchkommt. Ich lasse mich verwöhnen und bin froh, wenn man mir in praktischen Sachen hilft". Letter Ina Lohr to Ernst Gaugler of 5 September 1940, PSF-ILC.

52 "Ich kann Ihnen nur schreiben, was ich nicht gut sagen kann: dass ich Ihnen für Ihre Freundschaft immer dankbar bin, auch dann, wenn ich scheinbar unnahbar und verschlossen bin. Der Kampf mit dem Heimweh war diesen Herbst eben schlimm. Es geht jetzt besser und ich hoffe den Mut nicht wieder zu verlieren". Letter Ina Lohr to Paul Sacher of 27 December 1940, private collection, Switzerland.

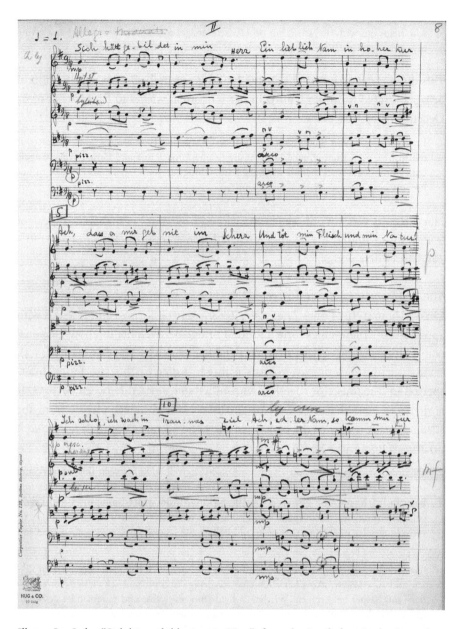

Ill. 5.4: Ina Lohr, "Sich hätt gebildet in min Herz", from the *Laufenberg Lieder*. Reproduction: PSF-ILC.

almost dance-like, based on a pronounced rhythm; and the third, superficially more re-
strained, leads to an inner intensification. The whole reveals an intimate knowledge of
the great melodic music of earlier times – while at the same time absolutely having the
effect of a modern creation – and gained the sympathy of the listeners through its naturalness, through its strong inner engagement and lack of pretension. It received warm
applause at the premiere.[53]

It was the generosity of acts such as this performance that reconciled Ina Lohr
to her work with Paul Sacher as his musical assistant, at least to a certain degree.
Directly after the performance on 9 May 1941, she wrote

> I still have to say to you on paper that which I otherwise would not be able to say to
> you calmly. It appears to be so absolutely easy to thank with words; at the same time, I
> have recently been so impatient and dismissive. I do hope, however, that I will at some
> point overcome the inner resistance that still stands in the way of a really good cooper-
> ation with one another. I increasingly believe that the main reason lies in the fact that
> you live from activity and I have a terrible need for quiet and reflection. When you are
> so active, then I think I have to continue working and cooperating in the same tempo
> and completely forgo my quiet. That then makes me unhappy and reproachful.
>
> But if you have enough patience, then it will perhaps get better, when I am clearer
> about everything. There are time and again moments that are so good, that they help
> often and for a long time. Such a moment was this evening. I thank you for your big in-
> vestment for the children of my mind and I want to devote myself with the same dedi-
> cation to your work – hopefully I will succeed.[54]

53 W.N. [Walter Nef?], "Die einstimmige Gesangsweise, der Kern der Komposition, wird
    auf Frauen- und Männerstimmen verteilt, die bald miteinander wechseln, bald zu schö-
    ner Fülle zusammentreten. Ein duftiger Streichersatz, aus dem bisweilen zwei helle Solo-
    violinen heraustreten, begleitet und verbindet den Gesang. Erzählend, dem Ton einer alten
    Ballade ähnlich, beginnt die erste Strophe, freudiger, fast tänzerisch, auf einen prägnan-
    ten Rhythmus gebaut, setzt die zweite fort, und die dritte, äusserlich wieder verhaltenere,
    führt zu einer innern Steigerung. Das Ganze verrät wohl intime Vertrautheit mit der gros-
    sen melodischen Musik der ältern Zeit, wirkt aber durchaus als neuzeitliche Schöpfung,
    die sich in ihrer Natürlichkeit, ihrer starken inneren Beteiligung und Prätentionslosig-
    keit die Sympathien der Hörer erwarb und bei der Uraufführung warmen Beifall erhielt".
    Under Basel in the rubric "Berichte aus der Schweiz und dem Ausland: Konzert Berichte"
    [Reports from Switzerland and abroad: Concert Reviews], in: *Schweizerische Musikzeitung*
    81/6, 1 June 1941, 165.
54 "muss ich Ihnen auf Papier noch das sagen, was ich nun einmal sonst nicht ruhig sagen
    kann. Es scheint so bequem einfach zu danken mit Worten; daneben war ich dann in letz-
    ter Zeit oft unduldsam und ablehnend. Ich hoffe aber wirklich, dass ich einmal die inneren
    Widerstände überwinden werde, die einer wirklich guten Zusammenarbeit zwischen uns
    immer noch im Wege stehen. Immer mehr glaube ich, dass der Hauptgrund darin liegt,
    dass Sie von der Aktivität aus leben und dass ich ein erschreckendes Bedürfnis nach Stille
    und Besinnung habe. Wenn Sie so ganz aktiv sind, dann meine ich, ich müsse im gleichen
    Tempo weiter schaffen und mitschaffen [sic] und meine Stille ganz opfern. Das macht mich
    dann unglücklich und vorwurfsvoll.

This letter demonstrates the extent of the bind in which Ina Lohr felt herself to be entangled. On the night after a successful performance of one of her own compositions, she still could not escape the fact that she felt entrapped by the situation, could not just say thank you. To the contrary, Paul Sacher's investment in her own composition made her simply feel guilty of not being equally generous and productive for him. It was just this unequal conflict – a moral comparison of incongruent aspects of their cooperation – that made it so difficult for her to make a clear inner commitment to her job as musical assistant.

This was compounded by Paul Sacher's financial generosity. For example, on 22 June 1941 he sent her some money in recognition of her composition, saying that he did this with all composers who have composed for him, be they friend or stranger. This in turn led to great inner compunctions on the part of Ina Lohr, as is revealed by a letter of 26 June 1941:

> When my parents went back to Holland a while ago, I vowed to belong to you and your circle and to fight against any sense of being an "outsider". Unfortunately, I have not been at all successful with this up until now, and for this I am very sorry, as, because of this, I am time and again the "difficult number" that I always was. Thus, for this reason I now, once again, find it difficult to accept the money (and so much money!) for the cantata. I had such pleasure in having given you something useful for once. And now it is not a present any more and I can never give you any presents again. With Beck and Burkhard it is different, as they live from their compositions and have already had commissions from you. And then there is the awful fact that I no longer work for you as I did before, or, better said, I do it for *you* and – with a heavy heart – do my best […] I cannot come to terms with these problems, even in peace and quiet, and you probably cannot even imagine why they are problems. This is what one becomes when one grows up with fairy tales and great beauty and only learns how to act as a benefactress.
>   And now I will bamboozle you and myself a little and take the money as a present from you, as an emergency fund should I become ill. This will remove a great worry from my [shoulders] and I thank you very, very warmly.[55]

Aber wenn Sie genug Geduld haben, dann wird es vielleicht besser, wenn ich mir klarer über alles das bin. Es gibt auch immer wieder Augenblicke, die so gut sind, dass sie lange und oft helfen. Ein solcher Augenblick war der heutige Abend. Ich danke Ihnen für Ihren grossen Einsatz für meine Geisteskinder und möchte mich mit der gleichen Hingabe Ihrer Sache widmen – Hoffentlich gelingt's!" Letter Ina Lohr to Paul Sache of 9 May 1941, private collection, Switzerland.

55 "Als meine Eltern damals nach Holland zurückfuhren, nahm ich mir fest vor, zu Ihnen und zu Ihrem Kreis zu gehören und jedes 'Fremdsein' zu bestreiten. Leider ist es mir bis jetzt gar nicht gelungen und das tut mir sehr leid, denn dadurch bin ich immer wieder die 'schwierige Nummer', die ich schon immer war. So fällt es mir jetzt wieder sehr schwer das Geld (und dann soviel Geld!) für die Kantate anzunehmen. Ich hatte eine solche Freude, Ihnen einmal etwas Brauchbares geschenkt zu haben. Und jetzt ist es eben kein Geschenk mehr und ich kann Ihnen auch nie wieder etwas schenken. Mit Beck und Burkhard ist es darum anders,

With the war and the concomitant separation from her family plus the retirement of her father, an additional factor entered the picture: the necessity of providing for herself. Most of her adult life, she had either been entirely or partially
supported by the generosity of her father. Now she had to face the fact of what
it really meant to be an independent woman and realize that she had financial limitations. This caused her at one and the same time to be fearful for her
future, as seen above, and to desire to prove to the world that she could support
herself. This, of course, only contributed to her emotional turmoil in regard to
her work with Paul Sacher.

On 30 June 1941, apparently after a discussion with him, she wrote once
again, somehow wanting to bring this long battle to an end:

> I only fear that you think that I could now also become difficult in a different way; this
> is, however, not the case. Our "musical marriage" has brought a very strong personal
> bond with it. It wasn't there at first, it has grown slowly, often [gone] through stormy
> periods and is thus stronger than most bonds. Through our talk, I have seen for the first
> time that you know that and that this is also true for you. That freed me from all hor-
> rible, mistrustful thoughts and I can now begin again with courage and feel myself less
> lonely and lost. Thank you for your trust and the great effort.[56]

Of course, this was only temporary, in that on 7 July 1941 she once again felt the
need for a few additional explanations. First of all, she thanked him for the additional financial support he had given her for her vacation quasi as a "placeholder
for her father", commenting that his generosity and stubbornness were greater
than her own, but also that it reminded her of her father. She promised to give

---

weil sie von ihren Kompositionen leben und schon Aufträge von Ihnen gehabt haben. Und
dann ist da die schlimme Tatsache, dass ich nicht mehr so für Sie arbeite, wie früher, oder,
besser gesagt, für <u>Sie</u> tue ich es und gebe mir, schweren Herzens alle Mühe. […] Ich werde,
auch in der Ruhe, mit diesen Problemen nicht fertig und Sie können sich wahrscheinlich
gar nicht vorstellen, warum das Probleme sind. So wird man eben, wenn man mit Märchen
und lauter Schönheit aufwächst und nur lernt, wie man sich als Gebende zu benehmen hat.
   Und jetzt beschwindle ich Sie und mich ein bischen [sic] und nehme das Geld als
Geschenk von Ihnen an, als Notpfennig für wenn ich einmal krank würde. Damit ist mir
eine grosse Sorge abgenommen und ich danke Ihnen sehr, sehr herzlich". Letter Ina Lohr
to Paul Sacher of 26 June 1941, private collection, Switzerland.

56   "Ich habe nur Angst, dass Sie meinen, ich könnte jetzt auch noch in einer anderen Art
schwierig werden; das ist nämlich nicht der Fall. Unsere 'musikalische Ehe' hat für mich
eine sehr starke menschliche Bindung mit sich gebracht. Sie war zuerst nicht da, sie ist langsam, durch oft sehr stürmische Zeiten gewachsen und ist darum stärker als die meisten Bin-
dungen. Durch unser Gespräch habe ich erst gesehen, dass Sie das wissen und dass es bei
Ihnen auch so ist. Das hat mich befreit von allen schlimmen, misstrauischen Gedanken
und ich kann jetzt wieder mit Mut anfangen und fühle mich weniger einsam und verloren.
Dank für Ihr Vertrauen und für die grosse Anstrengung". Letter Ina Lohr to Paul Sacher of
30 June 1941, private collection, Switzerland.

him back anything that she did not use. But she also felt the need to say why
she kept on turning down invitations to the Sachers' vacation house in Saanen.

> There are only very, very few people with whom I can really be myself; and they are all
> unreachable for me now. Otherwise it is always the case that I lose myself when I am
> with people that I like and who interest me. I would grow entirely accustomed to a place
> in your family, but would have very great difficulties giving it up again and finding my
> way back to myself. That's why I have to be by myself during the holidays, or with peo-
> ple I don't know; in order to gather myself together and rest.[57]

This is a very revealing passage, as in it she speaks of her difficulty of retaining a sense of self in the presence of those to whom she feels close. She had not
learned that personal boundaries were both acceptable and necessary, and so she
was constantly torn between wanting closeness with others and the necessity
of periods of quiet and isolation, in which she could process what had gone on
and return to herself. It also explains why she compartmentalized her relationships to such a great degree, as that was the only way she could deal with them.

The summer of 1941, however, was by no means spent resting. She first spent
a week in Interlaken, with a day trip on 17 July to visit friends and a former
student in Berne who were more in tune with her interests in church music.
Here, interest was expressed that she give an introductory course at the conservatory for teachers and students, and then another later in connection with
the instruction of *Hausmusik*. From 20–26 July she was in Winterthur for the
thought-provoking course on modes and solmization for organists and choir
directors mentioned in Chapter 3, where she gave six two-hour lectures. Immediately thereafter, from 28 July–2 August, she participated in a girl scout camp
in Adelboden, something that left her exhausted, as one can very well imagine.
Just three days later she went to Saanen to discuss the upcoming season with
Paul Sacher. Judging from the exchange of letters immediately thereafter, it
must have been a stormy session, with Ina Lohr – a bit giddy and excited by her
successes with the courses for theology students, organists and choir directors –

---

57 "Es gibt nur ganz, ganz wenig Menschen mit denen ich wirklich mich selbst sein kann; sie
   sind jetzt gerade alle für mich unerreichbar. Sonst ist es immer so, dass ich mich verliere,
   wenn ich bei Menschen bin, die ich gerne habe und die mich interessieren. Ich würde in
   Ihrer Familie mich ganz einleben, hätte aber nachher die grössten Schwierigkeiten diesen
   Platz wieder aufzugeben und mich selbst zurück zu finden. Darum muss ich in den Ferien
   allein sein, oder bei fremden Menschen; um zu sammeln und auszuruhen". The letter was
   dated 7 June 1941, but due to its place in the notebook and its content, and the letter of
   the same date from Paul Sacher mentioning the gift, it is clear that it was actually written
   a month later, private collection, Switzerland.

speaking of how she needed to free herself from some work with Paul Sacher in September in order to devote more time to her own work, and in the process overlooking his concerns, with, of course the corresponding results.

Already, on the following day, on 6 August 1941, Ina Lohr re-opened the discussion of their cooperation, commenting on how it must seem as if she were breaking her promises by returning to the question of whether she can continue working for Sacher. She said she had no choice but to do so, that for her, it was simply the question

> of whether I sacrifice my own work for you, this work that I do not merely as a profession, but really as a "profession", or our cooperation, (and therewith also your friendship and our close connection). This again belongs to the things that cannot easily be said. I do not do this work because it is my own work, or only because it seems easier to me than what you ask of me. It is only because sacred music gives me the sole possibility of answering the terrible questions of the time that I am involved in this work more fanatically than ever in the past two years. I cannot hate (this is not just a figure of speech, it would be easier, if I could), I cannot even judge, I can and must only continually praise, thank and pray in order to make up for what I have missed out upon for years. That's why everything becomes sacred music for me, as a girl scout quite correctly declared; and [why] a pastor from Winterthur spoke of my "tone theology". In these circles I can express my overflowing heart and that brings me again into balance. But I cannot forgo – although yesterday once again robbed me of my balance – your friendship and help. Do you really not know what you mean to me? I cannot leave you in the lurch; I would lose a part of myself with that.[58]

She then assured him that she would reorganize the schedule, so that she would not only do less for her own projects, but also be free at the times he needed her. And that she would turn to marking up the scores particularly carefully.

---

58 "Es handelt sich aber für mich einfach darum, dass ich entweder Ihnen meine eigene Arbeit opfere, oder unsere Zusammenarbeit, (und damit auch Ihre Freundschaft und unsere Verbundenheit), diese Arbeit, die ich nicht nur als Beruf, sondern wirklich aus 'Berufung' mache. Das gehört wieder zu den Sachen, die sich nicht gut sagen lassen. Ich tue diese Arbeit nicht, weil sie meine eigene Arbeit ist, oder nur, weil sie mir leichter fällt, als was Sie von mir verlangen. Dass ich seit 2 Jahren fanatischer als je dahinter bin, das kommt, weil die Kirchenmusik mir die einzige Möglichkeit gibt, auf die furchtbaren Fragen dieser Zeit zu antworten. Ich kann nicht hassen, (das ist wirklich keine Phrase, es wäre leichter, wenn ich es könnte), ich kann nicht einmal urteilen, ich kann und muss nur immerfort loben, danken und beten um nachzuholen, was ich Jahre lang versäumt habe. Darum wird jetzt alles bei mir zur Kirchenmusik, wie eine Pfadfinderin ganz richtig bemerkte und ein Pfarrer in Winterthur sprach von meiner 'Tontheologie'. In den Kreisen kann ich mein übervolles Herz äussern und das bringt mich wieder ins Gleichgewicht. Aber ich kann, obwohl der gestrige Tag mir das Gleichgewicht wieder nahm, nicht auf Ihre Freundschaft und Hilfe verzichten. Wissen Sie denn wirklich nicht, was die mir bedeuten? Ich kann Sie auch nicht im Stich lassen; ich würde damit einen Teil von mir selbst verlieren". Letter Ina Lohr to Paul Sacher of 6 August 1941, private collection, Switzerland.

That Paul Sacher had also been greatly affected by the confrontation is made evident by his letter of the following day, 7 August 1941. As this letter is so exemplary for their entire relationship, I quote it in its entirety.

Dear Miss Lohr,
Thank you for your letter. It found me after – for me – a sleepless night, or more exactly, after a sleepless hour.

For a long time now, I have given up all arguing and reasoning because it leads nowhere. If I rely only on my feelings for you, I have, for me, a very unusual stance: a mixture of indulgence and patience. But it is not completely new to me, this stance. I needed it once eight years ago.

In this hour awake in the night, I found this back & forth and up & down not worthy of us. To say nothing of the hurts, tensions & practical irritations that are connected with it. And then I decided, in accordance with your wish, to look for an assistant for the choir rehearsals in order to relieve you from this work. To be sure, I could only think of Hans Vogt. There is no need for a lot of imagination to see that new dangers for our cooperation could grow from this. If you want it, however, I will try it.

Love never morphs into indifference, and the abandonment of our cooperation! It would be a catastrophe. Again, apart from the objectively regrettable [aspect], for me it would mean the most drastic loss that I can imagine.

I still believe that the solution lies in the right dosage. I must not put too much pressure on you & must react to your "escapades" with indulgence rather than punishment. Nonetheless we would have to find a comparatively stable measure of constancy. In order to avoid the back & forth and also to ensure the dependability of the work. You want to try it again, according to your letter. I [want that] anyway.

I request that you only carry out those of your new plans that represent a very strong inner need, but to leave those out that do not push themselves impetuously to the surface. Actually, I thought the question about the rhythm of the songs was most clearly yours. The solmization is something that you can also do from the Schola [in reference to choices she spoke of in her letter]. Please orient yourself, in your work that is independent of me, not in accordance with the wishes of those that are besieging you, but in line with you own inner need. This is surely good advice and the most fruitful principle. I allow you all freedom [in this], as a matter of course. In your domain at the Schola anyway. I [would] even accept your resignation. Nonetheless, I shudder to think of the shambles that would then lie in front of us.

That was what came of that hour in the night. Now your letter has come in the meantime. It has taken the last trace of severity from my thoughts.

About everything else we can talk.

I will never beg you to maintain our cooperation. Everything that is done out of pity or against one's will, forced, or demanded is unfruitful and senseless. It has to be your own, autonomous decision. I am prepared to take full responsibility for my behavior. I cannot take away the responsibility for your decision from you. My concern for you remains. But I trust[ed] beneficent fate from the very first day.

Warmly yours Paul Sacher

1. Could you read this GP [season's program] text? Tell me, please, what you find bad.
2. In order to simplify the rehearsal work, do we want to choose, in place of Caldara, Friedrich II & Graun,

a) only Friedrich II & Graun

or

b) after all Lully?

Solution a) does appear quite possible to me. We would only need to rehearse Venite populi and the Te Deum until the Mozart concert, could actually take a vacation also with the choir in the fall vacation, or – should we get the music – rehearse Burkhard [the oratorio, *Das Jahr*], or also Praetorius or Bach.

3. The program of the 5th concert seems very good to me in our last version.

4. Thank you for "Volkslied". The other printed things are on approval, please send them back.[59]

59 "Liebes Fräulein Lohr,

herzlichen Dank für Ihren Brief. Er hat mich nach einer – für meine Verhältnisse – schlaflosen Nacht, genau genommen nach einer schlaflosen Stunde angetroffen.

Ich habe nun seit langem alles argumentieren & raisonieren aufgegeben, weil es zu keinem Ende führt. Wenn ich mich allein auf meine Gefühle für Sie verlasse, komme ich zu einer für mich ganz ausgefallenen Haltung: einer Mischung von Nachsicht und Geduld. Sie ist mir aber nicht ganz neu, diese Einstellung. Ich hatte sie schon einmal vor acht Jahren nötig.

In dieser wachen Nachtstunde fand ich dieses Hin & Her und Auf & Ab unserer nicht würdig. Nicht zu sprechen von den Schmerzen, Spannungen & praktischen Unzukömmlichkeiten, die damit verbunden sind. Und da habe ich mich dann entschlossen, nach Ihrem Wunsch eine Hilfe für die Chorproben zu suchen, um Sie von dieser Arbeit zu entlasten. Es ist mir allerdings nur Hans Vogt eingefallen. Es hat dann nicht grosser Phantasie bedurft, um einzusehen, dass daraus unserer Zusammenarbeit neue Gefahren erwachsen können. Wenn Sie es wollen, will ich es jedoch versuchen.

Liebe verwandelt sich niemals in Gleichgültigkeit, & die Aufgabe unserer Arbeitsgemeinschaft! Wäre eine Katastrophe. Abgesehen wiederum vom objektiv bedauerlichen, bedeutete dies für mich den einschneidensten Verlust, den ich mir denken kann.

Ich glaube noch immer, dass die Lösung in der richtigen Dosierung liegt. Ich darf Sie nicht zu sehr belasten & muss Ihre 'Eskapaden' mit Nachsicht, statt mit Strafe belegen. Trotzdem müssten wir eine einigermassen ruhige Linie der Beständigkeit finden. Zur Vermeidung des Hin & Her und auch für die Gewährleistung einer zuverlässigen Arbeit. Sie wollen es noch einmal versuchen, nach Ihrem Brief. Ich ohnehin.

Ich bitte Sie, von Ihren neuen Pläne nur diejenigen zu realisieren, die stärkstes inneres Bedürfnis sind, aber wegzulassen, was nicht stürmisch ans Tageslicht drängt. Eigentlich schien mir die Rhythmusfrage der Lieder Ihr eigenstes. Die Solmisation können Sie auch von der Schola aus durchsehen. Richten Sie sich in Ihrer von mir unabhängigen Arbeit bitte nicht nach den Wünschen der Sie Bestürmenden, sondern nach Ihrem inneren Bedürfnis. Dies ist sicher ein guter Rat und das fruchtbarste Prinzip. Ich lasse Ihnen von vorneherein alle Freiheit. In Ihrer Domäne Schola ohnehin. Ich akzeptiere sogar Ihre Kündigung. Allerdings graut mir vor dem Scherbenhaufen, der dann vor uns liegt.

Das hat sich in jener nächtlichen Stunde herausgeschält. Nun ist Ihr Brief dazwischen gekommen. Er hat meinen Gedanken die letzte Spur von Schärfe genommen.

Ueber alles andere können wir reden.

Ich werde Sie nie bitten, unsere Zusammenarbeit aufrechtzuerhalten. Alles mitleidig oder widerwillig Gewährte, Erzwungene und Gewaltsame ist unfruchtbar & sinnlos. Es muss Ihr eigener, autonomer Entschluss sein. Ich bin bereit die volle Verantwortung für

This letter reveals the degree to which Paul Sacher was also affected by the dis-
agreements, the squabbles. He could not sleep, he could not apply his normal
objectivity, but was forced to a stance of "indulgence and patience". Like Ina
Lohr, he spoke of how this reminded him of early times together, when in 1933
she was so upset about the idea of Palestrina in a concert hall that she refused
to travel to Paris with the Basel Chamber Choir and was considering returning
to Amsterdam. And also, like Ina Lohr, who genuinely had difficulties sleeping when such issues troubled her, he decided in a dark hour to cut through the
entanglements of the emotional swings in the cooperation, feeling they were
unworthy of them. He admitted in this letter to having resolved inwardly to
choose a new assistant for the choir, as she had requested, although that might
present new dangers to their cooperation. At the same time, he retained his
optimistic belief in the strength of their cooperation, being afraid of the consequences of its dissolution.

Nonetheless, as soon as he received word that she was willing to continue,
he tossed these plans aside, and once again began searching for the means to
give their work a certain stability. The only thing he asked of her was to try to
keep the scope of the projects outside of those for the BKO and SCB to those
that were of greatest need to her, to simply not react directly to the requests of
those around her. The degree to which he placed particular value on her freedom of choice is striking, in acknowledgment of the fact that, without it, no
creative work for either of them would be possible. It is noteworthy that he
considered this freedom to be self-evident in her domain at the Schola, striking evidence of her position there. Even while re-embarking in the coopera-

meine Haltung zu tragen. Die Verantwortung für Ihren Entscheid kann ich Ihnen nicht
abnehmen. Meine Sorge um Sie bleibt. Aber ich vertraue vom ersten Tag an einem gütigen
Geschick.
       Alles Herzliche Ihr Paul Sacher
       1. Können Sie diesen GP-Text lesen? Sagen Sie mir bitte was Sie schlecht finden.
       2. Wollen wir zur Vereinfachung der Probenarbeit anstelle von Caldara Friedrich II &
Graun
       a) nur Friedrich II & Graun
       oder
       b) doch Lully
wählen? Die Lösung a) schiene mir durchaus möglich. Wir müssten bis zum Mozart
Konzert nur Venite populi & das Te Deum üben, könnten nachher auch im Chor Herbst-
ferien machen, oder – falls wir das Material bekommen – Burkhard einüben, oder auch
Praetorius resp. Bach.
       3. Das Programm des 5. Konzertes leuchtet mir in unserer letzten Fassung sehr ein.
       4. Vielen Dank für 'Volkslied'. Die anderen Drucksachen zur Ansicht, bitte zurück."
       Letter Paul Sacher to Ina Lohr of 7 August 1941, PSF-ILC.

tion, he made clear that he would not oppose her resignation, if that was what she deemed necessary, in spite of the calamity that would bring. It was up to her to decide.

For the most part in the correspondence, Paul Sacher usually played the role of the strong, stable man who through his support for the sensitive, volatile Ina Lohr, provided her with the stability she needed to function socially in the world around her. She on the other hand, gave him the emotional and musical input he needed to be able to build up his career. This is one of the few letters in which he shows the same sort of inconsistency as Ina Lohr, the same sort of inability to stop a collaboration that was at one and the same time extraordinarily productive and contentious. And he, too, just as Ina Lohr always did, made the decision to continue, preferring to deal with their difficulties together rather than to give up their work, whose products gave him, and at times her, such satisfaction.

Common to the letters of both of them throughout this entire correspondence, is their ability to compartmentalize. The change in this letter, from the exhausted, almost shorthand language of the beginning to the highly efficient questions and comments of the final paragraph concerning the actual tasks at hand, is both noteworthy and characteristic of the issues involved.

In her answer to him of 10 August 1941, Ina Lohr opened by explaining how she has reorganized the coming month or two in order to facilitate the work with him. She then laid out her concept for the coming season:

> We will most likely obtain the stablest method of working if we adhere to a set day for our work. I want to reserve, as much as it is possible, two whole days for you in the coming semester, preferably Friday and Saturday and [in addition] Monday morning. Even if someone else helps you with the rehearsals for the Burkhard, I would study the score as soon as possible and often come to the rehearsals, so that we could speak about them, if you so desire.[60]

This is one of those paragraphs which makes the dimensions of the cooperation, the measure in which she was involved in the preparation of the BKO concerts

---

60 "Die beständige Linie in der Arbeit haben wir am ehesten, wenn wir möglichst an einem festen Arbeitstag festhalten. Ich will mir für das kommende Semester möglichst 2 Tage ganz für Sie reservieren, am besten Freitag und Samstag und den Montag morgen. Auch wenn ein anderer Ihnen mit den Proben für Burkhard hilft, würde ich die ganze Partitur baldmöglichst studieren und oft in Proben kommen, sodass [sic] wir doch darüber reden können, wenn Sie das wollen". Letter Ina Lohr to Paul Sacher of 10 August 1941, private collection, Switzerland.

palpable. The fact that she deemed two and a half days to be necessary for stable communication and work – whether or not this level of work was something she had regularly executed in the past – demonstrates the intensity of the cooperation (if that were not already self-evident from their correspondence). Given, however, the fragility of her health, as well as the number of hours she taught, to say nothing of her involvement in various church activities and the propagation of the *Probeband*, it also means that she was once again scheduling herself to the limits, if not beyond them, of her strength.

In this letter, she then went on to say how she perceived this offer to him:

> So, this is my "sacrifice". I have also thought about it. It is funny that I speak of a sacrifice in regard to a so well-paid job. But it would be the very worst, if I were to do this work because I am paid for it, just as if one pastes on stamps. No, then I would have to give it up and follow my real "profession". I can and may only do it, if I devote myself to it just as wholeheartedly as for my own things. When I realized that I should, for once, show that I can be true to my motto, "it does not matter *what* one does, but only *how* one does it", I suddenly had the courage to try it again. I actually always accept the wages as a present from you; I have difficulties connecting them directly to this work which I would prefer to and should give to you as a present.[61]

After apologizing yet once again for being difficult, and for her need for isolation to regain her inner strength, she declared:

> There is something that makes me happy and should reassure you: since you wrote in your letter that you shudder to think of the consequences of giving up our cooperation, I know that my friendship for you is much stronger than you or I thought. I will namely always be there for you, even if it were to ever come to our relinquishing the link outwardly. I would then not participate practically, but give lessons and courses and live very simply. But I would always be happy if you came. Perhaps I will choose this path in my life sometime; but for the meantime, let us try it this way.[62]

---

61 "So, da ist mein 'Opfer'. Auch darüber habe ich nachgedacht. Es ist komisch, dass ich bei einer so schön honorierten Arbeit von einem Opfer rede. Aber das wäre am schlimmsten, wenn ich diese Arbeit tun würde, weil ich dafür bezahlt bin, eben, so wie man Briefmarken aufklebt. Nein, dann müsste ich sie aufgeben und meinem eigentlichen 'Beruf' nachgehen. Ich kann und darf sie nur tun, wenn ich mich genau so stark einsetze, wie für meine eigene Sache. Als ich das einsah, dass ich jetzt einmal zeigen sollte, dass ich meiner Devise treu sein kann: 'es kommt nicht darauf an <u>was</u> man tut, nur <u>wie</u> man es tut', da hatte ich plötzlich wieder den Mut es noch einmal zu probieren. Das Honorar nehme ich eigentlich immer wie ein Geschenk von Ihnen an; ich kann es nicht gut direkt mit dieser Arbeit in Verbindung setzen, die ich eigentlich auch schenken möchte und sollte". Ibid.

62 "Etwas macht mich froh und sollte auch Sie beruhigen: seitdem Sie in Ihrem Brief schrieben, dass Ihnen vor den Konsequenzen der Aufgabe unserer Zusammenarbeit graut, weiss ich, dass meine Freundschaft für Sie viel stärker ist, als Sie oder ich gemeint haben. Ich werde nämlich immer für Sie da sein, auch wenn es je so weit käme, dass wir die Verbindung äusserlich aufgeben würden. Ich würde dann eben nicht mehr praktisch mitmachen,

It is doubtful that this statement was really a reassurance for Paul Sacher, as it is so evident that she was still leaving the possibility of resignation open, and that the coming season was just yet another attempt to make the cooperation function smoothly. But she was uplifted by the realization that he considered her work to be such a central part of the success of the BKO.

In the following days, Ina Lohr continued down the path of work as usual, writing a couple of short missives in answer to the questions at the end Paul Sacher's letter of 7 August 1941. On 17 August 1941, however, he answered the letter in greater detail, once again emphasizing how important her contribution was to him:

> I hope that the positive ideas that it contains will withstand [the test of] reality. Everything that I can do to help make [the execution of] your decisions easier, I will do gladly. The idea of the end of our cooperation is unbearable to me, from all points of view. It seems to me that the loss would go beyond that which is tenable, both humanly and objectively. But let us put these gloomy thoughts aside. We both want to try to do our best. As long as there is hope, I cannot doubt. I therefore also believe that you will find the means of doing everything in my realm as well as possible, without having to ask after the "what". Your motto encourages me![63]

The battle for this season was almost over, but this confidence on Paul Sacher's part that things would work out, made her fearful enough that she felt obliged to warn him on 19 August 1941 that she may overwhelm him and the choir with "religious vehemence" if she endeavors "no longer to be inhibited".[64] In conclusion, she wrote of the work she was planning to do: studying the choir scores and the text of the Mozart *Te Deum*, looking at the Burkhard score, as well as

---

sondern Stunden und Kurse geben und sehr einfach leben. Aber ich würde mich immer freuen, wenn Sie kämen. Vielleicht werde ich diese Lebensform einmal wählen; vorläufig aber probieren wir es so. Ich will versuchen in den nächsten 14 Tagen die so nötige Freude und Fröhlichkeit zu sammeln". Ibid.

63 "Ich hoffe, dass die guten Gedanken, die er enthält der Realität stand halten werden. Alles was ich zur Erleichterung Ihrer Entschlüsse beitragen kann will ich gerne tun. Die Vorstellung vom Ende unserer Zusammenarbeit ist mir unerträglich, von jedem Gesichtspunkt aus. Der Verlust erschiene mir menschlich und sachlich über das Verantwortbare hinauszugehen. Aber lassen wir diese trüben Gedanken. Wir wollen beide unser Bestes versuchen. Solange noch eine Hoffnung besteht, kann ich nicht zweifeln. Darum glaube ich auch, dass Sie den Weg finden werden in meinem Bereich alles so gut als möglich zu tun, ohne nach dem 'Was' zu fragen. Ihre Devise ermutigt mich!" Letter Paul Sacher to Ina Lohr of 17 August 1941, PSF-ILC.

64 "es kann sein, dass ich meine ganze religiöse Vehemenz über Sie und den Kammerchor loslasse, wenn ich mich bemühe nicht mehr gehemmt zu sein und wenn ich den natürlichen Auslass für diesen Bekenntnisdrang nicht mehr habe". Letter Ina Lohr to Paul Sacher of 19 August 1941, private collection, Switzerland.

slowly and systematically going through the complete edition of Praetorius and preparing her work for the Schola. Again, the discussion of personal needs must also be seen against the background of the work she was continually doing for the two institutions.

There were no more letters on this subject until the end of the year, when Ina Lohr sent her Christmas greetings on 22 December 1941. She addressed them – the only time she did such a thing – not to Mr. Sacher but to

> My dear closest one of all,
>   Also this year I come with empty hands, although I would love to give something. And also the only present that would be important for you has not been completed. How much I would have liked to promise you a quieter new year. I have fought more than ever in the past two weeks, and in spite of this, things don't get clearer. I only know one thing: that I won't go away from you, and that beyond all of the difficulties between us, the sense of belonging together remains, without which I can no longer exist. You are not my hostage, but the one closest to me, because I can't really be completely alone. But I have fought for years against my weakness and I no longer wanted to be needy and I can no longer successfully lay down my armor and the mask of a proud single woman. I cannot even write in the tone that I intended, namely how I speak with you in my thoughts, when I defend you against me. You have to believe me and patiently believe me that I fight for you and am searching for the correct form for our further cooperation. I cannot accept your help in this search, or only slightly. You would be frightened if you knew how dependent I could become. I only promise you that in the worst case, if I can no longer proceed on my own, I won't go to the Friedmatt [the psychiatric clinic in Basel], but then I will ask you for advice.[65]

65 "Mein lieber Allernächster
    Auch dieses Jahr komme ich mit leeren Händen, obwohl ich doch so gerne schenken würde. Und auch das einzige Geschenk, das für Sie wichtig wäre, ist nicht fertig geworden. Wie gerne hätte ich Ihnen ein ruhigeres neues Jahr versprochen. Ich habe in den letzten zwei Wochen mehr gekämpft als je und trotzdem klärt sich die Sache nicht. Nur etwas weiss ich: dass ich nicht von Ihnen weggehen werde, und dass hinter allem Schwierigen zwischen uns doch diese Zusammengehörigkeit steht, ohne die ich nicht mehr auskomme. Sie sind nicht meine Geisel, sondern mein Allernächster, weil ich doch nicht ganz allein sein kann. Aber ich habe Jahre lang gegen meine Schwachheit gekämpft und wollte nicht mehr hilfebedürftig sein und es gelingt mir nicht mehr meinen Panzer und die Maske einer stolzen Einzelgängerin abzulegen. Ich kann nicht einmal in dem Ton schreiben, wie ich es vorhatte, nämlich so, wie ich in Gedanken mit Ihnen rede, wenn ich Sie gegen mich verteidige. Sie müssen es mir glauben und geduldig glauben, dass ich für Sie kämpfe und die richtige Form für unsere weitere Zusammenarbeit suche. Ich darf Ihre Hilfe bei diesem Suchen nicht, oder nur wenig annehmen. Sie würden erschrecken, wenn Sie wüssten, wie abhängig ich werden könnte. Nur das verspreche ich, dass ich im allerschlimmsten Fall, wenn ich allein gar nicht mehr durchkomme, nicht auf die Friedmatt gehen werde, sondern dann werde Sie um Rat bitten". Letter Ina Lohr to Paul Sacher of 22 December 1941, private collection, Switzerland.

It is almost painful to see the degree to which she created an emotional prison for herself, one whose walls would open up momentarily when she was singing to the Lord. Lacking her family around her, she did not even know how to turn to those she considered closest to her for help, but insisted on finding her own path.

1942

The activity within the context of the Schola, for which there is no specific personal documentation, would be enough to keep anyone fully occupied. It must be remembered that it was only half of her work-life, the other half being devoted to the BKO, with all of its associated stresses and strains. Looking in from the outside it seems quite obvious that her own personal activities would have to be relegated to the sidelines, that there was no time for composition, even though she deemed it necessary for her own sense of inner balance.

It would therefore be understandable if the subject of her activities had come up at Ina Lohr's and Paul Sacher's regular meeting on Wednesday, 11 March 1942, as later that day Ina Lohr – with reference to their earlier conversation – felt compelled to write him about the real reason why she was so "difficult". It is namely at this moment in time that she chose to tell him that she had a third occupation, beyond those of working at the Schola and with him, namely that of carrying the burdens of other people, even strangers she met on the street, as mentioned above in Chapter 1. She even wrote that Basel was an escape, as "the foreign people in their foreign surroundings left me in peace for several months".[66] Once Basel became familiar, however, she was no longer able to keep these emotions at bay. She continued her story in the following manner:

> When it began again, I met you. Your first present after the first program was Rilke's "Malte", which helped me no end, for everything was in it. I also then read Rilke's letters and knew from then on, that one not only has to bear this hypersensitivity, but that it is also possible to employ it for a good cause. I tried that, and I am trying it still, and a portion of my work, for example some lessons, is a relief.[67]

---

66 "Mein Bleiben in Basel war eine Flucht. Die fremden Menschen in ihrer fremden Umgebung liessen mich einige Monate in Ruhe". Letter Ina Lohr to Paul Sacher of 11 March 1942, private collection, Switzerland.

67 "Als es wieder anfing, lernte ich Sie kennen. Ihr erstes Geschenk nach dem ersten Programm war Rilkes 'Malte', der mir unendlich geholfen hat, denn darin stand das alles. Ich las dann Rilkes Briefe und wusste von da an, dass man diese Ueberempfindlichkeit nicht nur ertragen muss, sondern dass es möglich ist sie zum Guten anzuwenden. Ich versuchte das und versuche es immer noch und ein Teil meiner Arbeit, z.B. gewisse Stunden sind erlösend". Ibid.

The protagonist in Rainer Maria Rilke's, *Die Aufzeichnungen des Malte Laurids Brigge* (Leipzig, 1910), also had this sort of hypersensitivity and it is clear that it was a comfort for Ina Lohr to know that she was not the only one in the world who experienced this, and also that Rilke had managed to put it to good use in his poetry. The degree that she was concerned about her mental health may be gleaned from her relief that Ernst Gaugler spoke of it "as if it were nothing awful, not a sickliness, but a personal characteristic". For her, the help came at the right moment, giving her a means to deal with the emotional burden which had escalated, due to the war and the separation from her family, to sheer insurmountability: prayer, particularly in song. Thus from her perspective, the issues with which she was contending in her work with Paul Sacher were existential, not only on the basic financial level, but also on that of her emotional health. The latter, however, was also tied up with the friendship that had come about over the years:

> You have really helped me, not only last fall and winter, but also for the last 12 years. First of all, because you did not count me among the psychologically ill, but to the contrary had such unwavering trust in me. And, in addition, you are the only person other than my youngest sister [Sally] who does not give me his sorrow to carry, but rather tries again and again only to lighten my own. I know that I am in good hands with you, and that you are my anchor, but I cannot become so dependent on you as I was before Christmas. When you went to Saanen [where the Sachers' had a vacation house], I felt as if I had been completely abandoned. The illness [which she had over Christmas] was thus a deliverance. In those weeks I then fought my way back to the old armored independence. I am alone and even lonely, and I have to make something right out of this loneliness without becoming a burden to you. And I also have a lot of help from the trust, friendship and love that the people here also give me.[68]

Thus Paul Sacher's very pragmatic approach, probably even his relatively detached manner, and his clear desire to concentrate on musical issues, was no doubt perceived by Ina Lohr as an affirmation of her abilities, of her person,

---

68 "Sie haben mir nicht nur im letzten Herbst und Winter, sondern 12 Jahre lang wirklich geholfen. Erstens dadurch, dass Sie mich nicht zu den Nervenkranken zählten, sondern im Gegenteil ein so festes Vertrauen zu mir hatten. Und daneben sind sie der einzige Mensch neben meiner jüngsten Schwester, der mir sein Leid nicht zu tragen gibt, sondern immer wieder probiert nur das meine zu erleichtern. Ich weiss, dass ich es gut bei Ihnen habe und dass Sie mein Anker sind, aber ich darf nicht so von Ihnen abhängig sein, wie ich es vor Weihnachten war. Als Sie nach Saanen gingen, kam ich mir vollkommen verlassen vor. Die Krankheit war insofern eine Rettung. In den Wochen kämpfte ich mich dann zur alten gepanzerten Selbständigkeit durch. Ich bin allein und sogar einsam und ich habe aus dieser Einsamkeit etwas Rechtes zu machen, ohne dass ich Ihnen zur Last werde. Und ich habe auch sonst viel Hilfe durch alles, was mir die Menschen hier auch an Vertrauen, Freundschaft und Liebe schenken". Ibid.

something that she was not used to receiving from the world around her. He did not treat her as a weak person, but was willing to engage in musical battle with her.

And it is just these musical issues that preoccupied her:

> It is only the feeling that we have failed in our all-too-big drive for activity, in that which is essential (I don't mean you and I, but the whole present-day world) and that it is high time that we start again from the beginning to build something up, not "like sheep [that] have gone astray; we have turned every one to his own way" [Isaiah, 53:6], but rather as knowing people who all share responsibility with one another and for one another. This feeling becomes so strong that much of our work becomes incomprehensible. Perhaps I will be able to untie this knot in time, before the long-lasting tension also becomes too much for you. The reason that I would also like to be formally independent from you, is only that I am so often disloyal to you when I am too preoccupied with this "third work". My lack of sleep is only due to the fact that I have no time during the day, only work superficially. Then the misery overcomes me at night. Only when I can pray while working, will it be resolved. Thus my monastic inclinations. But perhaps we will find a way.[69]

This letter is a key to understanding Ina Lohr, in that it states her motivation for so strongly pursuing her "tone theology". It provided her with her sole means for coping, for dealing with her hypersensitivity which made it so difficult for her to participate wholly in life; she always needed space in order to maintain her sense of self, and that in turn reinforced her loneliness. Within this personal construct, Paul Sacher was one of the few individuals who did not call her person into question, but rather supported her in her path through life. This was not entirely selfless, to be sure, as he derived great profit from her work in the pursuit of his own goals.

The next few months were perhaps more peaceful, for it is not until 7 July 1942 that Paul Sacher wrote in great irritation that he regretted that she was allowing herself to be pressured from all sides, complaining that this was "entirely

---

69 "Nur das Gefühl, dass wir im zu grossen Tatendrang versagt haben, im Wesentlichen, (ich meine nicht Sie und ich, sondern die ganze heutige Welt) und dass es höchste Zeit ist, dass wir wieder vorne anfangen etwas aufzubauen, nicht 'wie Schafe, die in die Irre gegangen sind, weil jeder auf den eigenen Weg sah', sondern wie wissende Menschen, die alle miteinander und für einander verantwortlich sind, dieses Gefühl wird so heftig, dass mir vieles aus unserer Arbeit unbegreiflich wird. Vielleicht gelingt es mir noch zur Zeit diesen Knoten zu lösen, bevor die dauernde Spannung auch Ihnen zu viel wird. Dass ich jetzt gerade so gerne auch äusserlich unabhängig wäre ist nur, weil ich Ihnen so oft untreu bin, wenn ich zu viel mit dieser 'dritten Arbeit' beschäftigt bin. Die Schlaflosigkeit hat nur den Grund, dass ich am Tag keine Zeit habe, oft nur äusserlich arbeite. Dann überfällt mich das Elend nachts. Erst wenn ich arbeitend beten kann, wird das gelöst sein. Daher die Klosterneigung. Aber vielleicht finden wir den Weg". Ibid.

against our agreement".[70] She was not consistent in what she said, they only had a little work to do, and he would have liked to talk to her quietly before their vacations started. And in addition, it was important to all concerned that her move to a new apartment take place peacefully. He stated his desires in this regard in the following manner:

> I therefore ask you to give up Berne, students and shake off other demands & to not do anything that you really know is too much for you. *Nothing* is so important that it will not work out somehow & everything else can just as well wait until after the vacation. This wish is not clouded by any egotism, but I just cannot watch while you ruin yourself with the power of the devil. Your loyal Capuchin[71]

This letter and her response illustrate, to a degree not seen elsewhere in the correspondence, the frictions between them that so strongly colored their cooperation. For she wrote on the following day thanking him for the flowers which no doubt accompanied his letter, saying:

> I didn't go to Berne, although I could have easily done it without slipping down again. These states are always the result of mental and emotional overexertion. That is terrible, but I can't deny it. There is also no point in us discussing it; I also had the impression, by the way, that you didn't want to.[72]

On both sides, there is this sense of exasperation that the other is not behaving as he or she should, just as in actual marital squabbles.

Once again, Ina Lohr resolved to clarify the situation during the summer vacation. She began on 12 July 1942 by apologizing to Paul Sacher for the fact that she felt compelled to return his gratuity for her holidays:

> I do not thank you any less warmly for the deed and the good intention. But I must do that now, which I should have already done last year: free myself both from within and from without. Perhaps I can begin again voluntarily in fall. If that doesn't work, then I will take on a half-day job with you until you have found a man who can carry out this

---

70 "völlig gegen unsere Abmachung". Letter Paul Sacher to Ina Lohr of 7 July 1942, PSF-ILC.
71 "Darum bitte ich Sie auf Bern zu verzichten, Schüler & sonstige Begehrlichkeiten abzuwimmeln & nicht all das zu tun, von dem Sie genau wissen, dass es über Ihre Kräfte geht. Gar nichts ist so wichtig, dass es nicht auch von selber ginge & alles andere kann ebensogut nach den Ferien getan werden. Dieser Wunsch ist von keinerlei Egoismus getrübt, aber ich kann es nicht mit ansehen, wenn Sie sich selber mit Teufels Gewalt ruinieren. Ihr getreuer Kapuziner". Ibid.
72 "Ich bin also nicht nach Bern gegangen, obwohl ich es gut hätte tun können, ohne wieder um zu sinken [sic]. Diese Zustände sind immer die Folge einer seelischen Ueberanstrengung. Das ist schlimm, aber ich kann es nicht leugnen. Es hat auch keinen Sinn, dass wir noch darüber reden; ich hatte übrigens [sic] den Eindruck, dass Sie das auch nicht wollten". Letter Ina Lohr to Paul Sacher of 8 July 1942, private collection, Switzerland.

cooperation objectively, without entirely exhausting himself emotionally. That is hardly possible for a woman; I, in any case, have not been able to do it.

You will hear little from me this summer, apart from the fact that I will send you the work bit by bit.[73]

On 27 July 1942, she then sent off a large batch of her work to him with the following commentary:

Herewith I am sending the ornamented Bach parts [Suite in B minor, BWV 1067, and the cantata *Non sa che sia dolore*, BWV 209, for the concert of 22 November 1942 with the Collegium Musicum Zurich] and the finished Senfl group [for the BKO concert of 15 October 1942, and the radio recording of 25 October 1942]. The Bach now looks quite different and I would like you to read it carefully to see whether it seems plausible to you this way. I should probably copy these two movements in score for you, otherwise you will not know what is happening. I will wait on that, however, until you have looked at it.

I have marked up the Senfl songs and written in the groups of three. This is primarily important in the instrumental pieces, because the [metric] unit has been reduced to an eighth note, so that the danger of syncopations is greater than otherwise. There is certainly too much added to them overall. That is only for you; we need to then go through the voices one by one and then only write that which is most necessary in the parts.

Erlebach [see Ill. 4.4] will soon follow, and by then we will hopefully have a report concerning [what music is available in print by] Lasso, for I will leave that program untouched until then.

I feel much better, I am for the most part quiet and can sleep. I have made myself a strict daily schedule and hold myself to it. One has created a hidden corner in the garden for me for my work and peace and quiet, and so I do not even need the lake. Probably this will also be the solution for Basel: that I live very quietly and for myself in my "cell" and do my work from there. That has been my idea since Christmas, but then, once again, it did not work at all. Perhaps this "cloister life" will make it possible.[74]

---

73 "Für die Tat und für die gute Absicht danke ich nicht weniger herzlich als sonst. Ich muss aber jetzt das tun, was ich schon letztes Jahr hätte tun sollen: mich innerlich und äusserlich einmal frei machen. Vielleicht kann ich dann im Herbst freiwillig wieder anfangen. Wenn das nicht geht, werde ich eine Halbtagesstelle bei Ihnen annehmen bis Sie einen Mann gefunden haben, der diese Zusammenarbeit sachlich leisten kann, ohne dass er sich menschlich dabei ganz ausgibt. Das ist für eine Frau kaum möglich, ich habe es auf alle Fälle nicht gekonnt.

Sie werden wenig von mir hören diesen Sommer, abgesehen davon, dass ich die Arbeit nach und nach schicken werde". Letter Ina Lohr to Paul Sacher of 12 July 1942, private collection, Switzerland.

74 "Hierbei die verzierten Bachstimmen und die fertige Senflgruppe. Bach sieht jetzt doch ziemlich anders aus und ich bitte Sie genau nachzulesen, ob die Sache Ihnen so einleuchtet. Wahrscheinlich sollte ich Ihnen diese 2 Sätze noch in Partitur schreiben, sonst wissen Sie nicht was geht. Ich warte aber damit, bis Sie es durchgesehen.

Bei den Senf[l]liedern habe ich bezeichnet u. die Dreiergruppen eingeschrieben. Das ist hauptsächlich wichtig in den Instrumentalstücken, weil da die Einheit auf ein Achtel gekürzt ist, sodass [sic] die Syncopengefahr noch grösser ist als sonst. Es steht jetzt sicher

This letter is once again indicative of Ina Lohr's value to Paul Sacher. First of all, she had begun doing, as a matter of course, the same work in the preparation of the parts and scores for the Collegium Musicum Zurich (CMZ), whose direction Paul Sacher had assumed in 1941, as she did for the BKO, in this case beginning by ornamenting the parts of Bach's works. In doing so, she changed the surface of the music sufficiently for her to ask him to check it over carefully to see if he were in agreement. She then also marked up the group of Senfl songs for the BKO. Also here, the extent of her musical influence becomes tangible, in that she – based on her understanding of texted music of the period – was advocating flexible rhythmic groupings rather than a strict "objective" performance of syncopations in line with the 20th-century understanding of meter. The habit of reducing the note values in transcriptions of music from earlier music enhanced this danger in her eyes.

This work, albeit during her vacation, lent structure to her secluded life in the garden of Hotel Belvédère in Spiez. It gave her something to hold onto, a tenuous connection to the outside world, while she attempted to find the inner quiet she needed in order to survive. At the same time, however, it robbed her of her independence, as she was not pursuing her own musical goals, was not composing, but instead preparing the music for Paul Sacher's orchestras in the time which should have been devoted to her own concerns. It was exemplary for the inner and outer conflict in which she found herself: her inner despair needed this external structure in order to keep herself above water; the specific external structure available to her, however, challenged something central within herself, without which she felt herself to be lost.

On the following day, Paul Sacher wrote thanking her for the scores, for her work. In addition, he declared himself to be happy that she was sleeping well, asking if she would not give him the "great pleasure" of being allowed to send her the money she had refused earlier as a birthday present. He could imagine

---

überall zu viel drin. Das ist aber nur für Sie; wir müssten alles dann einmal Stimme für Stimme durchnehmen und dann erst das Nötigste in die Stimmen einschreiben.

Erlebach folgt bald und dann haben wir hoffentlich Bericht über Lasso, denn das Programm lasse ich bis dahin noch liegen.

Es geht mir viel besser, hauptsächlich bin ich ruhig und kann schlafen. Ich habe eine ganz strenge Tagesordnung gemacht und halte mich daran. Im Garten hat man mir eine versteckte Arbeits- und Ruheecke eingerichtet und so brauche ich nicht einmal den See. Wahrscheinlich wird auch für Basel das die Lösung sein: dass ich ganz still und für mich in meiner 'Klause' lebe und von dort aus meine Arbeit tue. Das schwebte mir schon seit Weihnachten vor, nur ging es dann doch wieder gar nicht. Vielleicht macht es dieses 'Klosterleben' möglich". Letter Ina Lohr to Paul Sacher of 27 July 1942, private collection, Switzerland.

that spending another two weeks in the peace and quiet would be of great benefit to her health. He commented further,

> I cannot really understand what prevents you from accepting this gift from a friend. I like it when people who are close to me are content, and I am sad when I cannot contribute my share to this. Can you not separate friendship and work? I still hope for your understanding and consent.[75]

Once again, Ina Lohr felt compelled to turn him down on 29 July 1942:

> Unfortunately, I cannot give you the great pleasure. I cannot separate our friendship and our work, for since the time this work stopped interesting me sufficiently from the point of view of its content, it is only possible as an expression of my friendship. That is where the whole difficulty lies, and is that which makes me so sad. Something is no longer right and as long as that is so, I cannot accept anything.[76]

In her thank you note for the flowers he sent on 1 August 1942, she mentioned that she had been able to do nothing for the past few days. Apparently this was the beginning of a longer period of ill health, forcing her not only to extend her stay but, on 7 August 1942, also to ask Paul Sacher for financial assistance:

> And I must give up my pride after all and ask you for support! I had planned so carefully and paid my guesthouse for three weeks in advance, and I would have just gotten through to September with the rest. But now I had to go to the doctor, had to buy medicine and should stay here longer. The illness comes time and again to remind me that I cannot get through life completely alone! And it also finally forces me to rest and to some partially successful reflection.[77]

75 "Ich kann nicht wohl verstehen, was Sie davon abhält, diese freundschaftliche Gabe anzunehmen. Ich habe gerne wenn es Menschen, die mir nahestehen gut geht, & es betrübt mich, wenn ich meinen Teil dazu nicht beitragen kann. Können Sie persönliche Freundschaft & Arbeit nicht trennen? Ich hoffe noch immer auf Ihre Einsicht & Zustimmung". Letter Paul Sacher to Ina Lohr of 28 July 1942, PSF-ILC.

76 "Leider kann ich Ihnen die grosse Freude nicht machen. Ich kann unsere Freundschaft und die Arbeit nicht trennen, denn seitdem diese Arbeit mich sachlich nicht mehr genügend interessiert, ist sie nur noch als Äusserung meiner Freundschaft möglich. Da liegt doch eben die ganze Schwierigkeit und das, was mich so traurig macht. Etwas stimmt gar nicht mehr und solange das so ist, kann ich nichts annehmen". Letter Ina Lohr to Paul Sacher of 29 July 1942, private collection, Switzerland.

77 "Und jetzt muss ich meinen Stolz doch aufgeben und Sie um Unterstützung bitten! Ich hatte so schön disponiert und meine Pension für 3 Wochen im voraus bezahlt und ich wäre mit den Resten gerade bis September ausgekommen. Aber jetzt musste ich zum Arzt [sic], musste Mittel kaufen und sollte länger bleiben. Die Krankheit kommt immer wieder um mich daran zu erinnern, dass ich ganz allein im Leben nicht fertig werde! Und sie bringt mich auch endgültig zur Ruhe und zu einem einigermassen erfolgreichen Nachdenken". Letter Ina Lohr to Paul Sacher of 7 August 1942, private collection, Switzerland.

And to make matters worse, she had once again calculated too cautiously, so that the small sum she had requested did not cover her costs. She was thus obliged only four days later, on 11 August 1942, to turn to him again for help. She complained about her lack of energy, hoping that it would come again, going on to say that

> everything is connected together with a certain mental and emotional exhaustion. That is what makes me almost desperate on occasion. For me, all of our difficulties may be reduced to the question: if I am no longer interested in the work materially, are my mental and emotional strengths not capable of accomplishing that which you demand for friendship's sake? I fail in this again and again and it therefore – in view of this – seems difficult to accept your gifts as a friend.[78]

On 19 August 1942 she thanked him for this gift, remarking that she had to "definitively admit that I cannot budget and that life costs so frightfully much more than I thought".[79] And already on 2 September 1942 she was writing once again in gratitude:

> Hopefully you will not think that I now will suddenly just accept everything and not even really say thank you. I had resolutely resolved not to be "dramatic" any more and instead to laugh when tears are nigh, and therefore I can only tell you in writing that I am very, very happy for your help and that I honestly hope that you will never regret that you have made it possible for me to become Swiss. I cannot promise anything more, after all of those [promises] that I have been unable to keep. I will apply myself the best I can to once again make a useful whole out of the "shambles". I do not know whether I will succeed with this. I can only desire it honestly and hope.[80]

78 "Nur hängt es alles auch mit einer gewissen seelischen Erschöpfung zusammen. Das ist, was mich hie und da fast verzweifeln macht. Unsere ganzen Schwierigkeiten lassen sich für mich auf die Frage reduzieren: wenn ich sachlich das Interesse an Ihrer Arbeit nicht mehr habe, sind dann meine seelischen Kräfte nicht im Stande das, was Sie verlangen aus Freundschaft zu leisten? Da versage ich immer wieder und darum fällt es mir schwer Ihre Freundschaftsgaben trotzdem anzunehmen". Letter Ina Lohr to Paul Sacher of 11 August 1942, private collection, Switzerland.

79 "Ich muss endgültig zugeben, dass ich gar nicht rechnen kann, und dass das Leben erschreckend viel mehr kostet, als ich gemeint habe". Letter Ina Lohr to Paul Sacher of 19 August 1942, private collection, Switzerland.

80 "Hoffentlich meinen Sie nicht, dass ich jetzt plötzlich nur so alles annehme und nicht einmal mehr richtig danken kann. Ich habe mir aber fest vorgenommen nicht mehr 'dramatisch' zu sein und lieber zu lachen, wenn die Tränen in der Nähe sind und darum kann ich Ihnen nur noch schriftlich sagen, dass ich sehr, sehr froh um Ihre Hilfe bin und dass ich ehrlich hoffe, dass Sie es nie bereuen werden, dass Sie es mir ermöglicht haben Schweizerin zu werden. Versprechen kann ich, nach allem, was ich nicht habe halten können, nichts mehr. Ich versuche mit meinem allerbesten Willen aus den 'Scherben' wieder ein brauchbares Ganzes zu machen. In wiefern [sic] das gelingen wird weiss ich nicht. Ich kann es nur ehrlich wollen und hoffen". Letter Ina Lohr to Paul Sacher of 2 September 1942, private collection, Switzerland.

The decision to become Swiss was made for various practical reasons, among them – according to her autobiographical sketch – the facilitation of her participation in the introduction of the *Probeband*.[81] While certainly true, it was only one aspect of the picture, as is shown in an article about her family in the journal of the Provinciale Geldersche Electriciteits-Maatschapij in Arnhem, of which her father had been the director. About Ina Lohr they wrote that

> she was solely Dutch and although she wanted to stay in Basel, she was not allowed to busy herself with other work unless she had a permit specifically for it. Just at this point her work began to develop greatly, and she consequently had to request permits for all of her lectures, radio broadcasts, concerts, etc. Getting them caused such difficulty that she wanted to try to acquire Swiss citizenship.[82]

As we have seen, her father was unable to help her financially with this, so she was required to turn to Paul Sacher for support. In the eyes of the Dutch journalist, she was able to repay Paul Sacher through her work as a coordinator of the Dutch refugees passing through the Basel train station on their way from concentration camps. In any case, it was certainly true that she invested herself throughout the war in help for refugees, also those fleeing over the border. It must have required a great deal of willpower, and also contributed to her general inner turmoil, to be faced with the decision of becoming Swiss, at a time when she no longer had contact with her Dutch roots.

Apparently the sum total of all these experiences – the realization of the fragility of her existence, both financially and health-wise and the concomitant generosity of Paul Sacher, together with the inner sustenance she derived from her teaching – led to a successful cooperation in the BKO's first program of the season, as on 18 October 1942, Ina Lohr was able to write

> Our first concert gave me courage. If I can work not only for you, but also for the project, then it works. Then it would have to function the entire year. But I cannot promise [this], for my inner balance is very shaky.[83]

---

81 "Skizze zum Lebenslauf" II, 6.
82 "Zij was nu eenmaal Nederlandse en al mocht ze in Bazel blijven, haar werd niet toegestaan zich met ander werk bezig te houden dan waarvoor zij al een bepaalde vergunning bezat. Juist in die tijd begon haar werk zich echter sterk te ontplooien met het gevolg, dat zij voor alle lezingen, radio-uitzendingen, concerten, enz. vergunningen moest vragen". In: *Prelecta: Personeelsorgaan voor en door het personeel van de N.V. Provinciale Geldersche Electriciteits-Maatschapij te Arnhem*, June/July 1959, 7, PSF-ILC.
83 "Unser erstes Konzert hat mir Mut gemacht. Wenn ich, also nicht nur für Sie, sondern auch für die Sache arbeiten kann, dann geht es. Es müsste dann dieses ganze Jahr gehen. Aber ich kann nicht versprechen, denn das innere Gleichgewicht ist sehr schwankend". Letter Ina Lohr to Paul Sacher of 18 October 1942, private collection, Switzerland.

Paul Sacher responded with flowers and the following words:

> Our first concert also gave me great pleasure, because our cooperation was constructive
> & harmonious from beginning to end. But primarily, however, because *you* also thought
> that. It was accordingly also successful. I cannot express in words how happy I was about
> this. In any case, my warm thanks.[84]

The following weeks were seemingly very full and peaceful, as the few letters
in that period were almost entirely devoted to questions involving their work.

Musically, Christmas was always a time of great satisfaction for Ina Lohr,
for she derived deep pleasure, almost ecstasy, from the congregational singing
of songs rejoicing in the Lord's coming. This year she had two possibilities for
doing so, once in Arlesheim on 6 December 1942, and the second on the radio
on 21 December: "We all give thanks" ("Dank sagen wir alle"). The latter had
come about through the success of the broadcast with Conrad Beck in 1940. As
she told Jos Leussink in the interview in 1983, thereafter they had asked her always to

> take over the Christmas play. Because at Christmas they always invited a whole group
> of old and young people, whoever they might be, who had no Christmas party of their
> own. A professor could be seated next to a cleaning lady. Two hundred were invited.
> And there was a play [...], I had to provide the music; a couple of times I wrote the
> play myself, I really enjoyed that. I also once composed the complete Christmas gos-
> pel myself.[85]

But the holidays came yet once again, and with them the exhaustion so often
associated with the end of year. Her tiredness shed a relatively bleak light on her
life, leading her once again to reconsider her situation. Although she had managed to "balance" her workload by taking on more of her own projects, which
was successful from the point of view of reducing her internal stress, it left her
at her physical limits. Thus, it was only with great effort that she took up her
work again in 1943.

---

84 "Unser 1. Konzert hat mir eine wirklich grosse Freude gemacht, weil unsere Zusammen-
    arbeit vom Anfang bis Ende schön & harmonisch war. Vor allem aber darum – weil Sie das
    auch gefunden haben. Es ist dann auch entsprechend gelungen. Ich kann Ihnen nicht in
    Worten ausdrücken, wie froh ich darüber bin. Auf alle Fälle: herzlichen Dank". Letter Paul
    Sacher to Ina Lohr of 21 October 1942, PSF-ILC.
85 "voor het kerstspel wilde zorgen. Want met kerstmis werd hier altijd uitgenodigd een hele
    kring van oude en jonge mensen, wie ze ook maar waren, die geen eigen kerstfeest hadden.
    Daar kon een professor naast een werkster zitten. Tweehonderd werden er uitgenodigd. En
    daar kwam dan een spel [...], ik moest daar de muziek bij leveren; een paar keer heb ik het
    spel zelf geschreven, dat vond ik erg leuk. Ook (heb ik) het hele kerstevangelie eens zelf
    gekomponeerd". Interview with Jos Leussink, 24–25 March 1983.

1943

It is thus not surprising that a few months later Ina Lohr came up with yet another idea of how to deal with their difficulties, namely taking a complete break from her work with Paul Sacher from Easter on. She reconsidered that decision during the Easter vacation and concluded that it was, for various reasons, not really practicable. Therefore, on 4 April 1943 she once again wrote a long, searching letter:

> It has been a long time since I have had so much quiet for body and mind, as in this past week. The result is that I am physically better and also that I am inwardly quieter and see more clearly. To be sure, I also therefore worked very little for you and have in its place undertaken something entirely superfluous, but for me necessary and quietening: the copying of many compositions, scribbled down on all kinds of slips of paper. I am sending you something of the result, not because I expect that you perform it, but just because this small cantata came into being after our Senfl broadcast [25 October 1942]. It is made up of paraphrased, ornamented songs and I have tried to write a counterpoint which is "correct" and still allows for new possibilities.[86]

This must be the cantata "von der Liebe Gottes" (The love of God), *Domini sumus*, which opens with a fantasy over the Pange lingua melody, with the text taken from the Luther bible: "Herr, durch dein Blut" (see Ill. 5.5).

This piece is unlike anything else she had written since her student days, and shows a creative investment of energy and imagination, an urge to widen her compositional vocabulary. While clearly contrapuntal in approach, it once again exhibits an eclectic combination of stylistic elements – a cantus firmus, modal progressions, figuration in style of Bach, unison passages – which she melds together to create something truly her own. Together with the dissonances, the chromaticism at the word "Leiden" (suffer) gives musical expression to the text. The suffering then finds relief in the jubilant melisma at "Amen", first presented alone and then in octaves.

While composing, she was seemingly in that meditative space which often brings insight, so that afterwords she could write that much had become clearer

---

86 "Soviel Ruhe für Körper und Geist wie in dieser letzten Woche habe ich schon lange nicht mehr gehabt. Das Resultat ist, dass es mir körperlich besser geht und auch, dass ich innerlich ruhiger bin und klarer sehe. Allerdings habe ich dann auch sehr wenig für Sie gearbeitet und dafür etwas ganz Ueberflüssiges, für mich aber Notwendiges und Beruhigendes unternommen: das Abschreiben von den vielen, auf allerhand Zetteln gekritzelten Kompositionen. Etwas vom Resultat schicke ich Ihnen, nicht weil ich erwarte, dass Sie es aufführen, sondern weil gerade diese kleine Kantate entstand nach unserer Senflsendung. Es sind paraphrasierte umspielte Lieder und ich habe versucht einen Kontrapunkt zu schreiben, der 'richtig' ist und doch neue Möglichkeiten hat". Letter Ina Lohr to Paul Sacher of 4 April 1943, private collection, Switzerland.

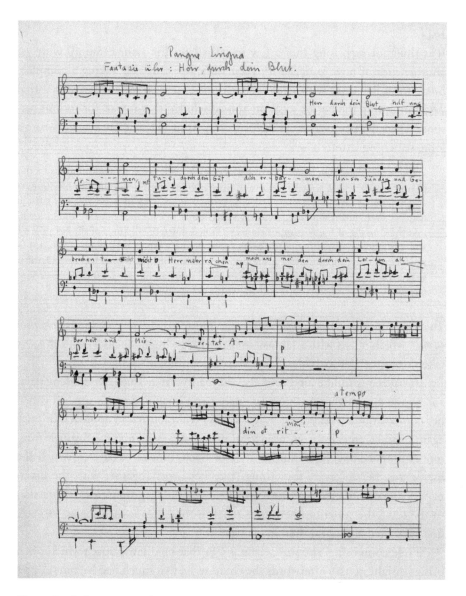

Ill. 5.5: Ina Lohr, opening of *Domini sumus*. Reproduction: PSF-ILC.

to her about their cooperation. She had come to the conclusion that her desire for a break when both were in Basel was impracticable and would only give rise to unwanted gossip. She did want a complete break, however, from mid-July to mid-September, where she had no desire "to be bound by the stupid money".[87] In the meantime she would continue her work on the scores for the concert of

---

87 "und darum will ich nicht einmal durch das dumme Geld gebunden sein". Ibid.

12 November 1943, as it had to be done anyway. Further she agreed to participate in the current season's last concert, as well as work on the programming for
the upcoming one. She did request, however, that she be freed from the obligation of evaluating modern music, whether at concerts or by reading scores, commenting that it is "not completely natural to always evaluate the work of other
musicians and to have to forgo writing my own".[88] This last point is noteworthy, as it reveals a further aspect of her work, not discussed in the previous chapter, namely that she was not only was preparing concert material for Paul Sacher
and assisting with the choir, but was also going to concerts of modern music and
evaluating what she heard in view of their own programming. What particularly galled her was that this inspection of other people's compositions, both in
score and in concert, took her away from composing herself, from her own creative processes, which in turn robbed her of an inner structure, an inner stability.

In concluding the letter, she came back to the metaphor of a "musical marriage", calling the concept itself into question:

> [This] letter sounds very categorical and I can only hope and trust that you will under-
> stand it as it is meant. I am at the critical point at which something will either fail or
> become really good. I must (which perhaps sounds very odd to you) find myself again
> and know what I can do without you. When a woman marries, it is right that she at-
> tempts to adapt her personality to that of her husband. The husband will also do this,
> one belongs together. You have compared our cooperation with a "musical marriage".
> The comparison is incorrect, because a marriage is something integral; you cannot limit
> it to one domain. I have put much, far too much of myself into this work; part of it,
> you have not even used, not even accepted. I must now know what I can do on my own,
> without you being the catalyst. Otherwise I will always put too much of myself into
> your things, and on the other hand, driven by a sense of self-preservation, too fanatically
> want and also do other [things]. I am thereby slowly losing my [inner] balance. God be
> praised that the other help is continually growing in me, which will perhaps make the
> apparently impossible possible for us.[89]

88 "Es ist wirklich nicht ganz natürlich immer die Arbeit anderer Musiker zu beurteilen und
dadurch das eigene Notenschreiben, was mir wirklich ein ganz persönliches Bedürfnis ist,
aufgeben zu müssen". Ibid.

89 "Der Brief klingt etwas gar kategorisch und ich kann nur hoffen und vertrauen, dass Sie
ihn recht verstehen. Ich bin an dem kritischen Punkt, an dem etwas entweder scheitert,
oder dann wirklich gut wird. Ich muss, (es klingt Ihnen vielleicht sehr komisch) mich selbst
zurücksuchen und wissen, was ich ohne Sie kann. Wenn eine Frau heiratet ist es richtig,
dass sie versucht ihre Persönlichkeit der des Mannes anzupassen. Der Mann wird das auch
tun, man gehört zusammen. Sie haben unsere Zusammenarbeit mit einer 'musikalischen
Ehe' verglichen. Der Vergleich stimmt eben dann nicht, weil eine Ehe etwas Ganzes ist;
man kann sie nicht auf ein Gebiet beschränken. Ich habe viel, zuviel von mir in diese Arbeit
hereingelegt; Sie haben es zum Teil gar nicht gebraucht, auch nicht angenommen. Ich muss
jetzt wissen, was ich aus eigener Kraft kann, ohne dass Sie der Anreger sind. Sonst werde
ich mich immer zuviel [sic] in Ihre Sache hineinbegeben und auf der anderen Seite, aus

We see here how clearly she was aware of the discrepancy between what she put into their cooperation and the final product, and how the definition of their cooperation as a "musical marriage" did not legitimatize that difference. As she pointed out, a wedded couple would ideally be adapting themselves to one another in all aspects of life, attempting to create an integral whole which was good for both of them. Where her comparison suffered, however, was in the fact that in the social context of the day, the woman was expected to forgo her own personal goals for the good of the family. Whereas she saw that this would not necessarily have to be the case in her work with Paul Sacher, she was again and again forced to acknowledge her need for that which her work for him gave her: mental and moral support; encouragement; her field of activity at the Schola; and last but not least, financial security. Ina Lohr was thus also continually being confronted with the fact that it would be difficult to survive in the outside world without his backing. The issues – so clearly articulated in this letter – are representative for the century-old conflict between men and women, expressed not on the sexual level, but on that of a cooperative partnership.

Evidently she kept her distance for the next few months, for in a letter accompanying some work for him, she wrote that she did not yet have the courage to simply eat with him.[90] But apparently she found it at some point before Paul Sacher went off on summer vacation, for which he expressed his gratitude.[91] She stayed in Basel a bit longer, according to the letter of 17 July 1943, busy with preparatory work for the concert of 14 November 1943, such as marking up the Buxtehude cantata, *Nimm von uns, Herr, Du treuer Gott*, ornamenting Carissimi's *Jepthe*, and rehearsing with the soprano soloist for that oratorio, Madeleine Dubois: "She is intelligent and musical, has a beautiful, but at times somewhat edgy voice, unfortunately sings entire passages too low and loved the ornaments".[92] She was also in touch with Ernst Haefliger and Eduard Müller about this concert. What she did not manage to do was prepare Handel's concerto grosso in D major for the CMZ concert on 4 November 1943, as she had a very bad headache due to a sinus infection.

Selbsterhaltungstrieb zu fanatisch etwas anders wollen und auch tun. Dadurch verliere ich langsam mein Gleichgewicht. Gott sei Dank wächst mir immer mehr die andere Hilfe, die vielleicht auch das scheinbar Unmögliche zwischen uns möglich machen wird". Ibid.
90 Letter Ina Lohr to Paul Sacher of 2 July 1943, private collection, Switzerland.
91 Letter Paul Sacher to Ina Lohr of 6 July 1943, PSF-ILC.
92 "Sie ist intelligent und musikalisch, hat eine schöne, hie und da etwas scharfe Stimme, singt leider streckenweise viel zu tief und fand die Verzierungen wunderbar". Letter Ina Lohr to Paul Sacher of 17 July 1943, private collection, Switzerland.

Before going on vacation, however, she once again wrote a very long, thoughtful letter on 17 July 1943 about where she saw the difficulties in their cooperation, shifting her focus from the disparity between their levels of activity to the differences between their approaches toward life, in that she could not keep up with his changes in direction, as she needed more time for reflection, for digesting experiences. As an example, she gave the performance of Igor Stravinsky's *Symphonie de psaumes* on 4 February 1943 where for the first time she had been able to "participate in a modern work with complete commitment and with a good result".[93] She had then been full of plans for the future which she had intended to discuss with him the following day, but he had canceled the meeting. And by the time they did meet up, Paul Sacher had already moved on to other things, leaving her feeling oddly dissatisfied. Another time, when she once again was feeling confident about embarking on a joint project, she joined others at a meal at Paul Sacher's home. Due to her physical and emotional exhaustion, however, she "felt herself to be a stranger" and thus excluded from the round of people enjoying themselves.[94] This in turn, although she knew it was unjustified and not part of their work arrangement, made her feel shortchanged, when in her opinion she was only doing the work for him out of friendship. At the same time, given the wartime situation, she became impatient with the fact that their weekly discussions were so insignificant in comparison with that which was happening around them. In addition, she disliked being one of the people he could pay to do jobs so that he could increase his own productivity, rather than going further in depth himself; at the same time, her two meetings with him a week were all she could deal with. Whereas she was aware her complaints were on one level entirely unjustified, as these acts of Paul Sacher were in no way intended to be directed against her, they nonetheless chafed her soul. It was almost as if she were using the relationship with Paul Sacher to come to terms with all of her despair about the wartime situation, about her position in life, about her loneliness. And while on a certain level this was certainly true, in that it involved her most innate expression, music, on another – which she also recognized – it was simply a reflection of her own battle against her inner demons.

93 "Ich war nach der Symphonie de Psaumes sehr glücklich, weil es das erste Mal war, dass ich auch in einem modernen Werk mit vollem Einsatz und mit gutem Resultat mitmachen konnte". Letter Ina Lohr to Paul Sacher of 17 July 1943, private collection, Switzerland.
94 "Es war ganz mein Fehler und mein Mangel an Vitalität, dass ich mich fremd und nicht zugehörig fühlte". Ibid.

Not unsurprisingly, Ina Lohr began the next season with trepidation. But her experience was different from that which she anticipated, as her letter of 2 September 1943 shows:

> It has been a long time since I have been so peaceful and calm as yesterday and today. I have often been thankful and glad and full of good resolutions when we have "cleaned things up". This time the thankfulness is greater, but quieter, as also the joy, and I have become leery of my good resolutions. Because I am not much at home in the active musical world, I am thus dependent on your generosity. With your help I have overcome my pride and [will now] accept for a year not to be "employed" by you, but rather to be "endowed". I can do nothing other than promise that I will do my best with the choir work.[95]

Paul Sacher responded two days later, remarking that he thanked both the heavens and her for this decision, concluding with "sometimes the weak are stronger than the strong. Never forget that in relation to us".[96] This makes it only too clear that he was aware of both sides of Ina Lohr's personality.

Although Paul Sacher had given her leave to do less for the BKO so that she could concentrate on her work for the *Probeband*, a letter of Ina Lohr's of 20 October 1943 – devoted entirely to organizational details concerning the concert of 14 November with works of Frescobaldi, Monteverdi, Carissimi and Buxtehude – clearly shows that she was still active as his musical assistant. Indeed, it is the first indication of a new field of work in this regard, one which would come to have increasing importance in the following years: writing program notes. In her notes for this concert, her ideals for the performance of this music shine through. She opened by mentioning that Carissimi, like other composers of the time had great confidence in the musical skills of the performers, in that the organist was expected to realize an unfigured bass and the singer to add ornaments. We know from her letter of 17 July 1943 that Eduard Müller was

---

95 "So friedlich beruhigt wie gestern und heute war ich schon lange nicht mehr. Schon öfters war ich dankbar und froh und erfüllt von guten Vorsätzen, wenn wir 'geputzt' hatten. Diesmal ist die Dankbarkeit grösser, aber stiller, wie auch die Freude und gegen meine guten Vorsätze bin ich misstrauisch geworden. Ich bin darum, weil ich [in] der tätigen Musikerwelt nicht sehr zu Hause bin, auf Ihre Grosszügigkeit angewiesen. Mit Ihrer Hilfe habe ich meinen Stolz überwunden und nehme es an ein Jahr lang nicht 'angestellt', sondern von Ihnen beschenkt zu sein. Ich kann nichts anders versprechen, als dass ich für die Chorarbeit meine besten Kräfte geben will". Letter Ina Lohr to Paul Sacher of 2 September 1943, private collection, Switzerland.

96 "Manchmal sind die Schwachen stärker als die Kräftigen. Vergessen Sie das nie, wenn es sich um uns handelt". Letter Paul Sacher to Ina Lohr of 4 September 1943, PSF-ILC.

responsible for the continuo realization and she for the ornaments. She went on to express her performing ethos in regard to this genre:

> A harmonically interesting accompaniment for the organ or orchestra can, to be sure, not kill the beauty of this music, but it is unnecessary and distracts from the essence of the plot and of the music. The only thinkable [exception] is the use of instruments to support the choir voices, which is [even] desirable under certain circumstances. This music seems to have come from the text, is not an addition or superficial layer. It should therefore be performed as simply as possible (although with ornaments!), thereby most easily communicating the tragic story of the daughter of Jephtha.[97]

In retrospect, this program documents publicly the degree to which Ina Lohr's ideas regarding the performance of early music influenced the BKO.

At the end of the year, Ina Lohr wrote to Paul Sacher with her usual mixture of thankfulness, renewed courage for facing the new year, and insecurity about whether she would be able to meet his expectations. On 31 December 1943 he replied that he looked forward to the future with confidence, as he could not believe that something as "meaningful and beautiful" as their work together could be "destroyed".[98] He went on to report some details regarding the re-programming of some concerts involving the genre of 'modern music', although she had been dispensed from it. Thus, it becomes clear that they were continuing their search for a means of cooperating together that was satisfactory to both.

1944

These remarks concerning contempory music led Ina Lohr to reflect on her ideas concerning this genre in a letter of 5 January 1944:

> Actually, modern music should be that which we most direly need and which is of greatest interest; but that of our time which is lasting should find expression in it, and that is almost never the case. My aversion is only so intense because I cannot understand that

97 "Eine harmonisch interessante Begleitung für Orgel oder für Orchester kann allerdings die Schönheit dieser Musik nicht töten, aber sie ist unnötig und lenkt vom Wesentlichen in der Handlung und in der Musik ab. Einzig eine Stützung der Chorstimmen durch Instrumente ist denkbar und unter Umständen erwünscht. Diese Musik scheint aus dem Text entstanden zu sein, ist keine Zutat, kein äusseres Gewand. Sie wird darum auch möglichst einfach (wenn auch mit Verzierungen!) aufgeführt und so am ehesten dem Hörer die tragische Geschichte der Tochter Jephtas vermitteln". Ina Lohr, "Das biblische Oratorium Jephta von Giacomo Carissimi", in: *Mitteilungen des Basler Kammerorchester*, Nr. 2, 6 November 1943, 3.

98 "Der Zukunft begegne ich mit Zuversicht. Ich kann nicht glauben, dass etwas so sinnvolles & schönes wie unsere Zusammenarbeit einmal zerstört werden könnte". Letter Paul Sacher to Ina Lohr of 31 December 1943, PSF-ILC.

music is still written and performed more or less as before – and that, while the whole world is turned upside down. Spiritual [*geistige*] people should either go within themselves and be able to speak of the eternal, or otherwise reflect the "voice of the time". Honegger and Geiser have given a bit of this, but it is not enough. [Frank] Martin escapes in his highly subjective, almost too cultivated music and Beck and Burkhard [just] continue writing. Abroad, most composers would not even be in a position to write down their music. Because it is still possible for us, our composers should be very serious about it and also the performers![99]

This is a much more differentiated expression of her difficulties with modern music, indicating that her stance was also related to the war, that she could not understand how musicians could simply continue on in their lives, as if the horrific bloodbath were not taking place next door. Originally, she had written this letter just to clarify her own standpoint, not because she had intended to send it to Paul Sacher. On the same day, however, she heard that he had been called up for military duty in Switzerland's militia army. She therefore both telephoned and wrote, saying that if he were really required for active duty, she would also indirectly join the war effort by helping out with the choir.

The first half of the year – as there are so few letters – was apparently relatively peaceful as far as their relationship was concerned. Another indication that things were going well is found in a letter of 17 March 1944, in which she communicated her decision to sing chant with the Basel Chamber Choir again, most likely for the concert on 3 December 1944 devoted to Guerrero's mass *Puer qui natus est nobis*, interspersed with chant, motets by Victoria, and organ intonations by Santa Maria and Cabezon. She recognized the inherent risk in this decision, as the problems with religious works remained, and also that she was being inconsistent, agreeing to work closely together with him again, after having striven for her inner freedom, and thus also his, for the past year. The question would be

99 "Eigentlich wäre die moderne Musik das, was wir am dringendsten brauchen und was am meisten interessiert, aber in ihr sollte das Bleibende aus unserer Zeit zum Ausdruck kommen und das ist fast nie der Fall. Meine Abneigung ist nur darum so heftig, weil ich es nicht verstehen kann, dass immer weiter Musik geschrieben und aufgeführt wird, so ungefehr [sic] wie vorher, und das, während die ganze Welt auf dem Kopf steht. Die geistigen Menschen müssten doch entweder in sich gehen und etwas vom Ewigen berichten können, oder dann die 'Stimme der Zeit' wider geben [sic]. Honegger und Geiser haben etwas davon gegeben, aber es reicht nicht aus. Martin flüchtet in seiner sehr subjektiven, fast zu kultivierten Musik und Beck u. Burkhard schreiben weiter. Im Ausland werden die meisten Komponisten gar nicht in der Lage sein ihre Musik aufzuschreiben. Weil das bei uns noch möglich ist, darum sollten unsere Komponisten erst recht ernst damit machen und die Ausführenden auch!" Letter Ina Lohr to Paul Sacher of 5 January 1944, private collection, Switzerland.

whether this will continue to be possible if we do something together that is so close to me. My "heaven" remains extraordinarily strong, but after a great effort for and with you, (which you do not at all feel as such), I am afterwards overwhelmed by a horrible exhaustion that I must deal with alone, as you neither know or understand it. Those are my "black moments" that make me harsh and severe towards you.[100]

In her letters of this period, she frequently speaks of the necessity of making her home a kind of refuge, a place to go when in spiritual need. In calling it her "heaven", she was perhaps referring to Friedrich Rückerts' *Ich bin der Welt abhanden gekommen*, set by numerous composers, among them Gustav Mahler for voice and orchestra, in which the poet speaks of how he has become so isolated from the world, that it is as if he were dead, concluding with the final couplet:

I live alone in my heaven,
In my love, in my song![101]

Not only does this poem epitomize her use of song for her spiritual regeneration, she herself set this text in August 1944, an indication of its significance for her (see Ill. 5.6). With its sensitive declamation, sharp contours, and combination of modally influenced melodic line with strikingly modern intervals, the song is an aural reflection of her mental state at the time.

It seems likely that the above-mentioned idea of a concert involving chant originated with Paul Sacher in his search to involve her once again more deeply in their work together. While agreeing to the suggestion, Ina Lohr felt the necessity of saying that she could not guarantee that it would work. And once again, she expressed her conviction that he should find an objective man for such work, one who would be able to deal with the aftereffects of a concert in a manner similar to Paul Sacher, absolving him from having to deal with her moods.

The summer had a different shape than in the past, in that the CMZ under Paul Sacher began to have regular concerts in the Engadine in July and in Lucerne in August. This also influenced Ina Lohr's activities in that she was involved in

---

100 "Ob das weiter möglich sein wird, wenn wir zusammen etwas machen, was mir so nahe geht, wird die Frage sein. Mein 'Himmelreich' hält allerdings wunderbar stand, aber nach einer grossen Anstrengung für Sie und mit Ihnen, (die Sie gar nicht als solche empfinden), kommt dann bei mir die schreckliche Müdigkeit, die ich allein überwinden muss, weil Sie sie weder kennen noch verstehen. Das sind meine 'schwarzen Augenblicke', die mich hart und grimmig machen Ihnen gegenüber". Letter Ina Lohr to Paul Sacher of 17 March 1944, private collection, Switzerland.
101 "Ich leb' allein in meinem Himmel, In meinem Lieben, in meinem Lied!"

Ill. 5.6: Ina Lohr, "Ich bin der Welt abhanden gekommen". Reproduction: PSF-ILC.

their preparation on various levels. She, of course, marked up the scores, but in this year the first concerts in Silvaplana on the 22 (open dress rehearsal) and 23 July 1944 were of her arrangement of the first part of Bach's *Art of the Fugue* for string orchestra, which the BKO had first performed in 1936. In connection with this, she also gave an introductory lecture on 21 July 1944. Of the performance she was able to confess the following to Paul Sacher:

> It was, perhaps, the first time that I so thoroughly understood that I could leave the thing in your hands and not merely judge the concert from my point of view. It was very, very beautiful on Sunday: the first group was much more uniform, the second beautiful both in sound and structure (apart from the too heavy bass in a couple of passages), IX brilliant but still quiet, and XI of a moving, inner intensity. If the tempo of this eleventh fugue is still almost intolerable for me (as also [that of] the chorale), this can only be attributed to my hypersensitivity to that which stands beyond the music. I still think that Bach would have communicated the dread more moderately by means of a faster tempo. But today one is accustomed to so much that perhaps only a few no-

tice everything that is said there. And unconsciously you respond to the audience's reaction. You are happy with the tempo; then that is all right for the moment. Until the
fugue has become "moderate" in me again, it does not leave me in peace, which in now
more or less the case!

Perhaps you thought I was somewhat cool after this really wonderful cooperation. I
was showing my embarrassment as one does in Basel, as I was very close to tears; it is a
good mask. My willingness to participate is, however, very great.[102]

So once again, Ina Lohr became immersed in the cooperation with Paul Sacher,
could identify sufficiently with what was going on that she did not feel the need
to distance herself from the process. This evidently took place on other levels
as well, as she was clearly evaluating contemporary music once again, as can be
seen by a review of a work by Albert Moeschinger, which was dedicated to Paul
Sacher:

> Very well made, but dark, restless, often very hard, although he attempts a large melodic
> line in the slow movement. It is too long for an improvisation on A. France's motto, too
> piecemeal in form for a cyclic work. A real Moeschinger and a typical expression of our
> time (unfortunately!). From this point of view a performance would be justified, which,
> however, would not bring the audience any redemption.[103]

In this somewhat ambiguous evaluation, she evidences a certain level of detachment, in that she is able to observe the quality of various parameters, the basic

---

102 "Vielleicht war es das erste Mal, dass ich so restlos verstand, die Sache Ihnen zu überlassen
und das Konzert nicht nur von meinem Standpunkt aus zu beurteilen. Es war am Sonntag
sehr, sehr schön: die erste Gruppe viel einheitlicher, die zweite klanglich und als Aufbau
wunderbar, (abgesehen vom zu schweren Bass an ein paar Stellen), IX brillant und doch
ruhig und XI von einer ergreifenden inneren Intensität. Wenn diese elfte Fuge für mich in
dem Tempo immer noch fast unerträglich ist, (wie auch der Choral), so ist das nur meiner Ueberempfindlichkeit zuzuschreiben für das, was hinter der Musik steht. Ich glaube
immer noch, dass Bach durch ein schnelleres Tempo das Schreckliche massvoller mitgeteilt
hat. Aber heute ist man soviel gewohnt, dass vielleicht nur wenige merken, was da alles
gesagt wird. Und unbewusst stellen Sie sich auf die Reaktion des Publikums ein. Ihnen ist
wohl bei dem Tempo; dann ist es vorläufig auch recht so. Die Fuge lässt mir keine Ruhe,
bis sie in mir wieder 'massvoll' geworden ist, was jetzt so ungefähr der Fall ist!
Vielleicht haben Sie gefunden, dass ich nach dieser wirklich schönen Zusammenarbeit
etwas kühl war. Ich habe mich Baslerisch geniert, weil die Tränen sehr nahe waren; es ist
eine gute Maske. Meine Bereitschaft mitzumachen ist aber wieder sehr gross". Letter Ina
Lohr to Paul Sacher of 21 July 1944, private collection, Switzerland.

103 "Sehr gut gemacht, aber düster, unruhig, oft sehr hart, obwohl er im langsamen Satz eine
grosse Melodik versucht. Für eine Improvisation über das Motto von A. France ist es zu
lang, für ein zyklisches Werk zu zerstückelt in der Form. Ein echter Moeschinger und ein
typischer Ausdruck unserer Zeit (leider!). Unter diesem Gesichtspunkt rechtfertigt sich
eine Aufführung, die allerdings dem Publikum nichts Erlösendes geben wird". This is
found on a piece of paper between the letters of 2 and 10 August 1944 of Ina Lohr to Paul
Sacher, and perhaps was enclosed in one of them, private collection, Switzerland.

compositional technique, questions of form, affect. And although she admitted that it fitted her criterion of being a "voice of the time", and therefore worthy of performance, she nonetheless still had her reservations, in that she would have really preferred some sort of redemptive conclusion. We will see later that she could become very enthusiastic when contemporary music reflected this aspect as well, for example in her reactions to Stravinsky's *Canticum Sacrum* and *A Sermon, a Narrative and a Prayer*, or the religious works of Sven-Erik Bäck.

During this summer, for once, her reflection on her participation with Paul Sacher was not solely a consequence of her own state of mind. In 1944, Dr. Robert Briner, a member of the council of the Canton of Zurich, offered Paul Sacher the directorship of the Zurich Conservatory with the perspective of being able to work regularly with the Zurich Tonhalle Orchestra. In his article about his connections to the city, "Ein Basler in Zürich", Paul Sacher simply comments that he had to turn down all offers for increased activity there, "because I wanted to continue my work in Basel".[104] A letter from Ina Lohr of 10 August 1944, however, gives an indication of how seriously he considered the invitation, how tempting it was to move on and devote himself to an elite ensemble that provided him with some of the greatest "artistic joys" of his professional career. In it, she spoke of some of the concerns she had in regard to the invitation:

> I had the impression that you cannot quite give up the Zurich plan because you are not quite sure of your closest colleagues in Basel. I can, of course, promise nothing for Walter Nef; for me, however, I have become convinced during these vacation weeks that I will not go back to Holland. What we have begun together in Basel is essential and necessary to me, because my best strengths are invested in it. But we need to be able to continue this work in a manner such that others can take it over. At the moment the Schola and BKO would cease to exist if you, Nef and I were to leave. In Holland I will only be able to do charitable work; my musical activities would be foreign there and not fit in. If we begin anew in Zurich, we will have gotten stuck in Basel half-way through. Beginning again is tempting in and of itself and I suddenly understood [what this] means for you, when I got to know the Collegium. For me, it would only be a part-time job. I can hope for lifelong cooperation solely [...] for Basel, and that I do with my entire heart. This time I am even thinking with joy about the work that is beginning again now. My attachment to you, to Basel, to all of Switzerland is far stronger than I knew.[105]

104 "weil ich meine Arbeit in Basel fortführen wollte". Paul Sacher, "Ein Basler in Zürich", in: *Vierzig Jahre Collegium Musicum Zürich*, Zurich: Atlantis Verlag 1982, 11.

105 "ich hätte den Eindruck, dass Sie den Zürcher Plan deshalb nicht ganz aufgeben können, weil Sie von Ihren nächsten Mitarbeitern in Basel nicht ganz sicher sind. Für Walter Nef kann ich natürlich nichts versprechen; für mich bin ich aber in diesen Ferienwochen zur Ueberzeugung gekommen, dass ich nicht nach Holland zurückgehen werde. Was wir zusammen in Basel angefangen habe, ist für mich lebenswichtig und notwendig, weil

Once again here, when given the choice, Ina Lohr decided to continue her work in Basel. Although she again and again called her cooperation with Paul Sacher into question, she could not imagine a life without it, would feel like she were giving up on an uncompleted task, just because there were difficulties, not because she was convinced that the goal was not worth pursuing. And so, their work in Basel continued.

Her decision to commit herself to Basel, however, did not mean that her difficulties with Paul Sacher stopped; but they were, perhaps, beginning to be take on a somewhat different form. On 9 December 1944 Ina Lohr wrote about her observations concerning the concert of 3 December in which Gregorian chant was interspersed between movements of a Guerrero mass, where she assumed the direction of a smaller half-choir made up of Schola students and selected members of the Basler Kammerchor for the chant numbers:

> First of all, I have to thank you for having made it possible for me and given me the space, for once, to sing from the depths of my heart. At the time, it absorbed me so deeply, that I could not judge whether the performance was good, nor whether you, on the whole, were happy. The performance was apparently good; I am still astonished daily by the reactions of listeners. I am not clear about the second question, and I am even very sad that we did not find the right contact, even in the concert. Otherwise, I always feel how much you are "in" something, but this time I was in my world, perhaps in my heaven, and you were in your world. For that reason, I cannot, as otherwise, be happy about a seemingly very beautiful concert. Our cooperation was certainly less good than usual. I was unable to understand that you simply left so much to me throughout the entire preparation period. Perhaps we would have communicated better if I had not been so closed and resistant. But you certainly [also] had so many other and different things to do. And I still believe that this is actually a danger for you; that is why I so often [feel I] cannot not continue and would prefer to just live very simply and not be your paid assistant, but only your adviser, as earlier, rather than contributing through this assistance to you being able to do as much as possible. If the work with the choir were to stop for the moment, then there would not be much other work [for

meine besten Kräfte darin stecken. Wir sollten aber im Stande sein diese Arbeit so weiter zu führen, dass sie andere übernehmen können. Jetzt würden Schola und B.K.O. zusammenfallen, wenn Sie, Nef und ich gehen. In Holland werde ich nur menschlich helfen können; meine musikalische Tätigkeit ist dort fremd und passt nicht zum Rahmen. Wenn wir in Zürich neu anfangen, sind wir in Basel auf halben Wege stecken geblieben. Neu Anfangen an sich ist verlockend und ich habe das für Sie plötzlich verstanden, als ich das Collegium kennen lernte. Für mich gibt es das wahrscheinlich nur noch als Nebenbeschäftigung. Lebenslängliche Zusammenarbeit [...] kann ich also nur für Basel hoffen, und das tue ich von ganzem Herzen. Ich denke diesmal sogar mit Freude an die Arbeit, die jetzt wieder anfängt. Meine Verbundenheit mit Ihnen, mit Basel, ja mit der ganzen Schweiz ist viel stärker als ich wusste". Letter Ina Lohr to Paul Sacher of 10 August 1944, private collection, Switzerland.

me] than that for the general programming. I am not striking, only fear a cooperation which we continue out of habit but which is basically unproductive.[106]

This passage makes it quite evident that in the past they had occasionally experienced that indescribable uplift of synergy when work together on a common project results in something greater than either of them could have produced alone, and that this powered their cooperation. Thus, Ina Lohr was just as dissatisfied with the thought that Paul Sacher perhaps had not received fulfillment from the concert, as if she herself had not done so. In addition, she obviously was missing the earlier real cooperation, the real fighting through of musical issues with him, and feared that she was contributing to a kind of efficiency which she found suspect. The resolution of how their differences in personal taste and in musical goals were be accommodated had yet to be found.

1945

The only substantive, truly personal letter in the first half of 1945, the last year of the war when everyone's nerves lay bare, was written on 4 January, as a reaction to her discomfort with her current task of evaluating the works of various composers. She opens by explicitly stating that she has tried to "do justice to each of them and to imagine what you [...] could get from these works". For example, she found *In Terra Pax* by Frank Martin, was made for him, that it was

---

106 "Erstens muss ich Ihnen danken, dass Sie es mir möglich gemacht haben und mir den Platz einräumten einmal so aus tiefstem Herzen zu singen. Es hat mich im Augenblick so sehr gepackt, dass ich nicht beurteilen konnte, ob die Leistung eine gute war und auch nicht, ob es Ihnen wohl war im Ganzen. Die Leistung war offenbar gut; ich bin noch täglich erstaunt über die Reaktion bei den Zuhörern. Über die zweite Frage bin ich nicht im Klaren, und ich bin sogar sehr traurig darüber, dass wir diesmal auch im Konzert den richtigen Kontakt nicht gefunden haben. Sonst spüre ich immer, wie Sie 'drin' sind, aber diesmal war ich in meiner Welt, vielleicht sogar in meinem Himmelreich und Sie waren in Ihrer Welt. Darum kann ich nicht wie sonst glücklich sein über ein offenbar sehr schönes Konzert. Unsere Zusammenarbeit war sicher weniger gut als sonst. Ich habe es während der ganzen Vorbereitungszeit nicht verstehen können, dass Sie mir soviel einfach überlassen haben. Vielleicht hätten wir uns besser verständigt, wenn ich nicht so verschlossen und abweisend gewesen wäre. Aber Sie hatten soviel anderes und verschiedenes zu tun. Und immer noch glaube ich, dass das für Sie sogar eine Gefahr ist; darum kann ich so oft nicht weiter mit und möchte viel lieber ganz einfach leben und nicht Ihre bezahlte Assistentin, sondern nur Ihre Beraterin, wie früher sein, als dass ich durch diese Assistenz dazu beitrage, dass Sie möglichst viel tun. Wenn die Chorarbeit vorläufig aufhört, gäbe es ausser der Arbeit am Generalprogramm nicht viel anderes. Ich streike nicht, habe nur Angst vor einer Zusammenarbeit, die wir aus Gewohnheit weiterführen, die am Grunde aber unfruchtbar ist". Letter Ina Lohr to Paul Sacher of 9 December 1944, private collection, Switzerland.

"fascinatingly interesting and masterly and very impressive".[107] But for her, this was insufficient because it hid "the sense of these texts, which have been assembled and edited in a rather high-handed manner".[108] Through remarks such as these, we see how she was now employing two sets of criteria in her reading of such scores for Paul Sacher, one purely musical, and the other based on the work's functionality in its religious context. Although she was aware that Paul Sacher would find favor in Martin's composition, her insistence that the work also come up to her own Christian principles meant that she could not consider cooperating with him practically in its performance. For this reason, she once again suggested that they go back to their original mode of cooperation, in which she would "gladly and with great resolve always attempt to know, to evaluate and to discuss your work with you",[109] going to the orchestra and choir rehearsals, and seeing one another once or twice a week. Although she offered to endeavor to continue evaluating the works of others, she felt that this was only successful if she were also working on her own compositions, saying that this enabled her to "better judge and appreciate the work of the others". Because this took time that should be dedicated to work for him, however, she had compunctions about doing this, remarking that her things were "worthless" for him.[110]

This letter gives some indication of the slow evolution of her work for Paul Sacher from being purely advisory in scope to something far more comprehensive, involving active practical involvement with the preparation of the choir, as well as the evaluation of new works in their constant search for stimulating programming. Due to the fact, however, that her obligations were never precisely defined, the work mutated in accordance with the needs of the moment, with new tasks being added to an already too long "to-do" list. At the same time, in particular with Ina Lohr's turn toward religion, their interests began drifting further apart, leading to her subsequent dissatisfaction with certain aspects of the cooperation, due to the differences between their musical ideals and goals. This letter once again represents an effort on her part to withdraw from that portion of the work which had come to drag her into conflict with him, with the hope of increasing the time available for her own work and of keeping the areas of friction between them to a minimum.

107 "es ist ganz ein Werk für Sie. [...] Es ist spannend interessant und meisterhaft und sehr effektvoll". Letter Ina Lohr to Paul Sacher of 4 January 1945, private collection, Switzerland.
108 "Für mich genügt das alles nicht, oder eigentlich ist es alles zuviel [sic], weil es den Sinn dieser Texte, die ziemlich eigenmächtig zusammengestellt und bearbeitet sind, verdeckt". Ibid.
109 "Ich will gerne und mit meinem besten Willen versuchen Ihre Arbeit immer zu kennen, zu beurteilen und mit Ihnen zu besprechen". Ibid.
110 "wertlos". Ibid.

5.3. The End of the War

The last few months of the war were so fraught that Ina Lohr apparently felt the need of having a daily outlet for her thoughts and emotions, perhaps in hopes of processing the events of the day before going to bed. She noted them down in a small diary in which she has often entered a quotation for the day on the left-hand page of each entry, while filling the right-hand one with her thoughts and activities.[111] The entries give a slightly different slant on her interactions with Paul Sacher, as they are not carefully worded documents, products of long periods of reflection, but merely commentaries on her day's activities for herself. In addition, they are written in Dutch, the language in which she expressed herself most freely. For example, on 31 January 1945, she wrote

> It is so sad that I can't find the old connection with P.S. I am too much absorbed in myself and can give good lessons from there [her own center], but no longer participate in the music scene. And he is becoming more and more the well-known conductor. I am always absolutely exhausted after such an afternoon with him. I composed it out [of my system] with Luther's prayer for peace "which the world cannot give". That was good.[112]

In three sentences she not only evaluated her own work and life, but also to saw how their paths were drifting apart, as well as illustrating how she used composition as a tool for maintaining her inner balance. By placing notes on paper, she calmed her soul.

But already two weeks later, on the 13 February 1945, she could exclaim

> Today it was already spring! I was free this morning and went therefore to work with Sacher. I strolled up there; the birds sang, and it smelled of earth and trees that were budding. Everything seemed so much lighter and more hopeful suddenly. The work also went well. P.S. himself wants to take something of mine into his programs. If I were not so completely exhausted and thus depressed, then everything would go so much better. But it is just this exhaustion that is the so necessary "thorn in the flesh".[113]

---

111   A few of these diaries are found in the PSF-ILC, and it is from them that the quotations in the text are taken.

112   "'t Is een echt verdriet, dat ik het oude contact met P.S. niet terugvind. Ik ben te veel in mezelf gekeerd en kan van daaruit goed les geven, maar niet meer meedoen in het muziek-leven. En hij wordt steeds meer de bekende dirigent. Ik ben altijd vrijwel uitgeput na zoo 'n middag met hem. Componeerde het uit met Luthers gebed om vrede 'die de wereld niet kan geven'. Das [sic] was goed". Diary entry of 31 January 1945, PSF-ILC.

113   "Vandaag was het opeens voorjaar! Ik was vanmorgen vrij en ging toen bij Sacher werken. Wandelde naar boven; de vogels zongen en het rook naar aarde en boomen, die botten. Alles leek zooveel lichter en hoopvoller opeens. Ook het werken ging goed. P.S. wil zelfs weer iets van mij in zijn programma's nemen. Als ik naar niet zoo gauw moe was en daardoor gedeprimeerd, dan zou alles zooveel beter gaan. Maar juist die moeheid zal wel de zoo noodige 'doorn in 't vleesch' zijn". Diary entry of 13 February 1945, PSF-ILC.

Work with him the following day was also harmonious and good, and he repeated his desire for compositions from her hand. Although she understood his wish as a compliment, a recognition of her ability, she – remaining firm to her faith – turned it down:

> He wants to perform something of mine, but it should be for the concert hall, and I can think of nothing for that! I find it easier to distance myself from this plan than he. Composition for composition's sake and for a concert does not tempt me any more.[114]

Once again, we see Paul Sacher, in his own way, trying to make the cooperation with him attractive to her by speaking to her creative side; he stayed, however, within his framework. This offer, while no longer being sufficient to engage her in compositional activity for him, did buoy up her spirits for a bit, as on 23 February 1945 she could write that she was living strangely, as part of her felt happy, since her work in both areas "was good and fruitful"; notwithstanding this, however, she remained in "never-ending anxiety and fear about home".[115]

It is at this point in the narrative that the inescapable events in the world also took over her life, as is made evident by her entry on 4 March 1945:

> This morning Basel was bombed. I heard it coming, saw the cloud and stood at the open window. But everything went so quickly that there was no time for fear. It is something appalling and absolutely unnatural. But I am now also completely at peace. "Wen's trifft, den trifft's". ["Whoever it hits, it hits".][116]

Although throughout this period she continued to meet with Sacher, with varying results, both positive and negative; her life – at least as revealed by the diary – became more centered on what she could do to help deal with the aftermath of war, how she could aid the survivors.

On 8 April 1945 a new path opened up for her, for she finally discovered an outlet for her charitable drive, alleviating her from her sense of helplessness in a world gone mad. She was, namely, invited to speak in Sunday school about the Netherlands, as the Protestant Church was planning to bring 3000 Dutch chil-

---

114 "Hij wil iets van mij uitvoeren, maar het is voor een zaalconcert en daarvoor valt me niets in! Ik doe makkelijker afstand van dit plan dan hij. Het componeeren om het componeeren zelf en voor een concert lokt me niet meer". Diary entry of 14 February 1945, PSF-ILC.

115 "Ik leef heel vreemd, gedeeltelijk bepaald goed en gelukkig in mijn werk dat nu op beide gebieden goed en vruchtbaar is, gedeeltelijk in nooit ophoudende zorg en angst om thuis". Diary entry of 23 February 1945, PSF-ILC.

116 "Vanmorgen werd Bazel gebombardeerd. Ik hoorde het komen, zag de wolk en stond voor het open raam. Maar alles ging zoo gauw, dat er geen tijd was voor angst. Het is iets ontzettend en absoluut onnatuurlijk. Maar ook nu ben ik volkomen rustig. 'Wen's trifft, den trifft's'". Diary entry of 4 March 1945, PSF-ILC.

dren to Switzerland to provide them with some necessary relief, both emotional and physical, from the bleakness of war. Less than a week later, on 14 April 1945, she met with Walter Robert Corti, the founder of the Pestalozzi Village for the accommodation of war orphans, to find out what she could contribute to the cause. The meeting was difficult, as she felt that Corti's interest, as a doctor, was primarily for the children's physical rather than their spiritual well-being and he was suspicious of those concerned about the latter. She reflected that "although there was much in what he said and his circumstances that repelled" her, that it was necessary for her to learn to "reject nothing and nobody, because everybody was needed".[117]

The death of Hitler was announced on 2 May 1945 and two days later the Germans surrendered Amsterdam, Rotterdam and Leiden. After so many years of longing for this day, Ina Lohr was left restless, between laughter and tears. It was typical for her that she lent significance to the fact that she was rehearsing "Christ ist erstanden" ("Christ is risen" by Samuel Scheidt) with her students at the moment when, on 7 May 1945, they heard that peace had been announced. She felt a heretofore unexperienced warm friendship with her students, concluding that "we must now, however, begin anew, and with great humility and thankfulness".[118]

On 9 May 1945, she met the first train with children from Holland and was responsible for the leaders accompanying the children until they left three days later. The occasion can best be described in her own words:

> Again, a day not to be forgotten. The train came at 11:30, with flags and the royal standard [of the House of Orange]; I could only keep up a good front with difficulty. And then the real work began in order to make sure everybody had a roof, and to forward letters, arrange for money, etc. In between I worked with P.S. and even sang my 2 cantatas [probably "Christus, der uns selig macht" and "Verleih uns Frieden genädiglich"] with Ursula D.[Dietschy] and Dr. Sch.[Schucan]! And this evening I heard so, so much about Holland. They are happy, even joyful and there is no place in their hearts for hatred, thanks be to God![119]

---

117 "hoewel veel in wat hij zei en ook in zijn omgeving me afstootte"; "dat ik niets en niemand afwijs, wat er ook iedereen dat gevraagd wordt". Diary entry of 14 April 1945, PSF-ILC.

118 "Maar nu moeten we opnieuw beginnen, en wel heel deemoedig en dankbaar". Diary entry of 9 May 1945, PSF-ILC.

119 "Weer een dag om nooit te vergeten. Om twaalf uur kwam de trein binnen met vlaggen en oranje; ik kon me maar met moeite goed houden. En toen begon een echt werken om iedereen onder dak te krijgen, brieven verder te sturen, voor geld te zorgen enz. Tusschenin met P.S. gewerkt en zelfs met Ursula D. en Dr. Sch. mijn 2 cantates gezongen! En vanavond veel, veel over Holland gehoord. Ze zijn blijmoedig, zelf vroolijk en voor haat is geen plaats in hun hart, Goddank!" Diary entry of 9 May 1945, PSF-ILC.

The following two days were full, with tea visits, teaching, a performance of Scheidt's "Christ ist entstanden" for the visitors, and her students distributing clothes. And then as suddenly as they came, they left on 12 May 1945, leaving Ina Lohr, the counsel and his wife and several Dutch-Swiss wives watching the departing train with a "longing heart".[120] Immediately thereafter, on the 12–13 May, Ina Lohr taught a weekend course together with Walter Nef, "Social Music of Earlier Times" ("Gesellschaftsmusik alter Zeit") with 37 participants. One can only imagine how exhausted she was by the time that was over.

Her life took on new meaning for her, gave her new elan also in her musical work, although her work with Paul Sacher seemed almost to become more difficult because he was aware of how much this other work meant to her. She came into contact with people from other classes, whom she was instinctively inclined to reject, but came to see how they also had something of value to offer. She learned that we "should not judge one another according to our habits or style of life. Each person can be God's tool for bringing about good and therefore merits our respect".[121]

After 22 May 1945 there are only a handful of diary entries, as she no longer had the energy to write at night; in addition to her teaching, her days were jampacked with meeting trains with displaced persons and with children, and with getting the Dutch children housed in Basel. These remaining entries are, however, of particular importance as they relate to her efforts to reconnect with her family. The first in this category, inscribed on the page for 24 May 1945 is particularly touching:

> Yes, on this day the letters came with the children's train. And they are all still alive, but Sally has a hunger tb [tuberculosis exacerbated by malnutrition] and mother is very weak. I write this on 31 XII 1946, and it is as if I experience once again the profound thankfulness and the overflowing need, for the time being, to give to others that which is due to my own beloved ones.[122]

---

120 "we stonden opeens weer op het perron, de consul en zijn vrouw en een paar Hollandsch-Zwitsersche vrouwen, die allemaal net als ik de trein met een verlangend hart nakeken". Diary entry of 12 May 1945, PSF-ILC.

121 "Ik heb er door geleerd, dat we elkaar niet naar gewoonten, niet eens naar levenswijze mogen beoordeelen. Iedere mensch kan Gods werktuig zijn om het goede te volbrengen en verdient daarom onze achting". Diary entry of 23 May 1945, PSF-ILC.

122 "Ja, op dezen dag kwamen er brieven met de kindertrein mee. En ze leven allemaal, alleen heeft Sally een honger t.b. en moeder is heel zwak. Ik schrijf dit op. 31.XII 1946 en 't is alsof ik het weer beleef die diepe dankbaarheid en de overstromende behoefte om voorloopig aan anderen te geven, wat mijn eigen lievelingen toekwam". Entered on 31 December 1946 on the page for 24 May 1945, PSF-ILC.

This moment had such meaning for her that she felt compelled to make this entry a year and a half after the fact, probably when passing her life in review on
New Year's eve of 1946. It is an indication of the degree to which she suffered from
being separated from her family. Although she had already been living in Switzerland for ten years when the war broke out, the fact that she could not reliably communicate with her family and see them whenever she wanted had been a
small torture for her. Hence her joy that they still lived and the gratification that –
if she could not help them in person – she could at least be of some use to others.

The next evidence of her activities is an exchange of letters between 17 and 22
July 1945 with Paul Sacher about the programming of the coming concert season. The discussions center primarily around the choice of Handel arias for the
concert of 12 October 1945. The alto soloist, Maria Helbling, clearly desired to
sing a scene from the opera *Orlando*. As this was too short, the problem was
finding an appropriate aria that fit with it. In the letters, they squabbled about
what would be best. Further, Paul Sacher asked whether she thought they could
exchange a piece by Stämpfli for one by Honegger in the concert of 15 February
1946. She was vehemently against this and in the end, neither piece appeared
on the program. And finally, she speaks of marking up the Bach *Magnificat* for
the concert of 25 November 1945 and Fux's Suite in D minor for 22 March 1946.

But this is a kind of background noise against which her real work was being carried out, the organization of lodgings for the refugees. At the same time,
she was using all possible contacts in her search for a possibility of returning to
the Netherlands to see her family before her mother died. On 17 July 1945 she
described her doings in the following manner:

> My travel has been postponed until the 24th. The Swiss train, which is sending 30 Swiss
> female escorts, is going then to pick up children. The difficulty now is that I do not yet
> have permission to stay in Holland until the next train, that is until 7 August. I am ac-
> tually only getting a visa to return with the children on the 27th. In this case, I couldn't
> even go home. I have asked everywhere, will only know in the last minute. I have re-
> ceived no additional news, but I am very peaceful. In any case, my little mother will
> now be able to die in peace. It is very sad, however, for my father; he is so dependent on
> her, and still so full of life. I must go to him in any case.
>
> Until yesterday I was traveling continuously to inspect various shelters. I now hope
> that I can quietly stay here [in Basel] for a week, for the innumerable impressions also
> tire me. At the consulate, all are working feverishly and are full of plans. My help is re-
> quired time and again, and more than ever I feel myself to be between two worlds, both
> of which place their demands upon me and that I cannot connect [with one another].
> Perhaps the trip to Holland will show me the way.[123]

123 "Meine Reise ist bis zum 24. verschoben. Dann fährt der Schweizerzug, der 30 Schwei-
    zerconveyeusen nach Nijmegen schickt um dort Kinder abzuholen. Die Schwierigkeit ist

Her higher-level students supported her in this work in that they, whenever necessary, took over her recorder lessons for children during this period, so that she could devote herself to the work with the refugees.[124] But even with that, this sort of organizational work, involving much travel and many meetings with people was simply too much for her, as one can see in her letter of 22 July 1945:

> Since yesterday, I have been living in tension. Friday I received notice that one can send telegrams to Holland, and I did that immediately, with a pre-paid answer. As I can't go to Holland, I'm much tormented by the uncertainty concerning my mother. I tried everything to pressure them to give me a Belgian or French visa for the train on Friday. Even the highest men at the Red Cross were of assistance, but the Belgian consulate remained callous. Then, when I wanted once again to take the first train to Berne on Thursday morning [19 July] in order to make a final attempt, my heart gave way anew and I was very miserable for 2 days. It is better now again, but it was worse this time and I know now that I cannot continue with this kind of work.[125]

Her plans were thus undermined yet again by the weakness of her health. Her passionate nature demanded that she give of herself fully, musically and personally; when she did, however, the payback was always immediate, in that her physical strength was not up to the exigencies of her will. In this case, this expe-

---

nun, dass ich noch keine Erlaubnis habe, bis zum nächsten Zug, d.h. bis zum 7 August in Holland zu bleiben. Eigentlich bekomme ich meine Visa nur, um am 27. mit den Kindern zurück zu reisen. Könnte in dem Fall gar nicht nach Hause. Ich habe alles angefragt, werde erst im letzten Moment Bescheid wissen. Nachricht habe ich auch keine mehr, aber ich bin sehr ruhig. Auf alle Fälle wird meine kleine Mutter jetzt in Ruhe sterben dürfen. Für meinen Vater ist es aber sehr traurig; er ist so abhängig von ihr und noch so vital. Zu ihm muss ich auf alle Fälle.

Bis gestern war ich ununterbrochen auf Reisen um verschiedene Heime zu inspectieren [sic]. Jetzt hoffe ich noch eine Woche ruhig hier zu bleiben, denn ich werde müde auch von den unendlichen vielen Eindrücken. Auf der Gesantschaft [sic] ist man fieberhaft an der Arbeit und voller Pläne. Ich muss immer wieder mithelfen und mehr als je fühle ich mich zwischen zwei Welten, die beide ihre Ansprüche an mich stellen und die ich nicht verbinden kann. Vielleicht zeigt die Reise nach Holland mir meinen Weg". Letter Ina Lohr to Paul Sacher of 17 July 1945, private collection, Switzerland.

124 Ina Lohr, "Skizze zum Lebenslauf", 6.

125 "Seit gestern lebe ich in Spannung. Freitag bekam ich Nachricht, dass man nach Holland telegrafieren kann, und habe das sofort getan mit Antwort bezahlt. Da ich nicht nach Holland kann, plagt mich die Unsicherheit über meine Mutter sehr. Ich versuchte alles um ein belgisches und französischen [sic] Visum für den Zug von Freitag zu erzwingen. Sogar die höchsten Herren vom Roten Kreuz haben geholfen, aber die belgische Gesandtschaft blieb verständnislos. Als ich dann am Donnerstag morgen noch einmal mit dem ersten Zug nach Bern fahren wollte um einen letzten Versuch zu machen, bekam ich wieder eine Herzschwäche und war 2 Tage lang sehr elend. Jetzt geht es wieder, aber die Sache war diesmal schlimmer und ich weiss jetzt, dass ich diese Art Arbeit nicht weiter machen kann". Letter Ina Lohr to Paul Sacher of 22 July 1946, private collection, Switzerland.

rience led her to decide to take two weeks vacation in St. Moritz, as the CMZ would be repeating the performance of her arrangement of the *Art of the Fugue* on 28 and 29 July 1945 in Silvaplana. At first, she stayed with a family who had taken in a Dutch child, getting comfort in the warm distractions of that life, while nonetheless all her thoughts were directed toward her dying mother. On 29 July 1945, she made the following entry in her diary:

> The *Art of the Fugue* was magnificent yesterday evening and again this afternoon. Sacher and the orchestra understand something of the world which stands behind such a work. I sat quietly above by the organ and felt Mother close to me. But I no longer can suppress my tears. It is therefore good that the family life demands something from me and distracts me in a good way.[126]

She spent her birthday, however, with the Sachers, together with the Honegger family which was visiting from France. And the last few days of her stay were also with the Sachers, as on 7 August 1945 she wrote from Basel to thank them for that peaceful interlude:

> Before the impending chaos starts, I must express my thanks once again in writing, because I couldn't quite put into words this morning, *how* good these days were. Like unexpectedly quiet, beautiful measures in a rather stormy movement. I really took "vacation from myself" at your place, from that "me" who is of the opinion that she only really belongs [there] in the role of your musical assistant. Perhaps, in spite of all the sorrow, it is a blessing for me that I no longer had the strength to remain independent. In any case, I felt it to be a blessing that I could sit at your table just as self-assuredly as Annettli and let myself be spoiled by you. Although I do not intend to become a "lame duck", I hope to retain some of this good trust when the vacation is over.[127]

It is clear that the Sachers saw her neediness, and just as with all of the other musicians they took under their wing, convinced her to take advantage of their

---

126 "De Kunst de Fuge was al gisteravond prachtig en vanmiddag ook weer. Sacher en het orkest beseffen iets van die wereld, die achter zoo 'n werk staat. Ik zat stil boven bij het orgel en voelde Moeder heel dicht bij me. Maar ik kan mijn tranen niet meer bedwingen. 't Is daarom goed, dat het familieleven iets van me eischt en me, op een goede manier afleidt". Diary entry of 29 July 1945, PSF-ILC.

127 "Bevor das drohende Gehetz anfängt, muss ich noch einmal schriftlich danken, weil ich es heute morgen nicht recht sagen konnte, <u>wie</u> gut diese Tage waren. Wie unerwartet stille, schöne Takte in einem ziemlich stürmischen Satz. Ich habe bei Ihnen wirklich 'Ferien vom Ich' gemacht, von diesem 'Ich', der meint, nur als musikalische Assistentin dazu zu gehören. Vielleicht ist es, trotz allem Traurigen, ein Segen für mich, dass ich keine Kraft mehr habe um selbständig zu bleiben. Auf alle Fälle habe ich es als Segen empfunden, dass ich mich so selbstverständlich wie Annettli an Ihren Tisch setzen durfte um mich von Ihnen verwöhnen zu lassen. Obwohl ich nicht im Sinne habe ein 'lame duck' zu werden, hoffe ich etwas von diesem guten Vertrauen fest zu halten, auch wenn die Ferien um sind". Letter Ina Lohr to Paul Sacher of 22 July 1946, private collection, Switzerland.

Ill. 5.7: Jet Lohr and Ina Lohr, 1932. Photo: courtesy of Aleid and Floris Zuidema, Lochem.

hospitality, giving her a few days of respite in this uncharted territory between war and peace, between life and death. Her mother died on 24 August 1945 (see Ill. 5.7).

At some later time, she made an entry in her diary commencing on that date and continuing over the pages of the following two days.

On this day Mother died. I only heard about it a couple of days later at the station. The telegram and the letters didn't arrive until the beginning of September. But I had known since the last days in Sils when I walked alone in the rain above Chasté and had a sense of the "other world", that God had taken her there and that we have no right to hold her back, even with our own wishes and thoughts.

Afterwards came the time that I felt her around me all the time. Especially in Zurich when I rehearsed the *Art of the Fugue* with Funk; and later sat in a dark corner of the Fraumünster to listen. Music, such music can connect God's world with our world. I do not wish to give up the quiet.[128]

128 "Op dezen dag is Moeder gestorven. Ik heb het pas enkele dagen later aan het station gehoord. Het telegram en de brieven kwamen pas begin September. Maar ik wist, sinds dien laatsten dag in Sils, toen ik alleen in de regen op Chasté rondliep en een besef van die "andere wereld" had, dat God haar al daarheen had genomen en dat wij geen recht hebben haar zelfs met onze wenschen en gedachten terug te houden.

Daarna kwam de tijd, dat ik haar aldoor om me heen voelde. Vooral in Zürich, toen ik met Funk de Kunst de Fuge repeteerde; en daarna in een donker hoekje van het Fraumünster zat te luisteren. De muziek, zulke muziek kan Gods wereld met onze wereld verbinden. Ik mag de stilte niet prijsgeven". Entered at a later date on diary page for 24 August 1945, PSF-ILC.

This entry, whenever it was written, opens a window on this no man's land of her existence at that time, where war was no more, but where the bureaucratic structures were still so rigid that such needs for personal contact could not yet be realized. Once again, she turned to God and to music for the comfort and peace she sought.

And her joy must have been immense when she finally received a visa. Paul Sacher immediately gave her a plane ticket to Amsterdam, so that she would not have to wait a single minute longer to see her family. In her letter of 18 October 1945, she turned anew to a musical image to express her feelings:

> Only now do I know how great the longing was, that was now suddenly fulfilled. Just like a long dominant with many secondary dominants which finally resolves itself in the tonic. The trip was like a miracle: we flew very quietly over a sea of clouds which opened up just above Holland. I was full of such emotion which then became even stronger when my father and my sister picked me up from the airport. We went with a car immediately to Haarlem in order to quickly be with my youngest sister. Everything was so inexpressibly good and is still so now. I will stay at my sister's in Amsterdam until Monday, then will go to Haarlem and must go to the minister in The Hague on Thursday. [...] I come from here and a part of me will always be at home here. But I belong now also in Basel and will begin again, hopefully with new courage, on the 29th.[129]

This was a time for new beginnings throughout the world, for putting the war behind oneself and moving on. The upheavals, however, had been so great that it was impossible to just go back to old ways of doing things; the structures of the past had collapsed, necessitating a renewal of civilized life. In this, music was no different than any other realm, the breaches in its customary cultivation within the European tradition revealed themselves throughout the world and on all levels. Not only were the schools devoted to the teaching of music, and the institutions dedicated to its performance forced to rethink their programs, but due to the increasing prevalence of the recording studio – utilized both by the radio and record companies – the market became wider, its base

---

129 "Erst jetzt weiss ich, wie gross die Sehnsucht war, die jetzt plötzlich erfüllt worden ist. Wie eine lange Dominante mit vielen Zwischendominanten, die sich endlich in die Tonika auflöst. Die Reise war wie ein Wunder: wir flogen ganz ruhig über einem Wolkenmeer, das sich gerade über Holland teilte. Das war schon eine Emotion, die dann noch stärker wurde, als mein Vater und meine Schwester mich doch am Flugplatz abholten. Wir fuhren mit einem Auto sofort nach Haarlem um schnell bei meiner jüngsten Schwester zu sein. Es war alles unsagbar gut und ist es auch jetzt. Ich wohne bis Montag in Amsterdam bei meiner Schwester, gehe dann nach Haarlem und muss am Donnerstag zum Minister im Haag. [...] Und ich komme von hier und ein Teil von mir wird immer hier zu Hause sein. Aber ich gehöre jetzt doch nach Basel und werde am 29. hoffentlich mit neuem Mut wieder anfangen". Letter Ina Lohr to Paul Sacher of 18 October 1945, private collection, Switzerland.

less elite and new financial factors became involved, particularly in regard to stylistic choices. Arguably, it could be said that musical performance on the whole became more standardized. With her return to Amsterdam and the con-commitant re-connection with her family, Ina Lohr, too could look forward to beginning again in Basel with new courage and perhaps new ambitions, now that she was no longer plagued by the dreads and the sorrows of war.

Chapter 6. Ina Lohr, the Schola Cantorum Basiliensis and the Burgeoning of Early Music

With the end of the war, the door to the world was once again opened, extending its invitation to the curious. This was no less true for Ina Lohr, Paul Sacher and all of their colleagues at the Schola Cantorum Basiliensis than anyone else. They thereby came increasingly into public notice throughout Europe, with Ina Lohr giving courses in the Netherlands, Paul Sacher receiving frequent invitations as a guest conductor, and the concert group of the Schola under August Wenzinger having ample opportunity to provide advertisement for the institution outside of Switzerland. For Ina Lohr and Paul Sacher this new activity also apparently reduced the need for correspondence. Accordingly, this chapter will turn less around their working relationship, but rather concern itself more with her activities within the SCB. This also reflects a greater sense of independence on Ina Lohr's part, both as a result of and impetus for a greater demarcation between their respective tasks within their cooperation.

6.1 The Schola Cantorum Basiliensis in 1945/46

The Schola, too, was bustling with new life, as is evident from its annual report, presenting a full roster of teachers and courses, as well as an increased number of events involving the institution; in addition, the number of students went up. Ina Lohr taught her normal courses (Gregorian chant, Gregorian chant choir, choir and ensemble exercises in *Hausmusik*, recorder, ensemble, Protestant church music, thorough bass, practical exercises and pedagogy), as well as three fall courses, and her students participated in seven recitals. In addition, the *Ensemble für Kirchenmusik* remained active, with four quite diverse concerts. The first, on 18 September 1945, was the beginning of an annual cooperation with the Munster organist, Fritz Morel, in his series of vespers concerts. On 30 November 1945, the ensemble joined with the SCB concert group in a benefit concert on behalf of a drive for postwar aid for academic institutions that had suffered during the war. The third concert reflected Ina Lohr's influence in the Swiss *Hausmusik* movement, in that her *Ensemble für Kirchenmusik*, together with one of her *Hausmusik* ensembles from the Schola, performed in the chapel of the Grossmünster in Zurich for the annual meeting of the Swiss Association for Folk Songs and *Hausmusik* on 2 March 1946.

The last of the four concerts took place in the reading room at the library of the University of Basel at the opening of an exhibition cleverly entitled *Drucker gegen Unterdrücker* ("Publishers against Opressors"). Organized by the press attaché at the Dutch embassy in Berne, J. B. Braaksma, the exhibition was devoted to the works published by illegal companies, such as "De Bezige Bij" ("The Busy Bee") which was active in the resistance against the German occupation. A facsimile of a broadsheet with a poem by Jan Campert, *Het Lied der Achttien Doden,* in honor of eighteen members of the resistance who were executed by the Germans in March 1941 is found in Ina Lohr's estate at the Paul Sacher Foundation. These facsimiles were produced specially for the occasion and were sold as a contribution to the health care of surviving members of the Dutch resistance. Given her attitude toward the war, and her connections with the Dutch population in Switzerland, it seems appropriate that she was invited to provide the musical accompaniment, with both her own works and those of Sweelinck, for such an event.

Her classes in Protestant church music in conjunction with the University and the Protestant Church of the City of Basel were also expanded, so that they took place during the entire academic year. While the course in the first semester was dedicated to the songs of the Reformation and their connections to Gregorian chant and to secular song, in the second, 16th-century psalms and their current use were the objects of study.[1]

6.2 Recognition in the Netherlands

It was, no doubt, one of these courses that the influential Dutch theologian and politician Gerardus van der Leeuw visited when, together with Kees van Dorp, he came to Basel to speak with Karl Barth shortly after the war. As a Dutch authority on comparative religion and also the minister of education from 1945–46, he had been persuaded by acquaintances that he must also take in one or two of her lessons. As Gerardus van der Leeuw was leaving, he told Ina Lohr: "we must have that in Holland too".[2] As a result, on 6 July 1946 she spoke in

---

1   "Die Lieder der Reformationszeit in ihren Beziehungen zum greg. Choral und zum weltlichen Lied" and "Die Psalmenlieder im 16. Jahrhundert und ihre Verwendung in unserer Zeit". *Jahresbericht der Schola Cantorum Basiliensis 1945/46,* 6. Archive of the Schola Cantorum Basiliensis.
2   "dat moeten wij in Holland ook hebben". Acknowledgment in the booklet for the celebration of her 80th birthday in the Netherlands, "Commissie ter voorbereiding van der viering van het tachtigste geboortejaar van I-NA LOHR", PSF-ILC.

Haarlem at a national conference devoted to the reformation of music within the Dutch Protestant church. At a much later date, she wrote of the difficulties surrounding this occasion. To begin with, her father was not convinced of her abilities as a speaker:

> He came in at the very last second, saw a yet empty chair next to another old man in the first row and sat down suddenly next to van der Leeuw, whom he knew only from the newspaper, who just then stood up in order to introduce us. "Us", because Ursula Dietschy, a young singer who was continuing her studies at the Schola Cantorum Basiliensis, had come along to support me, which she did outstandingly. But van de Leeuw introduced her astutely as "Fräulein" Dietschy, which caused a clear rumble from the audience (at that moment we were anything but a congregation). Our minister did not let himself be irritated and said with the same astuteness, that on this morning[3] we – now that we were looking at the songs of the reformers – would get to know the German language in a much different manner, and he added that "these ladies" spoke Swiss-German with one another and that I was Dutch by birth. As he went to sit down again, the mood was reserved and watchful and I went to stand in my place and knew "I am standing here and cannot do otherwise". My father was reassured by my stout-hearted bearing, pulled on the sleeve of his unknown neighbor and said audibly, "That's my daughter". Upon which van der Leeuw introduced himself just as audibly and assured him that he knew me very well. And this small incident changed everything: that mocking reserve made way for amused, well-meaning smiles and I still believe that this contributed more to the success of the morning than anything that I said or that we sang. But it turned out well, and afterward good questions were asked, and Kees van Dorp was able to announce that there would be a course about it in 1947. And van der Leeuw beamed and said: "Who knows what will come from this!"[4]

3 Although she wrote "middag" [afternoon], her talk took place in the morning; presumably she was confusing the time with the second presentation in Utrecht on 27 July 1946, which took place in the afternoon.

4 "Hij kwam op het laatste nippertje binnen, zag nog een lege stoel naast een andere oude heer op de eerste rij en zat opeens naast v.d. Leeuw, die hij alleen uit de krant kende. Die stond juist op om ons voor te stellen. 'Ons', want Ursula Dietschy, een jonge zangeres, die op de Schola Cantorum Basiliensis nog verder studeerde, was meegekomen om mij te ondersteunen, wat ze voortreffelijk deed. Maar v.d. Leeuw stelde haar opgewekt voor als 'Fräulein' Dietschy, wat een duidelijk gemor in het publiek wekte (we waren op dat moment alles andere als een gemeente). Onze minister liet zich niet storen en zei met dezelfde opgewektheid, dat we op deze middag, nu het om de liederen van de Reformatoren ging, de Duitse taal op een heel andere manier zouden leren kennen en hij voegde eraan toe, dat 'deze dames' onder elkaar Zwitsers spraken en dat ik Nederlandse van geboorte was. Toen hij weer ging zitten, was de stemming koel afwachtend en ik ging op mijn plaats staan en wist 'hier sta ik, ik kan niet anders'. Mijn Vader was door mijn kordaat optreden gerustgesteld, trok zijn onbekende buurman aan zijn mouw en zei hoorbaar 'Dat is mijn dochter', waarop v.d.Leeuw zich even hoorbaar voorstelde en verzekerde, dat hij mij heel goed kende. En dit kleine incident veranderde alles: dat mokkende afwachten maakte plaats voor een welwillend meesmuilen en ik geloof altijd nog, dat dat meer tot het slagen van die middag bijgedragen heeft, dan alles, wat ik vertelde en wat we zongen. Maar het werd goed, er wer-

The reaction to her presentation was overwhelming. Many years later, in a text for the 25th anniversary of the Centrum voor de Kerkgezang, entitled "De werkwijze van mej. Lohr acht ik de injectie waar de protestantische kerkmuziek in Holland op wachte" ("Miss Lohr's method of working is, in my opinion, the injection for which the Protestant church music in Holland was waiting"), the choral conductor Jan Boeke wrote that

> in the middle of her arguments about subjects such as "Can our choirs sing every Sunday in the service?" her manner of speaking-song and singing-speech hit us like a bomb. All confusion concerning questions of how music may or must function (congregation, choir, organ, precentor) were suddenly put into proportion by the sounding existential force of unisono singing. Our so beloved so-called cantus-firmus singing, in which the choir ornamented the congregation's song, fell by the wayside, the pseudo-"Gregorian" psalmody could not withstand the confrontation with a Luther psalm, sung in unisono.[5]

This effect was redoubled by their presentation of the same material on 27 July 1946 at the Organ Congress of the Dutch Organ Society in St. Jacob's church in Utrecht. The review of 30 July 1946 in the *Utrechts Nieuwsblad* reported that she spoke to the question of how we should sing our songs, answering with

> "for the moment in unison without accompaniment". She then sang Psalm 23 in a tempo suddenly as fast as the congregation had used for Hymn 98. According to Ina Lohr, it is really not about singing fast all the time; that is an opinion which at the moment one often hears expressed, but one has to start from the comprehensibility of the text. If the singing is to be good, then one has to not only listen to oneself, but also to that which one hears to the left and which one hears from the right, and that one can only do if one does not sing too loudly. In order to prove this by example and in order to indicate what one can achieve with other methods than the usual ones, the speaker had the congregation sing and this experiment produced a surprising effect. It was no

---

den na afloop goede vragen gesteld en Kees van Dorp kon aankondigen, dat er 1947 een cursus van zou komen. En van der Leeuw straalde en zei: Wie weet wat daar verder nog van komt!" In: "Commissie ter voorbereiding van der viering van het tachtigste geboortejaar van I-NA LOHR", PSF-ILC.

5   "Temidden van de betogen over onderwerpen als 'Kunnen onze koren elken zondag in den eeredienst zingen?' sloeg haar manier van sprekend zingen en zingen spreken als een bom in. Alle verwarring over de vragen hoe muziek in de eredienst mocht of moest functioneren (gemeente, koor, orgel, voorganger) werd hier plotseling gerelativeerd door de klinkende kracht van een existentieel eenstemmig zingen. De bij ons toen zo geliefde zgn. Cantus firmus-zang, waarbij het koor het gemeentelied versierde, viel door de mand, de pseudo-'gregoriaanse' psalmodieën hielden het niet, als zij werden geconfronteerd met een eenstemmig gezongen psalmlied van Luther". Jan Boeke, "De werkwijze van mej. Lohr acht ik de injectie waar de protestantsche kerkmuziek in Holland op wachtte…", in: *40 jaar protestantse kerkmuziek. Gedenkboekje ter gelegenheid van het 25-jarig bestaan van het Centrum voor de Kerkzang*, [Maasland]: Stichting Centrum voor de Kerkzang 1975, 8.

longer the expressionless singing, which we [...] still far too often hear, but music which gave the impression that it was sung by a veritable choir.[6]

These descriptions reveal the broad experience Ina Lohr had gained in Basel, not only from her teaching at the Schola Cantorum and her work with the Basel Chamber Choir, but also from her efforts to help propagate the *Probeband* in the early 1940s. She had clearly developed the stature to not only get up in front of a large audience and present her ideas clearly, but also to do so in such a manner that she immediately involved all in the process.

The response was so great that she was invited back to give courses in the following years, both in Haarlem and in Utrecht; in addition, the desire was openly stated in the press that she return to Holland. As the influential organist Hendrik Leendert Oussoren put it two years later: "It is to be hoped that Ina Lohr may be found willing to return to Holland in order to found a center for the performance of church music".[7]

6.3 Second Thoughts about Basel

Not unsurprisingly, this massive open support for her work within Dutch church circles made her reflect once again about her work with Paul Sacher, whether this was something that she wished to continue, whether she might not want to return to the Netherlands and embark on this new task, one very close to her heart. And so, after a year, on 29 September 1946 she once again wrote to Paul Sacher about her conflicted state of mind in regard to their work together.

---

6 "'hoe zingen we de liederen', beantwoordde zij met: 'voorloopig onbegeleid eenstemmig'. Zij zong daarop psalm 23 voor in eens zoo snel tempo als de gemeente gezang 98 ten gehoore had gebracht. Het gaat er echter niet om, aldus Ina Lohr, om altijd vlug te zingen; dat is een opvatting, die men tegenwoordig dikwijls hoort verkondigen, doch men moet uitgaan van de verstaanbaarheid van den tekst. Wil de zang goed zijn, dan moet men niet alleen zichzelf hooren, maar ook luisteren naar wat men links hoort en wat men rechts hoort en dat kan alleen wanneer men niet te luid zingt. Om de proef op de som te nemen en om aan te toonen wat met andere dan de gebruikelijke methoden kan worden bereikt, liet spreekster de gemeente zingen en deze oefening leverde een verrassend effect op. Die was niet meer de uitdrukkingslooze zang, dien wij [...] nog te vaak hooren, doch muziek, die den indruk maakte alsof ze door en behoorlijk koor werd gezongen". Music editor, "Een leerrijk orgelcongres in de Jacobikerk: Verrassend effect van gemeentezang", in: *Utrechts Nieuwsblad*, 30 July 1946.

7 "Het is te hopen, dat Ina Lohr bereid gevonden kan worden naar Holland terug te keren om hier een centrum van kerkmuziekbeoefening te stichten". H.L. Oussoren, "Het Nederlandse muziekleven in het heden", in: *Wending* 3 (1948), 628.

Her resolve to write stemmed from a renewed descent into depression, resulting from her general state of exhaustion and her longing for the contact with
people that she had when she was doing relief work, with the final "blow" coming, as "was almost always the case", from some interaction with Paul Sacher.
She lamented that when this happens

> something also lingers on, however, after I am once again calm and clear [of mind]: the
> impression that you, when it comes down to it, consider me to be hypersensitive, even
> not completely sound of mind. And that is what completely throws me, because I then
> believe it and am in despair about how you, and so many others, make such demands
> upon me which I will never be up to fulfilling. It is not that you say anything, to the
> contrary your "impersonal kindness" hurts far more, when you promise something and
> then behave differently later, because you never took the promise seriously with which
> you calmed me at the time.[8]

After the enthusiastic reception of her work in the Netherlands, accompanied
by serious suggestions that she return to the country of her birth and devote
herself to the renovation of the performance of church music, it must have
seemed almost unbearable to return to her unsatisfactory situation in Basel in
regard to her work with Paul Sacher. And in turn, this made her hypersensitive to what she perceived to be slights in the manner in which he dealt with
her needs, her world view. Indeed, her complaint about being perceived as
being hypersensitive even rings alarm bells, as in the letter of 11 March 1942 (see
p. 236) she had written that she was particularly grateful that he did not treat
her as being "psychologically ill". His remarks about her hypersensitivity may
have seemed to have taken a turn in that direction, and were probably particularly offensive to her.

She then turned the issue around, maintaining that her hypersensitivity had
the advantage that it gave her a "discerning ear for music" and thus the capability to study and mark up scores, while at the same time, making her "awk-
ward and unsuitable" for the larger practical tasks he desired. Accordingly, she
then reiterated her request that her work be reduced to its original dimensions

---

8   "Den letzten Stoss gaben Sie. Das war fast immer so [...] Etwas bleibt aber auch wenn ich
    wieder ruhig und klar bin: der Eindruck, dass Sie mich letzten Endes für übersensibel, ja
    eigentlich für nicht ganz zurechnungsfähig halten. Das ist was mich ganz umwirft, weil ich
    es dann glaube und daran verzweifle, dass Sie und so viele andere solche Ansprüche an mich
    stellen, denen ich nie gewachsen sein werde. Es ist nicht, dass Sie etwas sagen, im Gegenteil
    die 'unverbindliche Freundlichkeit' schmerzt viel mehr, wenn Sie etwas versprechen und
    nachher anders handeln, weil Sie das [sic] Versprechung, mit dem Sie mich im Moment
    beruhigten, nie ernst genommen haben". Letter Ina Lohr to Paul Sacher of 29 September
    1946, private collection, Switzerland.

with the original pay. In conclusion, she expressed her regret that it had come this far, saying "You cannot [...] change people according to [your] needs".[9]

Paul Sacher, on the other hand, had not been standing still either, but had also been receiving many more opportunities as a guest conductor and as a result, had gained much in musical confidence and stature. Thus this letter, although it on one level may just seem to be a repetition of ones she had written in the past, must also be seen in context of both of their successes in the wider world, leaving her in some way freer to make a decision to stop, simply because she had an alternative to remaining in Basel under what she felt to be the increasingly indifferent hand of Paul Sacher.

An exchange of letters between her and Paul Sacher and also Walter Nef, as assistant director of the Schola, around the end of year, make it clear that she had told both of them that she was thinking of leaving Switzerland, perhaps even at the end of the year. The communication between Paul Sacher and Ina Lohr had apparently become so onerous that Ina Lohr requested that she be left in peace after the concert on 1 December 1946. Some of her innermost thoughts during this interregnum concerning the matter are revealed in a "diary entry" made on the 31 December 1946:[10]

> The biggest difficulty is and remains the work with Sacher, perhaps also Sacher himself. He is now a conductor with much success, travels a lot and enjoys his own ability. Have I the duty, or perhaps not even the obligation, to pass judgment on that? That my part of the cooperation has become too much is a simple, clear fact and Sacher is prepared to take that into account and bring about some changes. But what hampers me far more is the new course that the BKO is now taking under his direction. Now that he conducts so much, he can no longer study works in depth as before. But then he cannot allow them to be prepared by me and then perform [them]. I rebel at this, much more than about the fact that my own participation is not mentioned and therefore not esteemed publicly. The most decent and best [thing to do], would be to take a leave of absence for a year in order to see if his development goes further in the direction of "guest conductor". Since the war, I have lost contact with that world. Must I not actually have gained enough inner strength to continue living in just that environment, to be a witness to God and his law, not so much with words, but simply through my existence? But I do not have the strength, at least not yet in any case. My flaw is that

9 "Diese Ueberempfindlichkeit hat vielleicht den Vorteil, dass ich hellhörig für die Musik bin und darum Partituren studieren und bezeichnen kann. Sie macht mich aber ungeschickt und ungeeignet für die immer grössere praktische Aufgaben, die Sie wollen. Sie können aber die Menschen nicht nach Bedarf ändern". Ibid.

10 Although the pages of her 1947 diary are filled with writing from 1 January to 13 February, in reality they represent the texts of only two separate days that overflow over consecutive pages, that of 31 December 1946 extending from 1 January to 30 January, and that of 4 January from 31 January to 13 February, PSF-ILC. Therefore, in this context I will be citing texts from one of these two days.

I take on too much, get too much involved with people, also out of some sort of vanity or perhaps more out of a need to get approval from others. A married woman gets that from her husband; it is, perhaps, difficult for us for that reason to hold fast to one direction, in that we want to expend too much love in all directions and also expect a response from all directions. I must, armored with this knowledge, draw strength and simplicity from [peace and] quiet.[11]

Many aspects of how she perceived her working relationship with Paul Sacher are revealed in this text. Somewhere within her she was outraged by a feeling that the work she was doing in preparation for the concerts was not receiving the attention and the care she considered necessary for the preparation of a performance. For her, this was even worse than the fact that her work was not receiving public recognition. This, of course, means that – notwithstanding all of her remonstrations to the contrary – deep down inside she was smarting because her work was not being openly acknowledged. She also laments her lack of moral fiber, that she is unable to just simply live her life dedicated to God, regardless of the external circumstances, simply because she also had the human need of support and approval. Interestingly enough, however, she once again implicitly compares their working relationship to a marriage, in that she reflects on how single women, unlike wedded women, do not have this source of strength in their immediate environment, and therefore give and expect too much in return from those around her. She sees her only answer in taking dis-

---

11 "De grootste moeilijkheid is en blijft het werk met Sacher, misschien ook wel Sacher zelf. Hij is nu een dirigent met veel succes, reist veel en geniet van zijn eigen kunnen. Heb ik de taak of misschien niet eens het recht daarover te oordeelen? Dat mijn deel van de samenwerking te zwaar geworden is, is een eenvoudig, nuchter feit en Sacher is bereid daarmee rekening te houden en er verandering in te brengen. Maar veel meer hindert mij de andere koers, die het BKO nu onder zijn leiding neemt. Nu hij zooveel dirigeert, kan hij zich niet meer in werken verdiepen zooals vroeger. Maar dan mag hij ze ook niet door mij laten instudeeren en dan uitvoeren. Daartegen kom ik in opstand, veel meer dan tegen het feit, dat mijn medewerking niet genoemd en daarom ook niet openlijk gewaardeerd wordt. Het zuiverste en best zou zijn, dat ik me een jaar terugtrok om te zien, of zijn ontwikkeling verder in de richting 'gast-dirigent' gaat. Met die wereld heb ik sinds de oorlog het contact volkomen verloren. Moest ik eigenlijk niet genoeg innerlijke kracht gewonnen hebben, om juist in die omgeving verder te leven en, niet zoo zeer met woorden als eenvoudig door mijn zijn van God en zijn recht op ons te getuigen? Maar die kracht heb ik niet, nu nog niet in ieder geval. Mijn fout is, dat ik te veel aanneem, te veel op menschen inga, ook uit een soort ijdelheid of misschien meer uit de behoefte om een toestemming van anderen te krijgen. Een getrouwde vrouw krijgt die door haar man; voor ons is het misschien daarom zooveel moeilijker, om één richting te houden, omdat we ons te veel aan liefde naar alle kanten willen uitgeven en ook van alle kanten een antwoord verwachten. Ik moet, met dit weten gewapend, kracht en eenvoudigheid uit de stilte putten". Diary entry of 31 December 1946, PSF-ILC.

tance from the world, of giving herself the time to come back to herself and to the "direction of her heart".

She then goes on to speak of her current life:

> After the liberation, I allowed myself to be carried away too much by the long-suppressed need to help and to do something noticeable and palpable. Because of this I got outside [the sphere of] my work. I was suddenly able to bring my own true vocation, singing – primarily sacred music – into harmony with my new, much broader world. It has become more alive, richer and more personal by this means, and the reaction of all involved is then also very positive. But I have more and more departed from the contact with official musical circles. Is it simply out of habit and desire for power that Sacher wishes with all of his strength to keep hold of me, makes a greater effort for this than actually corresponds with the work? Wouldn't he himself be much freer just in this stage of [his] development, if he were to let go of me? Or aren't we after all, after all the years of difficult, but also at times very wonderful and fruitful cooperation, tied to one another to such a degree that we have to attempt it again and again with one another[?][12]

Through her experiences, both at the end of the war for the various agencies providing relief, as well as through the recognition she had recently received in the Netherlands, she found herself in a different position in regard to Paul Sacher, perhaps a more objective one, in that she could compare it to other situations. This enabled her to question their cooperation at a much deeper level, really examine whether it was worthwhile to attempt to maintain it.

And then her return to the Netherlands brought other realizations with it, what bound her to her country, what it meant to her to see how both the citizens and her family were working together to rebuild it:

> They have begun anew and there is more, much more contact between the various circles and groups and everybody has learned to tackle things themselves and is not ashamed to do so. My own father is a magnificent example and I am proud of him and love him more than ever. To see how he cares for Pim [her sister Sally]; how he wants to compensate for mother, for that which he had neglected [(]can she not have always known in her deepest heart that all of this was in him?); and his love and interest in all

---

12   "Ik heb me na de bevrijding te veel laten meesleepen door de lang opgekropte behoefte om te helpen en iets merkbaar daadwerkelijksch te doen. Daardoor ben ik buiten mijn werk komen [te] staan. Mijn werkelijk eigen deel, het zingen en vooral de kerkmuziek heb ik meteen met mijn nieuwe, veel ruimere wereld in overeenstemming kunnen brengen. Het is er levender, rijker en menschelijker door geworden en de reactie van allen, die er aan meedoen is dan ook geheel positief. Maar het contact met het officieele muziekleven verlies ik meer en meer. Is het alleen gewoonte en gemakzucht, dat Sacher me met alle geweld wil vasthouden, zich meer moeite daarvoor geeft, dan eigenlijk met het werk in evenredigheid staat? Zou hij zelf niet veel vrijer zijn juist in die ontwikkelingsstadium, als hij mij losliet? Of zijn we toch door al die jaren van moeilijke soms ook heel mooie en vruchtbare samenwerking toch zoo aan elkaar gebonden, dat we het altijd weer met elkaar moeten probeeren". Ibid.

people and children around him; those are my most beautiful experiences of this year. And Pim, of course, in her still, constantly happy disposition and the country. I have never realized that I missed the whole Dutch landscape so much; nor that it was so much a part of me, and that I would experience such an intense joy in seeing it again. But perhaps I would have just as strong a longing for Basel and for the mountains if I were to live in the Netherlands again. I will always be between these two worlds. Or no, I must always try to be completely there, and to give of myself there, where I am at that moment and seize the day and pass on that which I have seized.[13]

Here, too, we see how she is torn between the two countries, how strongly she is aware that she has also established herself in Basel, and that no matter where she ends up living, both will be in her. This leads to her conclusion that she must learn to be in the moment, really live wherever she may find herself. As this was the difficult issue for her during the war, being able to be in both countries has given her a new perspective.

Paul Sacher evidently considered the case to be hopeless, that she would resign completely from her work with him and perhaps even return to the Netherlands, as a passage of his letter of 29 December 1946 indicates:

Your desire for seclusion caused me not to get in touch with you after my return home. Now, however, I want to send you my good wishes for the New Year.

It is a pity that the past year brought us such bad times and I am very sad about it. Your letter in fall was the most painful news in a long time. I do not understand that this decision was possible, given that we are bound together by such an old friendship. The cooperation, in spite of all its difficulties, was particularly good! But given your attitude, there is nothing left [to do] but to thankfully remember the past and to search for a new path. That is unfortunately not easy for me. I therefore hope that this gloomy decision at least brings something good for you.[14]

13 "Maar ze zijn opnieuw begonnen en er is meer, veel meer contact tusschen de verschillende kringen en groepen en iedereen heeft geleerd zelf aan te pakken en schaamt zich daar niet voor. Mijn eigen Vadertje is een prachtig voorbeeld en ik ben trotsch op hem en houd meer van hem dan ooit. Te zien, hoe hij voor Pim zorgt, hoe hij nu nog aan Moeder wil goed maken, wat hij haar te kort heeft gedaan, kon ze niet altijd in haar diepste hart geweten hebben, dat dit alles in hem was?) [sic] en zijn liefde en belangstelling voor alle menschen en kinderen om hem heen, dat zijn mijn mooiste ervaringen van dit jaar. En Pim natuurlijk in haar stille, altijd naklare blijheid en het land! Ik heb nooit beseft [sic], dat ik het heele Hollandische landschap zoo miste. Ook niet, dat ik er zoo mee vergroeid was en een zoo intense vreugde zou beleven bij het weer zien. Maar misschien zou ik evensterk naar Basel en naar de bergen verlangen, als ik weer in Nederland woonde. Ik zal altijd tusschen die twee werelden zijn. Of neen, ik moet probeeren altijd heelemaal daar te zijn en me daar te geven waar ik op dat oogenblik ben en de dagen te plukken en het geplukte verder te geven". Ibid.

14 "Ihr Wunsch nach Stille hat mich veranlasst seit meiner Heimkehr nichts von mir hören zu lassen. Nun möchte ich Ihnen aber doch alle guten Wünsche zum neuen Jahr schicken.

Little did he know that Ina Lohr had already written him on the previous day, confirming that she would be taking up her work together with him again at the beginning of the coming year, information which she communicated to him in the following manner:

It is not very difficult in a quiet room – which looks very festive and comfortable without the scores and other reminders of work – to make a new decision. The battle this time, however, was very difficult; perhaps the decision is more valuable as a result. I will stay and also continue to be your assistant. The offer from Holland, where they want me as a "qualified musician who stands on the foundations of the church", was tremendously attractive. My "piety" is perceived, at the very least, as superfluous and bothersome by you and by your circle; but for me, the "praise of God" is always, and in all activity, the final goal. In the Schola the various goals can be unified, in the BKO almost never. I am, however, deeply bound to the Schola and have also discovered that I have in part really become Swiss, and even more so, a *Baslerin*. Therefore, the decision will no doubt be right.

The problem with the choir will probably resolve itself correctly. I have now seen Lucas Wieser once in action and had an excellent impression. He has a sense for singing, particularly also for *a cappella* singing. Give him an honest chance, in that you give him your trust.

Apart from the choir, I would like once more to make a new attempt. We cannot change anything externally. If you would now designate me for the programming, that would only be a source of gossip. I want to avoid that at all cost. But it is also not necessary that I put so much of myself into the programming. That has as a consequence that I am only exhausted, dissatisfied and "pillaged" when the cooperation no longer can be as it was with Palestrina, Purcell, until ca. 1940. And that appears unlikely to me.

It is not possible to speak about the other difficulties. You do not understand them and that apparently cannot be changed. To be sure, however, I am increasingly driven into my own world by this experience, which makes the cooperation continually more difficult.[15]

Es ist schade, dass uns das abgelaufene Jahr so schlechte Zeiten gebracht hat & ich bin sehr traurig darüber. Ihr Brief vom Herbst war die schmerzlichste Nachricht seit langer Zeit. Ich verstehe nicht, dass dieser Entschluss möglich war, nachdem uns eine so alte Freundschaft verbindet. Auch die Arbeitsgemeinschaft war doch trotz allen Schwierigkeiten besonders schön! Aber es bleibt nun, angesichts Ihrer Haltung nichts anderes übrig als sich dankbar des Vergangenen zu erinnern & einen neuen Weg zu suchen. Das ist für mich leider nicht leicht. So hoffe ich, dass dieser betrübliche Entscheid wenigstens Ihnen etwas Gutes bringe". Letter Paul Sacher to Ina Lohr of 29 December 1946, PSF-ILC.

15   "Es ist nicht sehr schwer, im stillen Zimmer, das ohne Partituren und andere Arbeitsmahnungen sehr festlich und wohnlich aussieht, einen neuen Entschluss zu fassen. Der Kampf war aber diesmal sehr schwer, vielleicht hat der Entschluss darum auch mehr Wert. Ich werde also bleiben und auch als Ihre Assistentin weiter mitmachen. Das Angebot aus Holland, wo man mich als 'qualifizierte Musikerin, die ganz auf dem Boden der Kirche steht' will, war ungemein verlockend. Von Ihnen und von Ihrem Kreis wird meine 'Frömmelei' mindestens als überflüssig und lästig empfunden; für mich ist aber das 'Lob Gottes' immer und in jeder Arbeit das letzte Ziel. In der Schola lassen sich die verschiedenen Ziele vereinigen, im BKO fast nie. Ich bin aber der Schola zutiefst verbunden und habe auch entdeckt,

Paul Sacher was both pleased at this change of heart, as well as obviously a bit peeved, wounded, by what he clearly considers to be unjustified accusations, demanding also changes in attitude on her part in his letter of 30 December 1946:

> Yesterday I wrote you a melancholy letter which will reach you with some flowers on January 1ˢᵗ. Now, today, I receive your letter. Many thanks. If you would tell me what the "other difficulties" were, I could certainly understand them. But for years now, you have been very dismissive in this point. You make no use at all of my good will. In general, to my great sorrow, you consider me somehow as a "sated bigwig" who needs nothing, including you and your help. It is obvious that no grass can grow on this stony ground. Could you not let go of this defensive stance just a little, in order to seek a better "point de départ" for 1947? You yourself speak of a friendship for a certain P.S. This P.S. in question desires and is really searching eagerly for a good cooperation and is ready to take every consideration for his partner; should you really not know that? Can one be more than willing?[16]

dass ich zum Teil wirklich Schweizerin und vor allem Baslerin geworden bin. Also wird die Entscheidung schon richtig sein.

Das Problem mit dem Chor wird sich wahrscheinlich richtig lösen. Ich habe Lucas Wieser jetzt einmal in Aktion gesehen und hatte einen ausgezeichneten Eindruck. Er hat Sinn für Singen, gerade auch für a cappella Singen. Geben Sie ihm eine ehrliche Chance, indem Sie ihm Ihr Vertrauen geben.

Abgesehen vom Chor will ich nochmal einen neuen Versuch machen. Aeusserlich können wir nichts ändern. Wenn Sie mich jetzt für die Programmgestaltung nennen würden, gäbe das nur eine Anregung zum Klatschen. Das möchte ich um jeden Preis vermeiden. Es ist aber auch nicht nötig, dass ich soviel Eigenes in die Programme hineinlege. Das hat zur Folge, dass ich nachher nur erschöpft, unbefriedigt und 'ausgeplündert' bin, wenn die Zusammenarbeit nicht mehr so sein kann wie bei Palestrina, Purcell, ca. bis 1940. Und das scheint mir sehr unwahrscheinlich.

Ueber die anderen Schwierigkeiten lässt sich nicht reden. Sie verstehen sie nicht und das lässt sich offenbar auch nicht ändern. Allerdings werde ich durch diese Erfahrung immer mehr in meine eigene Welt hineingetrieben, was die Zusammenarbeit immer schwieriger macht". Letter Ina Lohr to Paul Sacher of 28 December 1946, private collection, Switzerland.

16   "gestern habe ich Ihnen einen melancholischen Brief geschrieben, der am 1. Januar mit einigen Blumen bei Ihnen ankommen wird. Heute erhalte ich nun Ihren Brief. – herzlichen Dank. Wenn Sie mir die 'anderen Schwierigkeiten' sagen würden, könnte ich sie bestimmt verstehen. Aber Sie sind leider seit Jahren in diesem Punkt sehr abweisend. Sie machen keinerlei Gebrauch von meinem guten Willen. Ueberhaupt betrachten Sie mich zu meinem grossen Schmerz irgendwie als 'Saturierten Bonzen', der nichts – auch Sie & Ihre Hilfe – nötig hat. Auf diesem steinigen Grund kann natürlich kein Gras wachsen. Können Sie diese Abwehr-Einstellung nicht ein wenig aufgeben, um einen besseren point de départ für 1947 zu suchen? Sie reden doch selber noch von einer Freundschaft für einen gewissen P.S. Dieser fragliche P.S. wünscht & sucht wirklich sehnlich eine gute Zusammenarbeit & ist zu jeder Rücksicht auf seinen Partner bereit. Sollten Sie das wirklich nicht wissen? Kann man mehr als guten Willens sein?" Letter Paul Sacher to Ina Lohr of 30 December 1946, PSF-ILC.

In a letter of 9 January 1947 to Walter Nef, Ina Lohr commented on Paul Sacher's response to the situation, saying that "Paul and I have made contact again, but now he is the disappointed one and he is not comfortable in that role",[17] a clear reference to the time in 1944 when he was considering moving to Zurich and abandoning both the SCB and the BKO (see p. 256). The discussions were quite profound, as is revealed by the entry in her dairy on 4 January 1947:

> P.S. came again today and we were now both much quieter and understood one another well again. He now has also understood and accepted there can be no other solution for the choir. I have to find another way to compensate him for this loss, for example with a better attitude. For that reason, I cannot allow myself to be "swallowed" by the Schola; nor by the great number of people. It is a new perspective that P.S. lives and works in a lonelier fashion that I [do]. But he is right. He can and wants to open himself up only to a few people who have at some point gained his trust.[18]

It is evident from Ina Lohr's short description of their encounter, that Paul Sacher had spoken about his predilection for working with a small group of trusted associates, which in turn made it important to him to maintain their cooperation. This provoked further acerbic reflection on her part – for the clarification of her own understanding of the situation – that for others he only had an "impersonal friendship" by means of which he kept people at a distance.[19] She traced this back to a lack of "general love for mankind" with a consequent negative effect on the spontaneity of his musicianship.[20] These thoughts, however, did not make her turn from him; but instead, the special nature of her position made her resolve to reserve enough time in her life to make the work together with him worthwhile.

She, too, once again attempted to explain to him what made their cooperation so difficult for her. In a carefully worded, typed text, with "Jan 1947" penciled

---

17 "Paul und ich haben den Kontakt wieder gefunden, aber jetzt ist er der Enttäuschte und die Rolle liegt ihm nicht". Library of the University of Basel, NL 212 (Estate Karl Nef), letter from Ina Lohr to Walter Nef, 9 January 1947.

18 "Vandaag kwam P.S. weer en we waren nu beide veel rustiger en hebben elkaar weer goed begrepen. Hij heefd nu ook begrepen en aanvaard, dat het met het koor niet anders gaat. Ik moet trachten hem dit verlies op een andere manier, b.v. door een betere stemming te vergoeden. Mag me daarom ook door de Schola niet laten 'opslokken'. Ook met door de al te vele menschen. 't Is een nieuw gezichtspunt, dat P.S. eenzamer leeft en werkt dan ik. Maar hij heeft gelijk. Hij kan en wil zich tegen over slechts weinig menschen, die nu eenmaal zijn vertrouwen hebben, uiten". Diary entry 4 January 1947, PSF-ILC.

19 "unverbindliche Freundlichkeit". Ibid.

20 "Eigenlijk is hij arm aan algemeene menschliefde en daarom is ook zijn musiceeren arm aan spontaniteit". Ibid.

in at the top in Paul Sacher's hand, she first described her inner state when creating a program, no matter whether it be for the entire season or a choir concert:

> The surfeit of work results from the fact that our work is not routine work. I would, to be sure, also be very unsuited to do such [routine work] and thereby also create for myself more bother than would be absolutely necessary. Because it is ever again new, each season's program is such an endeavor, each choir concert is almost like a "birth of a child". A program, such as the last one, gives me the same work, requires also, however, the same inner tension and exertion, as a composition.[21]

For her, programming was an act of immense creativity, calling upon all of her resources, musical, emotional, and – although not referred to here – her religious beliefs. She then goes on to describe her reactions when, either in rehearsal or performance, the work does not turn out as she has envisioned it. What is difficult for her is that she has no "status" in relation to her "mind-child", she has no recourse when it does not turn out as she desires. She contrasts herself to the composer, who

> remains the creator of his work, even if the musician who executes it understands and can form it entirely differently than he had imagined it while composing. The composer can stand up for his work, also defend it and explain, or even entrust it to another musician. I cannot do that and thus feel myself to be "at the mercy" of P.S. with my program. I am therefore also intolerant, because [I am] deeply unhappy and hurt when that which is essential to me in my program does not come through, is not even considered. And I cannot defend it or explain it, because "for the world" it is Sacher's program. Then there is nothing else for me to do but to make less personal programs and again to compose, which is also becoming for me an ever more urgent need.[22]

21 "Das Zuviel an Arbeit resultiert aus der Tatsache, dass wir keine Routinearbeit machen. Ich wäre allerdings auch sehr ungeeignet, solche zu leisten und mache mir dadurch sicher auch mehr Mühe, als unbedingt nötig wäre. Weil es mir immer neu ist, ist jedes Generalprogramm eine solche Anstrengung, jedes Chorkonzert sogar eine 'Geburt'. Ein solches Programm, wie das letzte, gibt mir die gleiche Arbeit, ist aber auch die gleiche innere Anstrengung und Verausgabung, wie eine Komposition". Private collection, Switzerland.

22 "Der Komponist bleibt aber der Schöpfer seines Werkes, auch wenn der Ausführende [sic] Musiker es ganz anders auffassen und gestalten kann, als er es sich im Komponieren vorstellte. Der Komponist darf weiter zu seinem Werk stehen, es auch verteidigen und erklären, ja sogar einem anderen Musiker anvertrauen. Das kann ich nicht und darum fühle ich mich P.S. 'ausgeliefert' mit meinem Programm – Darum bin ich dann auch unduldsam, weil tief unglücklich und verletzt, wenn das, was mir an einem Programm wesentlich ist, nicht durchkommt, nicht einmal beachtet wird. Und ich kann es nicht verteidigen oder erklären, weil es 'vor der Welt' Sachers Programm ist. Da bleibt mir nichts anderes, als dass ich weniger persönliche Programme mache und wieder komponiere, was mir auch ein immer dringenderes Bedürfnis wird". Ibid.

In this document, it becomes evident that one source of her constant conflicts with Paul Sacher stems from an inner predicament: she abhorred the limelight, but at the same time desired public recognition for her musical "children". By choosing the path of being Paul Sacher's assistant, she ensured that her programs saw the light of day, but in doing so she had given up control of their final form. As there was no recourse from this situation, if she were not willing to carve a path for herself in the musical world, she resolved to put her creative energy into composition and be more matter-of-fact about her work for Paul Sacher.

She went on to say that it is even worse when she participates in the choir rehearsals, both because of the physical exertion and their differing musical goals. She once again saw withdrawal from everything but the programming as being the only viable solution. Even if this required that she teach or write more, she would prefer it to pursuing a non-functional course. In conclusion, she maintained that

> Only if P.S. and the BKO desire and value my personal investment and perhaps also publicly acknowledge it to a somewhat greater degree, so that I can also stand up for my part of the work, will a further cooperation be possible. Otherwise it is only a mutual burden.[23]

And although she did not completely stop participating in the choir rehearsals until 1952, this marked the last of their major struggles concerning the form and content of their cooperation. Their correspondence becomes increasingly "business-like", in that it concerns itself to an ever greater extent with the programming of the BKO, with the notes for the individual concerts in the season, with evaluation of music, as well as with her preparation of the musical material.

6.4 The Beginning of the International Influence of the Schola Cantorum Basiliensis[24]

The 1946/47 school year was the beginning of a new awareness of the Schola Cantorum Basiliensis and its mission on many levels. Firstly, the number of stu-

---

23 "Nur wenn P.S. und das B.K.O. meine persönliche Arbeitsleistung wollen und schätzen und vielleicht auch etwas mehr öffentlich anerkennen, sodass ich auch zu meinem Teil der Arbeit stehen kann, wird eine weitere Zusammenarbeit möglich sein. Sonst ist sie nur eine gegenseitige Belastung". Ibid.
24 I would like to thank Madeleine Modin and Richard Sparks for their generous help in finding literature about the Swedish students at the SCB, and also Tore Eketorp for his help with translating.

dents increased significantly, in part because two of Ina Lohr's most favorite students, Ursula Dietschy and Elli Rohr, became available as teachers in the second semester, immediately after their mid-year graduation. But also, there was an increase in the number of students studying for a diploma; and their majors expanded from studying *Hausmusik*, recorder, organ and voice, to include harpsichord. Of particular importance for the future of the institution, but also the beginning of one of the highlights of Ina Lohr's pedagogical career was the advent of two young Swedes, who came for the summer semester in an eager search for new ideas after their comparative musical isolation during World War II: the violinist Nils Wallin and the keyboard player and musicologist Ingmar Bengtsson, both from Stockholm and both accomplished musicians. This was just the beginning of the advent of 32 musicians from Sweden between 1947 and 1962 (see Table 6.1).

Table 6.1: List of Swedish students who came to study at the Schola Cantorum.

Year	Name	Further Information
S.S. 1946/47	Ingmar Bengtsson (1920–1989)	Musicologist, organist, member of The Monday Group, co-initiator of the Lilla Kammarorkestern, studied musicology with Carl-Allan Moberg at the University of Uppsala and subsequently became his successor.
	Nils L. Wallin (1924–2002)	Violinist, as of 1947 member of The Monday Group, later studied with Carl-Allan Moberg, was director of the concert organization of the Stockholm Philharmonic Orchestra and founded the discipline of biomusicology.
S.S. 1948	Lars Frydén (1927–2001)	Violinist, teacher and musicologist. He studied baroque violin in Basel and recorded Bach and Mondonville with Gustav Leonhardt, and Rameau with Gustav Leonhardt and Nikolas Harnoncourt.
	Sven-Erik Bäck (1919–1994)	Composer, viola player, member of The Monday Group, Co-initiator of the Lilla Kammarorkestern.
	Eric Ericson (1918–2013)	Director of the eponymous Chamber Choir in association with The Monday Group, later a highly influential choir conductor, both in Sweden and throughout Europe.
S.S. 1949	Einar Lindstroem (Lindström?)	

Year	Name	Further Information
W.S. 1949/50	Sture Bergel (1923–75)	Recorder player. He published *Spela blockflöjt* in 1955, which employs solmization in a manner similar to that found in the tutor Ina Lohr wrote, as well as in theses written by two Schola students in completion of their diploma. Ina Lohr's personal copy has a handwritten dedication to "Ina Lohr, laid at her feet by her loyal child S.B".[25] According to Ina Lohr, he came to study questions concerning church music, harmony and pedagogy.[26]
S.S. 1950	Eva Nordenfelt (1936–1995)	Harpsichordist and the daughter of Birgitta Nordenfelt. Studied from 1954–57 with Eduard Müller and later with Ruggero Gerlin, Kenneth Gilbert and Gustav Leonhardt. Taught at the Royal College of Music in Sweden.
	Lars Edlund (1922–2013)	Composer, organist and teacher at the Royal College of Music in Stockholm. He was inspired by Gregorian chant and converted to Catholicism. He wrote the ear-training classics, *Modus Vetus* and *Modus Novus*. According to Ina Lohr, he came to study questions concerning church music, harmony and pedagogy.[27]
	Eric Ericson	
	Lars Frydén	
	Gunnar Hallhagen (1916–1997)	Pianist and professor at the Royal College of Music, Stockholm.
	Sven-Erik Bäck	
	Jan Crafoord (b. 1935)	He came to study gamba with August Wenzinger and later became a wine merchant.[28]
W.S. 1950/51	Gunno Sodersten (1920–1998)	Composer of sacred music (chorales, choir and organ music), choir director and organist. Music teacher at the Theological Seminary.
	Claude Génetay (1917–1992)	Cellist, conductor and music administrator. He taught several years at the Royal College of Music in Stockholm. He played in the Swedish Radio Orchestra and was later an administrator in its music department. He "provided performance opportunities for the composing members of The Monday Group through [...] a chamber orchestra".[29]

25 "Ina Lohr zu Füssen gelegt von Ihrem treuen Kind S.B", PSF-ILC.
26 Ina Lohr, "Gedanken über eine schwedische Generation und ihre Musik", PSF-ILC.
27 Ibid.
28 Telephone interview of 7 September 2016.
29 Ibid.

Year	Name	Further Information
	Karl Olof Nihlmann	These four played as a string quartet in Basel, with Frydén first violinist, Nihlmann second, Jonsson viola and Ericson cello. On 10 March 1951, with Frydén as soloist and Soldan Ridderstad as primus, they premiered Allan Pettersson's *Concerto pour violon et quatuor a cordes*.
	Axel Jonsson	
	Bengt Ericson	
	Lars Frydén	
S.S. 1951	Harald Göransson (1917–2004)	Church musician, cantor, organist and from 1953 harmony teacher at the Royal College of Music in Stockholm. He wrote the foreword to *Koralmusik* (1957), a hymnal that was the forerunner to the final version of the new hymnal of 1986, serving a similar function to that of the *Probeband* in Switzerland.[30] According to Ina Lohr, he came to study questions concerning church music, harmony and pedagogy.[31]
	Eva Nordenfelt	
	Birgitta Nordenfelt (1909–2000)	Mother of Eva Nordenfelt, well-known music pedagogue, came to the Schola Cantorum for a summer course to get new ideas. Her music school in Stockholm was open to performances of the works of The Monday Group. She also hired some of them, including Sven-Erik Bäck, Claude Génetay and Eric Ericson as teachers at the school.[32]
	Anna-Greta Nystig (b. 1922)	A student of Brigitte Nordenfelt, she came to study Gregorian chant, became fascinated by early instruments and studied early and modern *Hausmusik* with Ina Lohr.[33]
	Gunnar Hallhagen	
	Jan Crafoord	
	Rut Ericson	Recorded Nattvardsintroitus with the Danderyds Kyrkokör.

30 Harald Herresthal, "Das nationale Kirchenlied. Von Kantaten zu 'leichten Liedern'", in: *Musikgeschichte Nordeuropas: Dänemark, Finnland, Island, Norwegen, Schweden*, ed. by Greger Andersson, trans. by Axel Bruch, Christine von Bülow and Gerlind Lübbers, Stuttgart/Weimar: Verlag J.B. Metzler 2001, 76.

31 Per Broman, "New Music of Sweden", in: *New Music of the Nordic Countries*, ed. by John D. White, Hillsdale NY: Pendragon Press 2002, Part 5, 465.

32 Gunnar Larsson and Hans Åstrand, "Dödsfall: Birgitta Nordenfelt", Dagens Nyheter, 26 August 2000. (online://www.dn.se/arkiv/familij/dodsfall-birgitta-nordenfelt, last accessed 10 Ocober 2017).

33 Ina Lohr, "Gedanken über eine schwedische Generation und ihre Musik", PSF-ILC.

Year	Name	Further Information
1952/53	Ingmar Milveden (1920–2007)	Composer, musicologist and church musician. He was particularly interested in Gregorian Chant and later studied medieval Swedish liturgy and taught at the University of Uppsala.
	Eivin Andersen	
S.S. 1953	Selma Nordstrand	
W.S. 1954/55	Eva Nordenfelt	
	Jan Crafoord	
S.S. 1955	Maj Sehlmark-Ohlson	She became the director of music at a gymnasium.
	Eva Nordenfelt	
	Eva Eklund	According to Ina Lohr, she came to study questions concerning church music, harmony and pedagogy.[34]
	Jan Crafoord	
W.S. 1955/56	Synöve Lönell	
	Jan Crafoord	
W.W. 1958	Herbert Blomstedt	Violinist, at the time conductor of the Norköpring Orchestra (30 members), later internationally renowned conductor.
1958/59 ½ semester	Torsten Fåhréus	Violinist and music teacher who studied in Stockholm and Uppsala, and later worked primarily in Arvika.
1958/1959 ¾ semester	Christian Matthiessen	
1959/60 1 semester	Kerstin Johansson	She studied voice, and later was perhaps primarily active in the church.
W.S. 1960/61	Per-Olaf Johnson	A guitarist who played both folk and classical music, he later taught at the Royal Danish Music Conservatory and the Music School of Malmö.
1960/61 2 semesters	Sophie Falkenberg	She was enrolled in the *Hausmusik* program.
1961/62 1 semester	Eva-Lovisa Widenmeyer	She studied organ.

34 Ibid.

Many of them knew one another from their participation in The Monday Group (Måndagsgruppen). This loose organization of composers, performers, conductors and musicologists came together in the early 1940s and was named after the day on which they gathered together weekly in the small apartment of the composer Karl-Birger Blomdahl (1916–1968). The Swedish scholar Per Broman describes their main objective as being to learn "more about music and ideas that had been inaccessible during the war". They were not only curious musicians, but perceived themselves as revolutionaries of a sort, reacting "against the old national romanticism which as you know has controlled Swedish musical art forever".[35] In Broman's opinion, the significance of this group within the Swedish musical world should not be underestimated:

> Although it was a fairly heterogeneous group that hardly would constitute a school of composition in any stylistic sense, and although its meetings were informal in character, its impact on Swedish musical life would be enormous and would last well into the 1990s. The diversity of the individual members' talents, their eagerness for knowledge and new paths, and their capacity for work gave them important positions in Swedish musical life. [...]

In addition, in 1943 the Danish conductor Mogens Wöldike came to Stockholm for two years. He was particularly known for his cultivation of the performance of music of the Renaissance and the Baroque with his excellent Copenhagen Boy's Choir which he had founded in 1924. In Stockholm he spent time transcribing early music in libraries, but also was hired by the Swedish radio to conduct their choir and orchestra in concerts of Mozart and Bach, as well as *a cappella* choir music.[36] His work was followed with great interest by The Monday Group, and in particular by Eric Ericson, as it offered a window to earlier music than they were accustomed to hearing.

They, however, did not rest content with discussing and hearing this music, they also began performing it themselves with two entities associated with The Monday Group, Eric Ericson's Chamber Choir and the Lilla Kammarorkestern, initiated in 1942 by Ingmar Bengtsson, Claude Génetay and Sven Karpe. These ensembles played concerts devoted to works for *a cappella* choir, baroque chamber music, but also to contemporary pieces such as Stravinsky's *Dumbarton Oaks*. Thus, as they had practical experience in both early and con-

---

35 Per Broman, "New Music of Sweden", 464. Here Broman cites a letter from Blomdahl to a young Danish colleague.

36 Christina Tobeck, *Karl-Birger Blomdahl: En musikbiografi med inriktning på förhållandet mellan ord och ton i hans tidiga produktion*, Göteborg: Elanders Graphic Systems 2002 (Skrifter från Institutionen för musikvetenskap, University of Göteborg, Nr. 73), 135.

temporary music, they were curious about two institutions in the Basel musical scene: the Schola Cantorum Basiliensis and the Basel Chamber Orchestra.

Indeed, after the war, all of the members felt the need to break out of the isolation of Swedish neutrality, to go out in the world and widen their horizons, both musically and otherwise. It is ironic as well as understandable that all but two of them, Karl-Birger Blomdahl and Ingvar Lidholm, chose to go to Basel, i.e. to another country which remained neutral and therefore intact during the war. In a letter of 29 November 1946 to the Schola, Ingmar Bengtsson stated that his intention in coming to Basel for 2–3 months would be to gain "inspiration and knowledge" in order to be able to increasingly win the favor of the audiences in Sweden for earlier music. He wished to study the performance practice of early music, have lessons on harpsichord and clavichord, as well as delve into what Jacques Handschin had to offer in the department of musicology at the university.[37]

A letter from Nils Wallin to the musicologist Bo Wallner of 1 June 1947, a member of The Monday Group and later influential in the creation of a historiography of Swedish music in the 20th century, is highly revelatory not only concerning what fascinated and continued to draw Swedes to Basel, but also in what it says about Ina Lohr's instruction:

> And [there is so much that] one can barely speak about the (study) experiences. Now I'm only doing thorough bass and various theoretical exercises with Lohr, who is filling me to overflowing with all her ideas and subtle suggestions; violin playing on [works by] Rosenmüller and Corelli, and Biber (scordatura) with the just as wonderful (ask Ingmar) Marianne Majer; and finally, one or another ensemble class with the ever-traveling and absent Wenzinger. […]
>
> What Lohr has me do in thorough bass is invaluable. First of all, starting with all the old choir literature from Viadana to Bach, analyzing what is modal and not, the polyphony and its wonderful harmonious results, and finally from all this, improvising thorough bass. I have to say that as rich as this time is with questions, but above all with musical nuances, it's not the high baroque, but I am getting more confident that the 17th [century] will be my century.
>
> The Kindermann sonata I've dug up here and worked on, as well as recorded, belongs to the most beautiful I know, as well as the Italian things of Merulo, Marini etc. In addition, I have a slight hope that Wenzinger in Germany will find an old bow. Unfortunately, it's impossible to find a fiddle still in original condition, and I've tried to tune my Widhalm down, but it does not sound so good, because the lower tension only becomes too apparent. And everyone has such a brilliant interest in working with you,

---

37 Letter Ingmar Bengtsson to the Schola Cantorum Basiliensis of 29 November 1946, Stiftelsen Musikkulturens Främjande, The Nydahl Collection, Ingmar Bengtsson Archive, IB 1946 II 29.

so it's a joy. Lohr does everything for me, gives repertoire lists for us at home, gives tips right and left of how we can deal with this and that problem etc. Majer gets [us] materials that are unavailable, etc. And how Lohr did not lose patience [with me] at the beginning, when I did not really dare to depart from the rules of conventional harmony, is a mystery to me. But she just laughed and comforted me, that at least my mistakes were thought through and regretted that we in Sweden have such experts as the one who wrote out the thorough bass for Albrici (Sonata [Sinfonia?] a 6). She has a hard time forgetting that one. [...] I think they think it's fun with us because we are so phenomenally ignorant and so receptive.[38]

And we can gain an impression of what the experience meant to Ingmar Bengtsson from a long article he wrote for the *Svenska Dagbladet* of 11 June 1947. After commenting on some of the lacks of the Basel opera company, he observes that "one is, of course, especially interested in things that one can rarely or never hear at home in Sweden, and in Basel you especially find the cultivation of 'old' music, that is, the music from Bach and Handel's time and earlier".[39] He

38 "Och om (studie)upplevelserna kan man knappast tala. Sysslar nu endast med generalbas och diverse teoretiska övingar för Lohr, som proppar mig överfull med alla sina idéer och finesstips, fiolspel med Rosenmüller och Corelli samt Biber (förstämd) för den fortfarande lika underbara (fråga Ingmar) Marianne Majer samt slutligen en och annan ensembletimme för den evigt kringresande och tjänstledige Wenzinger. [...]
    Vad Lohr låter mig göra i generalbas är ovärderligt. Kommer för det första in i hela den gamla körlitteraturen från Viadana till Bach, analyserar i den vad som är kyrkotonartligt och inte, stämföringarna och dess underbara harmoniska resultat samt slutligen ur allt detta generalbasimprovisationer. Jag måste säga, att så rik som denna tid är på problem men framförallt på musikaliska nyanser, det är inte högbarocken, jag blir allt mer säker pa själv, att 1600 blir mitt tal. De Kindermannsonater jag här grävt fram och bearbetat samt spelat in, hör till det vackraste jag vet liksom de italienska sakerna av Merulo, Marini etc. Dessutom har jag ett svagt hopp om att Wenzinger i Tyskland skall finna en gammal stråke. Tyvärr är det omöjligt att finna en fela i originalmensur ännu, och jag har försökt stämma ner min Widhalm, men det klingar inte så bra, eftersom den mindre spänningen endast blir skenbar. Och alla har ett så strålande intresse av att jobba med en, så det är en fröjd. Lohr gör allt för mig, skafar repertoarlistor för oss därhemma, ger tips till höger och vänster om hur vi själva skola kunna klara det och det problemet etc. Majer skaffar på underliga vägar fram material, som är utsålt etc. Och att inte Lohr förlorade tålamodet den första tiden, då jag faktiskt inte vågade frångå den konventionella harmoniläran, är mig en gåta. Men hon bara skrattade och tröstade mig med att mina fel åtminstone voro überlegt samt beklagade att vi i Sverige har sådana experter som den som skrivit generalbasen till Albrici (Sonata [Sinfonia?] a 6).
    Den har hon svårt att glömma. [...] Jag tror att de tycker det är roligt med oss, därför att vi är så fenomenalt oplöjda och så receptiva". Musikverket: Musik- och Teaterbiblioteket, Archive Bo Wallner, letter Nils Wallin to Bo Wallner, Letter 1947–06-01.
39 "Naturligtvis följer man med speciellt intresse just sådant som man sällan eller aldrig kan få höra hemma i Sverige, och dit hör i Basel framför allt odlandet av "gammal" musik, alltså musik från Bachs och Händels tid och bakåt". Ingmar Bengtsson, "Industristaden Basel Bjuder all slags musik: Den gamla musikens högborg har plats för det dagsfärska", in: *Svenska Dagbladet*, 1 June 1947.

went on to speak of the Schola, mentioning that for fourteen years it had been "working carefully and insistently" towards the cultivation of early music and "has already achieved great results". This was followed by various examples of its activities in concert:

> [In a manner] as unpretentious as convincing, the school's *Ensemble für Kirchenmusik*, strengthened by recorders and violins, performed an exquisite 16th-century program in the form of a mass under the direction of Ina Lohr in the cathedral's Niklaus Chapel. [...] It was something of a revelation to hear this music in its proper context, performed with a living pulse and a spontaneous joy and naturalness that refuted any suspicion that this art would be forever dead and buried and of interest only as scientific research material.
>
> At least as surprising was to witness another occasion when the choir of the school, singing in the [church] choir could lead the whole congregation, without having rehearsed it beforehand and without organ accompaniment, in singing robust old Lutheran melodies in fluid 16th-century rhythms and lively tempi. Here one was dealing with a reconstruction of the entire Lutheran German mass from 1526.
>
> Another side of the institution is represented by August Wenzinger's gamba quartet, which together with singers and lutenists has brought 16th-century madrigals, songs and instrumental fantasies back to life.[40]

These remarks are of interest in that they underline the "spontaneous joy and naturalness" of the performance of the *Ensemble für Kirchenmusik* of 21 February 1947, something that essentially all those interviewed who have participated in concerts directed by Ina Lohr speak of as being the very essence of her music-making. It was that which also evidently fascinated Ingmar Bengtsson, experiencing it from the point of view of a member of the audience. In addition, the service with the Luther mass is another example of Ina Lohr involving the students in a demonstration of how a truly engaged cantor could lead an entire congregation in their joint praise of God. This service, which took place

---

40 "Lika anspråkslöst som övertygande framförde skolans kyrkomusikensemle förstärkt med blockflöjter och fioler ett utsökt 1500-talsprogram i mässform under ledning av Ina Lohr i domkyrkans Niklauskapell. Bland annat framfördes instrumentalsatser av Tomas de Santa Maria och körsatser av Ludvig Senfl och Joaquien des Prez. Det var något av en uppenbarelse att höra denna musik i sin rätta miljö, utförd med en levande puls och en spontan glädje och naturlighet som jävade varje misstanke, att denna konst skulle vara för alltid död och begraven och enbart ha intresse som veteskapligt forskningsmaterial.

Minst lika överraskande var det att vid ett annat tillfälle bevittna hur skolans kör genom att från koret leda sången kunde få hela församlingen att utan förövning och utan orgelackompanjemang sjunga friska gamla Luthermelodier i obunden 1500-talsrytm och livliga tempi. Den gången var det fråga om en rekonstruktion av hela Luthers tyska mässa från 1526.

En annan sida av verksamheten representerar August Wenzingers gambakvartett som tillsammans med sångare och lutspelare återuppväckt 1500-talets madrigal- och vissatser och instrumentala fantasier". Ibid.

on 2 March 1947, was the product of the last joint collaboration of Ina Lohr
with Wilhelm Vischer – and was the course for the theology students in that
school year – before he accepted a position in Marseille.

While commending these performances highly, Ingmar Bengtsson reserves
his highest kudos for the Basel Chamber Orchestra, thereby also revealing
where his foremost interest lay:

> The highlight of the performances, however, was the Basel Chamber Orchestra's last
> concert of the season [6 May 1947]. Slowly but surely the entire ensemble has grown
> into this music, [and] together has sought solutions to the stylistic questions and care-
> fully worked out every detail. One was amazed by and thoroughly enjoyed their perfect
> string playing, well prepared under leadership of the concertmaster Rodolfo Felicani;
> the dynamics were finely worked out and the ornamentation perfect!
>
> One could especially enjoy all this to the highest degree in an extremely imagina-
> tive Sinfonia in A major by Phil. Emanuel Bach, probably not performed in the last one
> hundred and fifty years, and an unknown – albeit well worth performing – Haydn sym-
> phony in D major entitled "L'Impériale".[41]

Coming to Basel as a harpsichordist and having founded a chamber orchestra
in Stockholm, what fascinated him most was what he heard from the BKO, its
mastery of dynamic and ornamental detail, its phrasing. Here, too, as we know
now, Ina Lohr played a significant role in the preparation of the orchestra, both
in marking the scores and in discussion with Paul Sacher.

He then concluded the article with an accolade for Basel:

> That is roughly the image of musical life in Basel today, with short shadows and lots of
> light that assiduously inspects forgotten angles and corners and at the same time casts
> an incomparable beam of light into the future. One thing is certain: Basel – with [par-
> ticular] emphasis on the Chamber Orchestra, Schola Cantorum and the regional group
> of the ISCM – is an active central and important source of inspiration in modern mu-
> sical life and an example that calls out for emulation in other countries![42]

41　"Höjdpunkten på framförandena blev emellertid Basler Kammerorchesters sista konsert för
　　säsongen. Sakta men säkert har hela ensemblen vuxit in i denna musik, gemensamt sökt
　　lösningar på stilproblemen och omsorgsfullt arbetat in varje detalj. Man häpnade och njöt i
　　fulla drag av deras perfekta stråkspel, väl förberett under konsertmästaren Rodolfo Felicanis
　　ledning, fint avskuggade dynamik och fulländade ornamentik! Särskilt kunde man glädja
　　sig åt allt detta i en ytterst fantasifull sinfonia i A-dur av Phil. Emanuel Bach, som troligen
　　inte framförts på de senaste hundrafemtio åren och okänd men spelvärd Haydn-symfoni i
　　D-dur kallad 'L'Impériale'". Ibid.

42　"Så ungefär ter sig bilden av basiliensiskt musikliv av i dag, med korta skuggor och mycket
　　ljus som oförtrutet söker sig in i glömda vinklar och vrår och samtidigt kastar ett oförväget
　　strålknippe in i framtiden. Ett är säkert: Basel – med tonvikt på kammarorkestern, Schola
　　Cantorum och ortsgruppen av ISSM – är en aktiv central och viktig inspirationskälla i
　　modernt musikliv och ett föredöme som manar till efterföljd i andra länder!" Ibid.

The enthusiasm with which both Nils Wallin and Ingmar Bengtsson reported of their stay in Basel was what led to the influx of Swedes over the following decade, both in classes at the Schola and in summer workshops under the aegis of Ina Lohr. In an interview with Helena Stenbäck on 2 July 1992, Eric Ericson said that they came back with the recommendation that the others in their group should "Buzz off to Basel!"[43] Not only Ericson took this advice, but also Sven-Erik Bäck, who with his wife Puck, and Lars Frydén had arrived in Basel a short while before him. This gave them the opportunity to greet Eric Ericson when his train pulled into the station with a recorder fanfare (see Ill. 6.1).

The significance of Basel as a musical mecca, a refuge in a culturally desolate world, is graphically described by Eric Ericson in an interview at the end of March 1997 with Hans-Gunnar Peterson and Karl-Erik Tallmo:

> Everything that happened in Stockholm and influenced me and many others got its natural continuation through the Schola Cantorum [...] Many of us were there the very instant the war was over. Switzerland had been spared the violence of war, and one could say that Basel had become a musical capital at that time. The large German publishing house Bärenreiter, which printed several volumes of renaissance and baroque music, had a branch office in Basel. And Paul Sacher was there, a very important and remarkably versatile man. Thanks to his marrying one of the richest ladies in Switzerland, he was financially independent and managed to run the Schola Cantorum at the same time as he led the Basler Kammerorchester, which was an important forum for new music. The contemporary radicals, like Hindemith or Honegger, wrote music for this ensemble ... The amazing thing with Basel was that it was not a small, self-absorbed, obsolete music city, but a sort of Mecca, a "*refugium*" after the war, where we in the evening could go out and listen to all of the important works.[44]

What is evident here, more so than in the reports of Nils Wallin and Ingmar Bengtsson, is the degree to which the Swedes were interested in the contemporary music being performed in Basel. They were not simply coming to the Schola Cantorum, but they were excited by the conjunction of the old and the new.

Interestingly enough, what Eric Ericson took away from Basel was not the choir sound; he recalls that he was "disappointed in the pure vocal sound down in Basel, [that] it was nothing compared to the Swedish [choir] sound".[45] Instead, the influences from Basel

---

43 "Stick till Basel!" Helena Stenbäck, *Svensk körpedagogik i ett kammarmusikaliskt perspektiv*, MA thesis, Centrum för musikpedagogisk forskning, MPC, Musikhögskolan i Stockholm / Stockholms Universitet 1992, 85.

44 Hans-Gunnar Peterson and Karl-Erik Tallmo, "Eric Ericson – 50 years with the Chamber Choir", http://www.art-bin.com/art/aericsone.html (15 July 2018).

45 "Jag minns att jag var besviken på det rent vokala ljudet nere i Basel, det var liksom ingenting mot den svenska klangen". Helena Stenbäck, *Svensk körpedagogik*, 85.

Ill. 6.1: Sven-Erik Bäck, Puck Bäck, and Lars Frydén at the station to welcome Eric Ericson. In: Oscar Hedlund, *Körkarlen Eric Ericson*.

were brought on by the instruments. By then harpsichord and recorder were new instruments with a totally different tone quality, and this was, of course, transferred to our singing practice. I am quite sure it came through the music, the music controlled the timbre, you cannot sing such things in any other way than in this lighter, rhythmical [manner].[46]

46 Interview Hans-Gunnar Peterson and Karl-Erik Tallmo, "Eric Ericson – 50 years with the chamber choir".

Although the composer Sven-Erik Bäck was very much part of the group of Swedes that came to Basel, he forged a much closer relationship to Ina Lohr than any of the others.[47] Indeed, there were few other musicians with whom she had such vibrant, intense discussions, as is evident not only from the following passage, but also from their correspondence. It was as if they were, on some level, kindred souls. His description of his first stay in Basel is as much a portrait of Ina Lohr as a woman, as a depiction of his time there. He saw facets of her personality that she only revealed to those closest to her; he respected her both as a composer as well as a teacher. He was obviously one of the few people around who were aware of her close contacts with composers such as Bartók, Hindemith, Honegger and Stravinsky. And he could only have learned about her knowledge of contemporary music through direct contact with her. In an interview with Oscar Hedlund in the 1980s, he interweaves his own experiences with his impressions of her as a person, thereby revealing the impact that she had upon him:

> For me, Basel is still something half dream-like, but it also signifies the tremendous substance that was offered us by the composer and music pedagogue Ina Lohr. She was a devout woman of the world, much more glamorous than her French counterpart, Nadia Boulanger. Under her tutoring we sang, for example, Schütz's *St. John Passion* [in actuality, Lechner's work was performed]. For a medieval concert with works by Dufay and Machaut she had ordered [the exhibition was in fact organized by the museum] old stained-glass paintings from Strasbourg [Mühlhausen] that had been buried and hidden during the war, to be displayed. They were exhibited at the Fine Arts Museum in Basel and created an intense experience with strong symbolism. And furthermore, without it being [explicitly] understood back then, it was a sort of epoch-making concert form – an interaction between sound and image. [...]
>
> She was a fairly unique person, a multitalented one. She was considered to be one of Europe's most distinguished connoisseurs of contemporary music, but she was also one of Europe's most distinguished connoisseurs of early [music]. She was a lecturer and selected the music to be played at Schola Cantorum Basiliensis and by Basel's chamber orchestra; since the 30s she had analyzed practically everything of importance in contemporary music. She spoke at least five languages and was a close friend of Bartók, Hindemith, Honegger, Stravinsky and others like that. She was, of course, quick to discover both Stockhausen and Pierre Boulez early on. She also taught Gregorian chant, Protestant church music, thorough bass, ensemble playing and [pedagogical] methodology – her educational genius consisted in integrating the old with the new. She seemed to have experienced the 14th century in a personal way. This remarkable person took care of all of us yokels from Sweden.[48]

47 See also Mattias Lundberg, *Sven-Erik Bäck*. Swedish Royal Academy of Music. Möklinta: Gidlund 2019.

48 "För mig är Basel ännu något halvt drömlikt, men det innebär också den massiva verklighet som erbjöds oss av tonsättaren och musikpedagogen Ina Lohr. Hon var en from världsdam, mycket flottare än sin franska motsvarighet Nadia Boulanger. Under hennes hand-

These enthusiastic responses, particularly that of Sven-Erik Bäck cannot have been other than a great pleasure and also stimulus to Ina Lohr. For the first time in her teaching career, she was able to teach on her level, was able to combine the old and the new. In addition, Sven-Erik Bäck's view of music was, as he himself admitted, "highly theocentric", so that "her profound understanding of the church music tradition, and not least what she taught me to see and hear in Dufay, Schütz and Stravinsky meant a great deal to me".[49] In addition, as the Swedes all knew one another from The Monday Group and were accustomed to analyzing music in discussion, had a common language, they formed a distinct entity within the Schola. Christopher Schmidt recalls going and sitting in on their classes with Ina Lohr, as the dialogue was so rich, at a level so high, beyond his level of competence at that point in his training, that he found it very rewarding.

This high level of interaction was confirmed in an article Ina Lohr wrote for the Swedish journal *Nutida musik* in 1967, in which she, in retrospect, attempted to describe her experiences with the Swedes from her own perspective:

> They came in February 1947: our first Swedes. They were called Ingmar Bengtsson and Nils Wallin and looked down upon us from way up high and wanted to learn everything that we knew and what we did not know. I was scared to death on the first day, not because these gentlemen were so big, but because they had such great expectations. How

ledning sjöng vi bl a Schütz' [Lechner's] Johannespassionen. Till en medeltida konsert med verk av Dufay och Machaut hade hon beordrat fram gamla glasmålningar från Strassburg som varit nedgrävda och gömda under kriget. De ställdes ut i Kunsthalle i Basel och gav en intensiv upplevelse med stark symbolverkan. Och dessutom: utan att man då begrep det var det en sorts epokgörande konsertform – samspel mellan ljud och bild. [...]

Hon var ju en tämligen enastående människa, en multibegåvning. Hon ansågs vara en av Europas mest framstående kännare av den nya musiken, men hon var också en av Europas mest framstående kännare av den gamla. Hon var lektör och valde ut den musik som skulle spelas vid Schola Cantorum Basiliensis och av Basels kammarorkester, alltsedan 30-talet hade hon analyserat praktiskt taget allt av betydelse inom den nya musiken. Hon talade minst fem språk och var bästis med Bartók, Hindemith, Honegger, Stravinskij och lite sådär. Hon var givetvis snabb att tidigt upptäcka båda Stockhausen och Pierre Boulez. Hon undervisade dussutom i gregoriansk sång, evangelisk kyrkomusik, generalbas, ensemblespel och metodik – hennes pedagogiska genialitet bestod alltså i att integrera det gamla met det nya. Hon verkade på något egendomligt sätt själv ha upplevt också 1300-talet. Denna märkliga person tog hand om oss bonnläppar från Sverige". Oscar Hedlund, *Körkarlen Eric Ericson*, Höganäs: Förlags AB Wiken 1988, 103–04.

49 Bo Wallner, "The Inspiration of Words and Gestures: A Conversation between Sven-Erik Bäck, Thomas Jennefelt and Bo Wallner", in: *Choral Music Perspectives: Dedicated to Eric Ericson*, ed. Lennart Reimers and Bo Wallner, Uppsala: Almqvist & Wiksell Trykeri 1992 (Publications issued by the Royal Swedish Academy of Music, No. 75), 218.

easy it is to be disappointed in such a case! [...] but already on the second day I knew that everything would be all right, for these tree-like and apparently so self-assured men sat there with our professional level students and amateurs in my *Hausmusik* class and sang and played along, as if it were their primary and most important concern. Naturally they had their own lessons, but they participated in everything as a matter of course [...]

The manner of teaching, also the works that we studied and played, were new to Ingmar Bengtsson and Nils Wallin and thus in that way they were our students; but we could also speak with them as colleagues and are indebted to them for numerous insights. We worked intensively until, in the very hot month of June, Nils Wallin became ill, because he was playing and writing eight hours of thorough bass exercises per day at a temperature to which he was unaccustomed! I have seldom felt so guilty, but also let myself later be captivated again and again by the peculiarly Swedish need to examine things thoroughly, to continually connect performance with reflection. Did we understand one another so well because I, a Swiss of Dutch descent, am also a musician with a tendency to brood?

Already in fall, the next group came [...] I was overcome by fear again, because there were now three[50] full-grown instrumentalists and a choir director in front of me, armed with great ability and a corresponding verve. But this time as well, the fear was unfounded, for these trained and excellent professional musicians adapted themselves as if they had always belonged to our "Schola family". Naturally they received their own lessons, in which not a single minute was lost, for their desire for knowledge was insatiable. The [lessons] were on the study of the literature, thorough bass in various epochs, but primarily on the discovery of monody in its most authentic forms: in Gregorian chant, in the secular songs of the Middle Ages, and in the songs of the time of the Reformation. The set of rules behind this melodic conception, as well as that of polyphony which stemmed from it was studied with the help of hexachord theory, which may be employed practically as "solmization". Then came the gist of the matter: the comparison with music of our own time, also with one's own compositions.

[...] And at that time, almost all of them composed and these compositions were criticized severely, always in relation to our discoveries in the field of pre-Classical, or even the earliest music. [...] With all of them it came to intense discussions about composition as the setting together (com-ponere) of traditional and still-used melodic figures; composition as a possibility of expression and representation by means of harmony, and as pure inspiration, which apparently cannot be traced back to rules. Almost all of the Swedes agreed with Luther's hypothesis that there is only freedom there where man voluntarily accepts the law. And that appears to me, now that I am looking back, characteristic. Does it not belong to the particularly Swedish character that they tame an uncommonly strong expressive desire, *have to* place it under regulation, in order to attain valid forms? Is this not connected with the large, little-populated, overwhelmingly beautiful country which almost offers too many possibilities? Was it a legacy of their home, that almost all of them had so many ideas, that not only the actual composers among them could just write down a string quartet, but also the violinist Lars Frydén and the cellist Bengt Ericson?

---

50 Actually, only two instrumentalists came in that second year. Gunnar Hallhagen whom she mentions in this context did not come until 1950.

This happened in the winter semester of 1950/51. […] We had strongly advised Lars Frydén to go and now really devote himself to becoming a virtuoso violinist in Vienna. But how I missed him, because the [other] three strings played with him in a quartet and would have liked to do that in Basel as well. And then, all of a sudden, at the very beginning of the semester, our good old concierge excitedly came into the room where I was working with a large group and called out in excitement: "Miss Lohr, Miss Lohr, our Mr. Frieden [with an implied different pronunciation] is here again!" And truly – there he was with Claude Génetay down in the corridor, and I scolded him from above, on the stairs, because he had not stayed in Vienna, until he, beaming at me, asked me disarmingly, whether I was not at all pleased to see him again. Naturally, I was actually highly pleased, but I also had a bad conscience. Then we worked more than ever in the semester, until late in the evenings, in my room which was actually too small, as it had not been built for so many and such big Swedes. And how we then analyzed two Bach solo sonatas as exactly as possible, and how he then played them, is something I will never forget. […]

But then also the two string quartets were practiced precisely and then played. The composers had not exactly made it easy for themselves and their fellow players. Then [the works] were remorselessly analyzed, even plucked to pieces and pruned, not by me, but by all the Swedes together. Critical, but friendly, true cooperation, as it now still exists in Sweden.[51]

---

51 "Im Februar 1947 kamen sie: unsere ersten Schweden. Sie hiessen Ingmar Bengtsson und Nils Wallin, schauten aus grosser Höhe auf uns herunter und wollten sich alles aneignen, was wir wussten und was wir nicht wussten. Mir war am ersten Tag angst und bange, nicht weil diese Herren so gross, sondern weil sie so erwartungsvoll waren. Wie leicht kommt es in einem solchen Fall zu Enttäuschungen! […] aber schon am zweiten Tag wusste ich, dass alles gut gehen würde, denn da sassen diese baumlangen, scheinbar so selbstsicheren Herren mit unseren Berufsschülern und Musikfreunden in meiner Hausmusikstunde und sangen und spielten mit, als ob das nun ihr erstes und wichtigstes Anliegen wäre. Natürlich hatten sie ihre eigenen Stunden, aber sie machten überall mit Selbstverständlichkeit mit […]

Die Art des Unterrichts, auch die Werke, die wir studierten und zum Klingen brachten, waren Ingmar Bengtsson und Nils Wallin neu und in sofern waren sie unsere Schüler, aber wir konnten uns mit ihnen auch als Kollegen unterhalten und verdanken ihnen manche Anregung. Es wurde intensiv gearbeitet, bis Nils Wallin im gar heissen Monat Juni krank wurde, weil er bei der ihm ungewohnten Temperatur acht Stunden im Tag Generalbassaufgaben spielte und schrieb! Ich habe mich selten so schuldig gefühlt, liess mich aber auch später immer wieder hinreissen vom speziell schwedischen Bedürfnis, den Sachen auf den Grund zu gehen, Musizieren und Ueberlegen dauernd zu verbinden. Haben wir uns darum immer so gut verstanden, weil auch ich, Schweizerin von holländischer Herkunft, eine Musikantin bin mit Hang zum Grübeln?

Schon im Herbst kam die nächste Gruppe […] Da packte mich die Angst von neuem, denn da standen nun drei ausgewachsene Instrumentalisten und ein Chorleiter vor mir, gewappnet mit grossem Können und entsprechendem Tatendrang. Aber auch diesmal erwies sich die Angst als unbegründet, denn diese diplomierten und ausgezeichneten Berufsmusiker fügten sich ein, alsob [sic] sie schon immer zu unserer 'Scholafamilie' gehört hätten. Natürlich bekamen sie ihre eigenen Stunden, in denen keine Minute verloren ging, denn ihr Wissenshunger war unersättlich. Um Literaturkunde ging es, um den Generalbass in verschiedenen Epochen, vor allem aber um die Entdeckung der Einstimmigkeit in ihren

With these anecdotes, we get a glimpse of the working atmosphere of the classes, of Ina Lohr's concern for the professional advancement of her students, and her delight in their creativity, their warmth of expression, both musically

echtesten Formen: im Gregorianischen Choral, in den weltlichen Gesängen des Mittelalters und in den Liedern der Reformationszeit. Die Gesetzmässigkeit dieser Melodik, sowie die der Polyphonie, die aus ihr hervorging, wurde mit Hilfe der Hexachordlehre, die sich praktisch als 'Solmisation' verwenden lässt, studiert. Dann kam aber das Wesentliche: der Vergleich mit der Musik der eigenen Zeit, auch mit eigenen Kompositionen.

[…] Und damals komponierten fast alle, und diese Kompositionen wurden einer strengen Kritik unterzogen, immer im Vergleich mit unseren Entdeckungen auf dem Gebiet der vorklassischen, ja der ältesten Musik. […] Mit allen kam es zu intensiven Diskussionen über das Komponieren als Zusammenstellen (com-ponere) von überlieferten und immer noch lebendigen melodischen Wendungen; Komponieren als Möglichkeit des Ausdrucks und der Darstellung mittels der Harmonik und als reinen Inspiration, die sich scheinbar auf keine Gesetzmässigkeit zurückführen lässt. Luthers These, dass es Freiheit nur dort gibt, wo der Mensch das Gesetz freiwillig auf sich nimmt, fand bei fast allen Schweden Zustimmung. Und das scheint mir heute, da ich Rückblick halte, bezeichnend. Gehört es nicht zur schwedischen eigen-Art [sic], dass sie einen ungemein starken Ausdruckswillen bändigen, einer Gesetzmässigkeit unterstellen muss, um zu gültigen Formen zu kommen? Hängt das vielleicht mit dem grossen, spärlich bevölkerten, überwältigend schönen Land zusammen, das fast zu viel Möglichkeiten bietet? […] War es ein Vermächtnis ihrer Heimat, dass fast alle so viele Einfälle hatten, dass es nicht nur den eigentlichen Komponisten unter ihnen, sondern auch dem Geiger Lars Frydén und dem Cellisten Bengt Ericson möglich war, ein Streichquartett nur so hinzuschreiben?

Das geschah im Wintersemester 1950/51 […] Lars Frydén hatten wir dringend nahe gelegt, sich in Wien nun wirklich ganz dem virtuosen Violinspiel zu widmen. Wie ich ihn aber vermisste, weil die drei Streicher doch mit ihm Quartett spielten und das gerne auch in Basel gemacht hätten. Und dann kam, ganz am Anfang des Semesters plötzlich unsere gute alte Abwartsfrau aufgeregt in mein Zimmer, wo ich gerade mit einer grossen Gruppe arbeitete und rief ganz aufgeregt: 'Fräulein Lohr, Fräulein Lohr, unser Herr Frieden ist wieder da!' Und wahr – da stand er mit Claude Genetay unten im Gang, und ich schimpfte oben auf der Treppe, weil er nicht in Wien geblieben war, bis er ganz strahlend und entwaffnend fragte, ob ich denn gar keine Freude hätte ihn wieder zu sehen. Natürlich hatte ich sogar eine sehr grosse Freude, aber auch ein schlechtes Gewissen. Dann aber wurde in dem Semester mehr gearbeitet als je, bis abends spät in meinem eigentlich zu kleinen Zimmer, das nicht für so viele und so grosse Schweden gebaut war. Wie wir zwei Solosonaten von Bach so genau wie nur möglich analysierten, und wie er sie dann spielte, das werde ich nie vergessen. […]

Aber auch die beiden Streichquartette wurden genau eingeübt und dann gespielt. Die Komponisten hatten es sich und ihren Mitspielern nicht gerade leicht gemacht. Dann wurde aber erbarmungslos analysiert, ja zerpflückt und zusammengestrichen, nicht von mir, sondern von allen Schweden miteinander. Kritische, aber freundschaftliche, echte Zusammenarbeit, so wie sie heute in Schweden noch besteht". Ina Lohr, "Gedanken über eine schwedische Generation und ihre Musik", typescript in PSF-ILC. Published in a Swedish translation in "Tankar om en svensk generation och dess musik", in: *Nutida Musik* 10/3–4 (1966/67), 26–30.

Ill. 6.2: Course in Stockholm: Jan Crafoord, Ute Freitag, Lennart Hedwall, Eva Nordenfelt, Bengt Ericson and Ina Lohr. Photo: courtesy of Anne Smith, Zurich.

and personally. It is not surprising then, with this sense of give and take, that the Swedes desired to show her their country, and thus invited her to come to Stockholm from 18–29 August 1952 to give a workshop, with four lectures, as well as a concluding concert which was broadcast on the radio on 3 September 1952. She was assisted in the practical work in this course by Eric Ericson, Sven-Erik Bäck, Lars Frydén and Gunnar Hallhagen.[52]

The course received considerable coverage in the daily newspapers, giving us insight into how, in spite of the concentration on Early Music, she managed to put everything into the context of *Hausmusik*, into a music-making that bridged the gap between amateur and professional, between performer and listener, to create a unified social experience (see Ill. 6.2).

> It has been said that a total of 23 Swedes in recent years has found their way to the famous institute for early music, the Schola Cantorum in Basel. The rumor of the experiences that can be gained there has spread like rings in the water. For all travelers to Basel, contact with Ina Lohr, one of the Schola's leading forces, has been particularly valuable

---

52 S.n., "Kurs om gammal musik", in: *Svenska Dagbladet*, 12 April 1952 and the radio program of the *Expressen* of 3 September 1952.

and stimulating. And right now, one of their dreams has come true. Ina Lohr has come to Sweden to give her old students a new injection and to help them broaden the circle.

For fourteen days, Ina Lohr, in the form of lectures, ensemble work and group teaching, will share her manifold knowledge of old music and how it is to be performed [...] But Ina Lohr's goal is not primarily to conquer new, that is, forgotten areas [only] for our aesthetic pleasure. Many wise instructions were given on practices from older times, based on contemporary statements. But for Ina Lohr, it is not enough to strive for a historically correct reproduction. Recapturing music from the epochs before 1700 is essential to her because there are spiritual values [in it] that are of importance and have actuality in our own time, and because the playing of that music is a valuable communal form that our current concert life lacks.[53]

The opening paragraph in this article is a public affirmation of the Swedes' appreciation of what they had received and learned from Ina Lohr in Basel and demonstrates how the initial contact with Ingmar Bengtsson and Nils Wallin had rippled out into a far larger circle of musicians. The measure of their influence can be seen in the fact that 22 of the 32 participants in the course were professional musicians.[54] The fact that amateurs were included in the course, however, indicates also an acceptance of her social mission through music. Like her, they were through and through professional musicians, but they also had a need of reaching out to others in society in order to attain full appreciation of music's powers. This may have been, as Ina Lohr suggested, a result of living in a so sparsely populated country, or perhaps due to the fact that so many of them grew up in highly religious families.

The final concert was true to the goals she set out to fulfill, in that the boundary between the performer and the audience "faded away", and music

---

53 "Det påstås att sammanlagt 23 svenskar under de senaste åren funnit vägen till det berömda institutet för gammal musik, Schola Cantorum i Basel. Ryktet om de erfarenheter som där kan vinnas har spritt sig som ringar i vattnet. För alla baselresenärer har kontakten med Ina Lohr, en av skolans ledande krafter, varit alldeles särskilt värdefull och stimulerande. Och just nu har en av deras önskedrömmar gått i uppfyllelse. Ina Lohr har kommit till Sverige för att ge sina gamla lärjungar en ny injektion och hjälpa dem att vidga kretsen.

Under fjorton dagar skall Ina Lohr i föredragets, sammusicerandets och gruppundervisningens former delge sina mångsidiga kunskaper om gammal musik och hur den skall utföras [...] Men Ina Lohrs målsättning är inte i första hand att erövra nya, det vill säga glömda, områden för vår estetiska njutning. Det gavs många kloka anvisningar om äldre tiders praxis, grundade på samtida uttalanden. Men för Ina Lohr är det inte tillräckligt med att eftersträva ett historiskt korrekt återgivande. Att återerövra musik från epokerna före 1700 är för henne väsentligt, emedan där finns andliga värden som har betydelse och aktualitet i vår egen tid och emedan utövandet av den musiken är en värdefull gemenskapsform som vårt gängse konsertliv saknar. LÅo". "Gammal musik väg till förnyelse", in: *Svenska Dagbladet*, 19 August 1952.

54 Letter Ina Lohr to Paul Sacher of 24 August 1947, private collection, Switzerland.

from the 15th to the 20th century was performed, including compositions by Ina Lohr herself, Ingvar Lidholm, Finn Høffding, Harald Saeverud and Sven-Erik Bäck.[55]

After this, things grew quieter as far as the Swedes were concerned in Basel; two of the younger ones, Eva Nordenfelt and Jan Crafoord, came to study for a longer stretch of time from 1954–57, the former continuing her harpsichord studies with Eduard Müller and the latter completing a diploma with August Wenzinger in viola da gamba.

The last of the main flood of visitors from Sweden was the now renowned conductor Herbert Blomstedt, who at the time took a leave of absence in the fall of 1958 from his first position as principal conductor of the Norrköping Symphony Orchestra, to spend six to eight weeks in Basel studying at the Schola.[56] He was fired by a sense of needing to know more about the performance practice of earlier eras, as the Norrköping Symphony was a small orchestra of about thirty musicians which performed Bach, Lasso, Schütz, Biber, etc. The choice of Basel was linked to memories of hearing August Wenzinger's gamba quartet play ear- and eye-opening concerts in Stockholm while he was studying there. His lessons with the gambist were devoted to string music, and he came to know August Wenzinger as a very fine and gentle man.

Herbert Blomstedt was no longer sure who had advised him to study with Ina Lohr; he suggested that the recommendation to do so might have come from Sven-Eric Bäck who not only shared her intense religiosity, but also got along well with her.[57] The conductor himself was enormously impressed by Ina Lohr, admired and respected both her and her great knowledge. He had individual lessons with her twice a week and may have attended some group lessons. In the lessons the focus was on the analysis of old music, Ockeghem, Dufay, etc. in a practical way, in the sense of how it was performed, as opposed to the theoretical approach in Uppsala. She was somewhat similar to Nadia Boulanger, and like her was offended when students did not agree with her or were

55 I.[ngmar] B[engtsso]n., "Hemmusik från fyra sekler", in: *Svenska Dagbladet*, 30 August 1952.
56 Telephone Interview of 20 June 2017. I am very grateful for Herbert Blomstedt for taking time out of his busy schedule and speaking so openly with me about his memories of the past. I was particularly touched, however, by his enthusiasm and desire of speaking about some of his recent musical decisions in a performance of Beethoven's 7th Symphony. It was a graphic demonstration of why he is so effective as a conductor.
57 This is substantiated by a letter from Sven-Erik Bäck to Ina Lohr of 7 May 1958, in which he recommended Herbert Blomstedt to her as a student, as well as asking if there would be a possibility for a conducting swap with Paul Sacher, PSF-ILC.

not serious enough. She was a stern educator, a type of mother-figure to the students. He had no difficulty dealing with this, given his age, religious background and disposition.

Later he read some of her articles on old Lutheran hymns, which showed that her interest was actually in the spiritual content of this music. She was "on fire" in her desire for presenting the information, was like a prophet. She was offended if something was wrong; she felt the necessity of being a witness to a truth that had been forgotten, that it was important that the treasures of the past should be passed on. Perhaps because of his own fundamentalist upbringing, he was one of the few people I encountered that was comfortable in speaking about the various sides of her personality – her fervent, knowledgeable teaching, her need to be right, and her dogmatic, evangelistic musical mission – accepting them all, while not needing either to identify with or reject any of them.

In a letter of July–August 1971 to Ina Lohr, Sven-Erik Bäck took the opportunity of the appearance of a book about The Monday Group, *40-tal*,[58] to pass review of this time at the Schola, to which a few pages had been devoted. He wrote that he hoped

> that now also people outside of "our circle" know that *you* – primarily – and the Schola Cantorum have meant an *enormous* amount to us and for musical life in Sweden. If I am allowed to sum up shortly – and dare to – I believe that there is now a need beyond ideological and confessional boundaries to find "spirituality". And there "we" have once again an "answer" – and *you* not only supported us, but also have given us above all material and arguments [and added in the margin in red with a line of dots leading to it] … and inspiration and demands – and give [them] to us again and again.[59]

These Swedish "students" must have meant a great deal to Ina Lohr in that she was able to bring all aspects of her being into her instruction: her love and knowledge of earlier music, both Gregorian chant and early polyphony; her compositional skills, both in analysis of early as well as contemporary music,

---

58 Bo Wallner, *40-tal: en klippbok om Måndagsgruppen och det svenska musiklivet*, Stockholm: Kugelbergs Boktryckeri AB 1971.

59 "Ich hoffe daß jetzt auch Leute, außerhalb 'unserer Kreise' wissen daß Sie – vor allem – und Schola Cantorum, enorm viel für uns und für das Musikleben Schwedens bedeutet haben. Wenn ich kurz zusammenfassen darf – und wage – glaube ich, daß es über ideologische und konfessionelle Grenzen jetzt ein Bedürfniß – 'das Geistige' zu finden, gibt. Und da haben 'wir' jetzt wieder eine 'Replike' – und Sie haben uns nicht nur gestutzt sondern vor allem Material und Argumente gegeben [and added in red with a line of dots] … und Inspiration und Aufforderung – und geben uns immer wieder". Letter Sven-Erik Bäck to Ina Lohr of July/August 1971, PSF-ILC.

and in her teaching of thorough bass; her ability to link her idiosyncratic theoretical understanding with performance issues; and her desire to express her faith through song. It was one of the few times in her life when she had no need of respecting or drawing boundaries in her work which for her were non-existent; she could simply be herself.

6.5 The Dutch Connection

The students from abroad, however, did not only come from Sweden. With all the attention garnered by Ina Lohr's presentations in the summer of 1946 (see pp. 272–75) in the Netherlands, she was eagerly sought after there, both for lectures and for workshops over the following years. Due to her greater presence in her native country stemming from her annual visits to her family, only a handful of students came to the Schola to pursue their studies. Her influence in the reform of Dutch Protestant church music – and thus indirectly early music – was nonetheless enormous. In addition, her work in *Hausmusik* was a model for the Dutch counterpart, and thus was also a source of students. Before looking at those that traveled specially to Basel because they were so fascinated by her approach, let us examine her work in Holland.

She gave the first of several courses, organized by the Vereeniging van Protestantsche Kerkmuziek (Society for Protestant Church Music) in the summer of 1947, from 7–11 July, entitled "Mensural Rhythm and the Church Modes" in the Lutheran Church at the Spui in Amsterdam.[60] In the following week on 16 July, she gave a concert together with Ursula Dietschy and the organist Dolf Hendrikse in the Nieuwe Kerk in Haarlem with a program which included a cantata of her own. P. Zwaanswijk, in his review of 17 July 1947, wrote that "a main characteristic of this concert was the great stylistic unity of the performances, both the vocal and instrumental, expressing itself in a simplicity, avoiding all expressivity that inclines toward romanticism".[61] A year later a follow-up course was held in the Remonstransekerk in Haarlem from the 5–9 July 1948.[62] Jan Boeke, the later director of Capella Amsterdam concluded that the

---

60 "Mensural rhythme en de Kerktoonsoorten". Jan Boeke, "De werkwijze van mej. Lohr", 8.
61 "Een hoofdkenmerk van dit concert was de grote stijleenheid van de vertolkingen, zowel van de vocale als instrumentale, zich uitend in een eenvoud, wars van elke naar romantiek zwemmende expressiviteit". P. Waanswijk, "Het oude orgel van de Nieuwe Kerk", in: *Haarlems Dagblad*, 17 July 1947.
62 The dates and titles of the courses are found in Jan Boeke, "De werkwijze van mej. Lohr", 8–10.

Ill. 6.3: Jan Boeke. Photo: courtesy of Anneke Boeke, Amsterdam.

singing of psalms, Gregorian chant and Lutheran songs that took place there "once again gave the assurance that the function of church music can only be achieved through singing. It is only by singing together that we notice how it must be sung, and it is certainly not the least of Miss Lohr's merits that she made us so aware of that".[63] A further course was held in fall of that year, also in Haarlem from 8–9 October 1948, on the subject of Psalms from Wittenberg, Strassburg and Geneva. Next, also in Haarlem, she dealt with questions concerning the sung forms of the Latin mass, Luther's German mass and Calvin's *La Forme des Prières* in July of 1949. In the following summer, from 17–22 July 1950, her course was about "Modern Composition in regard to Solmization" and "Liturgical Aspects of Church Hymns". Then in the subsequent year, another workshop was organized by the Centrum in Bergen on the 28–29 September 1957 on new hymns for the congregation.[64] Finally, on 4 October 1958 she gave a course in Amersfoort on "Reflections on Old and New Choir and Organ Music".

One of the prime movers behind these courses was Jan Boeke (1921–1993, see Ill. 6.3). Late in life, in the booklet prepared for the festivities being organized in her name in the Netherlands in honor of her eightieth birthday, she expressed her gratitude to the person who spearheaded the celebration,

---

63 "gaf weer de zekerheid, dat het Kerkmuzikale werk slechts zingende kan worden gedaan. Tezamen zingende merken wij pas hòe gezongen moet worden en het is zeker niet de geringste verdienste van Mej. Lohr, dat zij ons dat zozeer bewust heeft gemaakt". Jan Boeke, "Cursus Ina Lohr: (5–9 Juli 1948)", in: *Kerk en Muziek* 1 (1948–49), 63.

64 "Ina Lohr-Weekend in 'De Haaf' te Bergen (N.H.), 28–29 September 1957", in: *Het Orgel* (1957), 135.

Jan Boeke, who together with [his wife] Riek also saw to it that I obtained a large Dutch family with which I am very happy. The same thing has happened naturally in Basel diverse times, but there is a difference: Since the course in Holland in July 1947 was in the church on the Spui, I was dealing with a congregation, thus also with the church, and I was always concerned with sung prayer, praise and thanksgiving.[65]

But he did not only propagate her work, he and his family also developed an extremely close relationship to Ina Lohr, as is evidenced in an outburst in her interview with Jos Leussink in 1983 when she exclaimed that he was her "great support, and son and apprentice, but for a long time he has no longer been my apprentice, I have been far surpassed".[66] Jan Boeke, who officially had completed his studies with Anthon van der Horst at the Conservatory of Amsterdam only after the war, due to the institution being forced to close its doors by the Nazis, became the organist and choir director of Haarlem's Remonstranste Church in 1947. Toward the end of that year he came to Basel for a couple of months to study privately with Ina Lohr, albeit also taking part in the *Ensemble für Kirchenmusik*. Like the Swedes, he was thus actively engaged in her work with amateurs. An extraordinary bond was forged then, leading not only Ina Lohr to speak of him as her son, but also to him calling her "Moeder" or "Mother".[67] The depths of the relationship can also be measured by the regular, highly appreciated visits of the family to Basel, as well as by the large number of programs concerning the Cappella Amsterdam in her collection at the Paul Sacher Foundation. In addition, she gave him all of her early compositions, which were then passed on to Henk van Benthem, who donated them to the Vera Oeri Bibliothek of the Musik-Akademie Basel.

But he was not the only one to support her work in the Netherlands. An article in *Kerk en Muziek* by Hendrik Leendert Oussoren gives voice to his own experience with Ina Lohr in such courses, and also speaks of developments in the reform of Protestant church music throughout the Netherlands as a result of these courses. His first contact with her was in the 1948 course and left him

65 "Jan Boeke, die met Riek er ook nog voor zorgde, dat ik een grote hollandse familie kreeg, waar ik erg gelukkig mee ben. Dezelfde ervaring heb ik natuurlij [sic] ook verschillende malen in Bazel opgedaan, maar er is een verschil: In Holland had ik het vanaf die cursus in Juli 1947 in de kerk op het Spui met een gemeente te doen, dus ook met de kerk, en mij gaat het altijd weer om een gezongen bidden, loven en danken". Acknowledgment in the booklet for the celebration of her 80th birthday in the Netherlands, prepared by the "Commissie ter voorbereiding van der viering van het tachtigste geboortejaar van I-NA LOHR". PSF-ILC.
66 "is mijn grote steun, en zoon, en leerling, maar leerling is hij lang niet meer, ik ben ver overtrokken". Interview Jos Leussink, 24–25 March 1983.
67 "En op gevoel Jan, Kees [Vellekoop] en Jan zeggen moeder". Ibid.

totally convinced of the correctness of her path. He was nonetheless aware that this was not always the case, stating that "the odd thing here is that those which come into contact with her only rarely behave as neutral observers, but mostly either develop into a great proponent and advocate or into a furious opponent of her theories".[68] This polarization was something noticed by many, but rarely observed so objectively. He went on further to say that

the contact with Ina Lohr is such that one cannot leave an encounter with her without profit. One has to thoroughly realize why one sees her path as the right one or why one sees her path as a pernicious one and both reactions can lead to great profundity.[69]

He is also one of the few who attempted the task of expressing verbally how she affected him, noting that

It is very difficult to put into words what the essence is of the enrichment which Ina Lohr is capable of giving to someone. If one attempts to do so, however, then one would have to say that whenever one follows her theories or better said, puts her rules into practice, one takes on an entirely different attitude in respect to the music and to music-making on the whole; an attitude that can best be characterized by a feeling of liberation, a real release from all sorts of factors that normally have a restraining influence on joyful, but most of all, on meaningful music-making.

For that reason, it is so dangerous to make a judgment on the basis of written material alone. For that reason, it is so dangerous to deliver judgment merely as an observer, because the importance of that which one experiences comes to the surface from within and can only be judged if one has experienced certain things oneself. It is concerned less with a "knowledge" of various things than with an inner change of direction, by means of which one again acquires "faith" in music, and especially in sacred music.[70]

68 "Het merkwaardige hierbij is dat degene, die met haar in contact komt, zich maar zelden als neutraal toeschouwer gedraagt, maar zich meestal ontwikkelt òf tot een groot voorstander en aanhanger, òf tot een verwoed tegenstander van haar theorieën". Hendrik Leendert Oussoren, "Het kerkkoor in de praktijk (I)", in: *Kerk en Muziek* 2 (1950), 81.

69 "Het is eigenlijk met het contact met Ina Lohr zó, dat men aan een ontmoeting met haar nimmer zonder meer kan voorbijgaan. Men moet zich terdege realiseren waarom men haar weg als de juiste, of waarom men haar weg als een verderfelijke ziet en beide reacties kunnen tot grote verdieping leiden". Ibid., 81–82.

70 "Het is zeer moeilijk onder woorden te brengen wat de essentie is van de verrijking, die Ina Lohr iemand vermag te geven. Zou men dat toch trachten, dan zou men moeten zeggen dat men, wanneer men haar theorieën volgt of liever haar regels in de practijk brengt, ten aanzien van de muziek en het musiceren in het algemeen een geheel andere houding gaat innemen, een houding, die het beste gekarakteriseerd kan worden door een gevoel van bevrijding, een werkelijk los komen van allerlei factoren, die wezenlijk remmend werken op een vreugdevol, maar bovenal zinvol musiceren.

Daarom is het zo gevaarlijk om alleen op schriftelijke gegevens afgaande een oordeel te vellen. Daarom is het zo gevaarlijk om alleen als toeschouwer critiek te leveren, want het belangrijke dat men ervaart, is gericht van binnenuit en kan pas beoordeeld worden wanneer men bepaalde dingen meebeleefd heeft. Het gaat hierbij minder om een 'weten'

This experience of liberation, of becoming one with the music, is something that others mentioned, speaking of how it affected their lives not merely in the realm of music, but also opening up their worlds in other ways. Concretely in the Netherlands, however, it led to the desire to share this experience in churches throughout the country. It was recognized that to do so it would be necessary not only to have church choirs, but in addition to meet together with the congregation to give them the experience of this new manner of singing. Only in this way would they be able to bring across the necessity of singing the text with understanding, with the desire of expressing one's faith together with the entire congregation. In addition, quarterly meetings were organized, so that the leaders of such groups could discuss their experiences with one another, developing methods that were effective in bringing cohesion through music to the congregations. The totality of these measures is an indication of the effect that Ina Lohr's work had on music within the Protestant church throughout the Netherlands. Indeed, Jan Boeke traces the founding of the Centrum voor de Protestantse Kerkzang in Haarlem on 14 January 1950 with the goal of "cultivating the development of church music in general and the revival and, so far as possible, the renewal of church hymns in particular"[71] directly back to Ina Lohr's courses and their effect on the participants.

Her influence on the reform of Protestant church music in the Netherlands was highlighted by the theologian Adriaan Casper Honders who had first met Ina Lohr when she assisted Professor Julius Schweizer in his "Liturgical Seminar" in the summer semester of 1948 at the University of Basel, one of the highpoints of his stay there. He wrote, namely, of his disappointment that no mention was made in the introduction of the new hymnal for the Dutch Protestant church, the *Liedboek voor de Kerken* (1981), to what Ina Lohr had done for the renewal of the church hymns in the Netherlands, but only to the contributions of the men who had drawn their inspiration from her vision. He concluded that "it would be completely unjust, if her name were omitted in the future. Without her inspiring personality, we would not have gotten to where we are".[72]

---

van verschillende feiten als wel om een innerlijke ommekeer, waardoor men weer 'geloof' in de muziek en speciaal in de kerkmuziek verkrijgt". Ibid., 82.

71 "het helpen bevorderen van de ontwikkeling van de Kerkmuziek in het algemeen en van de verlevendiging en zo mogelijk de vernieuwing van de Kerkzang in bijzonder". Jan Boeke, "De werkwijze van mej. Lohr", 10.

72 "Het zou volstrekt onjuist zijn wanneer in de toekomst haar naam vergeten zou worden. Zonder haar inspirerende persoonlijkheid waren wij niet gekomen waar we zijn". Adiaan Casper Honders, "Een vrouw achter het liedboek", in: *Mededelingen van het Instituut voor Liturgieweteschaap van de Rijkuniversiteit te Groningen* 15 (1981), 28.

Ill. 6.4: Renske Nieweg directing an evening of Christmas music in Markthal, 1957. Photo: https://www. niekvanbaalen.net/Renske_Nieweg/ memorystick/images/1306 (21 November 2019). Photo: courtesy of Rijk Mollevanger, Oud-Bijerland.

In addition, as Jolande van der Klis pointed out in her groundbreaking book on the Dutch Early Music movement, *Oude muziek in Nederland* (Utrecht, 1991), her work not only served as a model for the Centrum, but also for those promoting *huismuziek*. During the pre-war and war years, *huismuziek* had been cultivated within the socialist youth organization, *Arbeiders Jeugd Centrale* (AJC), the Dutch equivalent of the German *Singbewegung*. In the period immediately following the war it was recognized that if one wanted to continue to develop and expand this type of amateur music-making, it would be necessary to train leaders of such ensembles, in order to promote and ensure a higher standard of musicianship. One looked to Ina Lohr in this, as well, as she was responsible for such a training program at the Schola Cantorum.

Renske Nieweg (1911–2002, Ill. 6.4), who had been extremely active in the AJC, also participated in Ina Lohr's workshops in the late 40s and closer contact was established between the two, as between kindred spirits. This can be seen, for example, in their correspondence about the best way to deal with a difficult situation which had come about as a result of Ina Lohr having given a talk about her way of teaching church music in Basel in Hilversum. This had been within the context of a course introducing Willem Gehrels' (1885–1971) music-pedagogical method for pre-schoolers, led by the Dutch innovator himself. The latter's work is often referred to in the Netherlands in the same breath

Ill. **6.5**: Evening of Christmas music in Martkthal, 1959. Photo: https://www.niekvanbaalen. net/Renske_Nieweg/memorystick/images/1273 (21 November 2019). Photo: courtesy of Rik Mollevanger, Oud-Bijerland.

as that of his better-known colleagues Zoltán Kodaly and Carl Orff. According to a letter from 11 October 1949 from Ina Lohr to Renske Nieweg, it had apparently been openly advocated on that occasion that the two methods be merged, complete with the suggestion that this be attempted in a *huismuziek* course Renske Nieweg was organizing for Ina Lohr in the spring of 1951. In that letter Ina Lohr clearly stated that this was impossible, expressing her gratitude that the two of them were of one mind about this, for Gehrels "sees that a link is not possible, but does not dare acknowledge the 'either or [situation]' with all of its consequences. Therefore, he acts as if it is primarily about the church modes; we know that our whole musical thinking and activity is changed by solmization".[73] Further, in 1965, Ina Lohr provided music for a Christmas concert of Renske Nieweg's Amerfoort group (see Ill. 6.5), with much detailed discussion as to the exact instrumentation. The closeness of the bond between them can be measured by the fact that in 1981 Ina Lohr offered Renske Nieweg the informal "jou". As we shall see, two other influential figures in the movement, Wim

---

73 "Hij ziet in, dat een verbinding niet mogelijk is, maar durft het 'entweder oder' nog niet met alle consequenties te aanwaarden. Daarom doet hij, alsof het alleen om de kerktoonsoorten gaat; wij weten, dat door de solmisatie ons heele muzikales denken en doen verandert". Letter of Renske Nieweg to Ina Lohr of 11 October 1949, kindly scanned for me by Rijk Mollenvanger, Oud-Beijerland.

Waardenburg and her cousin Henk Waardenburg, came to Basel in the 1950s to study at the Schola, contributing to Ina Lohr's influence in the Netherlands in this field as well.

6.6 The Triumvirate: Gustav Maria Leonhardt, Christopher Schmidt and David Kraehenbuehl[74]

Just at the same time that the Swedes began arriving in Basel, another grouping began to make itself felt at the Schola, for in the school year 1947/48 both Gustav Maria Leonhardt (1928–2012) and Christopher Schmidt (b. 1927) commenced their formal music studies there, the former in the first semester, the latter in the second. The former came to Basel, no doubt in part due to the activities of Ina Lohr in the Netherlands after the war, but also because their families knew one another and they had a common teacher, Anthon van der Horst. As she wrote to Paul Sacher on 3 August 1947, "The young Leonhard[t] is *very* talented and can already do a lot. He will already be in Basel for the fall courses".[75] The Dutch link to the Schola must have been part of the attraction of the institution for his father: he would be able to attain a professional degree on the instrument of his choice – something that could not be taken for granted with the harpsichord at that time – in a country which had not suffered the ravages of war, and where there was even a respected Dutch teacher who could be expected to keep an eye on him. And indeed, it was probably through her that he found lodging with Christopher Schmidt's family for the first six months. The harpsichordist was well-prepared both musically and technically. When he arrived in Basel in 1947 he was already a fan of Bach and Stravinsky, with a religious zeal to perform according to the composer's intentions, with an aversion to vain external display and a tendency to rely on articulation rather than rubato or any form of so-called "Romantic" expression.

Christopher Schmidt's contact with Ina Lohr went back to his childhood when as a ten-year-old he took recorder lessons from her. As he told the story

74 The material in this section is largely taken from Anne Smith and Jed Wentz, "Gustav Maria Leonhardt in Basel: portrait of a young harpsichordist", in: *Basler Jahrbuch für Historische Musikpraxis* 34 (2010), 229–44, as well as Christopher Schmidt, "Erinnerungen an Ina Lohr" and expanded immensely by the numerous conversations that I have had with Christopher Schmidt during the course of writing this book.

75 "Der junge Leonhard [sic] ist sehr begabt und kann schon viel. Er wird schon für den Herbstkurs in Basel sein". Letter Ina Lohr to Paul Sacher of 3 August 1947, private collection, Switzerland.

Playing the recorder was not important to me, but I loved the weekly pilgrimage to the Seidenhof, the location of the Schola at that time. The Seidenhof [...] seemed like a small castle to me, and Ina Lohr was its princess. How old was she? I asked myself. As old as my mother? older? younger? She was friendly – dignified; she would have fit well with my relatives that I had left behind in Germany. [...] I particularly liked her singing, even if I also found the bicinia which I had to practice with her somewhat bland; I myself preferred to sing Handel arias.[76]

He nonetheless learned much from her singing, coming to understand the link between the vocal conception of a melody and its instrumental execution that was of use to him in his later training on the violin and organ. As an adolescent he had come to love the music of Johann Sebastian Bach, and thus decided that he wanted to study the organ, which in Basel at that time meant with Eduard Müller, although he had had no previous experience with the instrument. This caused not inconsiderable upheaval at the Schola, as one can tell from a letter from Walter Nef to Paul Sacher of 17 March 1948:

I met with greater resistance with Miss Lohr than I had expected. She apparently wants to not only make a student out of the young Schmidt, but also a "disciple", who will later spread her idea of church music "throughout the world". Thus, she is particularly anxious to keep other "harmful" influences away from him, another reason for us, in the interest of the student, to be vigilant. I have nonetheless insisted, and I hope that it stays that way, that Mr. Schmidt in his first trial semester will major in organ, i.e. that he will have a whole lesson weekly with Müller. He must immediately and in a concentrated fashion begin with the organ, in order that it will soon become clear what his perspectives on the instrument are.[77]

76 "Das Blockflöten war mir nicht wichtig, aber ich liebte es, jede Woche zum Seidenhof, dem damaligen Domizil der Schola, zu pilgern. Der Seidenhof [...] erschien mir wie ein kleines Schloss, und Ina Lohr war das Burgfräulein. Wie alt war sie?, fragte ich mich. So alt wie meine Mutter?, älter?, jünger? Sie war freundlich – würdevoll; sie hätte gut zu meinen Verwandten, die ich in Deutschland zurückgelassen hatte, gepasst. [...] Ganz besonders aber gefiel mir ihr Gesang, wenn ich auch die Bicinien, die ich mit ihr zu üben hatte, etwas salzlos fand; ich selber sang mit Vorliebe Arien von Händel". Christopher Schmidt, "Erinnerungen an Ina Lohr", 159.

77 "Ich bin bei Fräulein Lohr auf stärkern [sic] Widerstand gestossen, als ich erwartet habe. Sie will offensichtlich aus dem jungen Schmidt nicht nur einen Schüler, sondern einen 'Jünger' machen, der später ihre Art der Kirchenmusik 'in den Landen' verbreiten soll. Da ist sie besonders ängstlich darauf bedacht, andere 'schädliche' Einflüsse von ihm abzuhalten, ein Grund mehr für uns, im Interesse des Schülers wachsam zu sein. Ich habe aber dennoch durchgesetzt und hoffe, es bleibt dabei, dass Herr Schmidt in diesem seinem ersten Probesemester Hauptfach 'Orgel', d.h. wöchentlich eine ganze Einzelstunde bei Müller hat. Er soll sich sofort und intensiv mit der Orgel auseinandersetzen, damit sich bald zeigt, wie seine Aussichten auf diesem Instrumente [sic] sind". Letter Walter Nef to Paul Sacher of 17 March 1948, PSF-PSC.

Ill. 6.6: Christopher Schmidt and Gustav Leonhardt with a cat. Photo: courtesy of Christopher Schmidt, Ennetbaden.

On the subject of recorder lessons, however, she remained hard, demanding that he have them from her, although at that time she had otherwise stopped teaching the instrument. This possessive, mothering instinct, combined with a messianic zeal, already mentioned above by Herbert Blomstedt, was referred to by a number of her former students and remembered by them either with gratitude or frustration, depending on the degree the students felt themselves to be limited or supported by her efforts. This letter is an indication that it was felt that it was necessary to keep a watchful eye out for the students' well-being, to make sure that they were free to make their own path through life.

His contact with Gustav Leonhardt at that time was very close, certainly facilitated through Leonhardt's having initially lodged in their home. Although Christopher Schmidt was not at the same level of proficiency as Leonhardt, the harpsichordist shared his love for Johann Sebastian Bach and recognized his innate musical ability, and was in a certain sense one of his teachers, helping him with the organ, accompanying him on the violin. Christopher Schmidt also is proud of being the one who introduced Gustav Leonhardt to the works of Frescobaldi. Something of the nature of their interactions can be seen in the photograph of the two of them with a cat (see Ill. 6.6).

The third member of this group, David Kraehenbuehl (1923–1997), was older and further advanced in his training and only came to Basel for the year

1949/50, but nonetheless established firm connections with both of his fellow students. He came with a rich theoretical and compositional background, having been one of the fortunate few chosen by Paul Hindemith to study with him at Yale, earning his MA in music in 1949, just before his mentor left for a year at Harvard to give the Norton lectures. Upon graduation he received a scholarship to study in Basel for a year at the Schola.[78] It must be mentioned that David Kraehenbuehl was involved in Paul Hindemith's Collegium at Yale and actually took part in the concert at the Metropolitan Museum of Art in 1948, in which instruments of the collection were employed, and thus had already had experience with earlier music as well.[79] David Kraehbuehl, like the Swedes, thus came as a fully trained musician and took Gregorian chant, performance practice, and harpsichord.

Christopher Schmidt still speaks with great enthusiasm of the classes with David Kraehenbuehl and Gustav Leonhardt where they worked on three-part chansons by Binchois, Dufay and pieces from the Glogauer Liederbuch, with the first two playing recorder and the Gustav Leonhardt playing gamba, in which they accompanied the voice of Ina Lohr. The three of them did not see themselves as students, they just got together to speak about music, with all of them bringing in their perceptions. They felt very free in the lessons and had no inhibitions about disagreeing with her, as their enthusiasm for the music was too great. At the end of the hour they often had a need to continue and then the three of them would organize a time on the weekend, and Ina Lohr would just say that she would come too. Nobody thought much of it, as they were not really lessons. The focus was simply on the music and thus if she sang something as an example, it was more than mere instruction in that it was in the context of her own participation in the music-making.[80]

In his reminiscences of her, he expressed himself in the following manner about the classes on the monodic sacred song:

> Here the influence of Ina Lohr extended far beyond the Schola, and she was the source for quite some disquiet in the world of the church. We, her students, participated in all sorts of lectures, courses, and church services. I still see the small woman in front of me; she stood like a rock there, singing and beating time. It was a confessional singing, but without being unctuous. Surely one had never heard the songs of Martin Luther in that manner before in our time, sung with their original rhythms, which were, however, of-

---

78 Background information concerning David Kraehenbuehl is taken from Charles Burkhart, "Remembering David Kraehenbuehl", in: *Journal of Music Theory* 41 (1997), 183–92.
79 Interview with Christopher Schmidt of 22 September 2014.
80 Interview with Christopher Schmidt of 31 July 2017.

ten too difficult for the members of the congregation she was leading: a primal singing that also gave rise to a revolution among some theologians.[81]

It is one of the few descriptions from that time of her presence within the church, once again one of those situations where one had to actually be there in order to understand the power of the medium and its potential for moving its auditors. Later he writes that

she had a somewhat acerbic, but wonderfully clear voice – a well-known organist dreamt of having its sound caught in an organ register; but she lacked the magic. She did not sing as a professional singer, there was no performance in her singing, but rather only devotion.[82]

She thus had the power to captivate you with her music-making, not because of its perfection, but because of its authenticity, its immediacy, its selflessness. Particularly memorable for Christopher Schmidt was the power of Leonhard Lechner's St. John Passion sung together with amateurs on 1 April 1949 in the church of St. Theodor in Basel. In spite of the success of the performance, neither Christopher Schmidt, nor Gustav Leonhardt were entirely happy about having to work together with people whose musicianship left something to be desired. It seems most likely that the story Leonhardt told to Jolande van der Klis about certain teachers in Basel "who found it suspicious if one played too well" must refer to Ina Lohr and that he "did not make himself well-loved" by ridiculing this point of view.[83]

Christopher Schmidt described what he learned from her as being a different kind of thinking, that with her he came to follow the compositional process along with the composer. It was something that could not be transferred to the realm of what could be said, being a kind of intuition rather than proof,

---

81 "Hier reichte die Wirkung von Ina Lohr weit über die Schola hinaus, und sie sorgte für nicht geringe Unruhe in der kirchlichen Welt. Wir, ihre Schüler, waren bei allen möglichen Vorträgen, Kursen und Gottesdiensten mit dabei. Noch sehe ich die kleine Frau vor mir; wie ein Fels stand sie da, singend und taktierend. Es war ein bekennendes Singen, aber ohne einen Hauch von Salbung. So hatte man die Lieder von Martin Luther in unserer Zeit wohl noch nie gehört, gesungen in ihrem ursprünglichen Rhythmus, der allerdings für die Gemeindeglieder, die sie anfeuerte, oft zu schwierig war: Ein Urgesang, der auch bei einigen Theologen eine Revolution hervorrief". Christopher Schmidt, "Erinnerungen an Ina Lohr", 160.

82 "Sie hatte eine etwas herbe, aber wunderbar klare Stimme – ein bekannter Organist träumte davon, ihren Klang in einem Orgelregister einfangen zu lassen –, doch die Magie fehlte ihr. Sie sang nicht wie eine Berufssängerin, es gab in ihrem Gesang keine Darstellung, sondern einfach nur Hingabe". Ibid., 161.

83 Jolande van der Klis, *Oude muziek in Nederland*, 123.

for not everything can be proved; but rather there is an inner line, which can be imagined, and it is either convincing or it is not. In music theory there is little room for proofs, as one cannot prove a vision.[84]

Gustav Leonhardt himself gave touching confirmation of the debt he owed to Ina Lohr in 1983, in a letter, written by him to her on the occasion of her 80th birthday:

> Here come my very best wishes (from Bruges, where the competition has just started) to you, who celebrates your 80th birthday [...] how many will be with you on the day in their thoughts, and in thankful remembrance review everything they have to thank you for. I am one of them and cannot begin to mention everything, perhaps because it is so interwoven with my entire musical development; however, I do want to mention here the enormous experience with melodic monophony [*melodische eenstemmigheid*] for which I have to thank you. Even a harmonist (which a harpsichordist principally is) can make use of that! I am very grateful to you for the place you took and take in my musical development and wish you joy and health from all my heart.[85]

Thus, like many others, he found it difficult to put into words exactly what he gained from the work with Ina Lohr, but recognized that it was largely in relation to her special attention to melody, no doubt in relation to text.

Ina Lohr also always spoke highly of the BKO and its director in her classes. In the case of these three students, however, it was made possible for them to take part in some of the performances, either by singing in the Basel Chamber Choir or playing in the BKO itself. Christopher Schmidt remembers that they all sang in Paul Hindemith's requiem, *Als Flieder jüngst mir im Garten blüht*, on a text by Walt Whitman, on 9 December 1949, and that on 27 January 1950 they participated in Marcel Mihalovici's Variations for Brass and String Orchestra. The latter was a very noisy piece, and Christopher Schmidt remembers Gustav Leonhardt's glee when he had managed during one run-through to play an

---

84 Interview with Christopher Schmidt of 8 March 2016.
85 "Hier komen uit Brugge, waar het concours zojuist begonnen is, mijn allerbeste wensen voor U die Uw tachtigste verjaardag viert [...]. Doch [hoe?] velen niet zullen op de dag in gedachten bÿ U zyn, en in dankbare herinnering alles aan zich laten voorbijtrekken wat zy aan U te danken hebben. Ik behoor bij hen en kan er niet aan beginnen alles op te noemen, misschien ook omdat het zo verwerven is met de hele muzikale ontwikkeling; toch wil ik hier de enorme ervaring van de melodische eenstemmigheid die ik U te danken heb, noemen. Zelf een harmonist (die een clavecinist toch grotendeels is) kan daar gebruik van maken! ik ben U zeer dankbaar voor de plaats die U in mijn muzikale ontwikkeling innam en inneemt en wens U van ganser harte vreugde en gezondheid toe. Brugge, 28. Juli 1983". Card Gustav Leonhardt to Ina Lohr, PSF-ILC.

entire Bach Suite without anybody having noticed that he was doing so, even though he was seated toward the front of the cello section.[86] In addition, both Christopher Schmidt and Gustav Leonhardt played in Boris Blacher's *Dialogue for Flute, Violin, Piano and String Orchestra* on 14 December 1951, as well as in many Haydn symphonies. Thus, here too, we see an intersection, a transcending of the boundaries between the old and new, rather than the strict separation that later came to be so prized.

This was pursued to a different degree with David Kraehenbuehl who composed two pieces for the orchestra, Variations for Piano and String Orchestra in 1951/52, which was performed on 26 March 1954 and his *Epitaphs Concertant*, a concerto for piano and orchestra in 1955, premiered on 14 March 1958. Although he otherwise – according to Christopher Schmidt, who later went and worked as his assistant at David Kraehenbuehl's New School for Music Study in Princeton – seemed to have put his experiences in Basel completely behind him, as not relevant to his current life, he did make use of the connection to get his works performed. Indeed, there are two letters from Ina Lohr that give an indication that it was partly through her influence on Paul Sacher that the Variations were taken up in the programming.[87]

Although David Kraehenbuehl did not maintain any connections with Ina Lohr or the Schola, there are aspects of his life plan that are strangely reminiscent of her own. In 1960, after having launched the *Journal of Music Theory* and receiving tenure at Yale, he gave up his job to go and co-found the New School for Music Study in Princeton, New Jersey, in order to improve the training of young piano students, getting highly involved in creating a body of compositions and a theory program for it. In addition, he also converted to Catholicism in 1956 and began composing works for the church, both for its new liturgy as well as for the concert hall. Although he did not give up his interest in concert music, like Ina Lohr he put his entire professional attention on functional music for pedagogical and liturgical purposes.

Gustav Leonhardt continued to maintain personal contact with her throughout his life, as is evidenced by the letter for her 80th birthday. She joined Gustav Leonhardt and others for the performance of some medieval and renaissance music at the party in honor of his parents' silver wedding anniversary at

---

86 Interview with Christopher Schmidt of 20 October 2017.
87 Letters of 11 January 1952 and 9 April 1954, MSS 79: III.9.162, The David Kraehenbuehl Papers in the Irving S. Gilmore Music Library of Yale University.

the beginning of 1950.[88] She also put together a pastiche in the form of a cantata for his wedding in June of 1953 with Marie Amsler, whom he had met when
she studied with Walter Kägi in Basel. It was performed by colleagues from their
time at the Schola at the celebration following the wedding, where Christopher
Schmidt had played the organ. And whenever he came through Basel, the harpsichordist either telephoned or visited her, as is evidenced by her diaries.

Christopher Schmidt, as he lived in Basel, at first remained within her realm of
influence, while continuing his studies on organ with Heinrich Funk. In 1952/53
he was hired for a trial year teaching recorder and theory at the Schola. Later
he was also given a position as an assistant to Paul Sacher. In the spring of 1958,
however, he felt the need to break away, of giving himself the opportunity of
finding his own musical stance by going far away from his personal and cultural center. As mentioned above, he went to the United States, first spending
a year and a half in California before going to Yale, and taking classes in their
summer program, and thereafter studying with David Kraehenbuehl for a year
in Princeton. When he returned to Switzerland in 1961, he first taught at the
Ecole d'Humanité in Hasliberg Goldern, a progressive boarding school. In 1972
he returned to Basel to teach Gregorian chant and ear-training at the Schola. In
spite of his long absence from Basel, Ina Lohr could not entirely abandon her
sense of being his teacher nor her hope that he would take over and nourish her
educational plan at the institution. As a result, Christopher Schmidt felt forced
to maintain a certain distance in his relationship to her, in order to be able to
pursue his work according to his own lights. He, in his turn, of course, shaped
and sharpened the ears of his own generation of students at the institution.

6.7 Finding a New Balance Between the SCB and the BKO

Although the Schola's reputation abroad was greatly augmented by the influx
of these highly competent musicians, the normal activities of the school – and
thus also those of Ina Lohr – continued. Notwithstanding her decision that
she would no longer take part practically in the BKO's activities, in actuality it
took years for both Ina Lohr and Paul Sacher to find a new mode of working
together that met their needs. These new students at the Schola, however, gave
her a reason that was acceptable to both Paul Sacher and the outside world to

---

88 Letter Gustav Leonhardt to David Kraehenbuehl, 3 October 1950. MSS 79: III.9.160, The
    David Kraehenbuehl Papers in the Irving S. Gilmore Music Library of Yale University.

invest more time into her teaching. What follows will attempt to paint a picture that in some way encompasses both her day-to-day life, as well as those events that were in some way out of the ordinary.

At the Schola, most of her time was invested in the *Hausmusik* program. As Walter Nef wrote in the annual report for the year 1953/54, more than half of the diplomas at the Schola had been awarded for *Hausmusik*, "which may be viewed to a great degree as an SCB diploma. It is, as the courses of study and exams have shown, not entirely unproblematic, but apparently fulfills a need of those students who feel a greater call to become a music teacher than a performing singer or instrumentalist".[89] As we have seen above, these students were also needed to fill the teaching posts of courses for children and lay adults, who provided the social, cultural and financial support required for the SCB's continuing existence. This category was made up mostly of local students, joined by a select few from abroad who had been inspired by her work in this field. Although perhaps less interesting to today's reader, the instruction of these students was high on her list of priorities, as they would carry her musical ethos back into the community. It is also the most difficult portion of Ina Lohr's life to write about, as it was characterized less by events of note, than by continuous, devoted work.

Perhaps her teaching of these courses is best captured by a passage in Wim Waardenburg's obituary for Ina Lohr, written long after the three years she spent in Basel. In it the former student tells her own story of arriving in Basel and going immediately to the Schola, and standing

> next to the impressive sign, "Lehr und Forschungsinstitut". The bell resounded through the stairwell. The concierge hung over the banister to see whether I wiped off my feet before I climbed her stairs. And at the end of the stairs lay Ina Lohr's workroom: spacious and bright, with windows that looked out over the garden to the Rhine, a table in the middle and an old keyboard instrument near the window. In the wall cupboard there was a chaos of papers with an invisible but strictly logical order. She came to meet me and while my suitcase still was at the station, I received my first recorder lesson.
>
> That Schola! … Above us Wenzinger analyzed Bach and below us the children sang and played on the recorder "'s goht öpper dure Tannewald" […] while their snowy shoes stood properly in a row in the corridor. On the days of Ina Lohr's house and church music ensembles, the tiled stove in the big front room was stoked up additionally. In those ensembles the students met the established citizens of Basel, who had already sung and

89   "das in besonderem Masse als SCB-Diplom betrachtet werden darf. Es ist, wie die Ausbildungen und Prüfungen gezeigt haben, nicht ganz unproblematisch, kommt aber offensichtlich einem Bedürfnis derjenigen Schüler entgegen, die sich mehr zum Musikerzieher als zum ausübenden Sänger oder Spieler berufen fühlen". *Bericht über das einundzwangzigste Schuljahr der Schola Cantorum Basiliensis*, 1. September 1953 bis 31. Juli 1954, 2. Archive of the Schola Cantorum Basiliensis.

played [in them] for years and who would continue in them for years after our departure. These were the best times of the week: Dufay, Isaac, Walter, Schein and the mighty
sound of Schütz.[90]

For those who went through the program happily, this description encapsu-
lates their experience, one divided between the individual instruction on their
instrument, theoretical courses primarily taught by Ina Lohr, performance practice from August Wenzinger, work in classes together with other students given
by both August Wenzinger and Ina Lohr, but also in the larger ensembles with
amateurs under the latter, and finally the teaching of children. The only documentation of her work in this field is found in the annual reports in which the
student recitals, exams and concerts are listed, and in her diaries.

At the same time, her work with Paul Sacher continued at the same intense pace
as before. In his typical fashion, he gave her some money in the name of the
Easter bunny to enable her father to come and spend a week or two with her in
April 1947, in a comfortable hotel in Vevey. In her birthday greetings later on
that month, she promised that she would actively take part in the rehearsals for
Allegri's *Miserere* for the concert of 7 December 1947 in which the *Ensemble für
Kirchenmusik* was singing the second choir. She was unwilling to go any further
than that, for it would be so awful for her

> if the good atmosphere between us, which is so necessary and beneficial for our coop-
> eration, would be lost again, as the over-exertion would make me harsh and reproach-
> ful. It is really very annoying for you that I am a woman, but that can't be changed! Just
> this vacation with my father has shown me how strong the need in me is to take care [of
> someone] and then enjoy things together. It doesn't bother me at all that I have missed

---

90 "Niet lang na bovengenoemde cursus reisde ik naar Bazel en stond daar voor de Schola,
    naast dat indrukwekkende bordje 'Lehr und Forschungsinstitut'. De bel galmde door het
    trappenhuis. Over de trapleuning hing de conciërge om te kijken of ik mijn voeten veegde
    voor ik haar trap besteeg. Aan het eind van die trap lag Ina Lohrs werkkamer: ruim en licht,
    met ramen die over die tuin uitkeken op de Rijn, een tafel in het midden en een oud toets-
    instrument bij het raam. In de muurkast een chaos van papieren met een onzichtbare maar
    strik logische orde. Zij kwam mij tegemoet en terwijl m'n koffer nog op het station stond,
    kreeg ik mijn eerste blokfluitles.
       Die Schola! ... Boven analyseerde Wenzinger Bach en beneden zongen en floten de
    kindertjes ''s goht öpper dure Tannewald' [...] terwil hun besneeuwde schoentjes netjes
    op een rij in de gang stonden. Op de dagen van Ina Lohrs huis- en kerkmuziekensembles
    werd de Kachelofen in de grote voorkammer extra opgestookt. In die ensembles ontmoet-
    ten de vakleerlingen de gevestigde Basler die daar al jaren zongen en speelden en daarmee
    nog jaren zouden doorgaan na ons vertrek. Het waren de grote uren van de week: Dufay,
    Isaac, Walter, Schein en de machtige klank van Schütz". Wim Waardenburg, "Ina Lohr:
    1903–1983", in: *Muziek & Onderwijs* 21 (1984), 85.

out a bit on this part of life, but I once again better understand *why* I get so impatient and harsh when there is nothing but work. When the balance is good, then I can put some of this "care" into the work, and I would very much like to try this out.[91]

As in previous times, he was more satisfied with the outcome of this cooperation than she, for on 26 December 1947, she was once again writing to say how difficult she found it to work together with him, even at the Schola, where he was becoming too dictatorial. She assured him that all of her plans and suggestions for the Schola were carefully thought through. Should she no longer be completely available to the school, it was for these "inescapable" reasons. But in 1948 things took a turn for the better, leaving her to comment in a letter of 15 June 1948 that "we also had some good hours recently".[92]

In addition to the concert with the Basel Chamber Choir, the *Ensemble für Kirchenmusik* took part in 14 other concerts during the school year 1947/48, including three performances in connection with an exhibition of "30 Master Works of Old German Masters" at the Fine Arts Museum Basel and four in connection with the exhibition of "The Medieval Stained-Glass Painting from St. Stephen's in Mühlhausen" mentioned above somewhat inaccurately by Sven-Erik Bäck. Christopher Schmidt recalls that performances together with Ina Lohr in such venues were particularly pleasurable in that they were not true "concerts". Ina Lohr felt much more at home in such environs and therefore the music was infused with a sense of spontaneity.[93] Moreover, there were two performances of Lechner's St. John Passion which were so well received that the program was included in the following year's Freunde Alter Musik Basel (Friends of Early Music Basel) concert series. And lastly, on 12 September 1948, together with Ursula Dietschy (soprano) and Marianne Majer (violin), she performed a con-

---

91 "Es wäre mir so schrecklich, wenn die gute Stimmung zwischen uns, die für die Zusammenarbeit nötig und fördernd ist, wieder verloren ginge, weil die Ueberanstrengung mich grimmig und vorwurfsvoll machen würde. Es ist schon sehr lästig für Sie, dass ich eine Frau bin, aber das lässt sich nicht ändern! Gerade diese Ferien mit meinem Vater haben mir gezeigt, wie stark in mir das Bedürfnis ist, ein wenig zu sorgen und es dann auch net[t] zusammen zu haben. Ich nehme es gar nicht tragisch, dass diese Seite vom Leben bei mir etwas zu kurz kommt, aber ich verstehe jetzt wieder besser, <u>warum</u> ich so unduldsam und grimmig werde, wenn es nichts als Arbeit gibt. Wenn das Mass richtig ist, kann ich etwas vom 'Sorgen wollen' in die Arbeit hineinstecken und das möchte ich sehr gerne versuchen". Letter Ina Lohr to Paul Sacher of 26 April 1947, private collection, Switzerland.

92 "wir hatten aber auch gute Stunden in letzter Zeit". Letter Ina Lohr to Paul Sacher of 15 June 1948, private collection, Switzerland.

93 Interview with Christopher Schmidt of 8 December 2017.

cert of modern *Hausmusik* under the auspices of the local section of the ISCM which included four responsories and a suite for solo violin of her own.

Just before leaving for her summer vacation in the Netherlands that year, however, she heard that her father was seriously ill. He died only days after her arrival there, on 29 June 1948. That summer was then bound up with the shared mourning of the three daughters, and the inner and outer reorganization of their lives. The death at one and the same time, intensified the bonds between the sisters and gave greater significance to her tie to Basel.

The cooperation with Paul Sacher was seemingly very peaceful in the 1948/49 season, with work continuing on the program for the following year in its wonted fashion. Paul Sacher was no doubt highly pleased by a remark in her letter of 12 July 1949, that "I actually have a very good work-year behind me, and I am not even too tired at the beginning of the vacation. Were you perhaps shortchanged?"[94]

She was perhaps justified in asking that question, judging from what she was doing at the Schola that went beyond the norm. For example, there were no courses in Protestant church music. Instead Ina Lohr was responsible for the musical aspects of Julius Schweizer's seminar on liturgy at the University, the main subjects of which were Luther's German mass and Zwingli's and Calvin's order of worship. The course was also open to the internal students at the Schola.

She also began teaching a course in Catholic church music at the behest of the Roman Catholic Commission for religious courses for the canton of Basel-Land. A similar course had been taught four years previously by August Wenzinger and they once again asked the Schola if it could provide such instruction in the winter semester of 1948/49. This time it was taken over by Ina Lohr. Interest in such courses remained over an extended period, as Christopher Schmidt has memories of seeing a group of black-clad priests disappearing into her teaching room.

Out of a desire to expand their knowledge and methodology in relation to the repertoire found in the school songbook, a group of young primary school teachers requested a course on sacred and secular song. As it was seen to be desirable to accede to such special wishes, in order to expand the influence of the Schola's approach to such music, Ina Lohr took over the course.

---

94 "Eigentlich habe ich ein sehr schönes Arbeitsjahr hinter mir und gehe nicht einmal zu müde in die Ferien. Sind Sie nicht zu kurz gekommen?" Letter Ina Lohr to Paul Sacher of 12 July 1949, private collection, Switzerland.

And finally, the *Ensemble für Kirchenmusik* participated in 11 events, two of them also in connection with an exhibition of the German Romantics at the Basel Art Museum. That which remained lastingly in the memories of many, however, was the performance of Lechner's St. John Passion within the context of the FAMB concert series.

She was equally active in the following school year, 1949/50, if not more so. Not only were her introductory courses in both Protestant and Catholic church music at various venues well-attended, but also her course in sacred and secular song for primary teachers was extended due to its popularity. The schedule of the *Ensemble für Kirchenmusik* was extraordinarily full: it took part in 17 concerts, again four of them in relation to exhibitions in the art museums of Berne and Basel.

This public success, however, was offset by a further blow to the Lohr family, when on 3 April 1950 her younger sister Sally died after many years of being bed-ridden with tuberculosis. As they had shared an affinity in religious matters that went beyond the practice of the family, this left Ina Lohr in greater emotional isolation. On that day, Ina Lohr later wrote one of her most touching songs, *Die mijn hartens vrede zijt* on a text by Jacqueline Elisabeth van der Waals (1909) adapted from a poem by Thomas à Kempis (see Ill. 6.7).[95] According to a note on the page, it was sung at Sally Lohr's grave in Haarlem by her friends, under the direction of Jan Boeke.

In this year – perhaps because of the intensity of her work, perhaps because of the death of her sister – she once again decided to terminate her cooperation with Paul Sacher, writing after an obviously stormy meeting on 31 May 1950, that the necessity of this pained her, but she had nothing more to offer him. In reflecting on the past, she knew "that that which was difficult was also good, because we both stood behind it". She felt nonetheless the need to reassure him that she would not go "into a cloister". Indeed, she was much more open to the world than in the past, but to "the world of the church and her students".[96]

But this, like all of her other previous decisions of this nature, was soon a thing of the past, as is evident from a letter of 18 March 1951. This time, however, she approached the matter with greater resolve, requesting that he reflect upon their conversation from the previous day, continuing that

---

95 A recording of Ina Lohr singing this song may be heard here: https://soundcloud.com/user-802211739-365337350/ina-lohr-die-mijns-harten.

96 "[...] Welt der Kirche und meiner Schüler". Letter Ina Lohr to Paul Sacher of 31 May 1950, private collection, Switzerland.

Ill. 6.7: Ina Lohr, *Die mijns harten vrede zijt* on a text by Jacqueline Elisabeth van der Waals. Reproduction: PSF-ILC.

This time I will stick to [my decision], that I will no longer take part in any manner of practical work. Our cooperation in this manner was always somewhat forced, and I am no longer able to allow myself to be persuaded and coerced. And the change cannot be all that large for you when, for example, in the case of the St. John Passion, the only thing that was a bit useful to you were the markings in the chorales. Then I have invested too much work, which I always do when only a portion of the picture is concerned that may solely be understood in the context of the whole. Perhaps you will find someone who can approach these questions with greater ease and skill, which would surely be more in line with your thinking.[97]

97 "Diesmal bleibe ich nämlich dabei, dass ich praktisch in keiner Art mehr mitmache. Unsere Zusammenarbeit war in dieser Art immer etwas erzwungen, und ich bin jetzt nicht mehr im Stande mich weiter überreden und zwingen zu lassen. Und so gross kann die Änderung für Sie nicht sein, wenn z. B. im Fall der Johannes Passion nur die Bezeichnung der Choräle Ihnen etwas genützt hat. Dann habe ich viel unnötige Arbeit geleistet, was ich immer tun werde, wenn es um ein Teilgebiet geht, das nur vom Ganzen aus zu verstehen ist. Vielleicht finden Sie jemanden, der diese Fragen leichter und geschickter anpackt, was sicher mehr

And while they once again revised their mode of working together, it was on a new basis. It is as if she had finally gained enough confidence to acknowledge to herself that both of their paths were valid, that it was not an abandonment of her own convictions, if she supported Paul Sacher in his course. To this end, she wrote on 22 April 1951 about how glad she was that it did not come to a breach between them. She went on to say that

> what you do not believe, and I believe also do not understand, is that I am finally so far that I can take you as you are and also can like you very much. I really [can] let you be free, as long as I do not have to go along your path in the musical world. If you are happy with that, that I remain entirely in my world and no longer identify myself with your work in any way whatsoever, then perhaps things can become much better and more peaceful.[98]

In allowing herself the liberty to be at peace in her world of church music, she was also able to accept Paul Sacher and his goals.

Thus, their cooperation continued very fruitfully, as evidenced by the fact that at the end of July she was comparing the manuscript score of C.P.E. Bach's *Magnificat* with the print of 1779 and the parts printed by Schirmer, with the intent of preparing the material for a performance of the BKO. In Illustration 6.8 one can once again see her meticulous emendations to the *Quia respexit,* ranging from specification of the timing and length of the appogiaturas, clarification of the dynamic indications, inclusion of a German translation of the Latin text, to the pasting in of a two-measure correction taken from one of the other versions of the piece. Thus, it is clear that she remained active in this aspect of her work for Paul Sacher, was still marking up the scores for performance, and not reducing it merely to her participation in the programming and the creation of the concert notes.

These emotional turbulences in her life, however, did not hinder her activities at the Schola. Although her students participated in fewer recitals and concerts, she gave numerous lectures for which they sang and played the examples. She herself also gave fewer outside courses, among them her traditional

---

in Ihrem Geist wäre". Letter Ina Lohr to Paul Sacher of 18 March 1951, private collection, Switzerland.

98 "Was Sie nicht glauben und, glaube ich, nicht verstehen ist, dass ich endlich so weit bin, dass ich Sie nehme wie Sie sind und auch sehr gern haben kann. Ich lasse Sie wirklich frei, solange ich nicht Ihre Wege im Musikleben gehen muss. Wenn Sie also damit zufrieden sind, dass ich ganz in meiner Welt bleibe, mich gar nicht mehr mit Ihrer Arbeit identifiziere, dann kann es vielleicht viel besser und ruhiger werden". Letter Ina Lohr to Paul Sacher of 22 April 1951, private collection, Switzerland.

Ill. 6.8: *Quia respexit* from C.P.E. Bach's Magnificat, score from 1779. Photo: PSF-PSC.

Ill. 6.8: (continued)

five-week course for theology students at the University; but she requested that some of her students and former students take over a surprising number of workshops for the Schola during the second semester of the school year, almost certainly in relation to the deterioration of her sister's health.[99]

Among the lectures were two, given in May and June 1951, for primary school teachers which dealt with the use of the recorder in their classes. These were illustrated by a recorder ensemble from her already existing course for such teachers. The lectures were a result of meetings between representatives of elementary school teachers, the Music School and Conservatory, and the SCB, in the hopes of not only raising the level of instruction of the recorder in schools, but also subjecting it to a certain degree of external supervision. It was agreed that both the SCB and the Conservatory would offer a two-semester course for beginners and a single semester for the advanced. Ina Lohr was, of course, responsible for the Schola course in the subsequent 1950/51 school year, and it was attended by 30 participants. The interest in these courses – which continued for many years – was great, and not only from the side of the students. In one of her rare diaries, Ina Lohr mentions again and again her great pleasure in these classes, going so far as to say on 5 May 1953:

> Sometimes I don't know what makes me happier; the really very intensive work with the professional students or that apparently simple search for possibilities with the primary school teachers. That which the "unmusical" Stutz and Merz [names of her students] notice and achieve in the field of children's songs is amazing.[100]

Her investment in the musical education of children can also be seen in her extensive involvement in the production of *Alles singt und springt,* the songbook for the Basel schools published in 1958.[101] Not only was she one of the few living composers who contributed a melody to the book, she also provided accompaniments to 24 of the 294 songs. In addition, she clearly had an influence on the choice and presentation of other songs, in that there are many Huguenot psalms and other melodies from earlier eras which cannot really be considered standard fare for children. If applicable, the modes of the individual songs are

---

99   Minutes of the teachers' conference of 2 May 1951, PSF-PSC.
100 "Soms weet ik niet, wat me gelukkiger maakt; het werkelijk heel intensieve werken met de beroepsleerlingen of juist dat schijnbaar eenvoudige peilen naar muzikale mogelijkheiden bij de onderwijzers. Wat de 'onmuzikale' Stutz en Merz op het gebied van kinderliederen merken en zelf volbrengen is verbluffend". Diary entry of 5 May 1953, PSF-ILC.
101 I wish to thank Margrit Fiechter for pointing out the extent of Ina Lohr's activities in the schools, and in particular in the songbook.

identified. In addition, suggestions of multiple possibilities of instrumentation or performance are often given for her arrangements.

Further, she wrote the music to a Christmas play for children on a text by Marianne Garff, *Das Öchslein und das Eselein*, which she originally published herself in 1950. It was sufficiently popular that a reprint of it was included by the Berne Teachers' Association in their journal *Schulpraxis*.[102] In her archive at the Paul Sacher Foundation, there are also letters and drawings from school classes from Riehen and Basel which performed the play in 1971 and 1974, long after Ina Lohr had stopped teaching these courses, a further indication of her influence in the local schools.

At the beginning of the 1951/52 school year, perhaps missing the Swedes, Ina Lohr remarked to Paul Sacher that "our Schola is running somewhat quietly at the moment".[103] There are, however, three events in that year that particularly stand out. To begin with, as mentioned above (see p. 244), she was asked by the radio to take over their Christmas programs for those living alone, the first of which was broadcast on 24 December 1951. Christopher Schmidt commented on the good atmosphere at the radio studio at such broadcasts, how the sound engineers were her friends and treated the musicians very warmly. As a result, everybody was relaxed, the music was performed particularly well and all were in a festive mood.[104] The program included works from earlier eras, but also pieces by Kodály and herself.

Then, on 17 February 1952, the *Ensemble für Kirchenmusik* took part in a concert in which music for the synagogue, and the Catholic, Lutheran, and Swiss reformed churches was performed under the auspices of the Christian-Jewish Society (Christlich-Jüdische Arbeitsgemeinschaft). The Jewish music was performed by a cantor and piano, whereas the ensemble was responsible for the music from the various Christian churches, which was not limited to Gregorian chant and Protestant music from the time of the Reformation, but also included that of various contemporary composers. Occasions such as this were always highlights for Ina Lohr.

Finally, on 7 May 1952, a recorder ensemble made up of teachers, and former and current students of the Schola (Christopher Schmidt, Ina Lohr, Valerie Kägi, Anita Stange, and Armin Lüthi) together with 2 violins (one of them Ro-

---

102 Special reprint included in *Schulpraxis*, Nr. 7/1961. Berne: Sekretariat des Bernischen Lehrervereins.

103 "Unsere Schola 'läuft' etwas ruhig momentan". Letter Ina Lohr to Paul Sacher of 29 September 1952, Private collection, Switzerland.

104 Interview with Christopher Schmidt of 8 December 2017.

dolfo Felicani, a Schola teacher), clarinet and cello (August Wenzinger) took part in the premiere of Bohuslav Martinů's *Stowe Pastorals* in celebration of the 25th anniversary of the Basel section of the ISCM. Although the piece cannot at all be said to be written in a pronounced avant garde style, it does indicate – together with the above-mentioned concerts – the freedom with which musicians at the time moved between the realm of the old and the new.

Her work for Paul Sacher in this season seems to have been untroubled. A reflection of this may be seen in her note to him of 21 January 1952 on the occasion of the 25th anniversary of the BKO:

> Warmest congratulations on the actual day of the anniversary! There would probably be a lot to write about that, but I don't have the time. And you don't have the time to read it! Only this much: I am thankful and happy that we can (hopefully) celebrate in peace with one another and that I can say in spite of all the difficulties: "I would do it again". Hopefully we still have some good years from now on ahead of us![105]

At this event she was named an honorary member of the BKO – appearing first on the list for 1952, followed by Maja Sacher, Béla Bartók, Conrad Beck, Willy Burkhard, Paul Hindemith, Arthur Honegger, Frank Martin, Bohuslav Martinů, and Igor Stravinsky – in recognition for her long-term services to the orchestra and its director.

Otherwise their correspondence in 1952 is once again dominated by questions of programming, as both of them were away for long periods of time, Ina Lohr in the Netherlands at Easter and in the summer, followed by her course in Sweden and a lecture on 2 September for the Association of Music Teachers at the Conservatory of Music in Copenhagen on "Early Music and Solmization in Today's Musical Instruction", whereas Paul Sacher was on an extended excursion to South America with his wife. A fragment of their communication on this subject in connection with the program for the BKO's 1953/54 season is found in Table 6.2.[106] From this it is evident that although certain elements of the program were fixed, often major changes took place after their initial brainstorm-

---

105 "Herzliche Glückwünsche zum heutigen, eigentlichen Jubiläumstag! Es wäre wohl allerhand dazu zu schreiben, aber mir fehlt die Zeit. Ihnen auch die Zeit zum Lesen. Nur so viel: ich bin dankbar und glücklich, dass wir in (hoffentlich) gegenseitiger Zufriedenheit feiern können und dass ich trotz aller Schwierigkeiten sagen kann: 'ich würde es noch einmal machen'. Hoffentlich sind uns noch gute Jahre von jetzt an zugemessen!" Letter Ina Lohr to Paul Sacher of 21 January 1952, private collection, Switzerland.

106 The planning of the program for the Collegium Musicum Zurich is discussed in equal detail, but Paul Sacher's first draft is lacking, thus making its evaluation more difficult.

Table 6.2: Programming discussion concerning the BKO 1953/54 season in comparison to the final outcome. The names of the pieces in the table reflect their nomenclature in the letters themselves.

	15 September 1952 (Paul Sacher)	25 September 1952 (Ina Lohr)	Final Program
Extra USA	Kraehenbuehl Variationen Copland Clarinet Concert	Does it need to be USA program? Good serenade by de Plessis, young South African.	No concert.
I 30 Oct. 1953	1. Haydn Notturno 2. Haydn Piano Concerto F major 3. Haydn Symphony 90, E-flat major Instead of 1. J. C. Bach, Symphony or Concertino Notturno Stamitz, Orchestra Quartet Instead of 2. Mozart, Oboe Concerto Mozart, Horn Concerto, KV 417 E-flat Sperger, Contrabass Concerto Zelter, Hoffmeister, Pleyel, Viola Concerto	Although a Haydn program is always attractive, we still have unresolved problems, thus perhaps the following: Stamitz, Orchestra Quartet Sperger, Contrabass Concerto Haydn, Notturno or symphony	Stamitz, Orchestra Quartet, F major, Op. 4/4 von Weber, Clarinet Concerto, E-flat, op. 74 Haydn, Symphony E-flat, H I:91
II 18 Dec. 1953	25th anniversary, Basel Chamber Choir J. S. Bach, Magnificat Honegger, Christmas Cantata	Questions the quick succession of II and III and III as being too much material for the choir, suggests switching III and IV, even though that would mean rehearsing Mozart and Burkhard in parallel.	Schütz, Historia von der Geburt Jesu Christi, SWV 435 Honegger, Christmas Cantata

	15 September 1952 (Paul Sacher)	25 September 1952 (Ina Lohr)	Final Program
III 29 Jan. 1954	Mozart, Idomeneo		Français, Orchestersuite "La douce France" Binet, "L'or perdu" for Voice and Orchestra Roussel, Small Suite for Orchestra Bartók, Suite Nr. 2 for Orchestra, op. 4 (version 1943)
IV 18 Feb. 1954	Fortner Tomasi, Div. Convica Binet, Printemps		Mozart, Idomeneo, Rè di Creta, KV 366
V 26 Mar. 1954	Purcell Suite or Rosenmüller, Scheiffelhut, Eckhard, Biber Vivaldi Concerto or Bonporti, Telemann Campra, Les femmes Rebel, Les Eléments or Handel, Concisi or Water Music	She has read the article on Rebel, but would first need to see the score or hear the piece. Would be particularly good together with Purcell's Fairy Queen because of the descriptions of nature. She is fighting with Vivaldi: she needs to look at all concerti that are considered to be "good" with him and make closer selection.	Purcell, Suite from "The Double Dealer" Vivaldi, Concerto 2 flutes, 2 oboes, bassoon, 2 violins and orchestra, FXII, Nr. 17 Kraehenbuehl, Variations for Piano and String Orchestra Hindemith, Concerto for Winds, Harp, Orchestra
VI 6 May 1954	W. Burkhard, Mass		Burkhard, Mass for Soprano and Bass Soli, mixed choir and orchestra, op. 85
Extra 13 June 1954	For Schweizer Tonkünstlerfest: As the contemporary music is primarily Swiss during the season, and as a counterpart to II, we could mix old and new. But if we manage to find a good 17th–18th century program, would prefer that.		Regamey, Music for Strings Binet, "L'or perdu" for voice and orchestra Robert Oboussier, Concerto for violin and orchestra Zbinden, Sinfonie Nr. 1 for chamber orchestra, op. 18

ing. Ina Lohr's questions here are largely of a basic nature, dealing with matters such as the actual number of rehearsals required for the choir to learn the music. As we see here, Paul Sacher not only acceded to changing the order of the third and fourth concerts as suggested, but in addition the Bach *Magnificat* was replaced by Schütz's Christmas Oratorio. With this Paul Sacher achieved two goals: 1) by having the woman's choir for the Schütz sung by the *Ensemble für Kirchenmusik*, he significantly reduced the role of the choir; and 2) at the same time he once again actively involved Ina Lohr in the choir concerts. A diary entry on 28 January 1953 makes it clear how her great enthusiasm for a specific musical project could overcome all doubts concerning her cooperation with Paul Sacher:

> P.S. enjoyed the thinking aloud and the programs for the coming season are almost finished. The question is whether I should perform the "soliquenten" of the Schütz Christmas Oratorio with the [women's choir] of the *Ensemble für Kirchenmusik*?! I would like to do it so much but am afraid that it will once again be seen as a craving for "recognition". P.S. does not consider that to be a reason.[107]

This short passage does much to explain the dynamics of their relationship. Whilst their correspondence is often used to clarify their difficulties with one another, here in the diary we see their common creative drive rising to the surface.

The Schütz Christmas Oratorio was to appear in the same program as Honegger's Christmas Cantata. In the interview with Jos Leussink, Ina Lohr speaks of her friendship with the composer stemming from hard work, first on *Jeanne d'Arc au bûcher*, followed by *La Danse des morts*, going on to say that

> at the end came his *Cantate noel*, that was his last work, [gets a book] … [a] photograph shows how Honegger came on stage to express his thanks, at the very end, deathly ill. Tears ran down my cheeks, when he felt his way back to his seat in the hall. And then I jumped up and took him by the arm, then he said: "*ma petite dame, vous êtes là*", as if that were not something to be taken for granted. [Leafs through *Alte und Neue Musik II: 50 Jahre Basler Kammerorchester* to photo on page opposing 350.] That is the old, actually already dying Honegger. Very serious, frightfully serious … except for the marvelous moment where the children sing "*freue dich, freue dich Israel, geboren ist Immanuel*". […] But then he became so ill, that he was [in the hospital in Liestal]; […] he couldn't orchestrate the end any more, but he had written everything down, so that his wife had to orchestrate it, which she did marvelously – he only gave her a sign at the

---

107 "P.S. genoot van het hardop denken en de programma's voor volgend jaar zijn bijna af. De vraag is, of ik de soliquenten van Schütz Weihnachtsoratorium met het Ens. f.k.M. zal uitvoeren?! Ik zou het dolgraag doen, maar vrees, dat het weer als 'geltungstrieb' zal worden opgevat. P.S. vindt dat geen argument". Diary entry of 28 January 1953, PSF-ILC.

very last word that the bassoon should sing very low: "Il est né le divin enfant...", and that is so gripping. Thus, I completely experienced the creation of it. [...]

And that was funny: Then he suddenly spoke in Zurich dialect ... as he told me about all the Christmas songs that were sung all mixed up together there – I do not know whether or not it is a very great work from the compositional perspective, I can no longer judge; for me it was a tremendous happening, to experience this. At that time he could come down from Schönenberg in order to say: "look, here are two more pages". All of that made such a powerful impression. And then he said once: *"oui, ca doit être comme ça, je sais: nous sommes sauvés ... Das isch wie ne Schleier vo Friede umd ganze Welt umme".* ["Yes, that should be like that, I know: we are saved ... That is like a veil of peace around the entire world".] That was really ... an experience. That was thus the friendship with Honegger, whom I still value highly.[108]

The composition of this piece must also have taken place in this time period and we see once again here how closely Ina Lohr was integrated into the whole BKO organization.

It must have been about this time that she had increased contact with Ernst Krenek, about whom she also spoke in her interview with Jos Leussink:

Ernst Krenek, [...] who was often here [...] has a very cerebral side, his number symbolism and all of that ... And then I found it so terribly nice when he said, I would so very much like to compose something simple. And there was a student of mine who has now been the director in a Catholic church for a long time, he was standing near by and

108 "totdat op het laatst kwam de 'Cantate noel', dat was zijn laatste werk, [gets a book] (een) fotografie laten zien van Honegger zoals hij toen op het podium nog kwam bedanken, op het laatst, doodziek, de tranen liepen me over de wangen, toen hij zich terugtastte naar zijn stoel in de zaal. En toen ben ik opgesprongen en heb hem aan zijn arm genomen, toen zij hij: 'ma petite dame, vous êtes la', alsof dat niet vanzelfsprekend was. [Leafs through *Alte und Neue Musik II: 50 Jahre Basler Kammerorchester* to photo on the page opposing 350.] Dat is de oude, eigenlijk al stervende Honegger. Heel ernstig, vreselijk ernstig [...] behalve dan het prachtige moment, waarop de kinderen zingen 'freue dich, freue dich Israel, geboren ist Immanuel'. [...] maar toen werd hij zo ziek, hij lag daar [in het ziekenhuis], [...] toen kon hij het laatste niet meer orkestreren, maar hij had het al zo opgeschreven, en zijn vrouw moest het orkestreren, dat heeft ze prachtig gedaan, hij heeft haar maar één wenk gegeven, heel op het laatst moet de fagot nog heel laag zingen: 'Il est né le divin enfant', [...] En hij geloofde daar ook in.

En dat was grappig: Dan sprak hij opeens Züridütsch ... zoals hij mij vertelde, al die Kerstliederen die daar door elkaar gezongen worden – of dat nou kompositorisch een heel groot werk is weet ik niet, ik kan dat niet meer beoordelen, het is voor mij een gebeurtenis geweest, dat mee te beleven: dan kon hij naar beneden komen op de Schönenberg, om te zeggen, kijk: er zijn weer twee bladzijden bijgekonmen. Dat maakte (alles) zo'n geweldige indruk. En toen zij hij een keer: 'oui, ca doit être comme ca, je sais: nous sommes sauvés [...] Das isch wie ne Schleier vo Friede um d'ganze Welt umme'. Dat was werkelijk een belevenis. Dus dat was de vriendschap met Honegger, die ik nog steeds erg waardeer". Interview with Jos Leussink, 25 March 1983.

he said: "O, for my church choir, because they really do sing in tune". So he went to listen and then wrote for them those things that you mentioned yesterday; they are beautiful [...] I did all of the music also with my choir, just so we could get to know it. It is so nice to sing, excellent for the voice. Krenek was one of the most musically erudite people I have ever seen, he knew nearly everything. It was difficult with him in conversation, because he always became very cerebral [...] and that is, alas, not my thing. [...] I know that I need it, I need that knowledge, to hold my feelings in check. But it is not so important to me, that I talk much about it. [...] But that, too, was a meeting that gave me much. Exactly those little things brought me to also compose such simple things for smaller choirs, which indeed resonated with them and which they were able to sing.[109]

One of the pieces that inspired her must have been *Veni sanctificator*, as in her estate there is a copy of the work which she had obviously studied and analyzed melodically by means of solmization (see Ill. 3.3). It is also known under the name of *Motette zur Opferung für das ganze Kirchenjahr*, op. 141 (1954) and was premiered under Ernst Pfiffner's direction on 27 March 1955 in Basel.[110] Ernst Pfiffner was the music director in St. Michael's Church from 1950–67 and also had instruction from Ina Lohr, as his name appears once in her diary as scheduled to have a lesson together with Rudolf Kelterborn and Walter Reinert on 13 November 1953. In addition, Ernst Krenek wrote the *Psalmverse* (work without opus Nr. 92) for soloists and choir, composed on 26 August 1956, "for Ernst Pfiffner in Basel" ("für Ernst Pfiffner in Basel"). This is again evidence of how she brought her students repeatedly into contact with the composers who came through Basel with their compositions for Paul Sacher. In this case – in spite of the fact she found the interpersonal contact with Krenek difficult – she her-

109 "Ernst Krenek [...] die vaak hier was [...] dus hij heeft natuurlijk een heel cerebrale kant, en getallensymboliek en alles dat. En toen vond ik het zo vreselijk leuk dat hij zei, ik wou zo graag iets heel eenvoudigs componeren, en daar stond die leerling van mij, die nu allang dirigent is van een katholieke kerk hier is, die stond daar bij, en die zei: 'O, voor mijn kerkkoor, want dat zingt heus heel zuiver'. Toen is hij gaan luisteren, en heeft daarvoor toen die dingen geschreven, die U gisteren ook noemde, die zijn prachtig [...] Dat heb ik ook allemaal met mijn koor gedaan, eenvoudig dat wij het ook leerden kennen. Het zingt zich zo goed, zijn voor de stem voortreffelijk [...] Krenek was een van de meest muzikaal belezen mensen die ik ooit gezien heb, hij kende bijna alles [...] In gesprek was bij hem dat het moeilijke, dat hij altijd in gesprek heel cerebraal werd [...] en dat is helaas niet mijn kant. [...] Ik weet dat ik dat nodig heb, de kennis heb ik nodig, om de gemoedskant in toom te houden. Maar het staat niet zo voorop, dat ik daar veel over praat. [...]. Maar ook dat was een ontmoeting, die me heel veel gegeven heeft. Juist die kleine dingen hebben bij mij er weer toe geleid, dat ik ook weer voor kleinere koren zulke eenvoudigere dingen ben gaan schrijven, die toch aanklang vonden en die ze konden zingen". Interview with Jos Leussink of 25 March 1983.

110 Many thanks to Simon Obert for bringing the connection between Ernst Krenek, Ernst Pfiffner and these psalm compositions to my attention.

self was inspired by his choral writing, leading to her composing similar things for her own choirs.

6.8 Six Weeks in the Life of Ina Lohr

On the whole, we have far more information about the balance between various aspects of her life in the first half of 1953 than at any other time in her life because she was once again keeping a diary. Therefore, the first six weeks of this year will be discussed here in greater detail, not so much for the specific importance of the material therein, but rather to illustrate how little breathing space there was from day to day. As so frequently, it began with a period of withdrawal, from which she drew great pleasure, devoting herself to reading and reflection:

> I always have to learn to be patient with students and friends after a vacation largely spent alone. It is as if I had gone on ahead on a walk and seen many beautiful things, and now I am suddenly together with the others again who have been talking throughout and did not see any of it. In the end, the wealth of reading and reflection must be of benefit to them.[III]

This desire for peace and quiet is understandable, however, in view of the diversity of her activities and the energy required for them. This was particularly an issue, as her health was once again an object of concern, leading to a decision on 5 January 1953 to have her infected tonsils and adenoids removed in mid-February. One has to be astonished at what she nonetheless managed to achieve in the meantime.

On the one hand, she was studying the music for the upcoming BKO concert, Rameau's Overture to the ballet *Zaïs*, Grétry's Concerto for flute and orchestra, and six dances from the opera *La Rosière républicaine*. In comparing them she came to recognize what a revolutionary Grétry was, flaunting all of Rameau's rules and instead paying attention to melody and sound. She also evaluated new scores for possible use in future concerts, among them a mass by Monteverdi, published in 1951, and then performed in Basel on 13 May 1955; and Stravinsky's *Cantata*, completed in August 1952 and premiered on 11 November of the same year. She was particularly taken by the latter as it reminded

---

III "Ik moet na een vacantie van veel alleen zijn altijd weer geduld leeren hebben met leerlingen en vrienden. 't Is, als of ik op een wandeling alleen vooruit liep en veel moois zag, en nu opeens ben ik weer met de anderen samen, die door gepraat hebben en dat alles niet zagen. Ten slotte moet de rijkdom van lezen en nadenken toch hun ten goed komen". Diary entry of 6 January 1953, PSF-ILC.

her of Schütz's Christmas Oratorio. It received its Basel premiere on 9 December 1955. Her attendance of a concert organized by the ISCM may perhaps be seen in the context of evaluating new music for the BKO. She was not overly impressed with it, writing:

> The ISCM concert was organized only around virtuosity and sound, except for a toccata for piano by Moeschinger, which was reminiscent of Frescobaldi's method of working: re-fa-mi-re, combined with a chromatic theme, but also with impressionistic passage work![112]

Noteworthy in both these examples is Ina Lohr's ability to make the link to earlier styles, a trait that Sven-Erik Bäck found so valuable.

In addition, she had her regular meetings with Paul Sacher, relishing his pleasure in them. She went to the rehearsal of the Rameau and Grétry on 19 January 1953, remarking that he led it excellently and that "he again did not need me for it today".[113] On January 22, she found Darius Milhaud's *Malheurs d'Orphée* to be "magnificent, seeming new and 'zeitgemäss' [timely], even in rehearsal."[114] The following day she was even more impressed by the piece, less so by the soloists:

> Milhaud was more than magnificent, even gripping, although the interpretation of Euridice left much to be desired. Also, Mollet tried to make too much of it, but he was honestly moved by it. [Especially] magnificent, primarily for its sound, was the trio for men's voices with this instrumentation. A composer only writes one such work in his life![115]

Again, this reveals her intense participation in Paul Sacher's world of contemporary music.

In this same month, she spent much time preparing a lecture on modern music for recorder, including examples played by a current student, Armin Lüthi, and Christopher Schmidt, for an audience of architects and other

---

112 "Het IGNM concert was, alleen op virtuositeit en klank berekend, behalve een toccata voor piano van Moeschinger, die aan de werkwijze van Frescobaldi deed denken: re-fa-mi-re, gecombineerd met een chromatisch thema, maar ook met impressionistisch passagewerk!" Diary entry of 11 January 1953, PSF-ILC.

113 "Daarvoor heeft hij me heusch niet weer nodig". Diary entry of 19 January 1953, PSF-ILC.

114 "Milhaud's Malheur [sic] d'Orphée is prachtig; werkt zelfs op een repetitie verbluffend nieuw en 'zeitgemäss'". Diary entry of 22 January 1953, PSF-ILC.

115 "Milhaud was meer dan prachtig, aangrijpend zelfs, al liet de interpretatie van Euridize veel te wenschen over. Ook Mollet probeerd er te veel van te maken, maar hij was er eerlijk door gegrepen. Prachtig, vooral als klank, was het terzet voor mannenstemmen met deze instrumentatie. Zoo 'n werk schrijft een componist maar eens in zijn leven!" Diary entry of 23 January 1953, PSF-ILC.

graphic artists at the university on 22 January 1953. She felt considerable anxiety concerning the lecture in the days preceding it, perhaps understandable in that she went out on a limb by illustrating how her own compositional style might be understood within that of her contemporaries. According to a review, she claimed that the expressive drive associated with modern music was "connected with the search for a new kind of melodic line, based on a new melodic language, taken from the spoken language as it is used today" and that one was "experiencing a new flowering of the sense for language". She then demonstrated, with a work by Alban Berg, how the voice was employed so that the listener was more attentive to the content than to the manner of performance, saying that "it was not beautiful, but authentic, in the effort to give a picture of the thinking and experience of our time. It is expected of the listener that he partake of it inwardly". With examples of Walther Geiser, Sven-Erik Bäck, and herself, she explained how these melodies were complete in and of themselves, without accompaniment. She then drew "a parallel to modern drawing with its renunciation of shading and color, but also to Martin Luther's translation of the Bible that was intended for reading aloud and listening".[116] Although very specific, directed towards a single aspect of the contemporary musical scene, it shows great deal of self-reflection about her own place in the 20th-century compositional world.

She was, of course, also fulfilling her teaching duties during this entire period. These included the rehearsal of the musical side of an investiture of two Dominican nuns in Riehen on 25 January 1953, in which her classes in Gregorian chant took part. Afterwards she reached the conclusion that although the music went very well, she was "a Protestant by conviction. The mass in its current form is

---

116 "Mit dem Ausdrucks- und Mitteilungswillen hängt das Suchen nach einer neuen Melodik zusammen, ausgehend von einer neuen Sprachmelodik, von der Sprache, wie sie heute gesprochen wird. Wir erleben ein neues Aufblühen des Gefühls für Sprache. An Alban Berg demonstriert die Vortragende, wie die Singstimme so verwendet wird, dass der Zuhörer mehr auf das Gesagte als auf die Art, wie es gesungen wird, achtet. Wer Klanggenuss will, nennt diese Musik spröde. Ist sie nicht schön, ist sie dafür echt, bemüht, ein Bild zu geben vom Denken und Erleben unserer Zeit. Vom Zuhörer wird erwartet, dass er an ihm innerlich Anteil nimmt. An Beispielen von Walter [sic] Geiser [...], Ina Lohr [...] und dem jungen Schweden Sven Erik Bäck [...] erläutert die Künstlerin, dass diese Musik in ihrer Einstimmigkeit vollständig ist, keiner Begleitung bedarf. Im Oratorium von Willy Burkhard singt der ganze Chor einstimmig und spielt das ganze Orchester einstimmig. [...] Ina Lohr erkennt eine Parallele dazu in der modernen Zeichnung mit ihrem Verzicht auf Töne und Farben, aber auch in der Bibelübersetzung von Martin Luther, die zum laut Lesen und Hören bestimmt war". p.h., "Moderne Musik", undated newspaper clipping from 1953 from an unidentified newspaper, PSF-ILC.

so overladen that it is impossible to consciously follow all of those concepts. It only functions through one's feeling and through observation. Is that enough?" thereby showing her own personal ecumenical limits.[117]

She also had to deal with Armin Lüthi's nerves as he prepared for his final exam. Leading up to it, she had organized a recital of old and new recorder music on 6 February 1953, in which various teachers and students participated. Afterwards she confessed that although the rehearsals had been good, "when she stood in front of the people she was so dead-tired that she had to pull her last strength together and sometimes really played incorrectly".[118] The two students, however, had played well.

Two days later she was able to write that "P.S. thought that our recital on Friday was very good. That says something. Then it was actually worthwhile, particularly for Woffer [Christopher Schmidt] and Lüthi".[119] The latter's final exams were on the 12 and 14 February, sandwiching a BKO concert. And on 15 February 1953 she entered the hospital for her tonsillectomy.

Is it then surprising that she had an occasional day where she was unable to do anything, or decided to buy a *Woman's Home Companion* to recover or escape from her daily pressures? What is perhaps astonishing, but also typical for her, was that she did wonder whether she would find peace in the hospital "without the stability of working, and without the order that music always creates".[120]

The operation went well and after a couple of weeks, she took up her normal busy schedule again. Shortly before the Easter break, however, she again became a bit ill, and was not in the best shape when she went to visit her sister Etty in Amsterdam. Her sister looked into the causes of Ina Lohr's poor health more thoroughly and finally decided that the basic problem was an underlying depression and prescribed dexedrine for it, which alleviated some of the immediate symptoms. Nonetheless, Ina Lohr was relieved when she discovered that by the end of June she could stop taking it without a recurrence of her depression.

117 "Maar ik ben toch overtuigd Protestant. De mis, zooals die nu is, is zoo overladen, dat het onmogelijk is al die gedachten bewust te volgen. Het gaat uitsluitend door het gevoel en door de waarneming. Is dat genoeg?" Diary entry of 25 January 1953, PSF-ILC.
118 "toen ik voor de menschen stond was ik zoo dood moe, dat ik mijn laatste krachten moest verzamelen en er soms echt naast griep". Diary entry of 6 February 1953, PSF-ILC.
119 "P.S. vond onze Vrijdagvoordracht heel goed. Dat zegt wat. Dan is het toch de moeite waard geweest, vooral voor Woffer en Lüthi". Diary entry of 8 February 1953, PSF-ILC.
120 "zonder de gestadigheid van dat werk, en zonder de orde, die de muziek altijd weer schept". Diary entry of 31 January 1953, PSF-ILC.

The *Ensemble für Kirchenmusik* had once again been very active during this school year, performing numerous concerts, as well as taking part in various church services and in the Christmas play for the radio. The high point was the concert for the FAMB series on 5 June; she was very satisfied with the results and with the cooperation of all those involved.

She spent her 50th birthday vacationing in Founex (Vaud), Paul Sacher's birthday present to her for that year. As revealed in a letter to him of 3 August 1953, it was also a time for her to reflect on the past and contemplate the future:

> I do both with a thankful heart. It is always a worry to me that your thoughts of the past cannot be free of feelings of resignation and disappointment. Oddly enough, in recent times I have repeatedly had the idea that the cooperation could perhaps become more intense again over time. [...] I am only sad when I think about how my best achievements are worthless to you. I am referring to certain insights in the field of music theory, which make it possible to compose something which is very pure or to bring people to a very pure kind of music-making. But all this is only possible in small forms which are not commensurate with the concert situation.[121]

It is once again fascinating how clearly she sees the differences between her musical interests and intents in comparison to those of Paul Sacher, and how, nonetheless, they both found the means of continuing together, in what will be seen to become an ever more amicable fashion.

The 1953 diary, in combination with the correspondence and annual reports, is one of the most revealing documents about her life, in that it is only in this period that we can truly begin to comprehend the amount Ina Lohr worked in relation to the pressures she perceived from the outside and as well as from her own internal ones. It puts her complaints to Paul Sacher into a different light. At one and the same time, her question about whether she would be able to find peace in the hospital without work and the solace of music indicates, however, the degree that professional self-discipline was also essential to her sense of well-being.

---

121   "Beides tue ich dankbaren Herzens. Dass bei Ihnen das Zurückdenken nicht so ohne Gefühle von Verzicht und Enttäuschung geht, ist auch mir immer wieder ein Kummer. Merkwürdigerweise kommt mir in letzter Zeit immer wieder die Idee, dass die Zusammenarbeit vielleicht auf die Dauer wieder intensiver werden könnte. [...] Traurig bin ich nur, wenn ich bedenke, dass meine besten Leistungen für Sie wertlos sind. Ich meine gewisse Erkenntnisse auf dem Gebiete der Musiktheorie, die mich im Stande stellen etwas ganz Sauberes zu komponieren oder Leute zum ganz sauberen Musizieren zu bringen. Das ist aber alles nur in kleinen Formen möglich, die nicht zum 'Konzertformat' passen". Letter Ina Lohr to Paul Sacher of 3 August 1953, private collection, Switzerland.

6.9 The Last Years of the *Hausmusik* Diploma: 1953–57

From the musical or pedagogical point of view, the school year 1953/54 was perhaps one of the least eventful in the Schola's history. On another level, it was one of the most momentous, in that it moved to what had formerly been a private house on Leonhardsstrasse 4 on 1 March 1954, as a first step in its fusion with the Music School and the Conservatory. This amalgamation into a single institution around a central courtyard under the name of the Musik-Akademie Basel took place officially on 1 August 1954. The annual report maintained that it was good to have been independent at the beginning, but now that a foundation had been laid that it was also good to have the greater stability provided by the larger organization. And, indeed, by means of the subsidies, teachers' salaries were assured, and it was later possible to establish a pension plan for them, just in time for those who had been there longest.

For Ina Lohr, however, the school year flowed on much as in the past, with numerous recitals, the Christmas play for the radio, and various activities with the *Ensemble für Kirchenmusik*. Not unsurprisingly the concert with the Schütz Christmas Oratorio and Honegger's Christmas Cantata did not go optimally from Ina Lohr's point of view. Her New Year's letter of 6 January 1954 to Paul Sacher revealed the situation from her perspective, but with a few differences in comparison to the past:

> For 2 years now, we are clear about the fact that we are dependent upon one another, and that the old bond can no longer be dissolved. I am glad about this, but I will have to speak to you now and again when things cannot be resolved merely by friendship.
>
> The practical participation in the Schütz showed me once again that our cooperation, even today still, cannot extend that far. We are too different in music-making. Your activity in the rehearsals, but even more so in the concert, just ruins something beautiful for me and I have to exert almost superhuman control over myself to remain quiet. I hoped to perhaps hear something of the inner peace when listening to the recording. But it then seemed even much worse to me. In addition, just on that day you brought so much vitality, activity with you, that it was almost impossible to really "listen". Those are moments of suffering for me. And then, when you then so mercilessly and coldly passed judgment on the Bäck [piece], of which you knew – and had just heard – that I liked it and found it beautiful, then there were "shards" again.[122]

122 "Seit 2 Jahren sind wir uns darüber klar, dass wir auf einander angewiesen sind, und dass sich die alte Verbundenheit nicht mehr lösen lässt. Ich bin froh darum aber ich werde es Ihnen doch hie und da sagen müssen, wenn es mit der Freundlichkeit allein nicht getan ist.

Die praktische Mitwirkung im Schütz hat mir gezeigt, dass unsere Zusammenarbeit, auch heute noch, so weit nicht gehen kann. Wir sind im Musizieren zu verschieden. Ihre Aktivität in den Proben, aber erst recht im Konzert macht bei mir einfach etwas Schönes kaputt und ich muss mich fast übermenschlich anstrengen um ruhig zu bleiben. Ich hoffte

The difference in their approaches to music-making once again was dissected. Instead of insisting on quitting this time, however, she refered to the fact that they had decided that their cooperation can no longer be called into question. Rather than just suffering the consequences, she wrote about the difficulties, saying that she would pick out pieces for the proper of the mass to be performed in conjunction with Monteverdi's ordinary, so that he can rehearse it all himself with the Basel Chamber Choir.

She nonetheless went on to speak also of the amount of work required to carry out that which was demanded of her, reminding him that he had said that an average of 12 hours/week should be enough for her work for him. She reported that since September, with the evaluation of scores, the preparation of Schütz and Idomeneo – discovering it would not work as conceived, and searching out something that would – could hardly be done in less than twice that much time. In addition, her 17 hours at the Schola were all different and needed about 12 hours of preparation and correction of assignments. And if she did other things in addition, it was because she wanted to do a bit of performing. She even enclosed a budget she had made, being concerned about her own extravagance, pointing out that it showed her that she actually had need of the extra bits of income. Of course, she included it *not* because she was seeking a raise, but only to demonstrate that the outside jobs were not pure luxury. Thus, although she still found it necessary to establish limits in her work for him, her argumentation was on a less emotional plane.

Another noteworthy event of the year was her participation in a concert on 25 May 1954, organized by August Wenzinger, for a performance of a Dufay mass with a proper for Trinity. It involved a complete cornucopia of the foremost musicians active in the field of early music at that time, as not only did the *Ensemble für Kirchenmusik* take part, but also the Alfred Deller consort; Christopher Schmidt, recorder; Fritz Hartmann, English horn (!); Emil Rudin, trombone; Otto Steinkopf, dulcian; Marianne Majer, fiddle; Hannelore Müller and Johannes Koch, viola da gamba; Fritz Wörsching, lute; with August Wenzinger responsible for the whole. Christopher Schmidt recalled that she pre-

---

auf das Abhören vom Band um vielleicht doch etwas von der inneren Ruhe zu merken. Aber es schien mir dann noch viel schlimmer. Dazu kam, dass Sie gerade an dem Tag soviel Vitalität, Aktivität mitbrachten, dass das wirkliche 'Zuhören' fast unmöglich war. Das sind für mich Leidensmomente. Und als Sie mir dann den Bäck, von dem Sie wussten und eben noch gehört hatten, dass er mir schön und lieb ist, so erbarmungslos und kalt aburteilten, da gab es dann wieder 'Scherben'". Letter Ina Lohr to Paul Sacher of 6 January 1954, private collection, Switzerland.

pared all of the students for the performance, and suspects that she also worked with Alfred Deller, as he was open to this sort of input for music of which he had little knowledge.[123]

As her health was very poor during the summer, she decided to take a leave of absence until mid-October. In spite of this, Paul Sacher wrote on 15 September 1954 requesting that she mark in some trills in four Handel arias for a recording with a singer who was untrained in such matters. She had, however, sufficient strength of mind to delay her answer for almost two weeks. And even then, on 26 September 1954, she replied tersely that it was "unfortunately not yet possible. I will still desperately need the last 3 weeks in order to able to take up work again *with pleasure*. I could not do that up until now. But you know the trills at the cadences just as well as I; you could in any case put them in".[124] This is the first time in their correspondence that she has refused to do such work, has refused to let her vacation time be taken up with work for Paul Sacher.

The following season seems to have been a quiet year on all fronts, with few courses and student recitals, although she was still quite active with the *Ensemble für Kirchenmusik*. For the continuation of her legacy in Basel, however, it was an important year, as Arthur Eglin, a printer by training, and a musician by vocation, joined the *Hausmusik* program. Although he apparently had difficulties integrating himself within the Schola, he was one of Ina Lohr's truest devotees, carrying on her mission of creating small groups of lay people with which one made music, with voices and instruments.[125] In 1957 he assumed the leadership of the *Stadtposaunenchor Basel* (Trombone Choir of the City of Basel) and in 1965, that of the *Ökomenischer Singkreis Basel* (Ecumenical Singing Circle Basel). To this end, he made use of his talents as a printer to prepare music in the form of piano reductions for both the choir and trombones, enabling them to perform together, and providing them with a wider range of literature from earlier centuries than generally available at the time.

---

123 Interview with Christopher Schmidt of 19 October 2013.
124 "Leider geht es noch nicht. Ich werde die letzten 3 Wochen noch dringend brauchen um die Arbeit gern wieder auf zunehmen. Das könnte ich jetzt noch nicht. Die Triller an den Kadenzen wissen Sie aber so genau wie ich; die könnten Sie auf alle Fälle einsetzen". Letter Ina Lohr to Paul Sacher of 26 September 1955, private collection, Switzerland.
125 Interview with Christopher Schmidt of 8 August 2017.

The 1955/56 school year was equally tranquil, although the documentation allows greater insight into her activities in that year. Her normal teaching load was reduced slightly that year because Julius Schweizer, a professor of theology, gave a two-semester introduction into the liturgy of the Swiss Reformed Church. As usual, she gave numerous extra courses and the *Ensemble für Kirchenmusik* participated in diverse events. Perhaps one of the most spectacular was the musical accompaniment for the return of the early 14th-century reliquary bust of St. Ursula – which had been auctioned off from the Treasury of the Basel Cathedral in 1836 – to the Basel Historical Museum on 17 September 1955. In a letter of 30 September 1955, Paul Sacher reported that Dr. Christoph Bernoulli was so taken by the performance, that he wondered whether the group would be prepared to perform an additional benefit concert, which they did on 20 November 1955.[126]

The eager presence of Henk Waardenburg, however, was of great significance to her, particularly in retrospect, as he was the last person to ever receive a degree in *Hausmusik* from the Schola. Over the years, he has remained an enthusiastic supporter of the concept of *Hausmusik* and has never stopped teaching it since returning to the Netherlands. He said that he and his cousin Wim Waardenburg, who had preceded him to Basel and also taught in Amerfoort, had similar ideas about how to teach *Hausmusik*, of how one had the individuals sit in a circle, how one chose the pieces, how one let a piece come into existence. One started with the outer structural voices, adding in the others, getting people to listen rather than to merely count. He reported that there are no more "Spielgruppen" today, they are all "ensembles", because "Spielgruppen" are too amateurish. For him, *Hausmusik* was something very normal, that he had already experienced with Wim Waardenburg and Jan Boeke. The concept behind *Hausmusik* was the playing with one another, not as a set ensemble, and not according to what the conductor says. Ina Lohr, in comparison, spoke more about how and why one did things than he does.[127]

He spoke of his great gratitude for her work, saying that he had to thank her for his entire life. He had begun to study school music in the Netherlands and then shifted to *Hausmusik* and gone to Basel. He would have otherwise become a math teacher, as he didn't have the necessary musical skills. He nonetheless

126 Carbon copy of letter Paul Sacher to Ina Lohr of 30 September 1955, private collection, Switzerland.
127 All information concerning his experiences stems from two interviews, on 15 December 2014 and 9 April 2015.

felt the need to ask me the same question again and again, "But what did I really learn from Ina Lohr?" As so many others, he found it almost impossible to express the effect of her teaching – on his work as well as on his life – in words.

Her cooperation with Paul Sacher seems also to have run very smoothly in this year, with many references to evaluating scores and discussing questions of programming. One example, where Ina Lohr brought in own personal experiences, was in regard to Willy Burkhard's chorale, "Ich liege, Herr, in deiner Hut" (1939), where the conductor expressed his displeasure in the fact that the dynamic markings for each strophe had not been included. Ina Lohr responded in detail on the following day, 20 August 1955:

> I fought a vain battle with the dynamic markings in the chorale by Willy Burkhard. It speaks for the composition as a congregational hymn that it does not tolerate any intentional dynamics. The whole song is a quiet reflection that only emerges from the text. If variety is needed for the concert, I only see the possibility of alternating between unisono and four parts. But that would be very good! Or, if you would prefer:
> Str.   1 four-part
>   2 two-part with some of the men's voices
>   3 two-part with some of the women's voices
> Str.   4 four-part.
> The two-part setting is found in a well-known songbook, *Mein Lied,* which I have 5x. I do not particularly like the setting, but Burkhard liked it. We sang it on the Sunday, 10 days before he died in Boldern.[128]

Paul Sacher then replied on 22 August 1955, wondering whether it might be nice to double the voices with the woodwinds.

The programming for the 1956/57 season also was quite peaceful. Noteworthy was a remark in a letter of 15 August 1956 where she expressed her concern

128 "Mit den dynamischen Zeichen im Choral von Willy Burkhard habe ich einen vergeblichen Kampf geführt. Es spricht für die Komposition als Gemeindelied, dass sie keine beabsichtigte Dynamik verträgt. Das ganze Lied ist eine stille Besinnung, die sich nur aus dem Text ergibt. Wenn für das Konzert eine Abwechslung nötig ist, so sehe ich nur die Möglichkeit vom Wechsel einstimmig-vierstimmig. Die wäre aber sehr gut! Oder, wenn Sie das lieber wollen:
Str.   1 vierstimmig
         2 zweistimmig einige Männerstimmen
         3 zweistimmig einige Frauenstimmen
Str.   4 vierstimmig
Der zweistimmige Satz steht in einem recht verbreiteten Liederbuch 'Mein Lied', das ich 5x besitze. Ich finde den Satz nicht sehr gut, Burkhard hat ihn aber gern gehabt. Wir sangen ihn an dem Sonntag 10 Tage vor seinem Tod auf Boldern". Letter Ina Lohr to Paul Sacher of 20 August 1955 and carbon copies of letters Paul Sacher to Ina Lohr of 19 and 22 August 1955, private collection, Switzerland.

that someone younger might be more suitable for the evaluation of the most recent compositions:

> Unfortunately, I have real difficulties imagining the music of the really recent compos-ers. I would have to hear them much more frequently. But when and how?! Shouldn't you really have a younger lector for this work? Not because I want to "get out" of it, but because you would be better served by it. I feel as if I were reading a book in a for-eign language and am only just able to guess what is going on. Then perhaps my judg-ment will be very unfair.[129]

I suspect that she is not the only musician for whom this is true. But what is perhaps more important to recognize here, is that while she is acknowledging her limitations, she is also confirming that she has fulfilled this job for him up until that point.

The 30th anniversary of the BKO was celebrated on 25 January 1957 with a con-cert of George Fridric Handel's *Music for the Royal Fireworks* and Michel Rich-ard de Lalande's *Te Deum*. For the latter she once again prepared the score and parts, adding in the ornamentation, complaining that this was "kilometer work" but was part of the job.[130] She then met with the soloists in Paul Sach-er's office where "they all eagerly took 'lessons' for trills, even for interpreta-tion, but I was exhausted and again convinced that I do not belong in the con-cert world".[131] On 22 January, she went to a rehearsal and found that the praise did not come out enough, [that it was] too "diligent and earnest, so that I once again became really intolerable and that towards P.S.! That's deplorable because it is not their *fault*, but their *lack*. But [the barritone] Pierre Mollet knows something of it, he also suffers from 'routine singing'".[132] Apparently her out-burst, however had an effect, for on the following day she reported that "when

---

129 "Leider fällt es mir doch sehr schwer mir die Musik der wirklich Jungen vorzustellen. Ich müsste sie viel mehr hören. Aber wann und wie?! Sollten Sie nicht doch einen jungen Lek-tor für diese Arbeit haben? Nicht, weil ich mich 'drücken' will, sondern weil Ihnen besser gedient wäre. Ich fühle mich, alsob [sic] ich ein Buch in einer Fremdsprache lesen würde und nur gerade ahnen kann um was es geht. Da wird das Urteil vielleicht sehr ungerecht". Letter Ina Lohr to Paul Sacher of 15 August 1956, private collection, Switzerland.

130 Diary entry of 2 January 1957, PSF-ILC.

131 "Ze namen alle 'lessen' voor trillers, zelfs voor interpretatie zelfs gretig aan, maar ik was geslagen en weer overtuigd, dat ik niet in het concertleven hoor". Diary entry of 5 January 1957, PSF-ILC.

132 "Een repetitie voor het Te Deum van Lalande was zoo weinig lovend, zoo vlijtig en braaf, dat ik er weer eens echt onverdraagzaam van werd en wel tegen over P.S! Dat is erg, want het is niet hun schuld, maar hun gemis. Maar Pierre Mollet weet er iets van ook hij lijdt aan 'routinezingen'". Diary entry of 22 January 1957, PSF-ILC.

P.S. came this afternoon, he had not only overcome his anger about my walking out of the rehearsal, but he had even understood it, at least partially. And he has discovered that the work concerned is a *Te Deum*, not a piece of music that might or might not be beautiful which is primarily in D major".[133] It also apparently impressed the singers, in that some of them came to her classes in the following days. She had the sense finally, in the second concert, that some of the sense of praise came through, "at least P.S. and I felt it that way and celebrated the 30-year existence of the BKO with gratitude".[134] This vignette sheds light on the interactions between Paul Sacher and Ina Lohr, gives some insight into where their battles lay, but also why they found work with one another interesting and satisfying.

At the end of the school year, on 26 and 27 June 1957, Henk Waardenburg took and passed his exam in *Hausmusik*. He recalled that before the exams he had discovered a volume of Victoria lying around in room 6, where the exams were to be held. He began practicing from it, not knowing whether it had been left there on purpose. Ina Lohr then chose from it for the exam and as a result he did all right on it. When asked about the composer, however, he dissembled and suggested that it might be Palestrina or one of his contemporaries.[135] As this degree was the last one of its kind awarded by the Schola, it represented the passing of an era.

With this, of course, also came the waning of Ina Lohr's influence at the Schola. The growing desire of early music musicians throughout the world of attaining the status of professional musicians, of detaching themselves from any whiff of amateurism, led to *Hausmusik* – and all it represented – being treated with disdain. This redefinition of "early music" came together with the aging of all those involved in the Schola's founding. Concern was beginning to develop about the future of the Schola and the direction it might take, with new allegiances being forged and others disbanded. At the same time, it was just beginning to become evident that if the school were to survive, its entire ethos, curriculum would have to be renewed. All of this led to Ina Lohr beginning to feel increasingly threatened, or out of place within the institution.

---

133 "Toen P.S. vanmiddag kwam, had hij niet alleen zijn boosheid over mijn weglopen uit de repetitie overwonnen, maar hij had het zelfs, tenminste gedeeltelijk begrepen. En hij heeft ontdekt, dat het om een Te Deum gaat, niet om een al of niet mooie muziek, die voornamelijk in D dur staat". Diary entry of 23 January 1957, PSF-ILC.

134 "En ieder geval hebben P.S. en ik het zoo gevoeld en het 30jarig bestaan van het B.K.O. in dankbaarheid gevierd". Diary entry of 25 January 1957, PSF-ILC.

135 Interview with Henk Waardenburg of 15 December 2014.

Chapter 7. A Time of Transition: 1957–70

7.1 Diverging of Paths within the Schola

Almost from its beginnings, two aspects of the nascent early music movement joined together in the Schola: that of the *Singbewegung*, represented by Ina Lohr with her interest in furthering music in lay circles; and that of the drive towards professionalization which came to prevail in the second half of the 20th century as represented by August Wenzinger. One expression of this division may be seen in Ina Lohr's decision to leave the concert group after only two years to concentrate on her teaching of amateurs. Thus, while she was building up the internal pedagogical aspect of the school, August Wenzinger was creating the public image of the Schola through concerts with his gamba consort as well as the concert group. This compromise functioned exceedingly well in the early days, in that it corresponded with the strengths and interests of those concerned. Indeed, on a certain level – if we take Ina Lohr's and Paul Sacher's appellation of their cooperation as a "musical marriage" seriously – the participation of two such disparate personalities in the Schola might be classified as a "marriage of convenience". It became, however, increasingly fragile after the war, as young cognoscenti of early music came to aspire to the standard of technical excellence of professional proponents of the modern instruments, rejecting the *Hausmusik* approach wholesale, with its inclusion of amateurs and focus on the function of the musical work. In spite of the many critical remarks about the diplomas for *Hausmusik* at the teachers' conferences during that period, the immediate impact of this new mode of thinking at the Schola was limited. It appears to have been dampened by the influx of the large number of excellent students from abroad whose prime teacher was Ina Lohr, perhaps to the hidden chagrin of August Wenzinger. In addition, through her workshops in Holland and work with theology students in Basel, Ina Lohr was feeling increasingly secure and happy in her chosen role within the church. Thus, it is a question of one's frame of reference, as to whether she later came to be seen as isolating herself, or merely found herself in increasing isolation, due to the fact that she did not adapt to the changes in the society around her. Walter Nef clearly was of the former opinion, as is evident from his letter of 4 September 1966:

> The main problem for the SCB lies for me in the fact that it for years has no longer had a center. We had the good fortune to be able to begin with a twofold center: Ina Lohr for theory and church music, August Wenzinger for instrumental music and concerts. Both worked together at the beginning, everything was connected together. In-

creasingly I.L. isolated herself and placed herself in opposition to everybody else, even
to me, and left, without a replacement. For A.W. teaching has long since only been a
marginal activity, he is in his element with concert activities, and he will also go one
day without a successor.[1]

What emerges from this is that there was nobody at the Schola in the 1950s and
1960s to give the institution a dramatic new set of bearings for the changing
cultural environment in which they found themselves.

The original equilibrium was lastingly upset by the employment of Hans-Martin Linde (b. 1930) – who could not possibly have had any premonition of the
difficulties that would ensue – as a recorder teacher at the Schola in 1957.[2] The
source of his training and inspiration on the flute was Gustav Scheck, Kon-
rad Lechner that for choir conducting and composition, both of whom taught
at the Conservatory in Freiburg in Breisgau. His first encounter with August
Wenzinger was at a musicological conference in Cologne. The gambist immediately invited him to participate in the concert associated with it. This led to a
further concert in Düren with the SCB gamba consort, in which he played the
Telemann A minor Suite with gamba accompaniment. This in turn gave rise to
August Wenzinger's declaration: "We need you in Basel!"

An interview with Paul Sacher was then arranged and he was invited, as a
trial, to give a recital at the Schola for the directors and teachers on 21 March
1957, in which he played works of Loeillet, Telemann, Barsanti on recorder and
C.P.E. Bach, Mozart and Henze on flute, accompanied on harpsichord and
piano by Valerie Kägi. On the following day, he met Ina Lohr and Elli Rohr in a
local restaurant, where, according to him, Ina Lohr was reassured to learn that he
was a Lutheran minister's son, had played lots of *Hausmusik,* and that he could
also sing. Shortly thereafter he played the 4th Brandenburg (in which he had to
play the first four measures of the second recorder part for Valerie Kägi, as she
found the high f‴s in them too difficult) in a FAMB concert on 14 June 1957.

1   "Das Hauptproblem für die SCB besteht für mich darin, dass sie seit Jahren kein Zentrum
     mehr hat. Wir haben das Glück gehabt, mit einem doppelten Zentrum beginnen zu kön-
     nen: Ina Lohr für Theorie und Kirchenmusik, August Wenzinger für das Instrumentale
     und die Konzerte. Beide haben zunächst zusammengearbeitet, alles war aufeinander bezo-
     gen. I.L. hat sich mehr und mehr isoliert und zu allen andern in Gegensatz gestellt, auch
     zu mir, und ist ohne Nachfolger(in) weggegangen. Für A.W. ist der Unterricht längst eine
     Randerscheinung, er geht im Konzertbetrieb auf, und auch er wird einmal ohne Nachfol-
     ger gehen". Letter Walter Nef to Paul Sacher of 4 September 1966, PSF-PSC.
2   All information about Hans-Martin Linde's first years at the Schola stems from an inter-
     view of 5 August 2013. I am grateful for the fact that he was willing to speak so openly about
     his experiences.

Ina Lohr was still able to perceive the situation somewhat dispassionately two months later, as is made evident in a letter of 3 August 1957 to Paul Sacher, by a passage dealing with the programming for the BKO in which she suggested that

> It would be good to introduce Linde as the person who he actually is: the recorder player who is bringing the instrument – with the music of the 18th century – completely into our times. That is what you are also, of necessity, doing with both orchestras and what Wenzinger is increasingly doing. In the long run the SCB will also have to do this. Nef and I are the only ones who still consciously experience early music from the viewpoint of the epoch concerned and who wish to place it *vis-a-vis* contemporary music. Perhaps this is already obsolete.[3]

This is most likely in reference to her desire to have music be heard in the context that it was originally conceived (cf. pp. 87–88). The specific program they were contemplating, however, then went in a completely different direction, so that it was not until 19 May 1961 that Hans-Martin Linde played the Vivaldi concerto in C minor with the BKO. But already on 14 October 1957, he was given the opportunity of introducing himself musically at the Musik-Akademie Basel with a program of chamber music involving the recorder, together with August Wenzinger, Hannelore Müller and Valerie Kägi.

And finally, it can be read in the minutes of the teachers' conference of 28 February 1958, in a passage which almost certainly reflected Paul Sacher's attempts at integrating him within the institution, that

> with Mr. Linde a new element has come to the SCB. As a wind player, he is primarily interested in his instrument. Therefore, his instruction will be different from that customary at the SCB. It is to be hoped that Mr. Linde will find time in order to get to know all of the efforts that have been pursued up until now at the SCB. His instruction is something complete in itself, and a supplement to that customary at the SCB. Difficulties may perhaps reveal themselves in the instruction of the aspiring primary school teachers, who desire to be introduced more to pedagogical aspects than solely to the technique of playing the instrument. Mr. Linde is very nice and amenable as a person. It was decided that Mr. Linde be recommended [to the directors] for a fixed position.[4]

---

3 "Es wäre doch gut den Linde vorzustellen auch als den, der er eigentlich ist: den Blockflötenspieler, der das Instrument mit der Musik des 18. Jhdts. ganz in unsere Zeit hereinholt. Das ist, was Sie mit beiden Orchestern notgedrungen auch machen und was Wenzinger immer mehr macht. Die SCB wird auf die Dauer das auch machen müssen. Nef und ich sind die einzigen, die ganz bewusst alte Musik ganz aus der jeweiligen Epoche erleben und sie der heutigen Musik **gegenüber** stellen möchten. Vielleicht ist das schon überholt". Letter Ina Lohr to Paul Sacher of 3 August 1957, private collection, Switzerland.

4 "Mit Herrn Linde ist ein neues Element an die SCB gekommen. Als Bläser interessiert er sich in erster Linie für sein Instrument. Darum wird sein Unterricht sehr verschieden sein von dem an der SCB gebräuchlichen. Es ist zu hoffen, dass Herr Linde die Zeit findet, um alle Bestrebungen, die bisher an der SCB verfolgt wurden, kennen zu lernen. Sein Unterricht ist etwas ganz für sich Bestehendes und eine Ergänzung zu dem an der SCB gebräuch-

Very soon after Hans-Martin Linde began teaching, however, difficulties arose with Ina Lohr stemming from their differences in approach. On hearing him accompany his students in a student recital, she not only objected to his pupil's virtuosity, but also to the ornamentation in Hans-Martin Linde's own continuo playing and had no inhibitions in expressing such criticisms openly. Troubled by this difficult situation, he went directly to Paul Sacher and complained that she was spreading rumors about the poor quality of his teaching and accompanying, speaking of things of which she could have no personal experience. Paul Sacher suggested that he simply question her about her motives. Although Hans-Martin Linde could not really conceive of doing something so outside the traditional bounds of etiquette, he gathered up his courage and placed the question. As a result, this specific manifestation of the internal dissension within the Schola stopped. It did not prevent this dissension from taking on other forms, however. One of the more absurd, if you take into account how much contemporary music Ina Lohr had not only discussed, but also performed with her students in the post-war years, was her objection that he was working on such music with his students. This led to a conversation between the flautist and Paul Sacher, in which the latter called the performance of a piece by Helmut Bornefeld (1906–1990) in a student recital into question. Hans-Martin Linde, however, defended his choice, saying that the work was of high quality. It was then decided contemporary works of high musical quality could be performed at the Schola, with Paul Sacher laying down the line in the teachers' conference of 18 June 1960, claiming that "it is conceivable that an entire student recital might consist of modern recorder music, so that the students get to know this literature. As there are apparently no good pieces with harpsichord accompaniment, good ones with piano accompaniment should be presented".⁵

Far more serious, however, was the effect that such battles between colleagues had upon the students, particularly upon those who were lacking self-assurance. They remained constantly torn between the demands of loyalty placed

---

lichen. Schwierigkeiten können sich eventuell ergeben im Unterricht an Lehramtskandidaten, die mehr in die Methodik als in die reine Spieltechnik eingeführt werden möchten. Herr Linde ist als Mensch sehr nett und zugänglich. Es wird beschlossen, Herrn Linde zur festen Anstellung vorzuschlagen". Minutes of the teachers' conference of 28 February 1958, PSF-PSC.

5   "Es ist denkbar, eine ganze Vortragsstunde mit moderner Blockflötenmusik zu füllen, damit die Schüler diese Literatur kennen lernen. Da es offenbar aber keine guten Stücke mit Cembalobegleitung gibt, soll lieber Gutes mit Klavierbegleitung geboten werden". Minutes of the teachers' conference of 18 June 1960, PSF-PSC.

upon them, limiting not only what they learned, but also diminishing their own self-confidence. In this time period, until Ina Lohr decided to retire from teaching professional students, only those who were strong enough to maintain their own sense of identity in conflicted situations and retain their awareness of what they wanted to learn, emerged from the experience relatively unscathed. But the tensions were evident to all. Symptomatic for this is Ina Lohr's apology to Paul Sacher, on 17 April 1958, for the dissension at the end of their meeting on the previous day: it seemed more difficult than ever to her to find a place in the official Schola world.[6] In all of this, it must be emphasized that no single person was responsible for this sudden worsening of relationships within the institution. It was much more that the very precarious balance between the various forces had been suddenly upset through situations of conflict caused by the advent of someone from the outside who was carrying out his job in line with his personal musical ideals, just as all the others were. Ina Lohr thereby suddenly saw herself being challenged in the one place in her professional life that she had felt relatively secure and reacted accordingly. Rather than leading to the reinstatement of her power, it generated further disruption, causing her in the end to decide to retire from teaching at the professional level at an earlier date than she had probably originally intended, feeling that there was no more room for her at the Schola.

Seen from the outside, however, things seemed to continue normally. Her students participated in recitals, she taught four courses on church music together with various pastors, and gave various lectures, the most prominent of which was for the board of the Swiss Music Teachers Association on "Recorder Pedagogy on the Basis of Solmization" on 2 March 1958. The *Ensemble für Kirchenmusik*, however, only performed on four occasions that year.

It may have been a result of the increased tensions within the Schola that she began to look more seriously for a small vacation apartment on the Lake of Lucerne as a regular retreat, in the hopes of more frequently being able to avail herself of the quiet and isolation she required in order to stay on an even emotional keel. That summer she stayed in Kehrsiten, a village directly on the lake, which also proffered her the wide views she so cherished. It was also an environment conducive to work, as can be seen from her letters to Paul Sacher, in

---

6   "Es ist mir leid, dass wir am letzten Mittwoch so im Missverständnis auseinander gingen. Im jetztigen [sic] 'Zustand' fällt es mir schwerer als je, mich in die offizielle Scholawelt hineinzufinden". Letter Ina Lohr to Paul Sacher of 17 April 1958, private collection, Switzerland.

which she spoke of studying and marking up scores, considered programming suggestions and also described concerts of modern music. And it was there that she once again decided to become practically involved in a BKO concert, in that she agreed to sing in the angels' choir in Schütz's Christmas Oratorio on 12 December 1958.

For her, the most momentous event of the year by far – particularly because it was connected to her instruction of theological students and her work in the church – must have been the awarding of an honorary doctorate for her work by the University of Basel:

> The department of theology of Basel has awarded Ina Lohr an honorable doctorate because she […] devoted herself to the study of earlier music for the church and, in particular, has significantly promoted the understanding of the Protestant hymn; because she, thanks to her broad knowledge, has influenced the liturgical-musical life of our congregations in a substantial manner; because she has concerned herself with great pedagogical skill to the education of Basel theological students in church music.[7]

The fact that Paul Sacher, Ina Lohr and August Wenzinger all received honorary doctorates from the university is a reflection of the degree of importance lent to the activities of the BKO and SCB in cultural and academic circles within the city. In spite of all of the difficulties throughout the years between the SCB and the university, the contacts stemming from the initial encounters in Karl Nef's seminar remained unbroken, as may be seen by the regular performances of the BKO at the annual *Dies academicus* ceremonies, in which Schola faculty members frequently took part. The honorary doctorates may be seen as a public expression of gratitude for their cultural contributions to the city.

Her teaching went on more or less as usual, albeit, as in the year before, with only a few outside courses and concerts with the *Ensemble für Kirchenmusik*. Also, the course she gave in Amersfoort in October (cf. p. 307) was limited to a single day instead of the weekend courses she had been wont to give in the past. Further, Hans-Martin Linde now took over the majority of students from the courses for aspiring primary school teachers. Nonetheless, there were various

---

7   "Die Theologische Fakultät von Basel hat Ina Lohr zum Ehrendoktor ernannt, weil sie sich […] der Erforschung der alten Kirchenmusik mit Hingabe gewidmet und insbesondere das Verständnis des evangelischen Kirchenliedes wesentlich gefördert hat; weil sie dank ihren weitreichenden Kenntnissen auf das liturgisch-musikalische Leben unserer Gemeinden massgebend einwirkt; weil sie mit grossem pädagogischen Geschick um die kirchenmusikalische Ausbildung unserer Basler Theologiestudenten besorgt ist". W.N., "Der Dies academicus der Universität Basel", in: *Basler Nachrichten* 29./30. November 1958.

highlights: a recording in the Basel radio studio for Radio Hilversum on "Singing in the Church in Switzerland"; participation in a service for the Women's World Day of Prayer in the Church of St. Martin; and finally, she was responsible for the event of 26 April 1959 within the Protestant Week of the Church of St. Elisabeth "Ihr seid das Salz der Erde!"

The lattermost was a "sociodrama" in which a series of sketches dealing with questionable moral behavior was presented with both sung and spoken Biblical commentaries. Throughout her professional life, Ina Lohr wrote a number of such plays for amateur groups, frequently church congregations or school classes or, upon request, provided the music for such works. In this one, she was actively supported in the performance by Arthur Eglin on trumpet, as we know from a letter of 15 March 1959.[8] In examining the work, we can see how she cleverly managed to manipulate her compositional style to accommodate the difference in musical ability and experience (see Ill. 7.1). The instrumental ritornello is highly chromatic and tonally ambiguous. The opening of the upper part suggests B minor, but this is immediately called into question by the syncopated b-flat in the second voice. The phrase ends in the middle of m. 3, perhaps in D minor, only to be immediately followed by its inversion ending in a sounding A major. The motive is taken up in its original form again, this time in E minor and then expanded, with a redoubling of the motive from m. 2, to land in B-flat major. Although the individual lines of the entire section are seemingly simple melodically, it requires considerable musicianship to perform it. The singers were presented their beginning notes on a platter, as they could just take over the final b-flat of the instrumental introduction. The vocal parts themselves are easy to sing, although in the context with the others some notable dissonances are created, for example, the diminished chord on b at the conclusion of the second part, before the da capo. The tonal ambiguity, also evident in this section, as exemplified by the move from B-flat major to this diminished chord, is a reflection of the sense of loss of orientation expressed by the text: "For the Son of man is come to seek and to save that which was lost" (Luke 19, 10). This work is illustrative of the degree to which her compositions were determined by her knowledge of who would be performing them. This was by no means "abstract music", but music written for a very specific function, from both the practical and spiritual perspectives.

As a respite from the stresses of that school year, she spent most of the summer again in Kehrsiten, among other things working hard – as one can tell from the considerable correspondence – on the programming for the 1960/61

8 Both letter and music were generously placed at my disposal by Arthur Eglin, Basel.

Ill. 7.1: Ina Lohr, "Des Menschen Sohn ist gekommen" from *Ihr seid das Salz*. Reproduction: collection of Arthur Eglin, Basel.

BKO season, as ever weighing off the advantages of one piece or order against another. In addition, she was preparing the material for the upcoming season, such as the Suite in D minor by Georg Muffat for the concert of 19 February 1960.[9] Her markings in this suite are particularly interesting, in that they not only reflect her original intentions, but also later decisions by Paul Sacher (see Ill. 7.2), either made alone or in discussion with her. For both of these pieces

---

9   Carbon copy of letter Paul Sacher to Ina Lohr of 13 July 1959, private collection, Switzerland.

Ill. 7.1: (continued)

Ill. 7.2: Georg Muffat, Suite No. 3, D minor, from the *Florilegium Primum (1695)*. Reproduction: PSF-PSC.

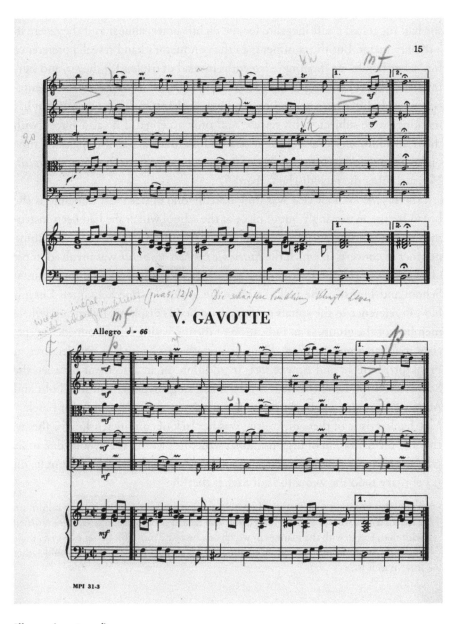

Ill. 7.2: (continued)

she had suggested a soft inegalité for the eighth notes, almost as if they were in a ternary meter. But the comments in the conductor's hand reveal a preference for "schwebende" or "floating" sixteenths instead of triplets for the air, and stating that a sharper dotting in the gavotte sounds better. The written documentation of such differences in opinion is telling, in that it makes it obvious that her markings were subject to his review, and only accepted if he also agreed with them. In addition, she also made it clear to him that she was also spending time on her own work, writing another of her numerous articles for *Singt und spielt*, "Versuch über die melodische Gebärde".[10]

The 1959/60 school year was undoubtedly one of her most difficult, as she began feeling increasingly out of place at the school which she had been instrumental in founding and developing. This can be seen in part at the declining number of concerts in which the *Ensemble für Kirchenmusik* was involved, most of which were part of a series of student recitals entitled "Music for Church, School and House". The nickname for the group, "Schneckentanteli Ensemble", in reference to the spirals of pinned-up braids displayed by certain female members of the group, is an indication of the increasing lack of outside acceptance for that group in Basel. She was nonetheless invited to give lectures in Frankfurt, Utrecht and Amersfoort. In addition, in an agreement between the Schola and Prof. Leo Schrade from the musicology departement, Ina Lohr and August Wenzinger taught the collegium musicum at the University of Basel.

Characteristic of these difficulties was her lack of comprehension for the increasing formalization of organizational structures within the Schola, due to its growth and to its being part of a larger subsidized institution. For example, on 11 February 1960 she wrote to Paul Sacher that she

> really does not want to be among those who get a guaranteed contract with a minimum fixed salary. I earn more than enough and will have a good pension. I am very satisfied with that, less so with the manner in which our institute must, for better or worse, present itself to the world. I therefore no longer wish to commit myself and would rather leave it as it is.[11]

---

10 Ina Lohr, "Versuch über die melodische Gebärde", in: *Singt und spielt* 27 (1960), 34–41. Letter from Ina Lohr to Paul Sacher of 12 August 1959, private collection, Switzerland.

11 "ich möchte wirklich lieber nicht zu denen gehören, die eine feste Anstellung mit Fixum bekommen. Ich verdiene mehr als genug und werde eine rechte Pension haben. Damit bin ich sehr zufrieden, weniger mit der Art, wie sich unser Institut wohl oder übel nach aussen zeigen muss. Darum möchte ich mich nicht mehr verpflichten und es lieber lassen, wie es jetzt ist". Letter Ina Lohr to Paul Sacher of 11 February 1960, private collection, Switzerland.

Paul Sacher ignored this request, placing higher priority on her receiving a regular income and a good pension, particularly in consideration of her poor state of health, than on her emotional sensibilities.

Her inner turmoil concerning the Schola is further revealed by a letter written a few days later, on 27 February 1960, by Walter Nef to Paul Sacher in which he describes some rather unpleasant conversations with Ina Lohr concerning

> the same problem as that from the first days of the SCB, but it has become more acute today. […] Miss Lohr says, among other things, that she will now definitively give up the collegium musicum [at the University], she will not even give the last lesson on the coming Wednesday. She will communicate her resignation to Prof. Schrade immediately. […] The collegium musicum is purely a matter of prestige. Also, the recorder courses for aspiring primary school teachers are only a matter of prestige.[12]

One gets a sense of a cauldron of emotions gradually coming to a boil, first being ventilated by little bursts of steam until the pot boils over. Judging from a letter of 12 May 1960 from Paul Sacher, something of the sort must have happened around that time:

> The injustice inflicted upon you is of imaginary nature. I am sorry that you tormented yourself with it. I am so open and loyal to you that there is really not the least reason for mistrust. Further, I am much too much indebted to you and I like you far too much & act accordingly. I always endeavor to help you & to proffer you the masculine protection that you are lacking since the death of your father [in 1948]. But your lively imagination often lets you see ghosts and your inflexible stubbornness leads you at times to an isolation, under which you suffer most – but your friends [suffer] with you.[13]

---

12 "Es dreht sich im Grunde immer um das gleiche Problem seit den ersten Tagen der SCB, aber es hat sich heute verschärft. […] Fräulein Lohr sagte unter anderem, das Collegium Musicum gebe sie endgültig auf, sie werde schon die letzte Stunde dieses Semesters am nächsten Mittwoch nicht mehr erteilen. Sie wolle ihren Rücktritt Prof. Schrade sofort mitteilen. […] Das Collegium Musicum sei eine reine Prestige-Angelegenheit. Auch die Blockflötenkurse für Primarlehramtskandidaten sei nur eine Prestige-Sache". Letter Walter Nef to Paul Sacher of 27 February 1960, PSF-PSC.

13 "das Ihnen zugefügte Unrecht ist imaginärer Natur. Es tut mir leid, dass Sie sich damit geplagt haben. Ich bin mit Ihnen so offen & loyal, dass wirklich nicht der geringste Grund für Misstrauen vorhanden ist. Ueber dies bin ich Ihnen viel zu dankbar & habe ich Sie viel zu gern & verhalte mich dementsprechend. Ich bin immer bestrebt Ihnen zu helfen & Ihnen den männlichen Schutz angedeihen zu lassen, den Sie seit dem Tod Ihres Vaters nicht mehr besitzen. Aber Ihre lebhafte Fantasie lässt Sie oft Gespenster sehen & Ihre starre Hartnäckigkeit führt Sie manchmal in eine Isolierung, unter der Sie am meisten, Ihre Freunde aber mit – leiden". Letter Paul Sacher to Ina Lohr of 12 May 1960, PSF-ILC.

Ina Lohr responded warmly, thanking him for the accompanying flowers,

> but still more for the very kind words! You know that such "shards" are so hurtful be-
> cause we are dependent on one another. And the more I admire your diplomatic ap-
> proach in the M.A. [Music Academy] (I know it would not work without diplomacy),
> the more I feel myself insecure in this institute. I will, however, try not to be mistrust-
> ful.[14]

Already in that letter, however, she apologized for her short scribble, as the act
of writing itself was physically painful. In the coming months things got worse:
both of her letters to Paul Sacher in July open with remarks about her new solutions for limiting the pain in her hand and arm while writing. In the first half
of the letter of 12 August 1960, which was typewritten, she spoke of how the
pain now seemed to have expanded its radius to include her right jaw. And by
19 August 1960 she sent a short note to say that she was now where she should
have been already awhile ago: in the hospital. He need no longer worry about
her.

Judging from her remarks three weeks later, her body collapsed under all of the
strains it was subjected to, from within and without. On 9 September 1960, she
explained to Paul Sacher how her sister Etty had visited her and was in total
agreement with the diagnosis, calling it a "manager illness". Another common
friend spoke of it as being a conductor's illnesss, "only far worse than with men".[15]
  That things were not quite as clear as this is revealed by a letter written to
Paul Sacher by Walter Nef on the same day:

> Yesterday I saw Miss Lohr for the first time in order to speak about the upcoming win-
> ter semester. She looks relaxed, the quiet, care and treatment in the hospital seem to be
> good for her. Both arms are still in bandages, but she can move her fingers, and a certain
> amount of progress seems to have been attained. Perhaps everything is nothing other
> than the consequence of years of overwork. But the type of illness remains quite unclear
> for outsiders (and maybe even for the doctors).[16]

14 "aber noch viel mehr für die sehr lieben Worte! Sie wissen es, dass solche 'Scherben' darum
    so verletzten, weil wir eben auf einander angewiesen sind. Und je mehr ich Ihr diplomati-
    sches Vorgehen in der M.A. bewundre (ich weiss, dass es ohne Diplomatie nicht ginge) um
    so mehr werde ich in diesem Institut unsicher. Ich werde aber versuchen kein Misstrauen
    aufkommen zu lassen". Undated letter Ina Lohr to Paul Sacher, private collection, Switzer-
    land.
15 "nur viel schlimmer als bei den Männern". Letter Ina Lohr to Paul Sacher of 9 September
    1960, private collection, Switzerland.
16 "Gestern sah ich zum erstenmal Fräulein Lohr, um mit ihr über das bevorstehende Win-
    tersemester zu sprechen. Sie sieht entspannt aus, die Ruhe, Pflege und Behandlung im Spi-
    tal scheinen ihr gut zu tun. Beide Arme sind noch eingebunden, aber die Finger kann sie
    bewegen, und es scheint ein gewisser Fortschritt erreicht zu sein. Vielleicht ist alles nichts

He went on to say that Ina Lohr was determined to resume her instruction at the Schola in the following year, perhaps with some reduction of her workload. As her return was still uncertain, he had also contemplated how one could deal with the situation if she needed a yet longer respite. He could see internal solutions for her ensemble classes and also for basso continuo. But he saw no substitution possibilities either within or without the SCB for her courses on Gregorian chant and Protestant church music. Indeed, finding a replacement for Ina Lohr was going to become one of the largest tasks faced by the Schola in the coming years.

Given these circumstances, it is not surprising that her activities were far reduced in the 1960/61 season, judging by the fact that she was only involved in four student recitals – three of which made up the entire activity of the *Ensemble für Kirchenmusik* for that year – and four external events involving a *Hausmusik* ensemble, including the traditional Christmas celebration for the radio. In addition, her correspondence with Paul Sacher about the BKO was limited. She did, however, teach her hymnology course at the University of Basel for the first time, where the response among the students was very positive. The few students who had her as a thesis adviser all remember her instruction enthusiastically, as being both inspiring and liberating.[17]

Her illness, together with her sense of alienation to what was going on at the Schola, obviously led her to consider the question of whether she wanted to continue to teach there. At times she must have felt that all of her principles were being called into question, as when she wrote to Hinrich Stoevesandt on 30 April 1961 that "here, i.e. at the Schola, church music has suddenly become a problem", saying that she let herself become unnecessarily upset by such things.[18] It is understandable that she should wonder why she should continue working at a school which she had helped to found, when all of a sudden those aspects of her teaching which she most valued were coming under fire.

This led to her resignation which Paul Sacher, after considerable inner struggle, announced at the teachers' conference on 25 June 1961.[19] She wrote Paul Sacher immediately after it was made public, saying that

anderes als die Folge jahrelanger Ueberanstrengung. Aber die Art der Krankheit bleibt für den Aussenstehenden (und vielleicht sogar für die Aerzte) recht undurchsichtig". Letter Walter Nef to Paul Sacher of 9 September 1960, PSF-PSC.

17 Various interviews with Hans-Jürg Stefan and that of 1 March 2016 with Peter Bürgi.

18 "Hier, d. h. an unserer Schola ist die Kirchenmusik plötzlich zum Problem geworden". Letter Ina Lohr to Hinrich Stoevesandt of 30 April 1961, Elisabeth Stoevesandt, Basel,

19 Letter Ina Lohr to Hinrich Stoevesandt of 25 June 1961, Elisabeth Stoevesandt, Basel.

last night, for the first time in a long time, I have once again slept very calmly. I am very thankful that you have now accepted and announced my resignation. Now we can prepare something and look with confidence into the future. It even appears possible to me now that I might even give some lessons afterward. But not for the professional students, but perhaps in the lay section.[20]

We are lucky to have her correspondence with Hinrich Stoevesandt, to whom she felt free to express her thoughts about the situation at the Schola – even obliged to, as his future wife was hoping to study with Ina Lohr – as he not only shared many of her views about the function of music in the church, but also her interest in contemporary Dutch theologians, in that he was translating the works of Kornelis Miskotte and Oepke Noordmans into German. Indirectly in this connection, she mentioned, in her letter of 2 July 1961, Sacher's similarity to Karl Barth:

> Whenever he says: "so that the church remains in the village" [a literal translation of an idiom meaning "we shouldn't get carried away"] (and he says it frequently), I ask myself whether he does not mean much more with it than he is now willing to admit. When I asked him what he was so fascinated by in Martinů's Greek Passion (the music is not at all modern), he said without hesitation: "the confession [of faith]. The Christ figure was Christ for him and, by the end, he had confessed [his faith] to him completely". For that reason also, church music shall remain a subject at the SCB: "the church shall remain in the village"![21]

Thus, for whatever reason, Paul Sacher stood by Ina Lohr in the question of whether church music should remain a part of the school curriculum. In the same letter, she declared she was increasingly "relieved that one was now speaking freely about her resignation and also [that one was] looking for a successor. Sacher seems transformed: he is making plans and wants to do everything

---

20 "Heute Nacht habe ich zum ersten Mal seit langer Zeit wieder ganz ruhig geschlafen. Ich bin Ihnen sehr dankbar dafür, dass Sie meinen Rücktritt nun angenommen und mitgeteilt haben. Jetzt können wir etwas vorbereiten und mit Vertrauen in die Zukunft schauen. Es scheint mir sogar wieder möglich, dass ich auch nachher noch einige Stunden geben würde. Nur nicht mehr an die Berufsschüler, ev. sogar an der Allgemeinen Abteilung". Undated letter Ina Lohr to Paul Sacher, private collection, Switzerland.

21 "Immer wenn er sagt: 'damit die Kirche im Dorf bleibt' (und er sagt das sehr oft), frage ich mich, ob er damit nicht viel mehr meint, als er jetzt gerade wahr haben will. Als ich ihn fragte, was ihn an Martinu's Griechische Passion so gefesselt habe (die Musik ist gar nicht modern), sagte er ohne zu zögern: 'das Bekenntnis. Die Christusfigur war für ihn Christus und er hat sich zuletzt ganz zu Ihm bekannt'. Darum soll die Kirchenmusik an der SCB als Fach auch bleiben: 'die Kirche soll im Dorf bleiben'!" Letter Ina Lohr to Hinrich Stoevesandt of 2 July 1961, Elisabeth Stoevesandt, Basel.

in order to have the instruction continue in the most similar manner possible".[22] She went on to say that she had written to Jan Boeke but did not think he would accept the job. David Kraehenbuehl was next on the list and only after he had been asked would a relatively unknown person, the organist Gerhard Aeschbacher, be invited to take over the position on the condition that he spend a year first learning her pedagogical method. She was relatively skeptical about this, thinking it unlikely that a mature musician would be willing to adapt himself to such a different approach.

In a letter of 13 August 1961, she communicated to Paul Sacher that Jan Boeke had turned down the offer:

> A wonderful letter came from Jan Boeke, but unfortunately a refusal. I regret it for us even more, as the letter shows again that he is really a personality with a sense of responsibility. For that reason, and also because he and his family are so utterly Dutch, he wants to remain in Amsterdam in the position that he likes so much. Will Leonhardt decide now in the same way? One can almost assume that from Boeke's letter. In any case, it is a very felicitous cooperation.[23]

The implication from this is that Gustav Leonhardt was also offered the job, but would probably also prefer to stay in the Netherlands and continue his collaboration with Jan Boeke. Ina Lohr went on to say that Elli Rohr had now completed a text on thorough bass and, as she had successfully taught the new professional students for a year, should be given that job, as it would take years until a Kraehenbuehl or Aeschbacher would have gained an overview of the material. She also wondered

> if we could not interest Linde more in our real concerns, if we were to give him the *Hausmusik* for professional students, the "sounding music history". You see, I return again and again to a division of the work, because I do not really see a "key figure".

22 "andererseits bin ich von Tag zu Tag mehr erleichtert, dass nun frei über meinen Rücktritt gesprochen und auch ein Nachfolger gesucht wird. Sacher ist wie verwandelt: er macht Pläne und will alles tun um den Unterricht möglichst in gleicher Art weiter zu führen". Letter Ina Lohr to Hinrich Stoevesandt of 2 July 1961, Elisabeth Stoevesandt, Basel.

23 "Von Jan Boeke kam ein grossartiger Brief, leider aber eine Absage. Ich bedaure es für uns um so mehr, da dieser Brief wieder zeigt, dass er wirklich eine Persönlichkeit ist mit Verantwortungsgefühl. Darum eben, und auch weil er und seine Familie so ausgesprochen holländisch sind, will er in Amsterdam auf dem Posten bleiben, den er sehr gerne einnimmt. Ob Leonhardt sich jetzt ähnlich entscheidet? Das kann man aus Boekes Brief fast verstehen. Auf alle Fälle ist das eine höchst gefreute Zusammenarbeit". Letter Ina Lohr to Paul Sacher of 13 August 1961, private collection, Switzerland.

Kraehenbuehl also has a pioneering project in Princeton which he will hardly relinquish. But you can ask him.[24]

From this, one can see that although she was retiring because she had come to feel out of place at the Schola, she wanted her legacy to continue, a vain hope given its lack of acceptance in the musical world around her.

She did, however, continue to receive support from within religious circles. Exemplary for this was her interaction with an American, Calvin Seerveld, whom she had probably originally met in the 1950s in Amsterdam, where he wrote his dissertation on Benedetto Croce's aesthetics. Although he later became influential in the reformational movement, devoted to the philosophical aspects of Neo-Calvinism, at that time he was a young, passionate student seeking to cast a new light on the Song of Songs by means of his own revolutionary translation. Inspired by his work with her, he asked her to set certain portions of his text to music, which she did in the summer of 1961 (see Ill. 7.3). On 1 April 1964, their combined production was premiered in Trinity Christian College, in Worth, Illinois as an Oratorio of Word and Song. In the remarks about the music in the program notes, one senses his investment in her ideas:

> The Dutch woman, Ina Lohr, truly a reformer in church music and hymnody, influential in both the Netherlands and Switzerland, teaches at [the] Schola Cantorum Basiliensis in Switzerland. Her students come to know her conviction that whenever people feel the need to speak together, in chorus, song is on the tip of their tongues. Song rises out of declamation. And when one would speak to God alone, yet is silent, when finally one dares raise his voice in prayer, then too, song is close by.
>   Would not lovers speaking their hearts intimately to one another also not naturally fall into song? In reply (August 1961), Ina Lohr wrote the song and music for sections of the English translation of the Greatest Song performed this evening. Notice how the tone follows the sense and mood of the words. Notice, too, that Solomon does not sing.[25]

Whereas her work remained somewhere between ignored and rejected in the larger musical world, her compositions continued to be received warmly within the church, as being highly appropriate for their function. Calvin Seerveld included these pieces in a luxurious publication, *The Greatest Song: in Critique*

---

24 "Ich frage mich, ob wir nicht Linde stärker für unser eigentliches Anliegen interessieren könnten, wenn wir ihm die Berufsschülerhausmusik anbieten würden, die 'klingende Musikgeschichte'. Sie sehen, ich komme immer wieder zum Aufteilen, weil ich die 'Schlüsselfigur' nicht recht sehe. Auch Kraehenbühll [sic] hat in Princeton eine Pionierarbeit, die er wohl kaum aufgeben wird. Aber Sie können ihn fragen". Ibid.
25 Program in his correspondence with Ina Lohr, PSF-ILC.

Ill. 7.3: Manuscript page from Ina Lohr's compositions for Calvin Seerveld's *The Greatest Song: in Critique of Solomon*. Photo: PSF-ILC.

of Solomon (The Hague: sypko + team, 1963 and 1967), complete with expressionistic wood prints by Flip van der Burgt.

As usual that summer, she and Paul Sacher had considerable correspondence about the BKO programming, as well as about Igor Stravinsky's *A Sermon, a Narrative, and a Prayer*, as she was to write the notes for its premiere on 23 February 1962 in a program devoted to his music in honor of his 80th birthday. She enthused: "Stravinsky preoccupies me to an almost worrisome degree. But it is a real liturgy: a reading from an epistle (of the mass), the associated reading from the Gospel (evangelium) and the resulting prayer!"[26] The degree of her enthusiasm for this work may also be perceived from how she spoke of it in the interview with Jos Leussink:

---

26 "Strawinsky beschäftigt mich fast beängstigend. Aber das ist eine richtige Liturgie: Lesung aus einem Brief (Epistel der Messe), daran bezogene Lesung aus der Apostelgeschichte (Evangelium) und daraus folgendes Gebet!" Letter Ina Lohr to Paul Sacher 19 August 1961, private collection, Switzerland.

Later, Stravinsky was also older, and no longer – I regret that I must say it – concerned so much with money and success. Of course, he also had to be, he had a family, and he was a faithful family man. [...] When he [Stravinsky] had grown very old, Sacher wanted something from him, actually a piece for his ensemble, for string orchestra. And then Stravinsky wrote back: I only compose Christian texts now, that is for choir with strings [...] I still do that with pleasure. He proposed *A Sermon, a Narrative and a Prayer.* [...]

And Sacher was at first shocked: it is so serious. And not only serious: Sacher had said, "It is an amateur choir, remember, it is an amateur choir, it is and will always be an amateur choir". "O", Stravinsky said, "that is constantly in my thoughts and that sound, the very pure, flawless sound, that is just what I want". And then we got it, and it is terribly difficult! Now, the nice thing was [...] I didn't do any rehearsing any more, I had overworked myself with that [...] But I still came to listen and the like, and once I had explained the texts (I could still do that) and also had explained how the music had grown from the texts [...], then they really wanted to sing that. It was terribly difficult, but they sang it beautifully [...] It is, for me, one of the most impressive works that I know.[27]

This is yet another indication of the degree to which she was actually still involved not only in the programming, but also in the performative aspects of the preparation of the BKO concerts.

In the fall of 1961, after a ten-year search for a place of her own in Lucerne to which she could withdraw from the stresses of her professional life, she finally found her "refuge": a one-room apartment, in a sunny and quiet location high above the city, with a view over the entire Lake. And it was from this retreat that she could write on 30 October 1962 to Hinrich Stoevesandt that

---

27 "En daarna werd Strawinsky ook ouder, en niet meer zo zeer op – ik moet het helaas wat zeggen – op geld en succes bedacht. Dat moest hij ook wel, hij had een familie, en hij was een trouwe familievader [...]. En toen hij werkelijk vrij erg oud werd [geworden was], toen wou Sacher nog iets van hem hebben, en eigenlijk een stuk voor zijn apparaat, voor strijkorkest. En toen schreef Strawinsky terug: ik componeer nu alleen nog maar christelijke teksten, dus voor koor, met strijkers [...] dat doe ik nog erg graag. En toen stelde hij voor: *A Sermon, a Narrative and a Prayer.* [...]

En Sacher kreeg eerst een beetje een schrik: het is zo ernstig. En niet alleen ernstig: Sacher had erbij gezegd, 'het is een lekenkoor, denk eraan, het is een lekenkoor, het is en blijft een lekenkoor'. 'O', zei Strawinsky, 'daar denk ik aldoor aan, en die klank, die heel zuivere, gave klank, dat is nou juist wat ik zo graag wil'. En toen kregen we dat: en dat is verschrikkelijk moeilijk! Nu was het leuke [...] Ik deed toen geen repetities meer, ik had me daaraan overwerkt [...] Maar ik kwam nog wel om te luisteren en zo, en toen ik de teksten had uitgelegd (dat mocht ik altijd nog doen) en ook erbij gezegd hoe die muziek uit de teksten was ontstaan [...], toen wilden ze dat werkelijk zingen. Het is een verschrikkelijke toer geweest, maar ze hebben het prachtig gezongen. [...] Het is voor mij een van de indrukwekkendste werken die ik ken". Interview with Jos Leussink, 25 March 1983.

after three very quiet months in Lucerne, I am so much better that I am again enjoying my work, [and] will surely continue with everything until July 1963 and afterward probably [with] the church music subjects, and in addition keep the school and *Hausmusik* courses! [...] But I am deeply thankful that I have much less pain and am again much more flexible. With 14 professional students that is very necessary.[28]

And indeed, for all intents and purposes the school year of 1961/62 followed its normal course, but Ina Lohr's activities there grew ever smaller in dimension. Her *Ensemble für Kirchenmusik* played in only two student recitals, her students sang at the funeral of the concierge, she was in charge of the Schola contribution to the annual festivities at the Musik-Akademie Basel, and her amateur *Hausmusik* group played in one external concert. This is a dramatic reduction from her heyday just a decade before. In addition, the number of theology students in her class at the university was considerably smaller, down to six, as opposed to 12–17 in earlier times.

Shortly before the beginning of the school year, it was also tentatively decided that the violinist, theorist, and composer, Wolfgang Neininger, should take over her courses upon her retirement. This latest Schola news was passed on to Hinrich Stoevesandt on 30 August 1961:

> I am supposed to train Wolfgang Neininger, so that he can take over my work in two years at the latest. The idea seems very good to me, but it will not be easy either for him or for me, if he must be present in all of my lessons, as Sacher envisions it. And the poor students, who need to pour out their hearts from time to time![29]

Paul Sacher and Walter Nef were even contemplating demanding that her successor obtain a degree in theory from the Schola. Walter Nef had his doubts about this proposal:

---

28 "Es geht mir nach 3 ganz ruhigen Monaten in Luzern soviel besser, dass ich mit Freude wieder an der Arbeit bin, sicher noch bis Juli '63 alles mache und nachher wahrscheinlich die kirchenmusikalischen Fächer, dazu die Schul- und Hausmusik beibehalte! [...] Aber ich bin zutiefst dankbar dafür, das[s] ich viel weniger Schmerzen habe und wieder viel beweglicher bin. Mit 14 Berufsschülern ist das auch sehr nötig". Letter Ina Lohr to Hinrich Stoevesandt of 5 November 1962, Elisabeth Stoevesandt, Basel.

29 "ich soll Wolf[g]ang Neininger einarbeiten, damit er dann meine Arbeit spätestens in 2 Jahren übernehmen kann. Die Idee scheint mir sehr gut, aber es wird weder für ihn noch für mich einfach sein, wenn er, wie sich das Sacher vorstellt, bei allen Stunden dabei sein muss. Und die armen Schüler, die doch hie und da auch ihr Herz ausschütten müssen!" Letter Ina Lohr to Hinrich Stoevesandt of 30 August 1961, Elisabeth Stoevesandt, Basel.

A degree in this case seems very difficult to me. It would primarily be a Lohr-diploma, and you know how uncompromising she is. Only those who "eat out of her hand" can obtain a degree from her. That is difficult enough for those she has raised herself. Neininger is too independent for that, too much of a finished personality; he must of necessity study her method of teaching, but he cannot copy it, but must afterward find his own path and proceed down it. I am afraid that the cooperation between them both will be difficult enough even without the degree. And concerning the "theory" degree itself, for the moment I cannot yet really imagine [what it might be].[30]

Due to this entire situation, Wolfgang Neininger experienced Ina Lohr rather differently than most others who knew her.[31] He found Ina Lohr to be a very interesting, very intelligent woman with an enormous sense for other people, being able to quickly read them. At the beginning she inquired of him how he dealt with music. He recalled that he played Machaut and the beginning of Bartók's 6th String Quartet for her, demonstrating the relationship between the two pieces. Apparently she found this very interesting – which one can well believe, as the Swedes spoke of her own predilection for such links – and considered it to be an aesthetic approach to music.

Wolfgang Neininger noted that there was a lot of singing in the classes and the students were constantly practicing solmization. Ina Lohr herself sang little in the lessons, preferring to let the students sing individually and then correcting them. She brought many of her own two- and three-part pieces to the lessons which were excellent didactic literature. He did not go to all of the classes, suggesting that his industry was perhaps not always commensurate with the sum Paul Sacher had paid him for freeing himself from other engagements, in order to be able to assume the position. But he learned a lot and was asked several times to teach the class; she was always pleased with the results. As far as he was concerned, however, it was inappropriate to apply solmization to all genres of music. In addition, there was too little ensemble work.

---

30 "Ein Diplom scheint mir in diesem Falle sehr schwierig. Das wäre in der Hauptsache ein Lohr-Diplom, und Du weisst, wie ausschliesslich sie ist. Ein Diplom kann bei ihr nur machen, wer ihr 'aus der Hand frisst'. Das ist schon schwierig genug für die 'Säuglinge'. Neininger ist dafür zu selbständig, zu viel fertige Persönlichkeit, er muss selbstverständlich ihre Unterrichtsweise gründlich studieren, aber er kann sie ja nicht kopieren, sondern muss nachher seinen eigenen Weg finden und gehen. Ich fürchte, dass die Zusammenarbeit zwischen den beiden schwierig genug sein wird auch ohne Diplom. Und was das 'Theorie'-Diplom selbst betrifft, so kann ich es mir vorhanden auch noch nicht recht vorstellen". Letter Walter Nef to Paul Sacher of 8 September 1961, PSF-PSC.

31 This and the following paragraph are based on information from an interview of Wolfgang Neininger with the author on 26 October 2015.

In time it became clear that their differences in approach were so great that if he were to teach these subjects, it would have to be according to his own lights, a necessity for any good teacher. Further, as he was aware of the tensions within the school, he told Paul Sacher that he did not wish to teach at the Schola, as long as she still had a position there.[32] But from Ina Lohr's perspective, this was just a further indication that her approach to music was slowly being abandoned at the school:

> Neininger has declared that under no circumstances does he want to teach alongside me. Sacher doesn't take that so seriously, also is of the opinion that N. cannot set such a condition, if he doesn't even want to give certain subjects. My impression is different: N. is opposed, without exactly saying it, to the "piety" and wishes to work "more on musical technique and style". Whether he will continue with solmization is also still very uncertain.[33]

And only a week later, she explained that

> Neininger has now withdrawn himself completely, however, in order to prepare himself for his new task, which he wants to shape in his own manner and in a completely new fashion. Sacher wrote to him that he expects a proposition in the near future, which can then be discussed. And he was also informed that, for the time being, I would continue giving the church music subjects.[34]

This, however, was not the only battle within the school that she was waging. She objected, for example, to the increasing regulation of the Schola administration, meaning she no longer could make autonomous decisions concerning the admission of students, writing to Hinrich Stoevesandt on 24 January 1963 that she was convinced after her last discussion with Walter Nef that it would be better to leave the Schola: "I just can't live and work according to scheme f".[35] Shortly thereafter she wrote a "Note of Opposition!" which was distrib-

---

32 Carbon copy of letter Paul Sacher to Ina Lohr of 23 July 1962, private collection, Switzerland.

33 "Neininger hat erklärt, er wolle auf keinen Fall neben mir unterrichten. Sacher nimmt das nicht so ernst, findet auch, N. könne eine solche Bedingung nicht stellen, wenn er gewisse Fächer gar nicht geben will. Mein Eindruck ist anders: N. wendet sich, ohne es genau so auszudrücken, gegen die 'Frömmelei' und möchte 'mehr musikalisch technisch und stiltechnisch' arbeiten. Ob er die Solmisation weiterführt ist auch noch sehr unsicher". Letter Ina Lohr to Hinrich Stoevesandt of 2 November 1962, Elisabeth Stoevesandt, Basel.

34 "Neininger hat sich nun ganz zurückgezogen aber: um sich auf seine neue Aufgabe vorzubereiten, die er in seiner Art und ganz neu gestalten will. Sacher hat ihm geschrieben, dass er in nächster Zeit einen Vorschlag erwartet, über den dann diskutiert wird. Auch wurde ihm mitgeteilt, dass ich vorläufig die kirchenmusikalischen Fächer noch gebe". Letter to Hinrich Sotevesandt of 9 November 1962, Elisabeth Stoevesandt, Basel.

35 "Ich kann nun einmal nicht nach Schema f leben und arbeiten". Letter Ina Lohr to Hinrich Stoevesandt of 24 January 1963, Elisabeth Stoevesandt, Basel.

uted to all of her colleagues after the teachers' conference of 10 February 1962, in which she laid out her distaste for the direction that the Schola was now taking:

I. Shall the SCB become a school only for the "talented", which (according to the explanations in the conference) will probably mean: for those with instrumental and vocal talents? Shall the cultivation of an audience with an understanding for music fall by the wayside, a special training of which we were once proud, that was fruitful and which some of us still take on with joy?

A harpsichord student who is inept may still perhaps have an intense need to make music, in order to better understand the music that she hears. She should therefore primarily learn to hear and then how she can play that which she heard (and also understood) with the possibilities given her. It is for just such people, in particular, that we should have – in the amateur division in any case – teachers (probably primarily female ones), who start from the capabilities of the student and develop them. Today it seems as if only the standards set by the teachers will allow admittance to the SCB. When in this connection, subsidies are mentioned, one could nonetheless wonder whether an audience which understands and loves music might be more important than a too large number of skillful instrumentalists whose awe for music has come to be lost through sheer technique.

II. We should, however, also not take on any students whose wishes we cannot fill. The two [students from] Oftringen want to study church music, as music for the church service. Such a [course of] study is based upon Gregorian chant and the German hymn and later proceeds naturally to larger forms. Solmization, mensural rhythm, thorough bass are basics of which they should have a sound knowledge and control. For such candidates, these are no longer "subsidiary" subjects. The very patient dealing with amateurs who make up a Christian congregation needs thorough training. If we do not find anyone who is particularly interested in this – and, let it be said, for the entire course of study – we should not take on such students.

It involves making music with choirs and instruments (also together with the congregation!) during the church service. This manner [of music-making] is foreign to almost all of the SCB teachers.

III. The name Schola Cantorum will then become meaningless if the instrumental instruction no longer is based on singing, and if, on the other hand, the vocal instruction is only measured in relation to voices of concert quality. Everybody at the SCB should learn that he can express himself with his own more or less good vocal capabilities and can join in an ensemble. If he is an instrumentalist or wants to become one, he learns to "make sounds" on his instrument. He should learn to use his vocal means in a healthy manner and make the greatest possible use of them. The vocal coach should therefore not so much prepare a "program" for the exam, but rather through singing in ensemble, as well as through sight-reading and simple songs, demonstrate that he has been able to awaken and intensify the[ir] joy in singing.[36]

36 "I. Soll die SCB eine Schule nur für 'Begabte' sein, was (nach den Ausführungen in der Konferenz) wohl heissen soll: für instrumental oder stimmlich Begabte? Soll folglich die Erziehung eines musikverständigen Publikums wegfallen, eine Spezialerziehung, auf die wir einmal stolz waren, die fruchtbar war und die einige von uns immer noch mit Freude auf sich nehmen?

On a certain level, there is nothing new in this document. Indeed, some of the points made in it are still valid today, for where will we draw our audiences, if we do not make an effort to introduce them into the process of music-making, of listening with understanding. It does, nonetheless, show her desperation and fear that that which she has spent her lifetime building up will now be discarded for ideals she cannot share. It must certainly have disturbed her sense of equilibrium – as is indicated by her physical breakdown – as well as her self-confidence. Her desire to leave an institution with which she no longer identified ideologically is thus very understandable.

Eine Cembaloschülerin, die ungeschickt ist, hat vielleicht doch ein sogar dringendes Bedürfnis Musik zu machen um die Musik, die sie hört, besser zu verstehen. Sie soll darum in erster Linie lernen zu hören und dann, wie sie das gehörte (und auch Verstandene) dann mit den ihr gegebenen Möglichkeiten spielen kann. Gerade für solche Leute sollten wir (auf alle Fälle an der allgemeinen Abteilung) Lehrer (wahrscheinlich vor allem Lehrerinnen) haben, die von den Möglichkeiten des Schülers ausgehen und diese entwickeln. Heute sieht es so aus, alsob [sic] die vom Lehrer zur Bedingung gestellten Möglichkeiten allein den Eintritt in die SCB erlauben. Wenn die Subvention in diesem Zusammenhang erwähnt wird, könnte man doch überlegen, ob ein musikverständiges und musikliebendes Publikum der Stadt Basel nicht wichtiger wäre, als eine zu grosse Anzahl geschickter Instrumentalisten, denen das Staunen über die Musik vor lauter Können abhanden gekommen ist.

II. Wir sollten aber auch keine Schüler annehmen, deren Wünsche wir nicht erfüllen können. Die zwei Oftringer wollen Kirchenmusik als Musik für den Gottesdienst studieren. Ein solches Studium geht vom gregorianischen Choral und vom deutschen Kirchenlied aus und kommt natürlich auch zu grösseren Formen. Die Solmisation, der Mensuralrhythmus, der Generalbass sind Grundlagen, die sie gründlich kennen und beherrschen sollten. Es handelt sich für solche Kandidaten schon nicht mehr um 'Nebenfächer'. Die sehr geduldige Beschäftigung mit den Laien, die nun einmal die christliche Gemeinde bilden, braucht eine minitiöse Vorbereitung. Wenn wir nicht jemanden finden, der sich gerade dafür besonders interessiert (und zwar für die ganze Ausbildungszeit), dü[r]fen wir solche Schüler nicht annehmen.

Es geht um ein chorisches Musizieren mit Singstimmen und Instrumenten (auch mit der Gemeinde!) im Gottesdienst. Diese Art ist fast allen Lehrern der SCB fremd.

III. Der Name Schola Cantorum wird dann sinnlos, wenn der Instrumentalunterricht gar nicht mehr vom Singen ausgeht, andererseits der Gesangsunterricht nur an dem Konzertgesang gemessen wird. Jeder soll an der SCB lernen, dass er mit seinen mehr oder weniger guten Stimmitteln sich au[s]drücken, auch in ein Ensemble einschalten kann. 'Töne Machen' lernt er auf seinem Instrument, sofern er ein Instrumentalist ist oder werden will. Seine Stimmittel soll er gesund brauchen lernen und sie möglichst viel einsetzen. Der Stimmbildner sollte darum vielleicht weniger ein 'Programm' für das Examen einstudieren, als durch Ensemblesingen, auch Blattsingen und durch einfache Lieder zeigen, dass er die Freude am Singen hat wecken und steigern können."

Included in the minutes of the teacher's meeting of 10 February 1962, PSF-PSC.

It is not surprising in this situation that she chose to have her students perform in private surroundings rather than in the regular Schola recitals in this school year, as well as organizing other possibilities for them. No activities of the *Ensemble für Kirchenmusik* are recorded. Later – in order to fill this gap on the institutional level – a vocal ensemble was created under the direction of Hans-Martin Linde.

Two letters remain extant that Paul Sacher sent to her in honor of her 60th birthday: one in his official role as director of the SCB and one in his role as director of the BKO. That concerning the Schola was obviously also intended as an acknowledgment of her immense contribution to the founding and development of the institution. He does not shirk in displaying his gratitude:

> For thirty years, you were the heart of the Schola: you formed all of those who obtained degrees and the innumerable other students as well, and shaped the Schola through your work and your personality. [...]
>
> I know that you always invested all the forces of your mind and heart and have never spared yourself. You have set the measure, and the young, who will be our successors, will have to make a tremendous effort in order to emulate your example. Everyone feels the greatest admiration for the inner vision that you were able to realize at the Schola, for how you worked from plenitude, [for] your musical, historical and musicological knowledge of early music and the sovereignty of your approach; and [feels] the deepest gratitude for your commitment. As an artist and a teacher at the Schola Cantorum Basiliensis, you have accomplished a creative feat, whose greatness we acknowledge and whose fruits surely bring you profound satisfaction.[37]

He then followed this up with further words of appreciation on the letterhead of the BKO, as he

> wanted to add his heartfelt personal thanks for her cooperation with the Basel Chamber Orchestra. As my "assistant" you have taught me to create meaningful and beautiful programs, and thereby stimulated the activities of the BKO in a crucial area. Draw-

---

37 "Sie waren während dreissig Jahren das Herz der Schola; Sie haben alle Diplomanden und die unzähligen übrigen Schüler geformt und durch Ihr Wirken und Ihre Persönlichkeit die Schola geprägt. [...]

Ich weiss, dass Sie an der Schola immer alle Ihre Kräfte des Geistes und des Herzens eingesetzt und sich nie geschont haben. Sie haben Mass gesetzt, und die Jungen, die unsere Nachfolger sein werden, müssen sich gewaltig anstrengen, um Ihrem Beispiel nachzueifern. Für die innere Schau, die Sie an der Schola verwirklichen konnten, für Ihr Wirken aus der Fülle, Ihre musikalische, historische und wissenschaftliche Kenntnis der alten Musik und Ihre souveräne Stoffbehandlung empfindet jedermann grösste Bewunderung und für Ihren Einsatz tiefste Dankbarkeit. Sie haben als Künstlerin und Pädagogin an der Schola Cantorum Basiliensis eine schöpferische Tat vollbracht, deren Grösse wir erkennen und deren Früchte Ihnen selber gewiss tiefe Befriedigung bringen". Letter Paul Sacher to Ina Lohr of 1 August 1963, PSF-ILC.

ing from your phenomenal knowledge of the literature, jewel-like programs came about which are now imitated everywhere.

Your participation in the Chamber Choir has not been forgotten, which unfortu-nately, to my great distress, already had to come to a stop many years ago.[38]

I think there can be no doubt about his sincerity in these letters, as he is very selective about that which he chooses to mention. In particular, there would be no reason to even speak of his sorrow over the fact that she was unwilling to continue sharing the rehearsal of the choir with him, if his regret were not genuine. There must have been yet a third, personal letter of congratulation, as in a thank-you letter of 15 August 1963, Ina Lohr speaks of having re-read the three birthday letters he had sent. She was particularly moved that for him, too, everything had been "very delightful":

> Even the painful [aspects] had to be. It was the price that we had to pay for the wonder-ful times that came later and that, as I hope, will still come. In any case, I am already again working with joy on the *Messiah* and on the Mozart program. And the Schola? Yes, we all called it into life, but it would not have been possible without your trust in my ideas, which were often quite fanciful. And I hope with my heart that the young will accrue sufficient fighting spirit, for that is the environment in which you can live! But it seems as if your needs will be met. And in the background, perhaps, I'll also still play along a bit.[39]

It thus would seem that both of them, notwithstanding all of the conflicts they had weathered over the years – or was it because of them? – had now come to understand their cooperation as one of the most meaningful aspects of their

---

38 "Ich möchte nämlich auch einen von Herzen kommenden persönlichen Dank für Ihre Mit-arbeit im Basler Kammerorchester anfügen. Sie haben mich als meine 'Assistentin' gelehrt, sinnvolle und schöne Programme zu gestalten und damit in einem entscheidenden Punkt das Wirken des B.K.O. befruchtet. Aus dem sagenhaften Schatz Ihrer Literaturkenntnisse schöpfend sind Perlen von Programmen zustande gekommen, die nun schon allenthalben nachgeahmt werden.

Unvergessen ist Ihre Mitwirkung im Kammerchor, die leider zu meinem grossen Schmerz schon vor vielen Jahren ein Ende finden musste." Letter Paul Sacher to Ina Lohr of 1 August 1963, PSF-ILC.

39 "Auch das Schmerzliche musste sein. Es war der Preis, den wir zahlen mussten für viel Schö-nes, das nachher noch kam und das, wie ich hoffe, noch kommen wird. Auf alle Fälle bin ich schon wieder mit Freude an der Arbeit am 'Messias' und am Mozartprogramm. Und die Schola? Ja, wir alle zusammen haben sie ins Leben gerufen, was aber nicht möglich gewesen wäre, ohne Ihr Vertrauen zu meinen oft recht ausgefallenen Einfällen. Und ich hoffe von Herzen, dass nun die Jungen für genügend kämpferische Tätigkeit sorgen werden, denn das ist das Element, in dem sich's für Sie leben lässt! Aber es sieht so aus, alsob [sic] Ihr Bedarf gedeckt sein wird. Und im Hintergrund spiele ich vielleicht auch noch etwas mit". Letter Ina Lohr to Paul Sacher of 15 August 1963, private collection, Switzerland.

lives. And one sees, that although she has recognized that there is no longer a place for her at the Schola, she would still like to be able to influence its future.

7.2 Semi-Retirement

New Outlooks …
Although she had withdrawn from the professional level at the Schola and many aspects of her life continued on as before, a space for new contacts and forms of interaction with diverse people was also opened up, as is also revealed by the source material. For example, Hinrich Stoevesandt, who had received important impulses in Basel and was working in Göttingen at the time, suggested that his fiancée, Elisabeth Roth, study at the Schola. Her mother had imposed a period of separation upon her daughter, believing her to be far too young at eighteen to be making such far-reaching decisions as marriage without taking some time and space to consider them carefully. The choice of coming to Basel to study with Karl Barth – together with the enriching benefit of being able to work with Ina Lohr – was seen in the eyes of the young couple as her preparation for the role of a pastor's wife. Thus, the distance was partially ameliorated by the bond of common experience and led to the inclusion of Ina Lohr within the family as the godmother to their first child. They lived in Germany until 1971, when they moved to Basel, where Hinrich Stoevesandt became the Director of the Karl Barth Archives from 1971–97. This familial and religious bond made their correspondence with Ina Lohr a prime source of information for this period of time. In music-making, with the professional students falling away, Ina Lohr became increasingly involved with Arthur Eglin's groups, the *Oekumenischer Singkreis Basel* and the *Stadtposaunenchor Basel*. As she wrote on 9 August 1969, "I am ever and again happy that the contact [with you] remains intact!"[40]

And finally she continued meeting new people in courses, such as one for a new group of Swedes in the summer of 1963, or at the one she gave in Arnhem on 7/8 September 1963 entitled "What can 'early music' mean to us".[41] It is probably at the latter that she met Kees Vellekoop, as in her first letter of

---

40 "Auf alle Fälle bin ich immer wieder froh, dass der Kontakt nicht abbricht!" Letter Ina Lohr to Arthur Eglin of 9 August 1969, Arthur Eglin, Basel.
41 See also her article "Wat kan oude muziek ons betekenen?" [Haarlem]: Stichting Centrum voor de protestantse Kerkzang/Vereniging voor Huismuziek 1964.

14 September 1963 she spoke of sending back a madrigal.[42] At that time, the young man, whose father Gerrit Vellekoop was a pioneer of the *huismuziek* movement in the Netherlands, was just beginning his studies on the gamba and in musicology. It is obvious that they had an immediate rapport, for they soon developed a correspondence over joint musicological interests, of which, with very few exceptions, only her letters are extant. These letters – although personal elements came to take an ever-increasing role – were full of advice. For example, on 17 November 1963, in response to a letter in which he had obviously mentioned that a professor at the university wanted him to write an article on numerology in 16th-century music, she warned against becoming too one-sided, withdrawn from society, as "our professor Handschin, who lived for his scholarship, but otherwise was a poor, lonely man".[43] As a countermeasure she recommended that he not give up his singing and playing for "this very special study".[44] He obviously questioned this response, wondering why his study of numerology should be so different from hers of solmization. Her response of 31 December 1963 was very candid:

> And you are right: with my solmization I am also outside the norm of all scholarly methodology. It is at times somewhat difficult when interacting with members of the field, but then also stimulating, because we must continually account anew for why we so stubbornly go our own way. By no means may it be a stubbornness "à tout prix". But it is not that with you. Whether we can really comprehend medieval man with the help of numerology or solmization, I do not know. It seems to me to be an illusion, that we think and act as if we could take on the style of whatever era whatsoever, or even approach it. We, whether we like it or not, live too intensely in our own time. And that is good![45]

42 Letter Ina Lohr to Kees Vellekoop of 14 September 1963. The letters were placed at my disposal by his widow, Jos Knigge, Utrecht, whom I wish here to particularly thank for her generosity in lending me the letters for this study.

43 "[…] onze Prof. Handschin, die in zijn wetenschap opging, maar daarnaast een arme, eenzame stakkerd was". Letter Ina Lohr to Kees Vellekoop of 17 November 1963, Jos Knigge, Utrecht.

44 "deze zeer speciale studie". Ibid.

45 "En je hebt gelijk: ik sta met mijn solmisatie ook buiten iedere gebruikelijke wetenschappelijke methode. In de omgang met lieden van het vak is dat soms wat moeilijk, maar dan ook weer animerend, want we moeten er ons steeds opnieuw rekenschap van geben, waarom we zo hardnekkig onze eigen weg gaan. Het mag in geen geval hardnekkigeid 'à tout prix' zijn. Maar dat is het bij jou ook niet. Of we werkelijk de mens van de middeleeuwen met behulp van getalsymboliek of solmisatie bereiken en begrijpen, weet ik niet. Het lijkt me een illusie, dat we denken en doen, de stijl van welk tijdperk ook, zouden kunnen overnemen of zelfs maar benaderen. We leven, of we willen of niet, te intens in onze eigen tijd. En dat is goed zo!" Letter Ina Lohr to Kees Vellekoop of 31 December 1963, Jos Knigge, Utrecht.

Only a few months later, she continued in this vein – on a certain level speaking of her relationship to musicological scholarship – in reference to some Gennrich transcriptions which she, like Kees Vellekoop, called into question:

> We shall never be able to say [who is right] with complete assurance, Kees, but it is for that reason that we should again and again remain seeking for that piece of truth, which presents itself to us now as the truth. And as long as you are honestly and seriously searching, nobody can demand or expect of you that you first reiterate what others say. It is just that searching for *yourself, daring* to judge yourself, that you must now learn as a student. Otherwise you will become an argumentative statistician who plays the one against the other, without coming to your own [means of] positively seeking and perhaps finding.[46]

In this recommendation, we see Ina Lohr reliving her own study days, in which she, as we have seen in Chapter 1, was regularly questioning the opinions of those around her, as well as keeping her distance from musical greats, in order to be able to develop her own style of composition without imposition from the outside world (see p. 136).

But the discussion did not remain on this abstract plane; throughout this initial period, they were continually discussing musical questions, in particular those that arose from Kees Vellekoop's research into numerology and rhetoric. Further, when he decided to teach solmization in a workshop, he apparently wrote to her asking how she would proceed. She in turn provided an eager summary of her approach, complete with examples.[47] After hearing about his experiences, she thanked him for his account, saying that "solmization has given me so many happy insights that I am once again happy when I notice and hear that a young person is once again walking on this path, and discovering flowers and grass to the left and the right and much living matter".[48]

---

46 "We zullen het nooit helemaal zeker kunnen zeggen, Kees, maar daarom zullen we toch altijd weer naar dat stukje waarheid blijven zoeken, dat zich nu aan ons als waarheid voordoet. En zolang je eerlijk en ernstig zoekt, kan niemand van je verlangen of verwachten, dat je vooreerst anderen napraat. Juist dat zelf zoeken, zelf durven oordelen moet je nu in je studietijd leren. Anders wordt je een strijdlustige statistieker, die de één tegen de ander uitspeelt, zonder tot een eigen, positief zoeken en misschien vinden te komen". Letter Ina Lohr to Kees Vellekoop of 10 April 1964, Jos Knigge, Utrecht.

47 Letter Ina Lohr to Kees Vellekoop of 10 April 1964, Jos Knigge, Utrecht.

48 "De solmisatie heeft mij zo veel blij inzicht gegeven, dat ik ook weer blij ben als ik merk en hoor, dat ook weer een jong iemand op dit pad loopt en links en rechts bloemen en gras en heel veel levends ontdekt". Postcard Ina Lohr to Kees Vellekoop of 21 September 1964, Jos Knigge, Utrecht.

It is not surprising that this sense of shared interests led Ina Lohr to suggest that Kees Vellekoop come to study at the Schola for a semester, also expressing a willingness to give a certain amount of financial support if necessary. Due to the reorganization of the Musik-Akademie Basel at this time, she recommended that he consider it for the fall semester of 1965/66.[49] When she went to Walter Nef to facilitate his coming, she was enraged to find out that she could no longer just say she wanted him as a student, but that there were now auditions: "I was completely out of my mind, when Dr. Nef told me all this, but now our institute has become a kind of factory, there is apparently nothing one can do".[50] She went on to say that if he did not want to go through the auditioning process, one could also organize it privately, complete with gamba lessons from August Wenzinger. In the end, he enrolled at the Schola for the entire school year 1965/66.

During that year, of course, there was little written correspondence, but soon after he returned to the Netherlands, he taught a course together with Jan Boeke in which he incorporated some of his new ideas. Seemingly, all did not go as he envisioned, as Ina Lohr wrote on 7 August 1966 saying that she had feared

> that the study week would not be easy. The difficulty therein is that we always want to offer that which we ourselves find fulfilling. And the two of you had two concepts that were totally unknown to the participants. For that, a week is too short and the whole [thing] then remains too vague. But if you start from what the participants can or cannot do, then you end up with Jöde and his countless arrangements, which we certainly don't want. I am curious how this work, and in particular [how] the cooperation with Jan [Boeke] will develop further.[51]

In this we see, on the one hand, how Ina Lohr clearly distinguishes her approach from that of Fritz Jöde of the German *Jugendmusikbewegung*, not deigning to lower her standards. It is also interesting to see also how two generations of

---

49 Letter Ina Lohr to Kees Vellekoop of 6 September 1964, Jos Knigge, Utrecht.
50 "Ik was erg uit mijn huisje, toen Dr. Nef me dit alles vertelde, maar nu ons instituut ook al een soort fabriek wordt, is er blijkbaar niets aan te doen". Letter Ina Lohr to Kees Vellekoop of 10 July 1965, Jos Knigge, Utrecht.
51 "Ja, dat vreesde ik al, dat die studieweek niet gemakkelijk zou zijn. De moeilijkheid zit hem hierin, dat we altijd dat aan bod willen brengen, waar we zelf van vervuld zijn. En jullie hadden dan dus 2 verschillende, voor de deelnemers geheel vreemde onderwerpen. Daarvoor is een week te kort en het geheel blijft toch vaag. Maar ga je uit van wat de deelnemers kunnen of niet kunnen, dan kom je bij Jöde en zijn talloze bewerkingen terecht, wat wij zeker niet willen. Ik ben benieuwd, hoe zich dit werk, en vooral ook de samenwerking met Jan verder ontwikkelt". Letter Ina Lohr to the Vellekoop's of 7 August 1966, Jos Knigge, Utrecht.

adherents to her approach to music came to join together in such projects, illustrating how strongly her work spoke to certain Dutch musical circles.

It must have been shortly thereafter that Kees Vellekoop wrote her a letter with the salutation, "Dear Second Mother", in which he revealed that he and Jos Knigge, whom Ina Lohr had met during the course of Kees Vellekoop's Basel sojourn, would soon wed and were expecting a child. She responded on 2 September 1966 with a letter to her "Dear Accepted Children", in which she expressed her joy, but also her concern and an admonition that he find the necessary time for his family within the constraints of his work. As with the Stoevesandts, this led to an intense participation and interest in their family life on her part, as she took her responsibility as a "second grandmother" seriously.

A letter of 27 October 1966 gives an indication of the intensity of their work together, in that she took three pages to respond to questions and criticism of her article, "Sprachmelodik im Gregorianischen Choral und in neuen, deutschen Messgesängen". Kees Vellekoop, like Sven-Erik Bäck, is thus one of the few people with whom she carried on long-distance, peer-level conversations about musical questions. He managed to present his own theories and opinions in such a way that she felt as if they were cooperating in their pursuit of a common goal; as a result, her walls of defense remained in abeyance.

And when his article, "Zusammenhänge zwischen Text und Zahl in der Kompositionsart Jacob Obrechts",[52] appeared, she was thrilled, writing on 30 April 1967 that it was "such a public, readable result of your time in Basel, Kees, of our work together next to one another, and it gives me such real courage and hope for a really good future".[53] Her influence is unmistakably evident in the solmization-based analysis of the cantus firmus of the motet *Parce dominus* which is used to illustrate his theories.

On 29 July of that year, he came to Basel for a week in order to discuss medieval quotations concerning rhetoric and to translate them into German. Writing to Arthur Eglin on 8 August 1967, she commented on how "it was fascinating to read that the orator is only allowed to raise his voice up to a fifth at the beginning, and even in the most important moments is not allowed to go be-

---

52   Kees Vellekoop, "Zusammenhänge zwischen Text und Zahl in der Kompositionsart Jacob Obrechts. Analyse der Motette Parce Domine", in: *Tijdschrift van de Vereniging voor Nederlandse Muziekgeschiedenis* 20/3 (1966), 97–119.

53   "Het is zo'n zichtbaar, leesbaar resultaat van je tijd in Bazel, Kees, van ons samenwerken naast elkaar, en het geeft me zo echt moed en hoop op een heel goede toekomst". Letter Ina Lohr to the Vellekoop family of 30 April 1967, Jos Knigge, Utrecht.

yond an octave. I have let myself be told!"[54] Some of this material must have served as the basis for his article of a much later date, "Emoties in de Meddeleeuwen". His discussion within it, concerning the affects associated with the individual modes was also clearly inspired by her ideas, and he was equally outspoken in his advocacy of performances reflecting the affective content of the text.

Thereafter, with his increasing familial and professional obligations, visits became rare, with the result Ina Lohr's letters begin concerning themselves less with music and more with her life in general.

And Continuity
It was for just such broadening of her horizons and new kinds of encounters that she blessed the effect of her "very exhausting 'retirement'" on her daily life, as she could leave burdensome subjects to the side, such as ornamentation and form studies, and concentrate on that which, for her, was the essence: music as the "means" of expression.[55] By the end of 1963, she went even further, writing that her "lessons at the Schola were gradually becoming pure joy".[56] Her work with Paul Sacher also continued apace: already in a letter of 15 August 1963 she speaks of her delight in working on the *Messiah* (concerts BKO of 20/21 March 1964) and the Mozart program (concert CMZ of 8 November 1963). In the second half of 1963, Paul Sacher himself was in poor health, having to cancel numerous engagements, and even underwent an operation.[57] As he himself was unable to conduct the BKO concert of Britten's music on 29 November 1963, it took place under the baton of Norman Del Mar. She wrote to him on 15 December 1963 describing some of her experiences in that situation, continuing on to speak of her frustrations with working with the choir on the *Messiah* with Mr. Watkins Shaw:

54 "Auf alle Fälle war es spannend zu lesen, dass der Redner seine Stimme am Anfang nur bis in die Quinte erheben darf und auch in den wichtigsten Momenten nicht über die Oktave gehen darf. Ich habe es mir sagen lassen!" Letter Ina Lohr to Arthur Eglin of 8 August 1967, Arthur Eglin, Basel.
55 "Da segne ich den, allerdings sehr anstrengenden 'Ruhestand'. Ja die Musik wird immer mehr 'Mittel', und darum scheinen einige Fächer wie Verzierungslehre, Formenlehre eine Belastung". From the further context it is clear that she is grateful that she no longer teaches these courses. Letter Ina Lohr to Hinrich Stoevesandt of 17 November 1963, Elisabeth Stoevesandt, Basel.
56 "Aber die Stunden an der Schola werden so nach und nach eine reine Freude". Letter Ina Lohr to Hinrich Stoevesandt of 31 December 1963, Elisabeth Stoevesandt, Basel.
57 Cf. letter Ina Lohr to Paul Sacher of 24 November 1963, private collection, Switzerland.

I am somewhat helpless, when I should be doing such a job for somebody else, merely hoping for the best, and therefore hopefully imagine that you will again be conducting the choir and orchestra for the first time [since his illness] with the Messiah. [...] In any case, I will now do the strings, so that they can be typeset. I'll do the wind parts myself. And I want to write about the form that came about because of the choice of the texts, and about the pieces that therefore cannot be omitted, although one usually does so still today.[58]

What this passage reflects is Ina Lohr's realization that she needs to start taking over responsibilities in the organization of this concert, in order to ensure that it will actually take place, with all of the accouterments, and with a maintenance of their established quality. This meant also, that at the end of January, she discussed the progress of the choir with the choir assistants and agreed to join in with them for two rehearsals in February, in order to be able to rehearse with divided sections of the choir.[59]

Her text for the *Mitteilungen des Basler Kammerorchesters* on the performance of the second and third parts of the *Messiah* is enlightening in regard to the extent that her ideas shaped and formed their programs:

Larsen, as a musicologist of our times, has analyzed the "Messiah", [and] as it were, discovered it anew. He began with the text and from the structure as a whole. If we compare his remarks with those of Handel's contemporaries, with the writings of Mainwaring, Burney, Mattheson, what is conspicuous is how often then that the "affect" of the music was central. The audience let itself be touched and moved, but did not think much about it, as the work came into being as an expression of its own time. [...]

Today we tend to assume that – with the help of musicology – we can penetrate to the innermost intentions of a composer. That this is an illusion is something we again and again experience anew. And nonetheless, the recognition that the conception of the composer must have been greater, more full of mystery than our interpretation ever can be, leaves us forever unsatisfied. Each generation attempts to take the work into its own time, to bring it close to its own audience. Mozart replaced Handel's sound ideal with his own, appropriate to his time. That was how the work became well-known to the 19th century: the sound became standard, the tempo was slowed for the benefit of the symphonic sound, abridgments were unavoidable.

---

58 "Ich bin etwas hilflos, wenn ich nun eine solche Arbeit nur so auf gut Glück für irgend jemanden machen soll, und stelle mir darum gerne vor, dass Sie gerade mit dem Messias zum ersten Mal wieder Chor und Orchester leiten. [...] Auf alle Fälle werde ich mich jetzt an die Streicherstimmen machen, damit die in Arbeit gegeben werden. Die Bläserstimmen mach ich dann selber. Und schreiben möchte ich über die Form, die aus gerade dieser Textwahl entstand, und über die Stücke, die man aus diesem Grunde nicht weglassen kann, auch wenn man das bis heute meistens tut". Letter Ina Lohr to Paul Sacher of 15 December 1963, private collection, Switzerland.

59 Letter Ina Lohr to Paul Sacher of 31 January 1964, private collection, Switzerland.

> We attempt in our performance to bring back the instrumentation of the orchestra intended by Handel, to derive the tempi from the forms and from the rules passed down to us from the 18th century, to avoid abridgments and to keep the original language which influenced the composition.[60]

Noteworthy here is not only the direction taken in their own interpretation, but also the modernity of Ina Lohr's recognition of the great difference between the approach of musicologists of the day in comparison to the critics of Handel's time, as well as her confirmation that the modern musician's aspiration for authenticity is but an illusion. It, too, is perhaps a reason why she did not react irritably to aspersions cast on her scholarship, in that she did not see her work as something abstract, but rather as research into aspects of the music necessitated by the desire to bring it to life practically within the current circumstances. She was aware that no matter when the work is performed, it is an expression of the time of the performance rather than of the composition itself.

Paul Sacher's score of the oratorio reveals the care with which Ina Lohr marked the entire work, as in the past clarifying details of the dynamics, ornamentation, articulation, as well as the rhythmic proportions between the individual movements; in addition, she included the Biblical references within the text. It is touching to see (see Ill. 7.4) the effort Paul Sacher made to execute these suggestions, as indicated by the annotation at the end of the chorus *All we like*

---

60 "Larsen hat als Musikologe unserer Zeit den 'Messiah' analysiert, gleichsam neu entdeckt. Er geht dabei vom Text aus und vom Aufbau im Ganzen. Vergleichen wir seine Äusserungen mit denen der Zeitgenossen Händels, mit den Schriften von Mainwaring, Burney, Mattheson, so fällt auf, wie sehr es damals um den 'Affekt' in der Musik ging. Das Publikum liess sich rühren und ergreifen, machte sich aber wenig Gedanken, da das Werk als Ausdruck der eigenen Zeit entstand. [...]
Wir sind heute geneigt, anzunehmen, dass wir mit Hilfe der Musikwissenschaft zu den eigensten Absichten eines Komponisten vordringen können. Dass es sich um eine Illusion handelt, erfahren wir immer aufs neue. Und doch lässt uns die Erkenntnis keine Ruhe, dass die Konzeption des Komponisten grösser, geheimnisvoller gewesen sein muss, als es unsere Interpretation je sein kann. Jede Generation versucht, das Werk in die eigene Zeit hineinzunehmen, es dem eigenen Publikum nahe zu bringen. Mozart ersetze Händels Klangvorstellung durch die eigene, seiner Zeit gemässe. So wurde das Werk dem 19. Jahrhundert vertraut: der Klang wurde massgeblich, das Tempo zugunsten dieses symphonischen Klanges verlangsamt, Kürzungen waren unvermeidlich.
Wir versuchen, bei unserer Aufführung das Orchester auf die von Händel beabsichtigte Instrumentation zurückzubringen, die Tempi aus den Formen und den uns überlieferten Vorschriften des 18. Jahrhunderts abzuleiten, auf Kürzungen zu verzichten und die Originalsprache, die auf die Vertonung von Einfluss war, beizubehalten". Ina Lohr, "Zu der Aufführung des zweiten und dritten Teiles des 'Messiah'", in: *Mitteilungen des Basler Kammerorchesters*, Nr. 113, 14 March 1964, 3.

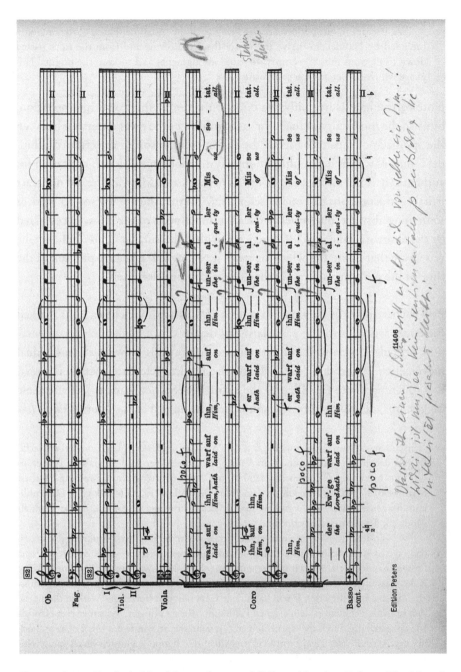

Ill. 7.4: Georg Friedrich Händel, conclusion of "All we like sheep" from *The Messiah.* Photo: PSF-ILC.

sheep: "Although IL wants an *f* ending, a *dim* comes of itself! It is only important that a sentimental *p* is not created and the intensity is maintained".[61] The performances of the work were clearly of great satisfaction to him, as in conclusion to his letter of 25 March 1964 he spoke of "still being gratified by our beautiful experience with the *Messiah*".[62]

Immediately thereafter she also taught a week-long course in Gwatt, five hours a day from 30 March to 5 April 1964, "Studies of Songs from the Church Hymnal" organized by the Evangelische Singgemeinde in conjunction with a course in choir direction. Participants spoke of the impact this course had upon them for their later work.

Around this time, she was also involved in further discussions concerning the theory and church music classes at the Schola, as her successor for these courses, Peter Benary, had decided to devote himself solely to his work at the Conservatory in Lucerne. In the end, in order to avoid any delay in the final exam for the students who had taken the course in Gregorian chant with either of them, it was decided that she should teach a *repetitorium* in the winter semester 1964/65, and that they be tested upon its completion.[63]

She profited from a warm and quiet summer, preparing for another course offered by the Center for Protestant Church Music in the Netherlands, this time in "Land en Bosch" in 's-Graveland on the weekends of 3/4 and 10/11 October 1964: "Rhythm as the Foundation for Music-Making".[64] In a letter of 19 October 1964 to Elisabeth Stoevesandt, she spoke of being very well, that she had even been able "to conduct a lot herself in Holland". The implication of this remark is that since her illness in 1960 she had been severely restricted in her activities as a choir conductor. Perhaps this was also a reason for the sudden reduction of the concerts of the *Ensemble für Kirchenmusik* in the early 1960s. She also confessed to looking forward to having professional students in her classes for Gregorian chant and Protestant church music. In addition, she was

61 "Obwohl IL einen f Schluss will, ergibt sich von selber ein dim.! Wichtig ist nur, dass kein sentimentales p entsteht & die Intensität gewahrt bleibt". PSF-PSC.
62 "Ich bin noch erfüllt von unserm schönen 'Messias'-Erlebnis". Carbon copy of letter Paul Sacher to Ina Lohr of 25 March 1964, private collection, Switzerland.
63 Minutes of the teachers' conference of 23 June 1964, 3, PSF-PSC.
64 "Rhythme als voor-waarde voor het musiceren", [Haarlem]: Stichting Centrum voor de protestantse Kerkzang/Vereniging voor Huismuziek 1964.

preparing for a French celebration of Calvin on 5 November 1964.[65] Further, she also wrote a long article "Handel's *Messiah* as a Liturgy" for the Sunday cultural section of the Basler Nachrichten on 6 December 1964 in preparation for the BKO's performance of its first part later that week. This is all evidence of the continuance of a high level of activity, albeit less well documented than before her partial retirement.

The following year was very quiet, in part due to her poor health in spring and summer. From her refuge in Lucerne she wrote to the Stoevesandts that she had

> had an extremely bad spring with an asthmatic cough that is only now slowly disappearing. Also the spondylosis and the pain resulting from it has gotten worse. But here everything will get better quickly, because I can completely relax. The rapid development of the Schola is, to be sure, very painful for me, even if I also can see that its coming was unavoidable. One is only concerned about [technical] ability now, not about the wonder and discovery, which was so important to us. […] My own lessons, *Hausmusik*, church hymns, etc., are very good.[66]

We know from another letter to Arthur Eglin that these hours of teaching, in spite of all of her physical complaints, amounted to ten hours a week.[67] And a month later she wrote to the Stoevesandts again, saying that she was beginning to get better,

> but I will only really be relieved when my blood values are once again in order. For someone with allergies, this summer has also been a test, one which I will only barely pass. Coughing and an elevated temperature remain faithfully loyal to me, but I have almost gotten used to it and am again working with pleasure. I am writing a series of short song analyses for the trombone choir [led by Arthur Eglin].[68]

---

65 "Ich konnte in Holland sogar wieder ziemlich viel selber leiten. […] Heute habe ich mich auf die französische Calvinfeier vorbereitet vom 5. Nov. und auf die 2 Stunden, an denen nun doch wieder Berufsschüler teilnehmen: Diplomkurs Greg. Choral und 'Vom Greg. Choral zum Ev. Kirchenlied'. Und ich freue mich auch wieder auf diesen Unterricht". Letter Ina Lohr to Elisabeth Stoevesandt of 19 October 1964, Elisabeth Stoevesandt, Basel.

66 "Ich hatte ein ausgesprochen schlechtes Frühjahr mit einem asthmatischen Husten, der erst jetzt langsam verschwindet. Auch die Spondylose und die daraus resultierenden Schmerzen haben sich verschlimmert. Aber hier wird alles sehr schnell besser, weil ich mich vollkommen entspannen kann. Die rapide Entwicklung der Schola ist für mich doch sehr schmerzhaft, wenn ich auch einsehe, dass sie unvermeidlich kommen musste. Es geht fast nur noch um das Können, nicht mehr um das Staunen, und entdecken, was uns doch sehr wichtig war. […] die eigenen Stunden, Hausmusik, Kirchenlied u.s.w., sind sehr schön". Letter Ina Lohr to Elisabeth and Hinrich Stoevesandt, 11 July 1965, Elisabeth Stoevesandt, Basel.

67 Letter Ina Lohr to Arthur Eglin of 17 June 1965, Arthur Eglin, Basel.

68 "Aber wirklich erleichtert bin ich erst, wenn das Blutbild auch wieder in Ordnung ist. Für Allergiker ist dieser Sommer auch eine Prüfung, die auch ich schlecht bestehe. Husten

Although the documentation for it is relatively sparse, this is one of indications that Ina Lohr was becoming increasingly involved, as an inspiration – if nothing else – in Arthur Eglin's work with the combined forces of the *Oekumenischer Singkreis Basel* and the *Stadtposaunenchor Basel*. Indeed, through it, he was carrying on her tradition of the performance of sacred music of the 16th and 17th (and also later) centuries as exemplified in the *Ensemble für Kirchenmusik*. In addition, remaining true to his own profession, he printed the music used by the groups, later distributing it in the Laudinella series. Arthur Eglin also honored Ina Lohr in these prints by publishing many of her settings of earlier melodies, particularly psalms.

Her last course at the university was about "'liturgical' (i.e. simply functional) singing, instigated by a theology student from Bremen [...] with 2 Israelis, 2 Catholic teachers, 1 Protestant teacher and 5 theology students". Here, too, she maintained her interest in ecumenical aspects of singing as an expression of faith.[69]

A letter to Kees Vellekoop of 11 September 1965 also demonstrates that she remained up-to-date in what was going on in the world of composition, as she mentions trying very hard to get into the music of Stockhausen in preparation for a concert on 18 October 1965 of his own works that the composer himself would be directing.[70]

Much of her later correspondence with Paul Sacher, beyond issues of programming, is concerned with her preparation of material for the *Mitteilungen des Basler Kammerorchesters,* for which she began assuming an ever-greater responsibility. Apparently the musicologist and music critic, the designated editor of the publication, Dr. Willi Reich, was not necessarily always happy about their interference, as is evident from a letter of Paul Sacher to Ina Lohr of 1 December 1965:

> Would you please read Dr. Reich's suggestions for the next *Mitteilungen* before our meeting this afternoon? He appears not to appreciate our meddling in his editorial ac-

---

und erhöhte Temperatur bleiben mir rührend treu, aber ich habe mich schon fast daran gewöhnt und bin wieder mit Freude an der Arbeit. Schreibe für den Posaunenchor eine Reihe von kurzen Liedanalysen". Letter Ina Lohr to Elisabeth and Hinrich Stoevesandt of 4. August 1965, Elisabeth Stoevesandt, Basel.

69 "'liturgisches' (also einfach dienendes) Singen, angeregt von einem Bremer Theologiestudenten, [...] mit 2 I[s]raeli, 2 katholischen Lehrern, 1 ev. Lehrer und 5 Theologiestudenten". Letter Ina Lohr to Elisabeth and Hinrich Stoevesandt of 14 October 1965, Elisabeth Stoevesandt, Basel.

70 Letter Ina Lohr to Kees Vellekoop of 11 October 1965, Jos Knigge, Utrecht.

tivity, because he disregards all of your suggestions. We should consider the situation this afternoon, so that I can speak in an appropriate manner to Mr. Reich.[71]

Although almost insignificant in itself, it speaks volumes about the extent of their cooperation in the planning and execution of the concerts, that they do not simply want to leave the conception of the program notes to someone else, but instead want to maintain control over their content.

At the beginning of 1966, Paul Sacher was hospitalized in Zurich for a simple tonsillectomy. An abscess behind the tonsils, however, was overlooked, and Paul Sacher then became very ill and thus was convalescent for a considerable period of time. A short letter of 19 January 1966 from Ina Lohr is revelatory concerning the regular rhythm of their work together:

> You will hardly believe it: I don't really know what to do with my "free" Wednesday afternoon, because it is in my bones that I lay out scores and my notes and brew you tea. I could, naturally, fill out my tax form, study the Spohr symphony (it is really beautiful) or deal with everything that lies on the desk. But that will only be possible once I have sent this greeting to you with my best wishes.[72]

It is a palpable sign of the extent of the interaction of their lives. A month later, on 19 February 1966, she was already once again writing about BKO concerns: about the choice of singers for future programs, the preparations for the upcoming choir concert, as well as her opinion of a performance of *Idomeneo* in his absence:

> The marking of the Haydn score [*The Seven Last Words of Our Redeemer on the Cross*, performed on 18 March 1966] took me a lot of time, but came out well (at least I hope so) and is clear. On Monday [21 February 1966] I will do the words in the choir rehearsal and then send you your page, with annotations, back to you. The work is much, much more beautiful than I thought.

71 "Können Sie wohl die Vorschläge von Dr. Reich für die nächsten Mitteilungen noch vor unserer Besprechung heute Nachmittag lesen? Er scheint unsere Einmischung in seine redaktionelle Tätigkeit nicht zu schätzen, weil er alle Ihre Vorschläge unbeachtet lässt. Wir wollen die Angelegenheit heute Nachmittag überlegen, damit ich auf geeignete Weise mit Herrn Reich sprechen kann". Carbon copy of letter Paul Sacher to Ina Lohr of 1 December 1965, private collection, Switzerland.

72 "Sie werden es kaum glauben: ich weiss mit dem 'freien' Mittwochnachmittag nichts Rechtes anzufangen, weil es mir in den Knochen sitzt, dass ich Partituren und Notizen parat lege und Ihnen einen Tee braue. Ich könnte natürlich meine Steuererklärung ausfüllen, die Sinfonie von Spohr studieren (sie ist wirklich schön) oder alles das aufschaffen [sic], was auf dem Schreibtisch liegt. Aber es wird erst gehen, wenn dieser Gruss mit den herzlichsten Wünschen an Sie abgegangen ist". Letter Ina Lohr to Paul Sacher of 19 January 1966, private collection, Switzerland.

Idomeneo, of course, was just again [performed], and particularly with these singers, a [true] experience, but I missed you greatly.[73]

Thus in his absence, Ina Lohr once again stepped in to assist in the preparation
of the choir, most likely discussing that which lay latent in the words. That Paul
Sacher was grateful for this care is evident from an undated card (probably sent
with flowers) after the performance, in which he declared "For me the Haydn
was [truly] an experience. I hope that you were not too displeased".[74]

She traveled to the Netherlands in the Basel carnival period at the end of February, where her sister Etty was in the throes of moving into a new apartment
for the elderly after her retirement in Utrecht. In addition, she went to Amsterdam where the school music department at the conservatory under Jan Boeke
("whom we would have so much liked to have had as my successor") had given
a concert, including, among other things, a work by her. It seems to have been
there that the plan was hatched for her to give a course in solmization for these
music teachers *in spe* at Whitsun. On 5 June 1966 she was able to write to the
Stoevesandts that the course had been very "exciting".[75] Sometime after that,
she performed a concert of 15th and early 16th-century German music with a
Hausmusik class in front of the breathtakingly beautiful Isenheim Altarpiece by
Matthias Grünewald in Colmar, once again attempting to place the music in
the cultural context of the time.[76] It must have been a moving experience for
all concerned.

At the beginning of the summer, she was also involved in preparing some
church services, as in the previous years for the Catholic church in Riehen, but
also in cooperation with the Dutch pastor ds. Wim Fijn van Draat who was
responsible for Dutch Protestants, as well as many lonely non-baptized compa-

---

73 "Die Bezeichnung der Haydn Partitur hat mir sehr viel Zeit genommen, ist aber (ich hoffe
es wenigstens) gut und deutlich herausgekommen. Am Montag mache ich die Worte in
der Chorprobe und schicke Ihnen dann Ihr Blatt bezeichnet zurück. Das Werk ist viel, viel
schöner als ich meinte.
    Idomeneo war natürlich auch jetzt wieder, und gerade mit diesen Solisten, ein Erleb-
nis, aber ich habe Sie schwer vermisst". Letter Ina Lohr to Paul Sacher of 29 January 1966,
private collection, Switzerland.
74 "für mich war der Haydn ein Erlebnis. Ich hoffe, Sie seien nicht zu unzufrieden gewesen".
Undated card, PSF-ILC.
75 Letters Ina Lohr to the Stoevesandts of 20 March and 5 June 1966, Elisabeth Stoevesandt,
Basel.
76 Letters Ina Lohr to the Stoevesandts of 8 February and 17 July 1966, Elisabeth Stoevesandt,
Basel.

triots, in Switzerland. On 31 July 1966 they held their fourth service together in which she took on the function of the organ, singing a psalm for the entrance of the pastor, singing one in alternation with his declaimed verses, and leading the congregation in a third. Perhaps most innovative was the decision to base the sermon on Psalm 117, with each strophe receiving an exegesis in advance of its singing, in response to questions posed by Ina Lohr, with communion being taken after the ninth verse.[77] On 8 August 1966 she reported to the Stoevesandts that

> the congregation was at first somewhat surprised, but then cooperated amazingly and sang very well, much better than otherwise with the organ. If my strength and voice still allow it, we want to dare to do this [again] from time to time. It remains risky, however, and I had palpitations before it, and was exhausted afterwards.[78]

What is so evident from this, is how she was eager to find new forms of liturgy in the hopes of engaging the congregation beyond the mere ritualistic attendance of the service itself. She was aware that she was going beyond the conventional structure, but took any chance to experiment, almost regardless of the effect on her own well-being.

The fact that such activities did have severe consequences for her health, no matter how outwardly successful, was revealed many weeks later, when in a letter of 12 October 1966, she explains that she

> actually had a so-called "depression" for about 7 weeks. As long as I didn't have to do too much and didn't have to continually dissemble to others, it doesn't bother me too much. Behind this curious "wall", which divides me in such a time from other people, I live very intensely, reading and thinking. There was no question of traveling and this is still the case, as I have only regained 1 of 4 lost kilograms.[79]

Once again, she was overwhelmed by one of those black periods in her life in which there seemed to be no other resource other than retreating from society.

---

77 Letter Ina Lohr to the Stoevesandts of 12 October 1966, Elisabeth Stoevesandt, Basel.

78 "Die Gemeinde war zuerst etwas verblüfft, machte dann aber erstaunlich mit und sang sehr gut, viel besser als sonst mit der Orgel. Wenn Kraft und Stimme mir noch erhalten bleiben, wollen wir hie und da so etwas wagen. Es bleibt aber ein Wagnis, und ich hatte vorher Herzklopfen und war nachher erschöpft". Letter Ina Lohr to the Stoevesandts of 8 August 1966, Elisabeth Stoevesandt, Basel.

79 "ich hatte tatsächlich ca. 7 Wochen lang eine 'Depression' wie das so heisst. So lange ich nicht zu viel unternehmen muss und mich andern gegenüber auch nicht dauern[d] verstellen, macht es mir nicht sehr viel. Hinter dieser merkwürdigen 'Wand', die mich in einer solchen Zeit von meinen Mitmenschen trennt, lebe ich sehr intensiv lesend und denkend. Von Reisen war aber keine Rede und das geht auch jetzt noch nicht, denn ich habe erst 1 von 4 verlorenen Kilo wieder zugenommen". Letter Ina Lohr to the Stoevesandts of 12 October 1966, Elisabeth Stoevesandt, Basel.

She went on to speak of how her sister and her partner came to visit her instead and how they had enjoyed themselves, but that she had suffered

> because my sister saw and treated me primarily as [her] poor sick sister. It helps me much more when my Basler friends, in spite of everything, exact something from me, place demands, because they know from experience that I *was* helped many years ago and that I find this help again and again in prayer.[80]

In retrospect, this is perhaps one of the reasons for the longevity of her cooperation with Paul Sacher. In that he continued to place demands upon her, even when she was raising walls between herself and society, he also gave her a handhold, a structure within which she could find her own way out of the depths and back into her normal life; he did not treat her as a lesser being, just because she was having psychological difficulties.

And that she found renewed strength and faith from such experiences is revealed by a description of a course she gave for roughly 30 directors of trombone choirs in the old "Ritterhaus" in Uerikon:

> It was a highly delightful occasion, because they absolutely wanted to know *why* they really play *what*. It was very contemplative but also light-hearted and we could sing so marvelously. And I could actually project more of the long absent light than would have been possible before this depression. I live once again wholly from gratitude![81]

The cooperation with Paul Sacher also continued unabated, with the usual discussions about programming, program notes, and soloists. On 26 August 1966 he also wrote to her in his role as the director of the Musik-Akademie Basel that he was enclosing a letter concerning the pension fund which was sent to all teachers for her information, in which obligatory retirement ages were introduced, 60 for women and 65 for men. He assured her that it was not valid for her, as she was already pensioned off and was only still teaching a few hours at the Schola. He then went on to say that he wished her to continue in this

---

80 "denn meine Schwester sah und behandelte mich vor allem als arme kranke Schwester. Es hilft mir viel mehr, wenn meine Basler Freunde trotz allem etwas von mir verlangen, Ansprüche stellen, weil sie aus Erfahrung wissen, dass mir schon vor vielen Jahren geholfen <u>wurde</u> und dass ich diese Hilfe im Gebet immer wieder suche und finde". Letter Ina Lohr to the Stoevesandts of 12 October 1966, Elisabeth Stoevesandt, Basel.

81 "Es war eine höchst erfreuliche Sache, weil sie unbedingt wissen wollten, <u>warum</u> sie eigentlich <u>was</u> spielten. Es ging recht besinnlich und doch auch heiter zu und wir haben herrlich singen können. Und tatsächlich konnte ich von dem lange entbehrten Licht mehr weiter geben als es vor dieser Depression möglich gewesen wäre. Ich lebe wieder ganz aus der Dankbarkeit!" Letter Ina Lohr to the Stoevesandts of 14 November 1966, Elisabeth Stoevesandt, Basel.

manner, as long as she had strength to do so.[82] And indeed, her teaching load remained at about 12 hours/week.[83]

At the beginning of 1967 there was a small flurry of letters, some concerning business, others quite personal. First of all, on 20 January Paul Sacher wrote to inquire whether Ina Lohr had an additional score and also a recording of Sven-Erik Bäck's *Favola,* which in all likelihood she was actively promoting. It was performed in the BKO concert of 18 January 1968. In another letter of the same day, he comments on the preparatory work for the *Mitteilungen des Basler Kammerorchesters* for their March performances of the St. John Passion. It clearly delineates her field of activity in regard to the program notes:

> With the enclosure, I am returning all of the material for the "Mitteilungen". I have put a plus or, respectively, a minus sign on all of them; but also the texts which received general approval are all too extended, so that we need to make a selection.
>
> In my eyes, it is a shortcoming that not a single article is about the St. John Passion, and I thus wonder whether a passage shouldn't be taken from Schering's text. Not everything he writes is out of date. When we perform the St. John Passion, there should really be at least one text that deals exclusively with this work.
>
> We will try to print the desired image from the book, but then the text selection will of necessity be still more limited. Incidentally, Dr. Vortisch [secretary of the BKO] prefers the image on page 37 to that found at the beginning of the book.[84]

Taking all this into consideration when looking at the final product (cf. Ill. 7.5), a single folded leaf, we can see the extent to which Ina Lohr's religious convictions also colored the public presentation of the BKO:

> Today his work is heard by an audience that cannot really imagine Bach's strong tie to Lutheran orthodoxy. And his mysticism, which also marks the work of many theologians of his time and found its expression in strictly formed orders, does, to be sure, touch us strongly, occupies musicologists, musicians and listeners, but remains for the most

---

82   Letter Paul Sacher to Ina Lohr of 26 August 1966, PSF-ILC.

83   Letter Ina Lohr to the Stoevesandts of 14 November 1966, Elisabeth Stoevesandt, Basel.

84   "In der Beilage gebe ich Ihnen das gesamte Material für die 'Mitteilungen' zurück. Ich habe überall ein Plus- resp. Minuszeichen gesetzt; aber auch die Texte, die allseitig Zustimmung finden, sind zu ausgedehnt, sodass wir uns zu einer Auswahl durchringen müssen.

     In meinen Augen ist es eine Schwäche, dass kein einziger Aufsatz von der Johannes-Passion handelt, und ich frage mich doch, ob nicht ein Stück aus dem Schering'schen Text genommen werden sollte. Es ist nicht alles, was er schreibt, veraltet. Wenn wir die Johannes-Passion aufführen, müsste doch wenigstens ein Text sich ausschliesslich mit diesem Werk beschäftigen.

     Wir wollen gerne versuchen, das gewünschte Buchbild zu bringen, nur wird dadurch die Textauswahl selbstverständlich noch beschränkter. Dr. Vortisch fände übrigens das Bild auf Seite 37 besser als das am Anfang des Buches stehende." Carbon copy of letter of Paul Sacher to Ina Lohr of 20 January 1967, private collection, Switzerland.

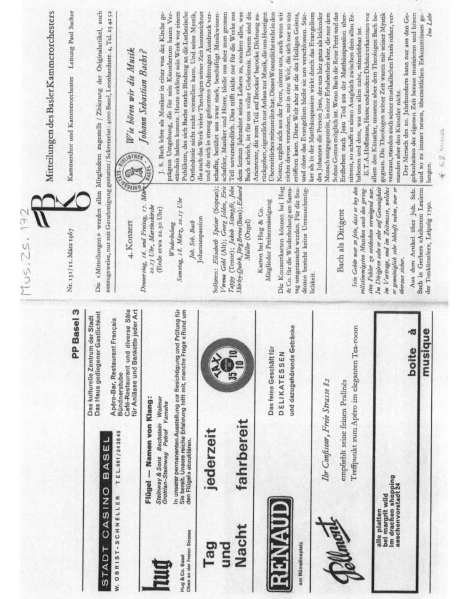

Ill. 7.5: *Mitteilungen des Basler Kammerorchesters*, 11 March 1967, Basel University Library.

Zahlenmystik bei J. S. Bach

J. S. Bach wurde als 14. Mitglied in die Mizlersche Sozietät aufgenommen, der als 11. Mitglied G. Fr. Händel angehörte. Der Canon triplex a 6 voci, auf dem Bilde in Bachs Hand, mit der Signatur J. S. Bach, ist Bachs meisterlicher Beitrag zur feierlichen Aufnahme in die Sozietät und stellt ein von Zahlen- und Namensymbolik erfülltes Rätselstück dar, dessen Entschlüsselung und Ausdeutung Fr. Smend verdankt wird. Dieser Canon triplex a 6 voci in verschiedensten Umkehrungen und Lesungen (Canon motu contrario) gestattet 480 Lösungen, in denen als Zahlen und Namenssymbole enthalten sind: SDGl. (Soli Deo Gloria) — J. S. B. — Johann Sebastian Bach — G. F. Händel und die Kreuzinschrift I. N. R. I. Die Gruppierung der stimmigen originalen Rätselauflösung des Kanons findet sich in J. S. Bachs Werk im Sanctus wieder. J. S. Bachs Mystik in der zeitvolligen drei Arten der Johannespassion haben zeitweilig drei Arten der Johannespassion angeboten und sind später wieder gefügt worden. Ob sie ursprünglich der verschiedenen «vierten» Passion angehört haben, ist nicht beweisbar. Neben diesen Veränderungen im Aufbau hat aber Bach im mittelalterlichen Kunstgeheimnissen der Dombauhütten, der Glasmalereien und der Farbtönnerung der grossen Maler zu vergleichen.

Nach Friedrich Smend in «St. Thomas zu Leipzig», Wiesbaden 1965.

Die Entstehungsgeschichte der Johannespassion

[...] mittelfing erneuter Nachprüfung. Sicher scheint, dass das Werk, so, wie man es heute kennt, nicht in einem Zuge und nicht nach einem von vornherein feststehenden Plan komponiert und dass es im Laufe einer Reihe von Wiederaufführungen zahlreiche Umgestaltungen sowohl im Aufbau wie in der Fassung der einzelnen Sätze unterworfen worden ist. Nach dem gegenwärtigen Stande der Kenntnis erscheint es jedoch, dass der Bestand an Sätzen in der ersten Fassung derselbe gewesen ist wie in der letzten. In einem Zwischenstadium stand am Anfang die Choralfantasie «O Mensch, bewein dein Sünde gross» als gewaltiges Exordium, die später an das Ende des 1. Teils der Matthäuspassion gerückt worden ist. Ähnlich hat in einer Zwischenfassung die Choralfantasie «Christe, du Lamm Gottes», die Bach, wohl noch vor der Entstehung der Passion, seiner als Probestück für Leipzig komponierten Kantate Nr. 23 «Du wahrer Gott und Davidsohn» angehängt hat, die Conclusio gebildet; in der letzten Fassung steht aber an ihrer Stelle wieder der schlichte Choralsatz «Ach Herr, lass dein lieb Engelein». Ausser diesen beiden Choralsätzen haben zeitweilig drei Arien der Johannespassion angehört und sind später wieder getilgt worden. Ob sie ursprünglich der verschiedenen «vierten» Passion angehört haben, ...

Langé der Zeit auch eine grosse Menge von Überarbeitungen im einzelnen vorgenommen, Transpositionen, Uminstrumentierungen usw., und da die Fassungen der Partitura wahrscheinlich bis in die 1740er Jahre hinein reichen, bieten die Varianten ein krauses Bild. Die mit W. Rusts Ausgabe in Bd. XII, 1, der Bach-Gesamtausgabe allgemein akzeptierte Gestalt entspricht der späteren Überlieferungsgeschichte, ohne dass sie als einer sich letzten Willen Bachs geschrieben werden könnte. Durch die Tonartenkomplexe klar gegliedert, baut sich das Werk in einer Folge von scharf zugespitzten und kontrastierenden Szenen auf. Gemäss dem saublich nüchternen Johannesbericht, der die stille Grösse des Gottessohnes in harten Zusammenwirken mit der Sinnwidrigkeit einer tobenden Menschenmasse stellt, überragt die realistisch aufgefasste Tragik des Geschehens die Betrachtung, die hier auf zwei Ariosi, sieben Arien und eine Arie mit Chor beschränkt wird (von ihnen gehören ein Arioso und eine Arie zu den Ersatzstücken für die gültigen Arien). Ausser dem Eingangssatz und dem Chorsatz «Ruht wohl» fehlen kontemplative Chöre; der Chor tritt nur in den Turbaätzen, den Choralen und, ein einziges Mal, in dem allegorischen Dialog «Eilt», ihr angefochtnen Seelen» in Tätigkeit. Auch kontemplative Rezitative fehlen gänzlich. Wie die Tonarten, so prallen die berücksichtigen Rezitative und die Turbae grell aufeinander. Sehr ausgebildet ist in ihrem zehnungslosen Naturalismus an die Kreuzigungsgebärtdillungen alttestamentlicher Maler erinnernd, bühneristen die Chöre der Juden, der Hohenpriester, der Kriegsknechte usw. vornehmlich gliedernde und regenerschliessende Funktion zu. Stärker als das Schwergewicht von 1739 betont damit die Johannespassion den Zusammenhang mit der Historie und den Arien wie ihrer bergleichlichen oratorischen Passion des 17. Jahrhunderts.

Friedrich Blume

In seiner «Geschichte der evangelischen Kirchenmusik», Kassel 1965.

Zahlenverhältnisse

Es gibt Augenblicke — vorzüglich wenn ich viel in das grossen Sebastian Bach Werken geleten —, in denen mir die musikalischen Zahlenverhältnisse, ja die mystischen Regeln des Kontrapunkts ein inneres Grauen erwecken.   E. T. A. Hoffmann

Aus seinem Artikel «Höchst zerstreute Gedanken», Erstdruck in der «Zeitung für die elegante Welt», 1814.

Hermann Hesse über die «Zeit der grossen Musikblüte»

Im Jahre 1935 schrieb Hesse über sein «Glasperlenspiel»:

«... Es kam mir eines Tages, manche Jahre bevor ich mit dem Versuch einer Niederschrift begann, die Vision eines individuellen aber überzeitlichen Lebenslaufes: ich dachte mir einen Menschen, der in mehreren Wiedergeburten die grossen Epochen der Menschheitsgeschichte miterlebt. Übriggeblieben ist von dieser ursprünglichen Intention, wie Sie sehen, die Reihe der Knechtschen Lebensläufe, die drei historischen und eine kastalische. Es gab übrigens in meinem Plan noch einen weiteren Lebenslauf, ins 18. Jahrhundert als die Zeit der grossen Musikblüte verlegt, ich habe gearbeitet und ihm mehr Studien gewidmet als allen anderen Biographien Knechts, aber es ist mir nicht geglückt, das Ding blieb als Fragment liegen. Die allzu genau bekannte und allzu reich dokumentierte Welt jener Jahrhunderts entzog sich dem Einbau in die mehr legendären Räume der übrigen Leben Knechts ...»

Ein maschinengeschriebenes Notizblatt Hesses ist uns neben zwei Skizzen erhalten geblieben:

Knecht wird Theologe, studiert in Tübingen mit Oetinger, schwankt zwischen Liebe zur Musik und zur Frömmigkeit, ist ohne Ehrgeiz aber voll Sehnsucht nach einem erfüllten Leben, einer Harmonie, einem Dienst am Vollkommenen.

Darum allmählich mit Theologie unzufrieden: zu viel Lehrstreit, Kirchenstreit, Parteien usw. Besucht Zinzendorf und die Inspirierten, ist sehr vom Pietismus erfüllt, aber das alles ist ihm zu kämpferisch, zu exaltiert usw.

Wird Pfarrer, findet aber kein Genüge dabei.

Spielt Orgel, erfindet Präludien usw., hört sagenhaft von Seb. Bach reden. Erst ganz spät, schon nicht mehr jung, findet ein Klang von Bach bis zu ihm: Einer spielt ihm ein paar Choralvorspiele usw. von B. vor. Jetzt «weiss» er, was er sein Leben lang gesucht hat. Der Kollege hat auch die Johannespassion gehört, erzählt davon, kann einiges reproduzieren, Knecht verschafft sich Auszüge aus diesem Werk. Er erkennt: hier hat, abseits von allen Lehrstreiten usw., das Christentum noch einmal einen neuen, herrlichen Ausdruck gefunden, ist Glanz und Harmonie geworden.

Er legt sein Amt nieder, wird Kantor, sucht sich Bach-Noten zu verschaffen. Bach ist eben gestorben, Knecht sagt: «Da hat nun Einer gelebt, der hatte alles, was ich suchte, und ich wusste nichts davon. Aber ich bin doch zufrieden, mein Leben war nicht umsonst». Er resigniert als stiller Organist.

Aus «Hermann Hesse: Der vierte Lebenslauf Josef Knechts», herausgegeben von Ninon Hesse, Frankfurt am Main 1965.

Ill. 7.5: (continued)

part incomprehensible to us. […] Therefore, the aria texts, which are partially based on Brockes' baroque poetry, are only an occasion for the music that should transmit the eternal to us today. This essential quality is in the notes, results from the form, [and] takes us, even if we understand nothing of it, into a world that can only reveal itself to us in this manner. This world is that of the Holy Spirit, and without the Gospel, it remains closed to us. […] Someone from the 20th century can only make music and hear it in accordance with the circumstances of his time, thus attaining ever new, eternal insights.[85]

This text, surrounded by various other passages about Bach's bent to mysticism and numerology – while on a certain level no doubt true – presumes a comprehension of the composer's religious and theological understanding that would certainly not only make many listeners of the 20th and 21st centuries uncomfortable, but also I suspect those of the 18th. Although not said in so many words, it implies that without true belief in the Lutheran faith, one is unable to adequately execute Bach's religious oeuvre, a creed of certain members of the early 20th-century Bach Gesellschaft and its Dutch adherents.[86] What is remarkable is the self-evident way that it characterizes the BKO performance of the work.

She not only wrote these notes, but she was once again also highly involved in the rehearsals of the choir. On 4 March 1967, she explained to the Stoevesandts:

There was not only [the task] of writing about the St. John Passion, but also much to discuss and to rehearse with the Chamber Choir. All help me, so that I do not overexert myself in the process, and it is now really getting better. But I am so tired that I canceled the course in Amsterdam after Whitsun, for safety's sake.[87]

---

85 "Heute erklingt sein Werk vor einem Publikum, das sich Bachs starke Bindung an die Lutherische Orthodoxie nicht recht vorstellen kann. Und seine Mystik, die auch das Werk vieler Theologen seiner Zeit kennzeichnet und die sich in streng geformten Ordnungen Ausdruck verschaffte, berührt uns zwar stark, beschäftigt Musikwissenschaftler, Musiker und Hörer, bleibt uns aber zum grossen Teil unverständlich. […] Darum sind die Arientexte, die zum Teil auf Brockes' barocke Dichtung zurückgehen, eigentlich nur Anlass zur Musik, die uns Heutigen Überzeitliches mitzuteilen hat. Dieses Wesentliche steht in den Noten, ergibt sich aus der Form, nimmt uns, auch wenn wir nichts davon verstehen, mit in eine Welt, die sich nur so uns eröffnen kann. Diese Welt aber ist die des Heiligen Geistes, und ohne das Evangelium bleibt sie uns verschlossen. […] Der Mensch des 20. Jahrhunderts kann nur aus den Gegebenheiten der eigenen Zeit heraus musizieren und hören und so zu immer neuen, überzeitlichen Erkenntnissen gelangen". Ina Lohr, "Wie hören wir die Musik Johann Sebastian Bachs?", in: *Mitteilungen des Basler Kammerorchesters*, No. 131, 11 March 1967, 1.
86 Jed Wentz, "On the Protestant Roots of Gustav Leonhardt's Performance Style".
87 "Über die Johannes-Passion gab es nicht nur zu schreiben, sondern auch viel zu reden und mit dem Kammerchor zu üben. Alle helfen mit, dass ich mich dabei nicht überanstrenge, und es wird nun auch wirklich besser. Aber so müde bin ich, dass ich den Kurs in Amsterdam nach Pfingsten sicherheitshalber abgesagt habe". Letter Ina Lohr to the Stoevesandts of 4 March 1967, Elisabeth Stoevesandt, Basel.

After all these years, given the correct composition, there was no stopping her cooperation with Paul Sacher in the preparation of the choir. There were two differences, however: she let herself be helped, so that she did not become over-exhausted (and it was recognized that this was not something she could achieve on her own); and she was happy with the results:

> The St. John Passion was much more than a beautiful concert, and that on all 3 evenings [16–18 March 1967]. The soloists were at first somewhat astonished by the conception and tempo and also by the fact that we asked them to stand while singing along with the final chorale. But just this transmitted to them the correct understanding of our "liturgy" already in the dress rehearsal, and the whole thing then became a true experience.[88]

And just shortly before this, at the beginning of the year on 21 January 1967, Ina Lohr had written in apology that she could not attend the celebration of 40 years BKO – no doubt due to ill health – declaring

> At least I must write you on the day of the anniversary, in order to congratulate you wholeheartedly. Actually, my complete memoirs should have come today too, but the work on them cannot be fit into [my] overfull days, and you have more from it, if I am there for the "daily business". And that I am: much more so than previously. And I wish with complete egotism for myself that our ever more beautiful cooperation may continue to last and flourish.[89]

In return Paul Sacher sent a small flowering tree in celebration of the BKO's birthday, thanking her "profoundly" for her letter.[90] On 27 January 1967 Ina Lohr sent her regrets for not being able to attend the concert of the previous day as she was still "barking", bringing the letter to a close by saying that she looked forward to the coming Wednesday, "for our 'everyday life' has in recent times also become quite festive".[91]

---

88 "Die Johannes-Passion war viel mehr als ein schönes Konzert, und zwar alle 3 Abende. Die Solisten waren zuerst etwas erstaunt über Auffassung und Tempo und auch darüber, dass wir sie darum baten den Schlusschoral stehend mitzusingen. Aber gerade das brachte ihnen schon in der Generalprobe das richtige Verständnis für unsere 'Liturgie', und das ganze wurde dann ein Erlebnis". Letter Ina Lohr to the Stoevesandts of 24 March 1967, Elisabeth Stoevesant, Basel.

89 "Wenigstens schreiben muss ich Ihnen am Jubiläumstag um Ihnen von ganzem Herzen zu gratulieren. Eigentlich hätten die vollständigen Erinnerungen auf heute kommen sollen, aber die Arbeit daran geht nicht in die überfüllten Tage hinein, und Sie haben mehr davon, wenn ich dann für die 'laufende Geschäfte' da bin. Und das bin ich: viel mehr als früher. Und ich wünsche mir ganz egoistisch, dass unsere immer schönere Zusammenarbeit noch weiter dauern und gedeihen möge". Letter Ina Lohr to Paul Sacher of 21 January 1967, private collection, Switzerland.

90 Undated visiting card Paul Sacher to Ina Lohr, PSF-ILC.

91 "Und ich freue mich auf den nächsten Mittwoch, denn unser 'Alltag' ist in letzter Zeit eigentlich auch recht festlich". Letter Ina Lohr to Paul Sacher of 27 January 1967, private collection, Switzerland.

All these messages demonstrate how their working relationship had become increasingly warm and trusting, as was corroborated by her letter to Maja Sacher of 31 January 1967 in which she explains that she could thank her husband on the following day when he came to "work", but that she wanted to "explicitly tell her that she really would have happily come this time, had looked forward to coming and belonging completely", referring back to times (see letter 7 June 1941, p. 226) when she did not allow herself to join in such festivities because she felt so out of place. Phrases in other letters from this period reinforce this impression, as when Paul Sacher speaks dismissively of a review of the St. John Passion, writing ironically that "Albertli [Swiss diminutive form of the name Albert] Müry also found *our* [my italics] St. John Passion 'breathless'. At least he writes that in a newspaper", obviously a commentary between colleagues.[92] Or when Ina Lohr calls the live recording of the performance (of 26 March 1965?) of Honegger's *Prélude, Arioso, and Fughette sur le nom de BACH* a "valuable memory".[93]

This, however, was only one aspect of her life, as is made all too evident by her version of the age-old lament of retired people: "I always thought that I would have time for everything in my *old-age*, but that is absolutely and completely untrue. It seems to me that I have more to do than ever, only that everything is much nicer and freer. And naturally everything goes a bit more slowly".[94]

She considered the restrictions caused by her health to be insignificant, reporting to the Stoevesandts that her depression was now completely a thing of the past and that she was once again "living and working" from a sense of deep gratitude.[95] This is significant in that it indicates that the depression of the previous year held its sway far longer than indicated by the letter of 12 October 1966. This, however, did not mean that her state of health was good, as on 3 July 1967 she wrote to the Vellekoops that her throat had been "swept out" twice and they had once again found degenerate diphtheria bacilli, just as in the pre-

92 "Nun hat also der Albertli Müri unsere 'Johannes-Passion' auch 'atemlos' gefunden. Wenigstens schreibt er das in einer Zeitung." Carbon copy of letter Paul Sacher to Ina Lohr of 6 April 1967, private collection, Switzerland.

93 "kostbare Erinnerung". Letter Ina Lohr to Paul Sacher of 15 June 1967, private collection, Switzerland.

94 "Und ich habe immer gemeint, im <u>Alter</u> würde ich für alles Zeit haben, aber das stimmt nun ganz und gar nicht. Es kommt mir so vor, alsob [sic] ich mehr zu tun hätte als je, nur dass alles viel schöner und freier ist. Und natürlich geht auch alles ein wenig langsam". Letter Ina Lohr to the Stoevesandts of 7 May 1967.

95 Ibid.

vious two years, which had caused her cough and tiredness. This necessitated that she go to the hospital in Lucerne for daily treatment.[96]

Her abhorrence of war surfaced once again with the Six-Day War between the Arabs and Israelis. She found relief from her own emotional turmoil in the same way as she had done at the end of World War II, in that she volunteered to lead the first meeting of the Children's Aid Fund for Israel.[97] She could not sit at home in despair, but rather felt called to do whatever was in her means to help those who suffered innocently from the consequences of belligerence.

Another aspect of her life is also reflected by short remarks in her letters to the Stoevesandts, namely an inner need for accompanying people through their terminal illnesses. She speaks of being there for parents whose first child was stillborn; for a friend and colleague who was terminally ill and wanted to discuss religious questions, but not with a pastor; or for a close friend from her student days, whom she visited over a considerable period once or twice a day until the woman found her final rest.[98] As we will see later, this activity became increasingly important to her when she moved into a residence for senior citizens, and she came to see it as a vocation, a part of her dedication of her life to God.

Although she always celebrated Christmas fervently, she had the sensation of never having had as much to do as in the 1967 season:

> We sang and played a lot, and my Christmas cantata – which I wrote in the garden in Haarlem in the summer vacation of 1947 – suddenly experienced a successful comeback. The *Hausmusik* (some of them, who were free) sang and played like real musicians in a hospital (with a real baby under the Christmas tree) and at the Christmas party which the University gave for the students from developing countries. That was impressive. They first listened, somewhat ill at ease, to the Gospel, to the exegesis and songs, but with increasing attention, so that it became gratifying for us all and it ended with Adeste fidelis being sung in at least 5 languages simultaneously, which was not beautiful, but convincing.[99]

96 Letter Ina Lohr to the Vellekoops of 3 July 1967, Jos Knigge, Utrecht.
97 Letter Ina Lohr to the Stoevesandts, 9 June 1967, Elisabeth Stoevesandt, Basel.
98 Letters of Ina Lohr to the Stoevesandts of 27 September 1967 and 13 October 1968, Elisabeth Stoevesandt, Basel.
99 "We hebben heel veel gezongen en gespeeld, en mijn Kerstkantate, die ik de zomervacantie 1947 in de tuin in Haarlem componeerde, beleefde opeens een succesvol come-back. De huismuziek (enige ervan, die vrij waren) zongen en speelden als echt muzikanten in een ziekenhuis (met een echte baby onder de Kerstboom) en op het Kerstfeest, dat die Universiteit gaf voor de studenten uit de ontwikkelingslanden. Dat was indrukwekkend. Ze luisterden eerst wat onwennig naar het evangelie, naat uitlegging en liederen, maar toen met steeds meer aandacht, tot het boeiend werd voor ons allemaal en eindigde met een niet

The year could not come to a close, however, without thoughts of the future. In her Christmas letter to the Sachers of 6 December 1967, she expressed the hope that "the biggest present that was granted to you both and to me during the past year endure in the new year: the knowledge of one another's existence [with a pun on the other meaning of "Da-sein": "being there"] and the gift of [our] cooperation".[100] Obviously they had reached a point in their lives where their awareness of their own mortality made them wish to express their gratitude for that which they had shared together in the past, and for all that might still lie in front of them.

Ina Lohr was having increasing difficulties with sinusitis and also with vertigo. Judging from their correspondence, it seems that it was thought that some of the problems might have been caused by some unspecified problem with her teeth, in that on 22 April 1968 Paul Sacher wrote "now we have also survived this tooth operation. I am glad that it is beginning to get better and wish you new strength".[101] To which Ina Lohr responded on the same day:

> After you left yesterday, I suddenly stood still in the middle of the room, completely filled with thankfulness for the fact we have once again received the gift of our cooperation. And today your letter and the wonderful cactus tree corroborate that you also experience this "new beginning" similarly. I have just reorganized my indoor garden, and this evening I will listen to the Mendelssohn recording in peace and quiet [he had sent it for her evaluation of the symphonies they were considering for a concert in the following season]. And the new tree removes any desire to go to Lucerne, so that we can work next Wednesday if you are free.[102]

mooi, maar overtuigend gezongen Adeste fidelis in minstens 5 talen tegelijk!" Letter Ina Lohr to the Vellekoops of 2 January 1968, Jos Knigge, Utrecht.

100 "Möge das grösste Geschenk, das Ihnen beiden und mir im vergangenen Jahr zuteil wurde: das umeinanders [sic] Da-Sein wissen und das Geschenk der Zusammenarbeit uns auch im neuen Jahr erhalten bleiben". Letter Ina Lohr to Paul Sacher of 6 December 1967, private collection, Switzerland.

101 "nun haben wir auch diese Zahnoperation überstanden. Ich bin glücklich, dass es anfängt besser zu gehen & wünsche Ihnen neue Kraft". Letter Paul Sacher to Ina Lohr of 22 April 1968, PSF-ILC.

102 "Als Sie gestern gegangen waren, stand ich plötzlich mitte [im] Zimmer still, ganz erfüllt von Dankbarkeit dafür, dass uns unsere Zusammenarbeit noch einmal geschenkt worden ist. Und heute bestätigen mir Ihr Brief und der wundervolle Kaktusbaum, dass auch Sie diesen 'Neuanfang' so erleben. Soeben habe ich meinen Zimmergarten neu eingerichtet und heute Abend werde ich die Mendel[s]sohnplatte in aller Ruhe anhören. Und der neue Baum nimmt mir jede Lust nach Luzern zu gehen, sodass wir nächsten Mittwoch, wenn Sie frei sind, arbeiten können". Letter Ina Lohr to Paul Sacher of 22 April 1968, private collection, Switzerland.

Apparently the operation "on the silly wisdom tooth lying with its roots leading up to her right ear"[103] did eventually result in an improvement in her res-
piratory problems, but the "cervical vertebrae and therefore also the attacks
of vertigo when riding in a car or train" remained very disturbing, so that she
was forced to renounce all travel.[104] The vertigo persisted for the rest of her life,
greatly reducing her radius of activity.

Although no longer working for the professional division of the Schola, she
had abiding concern for the institution's welfare. As yet, they had been unable
to find instructors to take over all of her courses at the school. But even worse,
as she reported to the Vellekoops on 11 August 1968, was the fact that there was
such internal dissension:

> After all of the discouraging things, Dr. Nef now wants to retire in 1½ years, when he
> is 60. Sacher, in the meantime, has been searching continually for someone who could
> give Protestant church music and now all of a sudden there is an outstanding musi-
> cologist [Dr. Rudolf Häusler],[105] who also has a diploma for choir directing and sing-
> ing (he studied with von Fischer and wrote his dissertation on Goudimel) who wants
> to work in the afternoon for us for a year, take a look at everything and then decide
> whether he wants to take "Gehörbildung" [ear-training], church music and the direc-
> torship upon himself.[106]

With this, one sees that Paul Sacher was still trying to find a solution that would
allow the Schola to continue along its established path, someone to replace Ina
Lohr's theoretical program. In aid of this, Ina Lohr gave both Rudolf Häusler
and Kurt Widmer, a bass who was also joining the staff, a few lessons in solmization, Gregorian chant, and French and German songs. In spite of all of this,

103 "De onnozele verstandskies lag met de wortels naar boven onder mijn rechter oor". Letter
       Ina Lohr to the Vellekoops of 23 June 1968, Jos Knigge, Utrecht.
104 "Aber, obwohl es mir nach der Kieferoperation vom letzten April sehr viel besser geht, blei-
       ben die Halswirbeln [sic] und damit die Schwindelanfälle beim Auto- und Bahnfahren
       sehr störend, sodass ich noch immer auf alle Reisen verzichten muss". Letter Ina Lohr to
       the Stoevesandts of 11 April 1969, Elisabeth Stoevesandt.
105 Minutes of the teacher's conference of 20 May 1968, PSF-PSC.
106 "Na al die ontmoedigende dingen wil Dr. Nef nu over 1½ jaar, als hij 60 is, zich laten pen-
       sioneren. Sacher heeft intussen aldoor gezocht naar iemand, die Evangelische Kerkmuziek
       kon geven en nu kwam daar opeens een uitstekend musicoloog, die ook een koordirectie
       en een zangdiploma heeft (hij studeerde bij von Fischer en promoveerde op Goudimel) en
       die wil nu een jaar lang 's middags bij ons werken, alles eens bekijken en dan beslissen, of
       hij 'Gehörbildung', kerkmuziek en de leiding op zich neemt". Letter Ina Lohr to the Vel-
       lekoops of 11 August 1968, Jos Knigge, Utrecht.

there remained a pressure, "a kind of guilt feeling in regard to Dr. Nef".[107] They had worked well together for 30 years, and she had not realized that she would be leaving him in the lurch by retiring from the professional division. At the same time, she asked herself whether "we can keep the Schola alive, which we started up in a time of almost frivolous enthusiasm, now that everything is so pragmatic, so focused 'on success'".[108] At about the same time, her successor in the theology department at the university had resigned, so that they once again offered her the job. As she was unable to take it on, it was decided to no longer offer a class in liturgy.[109]

At the beginning of 1969, Paul Sacher fought a long battle with flu, with four bouts within a comparatively short time period.[110] This necessitated, of course, finding a solution for the choir rehearsals in March and June involving Alessandro Scarlatti's *Passio D.N. secundum Joannem* and Igor Stravinsky's *The Flood*. On 4 January 1969 Paul Sacher was informed by Ina Lohr that the following disposition had been organized:

> I will take over the rehearsal of next Monday with [Frieder] Liebendörfer on the piano, for [Francis] Travis needs Vally [Valerie Kägi] in his orchestra rehearsal. The Scarlatti is much more beautiful than we thought. Unfortunately, the Dellers, father and son [Alfred and Mark], will hardly allow us to drive out their rubati. The Passion, particularly from the rhythmical point of view, is so full of surprises. But then the "integer valor" should be maintained! [...] On the 13th and 15th, Liebendörfer will then rehearse the Stravinsky, for in that week I have all sorts of things to do otherwise.[111]

It is obvious here, that once again she had no scruples about jumping in when necessary to ensure the preparations for a BKO concert. On 18 February 1969, Paul Sacher wrote that he would be "particularly grateful" if she would go and listen to one of the choir rehearsals at the beginning of March, as he would like

---

107 "een soort van schuldgevoel tegenover Dr. Nef". Letter Ina Lohr to the Vellekoops of 11 August 1968.

108 "of we de Schola, die we in een tijd van bijna lichtzinnig enthousiasme begonnen zijn, kunnen in leven houden, nu alles zo pragmatisch, zo 'op succes' gericht is". Letter Ina Lohr to the Vellekoops of 7 April 1969, Jos Knigge, Utrecht.

109 Letter Ina Lohr to the Vellekoops of 15 June 1969, Jos Knigge, Utrecht.

110 Letter of Ina Lohr to the Stoevesandts of 11 April 1969, Elisabeth Stoevesandt, Basel.

111 "Die Probe vom nächsten Montag werde ich übernehmen mit Liebendörfer am Klavier, denn Travis braucht Vally in seiner Orchesterprobe. Der Scarlatti ist noch viel schöner als wir meinten. Leider werden sich Vater und Sohn Deller kaum ihre Rubati austreiben lassen. Die Passion ist gerade vom Rhythmischen her so voller Überraschungen. Aber dann sollte der 'integer valor' bleiben! [...] Am 13. und 15. sollte Liebendörfer dann Strawinsky üben, denn in der Woche habe ich sonst allerhand zu tun". Letter Ina Lohr to Paul Sacher of 4 January 1969, private collection, Switzerland.

to know how the choir was progressing. The seriousness of his condition, however, may be elicited from a letter of 9 March 1969, in which she mentions how
she had discovered that he was in the hospital and commenting that no matter
what happens, they had had so many good and beautiful experiences, that they
could with a thankful heart reduce their workload somewhat, which would also
be good for his wife and for her.[112] This may have been true for the women, but
Paul Sacher recovered his strength and continued his career for many years to
come. In the same letter she also mentioned that the score of the passion was
full of errors, and that she had already spent four hours correcting them, and
that the work would continue the following day.

This time her participation in the concert yielded great pleasure, as is evident from her letter to the Stoevesandts of 11 April 1969:

> I had to actively take part in the rehearsals, with the choir as well as with the soloists,
> and it was actually very nice. It turned out, namely, that the father and son Dellers who
> sang the Testo (evangelist) and Pilatus, were not at all at home in the story of the pas-
> sion, so that Sacher continually and desperately requested me to "proselytize". And then
> Mark Deller, as the evangelist, sang the story movingly.[113]

It must have been particularly gratifying to her to have Paul Sacher requesting
her to do that which he had so much opposed in the past. It remains a question
of whether this was a purely musical decision, or whether they were also moving closer together on religious issues as well.

Over the years, she had developed a close relationship with Ursula Burkhard,
who was born blind in 1930, became a teacher, working with both blind and
seeing children. Together they created songs for children, with Ursula Burkhard
writing the text and Ina Lohr the melodies, such as those published in *Kleine
Biblische Balladen zum Singen und Sagen*,[114] or songs about the annual Basel fair
for children. In 1969 Ina Lohr also assisted her when it became necessary for
her to find a new place for her therapeutic work with deaf and blind children,
in conjunction with the Basel department of social work and the Children's
Hospital. Paul Sacher had come up with someone who was willing to under-

---

112 Letter Ina Lohr to Paul Sacher of 9 March 1969, private collection, Switzerland.
113 "Ich musste sowohl in den Chorproben wie mit den Solisten tatkräftig mitwirken und
     eigentlich war das sehr schön. Es stellte sich nämlich heraus, dass Vater und Sohn Deller,
     die den Testo (Evangelist) und den Pilatus sangen, in der Passionsgeschichte recht wenig
     daheim waren, sodass Sacher mich dauernd und dringend zum 'Frömmeln' aufforderte.
     Und dann hat Mark Deller als Evangelist die Geschichte ergreifend gesungen". Letter Ina
     Lohr to the Stoevesandts of 11 April 1969, Elisabeth Stoevesandt, Basel.
114 Basel: Hug 1973.

write the costs of this work, for which Ina Lohr thanked him in a letter of 18 July 1969, saying that he was "the friend who never turns one down nor forgets a request and who does whatever is in his capacity".[115]

As a product of her work with primary school teachers, Ina Lohr had written many songs for school classes. At the instigation of one of these teachers, Paul Lachenmeier, she put together a collection of 120 of these songs in *Sprechen, Lauschen, Singen*.[116] In the summer of 1969 she was writing the accompanying notes to these songs, explanations of how they could be used in the school classroom. She commented to Paul Sacher about this, saying that she had the feeling she was "very belatedly writing her own thesis".[117] On a certain level, this is very understandable, as the analogous pedagogical writings of her students certainly bore the stamp of her own teaching. This work apparently did her a world of good, because she also confessed that she had "slept 4 nights without sleeping pills; for the 1st time in about 16 years!"[118]

During this entire period, she was aware of the need of making space for future generations, as is revealed by her commentary in a letter to Paul Sacher of 7 September 1969, on the premiere of the concerto for flute, clarinet and orchestra by Hans Ulrich Lehmann in Lucerne. After some compliments about both the composition and its performance, she continued by reflecting upon the differences between the musical generations:

> We must take our young ones as they are, and give them the right to go their own way. [...] And who knows what will come from it, if we really only observe and leave the young ones their freedom, as we also seized it about 40 years ago!"[119]

At the same time, she lamented that the current students could not and would not play directly from a figured bass, as they contended that there were sufficient realized editions available, being supported in this by the current teachers

---

115 "dass Sie der Freund sind, der nie eine Bitte ausschlägt oder vergisst und der sein Möglichstes tut". Letter Ina Lohr to Paul Sacher of 18 July 1969, private collection, Switzerland.
116 Basel: Hug 1969.
117 "sehr verspätet meine eigene Diplomarbeit fertigstelle". Letter Ina Lohr to Paul Sacher of 18 July 1969, private collection, Switzerland.
118 "Habe 4 Nächte ohne Schlafmittel geschlafen; zum 1. Mal nach ca. 16 Jahren!" Ibid.
119 "Wir müssen unsere Jungen nehmen, wie sie sind und ihnen das Recht einräumen ihren eigenen Weg zu gehen. [...] Und wer weiss, was noch herauskommt, wenn wir wirklich nur noch zuschauen und den Jungen jede Freiheit lassen, so wie wir sie uns auch eroberten vor ca. 40 Jahren!" Letter Ina Lohr to Paul Sacher of 7 September 1969, private collection, Switzerland.

at the Schola. She thus brings the battle of the generations to the fore, and while identifying with the younger musicians' need to choose their own path through life, was still emotionally upset that her own was being left behind. Her time at the Schola, however, was also gradually coming to an end; in writing to Arthur Eglin on 9 July 1969, she mentioned she would have liked to retire with her 'boss', "but had then to acknowledge that it would not yet work now".[120] She did, however, reduce her workload to only two groups of *Hausmusik*.[121]

It is perhaps with one of those groups that she went to Strasbourg on 2 November to make some short recordings in the cathedral for an international Protestant broadcasting company: "I was completely free in the creation of 10 broadcasts, which were all accepted. But the female singer all of a sudden came down with a bad case of the flu and after a very enjoyable test broadcast, I was now also engaged as a singer [in addition to her function as director of the group]!"[122] This is evidence of the continuing strength of her influence within Calvinist circles around her.

In April 1970, she once again took over a choir rehearsal for Arthur Honegger's *Jeanne d'Arc au bûcher* when Paul Sacher was ill, promising not to proselytize too much, although it would be difficult.[123] He thanked her warmly for the unexpected help, and hoped they would be granted a few more years of such work together.[124] In June, they were once again planning to cooperate regularly in the preparation of the choir – much as they had done in the past – for a concert on 16/17/18 December, in which not only Dietrich Fischer-Dieskau, but also the Deller Consort were to take part. Among other things, Bach's cantata *Ich will den Kreuzstab gerne tragen* (BWV 56) and Handel's *Funeral Anthem on the Death of Queen Caroline* (HWV 264) were to be performed. Paul Sacher began negotiating the exact mode of their work together in a letter of 24 June 1970:

---

120 "Eigentlich wollte ich mich mit meinem Chef von der Schola zurückziehen, musste dann aber einsehen, dass das gerade jetzt noch nicht geht". Letter Ina Lohr to Arthur Eglin of 9 July 1969, Arthur Eglin, Basel.

121 Letter Ina Lohr to the Vellekoops of 29 January 1969, Jos Knigge, Utrecht, and to the Stoevesandts of 26 July 1969, Elisabeth Stoevesandt, Basel.

122 "Ik was volkomen vrij in het samenstellen van 10 uitzendingen, die allemaal werden aangenomen. Maar de zangeres kreeg opeens een zware griep en na een zeer plezierige proefzending, werd ik nu ook nog als 'zangeres' geengageerd!" Letter Ina Lohr to Erna van Osselen of 27 October 1969, Aleid and Floris Zuidema, Lochem, Netherlands.

123 Letter Ina Lohr to Paul Sacher of 26 April 1970, private collection, Switzerland.

124 Letter Paul Sacher to Ina Lohr, undated. PSF-PSC.

I only want to begin the choir rehearsals for our first concert (Handel) on 7 September. In the two following weeks [Frieder] Liebendörfer is in the military service, and I am on my vacation in the Engadine. Do you think that it would not be too much to ask the men, or respectively the women, to come once either on Monday or Wednesday, and let you take over these special rehearsals alone? All of the other rehearsals we would split. In this manner there would be a total of 13–14 choir rehearsals. I think that should be comfortable enough. If I were not able to be there for one rehearsal, because I have to conduct concerts, then Liebendörfer would take over one group and you the other, or you would not come at all and leave the rehearsals to Liebendörfer.[125]

Ina Lohr accepted this plan on 25 June 1970, placing her own demands:

The dates for the rehearsals have been noted down. I cannot do entire rehearsals, i.e. with breaks in which one really must speak with the people. I will work intensively from 8–9.30 and would be glad if you were to announce this in advance. We will have to see how we divide the other rehearsals. I really do not know, namely, whether I can direct the more difficult and to me unknown Stravinsky [*Perséphone*, for the concerts on 13/14 May 1971].[126]

After all the battles over the years about this sort of practical cooperation in relation to the choir, they have clearly reached a new point in their relationship, have come to a deep appreciation for that which they have achieved together over the years, which made it possible for them to enter in once again on such an experiment. It is a monument to their ability to work out the difficulties between them. At the same time, it is the end of another era, in that Ina Lohr retired completely from the Schola at the end of the 1969/70 school year, also giving up her apartment in Lucerne, which had so long been her refuge from the stresses of Basel.[127]

---

125 "Die Chorproben für unser erstes Konzert (Händel) möchte ich erst am 7. September anfangen. In den beiden folgenden Wochen ist Liebendörfer im Militärdienst, und ich bin in meinen Ferien im Engadin. Glauben Sie, dass es nicht zuviel ist, wenn man jeweilen am Montag und Mittwoch einmal die Herren, resp. die Damen bestellt und Sie diese Spezialproben allein durchführen müssen? Alle anderen Proben würden wir teilen. Insgesamt wären es auf diese Weise 13–14 Chorproben. Ich glaube, dass das komfortabel genügen sollte. Wenn ich einmal an einer Chorprobe nicht mitwirken kann, weil ich Konzerte dirigieren muss, würde Liebendörfer die eine Gruppe übernehmen und Sie die andere, oder Sie kommen überhaupt nicht und überlassen die Probe Liebendörfer allein". Letter Paul Sacher to Ina Lohr of 24 June 1970, PSF-ILC.

126 "Die Daten für die Proben sind eingetragen. Ganze Proben, d.h. mit Pausen, in denen man doch mit den Leuten reden muss, kann ich nicht machen. Ich werde intensiv von 8–9.30 arbeiten und wäre froh, wenn Sie das im voraus bekannt geben. Wie wir die andern Proben teilen, müssen wir dann sehen. Ob ich nämlich auch den mir unbekannten und viel schwereren Strawinsky in dieser Art leiten kann, weiss ich wirklich noch nicht". Letter Ina Lohr to Paul Sacher of 25 June 1970, private collection, Switzerland.

127 Letter Ina Lohr to the Vellekoops of 27 July 1970, Jos Knigge, Utrecht.

Chapter 8. Transcending the Final Boundary

8.1 Retirement

Even after the final disentanglement from the Schola, life for Ina Lohr went on much as before, just with less pressure, as she was no longer constantly confronted with approaches to music entirely antipathetical to her own. She remained Paul Sacher's musical assistant, although increasingly her actual activities were confined to participation in the programming and the search for material for the *Mitteilungen*. She maintained her work with amateurs at a modest level, continuing to teach two *Hausmusik* classes at a nearby church, the Zinzendorf House, and giving a few private lessons, all of which left her considerably freer.[1] Further, although more and more tied to Basel due to her poor health, she cultivated her contacts with the outside world through her immense correspondence and countless visits from friends (frequently metamorphosed former students) and family, as well as a few strangers. These included her sister Etty, the Vellekoops and the Boekes from the Netherlands, and the Bäcks from Sweden. It is, however, Ina Lohr's letters to her oldest friend from her schooldays, the graphic artist Erna van Osselen, that give us the greatest insight into this period of her life, as in them she speaks of the small pragmatic minutiae of life that are so telling, revealing her predilections, her worries, and her concern for others with an unparalleled openness.[2] In addition, her early dream of having a large family seemed on some level to have come into fruition, as a few of her former students adopted her themselves, either as an honorary mother, or as a godmother or second grandmother for their children. Although her physical health was poor during much of this period, she remained mentally and spiritually positive, as she was finally able to live her life entirely in the light of her beliefs. Without the structure of regular employment, however, there were fewer long-term projects, and her daily experience became increasingly enlivened by small incidents from the outside.

Many people who knew her commented on her infectious sense of humor, but this is rarely reflected in her writing. An example of it, however, may be seen in an anecdote that she recounted to Erna van Osselen in a letter of 7 December 1970. In Switzerland, St. Niklaus and his companion Schmutzli, who carries a

---

1   Letter Ina Lohr to the Vellekoops of 24 September 1970, Jos Knigge, Utrecht.
2   I am grateful to Aleid and Floris Zuidema, Lochem, for placing these letters at my disposal.

bundle of sticks as a threat of punishment for misbehaving children, go to the homes of children dressed up in traditional costumes, and hold court on the children's behavior during the previous year (having been informed by the parents in advance). The children recite poetry or play music to welcome them, and in the end are given goodies in order to encourage better conduct in the future. After explaining this tradition to her friend, Ina Lohr exclaimed:

> But imagine that such a person suddenly knocked on my door, while I, suspecting nothing, was writing. And the best [thing] about it was that I was completely bewildered when I saw that faithful friend with a long beard, but without "zwarte Piet" [the Dutch version of Schmutzli], on my doorstep. He told a magnificent story and it took 10 minutes before I noticed that it was the wife of my doctor who was bringing me a flowering Christmas cactus as a "roe" [the bundle of sticks that Piet always carried]. But then I turned the tables on her and asked whether St. Nick perhaps also was going to the slovenly doctor's family that never wrote bills and whether he then would take along the "roe" immediately in the form of an envelope with the payment. Then we both burst out laughing and it was a wonderful intermezzo.[3]

This story speaks volumes about the degree of her social integration within Basel, outside of her professional world, of her whole-hearted acceptance within the circles in which she felt at home.

She also spoke of the upcoming difficult concert with Dietrich Fischer-Dieskau and the Dellers, remarking that "for Sacher the concerts are still always high points, but I shy away from the many unexpected difficulties which have arisen over and over again in recent years. We have all become older and can therefore no longer count upon ourselves or upon one another as a matter of course".[4] So although she was still jumping in whenever necessary, she could also see, at

---

3   "Maar stel je voor, dat er zo iemand opeens ook bij mij aanklopte, terwil ik niets vermoedend zat te schrijven. En het mooiste was, dat ik er helemaal beduusd van was, toen ik die trouwe vriend met lange baard, maar zonder zwarte Piet op mijn drempel zag staan. Hij hield een prachtig relaas en het duurde 10 minuten, voordat ik merkte, dat het de vrouw van mijn doktor was die me een prachtig bloeiende Kerstcactus als roe bracht. Maar toen heb ik die spies omgedraaid en gevraagd, of de St. Nic. misschien ook naar die slordige doktersfamilie ging, die nooit rekeningen schreef en of hij dan de roe in vorm van een enveloppe met honorarium maar meteen mee wou nemen. Toen schoten we beide in de lach en het was een alleraardigst intermezzo". Letter Ina Lohr to Erna van Osselen of 7 December 1970, Aleid and Floris Zuidema, Lochem.

4   "Voor Sacher zijn die concerten nog steeds hoogtepunten maar ik zie op tegen de vele onverwachte moeilijkheden, die in de laatste jaren telkens opdoemden. We worden allemaal ouder en kunnen daarom nie meer zo vanzelfsprekend op ons zelf en op elkaar rekenen". Ibid.

least for herself, that this could not go on forever. While she was satisfied with the portion of the concert in which she was directly involved, this was not true for the rest:

> Our concert was very beautiful, as far as the Handel with the Dellers and the choir was concerned. Fischer-Dieskau with the Kreuzstab cantata was a fright. That's how the public [reception] can ruin a great singer, so that he almost makes a parody of one of the most beautiful Bach cantatas, in that he laid out all his skill for show. [...] A church concert with great soloists has become increasingly problematic for me, while Sacher finds such an experiment a failure, yet also always still interesting.[5]

Noteworthy here is that they were now in agreement about the result, if not about the consequences to be drawn from such a recognition. In her next letter to her friend of 2 February 1971 she continues on about her concerns in regard to her work with Paul Sacher, explaining that he "is still not yet prepared to give up some of his concert life, although his wife and I strongly 'nudge' him in this direction. Sooner or later I will really not be able to keep up any more, and after 41 years it will be very difficult [for him] to find another assistant".[6] Thus her retirement from the Schola has also made her look anew at her work with Paul Sacher, leading her to encourage him to reduce his workload, no doubt not only for himself, but also for herself. She does not question, however, continuing as his assistant, as long as her health allows her to do so.

One example of the difficulties she experienced in her work as an assistant, was a rehearsal that she took over from him, in which she explained the text of Stravinsky's *Perséphone*. As she admitted to Paul Sacher in a letter of 24 February 1971, she considered it to have been a failure:

> Unfortunately, the rehearsal was a fiasco. Poorly attended, joyless. And I am just not able to speak without also intervening. And I simply can't do it any more. Also my tape recording was not good enough for the big hall. That with the Handel Anthem was not louder, but the interest was greater. Handel and Queen Caroline were of greater inter-

---

5   "Ons concert was heel mooi, zover het Händel met de Dellers en het koor betrof. Fischer-Dieskau met de Kreuzstabkantate was een schrik. Zó kan het publiek een groot zanger bederven, dat hij uit één van de mooiste Bachcantates bijna een parodie maakt, omdat hij al zijn kunnen ten toon spreidde. [...] Een kerkconcert met grote solisten wordt voor mij steeds problematischer, terwijl Sacher ook zo'n experiment weliswaar mislukt maar toch altijd nog interessant vindt". Letter Ina Lohr to Erna van Osselen of 10 January 1971, Aleid and Floris Zuidema, Lochem.

6   "Sacher is nog steeds niet bereid om iets van zijn concertwerk op te geven, hoewel zijn vrouw en ik heftig in die richting 'opvoeden'. Binnen kort of lang zal ik het heus niet meer kunnen bijbenen, en na 41 jaar zal het heel moeilijk zijn om een andere medewerker te vinden". Letter Ina Lohr to Erna van Osselen of 2 February 1971, Aleid and Floris Zuidema, Lochem.

est than this Stravinsky, with its completely unknown goddesses and gods, which I had
so industriously studied.[7]

She was obviously frustrated that she was unable to animate the group in her
wonted manner, that she no longer had the physical resources to draw upon in
order to deal with such situations. Paul Sacher consoled her, saying that he "was
sorry that the rehearsal with the presentation of the 'Perséphone' recording did
not fulfill your expectations. The poor attendance, in particular, is to be regretted".[8] This is a telling reaction in that it does not confirm her conclusion that
the rehearsal was a failure, but rather sympathized with her frustration that she
could not meet her own self-set goals. Stravinsky's Perséphone was performed
together with his Ode in a concert that turned out to be a memorial for the composer, who had died just shortly before, on 6 April 1971. As Ina Lohr confided
to her friend, "We had so much to thank him for".[9]

Beyond her work for Paul Sacher, and the lessons she was giving, she also prepared a lecture "Man in the Psalms" ("Der Mensch in den Psalmen") about how
these poems still encapsulated human experience today; her ideas were limned
musically by Arthur Eglin's choir and trombone ensemble. This left her little
or no time for anything else, in particular as she was concerned how she would
survive a massive construction project that was soon to begin next to the house
she had been living in for many years, Leimenstrasse 80. It belonged to August
Wenzinger's sister Louise, and the new building would leave her with a view of
a brick wall from her windows. In order to be able to deal with the noise, she
found a one-room apartment nearby, in the house of one of the members of her
Hausmusik groups, where she could withdraw and work during the day during
the construction period.

7   "Die Probe war leider ein Fiasko. Schlecht besucht, freudlos. Und ich bin nicht im Stande
    nur zu erzählen und nicht auch einzugreifen. Und das geht einfach nicht mehr. Auch war
    mein Band doch nicht gut genug für den grossen Saal. Das mit dem Händel Anthem war
    nicht lauter, aber das Interesse war grösser. Händel und Queen Caroline interessierten mehr
    als dieser Strawinsky mit den so unbekannten Göttinnen und Göttern, die ich so fleissig
    studiert hatte". Letter Ina Lohr to Paul Sacher of 24 February 1971, private collection, Swit-
    zerland.
8   "Es tut mir sehr leid, dass die Probe mit der Vorführung des 'Perséphone'-Bandes Ihre Hoff-
    nungen nicht erfüllt hat. Vor allen Dingen der schlechte Besuch ist natürlich bedauerlich".
    Undated carbon copy of letter Paul Sacher to Ina Lohr, private collection, Switzerland.
9   "Wij hebben heel veel aan hem te danken". Letter Ina Lohr to Erna van Osselen of 16 May
    1971, Aleid and Floris Zuidema, Lochem.

In Amsterdam, the artist Erna van Osselen frequently attended concerts of the Concertgebouw Orchestra and then sent on the programs to her friend in Basel, knowing that they would provoke her curiosity. In her responses, Ina Lohr would then discuss them in the light of her own programming experience with the BKO. In general, she found them puzzling, even poor, as "apparently no account was given [to the fact] that listening to a specific work had an influence on the hearing of the following one. That is very important for us: a hobbyhorse perhaps, but our audience has been brought up very well by that little beast".[10] She was also very interested that a practice of having discussions after the concerts had been introduced at the Concertgebouw in the 1971/72 season, an idea which fascinated her, but which Sacher opposed.[11] Indeed, by 21 May 1972 she, too, had become convinced that the discussions were not fruitful, as evidenced by the summaries found in the programs.

She also intently followed what was going on in the Dutch Early Music community. For example, on 9 March 1971, she described her reactions to a recent recording by Sour Cream, the recorder trio with Frans Brüggen, Kees Boeke and Walther van Hauwe:

> It is all very musical, unbelievably together, and I am partial to the sound and also the articulation. But it also quite mannered and always with the same mannerism. How they manage to play the "fading tones" in tune is a riddle to me. It "sings" much more than with Linde and the ornaments "run" wonderfully, naturally. That which is not so natural, however, is that long notes have a free, large vibrato, and that the vibrato does not merge equally naturally into the following gesture. Playing a recorder well is actually just as difficult as playing any other instrument, even if the players are very capable. Moreover, the < > on long notes reminds me of the gamba playing of Wenzinger and his students. [...] Is there perhaps a record of all 3 Kuijken [brothers]? I lean more toward preferring those self-seeking musicians.[12]

10 "dat er blijkbaar helemaal geen rekening mee wordt gehouden, dat het luisteren naar een bepaald werk invloed heeft op het horen van het volgende. Dat is voor ons heel gewichtig: een stokpaardje misschien, maar ons publiek is door dat beestje toch heel goed opgevoed". Letter Ina Lohr to Erna van Osselen of 16 May 1971, Aleid and Floris Zuidema, Lochem.
11 Letter Ina Lohr to Erna van Osselen of 16 January 1971, Aleid and Floris Zuidema, Lochem.
12 "het is allemaal heel muzikaal, ongelofelijk goed als samenspel, en de klank, ook de articulatie is mij sympathiek. Maar het is wel erg gemanieerd en wel altijd op dezelfde manier. Hoe ze het klaar spelen om die 'fading tones' zuiver te houden is mij een raadsel. Het 'zingt' veel meer dan bij Linde en de versieringen 'lopen' heerlijk vanzelfsprekend. Maar niet vanzelfsprekend is het, dat lange Tonen een vrij sterk vibrato hebben, maar dat vibrato loopt dan niet zo vanzelfsprekend in de beweging verder. Eigenlijk is goed blockfluitenspelen net zo moeilijk als ieder ander instrumentaalspel, juist als de spelers veel kunnen. Trouwens doet het < > op lange tonen me aan het gambaspel van Wenzinger en zijn leerlingen denken. [...] Bestaat er misschien ook een plaat van alle 3 Kuijkens? Ik neig meer tot de keus

That fall she was quite ill, but by 30 November 1971 she could write that she was, "in the meantime, very much better, but am getting overwhelmingly many requests and commissions to compose and to write".[13] Among them, was an inquiry that was to bring her into national limelight, at least within religious circles, namely that of writing the music for the International Women's Day of Prayer for Switzerland,

> the day on which all women of the world who so desire, read and pray the same liturgy. This year the official text was so joyless (although the liturgy is based on the Bible text "Rejoice!") that the Swiss women had it written anew by Silja Walter, a Benedictine nun. I then wrote the music for it and now receive telephone calls from all parts of Switzerland from women who particularly want to sing and play it, and ask for advice. We first had 50 copies of the music made, but now more than 1000 have been sent out and more are continually requested. It is all very exciting, but also takes a lot of time and effort.[14]

In the end her music was performed in sixty churches throughout Switzerland on 2–3 March 1972.[15] She was not the only one who was astonished and delighted by the echo this liturgy unleashed in congregations throughout Switzerland; Leni Altwegg, the author of the sermon for the day, described it as a revolution:

> A revolution is taking place: In diverse Swiss churches, one danced and played ball in the service, also in my congregation. While throngs pushed their way into the church and it became too small, the pastor, wringing his hands, paced up and down in the sacristy: "If I had known that!" – Betwixt enthusiastic acceptance and bitter rejection, we pushed through with the dance liturgy created by Silja Walter, Ina Lohr and others in accordance with a sermon on Proverbs 8. Later the liturgy made its own way – it was repeated here and there, and some, who did not dare at first, carried it out later. The spark ignited – other sacred plays, liturgical dances followed.[16]

van deze muzikant-zelfzoeker[s]". Letter Ina Lohr to Kees Vellekoop of 9 March 1971, Jos Knigge, Utrecht.

13   "Ik ben intussen weer echt opgeknapt, maar krijg overstelpend veel aanvragen en opdrachen om te componeren en te schrijven". Letter Ina Lohr to Erna van Osselen of 30 November 1971, Aleid and Floris Zuidema, Lochem.

14   "Ik weet niet, of jij die dag kent, waarop alle vrouwen van de wereld, die dat willen, dezelfde liturgie lezen en bidden. Dit jaar was de officiele tekst zo vreugdeloos (hoewel de liturgie staat onder het bijbelwoord 'Freuet euch!'), dat de Zwitserse vrouwen opnieuw lieten formuleren door Silja Walter, benedictijnse non. Ik schreef er dus de muziek bij en nu komen er telefoontijes uit heel Zwitserland van vrouwen, die dat vooral willen zingen en spelen en raad vragen. We lieten eerst maar 50 exemplaren van de muziek maken, maar nu zijn er al meer dan 1000 weg en er worden er steeds meer aangevraagd. Het is allemaal erg boeiend, maar ook tijd- en krachtrovend". Letter Ina Lohr to Erna van Osselen of 16 January 1972, Aleid and Floris Zuidema, Lochem.

15   Letter Ina Lohr to Erna van Osselen of 2 March 1972, Aleid and Floris Zuidema, Lochem.

16   "Eine Revolution ist im Gange: in diversen Kirchen der Schweiz wird im Gottesdienst getanzt und Ball gespielt, auch in meiner Gemeinde. Während sich Scharen in die Kirche

The kernel of the liturgy was presented in a flyer (see Ill. 8.1) in which central elements of the whole, a melody of Ina Lohr's to a poem of Silja Walter's, were presented in their hand-written versions, side-by-side. In addition, she also became involved in the preparations for the celebration of the liturgy in the hall of the Salvation Army at Erasmusplatz in Basel, working together with the dancers and a group of singers, writing afterwards of her "sudden 'accidental' success as a composer" to Kees Vellekoop.[17]

Simone Staehelin-Handschin, a pastor's wife and part of the organizational board, recalls it as being an incredibly empowering period for the lay women within the church. It gave them the chance of exerting their creative forces in the shaping of the liturgy and with it the congregation, overcoming all threats from those opposed; it thus also called the male-dominated hierarchic structures of the church into question.[18] Silja Walter gave expression to that which she considered to be the value of Ina Lohr's music:

> Your participation anchored the idea and shape of the new form of the liturgy in the essence of the Christian church service, in praise and devotion. Perhaps you have – through your last work in the broader public – even created the basis for an official musical form for the church. Your music has lifted the old into the new and embedded the new in the eternal.[19]

Thus in a sense, this experience represents a culmination of Ina Lohr's life work, in that her drive to renew music in the Protestant church was directed toward making it a vehicle for bringing the congregation together as a unified entity,

---

hineindrängen und sie zu klein wird, läuft der Pfarrer händeringend in der Sakristei auf und ab: Wenn ich das gewusst hätte! – Zwischen begeisterter Zustimmung und erbitterter Ablehnung haben wir uns durchgesetzt mit der von Silja Walter, Ina Lohr und anderen nach einer Predigt über Spr 8 gestalteten Tanz-Liturgie. Später hat die Liturgie sich dann selber durchgesetzt – sie wurde da und dort wiederholt, und einige, die sich zuerst nicht getrauten, haben sie nachgeholt. Der Funke hat gezündet – auch andere gottesdienstliche Spiele, liturgische Tänze folgen". Leni Altwegg, "Die spielende Weisheit: Zu Sprüche 8, 22–31", in: *Ich spielte vor Dir auf dem Erdenrund: Frauen-Gottesdienste – Anleitungen und Modelle*, ed. Leni Altwegg, Margrit Huber-Staffelbach, and Simone Staehelin-Handschin, Freiburg, Switzerland: Paulusverlag; Basel: Friedrich Reinhardt Verlag 1990, 11.

17 "plotseling volkomen 'toevallig' succes als componiste". Letter Ina Lohr to Kees Vellekoop of 7 April 1972.

18 I would like to thank Simone Staehelin-Handschin here for the extraordinarily insightful interview of 6 March 2018.

19 "Ihre Mitarbeit hat Idee und Gestaltung der neuen Liturgieform in der Substanz des christlichen Gottesdienstes, im Lob und in der Anbetung verankert. Vielleicht haben Sie damit – durch Ihr le[t]ztes Werk in die Oeffentlichkeit hinein – die Ausgangslage sogar für eine offizielle kirchliche musikalische Form geschaffen. Ihre Musik hat Altes ins Neue gehoben und das Neue im überzeitlichen eingebaut". Letter Sijla Walter to Ina Lohr of 18 March 1972, PSF-ILC.

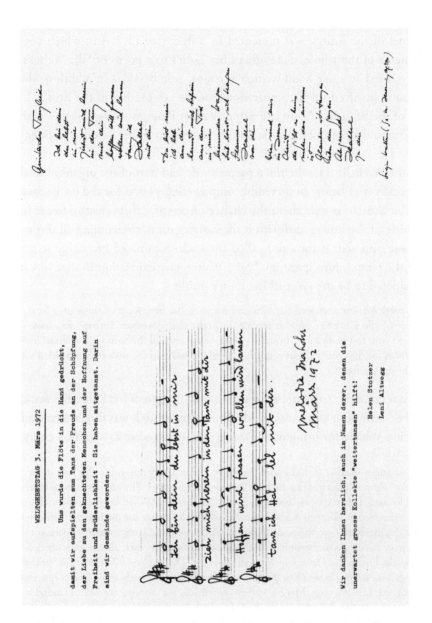

Ill. 8.1: Flyer for the liturgy of International Women's Day of Prayer, 3 March 1972.
Reproduction: courtesy of Simone Staehelin-Handschin, Basel.

so that it could, as it were, once again sing "as from one mouth". In everything she wrote in this regard, she was consistently searching for the means of giving the power back to the congregation, of speaking directly to God, so that it no longer lay solely in the hands of the pastor or the organist/choir director. Thus, both within the church, and within the musical profession, it was from her work with the lay population that she not only drew her strength, but also perceived her real success.

It seems almost serendipitous that, at about the same time, she was working at the behest of Sven-Erik Bäck on an article about Stravinsky's *Canticum Sacrum* for the Swedish journal for contemporary music, *Nutida Musik;*[20] serendipitous because her instinctive response to the work was associated with a secret desire to dance in San Marco in Venice as a young woman:

> With this work [Stravinsky's *Canticum Sacrum*] it became clear to me how all forms of art belong together in a church service. When, at the age of 19, I first entered the symmetrical circular rotunda in Venice [San Marco], I was almost overcome by vertigo because [its] great movement carried me away. I could have danced, but my too good upbringing did not allow that. When – many years later – I studied Stravinsky's *Canticum*, performed by Paul Sacher in Basel, this miraculous shared vibration repeated itself; it was also an experience of color, made visible by the symmetry. When – in the last movement – the music of the first movement is repeated in retrograde, that is from the end to the beginning, it is probably also perceptible for someone who is not aware of the process. But it is, however, not only a game; also skill is involved, as well as knowledge of the dogma.[21]

How much this association was influenced by the fact that she also heard the work performed in San Marco – perhaps at its premiere on 13 September 1956 – remains speculative.[22] The analysis that she wrote for the Swedish journal, how-

---

20 Ina Lohr, "Tankar om Stravinskys Canticum Sacrum", in: *Nutida Musik* 15 (1971/72), 19–22.

21 "An diesem Werk [Stravinsky's *Canticum Sacrum*] wurde mir klar, wie alle Kunstgattungen im Gottesdienst zusammengehören. Als ich mit 19 Jahren zum ersten Mal den symmetrischen Rundbau in Venedig [San Marco] betrat, überfiel mich fast ein Schwindel, weil die grosse Bewegung mich mitnahm. Ich hätte tanzen können, was meine zu gute Erziehung aber nicht zuliess. Als ich dann viele Jahre nachher Strawinsky's *Canticum* studierte, das Paul Sacher in Basel aufführte, wiederholte sich dieses wundervolle Gefühl des Mitschwingens, das auch ein Farberlebnis war, das die Symmetrie sichtbar machte. Wenn im letzten Satz die Musik des ersten Satzes im Krebsgang, d.h. von hinten nach vorne wiederholt wird, ist das wahrscheinlich auch für den, der den Vorgang nicht kennt, spürbar. Es ist aber nicht nur Spiel, sondern da geht es um Können, auch um dogmatisches Wissen". Untitled lecture text, PSF-ILC.

22 Letter Ina Lohr to Erna van Osselen of 7 May 1973, Aleid and Floris Zuidema, Lochem.

ever, once again exhibited an eclectic and idiosyncratic collection of methodo-
logical procedures, seemingly unsuited for this work; this notwithstanding, it
also reveals her intense study and radically personal understanding of the composition:

> The row contains the falling fifth la-fa-re and the ascending do-mi-sol [and] thus bears
> the minor and major triad within the melodic [sequence], as well as the possibility of
> [these notes] being sounded simultaneously within it. This possibility is that which
> Stravinsky, consciously or unconsciously, employed in the outer movements.
> Above the b-flat, g, b-flat (fa-re-fa in G [B in the original!] *molle*) in the bass [m. 10–
> 11, I: *Euntes in mundum*] lies the d of the trumpets and trombones, so that the la-fa-re
> *molle* is there in its entirety. But the d in the trumpets and trombones is also combined
> with b and f-sharp, thus has a double function: la-*molle* and re in a new hexachord,
> which has b as re, f-sharp as la, and also a as do. The second measure [upbeat to m. 11]
> brings e, g-sharp, b in the 2nd trumpet, g, b, d in the bass trumpet, while the 1st and 3rd
> trombones introduce the f. With the e-flat, for which we admittedly must wait until the
> 2nd trumpet inserts it in the 5th measure as the do of a new row: e-flat, f, g, a-flat (b-flat
> and c are already sounding). With that, all twelve notes are there, though now not line-
> arly, as a row, but in triads set in opposition and above one another. These triads arouse
> a diatonic impression of powerful simplicity in the listener, which is commensurate with
> both the commission [for a lay choir] as well as its performance.[23]

Nonetheless, it is her stubborn insistence on relating all of the musical activity in this passage to her own personal melodic analytical system, one borrowed
and adapted from medieval theory, that is deeply disturbing to a musician of
today. With this combination of solmization, tonal and serial theory, she in
the end sabotaged herself, in that her professional colleagues did not take her
seriously as a musician, did not listen to what lay beyond her words. Unfortunately, she herself did not feel the necessity of finding a language beyond that

---

23 "Die Reihe enthält die fallende Quinte la-fa-re und die steigende do-mi-sol, trägt also
    innerhalb des Melodischen schon den Moll- und den Durdreiklang als Möglichkeit auch
    des Zusammenklangs in sich. Diese Möglichkeit ist es, die Strawinsky bewusst oder unbe-
    wusst in den Ecksätzen verwendet hat.
        Ueber dem b, g, b (fa-re-fa im G. [H. in the original!] molle) im Bass liegt das d der
    Trompeten und Posaunen, sodass das la-fa-re-molle vollständig da ist. Aber das d wird in
    den Trompeten und Posaunen auch mit h und fis kombiniert, hat also eine doppelte Funk-
    tion: la-molle und re in einem neuen Hexachord, das h als re, fis als la und also a als do hat.
    Der zweite Takt bringt e-gis-h in der 2. Trompete, g-h-d in der trombe basse, während die
    1. und die 3. Posaune das f einführen. Mit dem es, auf das wir allerdings warten müssen, bis
    die 2. Trompete es im 5. Takte als do einer neuen Reihe: es-f-g-as (b und c klingen schon)
    einfügt. Damit wären alle zwölf Töne da, allerdings nun nicht linear, als Reihe gebracht,
    sondern in gegen- und übereinander gesetzten Dreiklängen. Diese Dreiklänge erwecken
    beim Hörer den Eindruck des Diatonischen, des kraftvoll-Einfachen, das dem Auftrag wie
    der Ausführung gemäss ist". German original of Swedish article, PSF-ILC.

of her own personal theory to communicate her understanding of the music; to her it was self-evident. Thus what she wrote was certainly how she herself heard the piece, and as a result required insight into her highly idiosyncratic system in order to understand it. Musicians were thus rebuffed because she refused to adapt herself to their language. This was largely a matter of unconcern to her, as her focus lay elsewhere.

Certainly, for various reasons, her life was moving gradually away from the circles of professional musicians. With her sinus problems and associated vertigo, her hearing was also affected; rooms full of people and loud music became a torture. The degree to which this disturbed her enjoyment of music is made evident in her letter to Paul Sacher of 4 August 1972, in thanks for his birthday greetings, in which she nonetheless gave expression to her hope that

> another few years of this now so untroubled cooperation will be given us [...] It cannot go on quite so nicely as before because I still hear fifths and had to turn off *Idomeneo* immediately yesterday. But perhaps this will be no obstacle in the creation of our programs and it also does not interfere with my work for the *Mitteilungen*.[24]

But this work, in any case, was not at the same level of intensity as before. In a letter to Erna van Osselen of 17 September 1972, she spoke of the never-ending stream of guests, both from the Netherlands as well as Switzerland; and how, beyond the few lessons she still taught, she still had "the work with Sacher that has now become quieter, and so many composition commissions that I can choose the best of them. That has never happened before in this measure".[25] Obviously, her difficulties with external sounds did not yet affect her ability to conceptualize music mentally.

She also had increased regular contact with people outside of the music world, in particular with the family of Christin and Walter Wehrli, and their three daughters. She had gotten to know them all through Christin Wehrli's participation in a *Hausmusik* ensemble. At some point, she became an un-

24 "Ja, auch ich hoffe, dass uns noch einige Jahre dieser jetzt so ungetrübten Zusammenarbeit geschenkt sein werden [...] Ganz so schön, wie es war, kann es nicht weitergehen, weil ich immer noch Quinten höre und den Idomeneo gestern sofort abstellen musste. Aber vielleicht ist das kein Hindernis beim Zusammenstellen von unseren Programmen und es stört auch nicht bei der Arbeit für die Mitteilungen". Letter Ina Lohr to Paul Sacher of 4 August 1972, private collection, Switzerland.

25 "En daarnaast heb ik nog wat lessen, het rustig wordende werk met Sacher en zo veel compositieopdrachten, dat ik er de prettigste uit kan kiezen. Dat is nog nooit in die mate voorgekomen". Letter Ina Lohr to Erna van Osselen of 17 September 1972, Aleid and Floris Zuidema, Lochem.

official grandmother to the children, having a special affinity with the youngest, who was handicapped. She ate dinner at their home on Saturday evenings,
where much was sung; she read books to the children, and her good humor and
infectious joy were appreciated by all. In addition, the older children later came
twice a month to her on Wednesday afternoons, and they spoke of Rembrandt,
Keats and the like, but also had the freedom to eat meals with bad manners
and make funny tape recordings; the youngest child also had her own regular
visits with her unofficial grandmother. It was also with them that Jan Boeke's
and Kees Vellekoop's families frequently stayed when they were in Basel, forg-
ing such bonds of friendship that the Wehrlis also spent various vacations in the
Netherlands visiting all those they had met through Ina Lohr. Thus in a letter
of 10 December 1972 to the Vellekoops, she inquired whether they were singing
Advent songs with their children, saying that

> We did that gloriously [last] Saturday at the Wehrli's […]! The Sunday before, the harp-
> sichord [played by Christin Wehrli] was inaugurated by and for the *Hausmusik* [ensem-
> ble]. Those are now my musical experiences, because I can no longer go to real rehears-
> als and concerts and I actually do not miss them either. The "social" or more generally
> human [aspects of life] are indeed becoming more important to me.[26]

This reduction in activity, however, was not entirely voluntary, in that she had
received a clear message from her body that things could no longer go on in the
wonted fashion:

> In any case, my insufficient heart found that it had now had enough and suddenly did
> very strange things just as I wanted to cross the Bahnhofstrasse in Zurich in order to
> speak about my music for the International Women's Day of Prayer 1973 and to sing it
> for them. I thought very matter-of-factly and without fear, "what a shame, I would have
> really liked to do this" and put one foot in front of another and actually got to the well-
> heated, very beautiful church, where it [the spell] passed after a ½ hour, so that I could
> sing and speak well and even travel back to Basel.[27]

---

26 "we deden dat Zaterdag heerlijk bij de Wehrli's […]! De Zondag daarvoor werd het clave-
    cimbel door en voor de huismuziek ingewijd. Dat zijn nu mijn muzikale belevenissen, want
    echt repetities en concerten kan ik niet meer aan en mis ze eigenlijk ook niet. Het 'sociale'
    of algemeen menselijke wordt voor mij in der daad steeds gewichtiger". Letter Ina Lohr to
    the Vellekoops of 10 December 1972, Jos Knigge, Utrecht.
27 "In ieder geval vond mijn insufficient hart, dat het nu wel welletjes was en deed opeens erg
    raar, juist toen ik in Zürich de Bahnhofstrasse wilde oversteken om in een kerk met 350
    vrouwen over mijn muziek voor de Wereldgebedsdag 1973 te spreken en die voor te zingen.
    Ik dacht heel nuchter en zonder angst 'wat jammer, dit had ik nog graag gedaan' en zette
    voetje voor voetje en kwam heus in die goed verwarmde, heel mooie kerk terecht, waar het
    na ½ uur weer bijtrok, zodat ik zelfs goed heb kunnen zingen en spreken en zelfs naar Bazel
    terug reizen". Letter Ina Lohr to Erna van Osselen of 6 November 1972, Aleid and Floris
    Zuidema, Lochem.

As a result of this wake-up call and many visits to doctors, it was deemed absolutely necessary that she move to an apartment where she no longer had to
climb stairs. Although Paul Sacher's staff and her own church congregation
were on the look-out for her, it took a while to find anything appropriate. In
the meantime, she only went out of her apartment once a day, reduced her visits to those needing her support, and sat when directing the small *Hausmusik*
ensembles she still taught.[28]

A sunny, two-room apartment was found for her on the fourth floor of Strass-
burgerallee 69 and the entire move was organized and undertaken for her by
the Wehrli family. They designed and created a garden for her balcony, in which
she never ceased to be delighted, raving over it in numerous letters.[29] A whole
stream of visitors came, from the Netherlands and Switzerland, partly to inspect
her new quarters and partly to see how she was faring. Although she missed the
regular evening chats with Louise Wenzinger, her health clearly improved.[30]
The rent, on the other hand, was higher than she could really afford, leading
her to sell some Asian miniatures stemming from her family, to give her the
financial cushion she needed.[31] The painting by Jan Toorop, *The Sea near Kat-
wijk*, which she had inherited on her father's death, however, she donated to
the Rijksmuseum in Amsterdam, where it now hangs as part of the permanent
collection.

The upheavals in her personal life did not prevent her from building upon the
previous year's success with the International Women's Day of Prayer, in that
she also composed the music for the liturgy of 1973, "Wachsam in unserer Zeit"
("Vigilant in our Time"), and directed it in the services of 2 March and 22 May
1973. In addition, she was involved in the rehearsals and preparations for the
repetition of the 1972 liturgy in Riehen on 16 June 1973.[32] Further, she remained
unwavering in her visits to the terminally ill, who were thankful for the "gratitude and joy" she brought to the hospital.[33]

28 Letters Ina Lohr to Erna van Osselen of 5 December 1972 and 28 January 1973, Aleid and
    Floris Zuidema, Lochem; letter Ina Lohr to the Vellekoops of 9 February 1973, Jos Knigge,
    Utrecht.
29 Letter Ina Lohr to Erna van Osselen of 25 February 1973, Aleid and Floris Zuidema,
    Lochem.
30 Letter Ina Lohr to the Vellekoops of 19 April 1973, Jos Knigge, Utrecht.
31 Letter Ina Lohr to Erna van Osselen of 18 June 1973, Aleid and Floris Zuidema, Lochem.
32 Letters Ina Lohr to Erna van Osselen of 25 February and 28 May 1973, Aleid and Floris
    Zuidema, Lochem.
33 Letter Ina Lohr to Erna van Osselen of 18 June 1973, Aleid and Floris Zuidema, Lochem.

Her link with Kees Vellekoop remained as strong as ever, as revealed by a passage in a letter of 10 July 1973 to Erna van Osselen, in which she spoke of her guilt feelings in regard to him when he and his wife stopped by on their return from Rome

> where he should have worked 3 months at the institute [Instituto Olandese] on his dissertation, but completely went off on a different track, because I had asked him to look up something about the *Dies Irae* in the Vatican Library. He remained busy with it there for a month and it fascinated him so much that he went back to it and he now wants to write his dissertation on this subject or … wants to completely abandon [his] doctoral studies and the academic world, because the practice of a musician's life and giving lessons is more attractive to him. I was taken aback, but understood him very well and in the end, Jos kept house for 2 whole days and Kees and I were totally involved in the rhetoric and music of the 13th century based on the *Dies Irae* [melody].[34]

Here we see she influenced him not only in his choice of subject matter, but that he was also tempted by the way she straddled the line between musicology and performance. In the end, however, he adhered to the path of scholarship, although the subject of his dissertation remained the *Dies Irae* sequence. Ina Lohr was involved in its writing up to the very end: not only were there several intense work sessions over the years, but in its final stages, as is evident from the extant material, she was answering pages of questions concerning both the language as well as the contents, correcting his German, to say nothing of providing her own input. In a nutshell: she served as an unnamed editor.[35]

And then on 1 August 1973, she celebrated her 70th birthday. Perhaps the most touching tribute of all came from Maja Sacher, who commented that she believed

> that the entire measure of your assistance has only completely dawned on Paul in recent years, just as he has only very slowly come to the recognition, and continues to do so

---

34 "waar hij 3 maanden op het instituut had zullen werken an zijn dissertatie, maar helemaal op een dwaalspoor kwam, doordat ik hem gevraagd had iets na te kijken over het Dies Irae in de bibliotheek van het Vatikaan. Daar bleef hij een maand mee bezig en het liet hem zo niet los, dat hij er weer op terug kwam en zijn dissertatie nu over dit onderwerp wil schrijven òf … helemaal van de promotie en proffenbaan af wil zien, omdat de praktijk van het muziekleven en het lesgeven hem toch meer aantrekken. Ik was onthutst, maar begreep hem erg goed en ten slotte deed Jos 2 dagen lang het huishouden en Kees en ik waren helemaal verdiept in de rhetoriek en muziek van de 13de eeuw naar aanleiding van het Dies Irae". Letter Ina Lohr to Erna van Osselen of 10 July 1973, Letter Ina Lohr to Erna van Osselen of 18 June 1973, Aleid and Floris Zuidema, Lochem.
35 Kees Vellekoop, *Dies ire dies illa. Studien zur Frühgeschichte einer Sequenz,* Bilthoven: Creyghton 1978 (Utrechtse Bijdragen tot de muziekwetenschap 10).

to an ever increasing degree, that he is excellent in bringing suggestions to fruition, but also has a particular need for these suggestions.[36]

Indirectly this is an acknowledgment, not only on Maja Sacher's part, but also on that of her husband, of the essential role Ina Lohr played in the success of the BKO, and ultimately in that of Paul Sacher as its director. It was perhaps something that he could not himself express openly, other than by his frequent gifts and the growing softness and warmth of his letters to her.

Her birthday, however, was not only celebrated on its official date, but also with a concert on 2 October 1973:

> A former student [Arthur Eglin], who is totally involved in church music, [both] vocal and for brass instruments, and who "dedicated" part of [the July/August] issue of his publication [*Der Bläserkreis*] to me, gave a vespers concert in the beautiful Waisenhaus church (do you know it, perhaps?) and insisted that I should come, albeit with my fingers in my ears when the trumpet or organ caused me pain. Even when he had said that, I still had not understood that what was involved was a belated birthday party, a real family party with about ± 120 people, of whom ± 30 were children. They sang magnificently and played well, Arthur held the nicest short speech and everything was really good and heartfelt.[37]

The number of people who came to the vespers, the contributions to his publication from many of those participating in Arthur Eglin's vocal and wind ensembles who knew and were influenced by Ina Lohr, make her position in these circles eminently clear. It was an open declaration of Arthur Eglin's intent to pursue her path.

And with the assistance of Arthur Eglin and his choir of voices and brass, she was still able to initiate and take part in the performance in Riehen of her cantata for advent, *Schuld, Busse und Verheissung* (1956/73). It was based on texts from the prophets Jeremiah and Isaiah, to which the choir and congregation

---

36 "Ich glaube, dass das ganze Mass Ihrer Hilfe, Paul erst in den letzten Jahren voll aufgegangen ist, wie er ja überhaupt langsam zur Erkenntnis gekommen ist und immer mehr kommt, dass er zwar wunderbar die Anregungen blühen lassen kann, aber auch dieser Anregungen besonders bedarf". Letter Maja Sacher to Ina Lohr of 1 August 1973, PSF-ILC.

37 "Een oudleerling, die helemaal in de gezongen en geblazen kerkmuziek zit en die ook dat nummer van zijn tijdschrift voor een deel aan mij 'besteed' had, gaf een avondmuziek in het mooie weeshuiskerkje (ken je dat eigenlijk?) en drong er op aan, dat ik zou komen, zelfs al zou ik mijn vingers in mijn oren moeten stoppen, als trompet of orgel me pijn deden. Ook toen hij dat gezegd had, had ik nog niet begrepen, dat het om een laat verjaardagsfeestje ging, om een echt familiefeestje met ± 120 mensen, waarvan er ± 30 kinderen waren. Ze hebben prachtig gezongen en goed gespeeld, Arthur hield een alleraardigste korte toespraak en alles was even goed en hartelijk". Letter Ina Lohr to Erna van Osselen of 7 October 1973, Aleid and Floris Zuidema, Lochem.

responded with songs from the Reformation. Attached to the work in her collection at the Sacher Foundation is the following notice concerning the work:

> It still only exists as a sketch on paper, and I almost certainly will not get around to orchestrating and notating it in a score. It was performed four times, always with the forces available to me (for the most part amateurs) and under my direction. On the radio, the narrators (once Leopold Biberti, once Hans Haeser) and Jeremiah (Ernst Denger) were professionals. The last time, in the Catholic church in Riehen (1973), a complete liturgy emerged, based on the text. The pastor took over the role of the narrator, the *Stadtposaunenchor Basel* (Arthur Eglin, director) most of the accompaniments. The *Oekumenischer Singkreis* supported my *Hausmusik*. The church was full to overflowing and the songs, supported by the brass, were sung excellently.[38]

Thus, even at this point in her life, she still took advantage of every opportunity of going out and celebrating the birth of Christ. Her cantata, however, is symptomatic for the difficulties encountered by scholars in evaluating her later compositions. As she grew older, she increasingly used her compositional skills primarily for her teaching, for her *Hausmusik* ensembles, and activities within the church, writing for specific individuals. As a result, not only is much of this music very simple, true *Gebrauchsmusik*, but it is also difficult to ascertain which compositions of this nature, now found in the Paul Sacher Foundation, she actually considered to be complete, finished works. Not only are there various versions, but also for her a mere melody, a song, could be a final product.[39] The cantata is exemplary for this, in that it had been performed four times without a finished score, differently each time. She left it in her collection, writing that she placing it "at the disposal of anyone who can use it".[40]

Throughout this entire period, she continued in her assistance to Paul Sacher, advising him on programming, providing material for the *Mitteilungen*, marking up scores, calculating the times of diverse works, determining the ranges

---

38 "Sie steht immer noch nur als Skizze auf dem Papier und ich werde kaum dazu kommen, sie genau zu instrumentieren und in Partitur zu bringen. Sie wurde vier Mal aufgeführt, immer mit den mir zur Verfügung stehenden Kräften (zum grössten Teil Laien) und unter meiner Leitung. Im Radio waren der Sprecher (einmal Leopold Biberti, einmal Hans Haeser) und Jeremia (Ernst Denger) vom Fach. Das letzte Mal ergab sich in der Katholischen Kirche in Riehen vom Text her eine geschlossene Liturgie (1973). Der Pfarrer übernahm die Rolle des Sprechers, der Stadtposaunenchor Basel (Leitung Arthur Eglin) die meisten Begleitungen. Der Oekumenische Singkreis (Arthur Eglin) unterstützte meine 'Hausmusik'. Die Kirche war überfüllt und die Lieder wurden, unterstützt vom Bläserchor, ausgezeichnet mitgesungen". PSF-ILC.

39 See the list of compositions, pp. 469–92.

40 "Ich stelle sie jedem zur Verfügung, der sie brauchen kann". PSF-ILC.

Ill. 8.2: Ina Lohr sitting at her desk, with a portrait of her father, painted by her sister Sally Lohr, and a photograph of her mother on the wall behind her. Photo: PSF-ILC.

of choral works and the types of voices needed for the solo works, etc. She no longer went to rehearsals or concerts, however, as her hearing did not allow for that.

Up until 1973, Paul Sacher had not given much consideration to the manuscripts, scores, letters and books in his possession that had come together over the years. In that year, however, Rudolf Baumgartner, the director of the Lucerne Festival suggested that a selection of autographs from his "collection" be exhibited at the Lucerne Art Museum in conjunction with the Festival, where the Collegium Musicum Zurich regularly took part.[41] The public interest in this

41 *Musiker-Handschriften: Originalpartituren aus der Sammlung Dr.h.c. Paul Sacher. Manuskripte der Werke von Schweizer Komponisten, die an den Internationalen Musikfestwochen Luzern, 1973, aufgeführt werden*, exhibition catalog, Kunsthaus Luzern, 19. August bis 8. September 1973, ed. Hans Jörg Jans, Lucerne: Kunstmuseum 1973.

exhibition was perhaps a contributing factor in his decision of that year to establish a foundation which was intended to take over and look after his musical estate which he had assembled in the course of his activities as the director of the BKO, the CMZ, and as a patron of the musical arts. In 1974, he then bought the house "Auf Burg", where his own library and collection were to be stored, together with the libraries donated by the historian Werner Kaegi, its former owner, and Ina Lohr. This was to be supplemented by a microfilm archive for "scholars from the whole world".[42]

The first evidence of Ina Lohr's active involvement in this project is found in a letter she wrote to Paul Sacher on 13 July 1974, presumably sometime shortly after he bought "Auf Burg", where she gleefully told him that

> My sister [Etty] was here and was so enthusiastic about the idea of a Sacher Foundation that she spontaneously offered the two Rembrandt etchings which actually belong to the Rembrandt-Bible [a facsimile of the original] as a bequest. I had actually left them as a bequest to her, but she no longer has any desire to accept them. [… My] books are already almost completely ordered, so that I can now make a comprehensive list.[43]

We thus see that room for Ina Lohr's estate was part of the orginal concept. A creation of a workspace for her may perhaps also be seen as Paul Sacher's attempt to ensure that she would still have access to her library if she were to be forced to downsize, as it was becoming increasingly evident that Ina Lohr no longer could live entirely on her own.

Not only were her hands and wrists beginning to make themselves unpleasantly known again, but by 25 May 1974 she was forced to admit to Erna van Osselen:

> No, I am not so well, but I experience this as a real crisis, as a transition to a new period of perhaps yet quieter, but therefore more concentrated existence. My right eye suddenly became dull which appears to come from my much too high blood pressure that, in spite of the medications, did not want to go down. Now I swallow still more and also different medications and even have weekly check-ups. And [although] it became somewhat better, they are still searching for the cause, because the angina pectoris is a conse-

---

42 Information about the origins of the Paul Sacher Foundation was taken from Hans Jörg Jans, "Paul Sacher und der Werdegang der Paul Sacher Stiftung", in: *Paul Sacher – Facetten einer Musikerpersönlichkeit*, ed. Ulrich Mosch, Mainz: Schott 2006 (Veröffentlichungen der Paul Sacher Stiftung 11), 203–36.

43 "Meine Schwester war da und hat sich über die Idee einer Sacher-Stiftung so sehr begeistert, dass Sie spontan anbot auch die beiden Rembrandt Radierungen, die doch eigentlich zur Rembrandt-Bibel gehören, im Vermächtnis zu lassen. Ich hatte sie eigentlich ihr vermacht, was sie aber jetzt gar nicht mehr annehmen will. [...] Die Bücher sind schon fast alle umgeordnet, sodass ich jetzt eine überblickbare Liste machen kann". Letter Ina Lohr to Paul Sacher of 13 July 1974, private collection, Switzerland.

quence of it. In any case, I now lie contentedly on my balcony, read and sleep a lot, allow all my good friends to go shopping for me, and can give my lessons with pleasure and spirit. But everything goes much more slowly.[44]

This decline in her health did not stop her, however, from pursuing her interests and rejoicing in her friendships. On 3 August 1974, she wrote to Paul Sacher thanking him for the wonderful thistles,

> which together with the score of the Art of the Fugue, full of scribbles, conjure up "our" time in the Engadine. I am no longer up to "new projects", but [our] old common ones were valuable, if also imperfect. [...] I await the Boeke's, who will stay 4–5 days and then I will remember that the *Mitteilungen* still exist and that you will come again on the 14th.[45]

Whereas it may be true that she no longer could undertake big projects with Paul Sacher for the BKO, she retained her musical interest and drive, selling two larger instruments so that she could buy a clavichord with such a light touch that even she could play it, therewith insuring that she still had a keyboard instrument at her disposal. And beyond the *Mitteilungen*, she was still evaluating music for the BKO, as well as discussing the programming of Paul Sacher's CMZ concerts involving Galina Vischnevskaja and Mstislav Rostroprovitch.

It goes without saying that her own personal projects did not stop. She had to confess to Erna van Osselen that she

> once again had more to do than ever; [it is] exhausting, but also very enjoyable and stimulating. Tuesday we [a *Hausmusik* ensemble] sang and played for 80–90 senior citizens in Riehen. Fall songs from that book with children's songs. [...] Requests for such "parties" with singing, playing and commentary come almost daily. But before Christmas I

---

44 "Nee, het gaat me niet al te best, maar ik voel dit echt als crisis, als overgang tot een nieuwe periode van misschien nog rustiger, daarom geconcentreerder bestaan. Mijn rechter oog werd opeens troebel en dat bleek aan die veel te hoge bloeddruk te liggen, die ondanks de middelen maar niet naar beneden wilde. Nu slik ik nog meer en ook andere middelen en ben zelfs wekelijks onder controle. En het wordt iets beter, maar ze zoeken nog naar de oorzaak, want de angina pectoris is het gevolg. In ieder geval lig ik zielstevreden op mijn balcon, lees en slaap veel, laat alle goede vrienden boodschappen voor me doen en kan mijn lessen met plezier en animo geven. Maar alles gaat veel, veel langzamer". Letter Ina Lohr to Erna van Osselen of 25 May 1974, Aleid and Floris Zuidema.

45 "die zusammen mit der vollgekritzelten Partitur der Kunst der Fuge 'unsere' Engadiner Zeit herauf beschwörten. 'Zu neuen Taten' bin ich nicht mehr fähig, aber die alten, gemeinsamen, waren kostbar, wenn auch mangelhaft.[...] Ich erwarte Boekes, die noch 4–5 Tage bleiben und dann werde ich mich daran erinnern, dass es noch Mitteilungen gibt und dass Sie am 14. wieder kommen". Letter Ina Lohr to Paul Sacher of 3 August 1974, private collection, Switzerland.

will not speak or sing myself any more, but only [prepare] programs for people who are independent enough to take the performance upon themselves.[46]

And the following week Jan Boeke came together with his daughter with the intent of working out a good repertoire for her future as a recorder player.

This level of activity, however, was too much for her system. Her body forced her to acknowledge her limits, in that she could no longer see clearly after 4 PM with her right eye. Her doctor was of the opinion that her eyes were fine

> but the general exhaustion, which my vitality deflects and apparently corrects, makes my eye muscle weak, so that I can no longer focus from the late afternoon on. Now I also understand why I walk a bit drunkenly on the street around that time. He urged me seriously to spend at least 10 of the 24 hours lying down, much of it with closed eyes. That makes my days short, especially the time that I would like to make available to others. There are so many people who really can use some of my vitality and trust.[47]

But her health did not improve; to the contrary, she found it almost impossible to change her lifestyle and her body continued to plague her, forcing her to the decision of moving into an apartment in the Dalbehof, a senior citizen's residence near a hospital, with a telephone next to her bed, so that help was available should she need it. And although she remained cheerful, she was reluctant to move and leave behind so much that was dear to her. At the same time, she could foresee that once she was there with her two rooms, and with all the amenities including the midday meal, that she would be able to read more and work less, and be very contented.[48]

By 15 February 1975 she was actually very relieved that she was moving, as life on the whole was becoming increasingly difficult. She therefore realized the

---

46 "ik heb weer eens meer te doen dan ooit; vermoeiend, maar erg prettig en animerend. Dinsdag zongen en speelden we (mijn huismuziek, [...]) voor 80–90 bejaarden in Riehen. Herfstliederen uit dat boek met kinderliederen [...] Er komen bijna dagelijks aanvragen voor zulke 'feestjes' met zang, spel en commentaar. Maar vóór Kerstmis spreek en zing ik zelf niet meer, maak alleen nog programma's voor mensen, die zelfstandig genoeg zijn om de uitvoering zelf op zich te nemen". Letter Ina Lohr to Erna van Osselen of 13 October 1974, Aleid and Floris Zuidema.

47 "maar de algemeene overmoeheid, die mijn vitaliteit opvangt en schijnbaar corrigeert, de oogspier slap maakt, zodat ik vanaf de late middag niet meer fixeren kan. Nu begrijp ik ook, waarom ik om die tijd soms een beetje dronken op straat loop. Hij drong erg aan op die minstens 10 van de 24 uur liggen, veel met gesloten ogen. Dat maakt mijn dagen kort, vooral de tijd die ik toch, graag voor anderen beschikbaar zou hebben. Er zijn zo veel mensen, die wel iets van mijn vitaliteit en vertrouwen kunnen gebruiken". Letter Ina Lohr to Erna van Osselen of 24 November 1974, Aleid and Floris Zuidema.

48 Letter Ina Lohr to Erna van Osselen of 27 January 1975, Aleid and Floris Zuidema.

need for haste and had begun to sort out what should go to the Paul Sacher Foundation:

> It is simpler than you think, because in that enormous, but very neglected house there are 2 rooms that are neatly in order and free, because Dr. Kaegi [Werner Kaegi's wife, Adrienne von Speyr] had to give up her practice just after they had moved in. He now has had all of the installations removed, emptied the bookshelves and on next Friday I will go for tea with him, in order to discuss the possibility of storing some of my furniture and books there that I cannot take with me. He himself wishes me to have a key and come and work there, if I so wish! "He" is, to be sure, Prof. Dr. Werner Kaegi, the friend and translator of Huizinga and the man who hopes to finish off the large new edition of the works of Jakob Burckhardt this fall. His library will remain there, that of Sacher + his own collection and that of [Sacher's] wife will come there, and then my 1 or 2 rooms.[49]

On 24 April 1975, all of the things she could not take with her were brought to "Auf Burg"; a few months later she received three keys, one for the outer door, one for the glass door and one for the room.[50]

8.2 Life at the Dalbehof

There is little extant correspondence for the rest of the year, other than that involving her work for Sacher, as evidently it took her time to adjust to the new situation and to regain her health. But she did write to Erna van Osselen on 24 August 1975, that she now felt at home, as had the 18 Dutch friends that had visited her up until then, and that another four were expected from the Netherlands as well as three Swedes and an American. An indication of how quickly she had become integrated in her residence is given by her description of a Christmas carol sing-along that she had organized, in which she, with the

---

49 "'t Is eenvoudiger dan je denkt, want in dat reusachtige, maar zeer verwaarloosde huis zijn 2 kamers keurig in orde en vrij, omdat Frau Dr. Kaegi haar praktijk moest opgeven, net nadat ze erin getrokken waren. Hij heeft er nu alle installaties uit laten halen, de boeken-kasten leeggehaald en volgende Vrijdag ga ik bij hem thee drinken, om te spreken over de mogelijkheid, dat ik daar dan nu al een deel van mijn meubels en die boeken, die ik niet mee kan nemen deponeer. Hij wil zelfs, dat ik een sleutel krijg en daar kom werken, als ik dat graag wil! 'Hij' is dus Prof. Dr. Werner Kaegi, de vriend en vertaler van Huizinga en de man, die de grote nieuwe uitgave van de werken van Jakob Burckhardt in de herfst hoopt te besluiten. Zijn bibliotheek blijft er in, die van Sacher + verzamelingen van hem en zijn vrouw komen er in en dan mijn 1 of 2 kamers". Letter Ina Lohr to Erna van Osselen of 15 February 1975.
50 Letter Ina Lohr to Paul Sacher of 7 April 1975, private collection, Switzerland.

help of her *Hausmusik,* had gotten 28 of the 40 fellow residents to join in, even with the less well-known songs, by holding a preparatory session in advance.[51]

One of the major events in her life in the following year was the celebration of Paul Sacher's 70th birthday on 28 April 1976. Radio Basel reserved an hour's time in his honor, allowing him to choose six friends to speak about him. As Ina Lohr wrote Erna van Osselen on 8 February 1976:

> He named 12 names, and I am the only woman in that illustrious company which must give their best. Fortunately, I am allowed to speak over our cooperation (almost 47 years!) and can draw freely from my memories. 3 prof[essor]s will be responsible for the official part! I have the material, but formulating it for something that should last only 5–6 minutes is tricky.[52]

The text for this broadcast is no doubt the one entitled "Zusammenarbeit mit Paul Sacher" in her collection in the Foundation. Apart from that, she did not partake in the festivities surrounding his birthday, except for going to one of the three concerts Mstislav Rostroprovitch gave in his honor, a program of three of the Suites by Johann Sebastian Bach in the Münster, where she knew, due to the size of the church and the compositions' low register that she would still be able to enjoy his playing in spite of the difficulties with her hearing.[53] This not-withstanding, Paul Sacher expressed his gratitude for their long-standing cooperation in the following manner: "You spoke very kindly about me on the radio, and the magnificent tulips long gave us pleasure. But the best thing is our long friendship and our working cooperation".[54]

In January of 1977 the 50th anniversary of the BKO was celebrated, in which Ina Lohr participated only at a distance, as her health and her ears were neither up to the concert nor the dinner. She did, however, send a message to the assembly, for which Paul Sacher thanked her greatly.

Correspondence concerning questions of programming for both the BKO and the CMZ continued on with great regularity. In response to her birth-

---

51 Letter Ina Lohr to Erna van Osselen of 2 January 1976, Aleid and Floris Zuidema, Lochem.
52 "Hij noemde 12 namen en ik ben de enige vrouw, die in dat illustere gezelschap iets ten beste moet geven. Gelukkig mag ik over onze samenwerking spreken (bijna 47 jaar!) en vrij uit mijn herinneringen putten. Voor het officiele zorgen dan 3 proffen! De stof heb ik, maar het formuleren voor iets, dat maar 5–6 min. mag duren, is een tour". Letter Ina Lohr to Erna van Osselen of 8 February 1976, Aleid and Floris Zuidema, Lochem.
53 Letter Ina Lohr to Erna van Osselen of 4 April 1976, Aleid and Floris Zuidema, Lochem.
54 "Sie haben am Radio sehr lieb über mich geredet & die prächtigen Tulpen haben uns lange erfreut. Aber das schönste ist unsere lange Freundschaft & Arbeitsgemeinschaft". Letter Paul Sacher to Ina Lohr of 17 May 1977, PSF-ILC.

day greeting of that year, he affirmed in a letter of 17 May 1977 that he "was glad that we, although no longer the youngest, still regularly get together and get to converse about things which have been of common interest to us in the past, and still, in part, in the present".[55] And on her own birthday, he confessed that "he did not know, how [he] could continue without" her.[56] She herself responded to the latter by saying that

> With the passing of the years, one increasingly comes to know that especially that loyalty which holds fast despite all differences is a miracle and a strength. In a week from today, rehearsals begin again for you, and I will give lessons again as of Monday. The vacations were not necessarily quiet, but the loyalty of friendship and the trust that also very successful musicians still demonstrate towards me today, have had a stimulating effect and have filled me with gratitude.[57]

These touching expressions of gratitude for what they have shared with one another over time now become a constant in their letters, as their brushes with ill health – as with all aging people – brought them more directly into contact with their own mortality.

Ina Lohr also encountered this in her daily life in the senior citizens' residence, where she carried out her self-imposed task of helping the sick and depressed. She not only did this with her visits to individuals, but she also once again contributed to the festive mood at the Christmas dinner in 1977, by having her small *Hausmusik* ensemble – the only one she still taught – come and perform some music, as well as support the residents in the singing of carols.[58]

She also wrote to Erna van Osselen about a project that was to begin in the new year, the cataloging of her books and music, for which a place had been

---

55 "Ich bin froh, dass wir, obwohl nicht die Jüngsten, noch regelmässig zusammenkommen und uns über Dinge unterhalten dürfen, die uns in der Vergangenheit und zum Teil noch in der Gegenwart gemeinsam interessieren". Letter Paul Sacher to Ina Lohr of 17 May 1977, PSF-ILC.

56 "Ich weiss nicht, wie ich ohne Sie weitermachen könnte". Visiting card [attached to box of chocolates] Paul Sacher to Ina Lohr around 1 August 1977, PSF-ILC.

57 "Man weiss es mit den Jahren immer mehr, dass gerade die Treue, die aller Verschiedenheit Stand hält, ein Wunder und eine Kraft ist. Heute in einer Woche fangen für Sie schon wieder die Proben an und ich gebe ab Montag wieder meine Stunden. Die Ferien waren nicht unbedingt ruhig, aber die Treue in der Freundschaft und das Vertrauen, die auch sehr erfolgreiche Musiker mir heute noch zeigen haben anregend gewirkt und mich mit Dankbarkeit erfüllt". Letter Ina Lohr to Paul Sacher of 10 August 1977, private collection, Switzerland.

58 Letter Ina Lohr to Erna van Osselen, Christmas Day, 1977, Aleid and Floris Zuidema, Lochem; and letter Ina Lohr to a former member of a larger *Hausmusik* ensemble of 31 December 1977, in the documents placed at my disposal by Arthur Eglin, Basel.

found in a bomb shelter (required by Swiss law at the time) in the Dalbehof, furnished with a carpet and folding table.[59] In the following letter of 22 January 1978, she spoke of how the "going back, ordering and cataloging of my books is the very best work therapy" for her, how it freed her a bit from her surroundings which had begun to be oppressing for her.[60] In this catalogization project she was aided by Ursula Karlhuber, who was paid for her assistance by Paul Sacher.[61] That these books were intended for the Foundation is also confirmed by an exchange of letters with him about the space available to her for her books.[62] She soon discovered, however, that she had an allergic response to the air in the basement room, due to the poor ventilation. By June, she was able to rent workspace in the ergotherapy room and it was foreseen that all of her books and music – including those which had been deposited for a while in the Foundation – would be brought there by the beginning of July. She looked forward to the prospect that her whole life, with all of its stylistic periods, would pass before her, in the process of organizing them.[63]

She sought integration in the daily life of the residence not only for herself, but also for her friends, as is evidenced by the homemade letter paper she used at Christmas that year. In the past she had created writing paper by making collages of images and poems, combined with her music. Erna van Osselen had expressed a desire to make a contribution of this nature. It thus came about that her drawing of a maple tree that stood in the courtyard of the Dalbehof inspired another inhabitant, Helen Schärr-Ammann, a long-term friend and participant in various *Hausmusik* ensembles, to write a poem about it, which Ina Lohr then set to music (see Ill. 8.3). She then sold this photocopied collage for 20 centimes/page to the residents, in order to be able to give her friend a small gratuity for her drawing. Apparently it was a source of great pleasure to all.[64]

59 Letter Ina Lohr to Erna van Osselen, Christmas Day, 1977, Aleid and Floris Zuidema, Lochem.
60 "Het terugvinden, ordenen en katalogiseren van mijn boeken is voor mij de allerbeste werktherapie en bevrijdt me een beetje uit deze omgeving, die me zo langzamerhand toch wel erg to pakken had". Letter Ina Lohr to Erna van Osselen of 22 January 1978, Aleid and Floris Zuidema, Lochem.
61 Letters Ina Lohr to Paul Sacher of 8 January 1978, 24 May 1979, and 7 March 1980, private collection, Switzerland.
62 Letter Ina Lohr to Paul Sacher of 1 May 1980 private collection, Switzerland.
63 Letter Ina Lohr to Erna van Osselen of 16 June 1978, Aleid and Floris Zuidema, Lochem.
64 Letter Ina Lohr to Erna van Osselen, Christmas Day, 1977, Aleid and Floris Zuidema, Lochem.

Unser Garten im Dalbehof

Ein alter Ahorn - moosbewachsen
die Äste knorrig, steil empor,
So steht er vor mir denkt gelassen
ist's weise so? bin ich ein Tor?

Ich trutze jedem Ungewitter,
der Wind zerzaust mein altes Haar,
viel Jahre schlugen mich zum Ritter
mein Panzer grünt noch jedes Jahr.

Und jeden Herbst streu ich die Blätter,
ein güldenen gelben Segen aus,
auch meine Sämlein noch viel netter
wie Helikopter fliegen aus.

Helen Schär-Amman

Ill. 8.3: "Unser Garten im Dalbehof", Letterhead created by Erna van Osselen, Helen Schär-Amman, and Ina Lohr. Reproduction: PSF-ILC.

Around this time, she asked Christopher Schmidt to lead a group of some of the people who had been in her *Hausmusik* ensembles. It started in one of the smaller rooms at the Schola; but then the director – at that time Peter Reidemeister – objected to so many people coming to the school for something outside the auspices of the Schola, that it was shifted to a local church. Although ostensibly in Christopher Schmidt's hands, she was unable to resist the opportunity of providing "clarification from the historical perspective" when called upon to do so.[65] Although originally about 15 in number, when they moved to

65 Letter Ina Lohr to Erna van Osselin of 22 January 1977, Aleid and Floris Zuidema, Lochem; and diverse interviews with Christopher Schmidt.

the church it expanded to about 30–40 members, mostly older women. For Christopher Schmidt it was an excellent opportunity to gain experience in singing the pre-Reformation and Reformation repertoire in unison with a motivated and experienced group.[66] For Ina Lohr, perhaps, it represented her last effort to pass on her legacy with that music.

The biggest events in her life in this year were the two celebrations associated with her 75th birthday, the more official one on the day itself, and the second instigated and organized by Arthur Eglin, this time with her cooperation. The latter was a mixed blessing, on many levels, as is revealed by her first letter of 9 April 1978 concerning it:

> Your loyal friendship and your continuing trust have been good for me, but your request once again showed me how threatening this birthday is for me. Five years ago, I could still listen to the music in the Waisenkirche with the help of earplugs and derive great pleasure from it. And the [concert of] 29 September of last year ["Der Mensch in den Psalmen", see p. 412] was also still a wonderful experience. But since then, the periostitis has remained and listening to music has become an increasingly great effort; also sitting and speaking [in front of an audience. …] High notes and also those that are only somewhat loud produce a terrifying cacophony for me, so that the music, as it actually is, no longer reaches me. This is then followed by a very unpleasant vertigo, which I should – if at all possible – avoid.[67]

After having counted up all the reasons against his suggestion, she then agreed to take part, saying that she would like to compose a version of Psalm 121, something she had long put aside because other more important things had intervened. A month later she wrote to Arthur Eglin, saying that she was working on it, but everything was going so slowly because it took so much time.[68]

---

66 Interview with Christopher Schmidt of 19 March 2018.
67 "Deine treue Freundschaft und Dein bleibendes Vertrauen haben mir gut getan, aber Deine Anfrage hat mir wieder gezeigt, wie drohend dieser Geburtstag vor mir steht. Vor 5 Jahren konnte ich mit Hilfe von Oropax eure Musik noch in der Waisenhauskirche anhören und meine grosse Freude daran haben. Am 29. Sept. letzten Jahres war das Zusammensein in dieser Art mir auch noch ein Erlebnis. Aber seither ist die Knochenhautentzündung geblieben und Musik Hören wird eine immer grössere Anstrengung; auch das Stehen und Reden. […] Hohe und auch nur irgendwie starke Töne erzeugen bei mir eine erschreckende Kakophonie, sodass die Musik, wie sie eigentlich ist, mich nicht mehr erreicht. Es folgt dann der sehr unangenehme Schwindel, den ich nach Möglichkeit vermeiden sollte". Letter Ina Lohr to Arthur Eglin of 9 April 1978, Arthur Eglin, Basel.
68 Letter Ina Lohr to Arthur Eglin of 5 June 1978, Arthur Eglin, Basel.

On 21 June 1978, however, she felt obliged to write that she had

> just torn up the entire sketch of the psalm. This music is no longer really good. I believe that my music up until now was, although simple, at least pure and authentic. But now I am no longer sufficiently in practice to be able to write down *that* which I envision. [...] I live today in the world of the aged, can no longer withdraw myself from their problems, can even really help. But I make and hear far less music and I am not even sad about it! Perhaps it proves that I never really belonged to the musicians' [world], although music was and is actually my strongest form of expression. But then it is a music which lives in the moment and passes, it cannot be captured on paper. In my old age, I am coming back almost exclusively to singing monophonically, retreating from the world of musicians, but would like to speak about how it was, [how it] changed again and again, and would be happy if you were to sing examples for it.[69]

It must have been a completely galling experience for her to discover that she could no longer do something that she took for granted, upon which she had based her entire professional life. But she nonetheless had the mental fortitude to admit to herself, and to the world, that she no longer met her own standards of musical competence in regard to composition. It is interesting in this context that she also questions whether she really belonged to the "world of musicians", for it was precisely in this context, whether with Paul Sacher or with those aiming for greater professionalization within Early Music, that she fought her greatest battles: her goals were different than theirs, but they shared the common language of music.

They then agreed on a program, which included a version of Psalm 121 based on a Martin Buber translation, which she had written earlier and no longer possessed herself. She then declared in a letter of 2 July 1978 that "as soon as I have moved my books here [presumably from the Paul Sacher Foundation], regular work will be done on my talk, which will be easily combined with my 'spiritual

---

69 "Es fällt mir sehr schwer Dir zu schreiben, dass ich soeben die ganze Skizze des Psalmes zerrissen habe. Diese Musik ist nicht mehr wirklich gut. Ich glaube, dass meine Musik bis jetzt zwar einfach, aber mindestens sauber und echt war. Jetzt aber bin ich nicht mehr genügend in der Übung um das aufzuschreiben, was ich mir vorstelle. [...] Ich lebe heute in der Welt der Alten, kann mich ihren Problemen nicht entziehen, kann sogar wirklich helfen. Aber ich mache und höre viel weniger Musik und bin nicht einmal betrübt darüber! Vielleicht beweist das, dass ich nie so ganz zu den Musikern gehörte, obwohl die Musik eigentlich meine stärkste Ausdrucksform war und ist. Aber das ist dann eine Musik, die im Moment entsteht und vergeht, sie lässt sich nicht aufschreiben. Ich komme also im Alter zu einem fast dauernden einstimmigen Singen zurück, ziehe mich aus der Welt der Musiker zurück, würde aber gerne erzählen, wie es war, immer wieder anders wurde und wäre glücklich, wenn Ihr dazu Beispiele singen würdet". Letter Ina Lohr to Arthur Eglin of 21 June 1978, Arthur Eglin, Basel.

advising' and with the completion of the card catalog".[70] She also mentioned that Paul Sacher was horrified to hear that the concert was scheduled for the same date as the BKO annual meeting, and asked whether the date for the festivity could be shifted.

Despite her discomfort at the thought of any celebration of her birthday, in her thank-you letter to Paul Sacher of 5 August 1978, after it had passed by, she had to admit that she had been gratified by the occasion, that it did her

> good to experience this friendship from all sides in such a concentrated fashion, although I am aware of it and am thankful for it every day. That is particularly true for you, when I think of all the years that we have experienced together, connected through music, through the good and the beautiful in the absolute sense, but also through the personal contact, which is clearer to me than ever before. The ordering of my books awakens many memories which show me how rich, in every way, the almost 50 years in Basel have been for me.[71]

With this, she once more took up a discussion begun years before, in a letter from Paul Sacher of 1 August 1940, also her birthday, about the relationship between beauty and goodness as absolutes (see pp. 209–210), in reply to which Ina Lohr had insisted on the priority of goodness. She went even further in answering Arthur Eglin's tribute to her, "Substanz vor Brillanz", drawn from words that she had once used in a lesson to draw attention to the content of a piece rather than to its surface: "I have more than once experienced that with the help of brilliance, the substance of a sacred work was so strongly conveyed to the audience that the concert became a church service".[72] In quoting an extended passage of this response in a letter to Paul Sacher of 28 September 1978, she thus completed a circle, admitting that he was right in their case, that

70 "Sobald ich meine Bücher hie[r]her gezügelt habe, wird regelmässig an der Plauderei gearbeitet, was sich gut mit der 'Seelsorge' und mit dem Aufarbeiten der Kartothek verbinden lässt". Letter Ina Lohr to Arthur Eglin of 2 July 1978, Arthur Eglin, Basel.

71 "Ich muss auch gestehen, dass es mir gut getan hat, diese Freundschaft von allen Seiten sozusagen konzentriert zu erleben, obwohl ich sie doch kenne und täglich dankbar dafür bin. Das gilt nun Ihnen gegenüber ganz besonders, wenn ich an die vielen Jahre zurückdenke, die wir mit einander erlebt haben, verbunden durch die Musik, durch das Gute und Schöne überhaupt, aber auch durch menschliche Kontakte, die mir heute klarer sind als je zuvor. Das Ordnen meiner Bücher weckt viele Erinnerungen, die mir zeigen, wie reich in jeder Beziehung die bald 50 Basler Jahre für mich gewesen sind". Letter Ina Lohr to Paul Sacher of 5 August 1978, private collection, Switzerland.

72 "Ich habe es mehr als einmal miterlebt, dass mit Hilfe der Brillanz die Substanz eines geistlichen Werkes so stark auf das Publikum übertragen wurde, dass aus dem Konzert Gottesdienst wurde". Arthur Eglin, "Substanz vor Brillanz", in: *Bläserkreis* 20/7, 1978, n.p. and her response in *Bläserkreis* 20/8, 1978, n.p.

indeed the personal contact, the acceptance of his means, had also proffered a possibility of attainment of her own goals.

In spite of this, she was so conscious of the distance between her musical world and that of Paul Sacher, that in the end, she felt forced to un-invite him to Arthur Eglin's concert of 31 August 1978. In a letter to Paul Sacher on the following day, she admitted that it had been very unpleasant to do so, but that it had been a correct decision, since although all had participated with fervor, only occasionally had there been moments that met concert standards. And while this did not disturb her, because she knew they were doing their best and providing pleasure for the audience, she knew that her worlds were far apart from one another and that she at one and the same time belonged to all of them and none of them.[73] This is a further expression of her essential loneliness, of never having really been able to find that compromise between remaining true to herself while simultaneously integrating herself within a social entity. Her means of transcending the boundaries between people, movements, religious beliefs, was to encapsulate them within herself, partaking of all of them to a lesser or greater degree, but not allowing them to claim her in totality. In doing so, however, she was never able to express herself – nor be understood by others – in her entirety.

This was also true in the last task she had set herself in life:

> helping in this senior citizen's residence, in various hospitals, and wherever. The task fills my days completely and – although I would love to have more time to listen to music, to sing myself and to read a lot – I am thankfully happy that my days, even in the 76th year of my life, still fly by. […] Naturally, I also have time for myself, but I really need it in order to find my way back to my own world each time by means of records and tapes, and through the ordering and cataloging of my many books, which will be saved for whomever might have interest in them later.[74]

73 Letter Ina Lohr to Paul Sacher of 1 September 1978, private collection, Switzerland.
74 "Mijn eigenlijke taak is nu het helpen in dit bejaardencentrum, in verschillende ziekenhuizen en waar dan ook. Die taak vult mijn dagen volkomen en, hoewel ik graag meer tijd zou hebben om muziek te horen, zelf te zingen en veel te lezen: ik ben dankbaar gelukkig, dat de dagen ook in mij[n] 76ste levensjaar nog om vliegen. […] Natuurlijk hebe ik ook tijd voor mezelf, maar die heb ik hard nodig om telkens weer mijn eigen wereld terug te vinden met behulp van platen en toonbanden, en door het ordenen en catalogiseren van mijn vele boeken, die bewaard blijven voor wie er later belangstelling voor mocht hebben". From a typed text of a letter to Ina Lohr's Dutch friends of 30 October 1978, used as a basis for reducing the backlog of her correspondence, sent to Erna van Osselen, with personal remarks following, Aleid and Floris Zuidema, Lochem.

Although Ina Lohr was a resident in the center, she kept herself also apart from it, having given herself the task to be there for others around her. Just as earlier in life, she then needed to withdraw to regain her sense of self, to retain her self-identity.

Another manner in which she came to use her musical skills to raise the spirits of and create social bonds between those residing in the center, apart from the singing at the Christmas dinner, was by holding weekly sessions in her rooms devoted to the listening of music. She herself selected the music, which could range from winter songs, known and unknown, Beethoven quintets, Mozart piano concerti, and 16th-century instrumental music from Basel. They discussed the music, the texts, sang at times, and spoke of the different ways of listening. And she conceded to Erna van Osselen on 28 January 1979, that her friend was right in saying that she helped herself just as much as she helped others.[75]

Her life continued on peacefully in this manner, with her battles against her various aches and pains, helping others, receiving visitors from near and far, as well as meeting with Paul Sacher. She was obviously doing less for him, but still involved in questions of programming, choice of singers, the *Mitteilungen,* and served as the mediator between him and Jan Boeke, whose soloists of choice were being considered for a concert in 1980, and Sven-Erik Bäck, whose *Signos* for percussion was performed on 23 September 1979 in the foyer of the Basel Theater. These two friends were also responsible for two of the high points of her year.

First Jan Boeke, who was on tour with Cappella Amsterdam that summer, had organized a concert especially for her, with twenty members of his ensemble, in the courtyard of the Dalbehof on 13 August 1979. It must have meant a great deal to her to have a renowned Dutch ensemble, led by one of her most loyal friends, sing for her and her fellow inhabitants.

And just a few weeks after that, the Bäcks came, a visit that brought her to life, as she admitted to Erna van Osselen, that transformed her into a musician again:

> Suddenly I am *also* completely in my own work again and lay one egg after another. The impulse to this came from Sven-Erik Bäck, who was here with his wife for 3 days. Last week Sacher directed a work by him for clarinet and percussion. [...] Bäck had the greatest success, was very happy and Sacher immediately gave him a new commis-

---

75 "En je hebt gelijk als je zegt, dat ik met dat helpen net zo veel mezelf help als de anderen". Letter Ina Lohr to Erna van Osselen of 28 January 1979, Aleid and Floris Zuidema, Lochem.

sion! And Saturday morning, Sunday morning and afternoon, and also Monday morning, Sven-Erik [and I] sat in front of my best [audio] devices and recorded a conversation between the two of us about the question of whether music can actually be spiritual music.[76]

The three and a half hours they recorded were to serve as a starting point for two broadcasts on the subject in Sweden and perhaps for a book. Being stimulated at this level clearly served as a catalyst for a little while, leading her back to her own personal projects.

She was, however, brought back down to earth again only shortly thereafter by a facial neuralgia. By 20 January 1980, she was complaining that she suddenly felt old and tired, no longer really able to go out and visit the sick as she had been wont to do. She decided then to restrict her efforts to the residence, in particular by continuing to host the Monday circle.[77]

Her work in ordering her books, too, began to take on a slightly different form, as a consequence of a gradual change in Paul Sacher's vision for his Foundation. In particular, the acquisition of further musical estates, most spectacularly that of Igor Stravinsky in 1983, both as purchases and gifts, necessitated a complete renovation of the building between 1982–85 and prompted a modification of its statutes in 1986. Its goal came to encompass not only the preservation of his musical estate and the possessions of the Foundation, but also the creation of an internationally recognized institution for the study of the works contained within it. One still intended to set aside a room for her books and valued possessions, as is evidenced by her concern about what her room would look like. She wrote to Paul Sacher, namely, on 1 May 1980 that although she could measure how many meters of books she had, it was of no use, if she could not visualize it in the space available, together with her furniture and paintings. She wondered whether it might be possible for the architects who were supervising the renovation, Katharina and Wilfrid Steib, to come by and look at the situa-

---

76 "Opeens ben ik weer helemaal <u>ook</u> in mijn eigen werk en leg het ene ei na het andere. De stoot daartoe gaf Sven-Erik Bäck, die met zijn vrouw 3 dagen hier was. Sacher dirigeerde verleden week een werk van hem voor klarinet en slagwerk. [...] Bäck had het grootste succes, was zielsgelukkig en Sacher gaf hem meteen een nieuwe opdracht! En zaterdagmorgen, zondagmorgen en -middag, ook nog maandagmorgen zaten Sven-Erik [en ik] voor mijn beste apparaten en namen een gesprek tussen ons beide op over de vraag, of muziek eigenlijk geestelijke muziek kon zijn". Undated postcard Ina Lohr to Erna van Osselen, Aleid and Floris Zuidema, Lochem.

77 Letter Ina Lohr to Erna van Osselen of 20 January 1980, Aleid and Floris Zuidema, Lochem.

tion themselves.[78] Although the room existed for a number of years, it eventually became impossible to continue treating her collection differently from the others, due to the enormous growth of the Foundation. Her room thus subsequently became one of those open to visiting scholars, like those around it; and her books and music are now found in the archives, as all the other material under its aegis, including Paul Sacher's own library.[79]

Shortly thereafter, on 14 June 1980, she wrote asking whether they might meet a bit later on the following Wednesday, commenting that "we do not actually have anything more [that is] pressing to discuss, which is a pity on the one hand, and on the other good. You seem to me to be in your element; I also am. But I am naturally pleased if the contact is not lost".[80] In spite, or perhaps because of this, soon thereafter Paul Sacher made an enormous step in creating a sense of increased closeness between them. It is in the all-important interview with Jos Leussink that Ina Lohr told the story about how they came to address one another with the familiar you form, and by their first names:

> Sacher and I have only called one another by our first names since we both retired from the Schola and the Music Academy; and then he just came in suddenly and said "Hello Ina" and I also said "Hello Paul".[81]

It is almost as if they could only enter into this closer form of communication – or was it only she that had problems with lowering this linguistic barrier? – when they were no longer working so regularly together. In writing the first letter to "Lieber Paul" on 2 December 1980, she recognized "how odd it is that we, simply in the excitement of our work, stayed with 'Sie'; also as a matter of convenience on my part. I will now practice diligently".[82]

---

78 Letter Ina Lohr to Paul Sacher of 1 May 1980, private collection, Switzerland.

79 Niklaus Röthlin, "Geschichte des Hauses 'Auf Burg'", in: *Paul Sacher Stiftung*, Basel: Paul Sacher Foundation 1986, 10–12; Hans Jörg Jans, "Paul Sacher und der Werdegang der Paul Sacher Stiftung", 203–36, especially 212–23 and 219–25.

80 "Wir haben eigentlich nichts Dringendes mehr zu besprechen, was einerseits schade, andererseits gut ist. Sie scheinen mir in Ihrem Element zu sein, ich bin es auch. Aber natürlich freut es mich, wenn der Kontakt nicht verloren geht". Letter Ina Lohr to Paul Sacher of 14 June 1980, private collection, Switzerland.

81 "Sacher en ik hebben elkaar pas bij de naam genoemd doen wij beide dus pensioniert waren van Schola en Musik Akademie en doen kwam hij opeens binne en zei 'Salüt Ina' en zei ik ook 'Salüt Paul'". Interview Ina Lohr with Jos Leussink of 25 March 1983.

82 "Als ich heute mit Hans Lanz im Casino zum Mittagessen war, fiel mir ein, wie komisch das ist, dass wir, einfach im Arbeitseifer beim 'Sie' geblieben sind; auch aus Bequemlichkeit meinerseits. Ich werde jetzt brav üben". Letter Ina Lohr to Paul Sacher of 2 December 1980, private collection, Switzerland.

Her health, however, was deteriorating and, with that, the radius of her activities was narrowing. Her vertigo was such, that she could not reliably travel by tram, heard people's voices in three octaves, and could no longer hear music clearly, so that she no longer went to concerts.[83] Thus she stayed at home as much as possible, devoting herself to her projects there, including her regular meetings with Paul Sacher to discuss the programming of the upcoming season. This work suffered a sudden interruption in April when she had a heart attack. Although she recovered from it "fantastically", was no longer dizzy, she also no longer heard music, but only overtones. She commented to Paul Sacher: "As everything still goes very slowly and makes me tired, I do not even miss the music".[84] It was also a catalyst for her to write her "Sketch of an Autobiography" and plan her funeral down to the address list.

Paul Sacher's various responses were quite touching. The first, on a visiting card accompanying some orchids, was simply: "It's a miracle that we made it again. I wish you further care & help, strength & blessing. If you need me: just telephone! Happy Easter! In thankfulness, Yours, Paul".[85] And sometime later, in a thank-you note after his 75th birthday: "The button roses and cowslips which I received from you were the most beautiful of the floral decorations. I just re-read your life up to the time you arrived in Basel. I often think of you & would like to come by again. Perhaps at Whitsun?"[86] Back in her own home, Ina Lohr received the letter with a mixture of joy and a bit of astonishment, as she had never considered the possibility that she should have called him, invited him; he had always taken the initiative himself in the previous 50 years. She warned him, however, that although she was receiving visitors and taking care of her own household, everything went very slowly.[87]

In spite of this, she managed to continue her labor on the fourth edition of *Solmisation und Kirchentonarten* upon which she had been working since the beginning of the year. This edition brought a few real changes with it, in that

---

83 Letter Ina Lohr to Arthur Eglin of 30 November 1980, Arthur Eglin, Basel.

84 "Da alles noch recht langsam geht und schnell müde macht, vermisse ich die Musik nicht einmal". Undated letter Ina Lohr to Paul Sacher, private collection, Switzerland.

85 "es ist gewiss ein Wunder, dass wir noch einmal davon gekommen sind. Ich wünsche dir weiterhin Schutz & Hilfe, Kraft & Segen. Wenn Du mich brauchst: Telefon genügt! Schöne Ostern! In Dankbarkeit[,] Dein Paul". Undated visiting card Paul Sacher to Ina Lohr, PSF-ILC.

86 "Die Rösli & Maierysli, die ich von Dir erhielt, waren mein schönster Blumenschmuck. Dein Leben bis zur Ankunft in Basel habe ich soeben wieder gelesen. Ich denke oft an dich & käme gerne wieder einmal vorbei. Vielleicht an Pfingsten?" Card Paul Sacher to Ina Lohr from May 1981, PSF-ILC.

87 Letter Ina Lohr to Paul Sacher of 31 May 1981, private collection, Switzerland.

she had decided – now there were a sufficient number of scholarly transcriptions of the chant melodies available – that she could notate much of the music as she herself would sing it rhythmically; she also added many new pre-Reformation and Reformation songs. She finished this reworking in autumn of 1981 and it was published by Hug in Basel. One of the catalysts for this new edition may have been the advent of Henk van Benthem in Basel in 1980. A former student of Jan Boeke, he came for about a year, with the primary intent of making a translation of this book into Dutch. He took a draft back with him to the Netherlands, where he and Jan Boeke then edited and published it in 1983, for Ina Lohr's 80th birthday. This translation of her book prolonged her influence in the Netherlands, in that it served as a basis for instruction in various conservatories.

In August [?] of 1981 she had also begun working "with almost obsessive joy" on her article on the relationship between text and melody in the Salve Regina antiphon and Hans Sachs's translation thereof for the book in celebration of the Schola's 50th anniversary, *Alte Musik: Praxis und Reflexion.*[88] In a letter of 10 October 1981 to Kees Vellekoop, she mentions the rush for completing the article for a deadline two years before the date of publication and regretted that she was no longer able to get to the University Library to consult the most recent literature. She acknowledged that her article no longer belonged to the more academic style at the Schola; nonetheless, it was representative of her contribution to the institution.

It is also clear, however, that her life was becoming increasingly circumscribed. She described it to Arthur Eglin on 4 April 1982 in the following manner:

> I can no longer go out much, only very little actually, but I experience each day given me with gratitude, even though there is so much misery in this world. As long as I can still help a bit in my world, which has become small, I still sing each morning from the psalms or also from other texts. [...] Monophony has once again taken total possession of me.[89]

---

88 "mit fast 'besessener' Freude". Letter Ina Lohr to Paul Sacher of 17 [August?] 1981, private collection, Switzerland. "Die Sprachmelodik und Zahlensymbolik des 'Salve Regina' als Antiphon (11. Jahrhundert) und als Meistergesang der Reformationszeit (16. Jahrhundert)", in: *Alte Musik: Praxis und Reflexion*, ed. Peter Reidemeister and Veronika Gutmann, Winterthur: Amadeus 1983, 125–43.

89 "ich kann nicht mehr viel ausgehen, sogar nur sehr wenig, aber ich erlebe jeden mir geschenkten Tag dankbar, wenn es auch noch so viel Elend in dieser Welt gibt. Solange ich in meiner klein gewordenen Welt noch ein wenig helfen kann, singe ich jeden Morgen

It was, of course, not only a case of she not being able to go out as much, but also visits to her grew more infrequent, as can be seen also with Paul Sacher. On a visiting card, perhaps sent with some flowers, for example, she congratulated him on his 76th birthday, but also asked: "Could you, at your convenience, inform me when you may perhaps come next? Otherwise, I will begin by mistake to give this time to others, or lose myself entirely in my books".[90] He responded on 12 May 1982 that he would be unable to come before 7 June, adding, however, that he naturally could always be reached by her; five days later he sent her his article on Bartók and the CMZ's program for the following season. But there are several other cards indicating that he had sent her flowers or even wine, clearly indicating that they remained in irregular contact with one another over various channels.

8.3 Psalm 90.10: Our days may come to seventy *years*, or *eighty*, if our strength endures

The frailty of Ina Lohr's health must have been evident to all, in that everybody seems to have been intent on making the celebration of her eightieth birthday particularly glorious. The festivities can be divided into various categories. First of all, there were all the people who came to visit her from near and far to congratulate her. For Easter, Paul Sacher had given her not only flowers but vouchers for restaurants so that she could freely entertain others without overextending herself either financially or physically. In addition, he obviously tried to put her life-long activities for him into perspective, endeavoring to convince her to suggest some sort of present for herself that would truly give her pleasure, as is revealed by her letter of 26 June 1983:

> I am very happy that you explained everything to me so exactly on Saturday, so that I can see and comprehend their true dimensions. And I even thought of a – to be sure – very expensive present that would make not only me thankful. (I am that anyway!) Do you remember the Japanese No mask (a specimen from the 16th century), which hung in my room in the Leimenstrasse and made such an impression on you back then? For several years now, it has been at the home of the artist Martha Pfannenschmidt, who made a very beautiful picture with this mask as a centerpiece. At the moment [the painting] is hanging in a small exhibition that Ursula Karlhuber installed in the bookstore,

noch aus den Psalmen oder auch andere Texte. [...] Die Einstimmigkeit hat mich wieder ganz". Letter Ina Lohr to Arthur Eglin of 4 April 1982.

90 "Meldest Du gelegentlich, wann Du vielleicht wieder kommst? Sonst fange ich aus Versehen an, diese Zeit sonst zu vergeben oder mich ganz an meine Bücher zu verlieren". Undated visiting card Ina Lohr to Paul Sacher, private collection, Switzerland.

Bücher Box Drachen, and costs CHF 4500!! If that, in my opinion, *very* beautiful picture were to hang next to the mask in your Foundation, that would be a remembrance of
my father, who gave the original to me for my 20th birthday, and also of my dear Marthi
Pfannenschmidt, with whom, together with Hans Lanz, I eat every [other] Tuesday in
the Casino. But it is a very expensive thing and I would easily understand it if it were to
go too far for you, and I am, as I have said, grateful to you anyway.[91]

Attached to the letter in the folder of correspondence is a note: "Mrs. Karlhuber will gladly deal with the picture for Ina Lohr's birthday". It was a rare move
on Ina Lohr's part, in that it brought portions of her life together that she otherwise had kept separate: Paul Sacher, her family, and her friends; and on the
other hand, it was also a typical gesture, because in the end, she was donating
not only the picture, but also the No mask to the Paul Sacher Foundation.

Her Dutch "family" – in this case, Jan Boeke, Wim Kloppenburg, Gerard van
der Leeuw (the son of the minister who originally instigated her first lecture
after the war in Haarlem), Kees Vellekoop and Henk Waardenburg – organized
a whole program of events from May through November in celebration of her
birthday. The program was highly varied and embodied many of the aspects of
Ina Lohr's life, and at least one that was not. It involved: 1) a *huismuziek* day for
strings and brass in Amersfoort, under the auspices of Henk Waardenburg, who
also invited Arthur Eglin's trombone choir to come and join them and to give
a concert; 2) a lecture on the performance practice of Gregorian chant given by

---

91 "Sehr glücklich bin ich darüber, dass Du mir am Samstag alles so ganz genau erklärt hast,
sodass ich die richtigen Proportionen sehen und begreifen kann. Und es ist mir sogar ein
allerdings sehr teures Geschenk eingefallen, das nicht nur mich dankbar machen würde.
(Ich bin es sowieso!) Erinnerst du Dich an die japanische No Maske (Exemplar aus dem
16 Jhdt), die in der Leimenstr. in meinem Zimmer hing und Dir damals Eindruck machte?
Sie ist seit einigen Jahren bei der Malerin Martha Pfannenschmid, die ein sehr schönes
Bild mit dieser Maske als Mittelpunkt machte. Das hängt jetzt gerade in einer kleinen Aus-
stellung, die Ursula Karlhuber im Bücher Box Drachen einrichtete und kostet fr. 4500!!
Wenn das, ich finde sogar <u>sehr</u> schöne Bild neben der Maske in Deiner Stiftung hängen
würde, wäre das ein Andenken an meinen Vater, der mir das Original zum 20. Geburtstag schenkte und an meine liebe Marthi Pfannenschmid, mit der und mit Hans Lanz ich
jeden Dienstag im Casino esse. Aber es ist eine teure Sache und ich begreife es gut, wenn
das Dir doch zu weit geht und bin Dir, wie gesagt, sowieso dankbar". Letter Ina Lohr to
Paul Sacher of 26 June 1983, private collection, Switzerland. Martha Pfannenschmid (1900–
1999) was a graphic artist known not only for her work in forensic medicine, but also as
an artist and illustrator (of among other works, Johanna Spyri's *Heidi* and Carlo Collodi's
Pinocchio). In the Ina Lohr Collection at the Paul Sacher Foundation, there are two post-
cards sent to Ina Lohr, which are representative for her work. Hans Lanz (1920–2004) was
associated with the Historical Museum in Basel for all of his professional life and was its
director from 1967–1984.

Christopher Schmidt at the University of Utrecht; 3) a symposium on tempo in the 18th century curated by two advocates of slow tempi (not one of Ina Lohr's chosen causes), Jan van Biezen and Willem Talsma at the University of Utrecht; 4) a concert at the Utrecht Festival with Cappella Amsterdam under the direction of Jan Boeke, entitled *De Mis in het Concertleven,* based on Ina Lohr's thoughts about the place of liturgical music in the concert hall; 5) a course for people who lead children's choirs and ensembles with Henk Waardenburg and Wim Kloppenburg; 6) four concerts for church and the home, to be given within a church environment by three different choirs and containing either music by or dear to Ina Lohr; 7) a concert of music by Johann Sebastian Bach and Johann Rosenmüller with Cappella Amsterdam in both Amsterdam and Kampen; 8) a lecture on Bach as a theologian by Gerard van der Leeuw; and last, but certainly not least, the publication and personal presentation of the translation of her book on 19 August 1983.[92] In addition, a course on the importance of solmization for the analysis of polyphony and the teaching of counterpoint – using the new translation as a basis – was organized at the Utrecht Conservatory in November 1983, taught by Jan Boeke, Henk van Bentham and Fritz Nijs.[93] The engagement and intensity of the preparation demonstrates both the depth and breadth of her influence on many aspects of Dutch musical life in that period, within the church, within the schools, within the home and within the conservatories.

And finally, Arthur Eglin's fidelity to her vision of the function of church music was evinced by three vespers services with music, in the Basel Munster on 26 August, in the St. Alban Church on 4 September, and the St. Elisabeth Church on 17 September. The first of these – as well as the vespers for her 75th birthday, and her funeral service – included her own version of Psalm 90 (see Ill. 8.4), whose 10th verse in the Luther translation clearly had meaning for her: "Our days last seventy years, or at the most, then eighty years; and if it were good, then it was through effort and work".[94] At the service for her 75th birthday she brought her commentary to a close by highlighting this verse, saying that "yes, it had been effort and work, but it was very good".[95]

92 "Commissie ter voorbereiding van de viering van het tachtigste geboortejaar van Ina Lohr", flyer in PSF-ILC.

93 Flyer in the collection of Ina Lohr's letters to Kees Vellekoop.

94 Psalm 90.10: "Unser Leben währet siebzig Jahr und wenn's hoch kommt, so sinds achtzig Jahr, und wenn's köstlich gewesen ist, so ists Mühe und Arbeit gewesen".

95 "Ja, Mühe und Arbeit ist es gewesen, aber es war gar köstlich". Documentation supplied by Arthur Eglin.

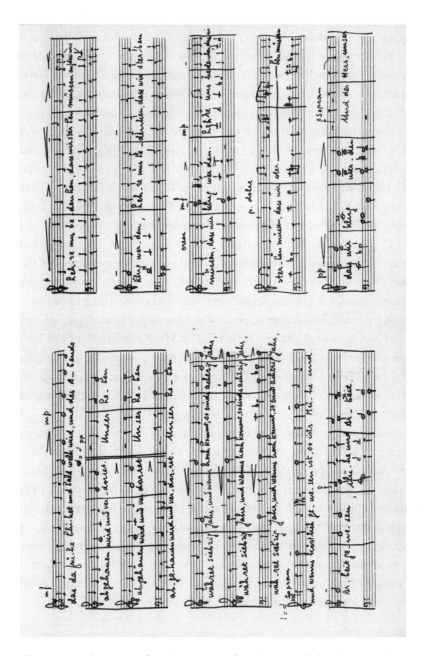

Ill. 8.4: Ina Lohr, excerpt from her setting of Psalm 90, including "Unser Leben währet siebzig Jahr". Reproduction: PSF-ILC.

From her expressions of thanks, one gets a sense of the wonder and gratitude that all this is happening to her. She was completely overwhelmed by the thought of all of the events organized in the Netherlands, exclaiming to Henk Waardenburg on 6 February 1983 that above all, she was "*thankful* for the long list of friends in the Netherlands!"[96] She admitted also to Paul Sacher on 7 August 1983 that she "had been very moved when Ursula Karlhuber had actually come in with the coveted painting and even hung it up", hoping that he also "found the painting good for the Foundation".[97] She went on to speak of her visitors, Erna van Osselen, Henk van Benthem and his wife, and later those responsible for the publication of the translation of her book, saying that she had "great difficulty in taking on the role of a V.I.P., but that she is happy with the many heart-felt letters".[98]

And it is with a sense of overflowing gratitude for friends that her life came to a close, dying on 6 October 1983 following a heart attack she had experienced the day before. As Christopher Schmidt wrote in his obituary, the memories of singing together with her would remain indelible.[99]

96 "Maar vóór alles ben ik <u>dankbaar</u> voor die lange lijst van vrienden in Nederland!" Letter Ina Lohr to Henk Waardenburg of 6 February 1983.
97 "Es hat mich doch sehr ergriffen, als Ursula Karlhuber tatsächlich mit dem ersehnten Bild hereinkam, es sogar aufhängte. [...] und hoffe nur, dass Du das Bild auch für die Stiftung schön findest". Letter Ina Lohr to Paul Sacher of 7 August 1983, private collection, Switzerland.
98 "Ich habe grosse Mühe, die Rolle einer V.I.P. zu übernehmen, bin aber glücklich mit vielen sehr herzlichen Briefen". Ibid.
99 "In der Erinnerung an Ina Lohr bleiben diese gemeinsamen Singstunden unauslöschlich". Christopher Schmidt, "Zum Gedenken Ina Lohr", in: *Basler Zeitung*, 13 October 1983.

Ill. 8.5: "Be still and know that I am God", Psalm 46.10. Ina Lohr's gravestone in the Hörnli Cemetery, Riehen. Photo: Anne Smith, Zurich.

Appendix 1: A Short Excurse on Solmization for the Intrepid

As it is difficult to comprehend the questions that arise in regard to Ina Lohr's introduction to the subject without an understanding of earlier solmization, its basic principles will first be discussed, based on those of 16ᵗʰ-century theorists. These will then applied to Clément Marot and Théodore de Bèze's version of Psalm 8, *O notre Dieu et Seigneur*, published complete with solmization in 1562.[1] This in turn will be compared to Ina Lohr's version from the 1981 edition of her book (see Ill. Appendix 1.1a and 1.1b).

In the theoretical framework of 16ᵗʰ-century music, the gamut – the range of music – extended from *gamma ut*, from low G in the bass to e", or *eelami* in the soprano. Each of these notes were given conjoint names consisting of Arabic letters, allied with solmization syllables from the three different kinds of hexachords, the *durum* on G, the *naturalem* on c, and the *mollem* on f. Each hexachord, made up as the name says of six notes, had the same structure: whole tone, whole tone, half tone, whole tone, whole tone. Thus a semitone lay at the center of each one. Although in singing one tried to remain in a single hexachord as long as possible, if the melody went beyond the sixth of the hexachord, one was then forced to mutate to another hexachord. At that time, pieces for the most part were considered to be in hard keys, i.e. with no staff signature, or soft keys with a b-flat. Pieces in hard keys were solmized with a combination of hard and natural hexachords, those in soft keys in a combination of natural and soft hexachords. When ascending the mutation always took place in the re of subsequent hexachord, when descending in the la of the subsequent hexachord.

The facsimile of 1562 of *O notre Dieu et Seigneur* consistently follows these customs of the time. Its first verse opens in the natural hexachord, mutating to the hard on re, on a, as was the rule for ascending melodies. The second verse stays in the hard hexachord until the la, a, at the end of the second staff, where it mutates to the natural hexachord, followed by a fa (super la). The mutation on la for the descending line was standard, as was also the fa super la for the b-flat. The third verse opens in the natural hexachord, changes in ascent over the leap of the fifth into re of the hard hexachord at the end of that staff. On the third to the last note, it mutates at the leap to g to sol, in preparation for the follow-

---

1   For a more complete introduction, see Anne Smith, *The Performance of 16ᵗʰ-Century Music: Learning from the Theorists*, New York: Oxford University Press 2011, Ch. 3.

Ill. Appendix 1.1a: Psalm 8 by Clément Marot and Théodore de Bèze, *Les Psaumes en vers français avec leurs mélodies*, Geneva: Michel Blanchier 1562, 21.

ing fa super la on b-flat, one not even signaled by a flat in the melody. The last verse opens in the hard hexachord, with a normal mutation to la at a for the final descent.

Ina Lohr's solmization exhibits two kinds of differences from that of the 16th century. One is rather trivial, the choice of mutating from the natural to the hard hexachord in the first phrase on the fifth rather than the fourth note; indeed it makes musical sense, in that it unites each clause in its own hexachord, "O notre dieu", in the natural and "et Seigneur amiable" in the hard, whereas the historical version reflects a relatively mechanical mutation practice. Her mutation at the end of the second line, however, actually contradicts the conventions of the

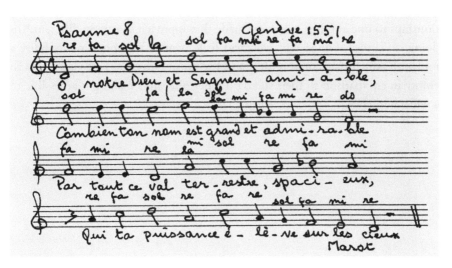

Ill. Appendix 1.1b: Psalm 8 with solmization of Ina Lohr, 1981. Reproduction: collection of Arthur Eglin.

16th century – which were, even then, not always obsequiously observed – in that it moves directly from the hard to the soft hexachord, which was explicitly forbidden. It also, however, is a musical choice, stimulated by the b-flat and reflecting a shift in the balance of melodic relationships between the notes, so that f becomes a local resting point; indeed in the four-part version by Goudimel there is a cadence on F at the end of this verse. Her mutation to the soft hexachord in the middle of the third line, instead of making the short excursion to the hard found in the Marot/ Bèze print, brings out the melodic parallel of the b-flat to a at the conclusion of the previous line. Interestingly here, the Goudimel four-part version has an open cadence on A major, which is somewhat more difficult to understand within the framework of a soft hexachord.

These distinctions exemplify at one and the same time, the inherent difficulties of her system as well as its brilliance. It could not work as a system for sight-singing because it depended on a level of musical and melodic understanding not usually found in the person needing solmization as a crutch, it did not have the needed consistency. But seen as a language used to investigate and describe the strengths and weaknesses of the relationships between the various notes in a modal melody, it is ingenious, as it allows for much more subtle differentiation in the kind of the links between the notes than that provided by the major and minor scales of functional harmony. Christopher Schmidt has come to the conclusion that this shift of attention away from the octave scale as an analytic unit – divided into a fifth and fourth – to the fifths and their relationships to one another, was what made this approach so utterly different.[2] In doing so, she gave musicians who had little contact to modal monophony a tool with which they could understand the music, which at first glance was so empty in comparison to their standard repertoire, thus making it accessible to a wider audience.

---

2   In many interviews during the years of writing this book.

Appendix 2: Compilation of the Schola's Activities 1933–39

Schoolyear	Teachers	Workshops	Concerts	Other
1933/34 Enrolled, 1st annual report: WS 40/30[1] SS 50/40 Enrolled, report of 1st three years: WS 29/24 SS 47/45	Cantus Gregorianus: Ina Lohr Voice: Max Meili, Dr. Arnold Geering Recorders: August Wenzinger (Ina Lohr) Violins 'in alten Mensuren': Walter Kägi Arm Viols (Rebecs, fiddles): Annie Tschopp Viola da Gambas: August Wenzinger Lutes (Guitars): Hermann Leeb Organ (Playing and Improvisation): Dr. Fritz Morel Harpsichord: Claire Levy, Dr. Fritz Morel Analysis with Examples: Ina Lohr Thorough Bass: practically Dr. Fritz Morel, theoretically Ina Lohr Bibliography of New Editions: Dr. Arnold Geering Ensemble: Paul Sacher	2–8 April 1934 Peterhof, Sarnen "Woche Alter Haus- und Kirchenmusik" Ina Lohr and August Wenzinger (20 participants) 7–14 October 1934 Peterhof, Sarnen "Woche Alter Haus- und Kirchenmusik" Ina Lohr and August Wenzinger (20 participants)	3 February 1934 festive opening reception with concert 3 concerts with chamber music group in Basel: 12–14 June 1934. 2 concerts in Zurich, 18–19 June	Negotiations with Otto Lobeck about loan of his instrument collection. Walter Nef chosen as substitute director during Paul Sacher's absence in 1934/35. Address: Wallstrasse 14, Basel

1   Number of inscriptions / Number of students (the students could enroll for more than one subject)

Schoolyear	Teachers	Workshops	Concerts	Other
1934/35 enrolled: WS 49/42 SS 52/44	New courses: • Clavichord (Valerie Kägi) • Vocal Ornamentation Practice (Arnold Geering) • Overview of Vocal Styles (Arnold Geering) • Introduction to Early Notation (Walter Nef) • The Early Instruments (Walter Nef) • Introduction to the Performance Practice of Early Music (Ina Lohr) • Introduction to Early Music (for amateurs) (Ina Lohr) • 3 new courses of recorder for children at the Waisenhaus, 6 children/course, not included in SCB student numbers [Ina Lohr] • Knabenchor (Ina Lohr)	23–25 November 1934, Basel "Alte Weihnachtsmusik" for church, school and the home, Ina Lohr and August Wenzinger (ca. 60 participants) 7–14 April 1935 Peterhof, Sarnen "Woche Alter Haus- und Kirchenmusik" Ina Lohr and August Wenzinger (ca. 20 participants) 3–10 August 1935, Rigi-Klösterli "Woche Alter Haus- und Kirchenmusik" August Wenzinger (ca. 20 participants)	First student concert: • 22 February 1935 Classes Ina Lohr and August Wenzinger Other concerts: • 3 October 1934 house concert for SMG (Schweizerische Musikforschende Gesellschaft) • 28, 29, 31 May 1935, Basel • 3, 4 June 1935, Zurich • 27 April 1935, Seidenhof Basel Benefit concert for the Basler Webstube (Weavers' Collective) • 24 June 1935, Munster Basel, Serenade of the Basler Studentenschaft (Basel Students)	Walter Nef assumed Paul Sacher's function as director of the Schola during the former's leave of absence Lobeck collection brought to Basel mid-October 1935 End of summer moved to Seidenhof, Blumenrain 34, Basel
1935/36 enrolled: WS 82/62 SS 78/58	• the enrollment numbers are without those in the choir (WS 19, SS 13) • the recorder class grew particularly, also because of classes for children • more humble growth in viola da braccio and viola da gamba classes New courses: • Chorübungen (WS 17, SS 13) • "Ausserliturgische Gesänge (Notker Balbulus, Adam de St. Victor, Hl. Hildegard)" (Ina Lohr)	First autumn courses for recorder: • 5 September–5 October 1935 (31/30), taught by Ina Lohr. Due to the number of students there were 2 parallel sessions. 4 special courses "Alte Haus- und Kirchenmusik" (26 to 48 participants): • 2–3 November 1935, Basel "Alte Weihnachtslieder und -spiele" (Ina Lohr and Walter Nef)	Student concert: 4 October 1935, classes August Wenzinger and Ina Lohr 3 concerts, 6–7 June 1936, Basel, directed by August Wenzinger with Max Meili, Arnold Geering, Gertrud Flügel, Valerie Kägi, Walter Kägi, Hermann Leeb, Ina Lohr (Gregorian chant choir), Fritz Morel, Annie Tschopp, Elsa Scherz-Meister, Nina Nüesch, Imre von Vépy, Joseph Bopp,	In new location, Seidenhof (see above) A school concert 23 March 1936 led to fall workshop in September 1936 (Ina Lohr) devoted to older "school music". Too few professional musicians registered for a proposed summer course, so it was cancelled. Ina Lohr gave a private week-long course for 7 participants in the

Schoolyear	Teachers	Workshops	Concerts	Other
	• "Lieder der Reformationszeit und ihre Beziehung zum gregorianischen Choral" (Ina Lohr) • Introduction to Early Music (Arnold Geering or Walter Nef?) • Introduction to the Notation of Early Music (Arnold Geering and Walter Nef) • SS 1936, no ornamentation for singers • SS 1936, Introduction to Early Music for Amateurs (Ina Lohr)	• 1–2 February 1936, Basel "Alte Haus- und Gesellschaftsmusik" (Ina Lohr, Walter Nef, August Wenzinger) • 7–8 March 1936 "Ostermusik" Ina Lohr, Arnold Geering • 2–3 May 1936 "Tanzmusik und Tanzlieder" (Ina Lohr, Walter Nef)	Willi Overhagen, Alexander Geld, Anton Wettengl, Ludwig Bertz, Maya Wenzinger, Emil Glatt, u.a. Musically but not financially successful. 15 March 1936, Basel Matinée with Prof. Dr. W. Altwegg "Musik und Dichtung aus dem alten Basel" 16 June 1936, Basel House concert for the benefit of poor schoolchildren. 6 July 1936, Basel Participation in event celebrating the 400th anniversary of the death of Erasmus.	"theory of the modes", thorough bass and ensemble. Participation in opening of international art history congress on 31 August 1936, repeated by demand on 4 September. For the first time it was attempted to present Renaissance dances according to the choreographies in treatises. Directed by Fräulein von Meyenburg; Otto Gombosi, Budapest was the advisor. Part of the program was presented at the international congress of chemists in Lucerne 20 August 1936. Swiss Music Pedagogical Association (SMPV) held its general meeting in Basel and viewed the Lobeck instrument collection on 26 March 1936. Walter Nef has almost completed a catalog of instruments. Paul Hirsch, Frankfurt a.M., loaned a selection of books and musical scores for study purposes and display to SCB.

Schoolyear	Teachers	Workshops	Concerts	Other
1936/37 enrolled: WS 103/75 SS 102/66	New teachers and members of concert group: • Gertrud Flügel (Violin) • Fritz Wörsching (Lute) New courses: • "Protestantische Kirchenmusik" instead of Gregorian chant (Ina Lohr) with Organ for the Church (Fritz Morel) • "Streichermusik" (direction for playing string music together for amateurs – August Wenzinger) • "Verzierungslehre" (Arnold Geering and August Wenzinger) • "Instrumentenkunde" (Walter Nef) • "Musikgeschichte in Beispielen" (Arnold Geering) SS "Alte Kinderlieder" (Ina Lohr, 18 participants) SS "Cantus gregorianus" again offered, but together with "Protestantische Kirchenmusik"	Autumn courses 1936 (Ina Lohr): enrolled: 45/35 5 special courses "Alte Haus- und Kirchenmusik": • 7–8 November 1936, Basel "Weihnachtsmusik" (Ina Lohr and Walter Nef) • 6–7 March 1937, Basel "Die deutschen, französischen und flämischen Psalmlieder der Reformationszeit" (Ina Lohr) • 22–23 May 1937, Basel "Pfingstmusik" (Ina Lohr and Walter Nef) • 14–15 November, St. Gall "Alte Weihnachtsmusik" (Ina Lohr and Walter Nef) • 13–14 March 1937, Basel "Alte Ostermusik" (Ina Lohr and Walter Nef)	Student concerts: • 20 December 1936 students of classes "Chorübungen" and "gregorianischer Chor" sang a Christmas mass (ordinary in German transcriptions from the Reformation, the proper in Latin), direction Ina Lohr • 25 February 1937 ensemble classes of August Wenzinger and Ina Lohr Concerts of concert group: • 11, 12, 13 June 1937 • Perceived as being most interesting were the following: – Monteverdi with the "Combatimento di Tancredi et Clorinda" – solo cantatas, organ and chamber works of Buxtehude (1637–1707) – The following musicians took part under the direction of August Wenzinger: Gertrud Flügel, Arnold Geering, Valerie Kägi, Walter Kägi, Hermann Leeb, Max Meili, Fritz Morel, Annie Tschopp, Fritz Wörsching, Margrit Vaterlaus, Philis von Salis, Sibylla Plate, Hans Theo Wagner,	In WS 1936 first internal student (professional) studying to become director of *Hausmusik* groups. in SS 1937, entrance of provisional internal student with harpsichord/organ as major Negotiations with the Education Department of Basel Stadt took place concerning a recorder course for talented, but poor pupils. No decision was reached, so that the SCB decided to launch a "Volksblockflötenkurs", as well as one for gamba, with 11 and 2 pupils respectively. On 25 April and 27 Juni, 1937, radio broadcasts of the concert group were transmitted. 6–7 February 1937, Lausanne Invitation from "Société des Concerts de la Cathédrale": lecture (Walter Nef) "Renaissance de la musique ancienne", and 2 concerts, one secular and one sacred.

Schoolyear	Teachers	Workshops	Concerts	Other
			Louis Fest, Peter Felix Jenny, Albert Klaus, Käthe Möller, Trudi Sutter, Maja Wenzinger	
			• 19 March 1937, Basel Concert group performed Schütz's "Sieben Worte" and J.S. Bach's "Actus tragicus", BWV 106. In addition to regular members, Dora Garraux, Maria Helbling, Hans Theo Wagner, Louis Fest, and Peter Felix Jenny took part.	
			• 29 May 1937, Schweizerisches Tonkünstlerfest, Basel Program: music of Senfl under the direction of Arnold Geering	
			• 18 October 1936, Basel "Spiel- und Hausmusik des Spätbarocks"	
			• 29 January 1937, Basel "Musik für Laute und Gitarre", Hermann Leeb	
			• 8 May 1937, Basel "Musik für Clavichord", with Valerie Kägi, together with Philis von Salis, soprano, and commentary of Walter Nef	
			• 29 June 1937, Abendmusik, Berne Munster Viola da gamba quartet	

Schoolyear	Teachers	Workshops	Concerts	Other
1937/38 enrolled: WS 115/75 SS 119/88 internal students: WS 2 SS 2	Annie Tschopp left the SCB SS introductory course in Gregorian chant (Ina Lohr) SS "Praktische Einführung in die Chorpolyphonie des 16. Jahrhunderts (für Chorleiter)" (Ina Lohr)	External courses, students not included in regular enrollment: There were Volksblockflötenkurse (enrollment WS 11/SS 13) taught by 2 supervised internal students, Gertrud Sutter and Mariane Majer, as practical training towards their degree. Ina Lohr taught 2 external courses in the SS: • at the Vincentianum, a Catholic orphanage (enrollment 23 nurses; 12 boys); • for the Kleinbasler choir (23 students) Marianne Majer taught a "Volks-blockflöten" course in the SS at the Vincentianum (12 students) August Wenzinger taught some gamba lessons in Winterthur Fall courses (enrollment: 56/55) with Gregorian chant, recorder, and ensemble (Ina Lohr)	• 30 June 1937, Biel General meeting of Biel music school, performance by part of concert group Student concerts: • 23 February 1938 "Kinder spielen alte Musik auf Blockflöten" (children's classes Ina Lohr) • 1 April 1938 "Passions- und Ostermusik" (Ensemble; Gregorian chant and choir classes of Ina Lohr) • 29 June 1938, Basel "Blockflötensonaten" (Recorder classes Ina Lohr) • 1 July 1938, Basel "Tanzlieder und Tanzsätze" (Children's classes of Ina Lohr) • 24 June 1938, Theodorskirche, Basel Students participated in a liturgical vespers of the Kleinbasler choir (Ina Lohr) • Summer concerts, 27 & 29 May 1938, Basel "Klänge und Klanggruppierungen" with Arnold Geering, Valerie Kägi, Walter Kägi, Hermann Leeb, Max Meili, Fritz Morel, August Wenzinger, Fritz	Gertrud Sutter was the first to pass an exam as an internal student at the end of WS 1937/38, receiving a diploma as "Leiterin von Sing- und Spielkreisen und Lehrerin für Hausmusik". Together with the music school and conservatory 3 lectures, "Alte Musikpraktiken" were presented with practical examples: • 5 November, 1937 Fritz Morel, "Die Darstellung von Bachs Klaviermusik auf dem modernen Flügel" • 21 January 1938 August Wenzinger, "Verzierungspraxis in der alten Musik" • 18 March 1938 Fritz Neumeyer (Saarbrücken), "Die Generalbassbearbeitung bei Händel und Corelli" Radio broadcasts: • 31 October 1937 "Klaviermusik aus fünf Jahrhunderten"

Schoolyear	Teachers	Workshops	Concerts	Other

		"Arbeitstage Alter Haus- & Kirchenmusik" (Ina Lohr and Walter Nef):
		• 23–24 October 1937
		  "Palestrina und Michael Praetorius" (22 participants)
		• 12–13 February 1938
		  "Heitere und gesellige Lieder und Instrumentalstücke" (16 participants)
		• 13–14 November 1937, Solothurn (22 participants), 27–28 November 1937, Biel (47 partcipants)
		  "Alte Weihnachtsmusik"
		• 4–9 October 1937, St. Gallen
		  "Arbeitswoche alter Musik" (33 participants)
		• 10–16 July 1938, Rigi-Klösterli
		  "Arbeitswoche alter Haus- & Kirchenmusik" (August Wenzinger, 22 participants)
			Wörsching, Elsa Scherz-Meister, Maria Helbling, Wilhelm Koberg, Marianne Hirsig-Löw, Margrit Gyger, August Sumpf, Felix Brodtbeck, a small choir, Franz Hindermann, Peter Felix Jenny, Albert Klaus, Marianne Majer, Gertrud Sutter, Maya Wenzinger, Georg Donderer, Albin Hendrich, Heinz Metag, Heinrich Wanschura, Ludwig Bertz, Anton Wettengl, Hans Balmer.
			1st concert: Telemann, Bach (solo violin sonata, Walter Kägi). Peri, the underworld scene from Monteverdi's Orfeo
			2nd concert: late medieval music.
			3rd concert: Schütz, Schein, Weckmann
			"The great number of participants, together with the variety and novelty of the instruments and several mishaps, led to not all portions of the concerts being at the artistic level of the previous years and lent them somewhat too much the character of an experiment. One did not quite succeed in joining the various foreign elements to an artistic whole in the tightly calculated
				Valerie Kägi (clavichord, klavier), Fritz Morel (harpsichord, organ), Walter Nef (introduction)
				• 19 June 1938
				Shortened version of Spanish, German, Italian program with Max Meili, August Wenzinger and Fritz Wörsching
				
				Three new instruments:
				Alfred von der Mühll gave the SCB a large unfretted clavichord from the estate of Gian Bundi. Pierre Pidoux gave the SCB a table pianoforte by Erard in excellent condition. And a tenor gamba in good condition by the Dutch maker Pieter Rombouts could be bought in England for the gamba ensemble.

Schoolyear	Teachers	Workshops	Concerts	Other
			– due to outside circumstances – rehearsal time. The concerts, however, provided rich fodder, which needs to be utilized and evaluated for the future". [2] • 16 October 1937, Basel "Alte Hausmusik auf dem Clavichord", Valerie Kägi with Philis von Salis and Gertrud Sutter • 22 March 1938, house concert, Basel August Wenzinger, gamba, and Fritz Neumeyer, harpsichord • 27 February 1938, Lausanne Invitation from "Société des Concerts de la Cathédrale": lecture (Walter Nef) "Renaissance de la musique ancienne", and 2 concerts, one secular and one sacred. • 16 December 1937, Berne & 17 January 1938, Basel Spanish, German, Italian program Max Meili, August Wenzinger and Fritz Wörsching	

2   "Die grosse Zahl der Ausführenden trug zusammen mit der Vielheit und Neuheit der Instrumente und einigen Missgeschicken dazu bei, dass die Konzerte nicht in allen Teilen die künstlerische Höhe der Vorjahre erreichten und etwas zu sehr den Charakter eines Experimentes an sich hatten. Es war in der aus äussern Gründen knapp bemessenen Probenzeit nicht ganz gelungen, die vielen fremden Elemente zu einer künstlerischen Einheit zu fügen. Die Konzerte lieferten aber reiche Erfahrungen, die es für die Zukunft zu nutzen und auszuwerten gilt".

Schoolyear	Teachers	Workshops	Concerts	Other
1938/39 enrolled: WS 79/137 SS 85/160 internal students: WS 4 SS 5	Fritz Morel resigned from the SCB due to being chosen as organist in the Münster and organ teacher at the Conservatory. Eduard Müller was hired as his successor. After acting as an assistant teacher for recorder and viola da gamba for children in WS 1938/39, Marianne Majer was officially hired as a new teacher for these subjects in SS 1939. The "Chorübungen" (Ina Lohr) were changed by request of various students to "Chor- & Ensembleübungen in Hausmusik", so that instruments could join in with the voices. It was so popular that Ina Lohr taught two groups of students in SS 1939. Ina Lohr supplemented her course, "Die Lieder der Reformationszeit und ihre Beziehungen zum gregorianischen Choral", with "Weltliche und geistliche Lieder der Reformationszeit". Experience showed that groups of 5 recorder students, particularly advanced ones, were too large, and so they were reduced to 4 students, and the fees raised from Fr. 40 to Fr. 50. The same	"Volksblockflöten- & Gambenkurse" 1938/39, used to give internal students practical teaching experience under supervision of SCB teachers: • WS 13/13 • SS 23/23 Autumn courses 1938: • Recorder (Ina Lohr and Valerie Kägi) • Gregorian chant and "Alte Schulmusik" (Ina Lohr) enrollment: 69/61 Workshops for "Alte Haus- & Kirchenmusik" (Ina Lohr and Walter Nef) • 24–25 September 1938, Biel "Palestrina" (32 participants) • 15–16 October 1938, Basel "Schütz & Praetorius" (18 participants) • 29–30 October 1938, Solothurn "Gregorianischer Choral & Kirchentonarten" (only Ina Lohr, 16 participants) • 19–20 November 1939, St. Gall "Alte Haus- & Gesellschaftsmusik" (27 participants) • 11–12 March 1939, Basel "Passionsmusik" (21 participants)	Student concerts: • 29 September 1938, Basel "Kinder spielen alte Musik auf Blockflöten" (Ina Lohr, Valerie Kägi) • 5 November 1938, Theodorskirche, Basel Participation of Ina Lohr's students in a church service • 16 December 1938, Basel "Weihnachtsmusik für Blockflöten" (Ina Lohr and Marianne Majer) • 24 March 1939, Basel Public recital of the recorder classes Ina Lohr and Valerie Kägi. • 23 May 1939, Martinskirche, Basel Liturgical service according to the words and melodies of Martin Luther, students of the classes of Ina Lohr • 6 July 1939, Bürgerspital, Basel "House music" classes of Ina Lohr Concerts: • Decided to move the concerts to September. The first concert was to be 17th-century madrigals and instrumental music;	Internal students WS: Fräulein Marianne Majer, Basel Frau Lena Schortländer, St. Gallen Fräulein Margrit Lüscher, Burgdorf Fräulein Mädlen Bregenzer, Lörrach In SS 1939: Frau Lena Schortländer, St. Gallen Fräulein Margrit Lüscher, Burgdorf Fräulein Mädlen Bregenzer, Lörrach Fräulein Susanne Graf, Berne Fräulein Marie Refardt, Basel Marianne Majer received her diploma as "Leiterin von Sing- und Spielgruppen und Lehrerin für Hausmusik" at the end of WS 1938/39. In WS 1938/39 students of the recorder classes of Ina Lohr, and various teachers demonstrated early instruments in an adult education course "our musical instruments" taught by Ernst Mohr and Walter Nef. A group of Ina Lohr's recorder students recorded music for the film "La Suisse Musicienne" for the Swiss national fair in Zurich in 1939.

Schoolyear	Teachers	Workshops	Concerts	Other
	was considered to be true for the new choir and ensemble classes, and so the fees here were raised from Fr. 5 to Fr. 20. Viola d'amore was explicitly not offered in WS 38/39. "Praktische Einführung in die Chorpolyphonie des 16. Jahrhunderts (für Chorleiter)" (Ina Lohr)	Arbeitswochen "Alte Haus- & Kirchenmusik" (August Wenzinger), 8–15 July 1939, Rigi-Klösterli. With the choice of the names of Palestrina and Bach, as well as an introduction to 18th-century performance practice, this workshop was directed more to the professional musician. The attendance of 23 students proved the "correctness" of this change.[3]	the second, music of the 11th to 14th centuries selected by Jacques Handschin; the third, a Telemann recorder suite with Gustav Scheck and Bach's coffee cantata. The outbreak of war in Europe caused the concerts to be postponed, although they had already been rehearsed before the summer vacation. • 1 October 1938, Biel-Bienne • 13 November 1938, Zurich • 21 December 1938, Basel 3 concerts of the Gregorian chant choir with members of the Basel Chamber Choir under Ina Lohr singing sections of the Gregorian proper between movements of Palestrina's *Missa Papae Marcelli*: • 4 November 1938, Frauenfeld Italian, Spanish, German program with Max Meili, August Wenzinger, Fritz Wörsching	There was a radio broadcast of German and English madrigals in Studio Basel on 28 June 1939. The SCB was present in the music pavilion of the Swiss national fair in the section "Music Schools and Conservatories". The planned concert of 26 September 1939 was another victim of the outbreak of war in Europe. It was, however, possible to display some of the instruments from the Lobeck collection.

3   "Mit der Wahl der Namen Palestrina und Bach und die Einführung in die Aufführungspraxis des 18. Jahrhunderts richtete sich die Arbeit diesmal mehr an den Fachmusiker. Der gute Besuch von 23 Teilnehmern erwies die Richtigkeit dieser Umstellung".

Schoolyear	Teachers	Workshops	Concerts	Other
			• 17–18 December 1938, Basel Concerts in memory of C.P.E. Bach who died on 14 December 1788. Alfred Kreutz (Stuttgart) played clavichord music and accompanied Ilse Wenzinger in some of the composer's songs. • 11 March 1939 Music for the inauguration of the museum Kleines Klingenthal • 20 May 1939 Old Swiss music for the opening of the first part of the exhibition "Zeichnen, Formen, Malen" in the Zurich Art Museum as part of the Swiss national fair in Zurich • 1 July 1939 and 2 July 1939 House concerts with members of the concert group • 8 July 1939 2 musicians provided music for the official celebration of Professor Fichter at the university.	

Books and Articles by Ina Lohr

Books:

Solmisation und Kirchentonarten, Zurich: Hug 1943.
Sprechen – Lauschen – Singen, Basel: Hug [1965?].
Solmisatie en Kerktoonsoorten, trans. by Henk van Benthem and Jan Boeke, The Hague: Stichting Centrum voor de Kerkzang 1983.

Articles:

"Der Gregorianische Choral auf Schallplatten", in: *Schweizerische Musikzeitung* 72 (1932), 594–96.
"Der Gregorianische Choral und seine Bedeutung für die Gegenwart", in: *Die Besinnung* 6 (1932), 79–84; reprinted in: *Schweizerische Musikzeitung* 72 (1932), 673–79.
"Neuausgaben alter Musik", in: *Schweizerische Musikzeitung* 73 (1933), 602, 662–64.
"Zur Wiederbelebung der geistlichen Monodie des Mittelalters im heutigen Chorkonzert", in: *Festschrift Karl Nef zum 60. Geburtstag*, Zurich: Hug 1933, 157–64.
"Weihnachts-Antiphonen", in: *Unser Weg: Schweizerisches Katholisches Jungmädchenblatt zugleich Werkblatt der Weggefährtinnen* 12 (1936), 278–79.
"Christus ist erstanden", in: *Volkslied und Hausmusik* 6 (1939), 19–23.
"Von einem Lied", in: *Volkslied und Hausmusik* 6 (1939), 115–18.
"Vom Reichtum des Kirchenliedes", in: *Volkslied und Hausmusik* 7 (1941), 168–72, 179–82.
"Wie ich meine Lieder schrieb", in: *Basler Nachrichten*, 3 May 1941.
"Vom einstimmigen Singen", in: *Volkslied und Hausmusik* 8 (1942), 99–102.
"Rhythmische Probleme im Choral", in: *Singt und spielt* 9 (1942/43), 51–56.
"Etwas von der Kirchenmusik im allgemeinen und von dem Kirchenlied im besonderen", in: *Singt und spielt* 9 (1942), 99–101.
"Der Probeband zum neuen Kirchengesangbuch in der Hausmusik", in: *Singt und spielt* 10 (1943/44), 3–6.
"Kirchenmusik im Konzert und Lied in der Kirche", in: *Singt und spielt* 10 (1943/44), 88–90.
"Was singen wir mit unsern Kindern in der Advents- und Weihnachtszeit?", in: *Singt und spielt* 10 (1943/44), 131–34.
"Das Gemeindelied zu Bachs Zeiten", in: *Singt und spielt* 11 (1944), 2–7.
"Etwas über die Blockflöte im Musikunterricht", in: *Singt und spielt* 11 (1944), 9–12.
"Die Zehn Gebote des Blockflötenspiels", in: *Singt und spielt* 11 (1944), 42–44.
"Das Gemeindelied einst und jetzt", in: *Singt und spielt* 11 (1944), 65–71.
"Der Dienst der singenden Kunst in der Kirche", in: *Singt und spielt* 11 (1944), 85–91.
"Hausmusik für die Weihnachtszeit", in: *Singt und spielt* 12 (1945), 34–35.
"Hausmusik um Bach", in: *Singt und spielt* 12 (1945), 54–56.
"Noch einmal: Hausmusik um Bach", in: *Singt und spielt* 12 (1945), 67–68.
"Hausmusik um Bach", in: *Singt und spielt* 12 (1945), 82–83.
"Stilfragen in der Hausmusik", in: *Singt und spielt* 13 (1946), 8–11.
"Hausmusik um Schütz", in: *Singt und spielt* 13 (1946), 34–37, 66–68.
"Hausmusik um Luther", in: *Singt und spielt* 13 (1946), 85–88.

"Hausmusik um Luther", in: *Singt und spielt* 14 (1947), 1–3.

"Feriengedanken über Hausmusik und über Zwinglis Lieder", in: *Singt und spielt* 14 (1947), 34–37.

"Wie singen wir die Hugenottenpsalmen?", in: *Musik und Gottesdienst* 1 (1947), 81–85.

"De liederen der reformatoren en hun betekenis voor dezen tijd", in: *Kerk en Eredienst* 2 (1947), 21–30.

"Een oud-nederlands 'Onze Vader'", in: *Musik und Gottesdienst* 2 (1948), 65.

"Moderne Hausmusik", in: *Singt und spielt* 14 (1947), 67–69.

"De gezongen psalmen van vroeger en nu", in: *Wending* 3 (1948), 50–55.

"Haspers Psalmberijming", in: *Kerk en Eredienst* 4 (1949), 115–19.

"Die biblischen Loblieder, wie sie in der Reformationszeit gesungen wurden", in: *Musik und Gottesdienst* 2 (1948), 2–7.

"Die Passionslieder des 16. Jahrhunderts", in: *Musik und Gottesdienst* 2 (1948), 44–48.

"Gedanken über einige Abendlieder", in: *Musik und Gottesdienst* 2 (1948), 113–17.

"Über die Bestattungslieder und ihre Tonarten", in: *Musik und Gottesdienst* 2 (1948), 132–36.

"Die Bedeutung der Kirchenmusik des 17. Jahrhunderts für die Hausmusik der Gegenwart", in: *Singt und spielt* 15 (1948), 18–21.

"Advents- und Weihnachtslieder", in: *Musik und Gottesdienst* 2 (1948), 153–59.

"Het rhythme der psalmmelodieën", in: *Kerk en Muziek* 1 (1948), 19–20.

"Enige gedachten over de studie van het oude kerklied", in: *Kerk en Muziek* 1 (1948), 52–54.

"De gezongen psalmen van vroeger en nu", in: *Wending* 3 (1948), 50–55.

"Zusammenfassende Gedanken über die Weihnachts- und Neujahrslieder", in: *Musik und Gottesdienst* 3 (1949), 8–12.

"Psalmen uit Wittenberg, Straatsburg en Geneve", in: *Kerk und Muziek* 1 (1949), 113–19.

"Lieder für den Gottesdienst bei Luther, Zwingli und Calvin", in: *Musik und Gottesdienst* 3 (1949), 65–74.

Review of Jürgen Uhde, *Der Dienst der Musik*, Zollikon-Zurich 1950 in: *Theologische Zeitschrift* (1950), 469–72.

"Vom Psalmensingen", in: *Unser Weg: Schweizerisches katholisches Jugendblatt, Werkblatt der Weggefährtinnen* 27 (1950), 10–13.

"Vom Psalmensingen (Fortsetzung)", in: *Unser Weg: Schweizerisches katholisches Jugendblatt, Werkblatt der Weggefährtinnen* 27 (1950), 48–51.

"Etwas über Hausmusik", in: *Unser Weg: Schweizerisches katholisches Jugendblatt, Werkblatt der Weggefährtinnen* 27 (1950), 121–22.

"Psalm 116, 1–14 (als gezongen lezing), Psalm 116, 15–19 (als intonatie)", in: *Pro regno pro sanctuario: een bundel studies en bijdragen van vrienden en vereerders bij de zestige verjaarag van Prof. Dr. G. van der Leeuw*, ed. Willem Jan Kooiman and J. M. van Veen, Nijkerk: G. F. Callenbach 1950, 317–21.

"Henry Purcell und seine Bearbeiter", in: *Schweizerische Musikzeitung* 91 (1951), 497–99.

"Textliche und melodische Zitate im Kirchenlied", in: *Musik und Gottesdienst* 5 (1951), 177–81.

"Einige Gedanken zum Thema 'Hausmusik – Konzertmusik'", in: *Singt und spielt* 19 (1952), 17–20.

"Der Dienst der Musik", in: *Singt und spielt* 17 (1951), 75–77.

"Zur Programmgestaltung", in: *Alte und Neue Musik [I]: Das Basler Kammerorchester (Kammerchor und Kammerorchester) unter Leitung von Paul Sacher 1926–1951*, Zurich: Atlantis Verlag 1952, 26–40.

"Die Kunst der Fuge", in: *Alte und Neue Musik [I]: Das Basler Kammerorchester (Kammerchor und Kammerorchester) unter Leitung von Paul Sacher 1926–1951*, Zurich: Atlantis Verlag 1952, 142–46.

Review of Max Brod's *Die Musik Israels*, Wizo, Tel Aviv 1951, in: *Rundbrief zur Förderung der Freundschaft zwischen dem Alten und dem Neuen Gottesvolk – im Geiste der beiden Testamente* 4.16 (April, 1952), 25.

"Kirchlicher Psalmengesang und Siegfried Redas Psalmbuch", in: *Musik und Gottesdienst* 6 (1952), 39–45.

"Nochmals vom Genfer Psalter", in: *Musik und Gottesdienst* 7 (1953), 73–79.

"Die Kirchenmusik als Lehrfach an der Schola Cantorum Basiliensis", in: *Musik und Gottesdienst* 7 (1953), 110–12.

"Die neuen Melodien im neuen Kirchengesangbuch", in: *Musik und Gottesdienst* 7 (1953), 161–64.

"Zeitgemässes Schaffen in der Musik", in: *Singt und spielt* 20 (1953), 49–53.

"Das Grammophon als Erzieher", in: *Basler Nachrichten* 110, Nr. 494/5, 20–21 November 1954.

"Das Gesangbuch in der Hausmusik", in: *Singt und spielt* 22 (1955), 73–79.

"Gedanken zum Musizieren in der Freiheit", in: *Basler Nachrichten* 111, Nr. 64, 11 February 1955.

"Zur Möglichkeit der Spontaneität im Gottesdienst", in: *Musik und Gottesdienst* 10 (1956), 161–64.

"Stimme und Gegenstimme", in: *Singt und spielt* 23 (1956), 2–4.

"Musik aus der Sprache, Musik aus dem Spiel", in: *Singt und spielt* 25 (1958), 65–76.

"Besuch bei den Meistersängern", in: *Singt und spielt* 26 (1959), 34–41.

"Versuch über die melodische Gebärde", in: *Singt und spielt* 27 (1960), 34–41.

"Inleiding over het onderwerp: 'Gebaar en toonsoort'", [Haarlem]: Stichting Centrum voor de protestantse Kerkzang, lecture given in Utrecht on 5 March 1960.

"Wat kan 'oude muziek' voor ons betekenen?", [Haarlem]: Stichting Centrum voor de protestantse Kerkzang, lecture given in Arnhem on 7–8 September 1963.

"Rhythme als voor-waarde voor het musiceren", [Haarlem]: Stichting Centrum voor de protestantse Kerkzang/Vereniging voor Huismuziek 1964.

"Vom Singen daheim", in: *Die Familie: Elternzeitschrift und Mutterblatt* 32 (1965), 177–78.

"Vom Singen in der Osterzeit", in: *Aus der Arbeit, für die Arbeit: Mitteilungsblatt der Christ. Verein Junger Frauen von Basel und Baselland*, Nr. 3, April 1965, page numbers unknown.

"Von den Psalmen in der deutschen Messe", in: *Die Schweizerin: Zeitschrift für Frauenart und Frauenwirken* 53 (1966), 134–36.

"Wär Gott nicht mit uns diese Zeit", in: *Musik und Gottesdienst* 20 (1966), 47–50.

"Sprachmelodik im Gregorianischen Choral und in den neuen, deutschen Messgesängen", separate print from the *Basler Volkskalendar*, Basel: Cratander 1967, 178–94.

"Von der 'natürlichen' zu der 'geschärften und polierten' Musica", in: *Schweizerische Musikzeitung* 108 (1968), 70–73.

"Über Jochen Klepper und Hugo Distler", in: *Singt und spielt* 35 (1968), 24–27.

"Tankar om Stravinskys Canticum Sacrum", in: *Nutida Musik* 15 (1971/72), 19–22.

"Vor- und Nachurteile", in: *Schritte ins Offene* 1/6 (1971), 10–11.

"Ein Altersnachmittag", in: *Schritte ins Offene* 4/2 (1974), 10.

"Musikalische Kreativität", in: *Schritte ins Offene* 5/4 (1975), 5.

"Können wir Alten einander helfen?", in: *Schritte ins Offene* 7/3 (1977), 28–29.

"Sven-Erik Bäck som tonsättare för kyrkan", in: *Svenskt Gudsbjansthir* 53 (1978), 3–5.

"Ouwe Neel, der Tod und das Kind", in: *Der schweizerische Kindergarten* 72 (1982), 16.

"Grundsätzliches zur Schulmusik" as a supplement to Elli Rohr, "Erfahrungen im Theorie-Unterricht an der Schola Cantorum Basiliensis", in: *Alte Musik: Praxis und Reflexion [I]*, ed. Peter Reidemeister and Veronika Gutmann, Winterthur: Amadeus 1983, 107–11.

"Die Sprachmelodik und Zahlensymbolik des Salve Regina als Antiphon (11. Jahrhundert) und als Meistergesang der Reformationszeit (16. Jahrhundert)", in: *Alte Musik: Praxis und Reflexion [I]*, ed. Peter Reidemeister and Veronika Gutmann, Winterthur: Amadeus 1983, 125–43.

"Was ist unser 'eigenes' Instrument?", in: *Der schweizerische Kindergarten* 73 (1983), 2–3.

"Die Krippe und die Krippenlieder", in: *Der schweizerische Kindergarten* 73 (December, 1983), 3–5.

Program Notes:

In many issues of the *Mitteilungen des Basler Kammerorchester*, Paul Sacher Foundation and the University Library of Basel.

Unpublished autobiographical sketch:

"Skizze zum Lebenslauf", Vera Oeri Bibliothek, Musik-Akademie Basel, Rara Sign. MAB Fb182.

List of Compositions

This list is by no means comprehensive, but reflects the prints and manuscripts of the Paul Sacher Foundation, the Vera Oeri Bibliothek of the Musik-Akademie Basel, and the Library of the University of Basel. As mentioned in Chapter 5, her pieces were often adapted for a particular situation, so that there are often many versions of the same piece. In addition, it is often difficult to distinguish between a melody that she considered to be complete in and of itself and a sketch. What the list does demonstrate is not only her commitment to teaching and working with the lay public, but also that she remained actively involved in composition throughout her life.

Vocal Works
I. German

Song Cycles:
Drei Lieder für Mezzosopran, Streicher, Flöte und Harfe nach Texten von Han Coray, Amsterdam/Basel, 1929–30, also in a version for mezzosoprano, flute, piano
1. Der Tod (H. Coray): Nur der Tod macht wunderbar
2. Das Leben (H. Coray): Das Leben ist das seligste Entzücken (Basel, May 1930; with obbligato flute)
3. Die Liebe (H. Coray): Wie ist die Liebe so wundersam! (Amsterdam, May 1929)

Drei Lieder nach Texten von Heinrich von Laufenberg, voice or unisono choir, published for the Basel Chamber Choir:
Es stoht ein Lind'
Sich hätt gebildet in min Herz, Leysin, Christmas, 1937
Ich wöllt, dass ich doheime, Basel, January, 1937

Four songs for baritone on texts by Hermann Hesse. Alto with flute and violin (or 2 violins) after texts by Hermann Hesse:
Einsame Nacht: Die ihr meine Brüder seid, flute/violin, violin, baritone
Glück: So lang du nach dem Glücke jagst, flute/violin, violin, baritone (but originally for alto)
Flötenspiel: Ein Haus bei Nacht durch Strauch und Baum, mezzosoprano and instrument
Allein: Es führen über die Erde, flute/violin, violin, baritone

Vier Winterlieder nach Texten von Hans Roelli, soprano and piano, private printing; there is also a version with string orchestra; the third movement also contains variations for the strings.
1. Das Land ist bis zur Ferne hart
2. Maria geht im Wald (Basel, 28 September 1930)
3. Weihnacht: Ein müder Wandersmann in seiner Dunkelheit
4. Jahreswende: In dieser Nacht ist jeder Mensch

Vom mönchischem Leben, Drei Lieder nach Texten von Rainer Maria Rilke for voice and piano or organ (Davos, November 1927), versions for baritone, soprano, and mezzosoprano with piano or organ
1. Alle, die ihre Hände regen
2. Ich finde dich in allen diesen Dingen
3. Wenn es nur einmal so ganz stille wäre

Von der Pilgerschaft 4 + 1 = 5 Lieder nach Texten von Rainer Maria Rilke (Stundenbuch), 1928
Ein Zyklus für Sopran und Kammerorchester (oboe, Eng. horn, bassoon, harp and strings), Arnhem, Basel 1932, in a privately printed version
1. In diesem Dorfe steht das letzte Haus (version with piano, 1927)
2. Manchmal steht einer auf beim Abendbrot (version with piano, 1928)
3. Er kam aus Licht
4. O wo ist er, der klare hingeklungen?
In the manuscript version, the next one is also numbered 4 in the original and the following one 5
5. Weihnacht: Ein müder Wandermann in seiner Dunkelheit
6. Jahreswende: In dieser Nacht ist jeder Mensch
Version for soprano voice and piano, in a clean score:
1. In diesem Dorfe steht das letzte Haus (Amsterdam, June 1927)
2. Manchmal steht einer auf beim Abendbrot (Davos, April 1928)
3. Es wird nicht Ruhe in den Häusern (Chernex Montreux, May 1928)

Larger Forms of Sacred Music for voices and instruments:
Die Geburt unseres Herrn Jesus Christus, voices, violins and viola, Bärenreiter=Ausgabe 2168, Kassel: Bärenreiter 1948.

Fünf geistliche Chorlieder für dreistimmige gemischten Chor a cappella. Performed 25 June 1931 at the Basel Conservatory, 1, 2, 5 by the Conservatory Choir, directed by Hans Münch, 3–4 by Helene Sandreuter, Pauline Hoch, and Hanns Visscher van Gaasbeek.
1. Jetzt wird die Welt recht neugebor'n (Text: Angelus Silesius)
2. Mir nach, spricht Christus, unser Held (Text: Angelus Silesius)
3. Fürchte nicht des Sturmes Toben (Text: Paul Zoelly)
4. Überall wölbt sich das Himmelsgewölbe (Text: Paul Zoelly)
5. In Ewigkeit, Amen

Herr, durch dein Blut, for 3-voice string orchestra and unisono choir (Pange lingua melody).

Psalm 104 (Schlusslied des Ebal): Die Ehre des Herrn ist ewig, solo soprano and tenor voices, choir.
Psalm 126: Die mit Tränen säen (Martin Luther), soprano, women's choir, flute or recorder, and violin.

Kantate nach Psalmtexten, soprano and barritone, and amateur choir and orchestra, 1937:
Einleitung
Psalm 94: Herr Gott, des die Rache ist
Psalm 126: Die mit Tränen säen

Psalm 67: Gott sei uns gnädig
Psalm 104: Die Ehre des Herrn ist ewig

Kantate von der Liebe Gottes: Domini sumus, small cantata for unisono choir and piano or organ, 1943/45, 2 manuscript copies with some performance suggestions.
1. Pangue Lingua: Fantasie über: Herr durch dein Blut
2. So die Blätter (Guido Gezelle)
3. Wohl dem, der den Herrn fürchtet (Psalm 112)
4. Ein geduldiger ist besser denn ein Starker (Proverbs 16, 32)
5. Wer will uns scheiden von der Liebe (Romans, 8, 35–39)

Kleine Kantate for soprano solo and women's choir (text Han Coray, 1931)
Alternating 3-part women's choir and soprano solo:
1. Unwandelbar von Anbeginn
2. Wenn es Nacht wird
3. Das Leben währt nur kurze Zeit
4. Wir müssen sehr leise durchs Leben gehn
5. Wir lieben
6. Das Leben ist das seligste Entzücken
7. Wenn Freunde fallen rings um mich her
8. O Herr

Liedkantate für die Advents- und Weihnachtszeit, unisono women's and men's choir with 3-part string orchestra, September 1943.

Schuld, Busse und Verheissung, cantata for Advent on texts from the prophets Jeremias and Isaiah to which the choir and congregation responds with songs from the Reformation, 1956/1973.

Weihnachtskantilene (after Matthias Claudius, 1953), alto recorder, discant gamba, unisono choir; abridged version played for Christmas festivities in Wildsches Haus, Basel, 18 December 1967.

Music for Festive Occasions:
Birthday Celebration:
Der Dirigent, Cantata for choir and strings, for Paul Sacher on his 50th birthday:
Es lebe hoch die Partituren
Getrost, wir sind noch da

Zwei Hochzeitslieder (for various couples):
Blaues Auge, blondes Haar (Christian Morgenstern), voice and instrument
Als die Münsteruhr sieben morgen schlug (Christian Morgenstern), voice and instrument

Hochzeit Alfred and Esther Rentsch-Loeliger:
Zu Lehen: Ich bin nicht mein (Werner Bergengruen), voice and instrument

Music for Plays:
Moses-Spiel (text Marie Rohner, music Ina Lohr, 1936), written for the retirement of Pastor
      Benz from St. Matthew's Church 1936
Die Zweite Meile, church play (text Pastor Marianne Kappeler, music Ina Lohr, 1956)
Christophorus-Spiel (text Caroline v. Heydebrand, music Dr. Ina Lohr, after 1958)
Ein Spiel von der Angst (congregation of St. Stephan, 22 May 1966)
Das Öchslein und das Eselein: Ein weihnachtliches Singspiel (text: Marianne Garff, music: Ina
      Lohr), in: *Schulpraxis: Monatsschrift des Bernischen Lehrerverein, 51/7* (1961)
Des Petrus Fischzug (text: Ursula Burkhard, music: Ina Lohr), for religious instruction
Die Eule (Heinz Ritter: Bärenreiter Laienspiele 109), voice and 2 instruments (recorders)
Frau Holle (play for children)
Freuet Euch!, Weltgebetstag, 3 March 1972
Ihr seid das Salz der Erde! (St. Elisabeth Church, Basel, 26 April 1959)
Two songs for *Der Kreis der Wahrheit* (play by Wilhelm Kutschbach) for voice and instrument:
      Wahre Freundschaft
      Sonne und Regen müssen wohl sein
Wachsam in unserer Zeit, Weltgebetstag, 2 March 1973

Songs with keyboard accompaniment:
Zwei altholländische Busslieder aus "Valerius Gedenckklank" [Adrianus Valerius, *Neder-
      landtsche Gedenck-clanck*], before 1626, arranged for high voice and organ or piano:
      Wie steht, O Herr
      Der du ausbreitest
An mein Klavier: Sanftes Klavier! (Chr. Fr. D. Schubarth), voice and piano
Augen, meine lieben Fensterlein (Gottfried Keller), voice and piano, Beilage zu *Singt und
      Spielt* 20/4 (1953), Zurich: Hug
Ausklang: Nun ist es still in meiner Seele (Medler), voice and piano (Arnhem, July 1928)
Gott lass leuchten den Regenbogen (Erwin Anderegg), voice, instrument, organ/piano. For
      the inauguration of the Friedmatt Ecumenical Center, 26 August 1973
Herr, gib uns Frieden (Dag Hammarskjöld), voice and organ, *Mitteilungen des Oekumeni-
      schen Singkreises Basel* and in manuscript
Ich muss die Creaturen fliehen, (text Joh. Fauler 1300?–1361), voice, instrument, piano/organ
Mit Gott tu alles fangen an (Hausspruch aus Ried bei Zürich), voice and organ, Beilage zu
      Singt und Spielt 20/4 (1953), Zurich: Hug
Neujahrsspruch: Wie die Blätter, (Guido Gezelle, Christmas 1944), voice with piano accom-
      paniment
O, lass mich trauern (Chr. Morgenstern), voice and piano (Basel, May 1930)
Osterlied: Ich, ich habe die Welt überwunden (Jesus Sirach 3, 21–24), voice and organ
O wo ist er (Rainer Maria Rilke), voice and piano (Basel, October 1930)
Passionslied: Herr, durch dein Blut, hilf uns Armen, voice and organ
So gehst du nun, min Jesu hin, voice and piano or organ
Mein Jesu, was für Seelenweh, voice and piano or organ
Vom menschlichen Leben: Denn der Herr ist der Allerhöchste (Sirach, 51, 38), voice and
      organ
Wandlung: Hältst, Stadt, Du nicht den Atem an? (Ursula Burkhard), voice and piano
Widmung: Glücklich die wissen (Rainer Maria Rilke), voice and accompaniment ad lib.,
      Beilage zu *Singt und Spielt* 20/4 (1953), Zurich: Hug
Wer mag uns scheiden von der Liebe Gottes?, voice and organ

Songs for more than one voice and/or instruments:
a) Collections
3 Lieder nach Texten von Rudolf Alexander Schröder:
Wir dürfen ihn bitten: Hilf, Vater und Herr! (also printed in *Mitteilungen des Oekumenischen Singkreises Basel,* No. 22, 2nd quarter 1973), versions for 1, 2 or 3 voices
Wir glauben Gott im höchsten Thron, 3 voices
Christ ist auferstanden, 3 voices

Vier Responsorien nach Sprüche aus dem "Cherubinischen Wandersmann" des Angelus Silesius, Laien-Musik, Blatt Nr. 13, Zurich: Hug 1938 for 3-voice women's choir or for one voice in the same range. Performed in 1948 under the auspices of ISCM in Basel, and at the Amsterdam Conservatory on 28 February 1966 under the direction of Jan Boeke:
Responsorium I: Alles gilt dem Weisen gleich, 2–3 voices
Responsorium II: Der Himmel senket sich, 2–3 voices
Responsorium III: Mensch, denkst du Gott zu schaun, 2–3 voices
Responsorium IV: Gott wohnt in einem Licht, 2–3 voices

6 Gesänge nach Texten von Kurt Marti, Basel 1973 (MS)
Ich wurde nicht gefragt bei meiner Zeugung
    voice and piano (organ)
    voice
    voice and 3 instruments in *Mitteilungen des Oekumenischen Singkreises Basel,* 27 (3rd quarter 1974)
Telegrammtext – Selig ihr armen, 4 voices, lower voices ad libitum
ich bin ihr seid – Der sagt ich bin, 2 voices, lower voice ad libitum
    nur einer tats – ich sterbe nicht, 2 voices
    das leere grab – ein grab greift tiefer, voice
    durch die tür – die könige berühren die türen nicht, 1–3 voices

Deutsche Messgesänge für sechzehn Sonn- und Festtage, vol. 1, Basel: Hug 1967, for unisono choir
Vierter Adventssonntag
Weihnacht: Messe in der Nacht
Dritte Weihnachtsmess (und 1. Januar)
3. bis 6. Sonntag nach Erscheinung
Sonntag Quinquagesima
Dritter Fastensonntag
Der hohe Ostertag
Vierter Sonntag nach Ostern
Christi Himmelfahrt
Pfingstsonntag
Dreifaltigkeitsfest (und Eidg. Bettag)
Dritter Sonntag nach Pfingsten
Siebter Sonntag nach Pfingsten
Vierzehnter Sonntag nach Pfingsten
Zwanzigster Sonntag nach Pfingsten
Dreiundszwanziger bis letzter Sonntag nach Pfingsten
Ordinariumsgesänge

25 dreistimmige Psalmsätze zum Singen und Spielen, (vol. 2 of *Deutsche Messgesänge*) Basel: Hug 1967, for organ, or 3 melody instruments, or for choir

1. Psalm 2: Was toben Völker
2. Psalm 8: Wie herrlich gibst du, Herr
3. Psalm 9: Von ganzem Herzen
4. Psalm 19: Der Himmel zahllos Heer
5. Psalm 22: Mein, Gott, mein Gott, warum
6. Psalm 24: Ihr Pforten, hebt
7. Psalm 25: Ich erhebe mein Gemüte
8. Psalm 31: Auf dich, O Herr
9. Psalm 33: Nun freuet euch
10. Psalm 34: Freund Gottes
11. Psalm 44: O Gott, auch unsre Ohren
12. Psalm 47: Singt mit froher Stimm
13. Psalm 66: Jauchzt alle Lande
14. Psalm 68: Steh auf in deiner Macht
15. Psalm 76: Seht Gott, der Herr
16. Psalm 78: Vernimm, mein Volk
17. Psalm 84: Wie lieblich
18. Psalm 90: Herr Gott, in allem Werden
19. Psalm 96: Sing, Erde, sing
20. Psalm 97: König ist der Herr
21. Psalm 98: Singt, singt dem Herren
22. Psalm 99: Gott ist's, der regiert
23. Psalm 100: Nun jauchzt der Herr
24. Psalm 110: Es sprach der Herr
25. Psalm 118: Nun saget Dank
26. Psalm 119: O selig sind
27. Psalm 130: Aus tiefer Not
28. Psalm 137: An Wasserflüssen Babylon
29. Psalm 139: Du Herr, mein Gott
30. Lobsang Mariae: Nun lobt mein Seel (Nikolaus Selnecker)

Arrangements of songs from the hymnal of the Swiss Reformed Church [GB]:

GB 6:	Ich erhebe mein Gemüte, 2-voice arrangement
GB 8	Psalm 32: O wohl dem Menschen, 2-voice arrangement
GB 13:	Seht, er fährt empor, 2-voice arrangement
GB 14	Psalm 57: Sei gnädig mir Gott, 4-voice arrangement
GB 16	Psalm 65: Man betet, Herr, 2 and 3-voice arrangements
GB 27:	Nun jauchzt dem Herren alle Welt, arrangement voice and piano/organ with additional high instrumental voice, or 2-voice arrangement
GB 43=46:	Nun danket all und bringet Ehr, violin and piano/organ or 4 voices
GB 63:	Bescher uns, Herr, das täglich Brot, 2-voice arrangement
GB 79=132	Neujahrslied: Nun lasst uns gehn und treten, voice and 2 instruments
GB 96:	violin and 4-voice arrangement
GB 106/ 91:	Mit Ernst, o Menschenkinder, 3-voice arrangement
GB 107:	Gott sei Dank durch alle Welt, 2 and 3-voice arrangements
GB 110:	Der Tag, der ist so freudenreich, 2-voice arrangement

GB 119:   Fröhlich soll mein Herze springen, 3 instruments or voices
GB 120:   Ich steh an deiner Krippe, 2 instruments and voice
GB 121:   Kommt und lasst uns Christum ehren, 3-voice arrangement
GB 126:   Dies ist der Tag den Gott gemacht, voice and piano/organ
GB 129:   Brich an du schönes Morgenlicht, 2-voice arrangement
GB 131:   Das alte Jahr vergangen ist, 2-voice arrangement
GB 142:   Wir danken dir, 2 instruments and voice
GB 148:   O Haupt voll Blut und Wunden, 3-voice arrangement
GB 149:   O Welt, sieh hier dein Leben (melody Heinrich Isaac, Innsbruck, ca. 1505),
            3-voice arrangement
GB 157:   Christ ist erstanden, 3-voice arrangement
GB 158/162: Erschienen ist, 3-voice arrangement
GB 160:   Gelobt sei Gott im höchsten Thron, 2 and 3-voice arrangements; instru-
            ment, voice and organ
GB 326/352/164: Nun freut euch hier und überall, 2-voice arrangement
GB 167:   Wach auf, mein Herr, 3-voice arrangement
GB 172:   Gen Himmel, voice and violin, voice and 2 recorders
GB 199:   Herr Jesu Christ, 2-voice arrangement
GB 246/265: Christi Blut u. Gerechtigkeit, 2-voice arrangement
GB 255:   Wie schön leuchtet der Morgenstern, 3-voice arrangement
GB 265:   Christi Blut und Gerechtigkeit, 2-voice arrangement
GB 275:   Befiehl du deine Wege, 3-voice arrangement
GB 281:   Wer nur den lieben Gott lässt walten, 4-voice arrangement
GB 293:   Herr, du weisst, arrangement for alto recorder or violin and voice
GB 310:   Wer nur den lieben Gott lässt walten, 4-voice arrangement for instruments
            and voices
GB 365:   Mit Fried u. Freud, 3-voice arrangement

Composition booklet on poems from Jochen Klepper's *Kyrie* (Witten: Eckart 1960):

1. Ambrosianischer Morgengesang: Schon bricht des Tages Glanz hervor, 2 voices
2. Morgenlied: Er weckt mich alle Morgen, in *Geistliche Lieder nach Worten von Jochen Klepper*, Laudinella-Reihe, Bl. 7, Basel: Arthur Eglin 1963, voice and 2 instruments
3. Mittagslied: Der Tag ist seiner Höhe nah, in *Geistliche Lieder nach Worten von Jochen Klepper*, Laudinella-Reihe, Bl. 7, Basel: Arthur Eglin 1963, voice and 2 high instruments / Dutch version: Gedenk op 't hoogste van de dag, 1983.
4. Abendlied: Ich liege, Herr in deiner Hut, in *Geistliche Lieder nach Worten von Jochen Klepper*, Laudinella-Reihe, Bl. 7, Basel: Arthur Eglin 1963, voice and 2 high instruments
5. Trostlied am Abend: In jeder Nacht, in *Geistliche Lieder nach Worten von Jochen Klepper*, Laudinella-Reihe, Bl. 7, Basel: Arthur Eglin 1963, 2 voices / Dutch version: In elke nacht 1983.
6. Das Kirchenjahr: Du bist als Stern, 3 voices
7. Weihnachtslied: Wer warst du, Herr, vor dieser Nacht. Voice and violin or alto recorder
8. Weihnachtslied: Die Nacht ist vorgedrungen, 3 voices
9. Weihnachtslied: Sieh nicht an, 2 voices and in *Geistliche Lieder nach Worten von Jochen Klepper*, Laudinella-Reihe, Bl. 57, Basel: Arthur Eglin 1967, voice and instrument
10. Weihnachts-Kyrie: Du Kind, zu dieser heiligen Zeit, 2 voices
11. Abendmahlslied zu Weihnachten: Mein Gott, dein hohes Fest des Lichtes, 3 voices
[12.] Weihnachtslied im Kriege: Nun ruht doch alle Welt, in *Geistliche Lieder nach Worten*

von Jochen Klepper, Laudinella-Reihe, Bl. 57, Basel: Arthur Eglin 1967, 2 voices
12.   [22.] Am letzten Sonntag des Kirchenjahres: Mein Gott, ich will von hinnen, 2 voices
      and in *Geistliche Lieder nach Worten von Jochen Klepper*, Laudinella-Reihe, Bl. 57, Ba-
      sel: Arthur Eglin 1967, voice and 2 high instruments
13.   [15.] Neujahrslied: Der du die Zeit in Händen hast, solo
14.   [13.] Silvesterlied: Ja, ich will euch tragen bis zum Alter hin, voice with organ, and
      in *Geistliche Lieder nach Worten von Jochen Klepper*, Laudinella-Reihe, Bl. 57, Basel:
      Arthur Eglin 1967, voice and instrument
15.   [25.] Geburtstagslied: Gott wohnt in einem Lichte, 2 voices
16.   [14.] Zur Jahreswende: Zuflucht ist bei dem alten Gott, 3 voices
17.   [20.] Reformationslied: Singt Gott, lobsinget seinem Namen! 3 voices
18.   [17.] Osterlied: Siehe, das ist Gottes Lamm, 3 voices
19.   [19.] Pfingstlied: Komm heilige Taube, 3 voices
20.   Der Herr ist nah: Wir wissen nicht den Sinn, 2 voices
21.   [16.] Gründonnerstags-Kyrie: Heut bin ich meines Heiland, 2 voices
22.   [26.] Tauflied: Gott Vater, du hast deinen Namen in deinem lieben Sohn verklärt,
      3 voices (für Pieter Lüthi, November 1954)
23.   [28.] Hochzeitslied: Freuet euch im Herren allewege!, 3 voices (für Beatrice von Salis,
      März 1955)

Entwurf Abendmahlsliturgie (text Prof. Julius Schweizer, melody Ina Lohr)

Laudinella and Bläserkreis Series:
Füge dich der Zeit (Friedrich Rückert) – Mir zum Geburtstag (1963), canon for 3 voices,
      Laudinella-Reihe, Blatt 1, [Basel: Arthur Eglin]
*Ein Lämmlein geht und trägt die Schuld: kleine Choralkantate für Chor, Instrumente und
      Gemeinde*, Laudinella-Reihe, Blatt 2, Basel: Arthur Eglin 1963
Dreistimmige Sätze zu Advents- und Weihnachtsliedern, Der Bläserkreis, Blatt 6, Basel: Arthur
      Eglin 1961:
      Nun komm, der Heiden Heiland (text Martin Luther), arrangement for 3 or 4 voices
      O Heiland, reiss die Himmel auf, arrangement for 2 or 3 voices
      Es kommt ein Schiff geladen, 3-voice arrangement
      Macht hoch die Tür, die Tor macht weit, 2-voice arrangement
Lieder zum Tageskreis nach Worten von Jochen Klepper, Laudinella-Reihe, Blatt 7, Basel:
      Arthur Eglin 1963:
      Morgenlied: Er weckt mich alle Morgen, 3 voices
      Mittagslied: Der Tag ist seiner Höhe nah, voice and 2 instruments
      Abendlied: Ich liege, Herr, in deiner Hut, voice and 2 instruments
      Trostlied am Abend: In jeder Nacht, die mich bedroht, voice and instrument
Psalm 149: Singt vor dem Herrn mit neuem Schalle, small chorale cantata for choir and instru-
      ments, *Der Bläserkreis*, Blatt 10, Basel: Arthur Eglin 1962
Dreistimmige Sätze zu Advents- und Weihnachtsliedern, Laudinella-Reihe, Blatt 22, Basel:
      Arthur Eglin 1964:
      Nun komm, der Heiden Heiland, 3-voice arrangement
      Es kommt ein Schiff geladen, 3-voice arrangement
      Uns ist geboren, 3-voice arrangement
      Mit Gott, so wollen wir loben, 3-voice arrangement
      Vom Himmel kam der Engel Schar, 3-voice arrangement

Das Gleichnis von den zehn Jungfrauen, choral reading for mixed voices, Laudinella-Reihe, Blatt 33, Basel: Arthur Eglin 1965

Psalm 8: Wie herrlich gibst du, Herr, pieces for choir and instruments, Laudinella-Reihe, Blatt 46, Basel: Arthur Eglin 1966

Geistliche Lieder nach Worten von Jochen Klepper, Laudinella-Reihe, Blatt 57, Basel: Arthur Eglin 1967:

Am letzten Sonntag des Kirchenjahrs: Mein Gott, ich will von hinnen gehen, 3 voices

Weihnachtslied im Kriege: Nun ruht doch alle Welt, 2–3 voices/instruments

Silvesterlied: Ja, ich will euch tragen, voice and instrument

Weihnachtslied, Sieh nicht an, was du selber bist, 3 voices

Drei Psalmfragmente for a solo voice or unisono choir, 1 to 2-voice accompaniment ad lib., Laudinella-Reihe, Blatt 57, Basel: Arthur Eglin 1970:

Psalm 42 (41), 12: Was betrübst du dich

Psalm 34 (33), 2–6: Ich will den Herrn preisen

Psalm 139 (138), 23–24: Erforsche mich, Gottesdienst

Vier Sprüche für Singgruppen, instruments ad lib., Laudinella-Reihe, Blatt 113, Basel: Arthur Eglin 1972:

Wer nun weiss Gutes zu tun, 2 voices and instruments

Des Menschen Sohn ist gekommen, voice and 3 instruments

Einer trage des anderen Lasten, voice and 3 instruments

Unser keiner lebt sich selber, voice and 2 instruments

Psalmverse, Laudinella-Reihe, Blatt 127, Pratteln: Arthur Eglin 1973:

Psalm 73, 23–26: Dennoch bleibe ich, voice and piano/organ or melody instruments

Psalm 128, 1–2: Wohl dem, der den Herren fürchtet, 2 voices

Psalm 90 (89): Herr, Gott, du bist unsre Zuflucht, for mixed choir a cappella, Laudinella-Reihe, Blatt 135, Basel: Arthur Eglin 1974

Drei- und vierstimmige Sätze zu Advents- und Weihnachtsliedern, Laudinella-Reihe, Blatt 155, Pratteln: Arthur Eglin 1975:

Nun komm, der Heiden Heiland, 3-voice arrangement with ad lib. instrumental upper voice

Lobt Gott, ihr Christen, 3-voice arrangement

Gelobet seist du, Jesu Christ, 3-voice arrangement

Nun singet und seid froh, arrangement for voice and 2 instruments

Wer will uns scheiden von der Liebe Gottes for solo voice or unisono choir and organ, Laudinella-Reihe, Blatt 179, Pratteln: Arthur Eglin 1977

Gebete um Frieden, Laudinella-Reihe, Blatt 247, Arthur Eglin: Aesch 1983:

Satz 1: Herr, gib uns Frieden mit dir, voice and organ/piano

Gebet um Frieden: Herr Gott, himmlischer Vater, voice and organ/piano, melody instrument

Satz 2: Herr, gib uns Frieden, voice and melody instrument

Vom menschlichen Leben: Vier kleine Chorstücke, Laudinella-Reihe, Blatt 345, Pratteln: Arthur Eglin ca. 1990

Man wird nicht besser mit den Jahren, voice or unisono choir

Denn der Herr ist der Allerhöchste, voice and three instruments

Füge dich der Zeit (Friedrich Rückert), 3-voice canon

Mein sind die Jahre nicht (Andreas Gryphius), voice or unisono choir

Passionsgebet for choir and instruments, Laudinella-Reihe, Blatt 397, Pratteln: Arthur Eglin 1996:

Barmherziger, ewiger Gott, with prelude for instruments, voice, violin, and organ, also
in an earlier version for voice and organ (1945)
In der Welt habt ihr Angst, Laudinella-Reihe, Blatt 411, Pratteln: Arthur Eglin 1997:
Jesus spricht: In der Welt habt ihr Angst
Christus ist erstanden (Martin Luther), 2-voice arrangement
Amen, Halleluja, 3-voice arrangement
Osterlied: Ich habe die Welt überwunden, voice with organ or piano

Psalms published in *Die Psalmen: Psalmen, Lobgesänge und geistliche Lieder der Christenheit*,
edited by Wilhelm Vischer, set by Ina Lohr, Trudi Sutter and Lili Wieruszowski (only the
pieces arranged by Ina Lohr are listed here), Zurich: Zwingli-Verlag 1944–46:
Christ, du bist das Licht und auch der Tag, 2-voice arrangement, vol. 8
Christ ist erstanden, 2-voice arrangement, vol. 5
Christ lag in Todesbanden, 3-voice arrangement (Martin Luther), vol. 5
Christ unser Herr zum Jordan kam (Martin Luther), 3-voice arrangement, vol. 7
Christe, du Lamm Gottes, 3-voice arrangement, vol 7
Christus, der uns selig macht (Michael Weisse), 3-voice arrangement, vol. 5
Christus, wir sollen loben schön (Martin Luther), vol. 4
Denk, Mensch, wie dein Heiland dich liebet (Petrus Herbert), 3-voice arrangement, vol. 5
Der du bist Drei in Einigkeit (Martin Luther), 3-voice arrangement, vol. 5
Dies sind die heiligen Zehn Gebot (Martin Luther), 3-voice arrangement, vol.7
Durch Adams Fall ist ganz verderbt, 2-voice arrangement, vol. 6
Ehre sei dir, Christe, der du littest Not, 2-voice arrangement, vol. 5
Erhalt uns, Herr, bei deinem Wort, 3-voice arrangement, vol. 6
Geht hin, die ihr gebenedeit, 2-voice arrangement, vol. 6
Gelobet seist du, Jesus Christ (Martin Luther), 2-voice arrangement, vol. 4
Gott der Vater wohn uns bei (Martin Luther), 3-voice arrangement, vol. 5
Gott sei gelobet und gebenedeiet (Martin Luther), 2-voice arrangement, vol. 7
Herr Christ, der einig Gott Sohn (Elisabeth Creutziger), 2-voice arrangement, vol. 4
Jesus Christus, unser Heiland (Martin Luther), 3-voice arrangement, vol. 5
Jesus Christus, unser Heiland (corrected version Martin Luther), 3-voice arrangement, vol. 7
Komm, Heiliger Geist, Herre Gott (Martin Luther), 2-voice arrangement, vol. 5
Komm, Schöpfer Geist, kehr bei uns ein (Martin Luther), 3-voice arrangement, vol. 5
Kommt her zu mir (Georg Grüenwald), 2-voice arrangement, vol. 6
Mensch, willst du leben seliglich (Martin Luther), 3-voice arrangement, vol. 7
Mit Fried und Freud ich fahr dahin (Martin Luther), 3-voice arrangement, vol. 4
Mitten wir im Leben sind (Martin Luther), 2-voice arrangement, vol. 8
Nun bitten wir den heiligen Geist (supplementeded by Martin Luther), 3-voice arrange-
ment, vol. 5
Nun freut euch, lieben Christen gmein (Martin Luther), 3-voice arrangement, vol. 6
Nun komm der Heiden Heiland (Martin Luther), 3-voice arrangement, vol. 3
Nun lasst uns den Leib begraben (Michael Weisse), 2-voice arrangement
Psalm 12: Ach Gott, vom Himmel sieh darein (Martin Luther), 3-voice arrangement, vol. 1
Psalm 46: Ein feste Burg (Martin Luther), 2-voice arrangement, vol. 2
Psalm 67: Es wolle Gott uns gnädig sein (Martin Luther), 2-voice arrangement, vol. 2
Psalm 124: Wär Gott nicht mit uns diese Zeit (Martin Luther), 3-voice arrangement, vol. 3
Psalm 128: Wohl dem, der in Furcht Gottes steht (Martin Luther), 3-voice arrangement,
vol. 3

Psalm 130: Aus tiefer Not schrei ich zu dir (Martin Luther), 3-voice arrangement, vol. 3
Vater unser im Himmelreich (Martin Luther), 3-voice arrangement, vol. 7
Verleih uns Frieden gnädiglich (Martin Luther), 3-voice arrangement, vol. 6
Vom Himmel hoch da kom ich her (Martin Luther), 3-voice arrangement, vol. 4
Vom Himmel kam der Engelschar (Martin Luther), 2-voice arrangement, vol. 4
Was fürchtst du, Feind Herodes, sehr? (Martin Luther), 2-voice arrangement, vol. 4
Wir glauben all an einen Gott (Martin Luther), 2-voice arrangement, vol. 7

Lieder zum Danke und Gratuliere (Anna Keller), Basel: Verlag von Heinrich Majer 1959:
Glick und Säge: wie still isch's worde, voice and violin
Sibzig: Im Läbe git's kai Stillestoh, voice and violin
Spruch: Wenn d'Sunne strahlt, voice and violin or recorder
Tanz: Me wird nit jinger, voice and alto recorder or violin
Troscht: O lueg zu dyne Fänschter uus!, voice and violin or recorder
I waiss, dass du kai Loblied witt, voice and vioin or alto recorder
Wenn äs näblet: Styg uffe, wenn's näblet, voice and instrument

Stimme und Gegenstimme: Zweistimmige Sätze für Kirche, Schule und Haus zu Psalmen und Geistlichen Liedern, Basel: Hug 1954 (2-voice arrangements by Ina Lohr):
1. GB 2, Psalm 5: Herr, höre doch auf meine Rede
2. GB 6, Psalm 25: Ich erhebe mein Gemüte
3. GB 11, Psalm 38: Straf mich nicht in deinem Grimme
4. GB 12, Psalm 42: Wie der Hirsch nach frischer Quelle
5. GB 13, Psalm 47: Singt mit froher Stimm
6. GB 19, Psalm 51: Miséricorde au pauvre vicieux / Sei gnädig mir, O Gott
7. GB 16, Psalm 65: Man betet, Herr in Zions Stille
8. GB 17, Psalm 67: Es wolle Gott uns gnädig sein
9. GB 18, Psalm 68: Steh auf in deiner Macht, O Gott
10. GB 19, Psalm 77: Herr, erhöre meine Klagen
11. GB 23, Psalm 93: Der Höchste herrscht in Majestät
12. GB 27, Psalm 100: Nun jauchzt dem Herren, alle Welt
13. GB 31, Psalm 117: Lobsingt ihr Völker allzugleich
14. GB 34, Psalm 124: Wär Gott nicht mit uns diese Zeit
15. GB 39, Psalm 138: Mein ganzes Herz erhebet dich
16. GB 71: Die helle Sonn leucht jetzt herfür
17. GB 72: All Morgen ist ganz frisch und neu
18. GB 84: Du höchstes Licht und ewger Schein
19. GB 74: Ich sag dir Dank, Gott Vater gut
20. GB 75: Aus meines Herzens Grunde
21. GB 79: Wach auf, mein Herz
22. GB 83: Hinunter ist der Sonne Schein
23. GB 84: Da nun der Tag uns geht zu End
24. GB 85: Mit meinem Gott geh ich zur Ruh
25. GB 86: Nun ruhen alle Wälder
26. GB 87: Der Tag ist hin
27. GB 95: Christus, du bist uns Licht und Tag

b) Individual Songs for several voices or voice and instruments:

Abendlied: Wann einst ich sterben soll (Pieter van Renssen), 3 voices
Aber, wie de gosch (J.P. Hebel), voice and 2 instruments
Ach bittrer Winter, wie bist du kalt, 3-voice arrangement
Das kleine Lied vom Brot: Das Stücklein Brot, voice and instrument
Das Antlitz: Wer kann noch wähnen (Margarete Susmann), voice and violin
Der Tod in Flandern (text and melody traditional), 4-voice arrangement for men's choir,
    Basel: Notenbureau Ernst Vogel [n.d.]
Du bist min, ich bin din, 3 voices
Einer trage des andern Last, canon
Füge dich der Zeit (Friedrich Rückert), for Ina Lohr's 60th birthday, canon
Fürchte dich nicht, 2 voices
Heb auf, was dir Gott vor der Tür legt, canon
Ich bin das Licht der Welt, 2 voices
Ich habe die Grippe, canon
In der kleinsten Arve harten Nadeln (Alice Stamm), voice and instrument
Lieben Liedchen: Auwe lip vor allem libe, 3 voices
Morgenlied (Dietrich Bonhoeffer): In Gottes Namen, manuscript melody
Nach grüner Farb mein Herz verlangt, voice and 2 instruments (1977)
O Heiland, reiss die Himmel auf, 3 voices
Osterlied (Werner Bergengrüen): Herr Christ will Ostern auferstehn
    manuscript melody
    manuscript and printed (Arthur Eglin?) 2-voice version for 2 high voices, melody in top
    part
    manuscript melody plus organ
Psalm 8: Wie herrlich gibst du, Herr, 2- and 3-voice arrangements and for unisono choir
    and organ
Psalm 10, 17–18: Der Elenden Verlangen hörst du, Gott, voice, Lenk, July 1955
Psalm 23: Der Herr ist Gott, 2-voice arrangement
Psalm 26: O herr, schaffe mir Recht (melody Geneva, 1551, German trans. Ina Lohr), 2 and
    3-voice arrangements
Psalm 34: Ich will den Herren loben, solo soprano and tenor, choir
Psalm 42, 12: Was betrübst du dich meine Seele, 2-voice arrangement
Psalm 50: Gott, der Herr, der Mächtige, 2 melody instruments, cornet, choir, guitar/viola,
    unisono choir, Lucerne, 1965
Psalm 65: Man betet, Herr, in Zions Stille (Hugenot melody, 1544), arrangement for 3-voice
    string orchestra with unisono men's and women's choirs
Psalm 67: Gott sei uns gnädig, 4 voices
Psalm 90: Herr, Gott, du bist unsre Zuflucht für und für, 1–4 voices
Psalm 104: Die Ehre des Herrn ist Ewig, 2 instruments, solo voice and unisono choir
Psalm 108: [Gott, es ist mein rechter Ernst], 2-voice arrangement
Psalm 117: Lobet den Herrn, alle Heiden, voice, flute and violin
Psalm 121: Zu den Bergen heb ich meine Augen (text Martin Buber), solo voice and choir,
    2 recorders, violin
Psalm 123: Ich hebe meine Augen auf zu dir, 3-voice arrangement, choir and instruments
Psalm 128,1: Wohl dem, der den Herren fürchtet
Psalm 134: Siehe, lobet den Herrn, voice and instrument
Psalm 139, 23–24: Erforsche mich Gott, arrangement voice and organ, or voice and 2 instru-
    ments

Siehe, lobet den Herren, 1–2 voices.
Wachet auf, 2-voice arrangement
Wegweiser: Weisch, wo der Weg zum Mehlfass isch (J.P. Hebel), voice, viola and cello
Weil wir denn solche Hoffnung haben, 3 voices
Wohl dem, der den Herren fürchtet, 2 voices

Christmas songs:
1st Sunday of Advent:
    Introitus (Ps. 24, 1–3): Zu Dir erhebe ich meine Seele, 2 voices
    Graduale (Ps. 24, 3–4): Alle, die Deiner Harren, 2 voices
    Offertorium: Zu Dir erhebe ich meine Seele
    Communio: Segen spendet der Herr, 2-voice arrangement
Bescheidene Hirten (text Helene Schär-Ammann), unison choir, 3 instruments (1971),
    printed by Arthur Eglin [n.d.]
Brich ein, O Gott (Arno Pötzsch, 1970), 3 voices
Bruder, ich geh auch mit dir, 3-voice arrangement
Chor der Engel: Merket empor und fürchtet euch nicht!, 3 voices
Der Tag, der ist so freudenreich, voice and instrument
Der Weihnachtsengel: Ehre sei Gott in der Höhe (Ursula Burkhart), voice
Die heiligen drei Könige (text Heinrich Heine), unison choir, 3 instruments, printed by
    Arthur Eglin 1971
Die Verkündigung: Es war eine Jungfrau auserkoren, 3-voice arrangement, 1973
Dr ängel singt vom Jesus-Kind, 2 voices
Es ist ein Ros entsprungen (melody Praetorius?), 3-voice arrangement, 1970
Es stoht ein Lind im Himmelreich, 1–2 voices
Freuen sollen sich die Wüste (Isaiah 35, 1–4), 2 voices, 1979
In dulci jubilo, 2-part arrangement
Isaiah 40, 1–5: Tröstet, mein Volk, 2 voices, organ or winds
Kleine Litanei für die Weihnachtszeit: Das Kindlein heisst Emanuel (Alice Stamm), voice
Leise rieselt der Schnee, 3-voice arrangement
Leuchte Erde! (Gertrud Kröncke), voice
Luke 12, 32, 35–40: Furchte dich nicht, version for 2 and for 3 voices
Matthew 25, 1–13: Dann wird das Himmelreich gleich sein, 2 voices and bass instrument
My Häzzli mecht säll Krippli sy, voice
O Leuchtelicht, 2 voices
O lieber Herre Gott, voice and piano/organ
O Sanctissima, for 3 violins; 2 violins and flute; or voice and 2 melody instruments, 1948
Reich und arm sollen fröhlich sein, 2-voice arrangement, 1974
Sei fröhlich und sing, Tochter Zion (Guillaume van der Graft, trans. Hinrich Stoevesandt),
    3 voices, lute or guitar
So sehr hat Gott die Welt geliebt (John 3, 16, 1963), 4-voice arrangement
Uns ist geboren in 4 languages, 2-voice arrangement
Was ist geboren, voice, alto and tenor recorders
Weihnachtsgruss 1972: Die heilgen drei Könige aus Morgenland (Heinrich Heine), voice,
    1971
Weihnachtslied: Als Eva Gottes Wort vergass (Ursula Burkhard), voice
Weihnachtslied: Bescheidne Hirten beugen sich (Helen Schär-Ammann), voice

Wenn d'Wiehnachtsglokke lytte (Anna Keller), voice, in: *Kinder-Sonntagsblatt*, December
    1971/12, 10.
Wie dunkel isch de Ärde (Anna Keller), voice, in: *Kinder-Sonntagsblatt*, December 1971/12,
    10.

Aphorisms:
Aphorismus (Marie von Ebner-Eschenbach): Die Grossen schatten das Grosse (for Otto
    Senn on his 80th birthday), voice, 1982
Du bist mein, ich bin dein, voice and organ, or for 3 voices
Geburtstagsspruch für Luggi [Louise] Wenzinger (for her 75th birthday): Weisst du wie's ein-
    mal war?, voice. Published in the *Schritte ins Offene* 6 (1976/1), 26
Glück und Unglück, voice
Glücklich, die wissen, dass hinter allen Sprachen (Rainer Maria Rilke), voice
Haussprüche, 1–3 voice choir, 2 flutes, 2 violins, cello and piano:
    Gott erhalte dieses Haus
    Wir müssen Gottes Kinder in der Jugend sein
    Das Hus, das stoht in Gottes Hand
    Eine kleine Kirch sei jedes Haus
    Menschengunst und Gottes Gnad ist gut
Neujahrslied: Gebe denn, der über uns wagt (Johann Peter Hebel), voice, 1971
Neujahrsspruch: Wie die Blätter / Zoo de blaren (Guido Gezelle), voice and piano
Neujahrswunsch: Ich wünsch Dir ein Jahr (Guido Gezelle), voice and piano, 1950
Sing, bet' und geh auf Gottes Wegen, voice and organ
Spruch: Unser keiner lebt sich selber, unisono choir, organ/piano
Spruchlied für das ganze Jahr 1980, voice and flute/violin, 1980
Spruchlied für die Adventszeit, voice and instrument, 1979
Um Bewahrung (Bergengrüen): Will ich aus meinem Hause gehen, voice and instrument
Unser Leben ist wie eines Sternes Bahn (Gerda Seemann), voice and alto recorder
Will ich aus meinem Hause gehn, voice and alto recorders
Wir bitten dich, sei unserm Haus, 3 voices (also used as a wedding song for Dieter and Gre-
    tel Leonhardt-Feldpausch)

c) Songs for voice or unisono choir:
17th Sunday after Whitsun, voice:
    Introitus: Gerecht bist Du, Herr
    Gradualis: Selig das Volk
    Offertorium: Ich flehte zu meinem Gott
    Communio: Löset ein, was ihr gelobt
Abenddämmerung: Wie eine Melodie ihr Ende findet (Ursula Burkhard), voice
Ach, dass nicht die letzte Stunde meines Lebens heute schlägt, voice
Alle Wiesen sind grün, voice
Allmächtiger, ewiger Gott (Martin Luther), voice
Als Licht und Hort, voice
Auf der Erde steh ich gern fest mit beiden Beinen, voice
Augen, meine lieben Fensterlein (Gottfried Keller), voice
Dafür sei Ehre dem Vater, unisono choir
Der Apfel ist nicht gleich am Baum (Hermann Claudius), voice, 1937
Der Regen rauscht (Johanna Russ), voice, 1935

Der Seligen werden Sänger sein (Martin Luther), voice
Die Seligpreisung (Matthew 5, 5–12): Selig sind, die da geistig arm sind, unisono choir, for
    the Sonnenhof, ca. 1962
Du bist das Brot des Lebens (Isaiah 55, 10–12), voice
Gewaltig endet so das Jahr (Georg Trakl), voice
Gebenedeit bist du unter den Weibern (Martin Luther), voice
Gedenke, Herr, deiner Kirche (Martin Luther), voice
Herr Gott, himmlischer Vater (Martin Luther), voice
Heut bin ich meines Heilands Gast, voice
Hilf Herr! Wir sind in arger Not (R.A. Schröder), voice
Ich bin dein, du lebst in mir (Silja Walter), voice, for the Welgebetstag, 3 March 1972
Ich wünsch dir ein Jahre, voice
Ihr Könige, hört einen König singen (Martin Luther), voice
Immer enger, leise, leise (Theodor Fontane), voice
In meines Vaters Garten (Hoffman van Fallersleben), voice
Kalenderblatt zum 1. August 1977: Man wird nicht besser mit den Jahren (Theodor Fon-
    tane), voice
Komm, heilige Taube, voice
Leuchten lernen: Könnte ich doch von den Sternen leuchten lernen (Ursula Burkhard),
    voice
Lobsang des Simeon (Luke 2, 29–32): Herr, nun lässest du deinen Diener, voice
Lobsang des Zacharias (Luke 1, 68–79): Gelobet sei der Herr, unisono choir or solo voice
Magnificat (Luke 1, 46–55): Meine Seele erhebt den Herrn, solo voice or unisono choir
Mein sind die Jahre nicht, voice, 1982
Mir selbst zum 80. Geburtstag: Sei heiter (Theodor Fontane), voice, 1983
Misslungener Versuch: Ein Mensch kann nicht versagen (Ursula Burkhard), voice, 1980
Präfation, voice
Psalm 34, 2–6: Ich will den Herrn preisen, voice
Psalm 105: Danket Ihm, ruft Seinen Namen aus (Martin Buber), voice
Psalm 121: Zu den Bergen, solo voice in alternatim with congregation (for Elisabeth Neu-
    mann), 1980
O lieber Herre Gott, wecke uns auf (Martin Luther), voice
Singt Gott, lob singet seinen Namen, voice
Sommertag! Sonnenschein! (summer 1980), voice
Über Nacht in die Frühlingspracht (Helene Schär-Ammann), January 1975, voice
Unser Garten im Dalbehof: Ein alter Ahorn (Helen Schär-Ammann), voice
Unser keiner lebt sich selber (The Romans 14, 1–8), voice
Unterwegs: Ein Mensch ist unterwegs (Mathilde Meng), voice
Vater, vollende was Christus begonnen (Silja Walter), voice
Vor der Wand (Mathilde Meng), voice
Woge, schweres Wasser!, voice

d) Composition Notebooks:
Sketchbook, Melodische oefeningen [melodic exercises]: Vorübungen zu den Liedern von
Laufenberg, Coray, Gertrud von Le Fort u. a. [First exercises for the songs of Laufenburg,
Coray, Gerturd von Le Fort etc.]
1. Glücklich, die wissen, dass hinter allen Sprachen das Unsägliche steht (Rilke), voice,
   Flims 1935
2. Ich wöllt, dass ich doheime wär (Heinrich von Laufenberg), melody with chords written
   in red pencil, and a melodic variant
3. Wenn es Nacht wird (Coray, *Das Leben*), Basel 1933, voice
4. Wir müssen sehr leise durchs Leben gehn (Coray, *Das Leben*), voice, Hilterfingen 1936
5. Das Leben ist das seligste Entzücken, voice
6. Ich muss die Creaturen fliehen, melody and long chords, 1937
7. Advent (Getrud von Le Fort, *Hymnen*): Singet es im Harren der Trühe, begins as solo
   voice and continues with 2–4 voices written on a single staff
8. Ich will ein Gloria singen, voice
9. Ich möchte mein Haupt eine Stille lang (Gertrud von Le Fort, *Hymnen*), voice
10. Zoo de blaren, die verdurden (Guido Gizelle), with suggestions of harmony as well
11. Vater unser, for SA, and sometimes suggestions for 3 voices
12. Ich sah die Unrast der Welt, (Gertrud von Le Fort, *Von den letzten Dingen*), voice
13. Sich hat gebildet in min Herz, with beginning in two parts (second for an instrument?),
    otherwise for one voice
14. Es stoht ein Lind im Himmelreich (Laufenberg)
15. Gouden stille kusten en de zee nog blauw, voice
16. Nun ist vorbei die finstre Nacht, voice
17. Steh auf, Herr Gott, die Zeit ist da, voice
18. Die Kirche ist ein armer Hauf, voice
19. Es ist ein Wort ergangen, voice
20. C'est que le fils de Dieu savait ("koor en solist"), voice
21. Ich, der Herr, bin sein Hüter (Eugen Henne, *Die Heilige Schrift*), voice, 1936
22. Wer will uns scheiden von der Liebe Gottes, first as melody, then as 3-part piece
23. Ich glaube an Gott den Vater, voice
24. Pays, arreté à michemin, voice with instruments sketched on one staff

Sketch book, 1940s, Sprüche zu den Reformationsliedern, voice:
Denn der Herr ist der Allerhöchste
Ihr Könige, hört einen König singen
Wann wird die goldne Zeit erscheinen
O lieber Herre Gott, voice with piano
Gebenedeit bist du, same as in composition book 1944/45 with augmented note values
Allmächtiger, ewiger Gott
Ja, ich habe die Welt überwunden (Martin Luther), also 2-voice arrangement
Gedenke, Herr, deiner Kirche
O Gott, du höchster Gnadenhort
Herr Gott, himmlischer Vater (Martin Luther)
Unterweis uns, O Gott (Johannes Zwick)
Wohlauf, du junges, fröhliches Blut (Ambrosius Blarer)
Fürchte den Tod nicht!
Die Seligen werden Sänger sein (Johann Walter)

Composition book 1944/45, voice:
Ich bin der Welt abhanden gekommen (Friedrich Rückert)
Wer mag uns scheiden (Romans 8, 35–39)
Ich stand auf Berges Halde
Psalm 121: Ich hebe meine Augen auf
Psalm 112: Wohl dem, der den Herrn fürchtet, Silvaplana, 1944
Ich muss die Kreaturen fliehen
O Lieber Herre Gott, advent prayer from the Babst Psalter, 1545
Ein Geduldiger ist besser denn ein Starker, (Proverbs 16, 32, Silvaplana, 1944)
Gebenedeit bist du unter den Weibern, same as in composition book 1944/45 with smaller
    note values
Meine Seele erhebet den Herrn
Psalm 92: Das ist ein köstlich Ding
Kanon à 3: Tag und Tag und aber Tagebuch
Ein Wald von Melden und Quecken
Herr Christ will Ostern auferstehn
Wir haben die Saat in den Acker gestreut
Weh und Leid
Dies ist der Zeiten grosse Wende
zu Lehen: Ich bin nicht mein
Denn der Herr ist der Allerhöchste

e) Childrens Songs, Compositions and Arrangements

Arrangements in *Alles singt u. springt: Liedersammlung für die Primarschule*, Basel: Lehrmittelverlag des Kantons Basel-Stadt 1958:

15. Das Lied vom Monde: Wer hat die schönsten Schäfchen?, 3-voice arrangement
27. Vor em Yschlooffe: Kumm Heiland, 2-voice arrangements
29. All Morgen ist ganz frisch und neu, 2-voice arrangement
36. Weisst du, wieviel Sterne stehen?, 3-voice arrangement
37. Psalm 136: Lobt den Herrn, 2-voice arrangement
65. Wollt ihr wissen, 3-voice arrangement
66. Der Gänsedieb: Wer eine Gans gestohlen hat, 4-voice arrangement
85. Des Gesellen Abschied: Es, es, es, und es, 2-voice arrangement
90. Der Postillon: Herr Postillon, arrangement with piano
94. Bauernlied: Im Märzen die Bauer, 3-voice arrangement
99. Lied eines Schmiedes: Fein Rösslein, composition for voice and recorder
141. Frau Schwalbe, arrangement with piano
170. Hopfenpflückerlied: Jetzt fahrn wir übern See, 3-voice arrangement
188. Wettstreit zwischen Sommer und Winter: Heut ist ein freudenreicher Tag, arrangement with piano
196. Mailied: Der Winter ist vergangen, 2-voice arrangement
204. Der Sommer ist da!, 2-voice arrangement
205. Geh aus, mein Herz!, 2-voice arrangement
207. Der Blümlein Antwort: In meines Vaters Garten, arrangement with piano
261. Gelobet seist du, Jesu Christ!, 2-voice arrangement
263. Ein Kinderlied auf die Weihnachten: Vom Himmel hoch, 3-voice arrangement
264. Zu Bethlehem geboren, 2-voice arrangement
265. Vom Himmel kam der Engel Schar, 2-voice arrangement

281. Wach, Nachtigall, wach auf!, 2-voice arrangement
290. Der grimmig Tod, 2-voice arrangement

Kleine Biblische Balladen zum Singen und Sagen (Ursula Burkhard), Basel: Hug 1973, voice:
Gottes Bund
Der Turmbau zu Babel
Abraham und Sara
Isaaks Opferung
Jakobs Traum
Das Gleichnis vom reichen Kornbauern
Jesus heilt einen Gelähmten, einen Taubstummen, einen Blinden
Stillung des Sturmes
Palmsonntag
Jesus hilft Thomas

Mässliedli fir Basler Kinder (Ursula Burkhard), later in an edition published by Hug, voice:
My Luftballon, du liebi Zyt
I bi e Ma, wie fein isch das
Lueg, dä rassig Helikopter
I ha kei Gält
Es schärbelet und deent so scheen
I bi scho gross
Wär gluschtet so und stoht und schmeggt
E Mogge han i geschter gha
Wie still ischs uff em Petersplatz
Guet Nacht, du liebi Mäss

Sprechen, Lauschen, Singen, Basel: Hug 1965. A recorder method for children.

Individual Children's Songs:
Ach lieber Herre Jesu Christ, voice and 2 instruments
Am Ygang in d'Schwyz, Nur klei isch unser Stibli, 2 voices
An di Haimetlose: Ihr Mensche ohni Dach und Brot, voice
Blumenrain und Totetanz, voice and 2 instruments
's goht öpper dure Tannewald (Helen Widmer), voice
Monatslieder für die Basler Schule, voice
Nun will der Lenz uns grüssen, voice and 2 instruments
Prolog zu jedem Weihnachtsspiel, unisono choir and 2 recorders
Uf dr Pfalz, instrument and piano
Unser Minschter, voice and piano
Wenn s'Martisgleckli lytet (Anna Keller) voice and instrument
Wohl zwischen zwei hohen Bergen

II: French

2 early songs ca. 1928:
Sur la Naissance de Noster Seigneur (Guillaume Colletet): Qui vit jamais
  C sharp major, high woman's voice and piano
Sur la Mort de Nostre Seigneur (Mathurin Renier): Cepandant qu'a la Croix
  C minor, woman's high voice and piano

Images (Lily Hirsch), Sept Mélodies, voice and flute (recorder), 1968
1. La Bougie: Flamme de la bougie
2. Le Soleil: Le soleil sort de la brume
3. La fumée: Dans le ciel de satin
4. L'Alouette: J'ai vu l'alouette
5. La Pluie: La pluie grise
6. La cerise: Une cerise Quelle surprise!
7. Le Pigeon: Sur le mur trottine un pigeon

Inscriptions sur les facades du Grand Châlet à Rossinières, for one or two women's voices, 1944
1. Veuille, O Dieu
2. Tu as été, Seigneur
3. L'homme, conduit par ses caprices
4. Que la vertu, que la sagesse
5. Que l'homme connaît peu la mort
6. Or donc, Seigneur apprend nous à comprendre
7. Si tout notre destin se bornait à ce monde
8. Espoir si consolant
9. O Seigneur, loué sera
10. Ne croyer point, amis,
11. En tes servant soit ton oeuvre apparente

La Laterne Magique (Maurice Carême), voice with piano or 3 instruments, 1968–69
1. Les Cloches: Il est des cloches dans la lune
2. Les Canards: Quels bavards, Ces canards!
3. Bonté: Il faut plus d'une pomme
4. Formulette: Brume, vole, efface l'école
5. Le Petit Soldat: Donc, ce vaillant petit soldat
6. Ronde: Dans cette ronde
7. Le Cerisier: Un cerisier se mit à rire
8. Liberté: Prenez du soleil

Petite Cantate de Noël on five old noels, woman's voice and strings, with a reduction for voice and piano and separate parts for strings

Incidental music for weddings:
For the weddings of François and Wen Billeter-Tsui and Jean Jaques and Marie-Claire Guinand-Billeter:
  Miracle de l'amour (Camille Belguise), 3 voices
  Nous deux nous tenant par la main (Paul Eluard), voice

Ce minuit-là nous fûmes les enfants d'hier (Paul Eluard), 2 voices
D'une main composée pour moi (Paul Eluard), voice
Nous deux nous ne vivrons pour être fidèle (Paul Eluard), 3 voices
Je voudrais associer notre amour solitaire (Paul Eluard), voice
Miracle de l'amour (Camille Belguise), 3 voices

Fragments du "Chateau des pauvres" de Paul Eluard mis en musique par Ina Lohr pour François et Wen Billeter-Tsui:
Il ne nous en faut pas plus, voice, tenor recorder, harpsichord
Il ne faut pas de tout, 2 voices
Nous entendons la fleur de la vie, voice and alto recorder
Le long effort des hommes, voice and alto recorder

Arrangements:
Centrum voor de Protestantse Kerkzang: Uitgave No. 1a :
Psalm 75, 2: O Seigneur, loué sera (text Theodore de Bèze, melody Pierre Dagent, ca. 1561), 2-voice arrangement; manuscript versions with new settings for each strophe, 2, 3 and 4-voice arrangements
Psaume 86: Mon Dieu, prête moy l'oreille (text Clément Marot, melody Loys Bourgeois), 2-voice arrangement, French-Dutch
Psalm 141: O Seigneur, à toy je m'escrie (text Theodore de Bèze, melody Pierre Dagent, ca. 1561), 2-voice arrangement, French-Dutch

Centrum voor de Protestantse Kerkzang: Uitgave No. 1b:
Psaume 138: Il faut que de tous mes espritz (text Clément Marot, melody Loys Bourgeois, 2-part arrangement, French-Dutch
Psaume 150:Or soit loué l'Eternel (text Theodore de Bèze, melody Pierre Dagent, ca. 1561), 2-voice arrangement, French-Dutch
Psaume 136: Louez Dieu tout hautement (melody Pierre Dagent, ca. 1561), 2-voice arrangement, French-Dutch

Agnus Dei: Christ, Agneau de Dieu (print from unknown source), 3-voice arrangement
Ah! si le ciel se déchirait! (Melody 1628), 3-voice arrangement, 1974
Cantique de Siméon: Maintenant Seigneur, tu laisses ton serviteur, 1970
Dans les ombres de la nuit (text 17th cent.), 2 instruments and alto
Il a paru, le jour béni (Requeil de Strasbourg, 1525), 3-voice arrangement
Jésus Christ s'habille en pauvre, 3-voice arrangement, c.f. in soprano
La nuit: O jour, ton divin flambeau (melody 17th cent.), 4-voice arrangement
Louange et Prière Nr 122, Psautier 196: Tu vas donc au supplice (melody Heinrich Isaac, Innsbruck, ich muss dich lassen in tenor), 3-voice arrangement
Louange et Prière Nr. 124: L'Agneau de Dieu va de bon coeur (text Paul Gerhardt, melody Strasbourg, 1525), 3-voice arrangement
Noël nouveau est venu (Savoie P. Arma, 127), arrangement 2 high voices and organ, c.f. in alto
Nous sommes trois souverain princes de l'Orient, 3-voice arrangement, 1945
Pour un maudit péché, 2 high voices and organ, c.f. in melody
Psaume 22: L'Eternel est mon berger, (melody Loys Bourgeois), 2-voice arrangement
Psalm 23: L'Eternel est mon berger, 2-voice arrangement
Pseaume 26: Seigneur, garde mon droit (text Theodore de Beze, melody Geneva, 1551), 3-voice arrangement, 1972

Pseaume 130: Du fonds de ma pensé (text Clément Marot, melody Strasbourg 1539), 2-voice arrangement

Psalm 140: O Seigneur, à toi je m'écri. 4-voice arrangement

Psautier 182 and 185: Roi couvert de blessures (melody Hans Leo Hassler 1601?), 3-voice arrangement

Quittez pasteurs (melody 18th century), arrangement for high voice and instrument

Seigneur, entends nos plaintes (text G.K. Chesterton, trad. Flos. Du Pasquier), 3-voice arrangement, 1970

III: Dutch

Song collections:
Drei Liederen naar Gedichten van A. Roland Holst, violin and voice
1. Gouden stillen kusten
2. Soms heerscht in een duin kom
3. Zij voorspelden mijn lied

Four Dutch songs
1. O Morgenstond, uw blij gelaat (Guido Gazelle), voice and piano, 1924
2. Al eer het licht ten avond raakt, voice and piano, 1927
3. O liefste Jesu zoet, voice and piano, 1927
4. O God, hoe moest ik dankbaar wezen (Guido Gazelle), voice and piano, 1928

All were performed in Zandvoort 2 July 1928, Nr. 1 in Hilversum 2 July 1928, all in Amsterdam, 26 May 1929, Nr. 2 in Arnhem, June 1929

Nieuwspreuk I: Zoo de blâren (Guido Gazelle, Dutch and German), voice and piano/organ

Nieuwspreuk II: Ik wensche u een jaar (Guido Gazelle, Dutch and German), voice and piano/organ

Oude nederlandse Geestelijke liederen, arrangements for voice and organ, Amsterdam 1928:
1. O Jesu soet
2. Compt al uit zuijden en uit oosten
3. Jesu, ons liefd' ons wensen
4. Waertoe laet gij u vervoeren
5. Ick wil mi gaen vertroosten
6. Heft op mijn cruijz
7. O Jesu mijn alderliefste Heer

Een Morgenlied, tafelgebeden, Avondliederen voor 2 en 3 stemmen. Uitgave van het Centrum voor de protestantse Kerksang, Nr. 103, ca. 1960:
1. Morgenlied: De zonne alreede is opgestaan, (Guido Gazelle), 2 voices
2. Tafelgebeden: Psalm 136: Looft den Heer, want Hij is goed, 2-voice arrangement
3. Psalm 146: Alle oogen wachten op U, 3-voice arrangement
4. Ons Vader, Godt ghepresen, 2-voice and 3-voice arrangements
5. Avondlied I: Wanneer ik sterven, 3-voice arrangement
6. Avondlied II: Sterkt mij ook, en geeft mij krachten, 3-voice arrangement; solo voice and keyboard/two low instruments

Tafelgebeden, getoonzet door Ina Lohr, publication of the Vereeniging voor Protestantsche Kerkmuziek
Psalm 136: Looft den Heer, want Hij is goed (melody Maistre Pierre), 2-voice arrangements
Psalm 145, 15–16: Aller oogen wachten op U, 3 voices
Het Gebed des Heeren: Ons Vader, Godt ghepresen (melody before 1609), 2- and 3-voice arrangements
Psalm 16, 8–11: Ik stel mij den Heere, 2 voices
Psalm 24, Des Heeren is de aarde en hare volheid, voice
Nu zijt wellekome, 2 voices
Psalm 118, 24–25: Dit is de dag, voice, Basel 1949
Psalm 23: De Heer is mijn herder, voice
Psalm 46: God is ons eene toerlucht en sterkte, voice

melodische gesprekken met en zonder woorden, gespräche und meditationen zum singen und spielen, Vereniging voor huismuziek, muziekbijlage n. 87, 2- and 3-voice pieces for instruments and voices:
1. Dialoog – Dialog
2. Gesprek I – Gespräch I
3. Overpeinzing I – Meditation I (text Jacqueline van der Waals: Daar ligt op de weiden een zee van licht)
4. Gesprek II – Gespräch II
5. Overpeinzing II – Meditation II (text Aart van de Leeuw: Lente de blonde)

Andermans nood doet ons deugd, voice
Christus is opgestanden, 2-voice arrangement
Daar ligt op de weiden (Jacqueline van der Waals), voice
Des Heeren is de aarde, voice
Die mijns harten vrede zijt (text Jacqueline van der Waals; melody written on 3 April 1950 on the death of Ina Lohr's sister Sally)
Een rieten dok met wilde wingerd, voice
Een rode ballon staat vlak voor de zon, voice
Ere zij God, voice
Gezang 14: Nu zijt wellekome, voice and organ, and also 2-voice and 4-voice arrangements
Gezang 57 (NHK): Christus is opgestanden, 1949, in: Centrum voor de Protestantse Kerkzang, Uitgave 6, voice
Godlof! Looft God in zijn heilig domein, voice
Halleluja! Ik zal den Heere van ganscher harte, 2 voices
Halleluja, looft den Heer!, 2-voice arrangement
Het was een maged uitverkoren, 3-voice arrangement, in: *kerstmuziek 1972*, ed. by Renske Nieweg and Chris B. Maasland, Vereniging voor huismuziek, no. 1010
Hij is de koning (for Renske Nieweg, 19 January 1976), 2–3 voices
Hij zal de redder zijn der armen, voice
In den beginne was het woord (Jan Willem Schulte Nordholt), voice
In elke nacht van angst en nood (Jochen Klepper), voice, 1983
Luid klinkt het lied van 't engelkoor, (melody, Erfurter Gesangbuch 1524), 3-voice arrangement; Christmas card for the Stichting Centrum voor de Kerkzang, 1968
Psalm 8: Heer, onze Heer, hoe heerlijk en verheven, voice and 2 recorders
Psalm 23: De Heer is mijn herder, voice

Psalm 47: Alle gij volken, 2 voices (for Renske Nieweg), 1976

Psalm 116, 15: Kostbaar is in de oogen des Heeren, 2 voices, in: Centrum voor de Protestantse Kerkzang, Uitgave 6, voice

Psalm 116: Ik heb den Herre lief, voice; in: *Pro Regno Pro Sanctuario: een bundel studies en bijdragen van vrienden en vereerders bij de zestigste verjaardag van Prof. Dr. G. van der Leeuw*, ed. by Willem Jan Kooiman and Jan Mari van Veen, Nijkerk: G.F. Callenbach 1950, 318–20

Psalm 90, 1b, 2, 12 and 14: Here, Gij zijt ons geweest, in: Centrum voor de Protestantse Kerkzang, Uitgave Nr. 11, voice

Psalm 118, 24–29: Dit is de dag, voice

Psalm 122: Ik was verheugd, voice

Psalm 126: Ik heb den Heer lief, voice

Psalm 130: Uit de diepte, voice, 1947

Psalm 145: Genadig en barmhartig, voice

"Op, waakt op!" zo klinkt het luide, voice and 2 recorders

Van vrouden ons die kinderkens zingen, 3-voice arrangement, 1965; in: the supplement to *Huismuziek,* November 1967, no. 6

Vanwaar zijt gy gekomen (for Renske Nieweg?), 2-voice arrangement, 1968

Wij delen verdriet en zorgen (Jan Wit), voice, in: Nr. 109, Stichting Centrum voor de Protestantse Kerkzang: The Hague

Incidental music for weddings:

For the wedding of Calvin Seerveld and Ines Naudin ten Cate:

Hooglied 4: Gans en al zijt gij schoon mijn liefste, 1 and 2 voices

Bruiloft [wedding] Henk en Connie Waardenburg-Swaan:

Wij krijgen elkander lief (Guillaume v. d. Graft), voice

Bruiloft [wedding] Gustav Leonhardt-Marie Amsler:

Mes Dames et Messieurs, chers amis (Rainer Maria Rilke), voice, 2 instruments and violoncello

Holland, gij ligt maar niet als een klein eiland (text from Gedroomd Gebeuren (fragment), Henriette Roland Holst), voice and violin

followed by a selection of older pieces

Latin Songs:

4 Cantus per Tempore Passione, for voice and organ

a.) Omnes amici mei

b.) Parce Domine

c.) Vere, languores nostros

d.) Deus meus

Performed in Kompositionsabend der Klasse Rudolf Moser, 3. Juni 1930, Helene Sandreuter, Gesang, Gertrud Sutermeister, Orgel

English Songs:

In Calvin Seerfeld, *The Greatest Song: in Critique of Solomon*, The Hague: Sypko + Team, musical settings for the high points of the Song of Songs.

Instrumental Music:

Avondluiden in Davos, piano
De Klokken van Amsterdam, piano
De Klokken van Luzern (voor moeder), piano, 1928
Praeludium [same as De Klokken van Amsterdam] und Kanon, piano; 2 further movements lost, 1931
Thema mit Variationen für Klavier, 1928

Streichquartett a-moll 1929, parts only, score lost
Lento – Fuga/Allegro – Vivace – Allegro con brio

Suite für Violine und Bratsche (diploma composition), Basel 1930
Pavane/Andante poco adagio – Gaillarde/Allegro – Allemande/Moderato – Courante/Vivace
Performed by Esther Semisch and Karl Schwaller, Schlusskonzert Musik-Akademie Basel,
    25 June 1931

Intonationen zu den Melodien im Gesangbuch der evangelisch-reformierten Kirchen der deutschen Schweiz, ed. Fritz Morel, Heinrich Funk and Kurt Wolfgang Senn, Berne: Krompholz & Co. 1955.
Intonations for the following hymns:
GB 7, Psalm 31: Auf dich hab ich gehoffet, Herr
GB 25, Psalm 25: Ich erhebe mein Gemüte
GB 42: Nun lasst uns Gott, dem Herren
GB 46: Nun danket all und bringet Ehr
GB 48: Sollt ich meinem Gott nicht singen, 2 versions
GB 65: Herzlich lieb hab ich dich, o Herr
GB 71: Die helle Sonn leucht jetzt herfür
GB 75: Aus meines Herzens Grunde
GB 78: Lobet den Herren, alle, die ihn ehren
GB 93: Gott der Tage, Gott der Nächte
GB 114: Gelobet seist du, Jesu Christ, 2 versions
GB 131: Das alte Jahr vergangen ist, 2 versions

Music for Alphorn
3-part arrangements:
Nun will der Lenz uns grüssen
Ach lieber Herre Jesu Christ
Wohl zwischen zwei hohen Bergen
Wie lieblich ist der Maien

3 kleine Stücke für grosse Alphornbläser, 3 alphorns
1. Für mutige Tage
2. Für übermutige Tage
3. Für friedliche Abende

Reigen in Re, 2 soprano recorders and percussion

Bibliography

1. Primary Sources:

Archival Sources of Unpublished Documents:

Archive of the Schola Cantorum Basiliensis, Basel
    Minutes of the board of directors
    Minutes of the teachers' meetings
    Correspondence of the administration with teachers
Amsterdam City Archives, Amsterdam
    Archive of the Vereniging Muzieklyceum: documentation of the Muziek-Lyceum, Amsterdam
Lohr Archive, Leidschendam, in the hands of Elisabeth van Blankenstein
    Letters and documents concerning the Lohr family
    Memoirs of Judith Schmitz
Netherlands Institute for Art History, The Hague
    Photo Collection RKD: portraits of Albertus Resink and Johanna Christina de Klerk Resink
Netherlands Music Institute, The Hague
    Documents concerning Hubert Cuypers and Anthon van der Horst
Paul Sacher Foundation, Basel
    Estate of Ina Lohr
    Correspondence of Paul Sacher
Vera Oeri Bibliothek, Musik-Akademie Basel, Ina Lohr Collection
    Documents concerning Ina Lohr
    Compositions by Ina Lohr
    Notebooks made by Margrit Fiechter with material for her classes with Ina Lohr in Gregorian chant and Thorough Bass
Floris and Aleid Zuidema, Lochem
    Photographs and documents concerning the Lohr family

Private Correspondence:

Bengtsson, Ingmar
    Correspondence with Schola Cantorum Basiliensis and Ina Lohr
    Basel: Paul Sacher Foundation, Ina Lohr Collection
    Stockholm: Stiftelsen Musikkulturens Främjande, The Nydahl Collection, Ingmar Bengtsson Archive
Eglin, Arthur
    Correspondence with Ina Lohr: Arthur Eglin, Basel
Kraehenbuehl, David
    Correspondence from Gustav Leonhardt, Ina Lohr, and Paul Sacher
    New Haven CT, Yale University, Irving S. Gilmore Music Library, David Kraehenbuehl Papers

Meili, Max
    Correspondence with Paul Sacher
    Basel: Paul Sacher Foundation, Paul Sacher Collection
    Zurich: Zentralbibliothek, Estate of Max Meili
Nef, Walter
    Correspondence with Paul Sacher
    Basel: Paul Sacher Foundation, Paul Sacher Collection
    Correspondence with various people
    Basel: University Library, Estate Karl Nef, NL 212
Nieweg, Renske
    Correspondence with Ina Lohr: Rijk Mollevanger, Oud-Bijerland
Osselen, Erna van
    Correspondence from Ina Lohr: Floris and Aleid Zuidema, Lochem
Stoevesandt family
    Correspondence from Ina Lohr to the Stoevesandt family: Elisabeth Stoevesandt, Ba-
    sel
Reinhart, Werner
    Correspondence with Paul Sacher and the Schola Cantorum Basiliensis
    Basel: Paul Sacher Foundation, Paul Sacher Collection
    Winterthur: Winterthur Libraries, Study Library, Depot Music Collegium Winter-
    thur
Vellekoop, Kees
    Correspondence from Ina Lohr: Jos Knigge, Utrecht
Willin, Nils
    Correspondence to Bo Wallner
    Stockholm: Musikverket: Musik- och Teaterbiblioteket, Archive Bo Wallner

Interviews:

The notes and recordings made in the course of writing this book are in the possession of the author. The following individuals were interviewed, some of them numerous times:
Wulf Arlt, Anneke Bailes-van Royen, Anthony Bailes, André Baltensperger, Henk van Ben-them, Elisabeth van Blankenstein, Herbert Blomstedt, Anneke Boeke, Edith Büchi, Peter Bürgi, Jan Crafoord, Arthur Eglin, Tore Eketorp, Stefan Felber, Margrit Fiechter, Veronika Gutmann, Veronika Hampe, Barbara Hasspacher, Christina Hess, Iris Junker, Elisabeth Kiessling, Jos Knigge, Evelyne Laeuchli, Petra van Langen, Jos Leussink, Hans-Martin Linde, Reina Lohr, Marianne Lüthi, Esther Nef, Hans Adam Ritter, Willy Rordorf, Chris-tina Rufenacht, Christian Schmid, Christopher Schmidt, Urs Schweizer, Richard Sparks, Theophil Spoerri, Simone Staehelin-Handschin, Hans-Jürg Stefan, Martin and Esther Stern, Hinrich and Elisabeth Stoevesandt, Marie Sumpf-Refardt, Monica Vischer Richter, Wolfgang Vischer, Henk Waardenburg, Bettina Wehrli, Christin and Walter Wehrli, John Wellingham, Peter Welten, Floris and Aleid Zuidema.

Recordings:

"Musik für einen Gast: Ina Lohr" on 30 November 1965 on DRS1, Archive of Swiss Radio and Television.

Interview Ina Lohr with Jos Leussink, CD 1–3, 24–25 March 1983, Vera Oeri Bibliothek, Ina Lohr Collection. The excerpts used in this book were transcribed by Albert Jan Becking; the translations were made by the author.

Paul Sacher: Ein Filmportrait, a documentary film by Leo Nadelmann, Swiss Television, 3 October 1971.

Secondary Sources:

Ahrens, Heinrich, *Die deutsche Wandervogelbewegung von den Anfängen bis zum Weltkrieg,* Hamburg: Hansischer Gildenverlag 1939.

Alte Musik I: Praxis und Reflexion, ed. Peter Reidemeister and Veronika Gutmann, Winterthur: Amadeus 1983.

Alte Musik II: Konzert und Rezeption, ed. Veronika Gutmann, Wintherthur: Amadeus 1992.

Alte und Neue Musik [I]: Das Basler Kammerorchester (Kammerchor und Kammerorchester) unter Leitung von Paul Sacher 1926–1951, Zurich: Atlantis Verlag 1952.

Alte und Neue Musik II: Das Basler Kammerorchester (Kammerchor und Kammerorchester) unter Leitung von Paul Sacher 1926–1976, ed. Veronika Gutmann, Zurich: Atlantis Verlag 1977.

Altwegg, Leni, "Die spielende Weisheit: Zu Sprüche 8, 22–31", in: *Ich spielte vor Dir auf dem Erdenrund: Frauen-Gottesdienste – Anleitungen und Modelle,* ed. Leni Altwegg, Margrit Huber-Staffelbach, and Simone Staehelin-Handschin, Freiburg (Switzerland): Paulusverlag and Basel: Friedrich Reinhardt Verlag 1990, 10–11.

Arlt, Wulf, "Zur Idee und Geschichte eines 'Lehr- und Forschungsinstituts für Alte Musik'", in: *Alte und Neue Musik II, Das Basler Kammerorchester (Kammerchor und Kammerorchester) unter Leitung von Paul Sacher 1926–1976,* ed. Veronika Gutmann, Zurich: Atlantis Verlag 1977, 37–93.

Baum, Paul Adriaan, *Indische mensen in Holland,* modern edition Amsterdam: Em. Querido's Uitgeverij B.V. 1963.

Baum, Richard, "Kabeler Kammermusik November 1933", in: *Zeitschrift für Hausmusik* 2 (1933), 100–01.

Bayreuther, Rainer, "Die Situation der deutschen Kirchenmusik um 1933 zwischen Singbewegung und Musikwissenschaft", in: *Archiv für Musikwissenschaft* 67 (2010), 1–34.

Bergé, A. C. M., Theo van der Bijl, et al., *Hubert Cuypers 80 Jaar,* Amsterdam: Huldigingscomité Hubert Cuypers 1953.

Bergeron, Katherine, *Decadent Enchantments: The Revival of Gregorian Chant at Solesmes,* Berkeley and Los Angeles: University of California Press 1998 (California Studies of 19th Century Music 10).

Berckenhoff, Herman Leonard, "Gewijde muziek", in: *Kunstwerken en Kunstenaars (Muziek),* Amsterdam: Maatschappij voor goede en goedkoope lectuur 1915, 66–72.

Berry, Mary, "The restoration of the chant and seventy-five years of recording", in: *Early Music* 7 (1979), 197–217.

Beukers, Th. M., *Korte en praktische Handleiding bij het instudeeren van den gregoriaanschen zang*, Haarlem: St. Jacobs-Godshuis 1914.

Biezen, Jan van, "The Rhythm of Gregorian Chant", http://www.janvanbiezen.nl./gregorian. html (4 September 2018).

Blankenstein, Elisabeth van, *Nieuwjaarsbrief Lohr, januari 2012*, Leidschendam [2012].

Bluher, Hans, *Wandervogel: Geschichte einer Jugundbewegung*, Vol. 1, Charlottenburg: Kampmann und Schnabel 1919[4].

Boeke, Jan, "Cursus Ina Lohr (5–9 Juli 1948)", in: *Kerk en Muziek* 1 (1948–49), 63.

Boeke, Jan, "De werkwijze van mej. Lohr acht ik de injectie waar de protestantsche kerk-muziek in Holland op wachtte...", in: *40 jaar protestantse kerkmuziek. Gedenkboekje ter gelegenheid van het 25-jarig bestaan van het Centrum voor de Kerkzang*, [Maasland]: Stichting Centrum voor de Kerkzang 1975, 8–12.

Brändli, Hans, *Ein Gesangbuch für Alle: kritische Betrachtungen und Vorschläge zum Probe-band für ein Gesangbuch der evangelisch-reformierten Kirchen der deutschen Schweiz*, Berne: Haupt 1942 (Religiöse Gegenwartsfragen, Heft 7/8).

Broman, Per F., "New Music of Sweden", in: *New Music of the Nordic Countries*, ed. John D. White, Hillsdale NY: Pendragon Press 2002, Part V, 445–580.

Burkhart, Charles, "Remembering David Kraehenbuehl," in: *Journal of Music Theory* 41 (1997), 183–92.

Brunner, Lance W., "The performance of plainchant: Some preliminary observations of the new era", in: *Early Music* 10 (1982), 316–28.

Bürki, Bruno and Martin Klöckner, eds., *Liturgie in Bewegung/Liturgie en mouvement*, Frei-burg (Switzerland): Universitätsverlag 2000.

Burght, Henri van der, "De Gregoriaanse kwestie", in: *Gemeenschap* 11 (1935), 536–51.

Butting, Max, "Die Musik und die Menschen", in: *Melos* 6 (1927), 58–63.

Cardine, Eugène, *Semiologia gregoriana. Note raccolte dalle lezioni*, Rome: Pontificio istituto di musica sacra 1968.

Carroll, Joseph Robert, *The Technique of Gregorian Chironomy*, Toledo: Gregorian Institute of America [1955].

Christ-von Wedel, Christine, "Basel und die Versprachlichung der Musik", in: *Basel als Zen-trum des geistigen Austauschs in der frühen Reformzeit*, ed. Christine Christ-von Wedel, Sven Grosse and Berndt Hamm, Tübingen: Mohr Siebeck 2014 (Spätmittelalter, Hu-manismus, Reformation 84), 127–34.

Christensen, Jesper Bøje, *Die Grundlagen des Generalbassspiels im 18. Jahrhundert: Ein Lehr-buch nach zeitgenössischen Quellen*, Kassel and Basel: Bärenreiter 1992.

Clough, Daniel, "Dom Guéranger's Influence on the Liturgy of the 20th Century; Especially Regarding Gregorian Chant", in: *Living Tradition: Organ of the Roman Theological Forum*, http://www.rtforum.org/lt/lt147.html (4 September 2018).

Combe, Pierre, *The restoration of Gregorian chant: Solesmes and the Vatican edition*, Washing-ton D.C.: Catholic University of America Press 2003.

Copalle, Siegfried and Heinrich Ahrens, *Chronik der Freien Deutschen Jugendbewegung*, Vol. 1, Bad Godesberg: Voggenreiter Verlag 1954.

Cuypers, Hubert, "Nieuw licht in het Gregoriaansche vraagstuk", in: *Caecilia: Maandblad voor Muziek en het Muziekcollege* 18 (1931), 52–57, 78–84, 100–10.

Eckart-Bäcker, Ursula, *Die Schütz-Bewegung: zur musikgeschichtlichen Bedeutung des "Hein-rich-Schütz-Kreises" unter Wilhelm Kamlah*, Vaduz: Prisca 1987.

Eckhart-Bäcker, Ursula, "Musikalische Erwachsenenbildung und Jugendmusikbewegung – Aspekte der Erneuerung in den 1920er Jahren", in: *Die Jugendmusikbewegung: Impulse und Wirkungen*, ed. Karl-Heinz Reinfandt, Wolfenbüttel: Möseler 1987, 185–96.

Ehrenforth, Karl Heinrich, "Musik will leben und gelebt werden: Anmerkungen zur Musikanschauung Fritz Jödes", in: *Die Jugendmusikbewegung: Impulse und Wirkungen*, ed. Karl-Heinz Reinfandt, Wolfenbüttel: Möseler 1987, 12–21.

Ehrhorn, Manfred, "Das chorische Singen in der Jugendmusikbewegung: Erneuerungsbestrebungen nach 1900", in: *Die Jugendmusikbewegung: Impulse und Wirkungen*, ed. Karl-Heinz Reinfandt, Wolfenbüttel: Archiv der Jugendmusikbewegung e.V. 1987, 37–55.

Eikelboom, Arie and van der Knijff, Jaco, "De vrouw van de kerktoonsoorten", 31 March 2008, http://www.refdag.nl/muziek/de_vrouw_van_de_kerktoonsoorten_1_252438 (9 May 2018).

Ellis, Katherine, *Interpreting the Musical Past: Early Music in Nineteenth-Century France*, Oxford: Oxford University Press 2005.

Eppinger, Heino, "Der Finkensteiner Bund und seine Zeitschrift", in: *Die Singgemeinde* 1 (1924), 1–2.

Erni, Jürg, *Paul Sacher, Musiker und Mäzen: Aufzeichnungen und Notizen zu Leben und Werk*, Basel: Schwabe 1999.

Felber, Stefan, *Wilhelm Vischer als Ausleger der Heiligen Schrift: Eine Untersuchung zum Christuszeugnis des Alten Testaments*, Göttingen: Vandenhoeck & Ruprecht 1999.

Fields, K.R. and L.S. Neinstein, "Uterine Myomas in Adolescents: Case Reports and a Review of the Literature", in: *Journal of Pedatric Adolescent Gynocology* 9 (1966), 195–98.

Frei, Hans A., "Ernst Gaugler (1891–1963): Charismatischer Diener des Wortes", in: *Theologische Profile: Schweizer Theologen und Theologinnen im 19. und 20. Jahrhundert*, ed. Bruno Bürki and Stephan Leimgruber, Freiburg (Switzerland): Universitätsverlag 1998, 133–45.

Fueter, Karl, *Vom Probeband zum Neuen Gesangbuch: das Urteil des deutschschweizerischen reformierten Kirchenvolkes und seiner Behörden über den Probeband als Vorstufe zum neuen Gesangbuch auf Grund der offiziellen, dem Vorstand des Schweizerischen Evangelischen Kirchenbundes eingereichten Akten*, [s.n., s.l.] 1944.

Funck, Eike, "Alte Musik und Jugendmusikbewegung", in: *Die Jugendmusikbewegung: Impulse und Wirkungen*, ed. Karl-Heinz Reinfandt, Wolfenbüttel: Archiv der Jugendmusikbewegung e.V. 1987, 63–91.

Funk-Hennigs, Erica, "Über die instrumentale Praxis der Jugendmusikbewegung – Voraussetzungen und Auswirkungen", in: *Die Jugendmusikbewegung: Impulse und Wirkungen*, ed. Karl-Heinz Reinfandt, Wolfenbüttel: Archiv der Jugendmusikbewegung e.V. 1987, 221–34.

Gajard, Joseph, *The rhythm of plainsong according to the Solesmes school*, New York, N.Y.: J. Fischer & Bro. [1945].

Garside, Jr., Charles, "The Origins of Calvin's Theology of Music: 1536–1543", in: *Transactions of the American Philosophical Society* 69 (1979), 1–36.

Gastoué, Amédée, *L'Art grégorien*, Paris: F. Alcan 1920.

Gastoué, Amédée, Review of Jules Jeannin, *Études sur le rythme grégorien*, Lyons 1926, in: *Revue de musicologie* 7 (1926), 218–20.

Geering, Arnold, "Schola Cantorum Basiliensis", in: *Mitteilungen der Schweizerischen Musikforschenden Gesellschaft* 1 (1934–36), 16–17.

Geering, Arnold, "Kurze Wegleitung zur Aufführung der Lieder Ludwig Senfls", in: *Volkslied und Hausmusik* 5 (1938), 182–86.

Geering, Arnold, "Musikwissenschaft in Basel", in: *Schweizerische Musikzeitung* 77 (1937), 299–303.

Geering, Arnold, "Volkslied und Kunstlied im 16. Jahrhundert in der Schweiz", in: *Volkslied und Hausmusik* 2 (1935), 19–23, 35–39.

Gerber, Walther, *Zur Entstehungsgeschichte der deutschen Wandervogelbewegung: Ein kritischer Beitrag*, Bielefeld: Deutscher Heimat-Verlag Gieseking 1957.

Görner, Rüdiger, "'… und Musik überstieg uns …': Zu Rilkes Deutung der Musik", in: *Blätter der Rilke-Gesellschaft* 10 (1983), 50–68.

Grosch, Nils, "Neue Sachlichkeit", in: *Die Musik in Geschichte und Gegenwart*, 2nd ed., Sachteil 7 (1997), col. 122–29.

Gutknecht, Dieter, *Studien zur Geschichte der Aufführungspraxis Alter Musik: ein Überblick vom Beginn des 19. Jahrhunderts bis zum Zweiten Weltkrieg*, Cologne: Concerto-Verlag 1993.

Haas, Robert, *Aufführungspraxis der Musik*, Wildpark-Potsdam: Akademische Verlagsgesellschaft Athenaion 1931.

Haberl, Franz Xaver, *Magister Choralis: theoretisch-praktische Anweisung zum Verständniss und Vortrag des authentischen, röm. Choralgesanges*, Regensburg: Friedrich Pustet 1866.

Haffter, E., "Kirchenchor und Singbewegung", in: *Volkslied und Hausmusik* 1 (1934), 103–106.

Hagmann, Elsbeth, "Die Finkensteiner Schule", in: *Volkslied und Hausmusik* 4 (1937), 166–68.

Halm, August, *Von zwei Kulturen der Musik*, Munich: Müller 1913.

Handschin, Jacques, "Die mittelalterlichen Aufführungen in Zürich, Bern und Basel", in: *Zeitschrift für Musikwissenschaft* 10 (1927–28), 8–22.

Handschin, Jacques, *Musikgeschichte im Überblick*, Lucerne: Räber 1948.

Handschin, Jacques, "Die historische Stellung von Gesang und Orgelspiel im Gottesdienst", in: *Gedenkschrift Jacques Handschin: Aufsätze und Bibliographie*, Berne: Haupt 1957, 161–65.

Handschin, Jacques, "Die alte Musik als Gegenwartsproblem", in: *Gedenkschrift Jacques Handschin: Aufsätze und Bibliographie*, Berne: Haupt 1957, 338–41.

Handschin, Jacques, "Die Musik in der deutschen Jugendbewegung", in: *Gedenkschrift Jacques Handschin: Aufsätze und Bibliographie*, Berne: Haupt 1957, 348–54.

Hanslick, Eduard, *Vom musikalisch-Schönen: ein Beitrag zur Revision der Aesthetik der Tonkunst*, Leipzig: Rudolf Wiegel 1854.

Hasper, Hendrik, *Verweerschrift tegen de aanvallen op "Het boek der psalmen": de psalmen van Israël op de oorspronkelijke melodieën uit de zestiende eeuw opnieuw naar het Hebreeuwsch bewerkt*, The Hague: Geestelijke liederen uit den schat van de Kerk der eeuwen 1937.

Haskell, Harry, *The Early Music Revival: A History*, Mineola, NY: Dover 1996[2].

Hedlund, Oscar, *Körkarlen Eric Ericson*, Höganäs: Förlags AB Wiken 1988.

Hendry, George S., "Barth for Beginners", in: *Theology Today* 19 (1962), 267–71.

Hensel, Walther, *Im Zeichen des Volkliedes*, Kassel: Bärenreiter-Verlag 1936[2].

Hensel, Walther, *Finkensteiner Liederbuch*, Kassel: Bärenreiter-Verlag, Vol. 1–10, 1923–1932/3.

Herresthal, Harald, "Das nationale Kirchenlied. Von Kantaten zu 'leichten Liedern'", in: *Musikgeschichte Nordeuropas: Dänemark, Finnland, Island, Norwegen, Schweden*, ed. Greger Andersson, translated by Axel Bruch, Christine von Bülow and Gerlind Lübbers, Stuttgart/Weimar: Verlag J.B. Metzler 2001, 63–85.

Hilber, Johann Baptist, "Singbewegung und Kirche", in: *Volkslied und Hausmusik* 1 (1934), 71–73.

Hiley, David, *Western Plainchant: A Handbook*, Oxford: Clarendon Press 1993.

Hill, Robert, "'Die Überwindung der Romantik' und die Rationalisierung der musikalischen Zeit in der Aufführungspraxis des 20. Jahrhunderts", in: *Alte Musik im 20. Jahrhundert. Wandlungen und Formen ihrer Rezeption*, ed. Giselher Schubert, Mainz, etc.: Schott 1995, 156–63.

Höckner, Hilmar, *Die Musik in der deutschen Jugendbewegung. Entwicklungsgeschichtlich dargestellt*, Wolfenbüttel: Georg Kallmeyer Verlag 1927.

Honders, A.C., "Een vrouw achter het liedboek", in: *Mededelingen van het Instituut voor Liturgieweteschaap van de Rijkuniversiteit te Groningen* 15 (1981), 21–28.

Hoondert, Martin J.M., "The Appropriation of Gregorian Chant in the Netherlands, 1903–1930", in: *Christian Feast and Festival: The Dynamics of Western Liturgy and Culture*, ed. P. Post, G. Rouwhorst, L. van Tongeren, and A. Scheer, Leuven: Peeters 2001, 645–76.

Horst, Anton van der, and Gerardus van der Leeuw, *Bach's Hoogmis*, Amsterdam: Holland 1941.

Horst, Anton van der, "Fragen der Chorerziehung", in: *Musik und Gottesdienst* 7 (1953), 1–10.

Jans, Hans Jörg, "Paul Sacher und der Werdegang der Paul Sacher Stiftung," in: *Paul Sacher – Facetten einer Musikerpersönlichkeit*, ed. Ulrich Mosch, Mainz: Schott 2006 (Veröffentlichungen der Paul Sacher Stiftung 11), 203–36.

Jeffery, Peter, review of Katherine Bergeron, *Decadent Enchantments: The Revival of Gregorian Chant at Solesmes*, Berkeley 1998, in: *Early Music* 27 (1999), 483–85.

Jenny, Markus, "Die Lieder Zwinglis", in: *Jahrbuch für Liturgie und Hymnologie* 14 (1969), 63–102.

Jenny, Markus, "Zur Pausenfrage in den Hugenottenpsalmen", in: *Musik und Gottesdienst* 7 (1953), 164–69.

Jöde, Fritz, "Hausmusik zwischen gestern und morgen", in: *Zeitschrift für Hausmusik* 3 (1934) 13–22.

Jöde, Fritz, *Musikalische Jugendkultur: Anregungen aus der Jugendbewegung*, Hamburg: Freideutscher Jugendverlag Adolf Saal 1918.

Juda, Jo, *De zon stond nog laag*, Nieuwkoop: Uitgeverij Heuff 1975.

Juda, Jo, *Voor de duisternis viel*, Nieuwkoop: Uitgeverij Heuff 1978.

Kater, Michael, *The Twisted Muse: Musicians and their Music in the Third Reich*, New York: Oxford University Press 1997.

Kaubisch, Martin, *Rainer Maria Rilke: Mystik und Künstlertum*, Dresden: Wolfgang Jess Verlag 1936.

Kaufmann, Walter, "Nietzsche and Rilke", in: *The Kenyon Review* 17 (1955), 1–22.

Kelly, Thomas Forrest, ed., *Plainsong in the Age of Polyphony*, Cambridge: Cambridge University Press 2009.

Kirnbauer, Martin, "'Tout le monde connaît la Schola' – Eine Spurensuche zur Vorgeschichte der Schola Cantorum Basiliensis", in: *Basler Jahrbuch für Historische Musikpraxis* 32 (2008), 145–57.

Kirnbauer, Martin, "Paul Sacher und die alte Musik", in: *Paul Sacher – Facetten einer Musikerpersönlichkeit*, ed. Ulrich Mosch, Mainz: Schott 2006 (Veröffentlichungen der Paul Sacher Stiftung 11), 25–56.

Kirnbauer, Martin, "'Aufs eindrücklichste für das Cembalo werben' – Wanda Landowska in Basel", in: *Notenlese: Musikalische Aufführungspraxis des 19. und frühen 20. Jahrhunderts in Basel*, ed. Martina Wohlthat, Basel: Schwabe Verlag 2013, 87–107.

Klatt, Fritz, *Rainer Maria Rilke: Sein Auftrag in heutiger Zeit*, Berlin: Schneider 1936.

Klis, Jolande van der, *Oude muziek in Nederland: Het verhaal van de pioniers 1900–1975*, Utrecht: Stichting Organisatie Oude Muziek 1991.

Koorneef, Arie, "Centrum voor de Kerkzang", in: *Huismuziek* 2 (1976), 11–14.

Kovach, Thomas, "'Du Sprache wo Sprachen enden': Rilke's Poem 'An die Musik'", in: *Seminar* 22 (1986), 206–17.

Krenek, Ernst, *Music Here and Now*, trans. Barthold Fles, New York: Russell & Russell 1939.

Kross, Siegfried, "Die Tagung 'Alte Musik in unserer Zeit' in Kassel", in: *Die Musikforschung* 21 (1968), 217–20.

Kurth, Ernst, *Grundlagen des linearen Kontrapunkts: Einführung in Stil und Technik von Bachs Melodischer Polyphonie*, Berne: Akademische Buchhandlung von Max Drechsel 1917.

Langen, Petra van, *Muziek en religie: Katholieke musici en de confessionalisering van het Nederlandse muziekleven 1850–1948*, Hilversum: Verloren 2014.

Lans, Michael Johann Anton, *Handboekje ten gebruike bij het onderwijs in den gregoriaanschen zang*, Leiden: van Leeuwen 1874.

Leeuw, Gerardus van der, *Bachs Matthaeus- en Johannespassion: met de complete teksten en hun vertaling*, Nijmegen: Sun 2000.

Leeuw, Gerardus van der, *Sacred and Profane Beauty: The Holy in Art*, Reprint of 1963 edition, New York: AAR and Oxford University Press 2006.

Linden, Bob van der, *Music and Empire in Britain and India: Identity, Internationalism, and Cross-Cultural Communication*, New York: Palgrave Macmillan 2013.

Löw, Hans W., "Die singende Gemeinde", in: *Volkslied und Hausmusik* 7 (1941), 6–10 and 19–23.

Louw, André van der, *Rood als je Hart: 'n Geschiedenis van de AJC*, Amsterdam: De Arbeiderspers 1974.

Lundberg, Mattias, *Sven-Erik Bäck*, Swedish Royal Academy of Music: Möklinta: Gidlund 2019.

Luther, Martin, *Luthers Geistliche Lieder und Kirchengesänge*, ed. Markus Jenny, Archiv zur Weimarer Ausgabe, Bd. 4, Cologne/Vienna: Böhlau 1985.

Marez Oyens, Gerrit de, "Solmisatie en Kerktoonsoorten in het onderwijs", in: *De pyramide: Orgaan van de Gehrels-Vereniging* (1949–50), 1–10.

Marti, Andreas, "Gesangbücher in der reformierten Deutschschweiz: Ein Überblick mit Auswahlbibliographie", in: *Ökumenischer Liederkommentar zum Katholischen, Reformierten und Christkatholischen Gesangbuch der Schweiz*, ed. by Peter Ernst Bernoulli, Freiburg: Paulus Verlag and Zurich: Theologischer Verlag 2001–2009, 6th part, unpaginated.

Marti, Heiri, "Die Singbewegung in der Schweiz", in: *Volkslied und Hausmusik* 1 (1934), 4–7.

Marti, Heiri, "Können wir noch singen?", in: *Volkslied und Hausmusik* 1 (1934), 14–15.

Maulpoix, Jean-Michel, *Kommentar zu Briefe an einen jungen Dichter von Rainer Maria Rilke*, Leipzig: Leipziger Literatur Verlag 2010.

Mersmann, Hans, "Alte Musik in der instrumentalen Musikerziehung", in: *Melos* 6 (1927), 322–27.

Mocquereau, André, *Le nombre musical grégorien ou rythmique grégorienne*, Rome/Tournai: Desclée 1908.

Mosch, Ulrich, "Paul Sacher und die Schallplatte", in: *Paul Sacher – Facetten einer Musiker-persönlichkeit*, ed. Ulrich Mosch, Mainz: Schott 2006 (Veröffentlichungen der Paul Sacher Stiftung 11), 94–99.

Müller-Blattau, Joseph Maria, "Die Beziehungen zwischen Kunstmusik und Volksmusik in Geschichte und Gegenwart", in: *Die Singgemeinde* 4 (1937), 33–39, 72–76, 103–09.

Murray, Gregory, *Gregorian rhythm: a pilgrim's progress*, Exeter [England]: Printed at the Catholic records Press [1930s].

Murray, Gregory, *The authentic rhythm of Gregorian chant*, Bath: Downside Abbey 1959.

Murray, Gregory, *Gregorian chant: according to the manuscripts*, London: L.J. Cary 1963.

Nef, Walter, "Wilhelm Merian zum Gedächtnis", in: *Die Musikforschung* 6 (1953), 143–44.

Nievergelt, Edwin, "Von der Arbeit am neuen deutschschweizerischen Gesangbuch", in: *Musik und Gottesdienst* 2 (1948), 49–54.

Neumann, Klemens, *Der Spielmann: Liederbuch für Jugend und Volk*, Mainz: Matthias-Grünewald-Verlag, 21st edition, [n.d.].

Nieuwenhuys, Rob, "Tempoe Deloe" in: *Tussen Twee Vaderlanden*, Amsterdam: G.A. van Oorschot Uitgever 1967².

Nievergelt, Edwin, "Zur Gesangsbuch Arbeit", in: *Musik und Gottesdienst* 2 (1948), 117–18.

Obert, Simon, "Der Direktor – zunächst aber Student und Anwärter: Paul Sacher und die Musik-Akademie der Stadt Basel", in: *Tonkunst macht Schule: 150 Jahre Musik-Akademie Basel 1867–2017*, ed. Martina Wohlthat, Basel: Schwabe Verlag 2017, 191–200.

Oost, Gert, *Anthon van der Horst 1899–1965: Leven en werken*, Alphen aan den Rijn: Canaletto 1992.

Otterstedt, Annette, "August Wenzinger", in: *Die Musik in Geschichte und Gegenwart*, 2nd edition, Personenteil 17 (2007), col. 772–73.

Oussoren, Hendrik Leendert, "Het Nederlandse muziekleven in het verleden", in: *Wending* 3 (1948), 559–64, 622–29.

Oussoren, Hendrik Leendert, "Het kerkkoor in de praktijk (I)", in: *Kerk en Muziek* 2 (1950), 81–86.

Oussoren, Hendrik Leendert, "Het kerkkoor in de praktijk (II)", in: *Kerk en Muziek* 2 (1950), 97–101.

Paap, Woulter, "Opkomst van de 'huismuziek'", in: *Huismuziek* 3 (1976), 19–22.

Paap, Woulter, *Huismuziek en Leekenmuziek: Muziek in Gezin en Vereeniging*, Bussum: "Ons Leekenspel" 1941 (De gulden regel, Nr. 11).

Pasler, Jann, review of Katherine Bergeron, *Decadent Enchantments: The Revival of Gregorian Chant at Solesmes*, Berkeley 1998, in: *Journal of the American Musicological Society* 52 (1999), 370–83.

Peterson, Hans-Gunnar and Tallmo, Karl-Erik, "Eric Ericson – 50 years with the Chamber Choir", http://www.art-bin.com/art/aericsone.html (15 July 2018).

Pfisterer, Immanuel, "Zur Frage der Begleitung einstimmig gesungener Choräle", in: *Volkslied und Hausmusik* 4 (1937), 8–11, 19–22.

Pothier, Joseph, *Les Mélodies Grégoriennes d'après la tradition*, Tournay: Impr. liturgique de Saint Jean L'évangéliste, Desclée Lefebvre 1880.

Potter, Pamela M., *Most German of the Arts: Musicology and Society from the Weimar Republic to the End of Hitler's Reich*, New Haven, CT: Yale University Press 1998.

Reidemeister, Peter, "Weite Felder für Schatzsucher und Pioniere – Paul Sacher und die Korrespondenzen zwischen neuer und alter Musik", in: *"Entre Denges et Denezy": Dokumente zur Schweizer Musikgeschichte 1900–2000*, ed. Ulrich Mosch with Matthias Kassel, Mainz: Schott 2001, 44–55.

Reimann, Hans, "Die Einführung des neuen Kirchengesangbuches: Ein Wort an die Pfarrer", in: *Musik und Gottesdienst* 7 (1953), 33–37.

Reinfandt, Karl-Heinz, "Fritz Jöde", in: *Die Musik in Geschichte und Gegenwart*, 2nd edition, Personenteil 9 (2002), col. 1074–76.

Richter, Christoph and Karl Michael Komma, "Walther Hensel", in: *Die Musik in Geschichte und Gegenwart*, 2nd ed., Personenteil 8 (2002), col. 1316–17.

Rifkin, Joshua, "Whatever Happened to Heinrich Schütz?", in: *Opus* 1 (1985) 10–14, 49.

Rilke, Rainer Maria, *Briefe aus Muzot: 1921 bis 1926 / Rainer Maria Rilke*, ed. by Ruth Sieber-Rilke and Carl Sieber, Leipzig: Insel-Verlag 1935.

Roberge, Pierre-F., "L'Anthologie sonore", http://www.medieval.org/emfaq/cds/ans99999. htm (13 May 2018).

Rosenstiel, Léonie, *Nadia Boulanger: A Life in Music*, New York: W.W. Norton & Company 1982.

Rössel, Willy, "Etwas von den Abc-Schützen und den Do-re-mi-Solisten", in: *Schweizerische Musikzeitung* 74 (1934), 599–601.

Rostroprovitch, Mstislav, ed., *Dank an Paul Sacher*, Zurich: Atlantis Verlag 1976.

Rothfarb, Lee A., *August Halm: A Critical and Creative Life in Music*, Rochester: University of Rochester Press 2009.

Rothfarb, Lee A., *Ernst Kurth as Theorist and Analyst*, Philadelphia: University of Pennsylvania Press 1988.

Röthlin, Niklaus, "Geschichte des Hauses 'Auf Burg'", in: *Paul Sacher Stiftung*, Basel: Paul Sacher Foundation 1986, 10–12.

Rubinoff, Kailan, "Authenticity as a Political Act: Straub-Huillet's Chronicle of Anna Magdalena Bach and the Post-War Bach Revival", in: *Music and Politics* 5, no. 1 (winter 2011). [http://dx.doi.org/10.3998/mp.9460447.0005.103].

Rutters, Herman, *Het Calvinistisch kerklied*, Delft: Sijthoff [n.d.].

Rutters, Herman, *J. S. Bach en onze tijd*, Amsterdam: Ploegsma 1941.

Sacher, Paul, "Musik und Schule", in: *Orchester Junger Basler*, Basel: Haupt 1927, 3–6.

Sacher, Paul, "Zur Frage der Verwendbarkeit liturgischer Musik im Konzert: Rundfrage durchgeführt von Paul Sacher", in: *Schweizerische Musikzeitung* 73 (1933), 11–15 and 51–55.

Sacher, Paul, "Ein Basler in Zürich", in: *Vierzig Jahre Collegium Musicum Zürich*, Zurich: Atlantis Verlag 1982, 11–14.

Saulnier, Daniel, *Gregorian Chant: a Guide to the History and Liturgy*, Brewster, MA: Paraclete Press 2009.

Scalliet, Marie-Odette and Koos van Brakel, David van Duuren, Jeanette ten Kate, *Pictures from the Tropics: Paintings by Western Artist during the Dutch Colonial Period in Indonesia*, Amsterdam: Koninklijk Instituut voor de Tropen 1999.

Schaal, Richard, "Jugendmusik", in: *Die Musik in Geschichte und Gegenwart*, ed. Friedrich Blume, 7 (1958), col. 286–306.

Schaik, Martin van, "In Memoriam Kees Vellekoop (1940–2002)", in: *Tijdschrift van de Koninklijke Vereniging voor Nederlandse Muziekgeschiedenis* 52 (2002), 115–17.

Schering, Arnold, *Aufführungspraxis alter Musik*, Leipzig: Quelle & Meyer 1931.

Schering, Arnold, *Musikalische Bildung und Erziehung zum musikalischen Hören*, Leipzig: Quelle & Meyer 1911.

Schmidt, Christopher, "Erinnerungen an Ina Lohr", in: *Basler Jahrbuch für Historische Musikpraxis* 32 (2008), 159–63.

Schoch, Max, "Dem Echten verpflichtet", in: *Quatember* 1987, 234–35.

Schoch, Max, "Karl Barth (1886–1968): Dialektische Theologie", in: *Gegen die Gottvergessenheit: Schweizer Theologen im 19. und 20. Jahrhundert*, ed. Stephan Leimgruber and Max Schoch, Basel: Herder 1990, 288–311.

Schoch, Max, "Eduard Thurneysen (1888–1974): Theologie der Seelsorge", in: *Gegen die Gottvergessenheit: Schweizer Theologen im 19. und 20. Jahrhundert*, ed. Stephan Leimgruber and Max Schoch, Basel: Herder 1990, 331–43.

Scholz, Wilhelm, and Waltraut Jonas-Corrieri, ed., *Die deutsche Jugendmusikbewegung in Dokumenten ihrer Zeit von den Anfängen bis 1933*, Wolfenbüttel and Zurich: Möseler 1980.

Schoute, Rutger, *De Nederlandse Bachvereniging 50 jaar*, [s.l.]: De Nederlandse Bachvereniging 1971.

Schoute, Rutger, *Het Muzieklyceum 1921–1976: een terugblik*, Hilversum: [s.n.] 1976.

Schwethelm, Hermann P., "M.J.A. Lans, ein Vorkämpfer des katholischen Kirchengesanges in den Niederlanden", in: *Fliegende Blätter für kath. Kirchenmusik* 43 (1908), 43–45.

Seerveld, Calvin, *The Greatest Song in Critique of Solomon*, Palos Heights, IL: Trinity Pennyasheet Press 1967.

Smith, Anne, "The Development of the Jugendmusikbewegung, its Musical Aesthetic and its Influence on the Performance Practice of Early Music", in: *Basler Beiträge zur Historischen Musikpraxis* 39 (2019), 471–514.

Smith, Anne, *The Performance of 16ᵗʰ-century Music: Learning from the Theorists*, New York: Oxford University Press 2011.

Smith, Anne and Jed Wentz, "Gustav Maria Leonhardt in Basel: Portrait of a Young Harpsichordist", in: *Basler Jahrbuch für Historische Musikpraxis* 34 (2010), 229–44.

Stählin, Wilhelm, "Die Bedeutung der Singbewegung für den evangelischen Kirchengesang", in: *Die deutsche Jugendmusikbewegung in Dokumenten ihrer Zeit von den Anfängen bis 1933*, ed. Wilhelm Scholz and Waltraut Jonas-Corrieri, Wolfenbüttel and Zurich: Möseler 1980, 836–40.

Stalder, Kurt, Eulogy of 23 January 1963 in: *Ernst Gaugler 1891–1963: Drei Predigten von Prof. Dr. Ernst Gaugler*, Allschwil/Basel: Christkatholischer Schriftenverlag 1964, 10–17.

Stefan, Hans-Jürg, "Markus Jenny: 1. Juni 1924 bis 22. Januar 2001", in: *Zwingliana* 28 (2001), 185–86.

Stefan, Hans-Jürg, "Der Genfer Psalter als Ausdruck von Calvins Spiritualität", in: *Musik & Liturgie* 134 (2009), 8–14.

Stenbäck, Helena, *Svensk körpedagogik i ett kammarmusikaliskt perspektiv*, MA thesis, Centrum för musikpedagogisk forskning, MPC, Musikhögskolan i Stockholm / Stockholms Universitet 1992.

Stephenson, Lesley, *Symphonie der Träume*, Zurich: Rüffer & Rub Sachbuchverlag 2001.

Stern, Alfred, ed., "Richtlinien der 'Schweizerischen Vereinigung für Volkslied und Hausmusik'", in: *Volkslied und Hausmusik* 1 (1934), 4.

Stern, Alfred, "Volkslied und Leben", in: *Volkslied und Hausmusik* 1 (1934), 9–12.

Strauß, Dietmar, *Eduard Hanslick, Vom Musikalisch-Schönen: Ein Beitrag zur Revision der Ästhetik der Tonkunst*, Mainz: Schott 1987.

Suñol, Gregorio Ma and G. M. Dunford, *Text book of Gregorian chant according to the Solesmes method*, Tournai: Society of St. John Evangelist, Desclée & Co. 1930.

Szeskus, Reinhard, *Das Deutsche Volkslied: Geschichte, Hintergründe, Wirkung*, Wilhelmshaven: Florian Noetzel 2010.

Tappolet, Walter, "Die Choralsingstunde", in: *Volkslied und Hausmusik* 1 (1934), 39–41.

Tappolet, Walter, "Gregorianischer Choral und Reformationslied", in: *Volkslied und Hausmusik* 7 (1941), 73–76.

Tappolet, Walter, "Singbewegung und Kirche", in: *Volkslied und Hausmusik* 1 (1934), 12–14.

Tappolet, Walter, "Über das Probeheft zum neuen schweizerischen Kirchengesangbuch", in: *Volkslied und Hausmusik* 2 (1935), 55–59, 69–71.

Tappolet, Walter, "Zehn Jahre Schola Cantorum Basiliensis", in: *Singt und spielt* 10 (1943/44), 138–40.

Taruskin, Richard, *Text and Act*, New York: Oxford University Press 1995.

Taylor, Jean Gelman, *The Social World of Batavia: Europeans and Eurasians in Colonial Indonesia*, Madison, WI: University of Wisconsin Press 2009[2].

Teulings, A.B.J., "Herman Lohr", in: *Biografisch Woordenboek Gelderland*, Hilversum: Verloren 2002, 94–97.

Thiele, Ulrike, *Musikleben und Mäzenatentum im 20. Jahrhundert: Werner Reinhart (1884–1951)*, Diss. Phil. University of Zurich, Zurich Open Repository and Archive, University of Zurich 2016, doi.org/10.5167/uhz-13409, publication forthcoming.

Thomas, Wilhelm, "Evangelische Kirche und Singbewegung", in: *Die Singgemeinde* 4 (1927), 1–7.

Thomas, Wilhelm, "Kirchenlied und Gesangbuch in der evangelischen Kirche Deutschlands", in: *Die Singgemeinde* 3 (1926), 33–38.

Tiggers, Piet, *Volksmuziek*, Amsterdam: De Arbeiderspers 1934.

Tobeck, Christina, *Karl-Birger Blomdahl: En musikbiografi med inriktning på förhållandet mellan ord och ton i hans tidiga produktion*, Göteborg: Elanders Graphic Systems 2002 (Skrifter från Institutionen för musikvetenskap, University of Göteborg, Nr. 73).

Vegt, Luuk van der, "Ina Lohr, 1903–1983", in: *De Pyramide* 38 (1984), 110–13.

Veldhuyzen, Marie, "Die Singbewegung in Holland", in: *Volkslied und Hausmusik* 4 (1937), 169–70.

Vellekoop, Kees, "Zusammenhänge zwischen Text und Zahl in der Kompositionsart Jacob Obrechts. Analyse der Motette Parce Domine", in: *Tijdschrift van de Vereniging voor Nederlandse Muziekgeschiedenis* 20 (1966), 97–119.

Vellekoop, Kees, *Dies ire dies illa. Studien zur Frühgeschichte einer Sequenz*, Bilthoven: Creygthon 1978 (Utrechtse Bijdragen tot de muziekwetenschap 10).

Vogelsang, Erich, "Jugendmusik und Kirche", in: *Die Singgemeinde* 4 (1927), 85–90.

Volksliederbuch für Männerchor, ed. Kommission für das Volksliederbuch, Leipzig: Peters [1906?].

Vollaerts, Jan W.A., *Rhythmic Proportions in Early Medieval Ecclesiastical Chant*, Leyden: E.J. Brill 1960.

Vötterle, Karl, *Haus unterm Stern: ein Verleger erzählt*, Kassel: Bärenreiter 1946, 1969[4].

Waardenburg, Wim, "Ina Lohr: 1903–1983", in: *Muziek & Onderwijs* 21 (1984), 84–85.

Wagner, Peter, *Einführung in die gregorianischen Melodien; ein Handbuch der Choralwissenschaft*, Freiburg (Switzerland): Universitätsbuchhandlung Veith 1895.

Wagner-Egelhaaf, Martina, *Mystik der Moderne: die visionäre Ästhetik der deutschen Literatur im 20. Jahrhundert*, Stuttgart: J.B. Metzler 1989.

Wallner, Bo, *40-tal: en klippbok om Måndagsgruppen och det svenska musiklivet*, Stockholm: Kugelbergs Boktryckeri AB 1971.

Wallner, Bo, "The Inspiration of Words and Gestures: A Conversation between Sven-Erik Bäck, Thomas Jennefelt and Bo Wallner", in: *Choral Music Perspectives: Dedicated to Eric Ericson*, ed. Lennart Reimers and Bo Wallner, Uppsala: Almqvist & Wiksell Trykeri 1992 (Publications issued by the Royal Swedish Academy of Music, No. 75), 207–18.

Weber, Jerome F., "The phonograph as witness to performance practice of chant", in: *Cantus Planus. Papers read at the Fourth Meeting. Pécs, Hungary, 3–8 September 1990*, ed. László Dobszay et al., Budapest: Hungarian Academy of Sciences 1992, 607–14.

Wegman, Rob, "'Das musikalische Hören' in the Middle Ages and Renaissance: Perspectives from Pre-War Germany", in: *The Musical Quarterly* 82 (1998), 434–54.

Weingartner, Felix, *Über das Dirigieren*, Leipzig: Breitkopf & Härtel 1920⁵.

Weingartner, Felix, *Unwirkliches und Wirkliches*, Vienna: Saturn-Verlag 1936.

Wendland, Ortwin, "Die Singbewegung und die Bünde der Jugendbewegung", in: *Die Singgemeinde* 4 (1927), 142–44.

Wentz, Jed, "H.R. and the Formation of an Early Music Aesthetic in The Netherlands (1916–1921)", www.forschung.schola-cantorum-basiliensis.ch/de/forschung/ina-lohr-project/rutters-and-the-early-music-aesthetic.html (4 February 2020).

Wentz, Jed, "Gustav Leonhardt, the Naarden Circle and Early Music's Reformation", in: *Early Music* 42/1 (2014), 3–12.

Wentz, Jed "On the Protestant Roots of Gustav Leonhardt's Performance Style", in: *BACH: Journal of the Riemenschneider Bach Institute* 48–49, No. 2–1 (2018), 48–92.

Wenzinger, August with Dieter Gutknecht, "Der Gesamtblick fehlt!", in: *Concerto* 3 (1986), 16–27.

Wenzinger, August, "Die Geige alter Mensur in der Kammermusik", in: *Zeitschrift für Hausmusik* 5 (1936), 121–23.

Wenzinger, August, "Ein Brief aus der Arbeit", in: *Zeitschrift für Hausmusik* 4 (1935), 144–48.

Wenzinger, August, "Über die Erneuerung der katholischen Kirchenmusik", in: *Volkslied und Hausmusik* 7 (1941), 163–68.

Wenzinger, August, "Über die instrumentale Ausführung alter Liedsätze", in: *Die Singgemeinde* 9 (1933), 106–08.

Wenzinger, August, "Über eine vergessene Gambenkunst", in: *Die Singgemeinde* 8 (1932), 24–26.

Winterhalter O.S.B. Beat, "Singbewegung und Gregorianischer Choral", in: *Volkslied und Hausmusik* 3 (1936), 155–57.

Wittkowski, Josef, "Katholische Kirchenmusik und Singbewegung", in: *Die Singbewegung* 4 (1927), 136–42.

Wohlthat, Martina, "'Ja, das war eigentlich der Hauptinhalt von meinem Leben …' – Die Institutsgeschichte der Schola Cantorum Basiliensis im Spiegel der Erinnerungen ehemaliger Lehrkräfte", in: *Basler Jahrbuch für Historische Musikpraxis* 32 (2008), 175–92.

Woolf, Vicki, *Dancing in the Vortex: The Story of Ida Rubinstein*, Amsterdam: Harwood Academic 2000.

Wyneken, Gustav, *Was ist Jugendkultur?*, Munich: Verlag von Georg C. Steinicke 1914.

Ziemer, Gerhard und Wolf, Hans, *Wandervogel und Freideutsche Jugend*, Bad Godesberg: Voggenreiter 1961.

Zon, Bennett, "Plainchant in nineteenth-century England: a review of some major publications of the period", in: *Plainsong and medieval music* 6/1 (1997), 53–74.

Zürcher, Hans Peter, "Die Probeband-Text-Kommission rein menschlich gesehen", in: *Reformierte Schweiz* 1, Heft 2 (February, 1944), 19–26.

Zwart, Frits, *Willem Mengelberg, 1871–1951: een biographie 1871–1920*, Amsterdam: Prometheus 1999.

Index

Schwabe Verlag's signet was
Johannes Petri's printer's mark.
His printing workshop was
established in Basel in 1488 and
was the origin of today's Schwabe
Verlag. The signet refers back to
the beginnings of the printing press,
and originated in the entourage of
Hans Holbein. It illustrates a verse of
Jeremiah 23:29: 'Is not my word
like fire, says the Lord, and like a
hammer that breaks a rock in pieces?'